Praise

'A bonkbuster in.   ,
                                              _aily Express

'Hold on to your hats – here comes the summer blockbuster'
                                              London Lite

'Perry is staking her claim to be crowned queen of the
blockbuster'   Woman

'*Guilty Pleasures* is an intelligent and stylish 21st-century take
on the Jackie Collins genre'   Red

'Summer wouldn't be summer without an OTT jet-setting
blockbuster'   The Gloss Magazine

Gold Diggers

'A sumptuously sexy book'   Elle

'A slick, uber glamorous cocktail of backstabbing beauties,
murder and sex'   Easy Living

'All hail the return of the beach bonkbuster'   Glamour

'A high-gloss soap opera of a story that will have you hooked'
                                                   InStyle

'The follow-up to Tasmina Perry's hugely successful *Daddy's
Girls* promises more glamour, lust and betrayal . . . Pick up
to read on the beach'   Bella

'Superior, provocative, almost tongue-in-cheek, sun-lounger
fun'   Good Housekeeping

'New York billionaire Adam Gold is moving to London and
the gold diggers are circling. Welcome to the world of sex,
murder and betrayal'   Heat

Daddy's Girls

'*Daddy's Girls* is the perfect beach read; a sexy guilty pleasure you devour like a caramel Magnum . . . A brilliant antidote to all those girl-seeks-boy-and-shoes chick lit books, this is glittering escapism that gives you a peek into the fabulous lives of the rich and powerful'   *Glamour*

'*Daddy's Girls* is the hottest holiday accessory this season. Slick, glossy and gloriously bitchy . . . The bonkbuster is back'
Elle

'Amid all the romping and camp one-liners, there are tart observations about race, class and family dynamics, too. The perfect beach read'   *Marie Claire*

'This glam and glitz, power and corruption romp of a book celebrates the genre of the great big beach read with no holds barred'   *Good Housekeeping*

'A sizzling summer read brimming with style, sex and sibling rivalry . . . A pacy bonkbuster that you won't be able to put down until its explosive climax is revealed'   *Closer*

'A sizzling debut . . . one to devour on the beach'   *InStyle*

'Tasmina Perry's *Daddy's Girls* is a hugely entertaining blockbuster that's impossible to put down'   *Image*

'A super-slick, seriously sexy murder mystery. Fantastic'
Company

'If you fancy some racy reading in the sun, Tasmina Perry's *Daddy's Girls* is the perfect choice for you. Packed with glamour, romance and intrigue, it'll keep you glued from the very first page'   *Heat*

TASMINA PERRY

Guilty Pleasures

HARPER

Harper
An imprint of HarperCollins*Publishers*
77–85 Fulham Palace Road,
Hammersmith, London W6 8JB

www.harpercollins.co.uk

This production 2012
1

First published in Great Britain by
HarperCollins 2008

A catalogue record for this book is
available from the British Library

ISBN: 978-00-0-792592-6

Set in Meridien by Palimpsest Book Production Limited,
Grangemouth, Stirlingshire

Printed and bound in Great Britain by
Clays Ltd, St Ives plc

MIX
Paper from
responsible sources
FSC® C007454

FSC is a non-profit international organisation established to promote the
responsible management of the world's forests. Products carrying the FSC
label are independently certified to assure consumers that they come
from forests that are managed to meet the social, economic and
ecological needs of present and future generations.

Find out more about HarperCollins and the environment at
www.harpercollins.co.uk/green

Acknowledgements

My continued gratitude to the wonderful HarperCollins team especially my editor and friend Wayne Brookes, Amanda Ridout, and the marketing, sales and publicity teams for their tireless work and enthusiasm. To the mighty Sheila Crowley, Linda Shaughnessy, Theresa Nicholls, Christine Glover and everyone at AP Watt.

Wendy Hinton pointed me in the direction of wonderful photographer Elise Dumontet. Thanks also to Susie Auty, Elizabeth Steele, Ian Johnstone, Marie, Liz and Sam for all your help and advice.

To my friends who understand when I go AWOL for three months when a deadline looms – I know I have been particularly elusive this time round. To my family for all their support and understanding, especially my mum, for all that she does and who made fifty thousand words in Whale Beach possible. My husband John is the best writer and editor in our house. Eternal thanks for all the hours of help, endless patience, wisdom and fabulous handbags – I can't do it without you. Finally, many friends and former colleagues shared their tales from the wonderful worlds of fashion and magazines. As I would hate to be responsible for anyone getting their discount cards revoked, these conversations will stay off the record. But you know who you are, and I'm incredibly grateful for all the colour and fantastic detail you gave me.

To Fin with love

Whenever you confront an unbridled desire you are surely in the presence of a tragedy in the making.

Quentin Crisp

PROLOGUE

Sometime in the 1980s

The residents of the South of France are too chic to consider themselves socially competitive, but in the villas that pepper the Côte D'Azur, one-upmanship was rife. Saul Milford, a man of not inconsiderable self-assurance, liked to think that *he* had the best villa in the whole area. An old mas in the foothills of Provence, Les Fleurs was not the biggest house but with its turrets and bright blue shutters, it was certainly the prettiest. Already that summer he'd had Princess Margaret, Mick Jagger and various other members of London's beau monde round the kidney-shaped swimming pool. They'd all seemed to enjoy themselves and it was easy to see why. The grounds were studded with fabulous bronzes, sculpted by his dear friend Christopher Chase, one of England's most prominent artists. There were olive groves, an abundance of poppies on the hillside, and in the sunshine, the Mediterranean sparkled like a sapphire in the distance. This evening, as dusk was settling on the grounds with a honey glow, it looked even more spectacular. It was excellent timing: tonight there was to be another party. Staff in white suits scurried around the pool plumping up cushions

3

and filling silver ice buckets with champagne. The smell of spices from the kitchen mingled with the strong scent of lavender and the air crackled with anticipation of a fabulous evening ahead.

Saul smiled to himself, sipping lemonade freshly made from fruit in his orchard, silently congratulating himself that his purchase of the villa the previous summer had been one of the best decisions he had ever made. He could certainly afford it. His company, the luxury goods house Milford, was doing well. For years the company's sumptuous leather products had been the preserve of the upper classes who ordered bespoke luggage for their exotic holidays. But the Eighties had seen the rise of a new, more democratic wave of millionaires riding on stock market killings. The City was awash with money and it was making Saul rich. Very rich. And what was the point of taking money to your grave?

Saul looked down from the terrace to where his two nieces Emma Bailey and Cassandra Grand were playing. From this distance, he could just about make out the dialogue between the two cousins. It was funny how personalities were set at such a young age. While the girls were similar in many ways, their differences were equally marked. So marked in fact, that Saul felt confident he could predict how their lives would unfold and the direction in which their desires and ambitions would take them.

Dangling her feet in the swimming pool Emma put a bookmark in her copy of *Jane Eyre*. At seven she was tall for her age, with clever, grey eyes that posed questions without the need to open her mouth.

'Do you want to play chess?' she asked her cousin.

'No,' replied Cassandra, rolling her eyes dramatically.

'What about hide-and-seek?' Emma persisted.

'No,' snapped Cassandra impatiently.

'Why?'

4

'It's for babies,' said Cassandra painting a coat of red polish on her stubby square fingernails. The twelve-year-old had been excited about the holiday for months. She loved hearing Saul's stories about rock stars and princesses and wanted to look perfect if she happened to meet any of them that evening.

'Why don't you go and ask Tom,' she added coldly, pointing to her three-year-old brother who was busily rummaging in a flower-bed getting soil in his hair.

'Tom's too young to play,' replied Emma, refusing to be fobbed off.

Cassandra looked up at her cousin, her eyes squinting up in the sun.

'Can't you see I'm busy?'

'Come on, Cass,' Emma persisted. 'There's loads of places to explore. We could go and look for butterflies. I bet there are *millions* in this garden. I've got a book in the villa that tells you how to identify them.'

'You are such a swot,' tutted Cassandra, smoothing down her long dark hair. 'We're on holiday. Can't you just relax by the pool like a normal person? Listen, I'll paint your nails if you give me fifty pence.'

'I haven't got fifty pence.'

'Well, you'd better go and find something else to do then,' said Cassandra, 'on your own.'

'OK then. I will,' said Emma. Above her on the terrace, Saul Milford smiled and then walked back into the house to get ready for the party.

She hadn't been able to sleep. How was she expected to with the music and turquoise light reflected from the swimming pool seeping through the shutters? She had crept out of bed and gone to watch the party from the safety of the terrace. In the glow of a thousand tea-lights the whole scene looked spectacular as

5

hundreds of impossibly glamorous people were laughing, drinking and dancing under an umbrella of moonlight.

Minutes earlier she'd been on the verge of going down to find her parents when Saul, taking a break from the action, had caught her.

'What are you doing here, I thought you went to bed hours ago,' he'd said sitting on the terrace next to her.

'How can I sleep with all this going on? It all looks so beautiful,' she had explained.

'There'll be time to enjoy all this when you're older,' he'd smiled, putting his arm round her. 'One day all this is going to be yours.'

'Really Uncle Saul?'

'Really,' he'd laughed, draining the last of his champagne and standing up. 'Now come on, off to bed! You know I can't protect you if your father finds out you're still up.'

What a wonderful holiday it had been! As it was the last night of the trip she had no desire to go back to bed. She waited until Saul had returned to the party and then wandered away from the house, walking deeper into the grounds, wanting to make the night last as long as she could.

The further she walked moving away from the candles around the pool and the buttery light spilling from the villa, the darker it became, only flecks of starlight peppered the tarry sheet of sky above her. The high rasp of frogs in the trees replaced the chirp of crickets and the air began to lose its floral scent. Still she carried on walking, the damp grass tickling her bare feet, drawn by a faint light in the distance. As she approached the light, she saw it was coming from the little wooden house she had explored with her cousin earlier in the week. She had wondered then what might be inside it, but it had been locked tight. She was not easily scared but for a moment her steps slowed as she wondered whether to turn back to Les Fleurs, now so far behind her that it was nothing more than a black shape in the distance. Suddenly she caught sight of a dim outline of a figure through the dusty glass of the outbuilding. Curious, she edged

6

closer, freezing when she heard a low moan from inside. She was now just below the shed's dirty window. Holding her breath, she slowly raised her head and peered inside. The glass was so filthy it was like looking through smoke. At first, she was unable to make out what or who was inside. But as she pushed her face closer she let out a gasp – at first in puzzlement and disbelief and then in horror, as she realized what was happening in front of her. Stumbling back, she fell and scraped her arm on a rock. She looked up at the window, then back to the villa. She knew she should leave – run back to her bed as fast as she could – but as if pulled by a force she could not control she looked through the window again, hoping against hope that what she had seen was just her imagination. But no: the vile image was still there. Shaking her head to rid it from her mind, tears streaming down her face, she turned and ran back to the villa, not yet aware that what she had just seen would change her life forever.

1

Twenty-three years later

Sitting in the passenger seat of an ink-black Mercedes, Emma Bailey turned round and watched the white Federal-style mansion fade from view, bringing to a close one of the most stressful days of her life. She blew out her cheeks, smiling to herself at a job well done. Emma had spent the last twenty-four hours charming and cajoling industrialist PJ Frost, attempting to persuade him that her company Price Donahue was the right one to advise him on a billion-dollar mergers and acquisition strategy. Emma's head was swimming. Not just from the pressure, but from dinner last night: a seven-course tasting menu with free-flowing vintage champagne that she had been in no position to refuse. Frost was from the old school where deals were brokered over food, liquor and preferably blood-sports, which she was glad to have been spared.

'We did it!' laughed Emma, sinking back into the leather and watching the frosty white landscape speed by.

'*You* did it,' said her colleague Mark Eisner, one of the partners at the firm as he turned up the heated seats. 'You were the one that got us the invite up here. You were the one who impressed him with the pitch. Price Donahue has been after the Frost business for years. You do realize that this is about twenty million dollars worth of fees?'

Emma smiled. She knew she had done well and it was good to hear her boss acknowledge it, but she had to admit a little bit of luck had helped: her chance meeting with PJ Frost at a business seminar had come at exactly the right time. PJ Frost had a vast industrial empire that took in everything from paper mills to food production. He was a billionaire, owned one of the finest homes in New England, a fleet of vintage sports cars and two Gulfstream jets, but when Emma had met him, he had just slipped out of the Forbes 400 and he was hell bent on re-igniting his business. Emma knew Price Donahue, one of the most prestigious management consultancy firms in Boston, were the firm to do it: they just had to convince Frost. Emma and Mark had made the long drive up to Vermont a day earlier and even if she did say so herself, they had done an amazing job presenting their ideas. The deal had been sealed on the Friday night. Unfortunately, then Frost had insisted they return to his mansion the next day and celebrate with a brunch of kedgeree, eggs Benedict and even more champagne.

'My blood feels like pure Dom Perignon,' groaned Emma, putting on a pair of sunglasses to ease her headache.

'I could think of worse things,' said Mark who'd had to stay sober to drive.

'It's not funny,' she said in a croaky laugh. 'I haven't had a hangover since college.'

'That was six years ago!' teased Mark.

'University not grad school,' she smiled, feeling herself flush. '*Eight* years ago.'

'Well, I particularly enjoyed it when you climbed on the grand piano to serenade Frost. I had no idea you were a gifted singer as well as a first-class brain.'

'I didn't!' she said sitting up and snatching off the shades.

'You did,' said Mark Eisner, a slow, lazy smile curling at his lips. 'You sang "Begin the Beguine". I like you like that. Less wound-up. Less serious.'

Emma stared at him, a look of horror on her face, until her foggy brain realized he was joking.

'Ow!' cried Mark, laughing, as she punched him on the arm. 'I could have you up on a discipline charge for that!'

He looked back at the frost-dusted road again and smiled.

'Hey, so you got a bit drunk. Don't look at it as over-indulgence, look at it as a necessary evil, Em. When you're a partner you'll soon realize that hollow legs are a pre-requisite of the job.'

Emma's buoyant mood softened.

'This weekend has got to have helped my chances, hasn't it?' she asked cautiously.

'Of what?'

'Partnership, of course.'

Although Emma had only been a Price Donahue manager for two years she felt sure she was in with a chance of being selected for partner. Yes, she was still not quite thirty, but she had brought in millions for the firm and her reputation alone had brought in a considerable amount of new business.

'Well, don't ask me, I don't know anything,' said Mark playfully. 'You're in the running but then you already know that.'

'You don't think they'll say I'm too young, do you?'

'If you're good enough, you're old enough,' he said seriously. 'Anyway, there's a partners' meeting on Tuesday before the final vote. I'll tell them what a fine job you did of reeling in that old buzzard PJ Frost with your sharp mind and fine singing voice,' he laughed.

It was getting dark as the soft-top SLK roared south, the trees and fields a blur.

'Hey, where are we going?' asked Emma, as Mark turned off the highway.

'To celebrate,' he smiled, reaching over and taking her cold hand. He pulled onto a side road through a thick forest of sugar maple and beech. Emma would have loved to have seen the glorious scarlet and orange of Fall, but the February frost, lying in a lacy veil on the trees, was just as beautiful. As they turned a corner, Emma could see that their destination was a log cabin by the shores of a small lake. Pulling up outside it, Mark got out of the car, went round to Emma's side and opened the door, taking her hand to help her out. As she stood, he pulled her towards him and kissed her on the lips. She responded greedily, pushing her body up against his.

'What *is* this place?' she asked when they finally came up for air.

'A hideaway for honeymooners and rich recluses.'

'Which category do we fall in?' she grinned.

'A little of both,' he winked. 'And wait until you see inside.'

The cabin was everything you'd want from a luxury bolt-hole in the wilderness. There were skis and Wellingtons in a rack by the door, while the main room was filled with big leather sofas draped with cashmere blankets. Velvet drapes hung at the windows and a stag's head hung over the stone fireplace. It was cosy and romantic, just perfect. Emma turned to look at Mark and felt herself blush: *perfect for an affair with the boss*, she thought.

Emma had always considered herself too cautious, too sensible for anything so clichéd as a workplace fling, especially with her own boss, but Mark Eisner was the most handsome, not to mention brilliant partner at Price Donahue. *But it was more than that*, thought Emma, looking at him, carrying in their bags: *Mark was good for her*. They had been dating for three months; getting together at a mutual friend's Thanksgiving drinks, and she still thought he was the most sexy man she had ever seen. With his dark brown hair and his smooth tanned skin, he looked more like a male model in a coffee advert than a city high-flyer. For the first time in a long time, Emma felt as if she was where she wanted to be. She loved her job, her life in Boston, being with Mark. And the cabin, she loved the cabin.

While Mark went to put their overnight bags in the bedroom Emma took off her coat and went to stand by the window to look out onto the lake.

The only thing that would have made it any more perfect would have been if they had spent a couple days up here. She'd have loved to have wrapped up in scarves and boots and gone for long walks together, plus there was some excellent skiing in Stowe, not too far from where they were now. But most of all, she wished she could stay here in bed, curled against Mark's strong back and sleep. She was frazzled, wound-up and anxious. It wasn't just the high-pressure sales pitch at PJ Frost's mansion, it was the constant demands of her job and the 18-hour days were finally catching up with her. The irony was that she *did* have the next three days booked off work but that was for another reason.

Mark came over with two glasses of chilled white wine and handed one to her.

'If the weather turns tonight we might get snowed in,' she said looking up at the ominous white sky.

'Chance would be a fine thing,' he said, snaking his arm around her waist.

'You do remember I have to be at the airport at four tomorrow afternoon.'

Mark reassured her with a smile.

'We'll make it even if I have to dig us out with my bare hands.'

'I wish you were coming with me,' she said, stroking her finger across his cheek.

'You know it will look odd if we both have time off at the same time,' he murmured. 'I'm sure my PA suspects us as it is. We don't want to rock the boat before partnerships are announced.'

Emma smiled.

'Well, I don't want anyone accusing me of sleeping my way to the top,' she joked, privately in complete agreement that she didn't want their relationship to become public. Not yet anyway. While office romances weren't expressly forbidden at Price Donahue, she didn't want to do anything that might harm her chances of promotion; wanting to minimize the recklessness of being with Mark in any way she could.

'Anyway, I don't exactly blame you for not wanting to come all the way to England for a funeral.'

'You sure know how to show a guy a good time.'

Mark saw her face fall and regretted the joke.

'Hey, Em, I'm sorry. I know how upset you were about your uncle.'

She nodded absently.

'After my dad died, Uncle Saul was more like a father to me than an uncle,' she said. 'He was the one who paid for my college fees. He was the only one to encourage me to go to university in the States. I spent a couple of summers working with him at his company and I think that helped me get into business school.'

'So why do I get the feeling you're not looking forward to going?' asked Mark.

Emma sighed.

'It's not Saul. It's the rest of the family . . .'

13

Mark waited for her to continue, but she remained silent.

'You never talk about them. Your family,' he prompted.

'There's nothing to tell,' she said turning away from him, but he pulled her back.

'Hey, save it for when you get back from England,' he said, stroking her hair. 'I want to know about them. I want to know more about you.'

Emma felt herself tense at the intimate gesture.

'You will call me if you hear anything about the partnership?' she asked.

'Honey, please just relax and try and forget about it, huh? For today, we're on holiday.'

As he held her she caught their reflection in the glass.

It had taken Emma time to grow into her looks but at twenty-nine even her own natural modesty could not deny that she looked good. At work, she always downplayed her attractiveness by wearing little or no make-up, but then she had a naturalness that suited it. Wavy, dark-blonde hair fell to her shoulders, her cheekbones were high, her mouth naturally full, and when she smiled it warmed up her intelligent grey eyes.

Moving closer, Mark slipped his fingers between two buttons of her shirt and under the lacy fold of her bra until his fingertips brushed her nipple.

Mark said, 'You're so beautiful.'

Emma would usually deflect compliments, deny them, or make them into a joke, but his touch seemed to sear her skin.

'I love you,' he whispered suddenly, looking into her eyes. Emma felt her stomach gallop.

'You mean it?' she said not knowing of any other way to respond.

He nodded, pushing back a loose strand of her hair behind her ear.

She let her body sink into his, and for the first time in weeks she felt such a sense of calm and belonging that she welled up with emotion.

'I love you too,' she whispered.

Mark moved his lips towards her neck running them down her skin.

'I'm sure I saw a bed somewhere around here,' he whispered, his voice hoarse with desire. 'I think it's about time we went and checked it out.'

She kissed him on the mouth, then started unbuttoning his shirt all the way down to his navel.

'Who needs a bed?' she asked, looking up and smiling wickedly.

2

Nothing as dramatic – or enjoyable – as getting snowed into a luxurious Vermont log cabin made Emma late for her uncle's funeral.

Her Sunday evening flight had been sitting on the runway for three hours and it was this that had thrown her entire schedule off kilter. That was the way Emma functioned: with order and precision and just a little margin left over as a safety net. But this time even her careful approach had let her down; by the time the taxi had made the fifty-mile journey from Heathrow to the tiny Oxfordshire village of Chilcot where the funeral was being held, she could already hear the rousing sound of hymns coming from inside the church.

'Shit, shit, shit, it's started,' she mumbled, making a dash for the church. Wincing as the double doors groaned loudly she squeezed inside and slipped into the end of the nearest pew.

'I am the resurrection and the life. He that believeth in me though he were dead yet shall he live.'

As she listened to the hollow sound of the vicar's voice echoing around the small church, Emma felt a pang of regret wash over her.

It had been three years since she had seen her Uncle Saul. Working at Price Donahue had meant that her holiday time was cut to a miserly two weeks a year. There was barely enough time to get to Martha's Vineyard let alone make the long journey to her family home. She should have made the time but she hadn't and now it was too late. Saul was dead, his coffin festooned with roses at the front of the altar. The life-force of the family, the bon viveur, the glue that had seemed to hold everyone together, was gone.

Emma's own father was buried in Chilcot church's grounds and it made the day seem even more poignant. She shut her eyes and for a split second she pictured herself running around Saul's villa as a little girl the summer before her father died. She could still almost smell Les Fleurs; the riot of scent from pine to jasmine, lavender to thyme. She remembered the wonder of seeing hilltop medieval villages for the first time and the illicit swigs of rosé smuggled from the kitchens by Cassandra. It had been the last perfect summer.

The service ended with 'Jerusalem', after which the coffin was carried down the aisle and the congregation streamed out into the grounds. Emma estimated there were over 200 people crammed into the narrow aisles; it was no wonder. Saul had been the patriarch of the village and Milford was still the main employer of most of its residents. It explained why so many of them were here, spilling out of the church, some of them in tears. Searching the crowd she vaguely recognized senior managers from the company. There was also a peppering of the London crowd that Saul had hung around with for four decades: elegant women with smart hats and impressive-looking husbands, well-known businessmen, politicians. She recognized Soraya, the Sixties supermodel, Terry O'Neill, even a handful of ageing rock stars.

'Finally,' said a disapproving voice behind her accompanied by a tap on the shoulder. 'Please tell me you were at the back of the church.'

'Yes, Mother, I was at the back of the church,' said Emma with a sigh, leaning in to kiss her mother Virginia. She was exquisitely dressed in a charcoal suit, her silver blonde hair swung in an elegant bob around her pinched disapproving face. At almost sixty, she was still beautiful in a way Emma was not, finely boned, elegant, regal.

'My plane was three hours late. You did get my message?'

'Your mother was worried sick,' snapped the man standing next to Emma's mother. Jonathon Bond was her mother's second husband. A stockbroker with pewter hair combed back in a slightly sinister style and a perpetually anxious expression, he had married Virginia within three years of Emma's father's death when she was still only ten. It was approximately at that point that Emma had begun to feel as if she were surplus to requirements within her own family. Emma liked to tell herself that she hadn't intentionally drifted apart from them, but the truth was she had wanted to leave England to escape from a mother who seemed to have no interest in anything outside her new marriage. But if she had subconsciously tried to punish her mother by moving to another continent, Virginia hadn't seemed to have been particularly bothered.

Today was the first time she had seen her mother in six months. She had invited her mother and Jonathon over to Boston for New Year, but Virginia had declined, saying Jonathon had to be at the office over the holiday. She'd since learnt from her cousin Tom that they'd actually spent New Year staying at the Four Seasons in Manhattan instead. Emma had thought she had stopped feeling disappointed with her mother but it seemed as if this was something she would never get over.

'Cassandra was here early,' said Virginia shortly, 'She had to come all the way from some fashion show in New York.'

'And I thought you had a boyfriend coming over?' said Jonathon looking around.

'Who told you that?' said Emma with surprise.

'Your mother said there was some chap at work.'

'Mum, please. It's nothing serious,' said Emma, suddenly feeling like a teenager.

'It never is serious, is it?' said Virginia, 'unless it's work.'

Seemingly tiring of the conversation, Jonathon grabbed Virginia's arm.

'Come along,' he said briskly, ushering them after the crowd, 'they'll be burying the poor sod.'

The mourners had collected around the grave with the family standing in a row behind the vicar. At the end of the line, Emma watched them. The head of the family, of the Milford dynasty, was now her Uncle Roger. Still a handsome man she thought, looking at his well-toned frame wrapped in a long black coat. His blond hair was well-trimmed, and just lightly flecked with grey even though he was in his mid-fifties. His beautiful wife Rebecca, a local girl who had tamed the company playboy stood behind him, tall, slender and blonde with wide feline eyes; the perfect accessory for the new Lord of the Manor. Tom, Cassandra's brother – all grown-up now, she noted – was dressed in something that only loosely qualified as a suit. Tom's mother Julia, an art dealer whose company Emma had always enjoyed, was at his side. And then there was Cassandra. Her eyes were obscured by the rim of an enormous black hat but that exquisite bone structure was still visible. She lifted her head and caught Emma looking over towards her; she gave Emma the hint of a smile. Moving to America had meant that Emma had got out from beneath the shadow of her charmed, more glamorous older cousin. But Emma had never been able to quite escape the voices. 'Cassandra is dating a rock star.' 'Did you see Cassandra on television?' 'Oh, Cassandra makes us all so proud.'

After Saul's body had been laid to rest, Emma went back inside the church to find the case she had stowed in the pew. As she walked out, the leafy grounds were almost empty as most of the crowd had taken advantage of the fleet of cars laid on to ferry the mourners to Saul's home Winterfold for the wake. But one striking figure was standing on the path. Cassandra.

Emma's heart sank. Cassandra's love of pretty skirts and beads when they had played together as children had translated into a career as one of the top editors in the world. Her magazine, *Rive*, was the most respected fashion publication on the planet and Cassandra was the living embodiment of it: elegant, poised and, to Emma's eyes, snooty and pretentious. Not much had changed there, she thought. Twenty-odd years on from Saul's villa and Cassandra still had the power to make Emma feel awkward and ungainly.

'Oh. Has everybody gone?' said Cassandra as Emma approached. 'I was just talking to the vicar about doing a Gothic shoot in the church grounds. Some of those overgrown tombs are stunning.'

Emma smiled nervously and motioned towards one of the Mercedes cars.

'Fancy jumping in this one?'

'This is actually my driver,' said Cassandra quickly. 'But feel free to join me. Donna Karan?'

'Sorry?' asked Emma as she struggled to get her case onto the seat next to her.

'Your suit. Donna Karan last season.'

'Er, yes. I think so,' replied Emma remembering how she

had bought the trouser suit because it was smart and black and for no other reason beyond that.

'Beautiful service, though,' said Cassandra. Her mind had already moved on: 'I got Robbie Van Helden to do the flowers. He does Elton's parties.'

Emma nodded nervously.

'How long are you staying?' she asked, filling the silence.

'Oh, I have to get back to London tonight,' said Cassandra. 'It's all rather inconvenient, slap bang in the middle of the collections. Never mind. When duty calls . . .'

She smiled and Emma thought how unusual it was that Cassandra seemed to be in such a buoyant mood. Emma found her spiky and was usually walking on egg-shells whenever she spoke to her. The slightest thing could send her into a hissy-fit.

'I'd leave now but I can't miss the big family pow-wow,' continued Cassandra ordering her driver to take them to Winterfold.

'Pow-wow? What do you mean?'

'Oh, didn't you hear? Apparently Saul wanted his will to be read, so it's happening tonight while everyone is still here.'

Emma frowned. 'How odd. I thought that the reading of the will died out about fifty years ago.'

'You know Saul, the old queen. He loved a bit of drama. Anyway, you shouldn't complain about it happening tonight. It saves you coming back from Boston,' smiled Cassandra.

'I suppose Uncle Roger will finally get his hands on the company then,' said Emma, wondering for the first time what would happen to Saul's extensive assets. Cassandra dipped her hat, so Emma couldn't see her face.

'Don't be so sure.'

They fell into silence as the car sped through the lanes

of the village. Past the Feathers pub where Emma had bought her first drink, past the park where her father had chased her and pushed her on the swings. There were many happy memories but some were still too painful to think about. She looked away.

The car swung into the avenue of lime trees that ran up to the manor house. A grand Georgian mansion, set in 800 acres of grounds, Winterfold had a haughty, almost severe beauty. Emma knew the story well of how the house came to be in her family; as a child it had been told to her at bedtime like a fairy tale of the beautiful aristocracy and their fantasy lives. The house had once belonged to the Greystone family, who had built the house from the proceeds of their merchant banking fortune. Merrick Milford, Emma's great-grandfather, was a local saddler's apprentice who had developed a reputation for being exceptionally skilled. The lady of the house, Lady Eleanor Greystone, was a keen horsewoman and had admired Merrick's work on her own saddles, so had asked to meet this young talent. Visiting the house, Merrick had been fascinated by a beautiful collection of trunks in the hall which Lady Greystone informed him were made by Goyard, the Parisian luggage house who supplied everyone from Indian maharajas to French aristocracy.

Buoyed by his mistress's praise and full of the arrogance of youth, the handsome young artisan had boasted: 'If you provide the materials, m'lady, I will make you a set of luggage even finer than this one.'

Taking him at his word, Lady Greystone delivered the finest leather, wood, brass pellets and canvas to Merrick's cottage on the outskirts of the village the following week. Six weeks later Merrick delivered six trunks that all neatly fitted inside one another like Russian dolls. The leather had been hand-stitched and coated with beeswax to seal it. Each trunk had a fine brass lock, forged by himself. The influential Lady

Eleanor told her friends and the young saddler was in business. When the First World War had passed and the upper classes resumed their travels, it was to the small Oxfordshire company Milford that they turned for exquisite bespoke luggage, not Goyard and Vuitton.

Twenty years and one good marriage later, Merrick Milford had elevated his position in society. The fortunes of the Greystone family, however, had not been so fortunate, so when Lady Eleanor's son Nathaniel gambled away the family fortune, the Greystones found a wealthy and eager buyer in the form of Edward Milford, Merrick's son. And in the Milford family, Winterfold had grown and thrived.

As Cassandra's car pulled up at Winterfold it was obvious, even now, that it was a well-tended and much-loved home. Flanking the pillars either side of the whitewashed steps were clipped bay trees and the black and white tiles on the pathway positively gleamed. The dove-grey brickwork and vast, sash windows looked well-kept, while spirals of smoke ascended from the four chimneys dotted around the roof.

'It really is a beautiful place, isn't it?' said Emma, almost as if voicing her own thoughts.

'Do you think?' asked Cassandra. 'It rather gives me the creeps.'

As they were shown inside, Emma had to admit Winterfold was an acquired taste, a unique house that was part home, part museum, adorned with an eclectic mixture of antiques, art and objets d'art from Saul's travels around the world. Crossed Maori war-clubs and grinning masks looked down disapprovingly over an exquisite Louis-Quinze writing desk; a stuffed lion's head shot on the Serengeti plains loomed over a roughly-carved French medieval fireplace that Saul claimed had once belonged to Gallic royalty itself. The owner's living environment reflected the man and Saul Milford had been an adventurer. So much so, that when Emma had heard about her uncle's death, she had been surprised that it had been something as ordinary as a heart attack, and that he hadn't been lost as he ballooned over the Pacific or been savaged by wild jackals in Tanzania. Emma smiled at the scene: amid all this chaos, this eclectic clash of cultures, tea and cake was being quietly, reverently served. Saul would have roared. Nevertheless Emma accepted an elegant bone-china cup from Morton, Saul's butler, and watched as visitors quietly stepped forwards to offer condolences to the family, the only note of drama being the swelling sound of Wagner in the background. The wake lasted barely an hour; the mourners seeming to disperse almost as quickly as they had arrived at Winterfold. Slowly the mourners left and Roger began ushering the family into Saul's study to the left of the grand staircase. Emma rubbed her red eyes; her jet-lag was kicking in and she would be grateful when the whole thing was over and she could get back to Boston.

'Em! How are you? I haven't managed to talk to you all day.'

A handsome young man in his mid-twenties nudged Emma's arm.

'Hello Tom,' she smiled, grateful for the first genuinely warm welcome she'd had since she'd arrived in England.

'How's the mistress of the universe? That's what they call you people, isn't it?'

Emma laughed. 'I'm a management consultant, not some Wall Street banker.'

'Oh yes, Mum did tell me,' grinned Tom, running his fingers through his hair. 'Sounds like a right old racket to me. You're brought in and paid millions of quid to tell the management team they're not good enough at their job?'

She tapped him playfully on the arm.

'It's a bit more complicated than that.'

She liked Tom. He was funny, sweet and handsome, with a scrub of dirty blond hair and a square chin that stopped him being pretty. She heard from him through emails full of smiley faces and barely legible missives about his latest line of work. Expelled from practically every public school that would have him, he had spent the time since he'd 'mucked up' his A-levels drifting round Europe and the US doing bar work in Amsterdam, photography in New York and some ill-defined 'business' or other in Dublin.

'Ah, but you would say it's complicated wouldn't you?' teased Tom. 'Can't have us cheeky little boys pointing at the Emperor's New Clothes, now can we?'

Emma tried to look severe, but just ended up giggling.

'So where are you working at the minute?' she asked.

'I'm considering my options,' shrugged Tom. 'Hey, maybe I need a management consultant to sort me out?'

'Maybe,' laughed Emma. 'Or maybe you just need to get up before noon!'

'Actually,' whispered Tom theatrically, 'I think I might be getting my big break at any moment. I'm sure Saul recognized my work ethic and business genius and is going to give me Milford lock, stock and barrel.'

'You too?' smiled Emma. 'He used to promise it to me whenever he was drunk,' she said remembering her uncle's words, *One day it will all be yours.* 'You know what Saul was like. He probably told Morton he was going to leave it all to him every time he made him a decent martini.'

She paused as she noticed her Uncle Roger beckoning them into Winterfold's study. Walking into the room with Tom she glanced around. It was a small room for a house of such size. There was barely enough space for the wide desk by the bay window and the two Chesterfield sofas on either side of the marble fireplace, but it certainly had all the trappings of the gentleman's retreat: there were leather-bound books lined up neatly along oak shelves, heavy midnight-blue velvet swags hung at the windows, and a creaky red wing-back club chair completed the picture. Outside it was gloomy and the wind made a whirling racket though the lime trees.

Tom nudged Emma as Roger walked in, taking his place in Saul's old club chair with an air of natural authority.

'I think someone else fancies his chances of getting his paws on Milford,' he whispered.

Anthony Collins, Saul's solicitor, had made the journey from Pimlico especially for the reading and was rather flustered. Sitting at Saul's desk and taking a sheaf of papers out of his briefcase, he fussed for a while, laying them in complicated piles and arranging his notes. Finally he looked up at Roger who inclined his head as if to indicate his permission to begin.

'Ladies and gentlemen, thank you all for taking the time to come to this meeting,' began Collins. 'I know it's not ideal having this meeting straight after the funeral, but Roger seemed to suggest it was the only time that we could guarantee everyone being here.'

Emma looked around at the family. Cassandra was perched on the arm of a Chesterfield, a high black stiletto dangling off one foot. Her mother was poised and dignified; Roger, regal and in control. They all had neutral, interested expressions, but she knew they must all be churning inside. And much as they tried to hide it, the buzz of expectation charged the air. Like vultures circling. The thought made Emma feel a little sick.

'Well, I'll keep it as brief as possible,' said Collins, shuffling his papers again and putting on a pair of reading glasses.

'The will is fairly straightforward. Of course I will answer any questions you have afterwards or you can always pop along to my office in London.'

Emma saw Cassandra give an impatient sigh, prompting Collins to clear his throat and peer intently at his notes. 'There are a few small bequests of watches, cuff-links, and smaller financial gifts. I needn't bother you with those. I will inform the beneficiaries first thing in the morning. Now. To the main part of the will . . .'

Collins paused, then began.

'My 1967 Aston Martin DB7, 1956 Mercedes gull-wing coupé, 1983 Alfa Romeo Spider, 1966 E-type Jaguar and 1963 Ferrari 250 have all brought me immense pleasure in life and I give them to someone who I know will experience the same sense of joy. I therefore bequest them to my nephew Tom, to be held in trust by his aunt Virginia until Tom reaches the age of thirty.'

'Thirty!' cried Tom, unable to contain himself. 'What's supposed to happen until then?'

Anthony cleared his throat. 'Well, they are to be held by your aunt,' he said simply.

'Is that legal?' he asked, dismayed.

'Tom, please,' said Roger sternly. 'We'd all like to get this over as soon as possible.'

I bet you would, smiled Emma to herself. Whoever was the majority shareholder was invariably the chief executive of Milford, and as Winterfold was officially a company asset, whoever was CEO of the company would be its de facto owner and resident. She could see Roger's wife Rebecca looking at the walls and carpets, no doubt planning what she was going to say to her interior decorators first thing in the morning.

'To my darling niece Cassandra,' continued Collins, 'I give Les Fleurs, my Provence villa, knowing how stylish she will keep it and that she will continue the tradition of throwing the most fabulous parties in Europe.'

27

Emma saw Cassandra smile and nod, but she was sure she had also gone a shade whiter.

'To my brother Roger, now head of the family, I bequest the chalet in Gstaad in the hope he will continue the tradition of a family Christmas in the snow.'

Roger looked straight at Collins, a frown on his brow. He looked as if he was about to speak, but thought better of it and simply nodded. A hush had now fallen over the room, as if everyone was holding their breath. The hiss and pop of the fire seemed unnaturally loud and Emma could hear Roger breathing through his nose.

'To my niece Emma, I give all my shareholding in Milford Industries. Over the years I have quietly watched her mature into a businesswoman of such force and reputation I feel safe in the knowledge that she will take the company to even greater heights than I have dared to dream. The wine cellar and art I also give to her in the hope that she will also find time to stop work once in a while and enjoy life.'

Emma felt stunned, then embarrassed and then a horrible creeping sense of guilt. She looked around to see the room shell-shocked. They were all staring at the fire, out of the window, at the floor; everyone was avoiding Roger's gaze. Roger, meanwhile, had turned pink.

'The residue of my estate, I give to my sisters Julia and Virginia,' concluded Collins. 'And that, ladies and gentlemen, is my client's last will and testament.'

'And you are absolutely sure this is the most up-to-date will in existence?' asked Roger, his brows compressed anxiously.

'Quite sure,' said Collins decisively, averting his eyes momentarily when he saw the fury in Roger's face.

'And what about this place?' asked Tom.

'Winterfold is officially a company asset,' said Collins. 'The CEO of the company has traditionally lived here.' He looked

28

over at Emma encouragingly who just looked at the ground and shook her head. Suddenly, everyone started talking at once. The family had started breaking into small splinter groups, whispering intently. To Emma they were deafening.

'He can't be serious, can he . . .?'

'I can't believe he would . . .'

'What on earth was he thinking . . .?'

'I felt sure he would have . . .'

Roger was standing over Collins, his eyes scanning the will keenly. Cassandra walked over to the window, pulled out her mobile phone and pressed it to her ear. Emma walked to Saul's club chair and sat down heavily.

'Wow, Em! Well done to you!' said Tom. 'I mean, I have to say I'm surprised, but hey, it's his money. So when's the party begin?'

Emma laughed nervously. 'I'm not sure everyone's in the mood to party,' she said quietly. She looked down and saw her hands were trembling.

'So?' Emma looked up to see Roger had moved over to her. He was a big man and his physical presence would have been enough to intimidate most people on a good day, but today he was bristling with barely-checked emotion, a little boy who has not been given the train set he had been promised. When she had been a little girl, Emma had always seen her Uncle Roger as a grown-up, as a rather strict figure of authority. But she was not a little girl now. Over the last few years, Emma had faced some of the world's most powerful men, telling them in so many words why their companies were failing, listing their shortcomings and weaknesses. She was not easily scared.

'Roger, please,' she said, 'I am as surprised as you. I can tell you that this certainly was not in my five-year plan.'

'So you're not interested in the shareholding?'

She bristled. *Did he expect her to give it to him?*

29

'Not in so much that I have time to run the company,' she said diplomatically, not denying to herself the prickle of excitement. 'I have my life in Boston, as you know.'

'So how much is it going to cost us?' chimed Rebecca, attempting a smile, but baring her teeth instead.

Emma shook her head and put her hands out in front of her.

'Roger, Rebecca. This is all a bit much for me to take in at the moment.'

'But you can't just sit there and . . .' began Rebecca, before being cut off by Tom.

'Exactly how much is "in remainder"?' he asked Collins.

The solicitor suppressed a smile. He could always predict the questions and from whom they would come; funny how the feckless son should be asking how much his doting mother would be getting. He sighed. There was nothing like money to break up even the most harmonious families.

'The remainder is what's left of the estate,' he said patiently. 'It will take some time to quantify, of course. Obviously death duties and fees and so on have to be paid.'

'What about the art at the Milford offices? There's a couple of Matisse sketches, a small Miro . . .' Julia added hopefully, looking up at a colourful abstract above the fireplace.

'I suspect they are Saul's own, in which case they pass to Emma.'

Julia's face said it all: ashen and tight-lipped. She had always coveted the eclectic art in Saul's home and had assumed he would send it her way, but not even the pieces in his office were destined to be hers. She looked as if she had been slapped. Cassandra, meanwhile, was sitting silently in the corner. Her face was expressionless. But she did not seem to be rejoicing in the gift of the villa in Provence.

Emma turned to see her mother. 'You can't possibly be

thinking of keeping the shares,' said Virginia slowly. 'Roger has been Milford's creative director for over twenty years.'

Emma gaped at her. She had never been very supportive as a mother, but this seemed a low blow even for Virginia. Saul's bequest had – presumably – made Emma a rich woman, but even now she could not be happy for her, in fact she was thinking of her brother and his position.

'I haven't made any decisions about anything, Mother,' said Emma shortly. 'But when I do, you and Roger will be the first to know.'

She moved away and walked up to Cassandra, who was looking ready to leave.

'You've got Les Fleurs,' said Emma softly. 'How wonderful!'

Cassandra smiled thinly. 'I couldn't have asked for better, could I?' she said. Emma noticed that her eyes were not shining. 'Now if you'll excuse me, I have to make an urgent call to the office.'

Emma flinched as Roger put his hand on her shoulder.

'To the victor the spoils, eh?' he said, with a forced jovial manner. 'I know you have business experience, so I know you'll weigh up the options and do what's right for Milford. I know you'll make the right decision. You take your time.'

He squeezed her shoulder and walked towards the door, leading Rebecca who was shooting daggers.

But Emma did not need to take her time. If Saul's will had just made her a rich woman, then that was something to be thankful for. But had Saul expected her to come back to Milford and run the company? The whole afternoon had been ghastly and she could only imagine what a lifetime back here would be like. She wanted to go back to Boston, to Mark and her own life as quickly as she could.

3

Cassandra Grand had a dream, a dream that she had been nurturing since the age of thirteen. She wanted to be the greatest fashion legend since Coco Chanel, a style maven whose name was a billion dollar brand. She wanted to be fashion's Martha Stewart, a female Tom Ford. She wanted it all and she wasn't going to let anyone stand in her way. Magazines were just the very start for Cassandra; she was already recognized as one of the top editors in the world and now she was ready to expand her empire. Some of the top luxury brands in the world had already come knocking, begging her to take on a consultation role, while her talent as a stylist meant she was still greatly in demand to style the hottest fashion advertising campaigns in the world. But there was one fly in the ointment: Emma Bailey. *That bitch.* Taking control of Milford had been a major part of Cassandra's carefully laid plans. She'd known for years that the company was ripe for re-invention and had planned to rebrand it *Cassandra Grand by Milford*. Obviously, after a few years she would drop the fusty *Milford* label entirely, but by then, Cassandra Grand would be the hottest name in fashion. But of course, it hadn't happened that way. Silly, foolish

Saul had put a stop to that and it made her almost physically sick with fury; all the time, energy and expense she had wasted playing the dutiful niece! All those lunches at Claridge's, the gifts on birthdays and at Christmas, the bottle of Petrus she had been sent by a French importer which had gone directly to Saul. And those dull family Christmas days spent with the family at Saul's chalet in Gstaad when she could have been on a lover's yacht in St Barts or at a friend's villa in Mustique.

And hadn't Saul promised the company to *her*? She remembered his words vividly.

'One day, all this will be yours.'

He had *promised* her. He *couldn't* just have meant the villa. Saul's treachery, for that is how she viewed it, was like a body blow so hard it made her muscles ache. It was she, Cassandra, who was in fashion! She was the one with the contacts, the vision! She could have made Milford into a global force. The new Dior – bigger! And now it was over.

The lift pinged, the light flicked to 'Floor 25' and Cassandra was brought back to the present. *This isn't over*, she thought, as the doors whooshed open and she strode into the *Rive* office. *This is just a setback.* Her spike heels clacked along as she looked out of the floor-to-ceiling windows at the north side of the office. At least she had her job; it would see her through while she regrouped and planned how she would seize Milford back. And no jumped-up, middle-management nobody like Emma Bailey was going to stand in her way. *Yes*, she thought smiling, *there was always another way.*

'Morning, Cassandra!' said a voice to her left. The smile dropped from her face and she glared back, annoyed by the interruption to her thoughts. She was unusually late for a Monday morning and the office was already buzzing. Normally she would have been first in, usually before 8 a.m., but she had been obliged to start the day with a breakfast with the

MD of Cartier. She enjoyed beginning the day alone, free from disturbances to collect her thoughts. To plan, to strategize. Cassandra was not a team player; she rated her talent and vision so far beyond the rest of her staff that she would gladly have crafted the whole magazine herself if time allowed. But even though she had cherry-picked her staff, she still sometimes felt as if she was dealing with amateurs and halfwits. As she passed through the glass doors into her plush office, her senior assistant Lianne met her halfway.

'Art need to see you immediately,' she said handing her a coffee; black, filter, scalding hot. Cassandra nodded and moved into her corner office to take her seat. It was a beautiful space, painted Dior grey and interior-designed to her specification, minimalist and chic. She sat down at her Perspex desk, uncluttered except for a white orchid, one in-tray full of layouts, another stuffed with party invitations and a pile of daily newspapers. Lianne had helpfully put the *Time* cutting announcing Cassandra as 'twelfth most important woman in fashion' in the centre of the glass. She picked it up and dropped it into the wastepaper bin without looking at it. *Twelfth,* she thought with annoyance.

Cassandra picked up the phone and punched Lianne's extension.

'Can you get Laura and Jeremy to step through as well. I want an update on the Friday's cover-shoot.'

She was behind and it was a feeling Cassandra hated. She loved doing the shows; she never believed those editors who said the collections were a chore that needed to be suffered, but it kept her out of the office for days at a time. Cassandra was a control freak, she hated even the smallest detail of *Rive* being passed to the printers without her express permission and she didn't let a minute go by when she didn't know exactly where the magazine was up to. She looked up at the wall in front of her where miniature pages from next month's issue had been pinned up: pages of glorious fashion by some of the world's best photographers, opinion pieces by some of London's most celebrated columnists. But there was one glaring hole: the cover story. She glanced at her calendar. It was down to the wire.

David Stern, *Rive*'s art director, came in first, wearing a black polo neck and holding a thick stack of photo paper.

'I hope that's the Phoebe shoot you have in your hands,' said Cassandra.

Stern nodded. 'I got Xavier to send over what he had. Awkward bastard. Said he wanted to retouch his selection before he would send anything.'

'To which you replied . . .' asked Cassandra.

'Send over everything you have *tout suite* before Cassandra makes sure you never work for any magazine in the company ever again.'

'Good answer,' she said with a thin smile. She hated the power which photographers seemed to bestow upon themselves. If it wasn't enough dealing with stroppy publicists, managers and agents, now she had photographers throwing diva hissy-fits. Well, Cassandra employed a zero-tolerance policy. If they wouldn't play ball – her ball – then they would be dropped without a backward look. *Rive* was bigger than the sum of its parts; they could get a pensioner with a Brownie camera to shoot a fashion story and he'd be hailed as 'the next big thing'.

David reverently laid three A4 prints on Cassandra's desk, the pick of the shots from the Phoebe Fenton shoot. She stood up, and rested the palms of her hands on the Perspex to examine them. They were sensational. All shot three-quarter length, with Phoebe wearing just a pair of high-waisted cream jodhpurs so tight that they looked as if they'd been painted on.

In two of the frames, her long chestnut hair was covering

her breasts, with just a cream triangle of navel visible. In the final image her hair had been blown away from her, fanning out like some Greek goddess. *Christ she looks good*, thought Cassandra. Phoebe Fenton had been *the* supermodel of the moment a decade earlier, but that was then and twelve months ago Cassandra would have laughed if she had been mooted to appear in British *Rive*. After Phoebe's surprise marriage to Ethan Krantz, a New York property billionaire seven years ago, Phoebe had retreated into a world of Upper East Side gallery openings and benefit dinners for land-mine victims. Far too conservative, far too worthy and way, way past it. Phoebe belonged to the US edition of *Rive* with their airbrushed fantasy versions of big Hollywood stars and wholesome celebrities. But things had changed. Choosing who to put on your cover was not just about *who* but *when*. Timing was everything and a sudden scandal in a cover model's private life could add 50,000 to a magazine's sales; much more if your timing made it an exclusive. And Phoebe Fenton's private life had suddenly gone into meltdown; her husband Ethan had run off with a Ukranian model thirty years his junior. Phoebe and Ethan were now in the throes of a nasty divorce and Ethan was fighting hard for the custody of their three-year-old little girl, Daisy. Rumours were everywhere of Phoebe's behaviour: drink, bisexuality, orgies, drugs. In the space of weeks, Phoebe had gone from all-American girl to all-American fuck-up. But up until now there hadn't been anything solid beyond one grainy long-lens paparazzo photograph taken in St Barts of someone who may, or may not have been Phoebe Fenton kissing a mystery brunette and thus Phoebe's public persona was as beautiful and gracious as it had always been.

Cassandra smiled. The images in front of her were the sexiest pictures she had ever seen of Phoebe. She congratulated herself for having picked Xavier to shoot her because these photos were fresh and fierce, erotic even. Shot by another photographer, Phoebe's naked breasts might have looked salacious, but in the hands of the man the fashion industry was calling the new Helmut Newton they looked delicate, exquisite, artistic. Pure fashion.

At that moment Laura Hildon, *Rive's* pretty blonde fashion editor, ran through the door, already talking.

'What do you think?' she gabbled. 'It was the best we could do, she hated everything except the jodhpurs.' She looked anxiously at Cassandra who was now holding the bare-breasted shot aloft.

'What happened to the Vuitton waistcoat?' she said icily. 'I told you we needed to get Vuitton on the cover this issue. They haven't had a cover credit in nine months and they are beginning to get tetchy.'

Laura looked stricken.

'Actually, I don't know what happened to the Vuitton top. I came into work to collect the clothes for the shoot on Friday morning and it had gone.'

'Gone?' asked Cassandra.

'I think someone took it from the rail on Thursday night,' said Laura, embarrassed. 'I should probably bring this up another time but I think Francesca has been taking things from my selection for her shoots.'

Cassandra flashed a look at David, back to Laura and then waved a hand to dismiss it. 'We'll sort this out later. In the meantime, what are the inside shots like?'

It was Laura's turn to shoot a look to David.

'Haven't you told her?' she asked breathlessly.

David cleared his throat before taking a seat on Cassandra's sofa.

'It started off normally enough. Laura managed to get her in a couple of dresses, then after lunch the stylist turns up.

37

Her stylist, I should add. Someone called Romilly, I've never heard of. They kept disappearing into the loos and they were glugging champagne like it was water. Phoebe went . . . well, she went a little weird after that. By five o'clock Romilly was saying that Phoebe wanted to show off her body. That she wanted to do her last great set of nudes.'

'I think she was drunk,' whispered Laura.

Cassandra couldn't stop herself from smiling.

'What's the copy like?' she asked, snapping back into business mode. 'Jeremy?'

Jeremy Pike, her features editor, was tall, slender and effeminate, dressed as always in a slim-cut suit and a neckscarf.

'Sorry I'm late, Cassandra,' he said deferentially. 'But I don't think you'll mind when you see this.' He waved a sheaf of typed paper in the air. 'I've just been waiting for Vicky's copy to come in. She called me up over the weekend to tell me how the interview had gone and she was beside herself. Anyway – she's just filed. Have a read of that.'

Cassandra read in silence, occasionally lifting her head to look at Jeremy, her eyes wide. Vicky Thomas had outdone herself this time. Vicky was one of the country's best celebrity interviewers. Over fifty and overweight, she was the antithesis of everything Cassandra usually demanded in a *Rive* reporter. But an appearance that suggested a jolly cuddly aunt was just a ruse she'd use to get celebrities to let their guard down. Many stars who should have known better had fallen into her honey-trap and admitted to things they had never told their own partners. Publicists hated her; it could take years to undo the damage she caused. And now it appeared that nice Auntie Vicky had weaved her magic once again.

'She interviewed her in Claridge's before the shoot on Thursday,' said Jeremy grinning. 'Apparently it was so dull,

Vicky said she might as well have handed her a press release. Luckily Vicky was at the shoot and suggested they go for a drink afterwards. That's when it got interesting.'

Cassandra looked up from the copy. 'I'll say it did. She asked her about the mystery brunette photo.'

Jeremy nodded.

'Yes, Phoebe actually admitted to being bisexual,' he squealed, clapping his hands in delight. 'She says *everyone's* at it these days. She even named names.'

'Was the tape running?'

'All the time,' smiled Jeremy.

Cassandra's eyes scanned the page, her eyes growing wider as she read Vicky's expertly-worded piece. It was perfectly balanced, managing to stay suitably fawning, while still letting the reader know exactly what was going on. She read out a passage to the stunned office.

'" . . . Accompanying us to Annabel's was the beautiful Romilly Dunn, the stunning New York stylist known for her colourful sex life, who proceeded to get cosy with Phoebe as the night rolled on."'

'Vicky says she can amend the copy to say Phoebe and Romilly were all over one another if you like,' said Jeremy, 'but she wanted to run it past you first.'

Cassandra knew she had more than a cover story here. Her passion and her expertise was fashion, but her journalistic skills were much wider than that. Ever since she had been parachuted in to British *Rive* three years earlier with a mission to bring the magazine back from the edge of extinction, she had constantly surprised the industry with what legendary *Vanity Fair* editor Tina Brown referred to as 'the mix', running beautiful fashion pages next to heavyweight intellectual essays, shopping tips next to campaigning reportage. Aware that the UK market was something of an also-ran in the fashion magazine arena compared to the mighty American publications, Cassandra had worked hard to harness London's creativity, mixing high society with high fashion and street-level cool, bringing in artists, philosophers, DJs and schoolgirls, including them all in the super-luxe *Rive* world. Each month she made *Rive* an event, each issue contained a surprise, whether it was running shocking photo-spreads among Moscow tenements, or convincing Damien Hirst to design the sets for her couture shoots. At a time when magazines were getting more anodyne with airbrushed photo-shoots and fawning celebrity interviews, Cassandra dared to push her luck, constantly delivering the surprising and the innovative. It was an audacious, not to mention expensive and highly risky approach, but it had paid off. *Rive* wasn't just the number one fashion magazine, it was the number one women's glossy. And this month Phoebe Fenton was going to take them to a new level.

'This is absolute dynamite,' said Cassandra in a low voice, eager to now end the meeting and run the copy past the company lawyer.

'OK, back to work,' she barked, waving a hand in dismissal and swivelling around in her chair. She snatched up the phone and was just about to call the legal department when she noticed the red light on her second line was flashing.

'I didn't want to disturb you while you were in the meeting,' said Lianne apologetically, 'but Phoebe Fenton has been on the phone twice in the last ten minutes. She's still holding.'

Cassandra groaned, holding her hand over the phone's mouthpiece as she debated whether to wait until she had called the lawyers. But curiosity got the better of her and it was nothing she couldn't handle.

'Put her through.'

There was a click, then Lianne's voice.

'I have Cassandra Grand for you, Ms Fenton.'

'Phoebe, darling,' purred Cassandra settling back into her ergonomic chair. She knew Phoebe a little, as they had met at numerous shows and fund-raisers over the years, but she wasn't a real acquaintance. Cassandra couldn't afford get too close to celebrities, for obvious reasons. One week they could be hotter than the sun, the next in fashion Siberia.

'Cassandra, honey, how are you?' said Phoebe warmly. 'Did you enjoy the shows?'

'Vintage Kors. Calvin was a little predictable. Some wonderful colours at Matthew Williamson and Zac Posen. It was a shame you were in London but then I'm sure you had great fun on our shoot.'

'Actually that's why I'm calling,' replied Phoebe.

'Yes, I'm so looking forward to seeing the shots,' said Cassandra enthusiastically. 'I love Xavier's work.'

There was a brief pause before Phoebe began again. Cassandra could tell Phoebe was picking her words very carefully.

'Cassandra . . . I'm a little concerned about how things went.'

A little late for that, darling, she thought.

'Oh, really?' said Cassandra, feigning surprise. 'I heard it went well. Xavier is a genius. We were very lucky to get him in London when the New York shows were on. He makes women look so strong. So beautiful.'

'Yes, I was wondering if we could talk about that. I'm nervous about the shots and the implications of the inter-view. I was wondering if I could . . .'

'Darling, you know we never give copy approval. Once we start, everyone wants it and then the whole magazine grinds to a halt,' replied Cassandra, cutting her short.

Phoebe paused again.

'Yes, I realize that. There's just a few things I'd like to

explain. In private? I was wondering if you could come over to my hotel for lunch.'

'I'd love to, Phoebe,' said Cassandra, beginning to enjoy herself, 'but it's London Fashion Week now. I've got to see the Paul Smith show and I have crisis after crisis to deal with here.'

'Cassandra,' said Phoebe, failing to disguise the annoyance in her voice, 'we go back a long way and that's why I'm calling. I don't want to get lawyers involved when we don't have to.'

'Lawyers?' laughed Cassandra. 'Why on earth would we need to involve lawyers?'

'Can you come to the Met for one o'clock? I'm in the penthouse.'

In that case I don't feel too sorry for you, thought Cassandra.

'I have a lunch at Cipriani but I could drop by at 12.30.'

'See you then.'

'Looking forward to it.'

You have no idea how much, thought Cassandra, and hung up.

Sitting in the back of the Mercedes, Cassandra flipped open her compact and put on some lip gloss. She allowed herself a small smile at the face looking back at her. Many women would feel inferior meeting a supermodel for lunch but Cassandra honestly didn't feel that way. She didn't have their freakish symmetry or gangly frame, but she was undeniably a beauty, with high cheekbones and a feline slant to her vivid green eyes. Her nose was a touch too long, her chin a little too pointed and at five feet eight inches tall she tipped the scales at eight stone dead – to go a pound over might mean not fitting into the sample clothes. And as a modern style icon, that would be career suicide. Not that she didn't have to work hard at it. Daily Pilates. Twice weekly tennis lessons. Three times a week Joel, *the* top session hair-dresser, came to her Knightsbridge apartment at 6.30 a.m. to blow-dry her long dark glossy hair. Plus she visited the Mayr Clinic in Austria once a year to eat spelt bread and Epsom salts for ten days, returning with glowing skin, a flat stomach and an uncontrollable desire for ice cream. No, Cassandra Grand was not a drop-dead beauty, but she was the pinnacle of chic. Impeccably dressed in a simple, under-stated style, she wore no jewellery except for a large diamond stud in each ear lobe, a gift from a lover. In fact, except for the La Perla underwear, she had paid for nothing she was wearing: her entire outfit were gifts from fashion houses and luxury goods companies desperate for endorsement from one of the world's most stylish women.

She snapped the compact shut as the car pulled up on Park Lane.

As Cassandra stepped out of the lift on the 10th floor into the penthouse of the Metropolitan, she could see the smudge of Hyde Park on the horizon through floor-to-ceiling windows. Phoebe was sitting on the cream couch wearing blue jeans and a white shirt. Long wavy hair the colour of coffee beans was tied in a ponytail. In her late thirties, Phoebe Fenton was still extremely beautiful, but her eyes looked tired and distracted.

'Phoebe, darling! You look wonderful,' said Cassandra, kissing her lightly on both cheeks.

'Mineral water?' asked Phoebe, reaching for a crystal tumbler.

Cassandra nodded. 'Still.'

Cassandra sat carefully on the sofa opposite Phoebe and crossed her legs elegantly under her. *I think I'm going to enjoy this* she thought, accepting her drink with a smile. Phoebe no longer had an agent – in fact negotiations for the cover-shoot had been done through her PA – and that instantly gave

Cassandra the upper hand. A big Hollywood publicist could get you over a barrel. If you upset one star on their roster, they could and would refuse access to any of their charges. You wouldn't even get photo approval for an ancient head-shot. But now Cassandra was in the driving seat.

'So have you read the interview?' asked Phoebe.

Cassandra gave a little deliberate laugh and shook her head.

'Wasn't the interview on Friday night?' she asked, 'Vicky won't even have transcribed the tapes yet. You need to give these big-name journalists at least a fortnight to get their copy in.'

Phoebe ran a finger around the edge of her tumbler.

'Well, I'm sure you've been told already, but I was a little, well, *manic* at the shoot on Friday.'

Cassandra raised an eyebrow.

Phoebe looked down at her glass again.

'You see, my friend Romilly popped by, she often comes to shoots with me. She dresses me for the red carpet and I feel comfortable with her, but she can be a bit . . . a bit wild. But she's a good friend and I need all the ones I can get at the moment.'

Phoebe looked up at Cassandra and the look of sadness in her brown eyes almost melted Cassandra. Almost. Phoebe sighed and continued.

'We had some drinks and I guess I was a little too loose-lipped.' She leant forward and put her elbows on her knees. 'Cassandra, I've just been diagnosed with bipolar disorder,' she said quietly.

'Manic depression?' said Cassandra. Phoebe nodded.

'I don't know if the separation triggered it, but the doctors say it's a chemical imbalance in the brain. It's a vicious circle. I'm depressed so I've been drinking, but drinking seems to bring on these extreme mood swings. I go a bit crazy. I say things I don't mean. I've just been put on lithium to keep it under control but it doesn't seem to have stabilized me yet.'

She stood up and walked over to the huge window.

'I've never met Vicky, your journalist before. She seems a nice woman but you never know, right?'

'Vicky is one of the best celebrity profilers in the UK,' said Cassandra with a hint of reproach.

'I'm just thinking she could paint an untrue picture.'

'I'm sure Vicky will be fair.'

Phoebe went over and sat down next to Cassandra, so very close that Cassandra felt uncomfortable.

'Cassandra, please,' she whispered. 'You don't understand. Ethan is fighting for custody of Daisy and he's fighting hard. Falling around in nightclubs, doing nude photo-shoots. If I look like a bad mom his team of very expensive lawyers are going to tear me apart. I did this shoot as a favour to *Rive*. I don't want it to make them take my baby away.'

Cassandra suppressed an internal snort. *A favour!* No one did anything in this industry without some ulterior motive. No doubt Phoebe wanted a set of sexy pictures to make her husband see what he was missing and come back to her. Well, the plan had back-fired.

'Phoebe honey, don't worry,' said Cassandra. 'I haven't seen the copy, but when I do, I'll make sure it's all completely complimentary. Our readers are going to love you.'

Phoebe huffed like a little girl denied her pony.

'Well I hope so, because I don't want to get difficult.' She flashed Cassandra a look that betrayed her simpering, girl-next-door persona. After all, thought Cassandra, no one got to the top of the tree in modelling by being a walk-over.

'I'm sure my attorney would go mad if he knew I was even talking to you. But I'll get an injunction on the magazine if I have to,' she said fiercely.

45

'Listen, I think we're all getting a little carried away,' said Cassandra smoothly, putting out a placatory hand. 'So you were a little drunk at the photo-shoot. Your friend may have been a little badly behaved. So what? *Rive* is a fashion magazine not the *National Enquirer*. We are here to celebrate people, darling, not destroy them.'

Phoebe looked a little more at ease.

'If you like I can email over the shots when I get them.'

'Is it all right if I look at the copy too?'

'You know we don't do that, Phoebe.'

'Please. For me?' she said, putting her head on one side.

Jesus, this woman is thirty-eight, thought Cassandra. *She'll be saying 'Pretty please, with sugar on top' next!*

'When are you back in New York?'

'Saturday.'

'We won't have layouts for at least a fortnight. How about I Fed-Ex something over to you then. Just so you can have a look at it?'

'I'm really grateful, Cassandra. I'm having a difficult time at the moment. My shrink says Romilly's not good for me. But it was tough being in that marriage. Claustrophobic.'

Cassandra touched her on the knee gently.

'He'll be sorry when he sees these photographs. You'll look amazing and everyone will be jealous. Trust me.'

In the back seat of her car Cassandra took out her phone. *An alcoholic, drug-taking bisexual and she blames it on bipolar! The nerve of it!* She punched in David Stern's number.

'David, I have a lunch and then the Paul Smith show so I won't be back until at least 3 p.m. But in the meantime there are a couple of things I want you to do.'

'Shoot.'

'Talk to Jeremy, talk to the subs. Tell them to rush the Phoebe Fenton copy through as it is. Then I want you to work on the cover. Go with the bare breasts image. Main cover-line: "Phoebe Fenton Bares All". I want "Bares All" in gold block foil across the cover; make sure it covers her nipples. I want this issue to *fly* off the shelves, not be *taken* off it.'

There was a silence at the other end of the line.

'Are you sure this is a good idea?' asked David.

Cassandra had asked herself that very question. It was a gamble, certainly. Some advertisers wouldn't be happy and some of her more conservative subscribers would be on the phone. But the fashion market was just the same as any other market: sex sells, and after a disappointing audit on last month's issue she needed to pull something big out of the bag. For, despite her position of power and influence as editor of *Rive*, Cassandra knew her kingdom rested on shifting sands. Editors were expendable, pawns used by management to cover their failings. And more than anything, UK glossy editors had a shelf-life; after forty, maybe forty-five, they tended to mysteriously disappear. It was a little better in the States. So the US *Rive* boss Glenda McMahon was still wielding her power at fifty, but a few dud issues and even she was instantly replaceable. What Cassandra was painfully aware of was that with the exception of perhaps Carmel Snow and Diane Vreeland, editors rarely left a legacy beyond their tenure. And it was a legacy she wanted.

'What do you mean "is this a good idea"?' snapped Cassandra.

David paused again, weighing his words carefully.

'Is this not going to crucify Phoebe? The tabloids will take this and rip her to shreds. I didn't think that was our agenda.'

'For a queen, you're very uptight, David,' she sneered. 'Our agenda is to *set* the agenda. To sell issues we have to be bold, we have to be provocative. We have to take chances.'

'Well this is certainly that.'

'Just do it, David,' she barked and snapped the phone shut.

And finally, after one hell of a gruesome week, she allowed herself a laugh.

4

'Good morning, Gretchen.'

It was 7.45 a.m. Although Price Donahue's working hours did not officially start until 8 a.m., there was already a hum of activity around the office. Emma herself had been there since 7 a.m., trying to get through a backlog of work which had piled up since her trip to England.

'Oh God, morning Emma,' said Emma's secretary breathlessly, rushing into her office and presenting her boss with a large bunch of red and yellow tulips. 'Sorry, I wanted to get in before you this morning so I could get these in a vase.'

'What's all this for?' she smiled, gathering the flowers up.

'Your birthday, silly. You make me remember when half of corporate Boston is born so I think I can remember my own boss's.'

Emma smiled and kissed her on the cheek. Gretchen was forgetful, disorganized and her time-keeping was atrocious, but she had a kind heart, a rare thing at any level in business, thought Emma as she watched the girl scuttle off to find a vase.

'Who's twenty-one again?'

Emma looked up to see her friend Cameron Moore, a

manager in the retail division, pop her head around the door. Her perfectly blow-dried mane of dark hair hung to one side, like a shampoo advert.

'Welcome back, sweetie,' she said. 'Here, a birthday gift.'

Cameron handed Emma a small orange box tied with a chocolate ribbon. She smiled. Emma usually bought clothes because they were smart, not because they were designer names, but she still recognized the famous bright orange of Hermès. She opened the box and a gorgeous silk scarf fluttered to the table.

'Oh, Cam, how wonderful! Thank you,' she said, getting up to give her friend a kiss on the cheek. 'I can't believe you remembered.'

'Are you kidding?' said Cameron, rolling her eyes, 'That secretary of yours has been bombarding everyone with emails for about a month! But enough of that, how was England?'

Emma sighed, looking down at the scarf, examining the stitching.

'Eventful. I've been given a company.'

Cameron's face lit up and Emma immediately regretted saying it. The news would be around the building in minutes and eyebrows would be raised. Total commitment had to be shown to Price Donahue at all times.

Cameron closed the door and hushed her voice.

'The family company? Milford?'

Emma nodded. As Cameron's area of expertise was luxury retailing she was interested to hear her friend's thoughts on the company even though she personally had little interest in her new shareholding.

'Your uncle *gave* it to you?' said Cameron incredulously. 'The whole thing?'

'A controlling interest, yes. It was a bit awkward really,' she shrugged. 'Still, it was nice to see my family, even if the circumstances could have been better.'

'Family?' hissed Cameron. 'Forget about the family! Jeez, Emma, you've got your own *company*! This is enormous!'

Cameron sat down on Emma's desk, as if stunned by the news.

Emma laughed at her friend's reaction, but it did make her think.

'So what do you think I should do?'

'Do? You should go straight in to see Davies right now and resign!'

'Resign? I have no intention of giving up work here, it's . . .'

Cameron interrupted, nodding her head.

'Yes, yes, I know, it's your life. But, Em, haven't you ever dreamed of getting off this merry-go-round? Haven't you ever wished you could stop telling fat old duffers how to run their companies and do it yourself?'

'Cam, I've even taken up golf to get this partnership,' she laughed.

'Golf? Emma! This is your big chance. What, you want to spend the rest of your life doing all the hard work for Daniel Davies and his little clique, hoping they'll throw you a bone someday?'

Cameron picked up Emma's scarf and waved it at her.

'OK, so Milford might not be Hermès right now. But honey, it *could* be.'

Emma looked her friend doubtfully.

'I don't think so.'

Cameron smiled.

'With you in charge, sweetie, anything's possible.'

Emma was sitting back at her desk at Price Donahue, trying to concentrate on a spreadsheet relating to a possible merger between two haulage companies, but for once, the jumble of figures was failing to hold her attention.

Looking at the orange Hermès box still on her desk she

51

reached into her handbag and pulled out a letter that had been given to her by Anthony Collins at Milford and which she had read once on the flight home.

Dear Emma,
If you're reading this letter it means I have gone, as JM Barrie would say, on an awfully big adventure. Here's hoping I had an interesting demise and that we managed to hook up for one last game of chess. We don't see each other as much as I'd like these days but I'm so proud of your accomplishments in America. You certainly grabbed the land of opportunity by both hands. By now, you'll also know about my plans for Milford. They may come as a surprise to some in the family but in my heart I know that you will know what to do with the company. We all know I am more bon viveur than businessman, but I believe this is one decision I have got right.

I hope you don't see the opportunity as a burden. There is great satisfaction to be had in working for yourself and your family rather than for other people.

I believe you can do great things if only you believe in yourself.

With much love,
Saul

She stared thoughtfully out of the window before a ping made her look up: an incoming email.

'How was it? Mark.'

She folded the letter, put it back in her handbag and began typing.

'Interesting, to say the least. How about dinner to discuss?'

There was an instant reply. *'Dinner it is for the birthday girl. Eight?'*

She looked at her watch and groaned. She'd been so

wrapped in her own dramas that she'd forgotten to send out an important letter. It wouldn't do to slip up on anything right now; the partnerships were due to be announced tomorrow. She called out to her secretary.

'Gretchen? Have you done that letter of engagement for the Frost Group yet? It was supposed to go this morning.'

Gretchen put her head around the door, a puzzled expression on her face.

'It's already gone,' she said. 'Mark came to speak to me about that a couple of days ago. Said the letter was going out in his name.'

'Really? When was this?'

'Tuesday. Sorry, Emma, but he's a partner. I didn't query it.'

'No, no, it's fine,' said Emma quickly. 'I'd just forgotten he was going to do it, that's all.'

When Gretchen had gone, she swivelled round to look out of the window. For some unaccountable reason, there was a sick feeling in her stomach. Was she being paranoid? Why had Mark sent the Frost letter out in his own name? OK. Maybe it was protocol because he was a partner but she had hustled hard for that piece of business.

She picked up the phone and dialled Mark's extension but it went straight to message.

'Emma. I thought you'd like to know,' said Gretchen popping her head around the door and whispering. 'It looks like partnerships are being announced today.'

'Today!' said Emma. 'I thought it was going to be tomorrow, Friday.'

Gretchen came into the office and closed the door. She was the hub of the PA grapevine; a better gossip than she was secretary and Emma didn't doubt that her sources were good.

'Jason Rich has already been seen coming out of Daniel Davies' office grinning like a Cheshire cat. Apparently a couple of other senior managers have just had meetings chalked in for after lunch.'

For the rest of the day Emma couldn't settle as all afternoon senior managers had been going up to see the managing partner Daniel Davies. When Gretchen put the call through at 5 p.m. asking her to go and see Davies, Emma could hardly stand the suspense.

This is it, thought Emma feeling sick. She stood up and smoothed down her skirt.

She tried to calm herself, but had never felt so nervous about anything in her whole life. Three years at Stanford. Another two at Harvard; Emma had always known she was not as academically gifted as her father, a Fellow at Oxford, so she had to work damn hard to the exclusion of everything else. No social life. No boyfriends. The work never stopped once she got to Price Donahue with six years of ninety-hour weeks, eleven and a half months a year. But a partnership at twenty-nine! It would mean instant respect around the city and instant respect in corporate America, not to mention a high six-figure salary. In ten years' time she could pick and choose board directorships at some of the biggest blue chip companies in the world. And best of all, it would have been all of her own making, not like the brash, young CEOs she met on the corporate circuit who only held the job because their daddies had held the position and their daddies before that. With a lurch, she realized that she was also thinking about Milford. *Handed to me on a plate*. Where was the victory, the glory in that?

She went to Daniel Davies' office on the top floor and tried to read his face the minute she walked through the door. He was sitting behind his desk, furiously scribbling on a yellow legal pad with a silver fountain pen. He was forty-five but his thick black hair was greying, making him look older. His gaze, when he looked up at Emma, gave nothing away.

'Ah, Emma,' he said, putting his pen down carefully.

'Daniel,' said Emma feeling her palms go clammy.

'Have a seat and I'll get straight to the point. You know we've been extremely pleased with you over the last twelve months. Client feedback has been excellent from many of your projects and we always like having a Harvard Baker Scholar on the team,' he said, referring to the prestigious award given to the top 5 per cent of students from the business school.

A flock of butterflies took flight in Emma's stomach.

'Thank you,' she said, trying to sound nonchalant.

'But despite my enormous respect for your abilities, I'm afraid you are not going to be invited to join the partnership this year.'

It was as if she had been kicked. She felt a thickness in her throat.

'I see,' she said evenly, fighting back her emotions. Now was not the time to fall apart – a tearful scene would only confirm their decision.

'I wonder if you could expand on that?' she asked. 'I know it was competitive this year, but some feedback might be useful.'

She was digging her nails into her palm, but managed to meet Davies' eyes.

He averted his gaze slightly.

'Of course,' he said slowly. 'Some partners simply felt that you were a little short of experience to make the jump to the next level. I'm sorry.'

Emma nodded. She had rehearsed a hundred times how she would respond to the news that she had not made partner. She knew the dignified response would be to thank him and leave the room immediately, but she had felt so sure. She had to know.

'Could I ask if it was a unanimous decision?'

She knew she was the strongest manager by a mile, she just *knew* it. But if the senior partners couldn't see it, then she was obviously wasting her time at the firm.

'I'm afraid so,' he said, examining his manicured finger-nails. 'Of course, the decision is taken by the board, but we take advice and recommendations from the partners you have worked most closely with.'

He paused and gave her a small encouraging smile.

'Everyone thinks you can do the job, Emma,' he said looking at her with his dark eyes.

'But some people think you could do with a little more maturity before you progress to the next stage.'

Emma could not hold it inside any longer.

'Who?' she asked weakly.

'Emma. Being a partner isn't just about doing the job. It's about bringing in business. Mark Eisner thinks you need to be more confident in social situations. You need to interact better with potential clients, be more aggressive with sales-manship.'

'Salesmanship?' repeated Emma, stunned. 'Only last week I brought in Frost Industries. I met PJ at a convention. He invited me to Vermont . . . It's worth a fortune in fees.' Her head was spinning. How could Mark, the man she was in love with, have betrayed her so brutally? He knew how much she had wanted this partnership. Only days ago, she had lain naked in his arms as he had told her she was the brightest talent in the firm. *Surely Daniel Davies was lying or mistaken?*

Davies raised an eyebrow. 'It was my understanding that Mark Eisner brought in that business and closed the deal. He told me so himself on Monday. We are grateful for your work on the pitch and I am sure you will be involved in the team that implements the work.'

She bit her lip knowing it was pointless to contest what David had said. She remembered how Mark had insisted on coming on the Vermont trip. At the time, she'd been flattered and excited. *'Bring me. Let's have a couple of nights in a five-star hotel on the company,'* he'd told her. But no: was he just looking for a way to steal her thunder? How much more of her work had he passed off as his own? *The bastard.*

'Emma. Given time, I, for one, think you have a future at Price Donahue,' said Davies sympathetically. 'You are only twenty-nine years old.'

'If you're good enough, you're old enough,' she whispered, her hands trembling.

They looked at each other, each knowing that Price Donahue was a company of Young Turks; you had your window of opportunity to make partner. If you didn't make it, you were history.

Without another word she got up and left the room.

She walked back to her office in silence, a short shake of the head all she needed to impart her news to Gretchen.

'Who did?' she asked, knowing Gretchen was popular with all the PAs and secretaries in the company.

'Pete Wise, Jack Johnson, Bob Hatch,' she said apologetically.

Pete Wise? The man was an idiot! And what business had Jack Johnson brought in? Despairing, Emma grabbed her coat and headed out into the cold Boston evening.

The tall office blocks of downtown soared up around her. In front, Boston harbour shimmered like a vat of ink. Suddenly she felt very small and alone.

Hearing footsteps behind her on the pavement, she turned to see Mark running after her, his breath puffing white clouds up to the skyline behind him.

'Em! Emma!' he called, panting as he caught up with her.

'I'm sorry. I'm so sorry you didn't make it,' he said, putting a hand on her shoulder. 'I only found out early today.'

She jerked her arm away from him.

'Don't give me that, Mark,' she said turning on her heel. 'You knew.'

'Emma. Don't get so worked up. What's the big hurry? You'll make partner next year.'

She stopped and turned back, her eyes blazing.

'Next year? Or perhaps the next? Or whenever you let Daniel Davies know that I've suitably matured?'

Mark went pale.

'What are you talking about?'

'Davies told me about your recommendation, that I wasn't ready for partner. Not quite the same line of bullshit you have been feeding me for the past two months, is it?'

'Now come on,' he said, putting out his arms towards her, 'that's not what I said.'

'Oh really?' she challenged. 'He seemed very clear about it.'

'He's obviously taken what I said the wrong way . . .'

The snake, thought Emma, walking off in disgust. Mark chased her, grabbing her arm.

'Davies thinks you brought in the Frost Industries as well. Apparently you told him so. Or did he take that the wrong way as well?'

'Come on Em, let's talk about this. I thought we were going to have supper.'

'You betrayed me, Mark,' she said her voice thick with emotion. She was desperate not to cry but she could feel the tears welling up and stinging the backs of her eyes.

Mark turned away then faced her.

He looked as if he was about to keep denying it but finally he simply shrugged his shoulders.

'OK. You're right. I happen to think you're not ready to be a partner,' said Mark flatly. 'You are a good business strategist, but you're too soft. You don't even have the balls to fire that dim secretary of yours. You're an academic, not a corporate player. You're too nice to make tough decisions. You're just not ready to play with the big boys.'

'And Pete Wise is ready? Jack Johnson is ready? Does being on your softball team make you ready for partnership? I'm good, Mark,' she pleaded. 'You know it.'

'You do well at Harvard and you think the world owes you a favour,' he laughed scornfully.

'I trusted you to tell the truth,' she said quietly. 'I trusted you to tell people like Daniel Davies that I was the best. But no, you surround yourself with yes-men, idiots who will make you look good.'

'Fucking you could have cost me my job and this is all the thanks I get,' he said sneeringly.

Droplets of rains began to fall. They were like slaps on the cheek.

'Fucking me,' she repeated quietly. 'Is that what it was to you?'

Mark glared at her, then waved a dismissive hand in the air.

'Ah, you needy women are all the fucking same: Davies is right, you probably do want to run off and have a baby.'

She looked at him. The man she had whispered 'I love you' to, the man she had admired and trusted, had withered to a sycophant and a liar, a man who lived off other people's hard work and talent. She knew she was better than him, but there was little doubt he had played the game better than her. The likes of Daniel Davies would never know how much she put into the company, how much profit was directly down to her efforts and talent because operators like Mark Eisner took the glory for himself.

Waves were beginning to whip up in the harbour and rain was beginning to fall more heavily. Lights on the skyscrapers behind her sent a muddled saffron glow into the shallow puddles. She was angry, confused, but she was sure about one thing.

'I don't ever want to see you again,' she said as evenly as she could.

'Emma, don't be ridiculous,' he said, the tone of his voice softening. 'We have to work together.'

'Do we?'

She thought of Winterfold, that crazy jumble of antiques and bric-a-brac, she thought of the lazy village and its single red telephone box, all of it a million miles away from this corporate jungle. Saul had trusted her to take over his entire company. Saul had faith in her. And suddenly so did Emma.

Suddenly she had a clear sense of purpose, a sense of belonging.

'Happy birthday, Em,' said Mark, hunching his back against the rain.

She didn't turn round. She just kept on walking.

5

Briarton Court, one of England's top boarding schools for girls, had phenomenal resources at its disposal. Its one hundred acres of grounds housed an embarrassment of riches: indoor and outdoor swimming pools, a lacrosse pitch, running track and tennis and petanque courts. In the classroom, Briarton's pupils – who included the children of politicians, tycoons, ambassadors, billionaires, minor European royalty and good old-fashioned English aristocrats – had the opportunity to study everything from Calculus to Mandarin, not to mention the wide range of extracurricular activities. Apart from the annual ski trip to Klosters, the most popular after-school activity by far was Briarton's monthly careers evenings which pulled in guest speakers to give the Oxford Union a run for their money.

That evening's guest speaker looked around the packed lecture theatre and took a sip of water. Cassandra Grand had been tempted to turn down the invitation to speak as it was slap bang in the middle of London Fashion Week, but when she had heard that in the last two years alone the speakers had included two cabinet ministers, a Nobel prize winner, Richard Branson and an Oscar-winning actress, Cassandra had found time in her diary.

She was glad she had; forty-five glorious, uninterrupted minutes talking about her glamorous life as a glossy magazine editor and – the girls hung on every word of this – how she had got there. Cassandra would reveal how she had left a similar school to this one eighteen years ago with the sole ambition of wanting to work for an upmarket fashion magazine. How her six months as an intern at US *Rive* almost killed her: lugging suitcases full of clothes to fashion shoots, unpacking them and ironing them, getting shouted at by the photographer, the art director and the models, running here and there to fetch coffee, batteries or pick up dry-cleaning, then repacking the suitcases, lugging them back to the office late at night before neatly folding the clothes back into padded envelopes for return to the fashion houses. She would tell them how she got her big break when she met Carla Miller, one of the hottest fashion names of the early Nineties, back in London. Carla styled shoots, catwalk shows and advertising campaigns for the likes of Calvin Klein and Versace and it was she who gave Cassandra a job as her assistant. She would tell them how Carla grew so confident in Cassandra's abilities that she would recommend Cassandra for small jobs that she was too busy, or simply too important to undertake. And she would describe how another chance meeting with Alliance Chairman Isaac Grey landed her a job as fashion editor on US *Rive* where she rose through the ranks to become their deputy editor and eventually seconded to salvage the UK edition as their editor-in-chief. Cassandra had loved talking about herself and reliving her apparently charmed life, leaving out the ruthlessness, the back-stabbing and political chicanery that was really at the heart of her success.

She was, however, unprepared for the onslaught of

questions from her eager audience, hands darting into the air like fireflies.

'How much money do you earn?' asked a blonde in the front row.

'What famous people have you met?' asked a Chinese girl further back.

'Do you get free clothes?'

'Do you have to be thin?'

Cassandra looked out onto the sea of eager faces wondering how many of them would make it. The fashion cupboards of glossy magazines, of course, were full of pretty young things like these who wanted to play with clothes all day long, killing time until a rich banker husband came to sweep them off their feet and out to the country.

'What do you need to get to the very top, other than a fabulous fashion eye?' asked a beautiful blonde girl. Now she looked more promising. Her blouse looked vintage YSL and she had that indefinable X factor. Stylish, confident, focussed. Cassandra smiled at her.

'Having a fashion eye certainly helps, but it's not essential. People who reach the very top know how to pick the best team, how to get the most out of other people's talent. What the editor-in-chief needs is passion, determination and a way of thinking commercially. Knowing what the reader wants. Knowing how to woo advertisers like lovers . . .' She paused, realizing she had overstepped the mark, but she gave the blonde a helpful, conspiratorial smile. 'If you want to make it to the top, my dear,' she said, perfectly seriously, 'you need to know how to make money.'

At that point, Miss Lamarr, head of the Sixth Form rose to her feet. 'I think that's enough questions now,' she said briskly. 'Miss Grand is a very busy woman. I'm sure she has plenty of fashion shows to attend,' she added light-heartedly.

A burst of eager applause bounced around the wood-panelled room. As Cassandra descended from the stage, she was surrounded by girls wanting to shake her hand or get an autograph. A flustered Miss Lamarr motioned to Cassandra who escaped through a side-door into a quiet corridor, shutting the pandemonium behind her. She took a deep breath, energy buzzing around her body. She felt like a movie star.

'Hiiiiiii,' squealed a loud voice to Cassandra's left. Before she could even turn, a lanky female body wrapped itself around her, almost toppling her over.

'Can you believe they wouldn't let me watch the lecture?' gushed the voice, not releasing the embrace. 'No year nines allowed, apparently. Rules are rules even if it's your mother speaking they said!'

'Darling, how are you?' said Cassandra, disentangling herself, before kissing the girl warmly on the cheek. Cassandra hadn't seen her daughter Ruby since Christmas and couldn't believe how much she had changed in only eight weeks. She had always been tall and gangly, but Cassandra was convinced she must have grown another inch since New Year. Already she was five feet eight and even the drab Briarton school uniform could not disguise her blossoming figure. *A size six*, thought Cassandra, trying not to feel envious: the perfect sample size. If there was one thing Ruby's father had given her, it was good genes, with olive skin, raven hair spilling down her back and eyes that could change from grape green to emerald depending on the light and time of day. She would have looked like Pocahontas were it not for a long vivid orange streak across Ruby's fringe.

'What on earth is that?' she exclaimed in horror.

'I know,' said Ruby, shrugging her shoulders. 'It didn't quite work out as I imagined. Sienna said I'd look good with some contrast in my hair. Now I look like a sun-tanned skunk.'

'What were you thinking? What the hell did you use?'

'Bleach.'

'Don't you know some of the best hairdressers are at my disposal? Do you never listen . . .?' she exhaled dramatically. 'Maybe Daniel Galvin will do a house call,' she said thoughtfully, still angry that this was yet another problem she had to sort out.

Cassandra had been twenty-one years old and on a photoshoot in Miami when she had met Narcisso, a half America/half Cuban male model. She had been too young to say no to sex with someone incredibly good-looking – and hell, why not? So they'd had a one-night stand. It was the most fantastic sex of Cassandra's life. It was not until five months later that she found out she was pregnant. As a rule, Cassandra ate very little to keep her rail-thin figure, which had sent her menstrual cycle haywire to say the least. Cassandra had thought it was the end of the world: it was too late to abort it, too far gone to hide it and she had no intention of contacting the father again. The thought of adoption had crossed her mind for a moment but – against all previous instincts – Cassandra found she had a maternal side. The baby was *her*. A part of her, a product of her. How could she give that up? She quickly came to regret such romantic thoughts. Holding Ruby in her arms was the first time she could ever remember feeling helpless and she hated the feeling. Added to which, almost immediately, having a baby interfered with her career. She couldn't travel, couldn't work late, couldn't attend all the parties so essential to maintaining a profile in the fashion world. Cassandra had no choice: she moved her daughter in with her mother and went back to work. At eight, Ruby was sent to boarding school. Ruby had her own room at Cassandra's Knightsbridge apartment, although it was rarely used.

Cassandra had fought hard to hold onto her career, but now she was glad she had Ruby. Unlike thousands of career women her age she didn't have to worry about the ticking biological clock or finding the right man because she *had* a child, one that was becoming more self-sufficient by the day. They climbed into the back seat of the Mercedes and Cassandra ordered the driver to take them into Rye.

'Here. Some of the older girls asked me to give you these.' Ruby thrust her hand into her Marni tote bag and pulled out a handful of CVs. 'You've made me very popular with the upper sixth.'

They drove out of the school gates and made the twenty-minute journey into Rye. Andrew dropped them outside the Mermaid Inn, the best restaurant in town. It had a slightly run-down rickety feel, with uneven floors and low beams, the sort of place you could imagine well-heeled smugglers frequenting. Sitting by the window, Cassandra could see up towards the medieval church and the half-timbered houses. There was an undeniably eerie beauty to the town. *Not quite Nobu*, thought Cassandra, *but charming nonetheless.*

'Isn't it great?' said Ruby, bouncing in her window seat, 'Johnny Depp stayed here once.'

'Did he?' said Cassandra, slightly mollified. 'I'm not at all surprised.'

'So how was the funeral?' asked Ruby, her young mind already on other things. 'I still don't understand why I couldn't have gone. I saw Uncle Saul more than you did and I really wanted to go and say my goodbyes.'

'Roger thought it best if there were no children and for once I agreed with him.'

'Mother, I'm not a child,' said Ruby, affronted. 'I'm thirteen years of age.'

'By the way,' said Cassandra crisply, 'Saul left you £10,000 in his will.'

'Wow! Brilliant!' squealed Ruby slurping her drink. 'Can I have it now?'

'Of course not,' said Cassandra fiercely.

'And did you get the company?' she replied playfully.

Cassandra almost smiled at her daughter. *Straight to the point, just like her mother.*

'No. Saul, in his infinite wisdom, gave it to my cousin Emma.'

'Ah, so that's why you're in a really shitty mood,' she smiled cheekily.

'Ruby!' said Cassandra. 'I don't pay £25,000 a year for your education to hear you swear.'

Ruby leant forward and held her mother's hand.

'What did you want that boring company for anyway?'

'I wanted it for us, darling,' said Cassandra, squeezing her daughter's fingers with a warmth that surprised her.

'But why?' asked Ruby. 'You have a cool job. We have money. If you'd got the company, we'd have had to move back to the village. Uncle Saul used to tell me that it was a perk of owning the company living in that house. Some perk! It's so creepy! I bet it's got ghosts.'

Cassandra moved her hand from her daughter's grip, smarting at her daughter's casual dismissal of her ambitions. What did that ungrateful wretch think she did this all for? How did she think she got such an expensive education? A few ghosts was the least of it. Cassandra took a deep breath, trying to get her emotions under control. Only Ruby could make her shake like this, she thought.

'So . . . what did you think of the March issue?' she asked, trying to change the subject.

'It was great. Although I think you do too much modern art.'

'Darling, lots of our readers are collectors or fancy themselves as collectors.'

'But it's all a bit rubbish, isn't it?' laughed Ruby. 'I mean the way you called that painter who does the orange circles a genius. How is he a genius compared to say Leonardo da Vinci? Did you know Da Vinci was probably one of the most all-round talented people ever? He designed helicopters, solar heating, rockets, everything.'

Cassandra smiled.

'Am I to assume you're studying the Renaissance period at the moment?'

'You got it,' grinned Ruby, happy her mother had taken the bait. '. . . And seeing as I got an A in my paper, are you going to take me to Paris? You did promise at Christmas . . .?'

The fact that Cassandra was the mother of a thirteen-year-old girl was an open secret in the industry, but it was not something she flaunted. There was no shame; over the years, Anna Wintour's child Bee Shaffer and French *Vogue* editor Carine Roitfeld's daughter Julie had been seen on the front row. But Ruby looked nearer eighteen than thirteen; Cassandra was only thirty-five, and did not want people doing the maths and getting it wrong.

'Now, darling, I know I promised you could come to a couple of shows this year but *Rive* is throwing a big party in Paris and I don't think it would be appropriate for you to be there. Maybe for couture in July, mmm?'

'I really wanted to go to the Louvre,' said Ruby in a low, disappointed voice.

Cassandra so wanted to please her daughter, to give in to her demands. She'd love to show Ruby off, but she had to be strong. She couldn't let Ruby's disappointment interfere with her plans, not now. She was doing it for both of them – didn't she understand that? Sometimes she felt so close to her daughter that she was almost part of her, other times it seemed as if they lived on different planets.

'When am I going to see you again?' said Ruby grumpily.

'I'm away for a little while. Milan, Paris and then I have to go to Mexico. But I think your grandmother is coming next weekend.'

Ruby looked up at Cassandra; her teenage barriers were all stripped away now and she was just a little girl who needed her mum.

'I miss you,' she said.

'I miss you too,' said Cassandra, her voice wobbling. 'But you know why I work so hard, don't you?'

'For us?'

Cassandra nodded, then reached under the table for a stiff paper bag.

'Here,' she said, 'I've been saving this.'

Ruby peeked inside, rifled through the tissue paper and then looked up beaming.

'Groovy. A Chanel quilt!' she said.

'The Chanel 2.55,' corrected Cassandra. 'So named because . . .'

'. . . because it was introduced by Coco Chanel in February 1955, I remember,' said Ruby quietly.

Cassandra felt a pang of disappointment and concern at Ruby's interest in the works of Leonardo da Vinci above those of Coco Chanel. While her daughter's quick-wittedness and spirit suited Cassandra's image of herself, to be too academic might be detrimental to Ruby's long-term prospects. Intelligence put too many men off, which was why brainy bluestockings like Emma Bailey ended up alone.

Cassandra had such high hopes for her beautiful daughter. She wanted her to be the belle of the Crillon ball. She wanted her to have a good marriage; a spectacular marriage, perhaps the son of an oligarch or the scion of some great American family. She wanted her to have glamour and power and money. She wanted her to have everything.

69

The car stopped back outside Briarton Court and they got out.

'Are you coming in to say goodbye?' asked Ruby. 'I have to be back in the dorm by nine.'

'I won't come to the dorm. I might get accosted for more autographs,' said Cassandra following her into the entrance hall.

'Don't pretend you don't love it,' smiled Ruby, twisting the chain strap of her bag around her fingertips. Cassandra kissed her daughter on the cheek and felt a shot of warmth course through her body. As Ruby ran down the corridor, her mother watched her go, only turning round when she heard the tapping of shoes coming down the stone floor towards her.

'Miss Broughton,' smiled Cassandra extending a hand to the matronly headmistress of Briarton.

'A wonderful talk, Miss Grand,' she said, although Cassandra detected a look of disapproval in the woman's expression. 'I have a love-hate relationship with the career talks. On the one hand, it's wonderful to be able to make use of the resources our parents offer us, but it does make the girls rather giddy.'

'Well, I have a handful of CVs to show for it,' said Cassandra, tapping her bag. 'It's the sort of initiative I like to see,' she lied.

Miss Broughton smiled. 'I'll walk you to your car.'

They stood in the doorway. Outside it was cold; frost was sitting on the ground and creeping fog was settling in the darkness in front of them.

'We didn't see you at parents' evening last month,' said Miss Broughton, a little too casually.

'I was in Paris, I'm afraid,' said Cassandra, refusing to rise to the bait. 'I believe my mother attended.'

'When we work so hard we have to work twice as hard not to be a stranger to our children.'

Cassandra bristled. *The cheek of the woman!*

'Until last month, *Miss* Broughton, I have never missed a parents' evening since my daughter started her education. But her last school didn't have parents' days during couture.'

There was the crunch of car tyres as Andrew her driver drove the Mercedes in front of them.

'I must go,' said Cassandra quickly tightening the belt of her cashmere overcoat.

Miss Broughton nodded, but continued to talk. 'You are aware that Ruby is one of the most able pupils in her year? Independent, although you would expect that from someone who has boarded for so long. Very bright too. But there is a definite rebellious streak there we must keep our eye on.'

Cassandra gave a small laugh. 'If we are referring to the orange stripe in her hair I'm going to get that sorted out immediately.'

The headmistress shook her head. 'I've always felt thirteen is a watershed age. The cusp of womanhood. She needs her mother to guide her along the right path.'

Cassandra felt herself stiffen. Was there the suggestion in the woman's words that she was not a good mother, or was she being overly sensitive?

'I thought that's what I paid you a great deal of money to do,' said Cassandra, pursing her lips.

'We like to think we have excellent pastoral care at Briarton but we can't be all things to all children.'

You hypocrite thought Cassandra, narrowing her eyes. *You charge the highest fees to make parents feel better about themselves but at the slightest hint of trouble, you throw the blame straight back at them.*

'Ruby has an enormous amount of love and attention from her family, Miss Broughton, I can assure you of that. I can also assure you that there are other schools who would be only too glad to take responsibility for a bright, capable pupil like Ruby.'

She opened the car door and climbed inside.

'As I said, a wonderful talk, Miss Grand,' Miss Broughton said as Cassandra slammed the door.

Through the tinted windows, she looked up at the Gothic beauty of Briarton Court and shivered. For a moment she thought about taking her daughter away. *That would show the old bitch*, thought Cassandra. She wouldn't want to lose the high grade exam results Ruby was likely to chalk up, would she? But then the reputation of the school was unparalleled and more importantly, the calibre of the pupils, of the friends that her daughter would forge, was also excellent. Besides, she didn't want the inconvenience of moving Ruby again. She looked away from the school and told Andrew to drive to London as fast as he could. She then turned her attention to dissecting the new issue of *Vogue* as it started to rain.

6

Emma told the taxi to go slowly. Past Prada, Gucci and Yves Saint Laurent. Past Hermès, Celine and Louis Vuitton. Past the window displays of grand twinkling diamonds: De Beers, Tiffany and Cartier. Past some of the greatest, most desirable luxury brands in the world. London seemed to have grown so much richer since the last time she had been shopping in Mayfair. Bentleys and high-end Audis lined the road, beautiful women with expensive haircuts and winter tans floated out of jewellers with big smiles and sparklers.

'So where d'you want dropping, love?' asked the cabbie, now visibly annoyed. He'd spent the last ten minutes snaking up and down Bond Street, with Emma pressing her face up against the window.

'Do you know the Milford shop?' she asked.

'Not the foggiest, love. What's it look like?'

Emma knew how he felt. It had been so long since she had last visited the Milford store that she could scarcely remember it either, and now having gone up and down the length of Bond Street, she was no wiser. Milford had four stores worldwide, all in prime locations; Rue St Honoré in Paris, Fifth Avenue in New York and Via Condotti in Rome, but the London shop was the flagship. Strange, then, that it seemed impossible to locate.

'There it is,' she said finally, and the taxi pulled up outside an anonymous-looking store on the lower stretch of New Bond Street.

'It's my shop. Well, sort of,' she explained to the cabbie as she handed him a crisp twenty pound note.

'Yeah, right,' said the taxi driver under his breath as he roared off. Emma loitered on the pavement, unsure whether she really wanted to go in. It was a rather forbidding place, painted in a dark blue with a tiny window display of some not terribly exciting wallets and gloves. Taking a deep breath, she pushed the mahogany door but it wouldn't open. She tried again, this time harder, but still it wouldn't budge. Then she noticed a bell to the side of the door and after pressing it twice, a buzzer sounded and it opened with a creak. The ghostly quiet which greeted her reminded Emma of going into a church. The store was dingy and very old-fashioned and it smelt slightly musty, like a country house boot-room. *Where's the glorious smell of leather?* she thought distractedly. There was a beautiful staircase in the middle of the room leading to a mezzanine floor, but the rest of the store was dark and depressing, with small windows which let in very little light. Behind the counter, an old man with a pince-nez eyed her curiously, then continued with his telephone conversation. Emma had the curious sensation of feeling both intimidated and ignored at the same time.

Since leaving Price Donahue, Emma had dealt with her sadness and anger in the only way she knew how – by losing herself in work. She had requested Milford's press cuttings and financial reports to be Fed-Exed over and had examined them with forensic thoroughness. She had quickly discovered that the company's financial position was dire. While the luxury leather goods industry was now a multi-billion dollar business – in the last two decades designer handbags had been one of the biggest growth areas in the whole of the fashion industry – Milford was barely staying afloat. Looking around, she knew exactly why. It was a Saturday afternoon and the shop was deserted. Emma wandered over to the nearest shelf and picked up a leather bag. She pulled a face. You didn't need to be a fashion expert to know that it was ugly. It was dark brown but it wasn't the warm, rich brown of milk chocolate; it was sludgy like mud. She ran her fingers over the bumpy leather – *ostrich* she wondered – it was obviously expensive but it wasn't an item she'd want in her wardrobe in a month of Sundays.

'Can I help you?' asked a stern-looking shop assistant with blonde hair the texture of candy-floss and a brass name-badge announcing her name as 'Barbara'. She looked at Emma's fleece and jeans with undisguised distaste.

'I'm just looking,' said Emma as brightly as she could.

'For anything in particular?' asked Barbara snootily.

'Actually, can you tell me which is your most popular bag?'

The woman looked stricken that anyone should base a choice on anything as vulgar as popularity.

'It's this one,' she said, indicating a brown leather tote. 'It's called the "Rebecca".' *I wonder where that came from, thought Emma.* She picked it up. The leather was certainly beautiful but the materials could not disguise the frumpy shape and the overcomplicated knotted tassels.

'It's rather expensive,' said Barbara.

Emma picked up the price tag. *£3,000! For that?* she thought to herself.

As if reading her thoughts, Barbara added: 'The crafts-manship on all the Milford range is superb.'

'Hand-stitched?' asked Emma remembering the summer after school she had spent working at Milford. In actual fact, the time she had spent with the workmen in the factory had been the part she had enjoyed the most. It had been a fascinating place. She remembered the wonderful smell of the warehouse where thousands of rolls of leather were kept; there were crocodile skins from Australia, python skins from India, calf skins from Brittany and goatskin from Scotland which was used to line all the handbags. She remembered watching Jeff Conway, Milford's head *cuireur*, stretch and beat leathers until they were butter soft and the white-coated artisans hunched over their work-stations, crafting the bags from start to finish, using needles, awls and *pinces de cuir*. Creating a bag had seemed like creating a work of art, not something that rolled off an assembly line.

'There is some hand-crafting involved,' said Barbara cautiously.

'But not hand-stitching?' repeated Emma, making a mental note.

Barbara was getting visibly irritated.

'If madam requires hand-stitching then perhaps you'd like to consider our bespoke service. But the price is considerably higher.'

'I didn't really want to pay too much,' said Emma.

'Then perhaps madam would be better off in another store. Oxford Street has an excellent selection of mid-market accessories.'

What a cow thought Emma. *No wonder the shop was empty.* Luxury retail wasn't just about the product, it was about the experience. If you were spending that much on something, you wanted to feel pampered and flattered, as if the luxury reflected back on you and your incredible good taste.

Emma handed the Rebecca back to Barbara and left the shop. As the door closed behind her, Emma inhaled a deep draught of fresh air.

'Thank you, Barbara,' she whispered to herself as she walked off towards the brighter, glossier shops of London's most fashionable street. The snooty assistant didn't know it, but she had done Emma a huge favour, because now she knew exactly what she needed to do.

Julia Grand sat in her daughter's spacious Knightsbridge apartment, drinking a chilled glass of Pouilly Fumé, thinking there could be few more pleasant places to spend a Sunday afternoon. A sprawling lateral Regency conversion, the flat had been decorated in Cassandra's favoured dove grey, chocolate and cream and was being flooded with lazy winter light from Hyde Park which lay beyond the floor-to-ceiling windows. The long walnut dining table had been set with Meissen porcelain – Julia noted that it was a different set from the one she had seen on her last visit – while Lucia, Cassandra's housekeeper, was preparing a light lunch of poached salmon and asparagus. Julia considered for a moment how much Cassandra must be earning to afford this luxury and felt a burst of pride at her daughter's accomplishments. Of course, Julia liked to think she'd had a considerable hand in Cassandra's success: raising her as a single mother, the years of looking after Ruby, but she was sure her daughter wouldn't think of it that way.

She looked over at Cassandra, wearing what she called her 'après yoga' look of cashmere jogging pants and a skinny white vest. Cassandra was leaving for Milan that afternoon and so she was taking armfuls of clothes from her cedar-lined wardrobes and folding them between tissue paper before putting them into two Louis Vuitton trunks. Julia had kept a fascinated inventory as she watched Cassandra pack: ten pairs of red-soled shoes, most of which looked unworn. Twelve skirts, twice as many dresses, cashmere sweaters in a rainbow of complementary colours and finally, almost a dozen coats, one each from the main designers showing at the Milan collections, which she would wear to the corresponding show. There must have been hundreds of thousands of pounds of clothes in those trunks which, according to Cassandra, would be completely redundant by the time the shows were over. Julia considered it an abject waste of money; think of what all that money could really buy! A Picasso sketch, perhaps, or a Corot landscape. Now that would be something worth having.

'So. Tell me again what Roger told you?' asked Cassandra, finally fastening the latches on the trunks and taking a seat at the dining table. Julia tried not to smile; Cassandra had a habit of making every conversation feel like a business meeting.

'He said that Emma has come back from Boston in time for the shareholders' meeting tomorrow.'

'And do you think it's significant?'

Julia shrugged.

'She's already told Roger she doesn't want to be CEO. I suspect she's just there to show willing and formalize Roger's appointment so we can all move forward.'

Cassandra frowned slightly.

'So everyone is happy with Emma's share in the company?' she asked.

'I never said that,' replied Julia diplomatically, knowing that her daughter had not been pleased with Saul's bequests. 'But what can we do? Roger has already engaged a lawyer; apparently we can't contest the will simply because we don't like what it says.'

Cassandra was silent for a moment and Julia reached across the table to take one of her hands.

'I was desperately disappointed at the reading of the will. It should have been you, darling. We know that. But there seems to be very little we can do.'

'Is this the sort of fight you put up when Dad left you?'

snapped Cassandra, pulling her hand away. Cassandra was angry. She was already well aware of the legal situation with Saul's will; her own lawyers had taken the full force of her fury when they had explained it was watertight. So Cassandra had contacted her financial advisers to explore the possibility of buying Emma's shareholding should she decide to sell, but even with a conservative valuation on Milford, they were talking very big numbers indeed. Cassandra might be the highest-paid editor in London, but it was still way out of her financial grasp.

Julia looked at her daughter wondering how she could be so fearsome. She blamed Cassandra's emotional detachment on herself of course, for allowing her husband Desmond to leave. She had tried to put *that* day in a box at the back of her mind. The day Desmond had left her for another woman, leaving her to bring up Cassandra and Tom by herself. In the years that followed Desmond had given very little financial support to Julia; maintenance payments dwindled to nothing once he'd moved to South Africa twelve months after their divorce. But it wasn't money Cassandra wanted from her father; it was love, support, approval. So Julia had spent the last two decades trying to make up for it. That was why she had volunteered to bring up Ruby when Cassandra had made the move to New York and it hadn't been easy. Suddenly burdened with a three-year-old grandchild, Julia had been forced to cut her time back at the Oxford gallery she owned with the result that it had almost gone under. It had taken the business a decade to recover but Julia had taken the sacrifice on the chin: everything she did was for her children.

Julia held her hand to her breast as if she had been stung.

'I'm sorry,' said Cassandra with an unusual tone of softness. 'I didn't mean it to sound like that. I'm just incredibly frustrated by the whole thing.'

'I could sell my shareholding to you, if that's what you want, darling?' replied Julia. 'A gallery space I'd love is coming up soon on Cork Street. The money would certainly come in handy.'

'Mother, you have 5 per cent stock,' sighed Cassandra, 'and 5 per cent is neither use nor ornament.'

They fell into silence as Lucia entered to serve the poached salmon with a spoonful of hollandaise sauce on the side. Julia used the interruption to change the subject – the situation at Milford was all anyone in the village could talk about and for Julia it was getting a little trying – and besides, she was keen to move on to matters even closer to home. 'Darling, the reason I wanted to see you today is that I'm very concerned about your brother,' she said.

'What's the matter this time?' asked Cassandra. She was aware that Tom had moved back into her mother's house and expected a tirade about cigarettes, loud music and mountains of washing.

'He wants to go to Goa. Next week. And he wants me to pay for it,' said Julia, a tone of exasperation in her voice.

'I should think it will do him good to get out of the country for a while,' said Cassandra.

'But I've read about these places in the *Daily Mail*,' Julia insisted. 'It's rife with disease and drug trafficking and heaven knows your brother doesn't need any encouragement in that department. Cassandra, can't you speak to him? Sort him out with a job or something to keep him in the country?'

Cassandra took a deep breath. It sometimes pained her to think how the role of parent and child had reversed so quickly. Increasingly Cassandra now felt like the head of the family and for once, it was not a position of authority she relished.

'You make me feel like a babysitter,' she snapped. 'I'm not here to entertain Tom just to keep him out of trouble.'

'I appreciate that, darling,' said Julia.

Cassandra snorted.

'I mean, remember the time I got him work in Xavier's studio.'

'He really wasn't cut out for photography,' said Julia.

'It was nothing to do with his talent behind the lens,' said Cassandra, dipping her fork into the fish. 'He was caught having sex with a model in the darkroom.'

'He's a boy, he's got hormones.'

'He's twenty-six, not some randy teenager.'

Julia met her daughter's eyes. 'Darling, please.'

Cassandra was tempted to say no. She was sick of Tom's feckless ways, drifting from one half-baked 'career' to another and she was annoyed that her mother expected her to pick up the pieces. It wasn't as if she didn't help out the family as it was. She introduced Julia to wealthy art patrons on London's society circuit and constantly promoted artists exhibiting in Julia's gallery, billing them as the next big thing in the pages of *Rive*. But there was always something else.

'OK, Mother, I'll see what I can do,' she said finally. 'But this is absolutely the last time: I mean it.'

Julia patted Cassandra's hand. 'Thank you, darling. He won't let you down.'

'Oh, I am absolutely sure he will,' said Cassandra. 'Now let's eat. I don't want to be late for my flight.'

Roger Milford never liked Monday mornings, but today he had woken up in a particularly anxious mood. From the bedroom window of the Old Rectory he could just see the iron entrance gates to Winterfold and it made his stomach ache. Roger was by nature a decisive, 'to hell with the consequences' kind of man, but for once, he was at a loss for what to do. On the one hand he had no intention of going into Milford this morning; the last thing he wanted to see

81

was that smug bluestocking niece of his sitting behind Saul's old desk. *My desk*, he corrected himself. On the other hand, much as it pained him to do so, he had to put on a good show for Emma, to impress her, to convince her that with himself installed as CEO her majority shareholding was in good hands.

Rebecca was sitting propped up in the four-poster bed, her mane of pale blonde hair falling perfectly over her shoulders. A tea tray was perched delicately to her side containing a china teapot, smoked salmon and egg-white scrambled eggs which Latvina, their Polish housekeeper, had prepared.

'I don't know why I can't come to the meeting,' she said, her lower lip pouting. 'I am a member of this family.'

'It's for shareholders and directors, honeypot,' said Roger, going over and stroking her cheek. 'I wish you could be there too, but my hands are tied.'

'What is the meeting actually for anyway?' asked Rebecca. 'She's told you she doesn't want to be CEO, hasn't she? So is this meeting to rubber-stamp your appointment?'

'It better bloody had be,' growled Roger.

His wife looked at him sharply, recognizing the note of doubt in his voice. The disappointment of not getting Saul's shareholding had been crushing, but at least it had gone to Emma – having such a good job in Boston, she surely wouldn't want to leave it for some muddy backwater? But it could so easily have been Cassandra and that . . . well, that would have been a disaster for Roger. She looked at him again, and squeezed the balls of her fists together. Roger *had* to be CEO. As comfortable as their present home was, it wasn't anything very special. She didn't want to live in the Old Rectory for the rest of her life like some vicar's wife holding dinner parties and making jam. They had to live in Winterfold. He had promised it to her ever since he had proposed at the Hotel du Cap eight years earlier. She thought back to their wedding day in the tiny church in Chilcot. Half the pews had been stuffed with her friends from the rich, fast social set she had fallen into when she had moved to London to model. The other half were her family from the villages surrounding Chilcot; uncles in cheap suits, cousins in hats from the charity shops. At the time, she hadn't been embarrassed because she had seen the ceremony as a farewell to her past as she moved to her rightful position in the upper classes. Back then, driving up the gravel drive to Winterfold where Saul had allowed them to have their reception, Rebecca had felt a quiet sense of satisfaction. Despite the twenty-year age difference she had been happy with Roger. He was a dynamic and incredibly attractive man and one day Milford would be his. But that was then and eight years was a long time. Life with Roger was going nowhere fast and it made her almost physically sick.

'Honey,' she asked, 'when do you think we can move in?'

Roger squeezed her fingers and gave her the most reassuring smile he could muster. He wished he could give this beautiful woman everything she wanted. From the second he had met her in Annabel's nightclub in Mayfair, he had wanted nothing else. Sure, he had known what she was – a two-bit model who had never had the breaks to make it into the big league, a beautiful hustler charming her way around the elite nightclubs of London – but he had pulled her up to his level and turned her into the creature in front of him; poised, elegant and respectable. She looked like the Lady of the Manor. He glanced out of the window towards the gates of Winterfold.

'Soon, my darling. As soon as we get it all sorted we'll be moving straight into Winterfold.'

I'll make sure of it, she thought biting her lip so hard she drew blood.

* * *

The Milford offices were in Byron House, a converted Regency villa a mile outside of Chilcot village. It was a striking building on its own with tall, thin windows and fluted columns either side of the entrance but Byron was all the more remarkable for the adjoining factory building. Built from glass and concrete in the early 1930s in the then-futuristic Art Deco style, it should have been an architectural disaster, but somehow the juxtaposition worked, each style complementing the other. The same principle of mixing the old with the new was visible in the company's boardroom, situated on the top floor of the old house. It was a truly magnificent space. Silk wallpaper lined the walls, a huge chandelier hung regally above a long mahogany table with tapered dress-legs and twelve toffee-coloured leather chairs. It was more like the dining room in a palace than a corporate meeting room, but offsetting the grandeur was a modernist steel and glass bar stocked with the finest spirits and champagne and a state-of-the-art audio-visual system set into the far wall, on which Bloomberg, the business channels and ticker-tape information was constantly beamed in from the world's money markets. Emma winced as she entered: this was clearly where Saul had spent Milford's wafer-thin profits. She walked around the room, trailing her fingertips along the table, gazing up at the dancing crystals in the chandelier, thinking of her Uncle Saul, putting off the moment: the moment when she'd have to sit in his chair.

It felt too big, and she felt an impostor sitting there at the head of the table, but she forced herself: the rest of the shareholders would be arriving at any moment and they would expect her to sit there. Emma could feel her nerves getting the better of her. She had tried to look the part of confident businesswoman, but she wasn't even sure if she could pull that off. Her red dress was an old stand-by for when she had to speak at conferences or in front of company directors. Back then it was like armour; confident and bold, but here at Milford HQ, it felt false and showy. Her hair had been blow-dried and she'd taken extra care with her make-up; not so much that she looked overdone but the tinted moisturizer and glossy lips made her feel ready for the day. *It's not what you look like, but what you say,* she scolded herself as people began to file in, smiling and murmuring a few words of greeting. Emma's mother and her Aunt Julia sat to her left halfway down the table. Julia gave Emma an encouraging smile, her mother looked down, playing with her wedding ring. Slowly the room filled: Anthony Collins, Saul's solicitor, then Ruan McCormack who was Milford's Head of Merchandising, followed by Abby Ferguson who looked after marketing. There was a hum of pleasant conversation and cordialities. And finally, in came Roger, his gaze lingering on Emma sitting at the head of the table. Emma felt her palms tingle with sweat and she played nervously with the gold bangle on her wrist. Since her first day at Harvard business school it had been Emma's dream to run a company one day. But as she prepared to address her board of directors, it wasn't a wave of euphoria she felt, but a rush of nausea.

'Hello, everyone,' she began, hoping they wouldn't hear the tremor in her voice. 'Thank you all for coming. Can I begin by saying that it was a great honour – although an enormous surprise – when Uncle Saul left me his share-holding. My first response was that the company didn't belong to me, that I had a life elsewhere, that I didn't belong here. So I felt that I should offer to sell my 70 per cent stake to the other shareholders.'

Emma could feel the tension and anticipation around the

room pressing in towards her. She glanced at Roger who was looking at his hands and nodding cautiously.

'But I have been thinking about this long and hard. Uncle Saul gave me those shares for a reason and I want to make him proud. We *all* want to make him proud. This company has a wonderful heritage and enormous potential.'

She took a deep breath.

'That's why I have decided to keep the shareholding and take the post of Chief Executive.' Emma paused momentarily, waiting for a reaction. She was greeted by silence. It was as if everyone in the room had stopped breathing.

'Well, I think there are various formalities and paperwork we'll need to deal with to authorize it, but . . .'

She looked at Anthony and the solicitor nodded.

'But the directors choose the CEO!' interrupted Julia suddenly. She turned to Roger. 'Isn't that right?'

Emma didn't wait for an answer.

'As 70 per cent shareholder I effectively control membership of the board,' she said.

'What she means, Julia,' said Roger, 'is that she can get rid of us in a heartbeat if we don't go along with what she says.' His lips were set in a thin line, his gaze stony. 'Is that not correct, Emma?'

Emma steeled herself. She'd hadn't expected this to be easy. *You have to be tough, you have to be tough*. She had spoken in front of CEOs of Forbes listed companies before now, but this audience, particularly Roger, who always intimated her even as a child, was making her feel sick. Emma leaned forward and put her hands on the table.

'I know this may come as a surprise, Roger,' she began, as levelly as she could. 'And I know some of you might not even think I should be here. But I think I can bring a lot to Milford. Yes, I don't know the company as intimately as most people in this room, but perhaps that's a good thing. Maybe we need to start thinking out of the box if Milford is going to recover.'

'Spare us your management consultancy,' said Roger tartly.

'And what do you mean by *recover*?' asked her mother, who had a cold look of disapproval.

Emma sat up in her chair, grateful for the opportunity to show them what she was good at.

'Since my arrival in England I've spent time getting up to speed with the company and where the luxury goods industry is, at large.' She opened a folder and passed some charts around the table.

'I've prepared these for you to look at. Milford's market share in the luxury leather goods is now, well, negligible. In the early 1980s we were competing with Gucci. I hardly need to point out that they and many other companies have now eclipsed Milford by a country mile. We have to modernize quickly if we're to survive but I really believe we can recapture some of our old glory.'

'Perhaps we haven't had the best couple of years,' interrupted Roger, looking around for support. 'But the new Autumn/Winter line is strong. At our last meeting Saul talked about increasing the marketing budget and we all agreed that that was the way forward.'

Emma noticed that Virginia and Julia were nodding, while Ruan and Abby looked less convinced.

'Unfortunately I think the problem runs a little deeper than that,' said Emma. She leant under the table and came up holding a handbag which she placed on the table top.

'I think I'm right in saying this is the most popular bag from our current line. The "Rebecca"?'

'That's right,' said Ruan.

'It's an elegant bag for our existing customer-base,' said

87

Emma as diplomatically as she could. 'But that customer-base is ageing. We're seen as a traditional company. *Too* traditional.'

'You're saying that people don't want our merchandise?' snapped Roger. His tone was sharp and defensive.

'Roger, I respect your experience but we have to look at the figures ruthlessly,' said Emma. 'Milford's sales and profits are on a steep downwards turn and yet the high-end accessories market is booming. You can blame marketing if you like, but the buck has to stop at the product.'

Roger barked out a hollow laugh.

'Since when have you been an expert in accessories design?' he said. 'I thought Cassandra was the style guru in our family.'

'I'm not an expert on fashion, no,' she said candidly. 'But I do know about business and I know about the people who can afford super-luxury products. They're a cash-rich, time-poor demographic. Women who can afford £2,000 handbags have busy lives. They want bags that are beautiful and functional, not stiff and formal. They want bags that make them feel sexy. Lifestyle statements. We need sleek, discreet luggage that can go from the airport to the boardroom. We need to update our products for the new millennium.'

She moved the Rebecca bag to one side and opened her laptop which was connected to one of the video screens in the wall. She pressed a key and a huge image of a Hermès 'Birkin' bag appeared.

'We sold 55 Rebecca bags last year,' said Emma. 'Hermès on the other hand has a waiting list of up to five years for Birkins and Kelly bags.'

'We're well aware of the competition,' said Roger dismissively.

'And why does everyone want to buy into Hermès?' she asked, turning her gaze from Roger to Abby. She needed support, she needed confirmation that what she was saying was right.

'Well, um, they're beautiful bags. They're entirely hand-crafted using the highest quality of workmanship,' said Abby cautiously.

'And they're pitched higher than other companies in the sector,' added Ruan. 'More expensive, more elite. They manage to be both classic and fashionable at the same time and, well, they just have a magic that everyone wants to buy into.'

Emma smiled and nodded. At least she had managed to get two people to understand what she was saying, even if they were only kowtowing to their new boss.

'And that's exactly where we should be aiming Milford,' said Emma firmly.

Roger laughed.

'Well, if our problem is a lack of sales, shouldn't we be pursuing a policy of more *inclusive* luxury to increase sales?' he asked, his voice heavy with sarcasm.

Emma took out another pile of papers from her leather folder.

'I have had this faxed through from a ex-colleague of mine at Price Donahue. She's an expert in the luxury sector.'

Emma began passing the crisp white documents down the table. *Thank goodness for Cameron,* she thought.

'Her analysis of the luxury goods market is that the sector is becoming devalued. When so many designer goods are now made in China, the very top end of the market, the growing numbers of high-net worth individuals, want a return to traditional craftsmanship. With that in mind I believe we need to be *more* exclusive, we need to be right at the very top end, the most luxurious on the market. We don't want to be in the business of churning out 'it-bags'. We want to make *heirlooms* for fashionable women.'

Emma stood and walked over to the video screen which

was now showing a black and white photograph of a white-coated artisan bent over a work-bench, making tiny holes in the leather enabling a bag to be hand-stitched.

'We need to get back to this. Gorgeous design and beautiful craftsmanship. Ruan, after this meeting can we discuss reverting production to hand-stitching?'

Her mother was laughing gently.

'Darling, I know you're only trying to help but you really don't know anything at all about the company. We've just spent thousands putting in the new machines to increase productivity.'

Emma stared back at her mother, her lips pursed.

'As it happens, I do know about the factory machines and every other part of the company,' she said, her anger making her rush her words. 'I have been over every inch of the company books and I know that money has been wasted on poor decisions in every area. That doesn't mean we should continue to do so.'

'This is preposterous,' said Roger slamming his hand on the table. 'Anthony?' he said looking over to the lawyer. 'Must we endure this, this . . . piffle?'

'Roger, please. Calm down,' interrupted Emma. 'This is not personal, it is simply what needs to be done to save this company from going under.'

'Emma, show some respect to your uncle!' said Virginia sternly. 'How dare you speak to him like that!'

'I think perhaps we need a short break?' said Anthony, quickly fiddling with his glasses.

'Fine,' said Emma, gathering her papers. 'I will be in Saul's office. Sorry, *my* office.' And she walked out, her head held high, but her heart sinking.

'This is totally outrageous,' shouted Roger storming into the office, just as Emma was sitting down. 'Are you deliberately trying to humiliate me in front of everybody?' he said, leaning over the desk and glaring at her.

Emma was taken aback by the force of his fury, but she felt protected by Saul's desk between them and she was tired of being bullied, especially by Roger.

'I don't mean any of this as a personal attack, Roger,' she said, her voice cold. 'But the business is on its knees. I saw the designs for the Autumn/Winter line and my gut feeling is that we're going to have to go again with them.'

'Go again! There's absolutely nothing wrong with them,' he spluttered. 'What exactly do you propose we do instead?'

Emma looked at him, her eyes narrow. She had made the decision about what she was about to say the moment she had left the Milford shop.

'I propose we get a new creative director.'

'But, but – I am in charge of design,' he said, panic in his voice.

'Roger, we can discuss this later.'

'We can discuss this in court!' he bellowed, marching towards the door.

'Roger, please.'

'Please? *Please?* That's all you can say?' he shouted, turning back, the fury blazing in his eyes. 'You come in here with your prissy little business school theories with zero experience in the real world and start telling us that a business we've been running for decades is worthless. How *dare* you!' he hissed. 'You're playing with people's lives!'

Emma began to feel the situation spiral out of control before her. Suddenly she could hear Mark's words in her head. *You're too nice. You're an academic, not a corporate player.*

'I dare, because I have to!' shouted Emma, stopping Roger in his tracks. She grabbed a thick file and threw it down on the desk between them. 'You look at the figures, Roger: they're all there in black and white. If we don't do something pretty radical, Milford is dead before the end of the year. How's that for the real world?'

Roger's face drained of colour and his mouth worked without sound.

'I am still a large shareholder of this company, young lady,' he finally managed. 'I know what the figures say and with a marketing budget . . .'

'Roger, you have a 20 per cent shareholding,' said Emma, stabbing a finger onto the spreadsheets. 'And 20 per cent of nothing is nothing.'

She stood up and inhaled deeply. There was no going back now.

'I give you my word, Roger, that by the time I have finished, your stake will be worth fifty times what it is now. Twenty years ago Gucci was almost bankrupt, now it's a multi-billion dollar company. A great designer turned Bottega Veneta around in months, not years. Chanel was once in the doldrums, so was Burberry, the precedents are all there. But we need to be brave, we need to *try*. Give me a chance, Roger. I can do this, I know I can.'

'And what makes you think we can trust you?' said Roger slowly.

Emma almost smiled.

'Saul did,' she said. 'That's a start, isn't it?'

7

The showroom of designer Guillaume Riche's Parisian atelier was alive with colour. Stork-thin models strutted down the makeshift catwalk with smoky eyes and hair so straight it swung in time to the music. Each girl brought out a look which was more beautiful than the last: a cashmere wrap coat in cyclamen pink, a bone white chiffon blouse with a graphite wool pencil skirt, a voluminous evening dress in amethyst. This was ready-to-wear at its most bold and luxurious. Finally Alexia Dark, one of the industry's hottest models, walked past in a gown sculpted in layers of primrose tulle so delicate it looked like the ripples of water on a tropical beach. Tomorrow, the unveiling of Guillaume Riche's Autumn/Winter collection would be the hottest show in town, but tonight it was a dress rehearsal and a private view for the luckiest, most talented fashion magazine editor in Paris: Cassandra Grand.

Standing at the end of the catwalk was a small man in tight charcoal jodhpurs. From the back he looked like a jockey except for the long grey hair that fell down between his shoulder blades. As the music died, he spun around dramatically to face the woman sitting in the front row and threw his hands into the air.

'Cassandra!' he cried. 'You are not clapping! Tell me why you are not clapping? You hate it! You hate the show!'

Cassandra laughed. She stood up and pulled on the little mink shrug that had been sitting on her lap.

'The beauty of the dress rehearsal, Guillaume,' she said, linking her arm through his, 'is that I don't have to clap. I've spent the last four weeks of shows clapping. I can't stop clapping because some devious design houses such as yourself have been known to film the audience to make sure they are clapping and withhold advertising if you do not show sufficient ardour. I'm sick of clapping. I practically have RSI.'

'So you hate the show?' Guillaume said nervously.

'As we both know, clapping is really no indication of the quality of a collection.' She paused dramatically and gave him a playful smile. 'But in this case I think the show is absolutely sensational.'

Guillaume stopped in his tracks and collapsed to his knees, offering a silent prayer of thanks to the god of fashion.

'Sensational. Do you mean that?' he said, slinking into a Louis Ghost chair next to the catwalk. 'I am not sure the hair is absolutely right. I think maybe the girls need white lips. *Merde*. I wish the venue would be ready so we could have a full dress rehearsal. But the sets aren't ready. They are *imbeciles*. Useless.'

Cassandra sat down and put her hand on his knee to reassure him. Guillaume Riche, one of the world's most beloved designers, really did not need overblown sets or white lipstick to show off the brilliance of his latest collection – it was amazing. Although he was nearly sixty, Guillaume was a designer at the peak of the game. In twenty-four hours' time, celebrities, editors and buyers from all the top retail stores in the world would throw themselves at his feet and scratch each other's eyes out to get hold of their favourite pieces. But tonight,

Guillaume's genius was for Cassandra's eyes only – as his collection always was in the final hours before it was unveiled. Her position as editor-in-chief of *Rive* meant she could not be Guillaume's official muse – other advertisers would not be happy – but she would always be called upon to make final suggestions, perhaps a change of shoes or accessories, or change the running order. Occasionally Cassandra actually recommended the axing of a look entirely and although Guillaume would naturally throw a hissy-fit to register on the Richter scale, he trusted her implicitly. And why wouldn't he? Wasn't it Cassandra who, almost single-handedly, had resurrected his career? The Nineties minimal aesthetic had very nearly killed off the flamboyant Guillaume Riche brand entirely, until Cassandra, then a junior stylist, had championed him on every shoot she styled. But much more significantly, when Cassandra had graduated to dressing up-and-coming starlets, she had used Guillaume's designs to dress them for the red carpet – and Hollywood needed little encouragement to fall back in love with Guillaume; his luscious clothes were old-school, movie-star glamour that flattered the legends and made the younger generation look sophisticated and worldly. And where the A-listers led, the rest of the fashion industry followed. Today Guillaume was now one of the most important designers in the world, a flamboyant foil to Lagerfeld's commercial brilliance and this show, Cassandra was sure, would be his biggest triumph yet.

'But how can we improve it?' said Guillaume, getting up and pacing around.

Cassandra flipped open her Moleskine notebook and reviewed her scribbled comments. Even in a mediocre collection she could pick out the one gem that could make a woman beautiful and elegant.

'I adored the inverted pleating, the volume of the skirts. However . . . the penultimate exit . . .'

'What is wrong?' said Guillaume, his eyes blazing. 'What?'

'The obi-belt on the amethyst dress, perhaps you should try it in pumpkin rather than black? It's just a little too predictable.'

For a moment, it looked as if Guillaume would explode. Then he reached out and pinched Cassandra's cheek affectionately.

'Ma cherie, you are always right.'

He clicked his fingers in the air and an assistant came running with two cups of espresso. Cassandra glanced at her watch. It was time to go back to her suite at the Plaza Athénée and prepare.

'You are coming to the party?' she said, downing the coffee in one.

'Of course, but only for a short time, I'm afraid. Your timing before my show is very bad and then . . .' he threw his hands in the air again, '. . . you request pumpkin obi-belts! But don't worry, the rest of Paris will be there.'

'Not all of them. Only those who are lucky enough to have been invited,' she smiled.

'Is Glenda coming?' he asked. Glenda McMahon was the editor-in-chief of US *Rive* and therefore one of Cassandra's most bitter rivals, despite the fact that she was Cassandra's former boss and mentor.

'Darling Glenda!' she exclaimed, without a hint of irony. 'I know she's in Paris. I saw her at Lanvin yesterday. Whether that means she will turn up tonight is anyone's guess.'

Her offhand comment switched Guillaume into a playful mood.

'I see she was only one place above you in *Time*'s "Most Powerful Women in Fashion" . . .'

'Will people stop mentioning that silly list?' replied Cassandra, standing up and handing her coffee cup to a make-up artist.

'One place,' said Guillaume gleefully. 'She is surely going to feel the breath on the back of her neck.'

'Guillaume . . .'

'My prediction is that in twelve months' time that job will be yours.'

'Guillaume, stop it! Glenda is a very gifted editor.' *But not as good as she was*, added Cassandra silently. As close a friend to Guillaume as she was, she simply couldn't admit that she wanted Glenda's job – Guillaume was as indiscreet as he was gifted. US *Rive* was where Cassandra had started her magazine career and it only seemed right that she should finish it there because New York was undeniably the centre of the media world, where money men, models and insiders collided and formed alliances. That was where she would make her next move, she was sure of it. She'd been at UK *Rive* for three years and knew it was already too long. She often lay awake at night thinking ahead to the day when she would be given the US *Rive* job, planning how she would finally take it beyond US *Vogue* to become the greatest fashion magazine on earth – and how she would make herself a legend at the same time.

'Well, if you are not interested in that job,' said Guillaume slyly, 'what about another one I hear of in New York?'

Cassandra looked at him curiously. She thought she knew every magazine move that was being made or plotted. She thrived on gossip, it was the lifeblood of the industry, running up and down the front row, crackling between the tiny tables of the fashionistas' favourite Parisian restaurant Chez George, at art previews and society weddings. For Cassandra it was not just idle tittle-tattle, it was professional ammunition.

'And what job would this be?' she asked.

'The launch of the AtlanticCorp's US fashion weekly,' said Guillaume, 'they have an editor-in-chief already but . . .'

'Carrie Barker – I know. She was drafted in from their newspaper division.'

'Yes. But they are not happy at all with the dummy and frankly my darling, I'm not surprised. The publishers presented it to me last week and it was . . . How do you say, *shit*.'

Cassandra caught her breath. This was gossip of the highest quality.

'So they are firing her?'

Guillaume nodded. 'I told them they could do better.'

He clapped his hands as if he was already bored with the conversation and an assistant appeared carrying a long plastic bundle.

'Now, ma cherie. What are you wearing to the party?'

'What? Oh, I haven't decided . . .' said Cassandra, still lost in thought.

'Well perhaps I can help,' said Guillaume with relish, tearing the layer of plastic off the package. Cassandra gasped.

'For you,' smiled Guillaume. It was a beautiful sculpted tulle gown, the very same show-stopping gown Guillaume had used to end the catwalk show, except this version had been created in the most glorious pale biscuit colour, its neckline sprinkled with delicate seed pearl embroidery. She reached out a finger to touch the beading.

'Lesage?' she said recognizing the work of the great French artisan house.

He nodded and she beamed. The colour was the perfect complement to her skin.

But it was more than that: this was a dress that would be fêted by journalists in thousands of column inches and be worn by A-list stars on the red carpets of the Oscars or Cannes – except they wouldn't be the first to wear it. Cassandra Grand would be, even before it had its official debut at Guillaume Riche's Autumn/Winter collection.

'It's beautiful,' she said, 'just so, so, beautiful!' Carried away by the moment, Cassandra dropped her guard and embraced Guillaume, kissing him on both cheeks.

'And it will fit perfectly.'

Cassandra smiled. She knew it would. It would fit her lithe body perfectly and it would fit her new plan perfectly, her new plan which started tonight.

'Maintenant,' screamed the sexy blonde, grabbing onto the bedsheets.

'Sure thing, baby . . .'

Tom Grand had dropped French as soon as he could at Shrewsbury school and he could barely remember how to say hello let alone decipher the ramblings of someone in the throes of orgasm, but he didn't need a dictionary to know the girl currently astride him was having a good time. Her small tits, glistening with sweat, were jiggling up and down as she slid herself along his cock, twisting her pelvis to grind her springy bush into him. Frankly, she was a wild-cat. Her name was Sophie. She was French, an actress, and when he had met her that afternoon in a café in the Bastille, where she'd been drinking espresso and painting her finger-nails black, he'd suspected she'd be a right goer. He hadn't minded that she wasn't the most groomed girl he had ever seen. She had stringy blonde hair tied back in a ponytail and had been wearing a green parka coat and flip-flops despite the cold. But she had a delicious way of holding her cigarette, a filthy laugh and beautiful, dark, flinty eyes. Almost immediately he'd wanted to take her back to his swanky room at the super-chic Hotel Costes. It was being paid for by *Rive* magazine and he wanted to make full use of the mini-bar and room service. But Sophie wasn't impressed and besides, she wanted to feed her cat. So before Tom knew where he was, they were in bed in her tiny one-bedroom apartment in Montmartre improving Anglo-French relations.

Sophie lifted herself off him, stroking her clitoris with the tip of his throbbing cock. When Tom could stand it no more he grabbed her hips, pulling her back down so that they were rocking in tandem harder and faster until they both came together in a spine-jolting explosion that made Tom cry out so loudly, it made his throat hurt.

'You're fucking good,' he said finally, exhaling deeply and collapsing onto the mattress.

'Good at fucking?' she replied in rather rickety English.

Tom laughed.

'Yes, I suppose that's exactly what I meant,' he said, propping his head up on the pillow and thinking that if it hadn't been for his mother he'd be halfway to India by now. He'd been finally evicted from his Camden flat for non-payment of rent just before Christmas and while he'd managed to extend his time in London looking up old girlfriends, he'd finally accepted his fate and moved back in with his mother just before Saul's funeral. When the chance of a trip to Goa came along – his friend Mungo said he could get him work at an 'amazing' full moon party – Julia had given him such a hard time about it all that when Cassandra had asked him to DJ at some do in Paris he'd quickly accepted. He knew his mother would have put her up to it, but he was slightly less angry when Cassandra had indicated that she could introduce him to fashion show producers and other people who might finally get his music career going. Plus, *Rive* were putting him up at the Costes, which was never a chore.

Although he and his sister weren't particularly close – Cassandra was too wrapped up in her shallow little world to really care about anyone else – every now and then she would throw him a bone. His mother and his friends were forever reminding him how lucky he was to have someone that connected and that powerful as a sibling, but Tom didn't see it that way. Yes, he had a wardrobe full of Dior Homme suits, Tom Ford shirts and Bill Amberg bags, none of which he had paid a penny for. His friends called him the best-dressed loser in town and that was exactly the point. Every opportunity Cassandra gave him, simply fuelled his sense of inadequacy and every job he fucked up just showed him up in sharp contrast to his sister's brilliant career. He used to think that he was just as creative as Cassandra and that he just hadn't found the right outlet yet, but at twenty-six, finding himself jobless and back at his mother's, well, maybe he wasn't really good at anything. Still, at least he was successful with the ladies.

Suddenly he remembered the party and sat up.

'Shit! What time is it?' Predictably, he didn't have a watch.

Sophie shrugged. 'Perhaps 9 o'clock.'

He was due at the *Rive* party at 10 p.m.

'Bugger. How far is the Marais? I have to be at this party for ten.'

Sophie's apartment was up eight flights of stairs in a run-down block overlooking Sacre Coeur. She shrugged again. 'Ten minutes. Maybe.'

He pursed his lips. He wasn't exactly sure where Montmartre was but he had a clue it was in the north of the city. The Marais was also on the right bank but closer to the Seine. Fuck it, he had to trust the local when she said it was close by, didn't he?

'Are you sure about that?'

Sophie didn't even bother to shrug this time, simply rolled towards him and took his nipple between her lips.

'Ooh,' he smiled to himself, 'no reply necessary.'

He put his arm behind his head and watched her slide off the futon.

Light poured in from the illuminated Sacre Coeur behind

them. She had a beautiful long body, a slim, sinuous back and smooth round buttocks that looked like marble in the half-light.

'Do you want some . . . 'ow do you say in English – GHB?' she said, fiddling with a glass vial on her cluttered dresser.

Tom guffawed. 'Shit, you get better all the time.'

Then he froze. There was a head poking round the bedroom door.

'Allo.'

Tom sat up and grabbed the duvet to cover his exposed body.

Christ! Who's this? He thought in a panic, imagining all sorts of knife-wielding boyfriend scenarios. Then he got a better look at the intruder. *Hey, she's a corker.*

'This is Sabine,' said Sophie distractedly.

Sabine was even more startling than Sophie, her black hair looked as if it had been cut with a pair of shears into an uneven bob, but her face was exquisite enough to take it. She walked into the room holding a ginger cat which Tom could see had three legs.

Sabine saw Tom looking and smiled. 'She fell from the window there onto the street. She survived so we call her Lucky.'

He liked this one too.

'Er. Who is she?' he asked, turning to Sophie. 'Your flat-mate?' It was, however, a one-bedroom apartment.

'My girlfriend,' she said casually putting the GHB into a small tumbler of water and handing it to him before lying naked across the bed.

Blimey, thought Tom, *I can't remember getting a hard on again so quickly.*

Sabine put the cat on the floor and kicked off her shoes before joining them on the bed, reaching over to kiss Sophie gently on the lips.

'What time did you say it was again?' said Tom, in no rush to leave.

Sabine looked at her watch. '9.15.'

The Marais was only ten minutes away Tom thought to himself as he moved forward to lie beside Sophie. She reached towards him and curled her black-tipped fingers around his hand and Tom knew that, for a short while at least, he wasn't going anywhere.

Giles Banks, *Rive* magazine's editor-at-large, stepped from the limousine outside the gorgeous Parisian *hôtel particulier* and offered a hand to the woman still in the car. As one pale caramel Manolo heel hit the pavement, even Giles, who had no interest in the opposite sex, recognized that she was a magnetic beauty. Dozens of flashbulbs went off like firecrackers. He stepped back out of the line of the cameras, knowing that nobody wanted a picture of him. This was Cassandra's night. The final part of a quartet of big nights held during the international collections that had seen her host parties in New York, London, Milan and Paris to celebrate *Rive*'s tenth anniversary. Sure, Giles himself had been the one she had entrusted to organize the parties and it had been a mammoth operation pulling in every contact to make sure every A-list star in town was going to be there, but tonight it would still be Cassandra at the centre of everyone's attention. So far the parties had all been enormous successes. The supper in New York, in a yet-to-be-opened restaurant in the Meatpacking District. In Milan, Cassandra's good friends, the Count and Contessa of Benari, had lent her their pocket-sized palazzo on the shores of Lake Como, while in London she had taken over Spitalfields Market for the night, draping the vast Victorian warehouse with white silk. They had all been very, very exclusive with invitations strictly specifying 'No plus ones' and they had all been a triumph. His efforts had been worth it.

Giles was aware that his boss had a difficult reputation; she was the most demanding and particular woman he had ever met, but she was also brilliant and had been good to him: very good. He had learnt so much from her, been given so many opportunities and in helping transform UK *Rive* he now had an international reputation as one of the most talented fashion journalists in the world.

He watched Cassandra's face break into a small composed and elegant smile as they walked through the doors of the beautiful hotel. Its grand atrium was twinkling in the glow of a thousand tea-lights. Huge glass vases were filled with scarlet and gold pomegranate halves and the perfumed air smelt like spiced nectar, sweet, rich and heady.

Giles could see Cassandra's eyes scan the crowd, looking for names. There were plenty to choose from. François-Henri Pinault and Salma Hayek. Sonia Rykiel, perched on a hot-pink sofa laughing with a friend. Bernard Arnault, CEO of LVMH and his beautiful daughter Delphine were talking to John Galliano whose elaborate plumed hat set him apart from the crowd – as usual.

Everyone knew the importance of tonight's party. Paris was fashion. All its main players were here. Nothing could go wrong.

'Oh, darling. Everybody's here.'

Cassandra kissed him on the cheek.

'You've outdone yourself,' she purred, swinging her dark hair over her shoulders. 'Although didn't Muffy Dayton have pomegranate vases at her divorce shower?'

Giles flushed a little. 'Did she?'

Still looking nervous, Giles's eyes darted behind her.

'Look out. Toxic is coming this way,' he said quickly.

Cassandra had just accepted a flute of pink champagne

from a waiter when her publishing director Jason Tostvig, also known as 'Toxic' due to his unpopularity with the editorial team, appeared at her side.

He kissed Cassandra on the cheek and shook Giles's hand awkwardly. Despite – or perhaps because of – his job, Jason was not a man completely comfortable in the world of fashion. He'd been drafted over from newspapers, was resolutely heterosexual, bullishly macho and seemed to think that even talking to somebody openly homosexual would somehow impact on his own masculinity.

'Quite impressive,' he smiled thinly looking around the room before raking his eyes over her dress. 'How much is this shindig costing me?'

'Whatever the invoice says, it's worth it,' smiled Cassandra, still glancing around the room. 'Throwing parties is a branding exercise.'

'Yes, but did we need four of them in as many weeks?'

'Perhaps you don't want to send the message that *Rive* is rich, exclusive and international. Perhaps I'll bring that up with Isaac Grey next time I see him,' she said, namechecking the CEO of their company.

Jason narrowed his dark eyes. Traditionally publishers and editors were mortal enemies, regarding each other as tight-fisted Neanderthals and irresponsible decadents, respectively. But Cassandra had a particular loathing for Jason. Not only did she think he was mediocre at his job, he had no handle on the fashion world beyond his cack-handed attempts at picking up models.

'Is that a threat?' he hissed.

'Merely an observation that you and I might have different agendas,' said Cassandra coolly. 'Personally I don't think you can put a price on goodwill.'

Jason puffed out his chest and popped a canapé into his mouth.

'Well, I hope some of that "goodwill" is directed at Oscar Braun,' he said, nodding his head over at the CEO of the Austrian fashion house Forden. 'They're threatening to pull £250,000 worth of advertising over the next two quarters. Perhaps you'd like to tell Isaac Grey *that* the next time you see him.'

Cassandra chuckled.

'Oscar is always saying that,' she said. 'Perhaps he'd help his own cause if he started showing decent collections. I have to put the fashion team in a headlock to get Forden's revolting things in the magazine.'

'I think we managed to get the mint bouclé jacket into the March issue,' said Giles helpfully.

'This time I think he's serious,' said Jason with a hint of relish. 'You'd better do some serious schmoozing because if his ad revenue gets pulled we're going to have to start looking at cutting editorial budget.'

Finally Cassandra turned to look at him.

'Leave the editorial out of this,' she snapped.

'Speaking of which,' said Jason looking up at the giant Phoebe Fenton cover. 'Has anybody actually read that interview yet?'

'It's embargoed till Monday,' said Cassandra quickly.

'Funny, I thought the plan was to give the issue out to guests after the party.'

'We never agreed that.'

'Well, I read the issue on the Eurostar and you gave poor Phoebe a right old kicking, didn't you? I was just thinking that perhaps you might be nervous about all these actors and models and socialites reading about their friend and what a coke-snorting whore she is, when you're right there to take the flak? I mean, Phoebe might be down, but she's not out. There's still a lot of "goodwill" around for her.'

Cassandra flashed him a furious look, then took a breath

to compose herself. What did Toxic care about 'poor' Phoebe Fenton? More likely he *wanted* there to be an uproar. He wanted trouble from the Fenton camp and wanted Cassandra to be held accountable. She was convinced he didn't like the fact that she was the star of the *Rive* operation while not one celebrity or CEO in this room would even know his name. He was a snake. She knew she was going to have to get rid of him at some point but Cassandra always thought tactically. While Tostvig was ambitious and spiteful, he wasn't the brightest candle on the cake and she'd rather be up against someone toxic and foolish than someone ruthless and clever.

'Cassandra, could I have a word?'

'What's wrong?' she said impatiently, turning see Sadie her junior assistant holding out a mobile phone. Jason looked over, his lips curling gleefully as he smelled trouble. Satisfied that Cassandra's perfectly-groomed feathers had been ruffled, he took a flute from a waiter and headed off to try and chat up Naomi Campbell.

'It's your brother,' whispered Sadie when he had gone.

'What on earth is the problem? Why is he on the mobile? Shouldn't he be here?'

She glanced at the DJ booth where a man with long dreadlocks appeared to be packing up his records.

'That DJ finishes in ten minutes,' explained Sadie. 'Your brother is on until twelve and Jeremy Healy has only just got off the Eurostar and won't be here for at least another forty-five minutes.'

'Well, get that man to stay,' she snapped, pointing up to the DJ booth.

Sadie had a look of sheer panic on her face.

'I've tried that! He's playing at Les Bains Douche in half an hour. His car is already outside waiting to take him there.'

Sadie thrust the phone towards Cassandra again. 'Do you

want to speak to Tom? He says he's stuck in traffic near Galeries Lafayette.'

Cassandra shut her eyes momentarily, willing herself to be calm but feeling such a sense of fury and betrayal that she felt her cheeks begin to sting hot. He was her *brother*. How could he let her down so badly yet again?

'Tell him that if he's not here in five minutes not only will *Rive* refuse to pay his expenses at the Hôtel Costes but that I, personally, will make sure that everyone even remotely connected to the music industry knows what a irresponsible moron he is. He won't be able to get a job sweeping the floor of a rat's cage by the time I've finished with him.'

'You want me to say all that to your brother?'

'If you don't, you can join him in the cage.'

Giles was already making calls on his mobile.

'I've just called Queen,' he said, covering the mouthpiece. 'They're sending one of their DJ's over immediately. He only lives on the Rue des Rosiers, so we should be OK.'

Cassandra grabbed Giles's hand and mouthed 'Thank you'. Then, in the blink of an eye, her legendary poise was back and she was gliding away smiling and waving at people in the crowd, as if nothing had taken place.

'Marvellous party, Cassandra. I don't think there is anybody more beautiful at the party.'

Cassandra turned to see Jean-Paul Benoit, chief executive of the Pellemont luxury goods house. Major advertiser. Major sleazeball.

'Jean-Paul!' she cooed, 'I was just telling Giles how we need to get fashion's most glamorous tycoon inside the pages of *Rive* magazine.' She took his arm and steered him away from Sadie. 'How would you feel about doing an "At Home"? You do still have your adorable house in Ile de Ré? It's one of my favourite places in the world. I've found this new photographer. I think he could be the new Testino. Someone like that could really do it justice.'

'Will you be coming along in person?' asked Jean-Paul, a wolfish grin on his face.

Cassandra smiled sweetly.

'I'm sure something could be arranged . . .'

Am I mad? thought Emma as she stepped out of the taxi. Paris; the city of lovers. It had magic. She and Mark had talked about coming together at New Year. That seemed so long ago now and here she was outside a glittering party alone. She looked at the paparazzi crowding around the entrance, their flashbulbs lighting up the red carpet leading into the *Rive* party and thought that the gates of hell themselves might not be quite so intimidating. In front of her, a long queue snaked down the street while two girls with stern expressions and clipboards either waved people through or condemned them to ridicule. She shivered. What had made her come without a ticket? *Desperation,* she thought, moving towards the entrance, holding her clutch bag in front of her like a shield. Emma was in trouble with Milford already. After a long and heated meeting with Roger she had agreed to create the new position of Director of Bespoke Services for him. If she'd truly had it her way, she'd have dispensed with him entirely but as she'd definitely rocked the boat enough since her arrival, she'd decided that a sideways move for Roger was the best solution in the short term. That left the glaring vacancy of head designer to revamp the collection and if she'd thought it would be an easy appointment she was very much mistaken. In the last week, she'd make clumsy attempts at poaching big design names from other fashion houses, but despite hitting the phones for hours on end, she'd rarely made it past the company switchboards. At the factory, staff morale was low and the atmosphere around the village wasn't just icy, it was glacial. Only yesterday she had driven up to the Milford factory gates to see that someone had spray-painted 'Bailey Out' on the wall outside. Emma knew she needed to make changes fast if she was to head off a meltdown within the company, but she seemed to be banging her head against a brick wall: Milford's image as a luxury brand was far worse than she had ever imagined. But there was one person she knew who could penetrate fashion's inner circle: Cassandra. But even she had proved elusive. Every phone call to her cousin's office was politely but firmly rebuffed. Cassandra was unavailable. Thinking laterally, Emma had contacted her aunt, Julia, but she had merely sent a message that Cassandra was in Paris for the week and would contact her on her return. Emma didn't have a week. Production of samples for the Autumn/Winter line had been halted and could not begin until a new designer was in place. With a press show scheduled for six weeks' time, they'd have to show Roger's designs if she didn't take action immediately – and she didn't think the company would survive that. So when Ruan heard through the grapevine there was a *Rive* party in Paris she had booked her Eurostar ticket at once, telling herself she would sort out the details when she got there.

Well, now I'm here, she thought. Emma took a deep breath and walked as confidently as she could up to the clipboard desk.

'Emma Bailey,' she said, smiling.

'Sorry. No,' said the girl, dismissing Emma instantly and looking down the line to the next poor sap.

'But I'm Cassandra . . .' began Emma, then stopped herself, immediately realizing that 'I'm Cassandra Grand's cousin' sounded like the whine of a gate-crasher – they'd probably already had a dozen people claiming to be relatives tonight.

'Can you look again?' said Emma politely, reaching into her clutch bag and placing her freshly-printed Chief Executive business card on the clipboard.

'Perhaps it's under Milford Luxury Goods,' said Emma with an air of authority. 'I might be on the advertisers' guest list.'

The girl looked at Emma for the first time and she saw a cloud of doubt cross her face.

'I'm sorry, Miss Bailey,' she said, lifting the velvet rope. 'Enjoy the party.'

Emma felt a little thrill of triumph. *Maybe I can pull this off after all,* she thought.

She walked into the impressive atrium mentally running through the questions she needed to ask Cassandra. Emma had even mulled over the idea of Cassandra joining the board as a non-executive director, although she had a nagging reservation. She wasn't entirely sure she wanted to invite a fox into her henhouse.

Emma had never been to a fashion party before. She was surprised to see food. Waiters drifted by with trays laden with delicate bites: savoury tartlets, crab claws and mini Fauchon éclairs, although for the most part the guests waved them away, as if taking a single one would show weakness. Emma felt as if she had crossed into another world.

It's only a party. They're only human, she said to herself, but it was hard to believe. Everywhere she looked there were impenetrable cliques of beautiful and powerful-looking people, talking, laughing and drinking champagne. Had Emma a better grasp of pop culture, she would have recognized that she was surrounded by actresses, models and big-name designers. Up close, many of them weren't actually beautiful, she thought with detached interest. But they had something, a worldliness and polish, a superiority. These people had 'it', whatever 'it' was. And Emma most certainly did not. She felt a sudden sense of inadequacy she hadn't felt since boarding school when she was known as Cassandra Grand's geeky little cousin, a bookworm with mousy hair and clumpy shoes. That bookworm, of course, went on to get an MBA and work alongside the CEOs of multinational blue-chip companies. In Boston Emma had felt on a level pegging with even the most impressive businessmen because she knew her intellect and business skills matched theirs. *But here!* For a second, Emma felt so far out of her depth, she should just turn round and go back to America. 'Bailey Out' – that said it all. But she was not a quitter. She grabbed a flute of champagne from a waiter and took a longer gulp than was polite. From a distance she could see Cassandra receiving guests like the Sun King granting an audience with the peasants.

'You look a little lost, can I help you?'

Emma turned to see a tall man in a lavender woollen suit. He extended a hand with a genuine smile.

'Oh, I hope so,' said Emma, taking his hand gratefully.

'Giles Banks. How nice to meet you.'

She smiled at his eccentric formality and relaxed. 'Emma Bailey – very nice to meet you too. I was beginning to feel invisible.'

'Oh, don't worry!' laughed Giles, leaning in as if to impart a secret, 'I felt like that for years at fashion parties, then I realized that almost everyone feels the same way. They spend their whole time looking around for someone more important or famous than them, worried that everyone else is looking more fabulous or having a brilliant conversation with someone amazing on the other side of the room. No one ever is, they're all talking about who else is here and who they're talking to.'

'So why does anyone come?' asked Emma, fascinated.

'Because you *have* to darling! This is the hottest party in

112

town, if not the whole planet! Who wouldn't want to be here?'

'So it gets better?'

'When you have the right friends. I'm a colleague of Cassandra Grand's and she's introduced me to everyone. Now I know who's going to be fun and who's going to be a crashing bore. Anyway, I always seem to find the most interesting person in the room.'

'Cassandra's my cousin.'

Giles raised his eyebrows.

'How extraordinary. Are you *that* cousin?'

'Which cousin?' asked Emma suspiciously.

'Oh, come now, Emma Bailey, don't be coy. The new CEO of Milford?'

'Did Cassandra tell you?'

Giles clapped his hands in delight. 'You *are* that cousin, how wonderful!' he cried. 'No, Cassandra's been very tight-lipped on the whole business, but fashion is a very small world, word gets around,' he said with a small smile. 'See? I've done it again.'

'Done what?' asked Emma.

'Found the most interesting person in the room.'

What is she doing here? thought Cassandra, seeing Emma's pale face move through the crowd towards her. *And what's she doing with Giles?* She instantly felt furious with Giles, then checked herself when she remembered she hadn't actually told him about Milford, Saul and Emma. Giles was a close friend and trusted confidant, but there were limits. To Cassandra, self-publicity was everything. She had to maintain an air of superconfidence and invulnerability at all times, even when she was cut up inside, even in front of friends. She certainly couldn't admit that she'd been passed over in favour of the geek who knew nothing about fashion. That would have been the ultimate humiliation.

113

Cassandra took a breath to compose herself. Ever since her mother had told her about the events of the Milford board meeting held earlier that week, how Emma had installed herself as CEO and deposed Roger in the process, Cassandra had been calculating her next step. She knew Emma had to be disposed of – and quickly – but she hadn't imagined a confrontation with her cousin would come so soon. Nor did she welcome the distraction on such an important night.

'Look who I found!' smiled Giles, pushing Emma forward, then darting to the right and embracing Sonia Rykiel who treated him like a long-lost friend.

'Emma. What a surprise.'

'I'm a gate-crasher I'm afraid, before you ask, I'm sorry, but I needed to speak to you,' garbled Emma, almost tripping over her words. There was something about Cassandra that had always unnerved Emma, though she had never been able to put her finger on it. The effect was magnified tonight: Cassandra was looking so otherworldly and glamorous in her amazing gown and everyone in the room was craning their necks just to look at her.

'Listen, Cassandra, I won't stay long,' she continued quickly, 'but there was something urgent I needed to ask you.'

'Nothing serious I hope?'

'It's the company.'

'Ah. Well, congratulations, if that's appropriate. I was surprised to hear you'd given up that job in Boston. It's one thing to be given a majority shareholding in a company; it's quite another to give up your life to become its CEO.'

Cassandra began walking out towards the hotel's courtyard. She didn't know why Emma was here, but she had no intention of any of the industry overhearing it.

'Yes, I surprised even myself. I never really saw myself being the sort to be in the fashion business,' said Emma, trying to smile. 'I've never really been bothered about clothes.'

Cassandra gave a hard, brittle laugh as they stopped in front of an ornate fountain.

'Clothes?' she said loftily. 'This business isn't about *clothes*, Emma. Clothes are just something to keep you warm. This business is about fashion, and fashion is a language, a lifestyle, a huge, billion-pound global phenomenon.'

She turned and pointed at a woman on the far side of the courtyard who was wearing a pair of high-waisted trousers. 'Fashion is the genius of that Balenciaga tailoring. Fashion is the feeling it gives her when she dresses and the sense of taste and sophistication other people see in her when they watch her float by.' Cassandra reached down and pulled up a piece of her gown. 'Fashion is this dress, a dress that will be first seen commercially on a catwalk tomorrow and whose photograph will be seen on front pages around the world. This dress won't even be in the stores until September and the copies of it won't filter down into the high street until weeks, maybe months later. But this one dress will generate thousands, perhaps millions of pounds in revenue and in its watered-down version, it will change the lives of thousands of women. It will get them laid, make men propose, it will make them miss lunch for a month just so they can afford it. This dress will transform them, make them feel wonderful, take them to a different place. Fashion has that power – it is magic.'

Cassandra took a breath, surprised by the passion of her speech, knowing that it would serve no purpose to vent the force of her anger on Emma. *Not yet anyway.*

'Although, strictly speaking, Milford isn't about fashion. It's about luxury leather goods,' stuttered Emma feeling completely out of her depth. 'It only really makes handbags.'

Cassandra nearly laughed out loud. What did Emma Bailey know about any of this? *Look at her in those navy trousers and sensible shoes!* This was the most glamorous party being held in Paris over Fashion Week and she looked like an estate agent.

Cassandra gave a little superior laugh.

'Oh, Emma, darling, handbags are the bedrock of the fashion industry. It's where the most profit is made. They can account for 70, 80 per cent of a fashion company's revenue. Do you think Louis Vuitton makes most of its money from ready-to-wear? They make it from Japanese girls spending half their salaries buying three handbags at a time. They make it from average Joe saving up for six months to afford a purse. Handbags are fashion's golden goose.'

Cassandra looked at Emma's clutch bag with barely concealed distain. 'At least, sometimes.'

Emma bristled. She hated being bullied by Cassandra and her style knowledge; she'd always felt like a scarecrow in comparison.

'We're getting off the point.'

'Which is?' asked Cassandra.

'I need a new designer.'

'Yes. Poor Roger.'

Emma bit her tongue and refused to rise to the bait.

'I wondered if you might be able to suggest someone?'

'Why don't you pencil in an appointment with my PA?' Cassandra replied, looking a little bored.

'Cassandra, I tried, but the soonest she could give me was in five weeks' time!'

'Well, I'm very busy as you can see. I'm off to Careyes next weekend. Have you ever been? You must. In the meantime, this is my party and I must go and attend to the guests. It's been lovely to see you and maybe we can put in that lunch?'

Cassandra began to move away.

'Please,' said Emma more forcefully. 'Even if you haven't got time to help me, remember this is also your mother's company.'

Clever bitch thought Cassandra. She exhaled heavily.

'All right. Good accessories designers are hard to find,' she said finally. 'The best ones get poached to head up the womenswear of big houses like Frida Giannini at Gucci. The alternative is to recruit a big name stylist and team them with a technically competent designer.'

'I want the biggest name we can get. Where do I begin?'

'Unless you have personal contacts, which I suspect you do not, the big appointments are made through fashion and luxury headhunters like Claude Lasner. He fixes up the right talent with the right company. Now I don't wish to be impolite, Emma, but this is a working event. A very important night for me. I'm going to have to go.' She looked down pointedly at the narrow gold watch on her wrist.

'Can I tell Claude you told me to get in touch?' asked Emma.

'Of course. He's a very dear friend. Now I really must go.'

As she turned, Cassandra walked straight into a body.

'Do you mind if I join in?' said a deep voice.

Jean-Paul Benoit handed Cassandra a glass of champagne and curled his fingers around her waist as he kissed her cheek. Cassandra pulled back from the strong scent of cologne.

'Don't worry, I was just leaving,' said Emma.

'And who was that?' leered Jean-Paul, as he watched Emma's behind disappear into the crowd. At the creative end, the world of fashion was largely homosexual. But the money men and the business brains were not. Jean-Paul had made it clear that he wanted sex with her. While sex, or the promise of sex, was a tool in Cassandra's repertoire it was one that needed to be used with care.

'That was my cousin needing advice on her little company,' she said boastfully. 'She fancies herself as the next Rose Marie Bravo.'

'Really,' replied Jean-Paul, looking after Emma with interest. 'And what company would that be?'

'Milford,' she said quickly.

'I didn't realize that was in your family. A good heritage.'

She saw the interest on his face and felt a stab of panic.

'A company in its death throes, I'm afraid.'

What was happening? This was supposed to be her perfect night, the pinnacle of her achievements so far and a springboard to the next stage, yet here she was, being ambushed by a mousy upstart, while the CEO of a major luxury goods conglomerate appeared to be interested in both Emma and the company. She felt like all her careful plans were coming unravelled.

Giles appeared and tapped Cassandra lightly on the arm.

'What?' snapped Cassandra, not trying to hide her annoyance.

'Sorry to interrupt,' he said, flashing a look of disapproval in Jean-Paul's direction, 'you're wanted at the door.'

'Excuse me, Jean-Paul. Duty calls,' she said, with a winning smile. 'Perhaps we can take this up again later on?'

She walked towards the entrance and through the sea of faces she could make out her brother Tom, arguing with a security guard. Their eyes locked through the crowd. She saw him mouth something to her but she turned her head away from him. *All people wanted to do was take, take, take,* she thought bitterly. *What had anybody ever given to her?* Without a backward glance, she turned to Giles.

'Make sure security throw him out onto the street. Publicly.'

Giles opened his mouth to object before he saw the fury in her eyes. He turned towards the door.

As Cassandra moved back in to the party, she saw Emma leaving the cloakroom with her coat. She breathed a small sigh of relief when Jean-Paul passed her without any sign of recognition. The last thing she needed was a major luxury goods conglomerate interested in Milford. Now Cassandra knew what needed to be done. She could not allow Milford to get off the starting blocks. It had to fail so she could rescue it and gain control of it herself. But how to begin?

Then she smiled; the answer was right in front of her. This room was packed with fashion's power players: executives, agents, photographers, art directors, stylists, PRs, journalists. All people Emma needed, people who needed to know that Milford was in the hands of an amateur who wore ballet pumps to the hottest party in Paris. People who needed to know that Milford was on the edge of bankruptcy. Fashion was a fickle world; it couldn't stand to be associated with failure. And she knew exactly where to start: in the distance she could see Claude Lasner. It was only fair to warn him, she reasoned. She thought of her mother's small shareholding in the company and shrugged the idea away. She had things to do. She had to make the night count.

8

'It's useless,' said Emma throwing down another portfolio on the oak kitchen table. 'This one only left St Martin's six months ago. How can I appoint someone like that to be the head designer of Milford?'

'It doesn't mean to say they're not any good,' said Ruan McCormack, pouring out coffee from the stove in the warm kitchen of Winterfold. Emma had invited Ruan and Abby Ferguson around for some supper, hoping to sift through the pile of applications for the job of head designer. Claude Lasner had politely but firmly told her that he only dealt with the 'top end of the market', while a contact of Emma's friend Cameron, who had been deputy design director at Gucci, had turned them down flat.

'I don't understand how you can call this good,' said Emma, holding up a photograph from one applicant's graduate show. 'This model is wearing a straitjacket! She looks like she's escaped from an asylum!'

'St Martin's is very creative,' said Abby, taking the photograph from Emma and looking at it as if she really understood it. She had only just left university herself; her father was a friend of Saul's which is how she got

120

the job but Emma was now beginning to doubt the wisdom of having invited her along at all. Although Emma liked her a great deal, her bubbly enthusiasm couldn't disguise her inexperience. In fact, so far she had brought very little to the evening's proceedings beyond throwing the odd lingering look in Ruan's direction.

'Look, this is serious,' said Emma. 'Obviously we've got to make the right appointment but I've got meetings with the banks next week and they are going to want to know who our management team are.'

'What about going back to Roger?' said Abby, trying to fill the silence.

'I'm not sure that's the best way forward,' said Emma diplomatically, although she knew the choice was narrowing between Roger and Mr Straitjacket.

'How about I open a bottle of wine?' said Ruan looking in his bag. 'I swiped this from the boardroom.'

'Great idea,' smiled Abby, jumping up to fetch some glasses. 'By the way, did you find out who wrote "Bailey Out" on the wall outside Byron House?' she asked as she was rummaging in a cupboard.

Emma shook her head sadly. She was beginning to find running her own company less of a dream and more of a nightmare that she couldn't wake up from. She understood why people in the factory and the village as a whole were nervous of change, but they hadn't seen the Milford accounts. If Emma couldn't find a way to reverse the company's fortunes, the factory would close and they would all be out of jobs. And at the moment, she didn't need the pressure of that responsibility to add to her worries.

'I've spoken to Johnston, the floor manager,' said Ruan briskly. 'He says he will launch a discreet inquiry but doesn't reckon any of his lot would do anything like that.' His voice had a note of reproach that caught Emma unaware. Ruan had been supportive of her plan to modernize the products and the working practices, and she'd rather assumed that Ruan was on her side all the way. But his protective attitude towards the factory floor – people he'd worked alongside and probably grown up with – was only natural. Emma made a mental note: *Must remember that this is life and death for some people.*

'It was probably some pissed kids from the pub,' said Abby, trying to make light of it. Emma smiled at her, but she was unconvinced.

'Perhaps,' said Emma feeling her voice wobble. Abby caught the gesture and looked uncomfortable and embarrassed. She put the glasses on the table.

'I'm just going through into the other room to phone my boyfriend,' she said with mock cheeriness. 'It's 8 p.m. He'll be wondering where I am.'

When they were alone, Ruan walked over and awkwardly put an arm around her. Emma had known Ruan McCormack almost all her life. Both his mother and father had been artisans at the factory. He had been a couple of years ahead of her at the local primary school, but at such a small village school, the kids all played together, plus Saul had allowed the children of Milford employees to swim in the lake at Winterfold, so Ruan had taught her to swim the front crawl and to dive. As they grew older they had drifted apart; just awkward smiles across the street when Ruan was with his friends. By the time Emma moved away to boarding school, Ruan had grown into a handsome young man; moody and super-cool; the hunk of the village. Whenever she came home in the holidays, if Emma saw him, she would blush furiously and run away.

She had hardly seen him in the last ten years but she had heard about his rise through the ranks of Milford to become head of merchandise. She knew he was well thought of and in the last two years he had been given a position on the board. He was still sexy, she thought with a smile. Dark wavy hair curled round the top of his white shirt. He had colouring that whispered of pirate ancestry; deep brown eyes, lightly-tanned skin and a strong mouth.

She dismissed the thought, feeling herself flush – she hoped it was the heat from the Aga. Today she was just grateful for his reassurance rather than his good looks. Ruan had been a tower of strength since the day she had arrived at Milford and he was about her only friend out here in the middle of nowhere.

'Are you OK?'

'I'm fine. It was just a bit of silly graffiti,' she lied.

Ruan had uncorked the bottle of wine and handed her a glass.

'I feel as if I'm stumbling around in the dark here,' she smiled. 'Tell me if you think we're wasting our time.'

'With the revamp?'

She nodded.

'A revamp is exactly what Milford needs,' said Ruan with such confidence it instantly buoyed Emma. 'Our manufacturing is good. Our leather is even better than what they use at Connolly or Valextra. We just need a break.'

She leant into him just a fraction.

'You could always cancel the meetings with the bank until we get a designer,' said Ruan.

'And prolong the agony?' said Emma, shaking her head. 'The longer the downward spiral continues the more difficult it's going to be to climb out of it.' She didn't want to tell him the whole truth, that suppliers hadn't been paid in three months, that unless something decisive was done, the company would be bankrupt within twelve months. Milford was Ruan's life and home and there was little other work in the area beyond agriculture, which in any case wasn't terribly healthy either after a series of environmental and political disasters. Theoretically, Ruan could find similar work elsewhere, but the reality was that Britain's manufacturing industry was on its knees. Whatever you needed, it could be made cheaper and faster in the Third World. It would be even worse for Milford's two hundred or so employees and Emma felt she had to protect them from such dire news until she was sure it was inevitable. But who could she share the burden with? She could hardly tell Roger – he probably hadn't ever looked at the company accounts in twenty years – and besides, he would feel vindicated if the ship went down with Emma at the helm. 'Oh, if I'd been in charge, I could have done something,' he would tell his cronies. 'But what hope did old Saul's legacy have with some young floozy playing shop?' Or her mother? She'd only care about Emma's problems as they impacted on her, specifically her shareholding and any awkwardness it would cause at dinner parties. Her Aunt Julia? It was reasonable to assume she would believe that the company should have gone to her own daughter. No, the bottom line was that Emma was all alone in this and would have to face it by herself. She was grateful when she heard the doorbell chime.

'Is that the food already?' said Ruan. 'They usually take hours.'

Along with Milford, Emma had inherited Morton, Saul's septuagenarian butler whom she could ill afford to keep on but who was a Cordon Bleu standard chef. As it was his night off and as the only things in the fridge were duck and lamb shanks, (none of which were right for Emma's single signature dish of spaghetti bolognaise) so she'd done the decent thing and ordered Chinese food from the village take-away. 'I'll go and see.'

Emma had to yank hard on the brass doorknob to open the door and cold night air rushed in. There was an old man standing there, not a delivery boy. At first she didn't recognize him as his face was lined and creased.

'Uncle Christopher?' she said flatteringly. 'Is that you?'

Christopher Chase was not a real uncle, rather one of Saul's oldest friends, often appearing at family gatherings and at Saul's villa. He was also one of the country's most famous sculptors: one of the few surviving members of the St Ives movement. As far as Emma could remember, he still lived in Cornwall, in fact she always thought of Uncle Chris in terms of the old nursery rhyme: 'As I was going to St Ives/I met a man with seven wives . . .'. Christopher was on his fourth wife and had three children aged from 24 to 50.

'It is indeed,' said the old man, taking off his hat with a dramatic gesture. He was still a debonair man now. His face was wrinkled, but his eyes were still bright blue and twinkly, and he was wearing a rakish maroon cravat at his neck.

'Gosh, well, you must come in,' said Emma, moving aside. 'It's been a long time.'

'Provence, I think, maybe fifteen years ago?' smiled Christopher as he took off his coat. 'As I remember, you told me off for not reading and you gave me a book. What was it? The one set in the South of France.'

'*Tender Is the Night.*'

'That was it!' he exclaimed, snapping his fingers. 'It was excellent.'

'I was so pompous,' laughed Emma, her earlier gloominess melting away. 'Anyway, have a seat and I'll nip through to the kitchen, I have some friends round for supper.'

'Oh, I don't want to intrude. I'll only be a few minutes.'

'No, it's fine,' she said waving her hand. 'Let me go and tell them to entertain themselves for a while.'

By the time she returned Christopher had wandered into the library.

'I see you've added a few feminine touches.'

She smiled. There hadn't been a great deal of time to do anything with the house, but she had removed a few of Saul's slightly more masculine decorations: the dented blunderbuss on the mantelpiece, the antique pistols, the buffalo skin Zulu shields, the rather severe-looking stuffed stag's head which looked down from the eaves.

'I tried to tell myself that poor stag had been dead for twenty years, but his eyes still seemed to be following me around, giving me evil looks,' she smiled.

Christopher laughed. 'I was there when Saul shot it. Perhaps I should have taken it myself and pickled it; I could have appealed to a whole new generation of art lovers.'

They both found themselves looking at the grand portrait of Saul above the fireplace. 'I do miss that old rogue . . .' said Christopher quietly. 'I didn't see him enough over the last few years. I regret that.'

'We all do,' said Emma.

Christopher nodded, then shivered, shaking his shoulders like a dog.

'Anyway, sorry for dropping by unannounced. I was on my way to London and thought I'd take a detour into Chilcot. I've just been to the church to pay my respects to Saul. I couldn't make the funeral: Chessie my wife was in hospital.'

'Oh, I'm sorry. Nothing serious I hope?'

Christopher shook his head.

'Everything's fine.'

He wandered over to the mantelpiece and picked up a silver frame containing a black and white photograph of Saul and himself in Egypt, and another of them arm-in-arm at the top of Mount Cook.

'Look at him,' said Christopher with affection, 'he always was a big showman.'

'You noticed he has the biggest gravestone in the church grounds?' smiled Emma.

'Of course he has,' laughed Christopher. 'He should have been an entertainer, not a businessman. I know he wouldn't mind me saying that. But he was shrewd enough to give the company to you. That news filtered down as far as St Ives.'

'Shrewd? Not everybody sees it that way.'

Christopher looked at her, rubbing his chin with his hand. Emma was startled to see that his artistic fingers were now twisted and gnarled by arthritis.

'I wanted to drop by and see if you were OK,' he said with a note of concern. 'How is it going so far?'

'Difficult,' she said honestly.

'Roger?'

Emma caught the co-conspirator's smile.

She grinned back and nodded.

'Roger always had a high opinion of himself. Always been the failing of this company in my opinion. Saul allowed him to get away with far too much, indulged Roger's ego. Actually, I think he was a little afraid of him. As I'm sure you know, Roger can be very charming, but he's also very manipulative. Saul made him creative director at twenty-five because, well, because that's what Roger wanted. And the company has been going downhill ever since.'

'Well, he isn't creative director of Milford any longer.'

'You fired him?' said Christopher, surprised.

'Not exactly. Moved him along.'

'Well, good for you,' said Christopher. 'But watch out for that one. You know what a rat will do when it's cornered.'

Emma frowned. *A rat?* It was obvious Christopher didn't think much of Saul's younger brother, but that last comment was laced with venom.

'Sorry, Emma,' interrupted Christopher, glancing at the clock on the wall, then at his own wristwatch, 'I really must be going. Chessie is at the Feathers. We're staying there tonight and then we're off to London.'

'Oh. OK, if you must,' said Emma, following him out of the library towards the door. 'It's always lovely to see you. How are the children, by the way?'

'All fine. Well, I think they're fine. I don't see as much of them as I'd like. My two eldest live in Scotland. Stella, my youngest, lives in the States now. She's a fashion designer. I tried to get her to follow in her old man's footsteps – she studied sculpture at the Slade, but it seems she prefers working with cloth rather than clay.'

Emma's ears had pricked up.

'She's a designer. Really? Who does she work for?'

'Oh, some trendy American company in LA. Can't even remember the name,' he laughed.

'LA?'

'"La-la-land", I know, but her mother lives on the West Coast. Stella went over there after college and never came back.'

'Is she a good designer?' asked Emma cautiously.

He laughed heartily. 'How could she fail with my genes? Hey, maybe you should give her Roger's old job? I'd be glad to have her back in the country.'

Emma smiled weakly. 'Maybe it's not such a crazy idea,' she said under her breath.

'Really?' said Christopher, pulling a black leather diary from his inside pocket.

'Then maybe you should give her a ring,' he said, writing something down. 'She doesn't call me much, but the last time I heard she seemed to be quite happy out there – takes all sorts, I suppose. Here's her number, anyway. You'll get her answer machine, she's never there. But if you leave a message she usually calls you back.'

Christopher hugged Emma then stepped back, holding her by the shoulders.

'You stay strong, young lady,' he said. 'Saul gave you the

128

company for a reason. Saul was many things, but he wasn't a fool and he chose you to carry on his legacy – not any of those vultures in your family. I, for one, think he made a splendid choice and I know you'll make him proud.'

He pulled down his hat and tipped a salute back inside the house, then he was away into the darkness and gone.

Emma stood there on the doorstep, feeling a distant wave of hope.

'Who was that?' asked Ruan, coming behind her with a glass of wine.

'Milford's lifeline,' said Emma.

9

'She is such a *bitch*!' said Stella Chase indignantly. 'Have you seen this shit?' She thrust a copy of US *Rive* towards her friend Tash, stabbing a finger at the page. Moments earlier, the two girls had been sitting quietly in Venice Beach's Fig-tree Café, eating frozen yoghurt and idly leafing through the latest fashion magazines. Then Stella had come across a twelve-page photo story on handbag designer Cate Glazer. Alongside a series of sumptuous photos of her palatial Hamptons home, the article gushed about Glazer's life: how she had started as a bit-part soap actress, fallen in love with and married Hollywood producer Lance Glazer, then launched her must-have range of bags and purses. The cherry on the cake, said the article, was Glazer's recent triumph, being crowned CFDA Accessories Designer of the Year.

'Which bit are we referring to?' asked Tash, taking a lick of double-berry yoghurt while she scanned the feature. 'The photo of their new forty-million dollar home in Sag Harbor or the roll-call of her former boyfriends? There's some pretty cute guys in that list, you know.'

'This bit,' said Stella, pointing at the page so hard her fingernail almost went through the paper. 'That entire section boasting about the "Beverly" bag. How the design came to her in a dream. A *dream*!'

Stella jumped up, grabbed her things and barged out from the air-conditioned cool of the café into the bright heat of early spring afternoon in Los Angeles. She dumped the paper sack bulging with groceries she had bought from Whole Foods that morning into the basket of her bicycle as Tash tagged along behind her, the magazine fluttering in her hand.

'Are you going to bring it up with her?' asked her friend.

'I won't even be seeing her until Wednesday. You know it's the Oscars tomorrow; she always takes the next two days off to recover.'

'Cate loves to party,' said Tash weakly.

Stella stopped dead on the boardwalk, causing a muscled in-line skater in only shorts and headphones to swerve dangerously to avoid her.

'Three years!' she said. 'Three bloody years I've been working for that company! And what thanks do I get?' she continued, determined to get it off her chest. 'I work 14-hour days. I design every purse, dress and shoe for that company and she tells the world the idea for her latest It-bag came to her "in a dream".'

'What you need is a good night out,' replied Tasha, putting a reassuring hand on her friend's shoulder. 'Apparently there's this great party in the Hills tonight. Like an unofficial pre-Oscars party. I hear Brad's gonna be there and . . .'

'You know Lance is gay, don't you?'

Tash threw her frozen yoghurt in the trash.

'Stella, honey! Let it go! It's bad for your karma.'

Stella didn't seem to hear her, starting to push her bicycle along the beach again. Across the wide expanse of sand, the sea twinkled in the distance.

'Maybe I'll go to that good tarot reader on the boardwalk

on the way home,' mused Stella vaguely, 'I think I need some psychic intervention to tell me what to do.'

'What you need to do is come out tonight,' said Tash firmly. 'Go home and get ready.'

Stella shook her head. 'I'd love to, but I can't.'

'What's more important than a party on Oscars weekend?' asked Tash seriously.

'Oh, a friend of the family is in town,' she said.

'So bring her to the party.'

Stella grimaced. 'I really don't think she's the partying kind.'

'Orlando is going to be there,' persisted Tash.

'Well, I'll think about it,' said Stella already on her bike, 'call you later.'

'Brad! Orlando!' called Tash after her, 'that guy out of the OC?'

Stella just turned back and waved, knowing that not even the cutest boys in Hollywood could lift the black cloud surrounding her today.

The two-mile cycle ride back to Santa Monica did little to clear Stella's head. The Santa Ana winds were blowing making it artificially warm for an early spring day. To her left the Pacific Ocean sparkled silver while in the distance, as if to welcome her home, the pier jutted out into the sea looking every bit as magical as it had the first time she had seen it almost four years earlier. *And look how far I've come*, she thought, with just a hint of irony. She had come to California six months after she had graduated, ostensibly to be nearer her mother who had moved from Cornwall to Montecito to 'reinvent' herself as an aromatherapist. But within weeks Stella had drifted down to LA, got a flat in Santa Monica and a job in a boutique on Melrose. Her wage was a pittance; the trade-off for them turning a blind eye to her lack of a green card. The boutique was hip and Stella was pretty which meant that she was often invited to parties. She went along for the free food and drink, but even at the most chic Hollywood Hills soiree, Stella was always the most stylish person there in the little dresses she customized from thrift shop finds or rolls of spare fabric from the shop. It was at one of those parties that Stella had met Cate Glazer, wife of the famous movie producer Lance, who had ambitions to be LA's answer to Kate Spade. Cate Glazer had been knocked out by the beautiful blonde Brit, but was more knocked out by the white jersey T-shirt dress she said she had run up that afternoon. It was simple but chic, cleverly using the material to show her figure off to best advantage. The kid clearly had talent.

'Can you design handbags?' Cate Glazer had asked her.

'I'll try anything once,' smiled Stella. What the hell, why not? She shrugged. And it was that easy: the next Monday Stella began work as 'design executive' for fledgling LA fashion house Cate Glazer. She hadn't realized when she signed on, however, that it was a workforce of two: Stella designed the bags which were produced by a company in Mexico, Cate handled the PR. Their first venture involved Stella making 100 totes from white sail canvas. Cate gave them to a selection of Lance's actress friends each of whom had been photographed carrying them. The photos ran in every magazine from *US Weekly* to *Vogue* and suddenly Cate Glazer was on the map. The orders poured in so fast that within six months they had to open a factory in Mexico. Three years later, Cate Glazer was one of America's hottest lifestyle labels, a multi-million-dollar business, branching out from accessories into fashion and interiors, while Stella was in pretty much the same place. Sure, she had an office with 'Design Executive' on the door, but despite her talent, she had never received a single job offer because everyone believed Cate Glazer was the talent behind the stylish Cate Glazer merchandise.

The sky was beginning to darken by the time Stella pushed her bicycle through her apartment door. *What a mess*, she thought, leaving the bike against the wall and stepping over the piles of laundry in the kitchen and books on the carpet. She opened the shutters to let the warm, salty scent of the Pacific fill the room. She had just put on a pot of coffee and was just contemplating transferring the huge mountain of plates into the dishwasher when her intercom buzzed.

'Who is it?' said Stella wearily.

'Emma Bailey.'

'Oh shit,' she said, before realizing her finger was still on the buzzer.

'I can come back,' said a crackling voice.

'No, no, come on up,' she said quickly, before rushing around scooping up everything cluttering the floor and flinging it all into a laundry bag. Then Stella stopped in her tracks. 'Oh shit!' she said, as the penny dropped. *This woman may be here to offer me a job.* Emma had called the previous day and after some polite pleasantries about Saul's death, Emma had muttered that there might be some design opportunities opening at Milford and that she was very keen to talk to Stella in person about them. Stella had been up for three days putting the finishing touches to a dozen clutch bags which a certain A-lister had requested for the Oscars red carpet. One bag would not do, Stella had been told, because the notoriously diva-esque actress could not possibly decide which dress she was going to wear until the afternoon of the event. Her mind fuzzed from lack of sleep and overwork, Stella had failed to take in the meaning of Emma's words. In fact, until this moment, she had failed to consider why Emma Bailey, new CEO of Milford Luxury Goods, would take the time and expense to fly six thousand miles to see her. 'Oh, SHIT!' she cried and ran for the bathroom.

Stella looked at herself in the mirror, wishing she had

time to change out of her shorts and vest-top. But she didn't look *too* bad. Her skin was lightly tanned and clear. She had a wide mouth, sun-kissed blonde hair in a Jean Seberg crop which suited her petite frame and height. She did not like to think of herself as beautiful although she suspected it, given the number of people who assumed she was an actress and men who made passes at her every time she went out. She ruffled her hair and pinched her cheeks. *Well, it'll have to do*, she thought. *She's not after me for my pretty face.*

'Come in. Come in,' said Stella, opening the door as she kicked her sneakers behind the magazine rack. 'Sorry it's a bit of a mess.'

Stella was slightly relieved to see that Emma seemed equally flustered.

'Don't worry, my fault for being early. The LAX immigration Gestapo waved me through without too much interrogation and the taxi driver seemed to have a death wish,' she smiled.

Emma took in the chaos of Stella's flat: the piles of magazines, the rolls of fabric, the precarious tower of DVDs by the TV, most of which seemed to be rom-coms or weepies. 'What a lovely view!' she exclaimed.

Stella burst out laughing and Emma couldn't help but join in. Stella decided immediately that she liked this crazy woman who had flown halfway around the world to see her. She could barely remember Emma from a holiday in Provence when they were both very young, but her mother still kept in touch with Julia Grand. From the snippets of gossip that occasionally filtered her way, Stella had gathered the impression that Emma was the black sheep of the Milford family: someone tough and independent and mysterious. But the woman in front of her was sweaty and creased and had more than a hint of vulnerability about her. *Well, that can't be a bad thing*, she thought.

'Well, I guess I'd better offer you a drink after you've come all this way,' smiled Stella, taking Emma's bag and plopping it on an already overladen armchair.

'Soda or vodka, I'm afraid,' she said, rummaging around in the fridge. 'Or I bought mint from the farmers' market so we could have fresh tea?'

'Mint tea would be lovely,' said Emma, wandering to the window and gazing out. 'So your father never made a sculptor out of you after all?'

Stella laughed. 'He tried – oh, he tried. And for a little while I went along with it. I studied sculpture at the Slade,' she called from the kitchen as she banged about preparing the tea.

'I fell into fashion design by mistake although it's not a hundred miles away from sculpture. All about form and shape. I took a course in pattern cutting but I'm pretty much self-taught.'

'And now you're a design executive at Cate Glazer.'

She looked at Emma wondering how much – or little – she knew about her life, not knowing that Emma had spent the entire twelve-hour flight to LA reading an inch-thick file on the growing Cate Glazer empire that she had obtained from a London press agency.

'Well, officially I'm the design executive, which means I help Cate design the products.'

'And unofficially?' asked Emma, immediately reading between the lines.

Stella hesitated and looked a little embarrassed.

'Cate is the front-person for the products, but I design everything. It's a little like a ghost-writer doing novels. She OKs everything and she knows what she likes. Plus however much I moan about her, I have to admit she's a great business brain and a marketing genius.'

The truth, thought Stella, was that Cate Glazer was a

136

nightmare. Controlling and arrogant, she was paranoid to the point of forbidding her staff to have telephones, in case they should be tempted to make personal calls on company time. Stella knew Cate was also terrified that her star designer might be poached, but instead of incentivizing her, she kept Stella locked away in a windowless office with her drawing boards and swatches, ensuring that no one outside the company ever met her. Stella brought the tea things out on a dusty tray and pushed some magazines off the sofa so they could sit down.

'So tell me, is this an interview or a chat?' asked Stella, handing Emma a cup. 'I take it from your call yesterday you're looking to boost your design team?'

'No. I'm actually looking for a head designer. I want someone to run the whole operation.'

'No way!' gasped Stella, almost spilling her tea. 'You haven't flown all the way from London just to speak to *me* have you?' she said incredulously.

Emma nodded.

'*Why?*' said Stella with a half-laugh.

Emma hesitated before she spoke. 'Well, because none of the big names are interested. Because I need to make an appointment very, very quickly before my family's company goes down the pan. Because I've done my homework and know you spent three summers working in the Milford factory, because I know you're the unsung hero of Cate Glazer and because I hope you care as much about Milford as I do.'

'Blimey. You're very straight-talking,' laughed Stella, not expecting such an honest answer.

'I used to be a management consultant,' smiled Emma. 'I'm used to speaking my mind.'

Stella took a sip of her tea, her heart suddenly thumping.

'You work in fashion now, honey. Nobody says what they really think.'

She paused, put down her mint tea and waved Emma over.

'Come through,' she said leading her to the second bedroom which had been converted into a studio. In stark contrast to Stella's living space, there was a clear order to this room. There was a tailor's dummy in the corner of the room and a sewing machine in front of the French window. Hung up on a wooden rail were a dozen squares of leather. Stella moved over to a white sofa near the window and sorted through a pile of bags.

'Some of this season's Cate Glazer bags,' she explained. 'No doubt you've seen all these . . .'

Emma picked one up and examined it. It was lovely. A perfect balance between the formal and the avant-garde, you could take it into the boardroom then out to a club without a worry. This girl was good.

Stella straightened up, holding out a taupe leather tote bag. 'This one, however, is my own. I make them for friends mostly, although Fred Segal might carry them in the Fall.'

'This is beautiful,' said Emma honestly. It was made from luxurious butter-soft leather and she had used the material as the starting point − it was somehow structured but relaxed. The bag seemed to mould itself around Emma's hands.

'But this is what I really wanted to show you,' said Stella, opening a cupboard.

'Vintage Milford bags,' she said, handing Emma a snakeskin clutch.

'Some used to belong to my mum, a couple were even my grandmother's, I think. This one . . .' she held up an amazing crocodile-skin day-bag, like a mini-Gladstone bag, '. . . I found this in Decades, a super-cool retro shop on Melrose. It cost me half my wage packet but I had to have it.' Stella talked quickly − the words bubbling from her mouth as if she was unable to stop them. She ran her hand over the bag as if it was a precious jewel.

'Can you see? The craftsmanship is amazing. Handbags were tiny in the 1950s. Women didn't carry their entire life around inside them as they do now. Look, there's an inside pocket for a compact. That could be adapted to hold a mobile phone, don't you think? And the curve of this buckle here is like a Barbara Hepworth sculpture. It's stunning – it's actually been die-cast. That sort of thing doesn't happen now, but I think it would be so great to reinstate it.'

Stella realized she had been babbling. She looked up at Emma and Emma was grinning from ear to ear.

'Honestly Emma,' she said, smiling back, 'you don't need me. Just look in Milford's archives or hunt down every single vintage bag you can get your hands on; private collections, vintage shops, even jumble sales. You don't need a star designer – everything you need is here.'

Emma held up Stella's own tote bag. 'No, what I need is this,' she said seriously. 'I'm no expert on design – God knows, look at the state of me,' she laughed, indicating her travel-crumpled suit, 'but even I can tell that what you have done with your own bags is special. Yes, the vintage bags are wonderful, but as you say, they were designed for their time. Women today want something that is right for now, something that in fifty years people will be looking at and saying "Wow, they were so stylish back then". I want you to take the Milford heritage as a framework and add this,' she waved Stella's bag again, 'the Stella Chase magic.'

Stella laughed out loud. 'You actually want me to do this?'

'Absolutely.'

Stella's head was reeling.

'But how can I . . .?'

'Listen to me, Stella,' said Emma, her face deadly serious,

'I came here because I was desperate. I couldn't get anyone to design Milford's collection and the bank is breathing down my neck. You were my last option. But since the moment I pressed that buzzer, I have been convinced that, given the choice of every top designer from Hermès to Vuitton, I would still choose you.'

Stella gaped. 'Are you on drugs?'

Emma laughed. 'Not quite, but it's how I feel. Call it a gut-feeling if you like, but I just know no one else could do the job better than you.'

'But I have my whole life here . . .' said Stella lamely, suddenly frightened by the sudden notion that she might actually want the job. Emma put her tea down.

'OK, let me tell you why you should do this,' she said, ticking the points off on her fingers. 'One, you'll have complete control over the designs – complete control. No ifs, no buts, you're in charge. Two, I'll get you all the support staff you need – no more late nights, well, not so many anyway,' she smiled.

'Three, I'm guessing you're on a salary at Cate Glazer? I'll beat it by 50 per cent and if it all works out we can talk about taking a shareholding. And four, you'll get 100 per cent credit for your designs, and I do mean 100 per cent. I want people to know you're behind the creative rebirth of Milford.'

Stella frowned, trying to take it all in, her little nose wrinkling up. She thought back to the CFDA awards when the name Cate Glazer had been called out for Accessories Designer of the Year. Stella had only been invited at the last minute when one of Cate's Hollywood friends had dropped out and she had almost been sick when Cate went up to accept the award alone. Behind every designer was a team of design assistants, pattern cutters, seamstresses, stylists and money men who all made it come together. But in the creative process, Cate hadn't so much as lifted a pencil.

'All I want to know is if you'd be interested in the job,' said Emma.

'Can I just check this?' asked Stella, a goofy smile on her face, 'You want me to work for Milford?'

'Yes.'

'As head designer?' she said, suddenly coughing.

'Yes. And of course you'd get to work in a beautiful green English village. No smog, no traffic, and not one mugging since they caught Dick Turpin.'

Stella snorted. Emma was a clever woman. She seemed to understand how Stella was feeling. She could see she wanted to get out of the trap she'd built for herself, to show the world exactly what she could do. But still . . .

She looked around her flat; the cheap white furnishings, paper lampshades and bamboo blinds, and wondered if it really was time to go back to England. She looked out of the window, where Santa Monica was disappearing into the dusk. Of all the places in LA, it was the place she loved best; there were English pubs, a large expat British community, it was close to the sea. But was that simply because it reminded her of home? Emma seemed to read her thoughts.

'Do you have a notice period on your contract?' she asked.

Stella laughed. 'A week, I think. When Cate took me on I think she wanted me to be quickly dispensable and the contract has never been changed.'

Emma stood up. 'Stella, I need you to help me do this. Together I really think we can turn Milford around. Make it the exclusive luxury brand it once was.'

Stella listened to Emma with an almost eerie detachment. She was talking a good game and she was clearly confident in her abilities, but there was a tiny flicker of fear in Emma's voice. For Stella, this was something new. Cate Glazer's self-belief had never wavered for a second. She shouted and ranted and demanded the very best, never for a moment contemplating failure. But Emma was different. She was honest and forthright and she was painfully aware that the whole thing could go tits up at any time. I like her, she thought, reaching out to shake Emma's hand.

'OK, boss, see you in a week.'

It was Emma's turn to gape.

'Really?' she replied.

'Really!' said Stella. 'Only, can I ask for one thing?'

'Name it.'

'Can I have my own phone?'

10

Sitting in the meeting room of the book publisher Leighton Best, Cassandra Grand was having trouble keeping her temper. She did her best to ignore the plate of cheap biscuits and ugly mug of milky tea that had been pushed in front of her, she could even overlook the IKEA furniture and magnolia walls. But what was driving her to distraction was listening to the company's art director Paula Mayle run through her so-called vision for the design of her new book *Cassandra Grand: On Style*.

'I hope you like it,' said Paula, putting down her mock-up board. 'We think the pillar-box red jacket is very strong.'

Cassandra just stared at her. *Who are these people?* she thought. *What do they do with their lives?*

'You're obviously not aware that red was something of a signature colour for Diana Vreeland.'

'Erm, Diana Vreeland?' asked Jenny Barber, the book's commissioning editor.

Cassandra rolled her eyes heavenward.

'US *Vogue* editor 1963 to 71. One of the most influential magazine editors of the twentieth century. She was at least

143

twenty years ahead of her time, completely understood the concept of brand – just as we must grasp it now. This book is a brand statement. *My* brand statement. Consequently, red is unacceptable. I would suggest lucite.' She turned a wintery smile towards Paula. 'It's a platinum, Pantone number 1032.'

'Paula, maybe you can look into that,' said Jenny to her assistant, quavering under Cassandra's gaze.

'I've also been making a few notes as we go along,' continued Cassandra taking a sip of water. She winced. It was semi-flat, sparkling mineral water.

'Fonts. Helvetica is an absolute no. My readers are going to be extremely design-conscious and I think they would appreciate something more unusual. I will send you the number of David Sellers, one of the country's best typographers, to create something new. We can use Tahoma or Trebuchet as a template.'

'So are you happy otherwi . . .'

Cassandra cut Jenny Barber off mid-sentence.

'My name Cassandra Grand should be bigger than the title,' she continued as if the interruption had never occurred. 'Lift it several point sizes. Also when I said coffee-table book, that's what I meant. Something of size. This has to be a book in people's libraries, a gift for people to treasure.' She held her hands apart to indicate the size of the book she had in mind. 'Roughly the size of a large picnic basket.'

'Well, I'm glad we've made progress here,' said Jenny when she was completely sure Cassandra had finished. 'One final thing though, Cassandra? When do you think we'll be seeing any copy? For a September publication date we're getting a *little* tight.'

Cassandra dismissed it with a wave.

'Don't worry about that. You'll have it within the fortnight.'

She glanced at her mobile which was suddenly glowing an elegant emerald green. 'Now if you'll excuse me,' she said politely, stepping outside the meeting room to collective sighs of relief from the Leighton Best editorial team. It was Lianne.

'Can you come back to the office immediately?'

'What is it? I'm at Linda Meredith for my facial in forty minutes.'

'I think it's important: Jason Tostvig and Greg Barbera.'

Cassandra caught her breath. *Greg Barbera? What did the Managing Director of the company want? He was on the international board.*

'Did they give any clues?'

'I'm just guessing, but there was a letter from a London solicitor acting for Phoebe Fenton in today's post. It's quite angry.'

Cassandra gave a long hard sigh.

'Fine. Tell Toxic and Greg I will meet them at twelve. But first, I need you to do something for me . . .'

Cassandra stood in front of the mirror, touching up her make-up. She had made a detour from the lift to the bathroom before she went into the *Rive* office. A sweep of mascara and a slick of gloss was all she needed to look like a model who had just stepped off the catwalk. There was a light smell of vomit coming from the cubicle behind her. It was a familiar smell at noon; there were at least half a dozen bulimics in the office. She took a little vial of her bespoke scent out of her purse and dabbed it on her pulse points. She was as ready as she'd ever be.

'Cassandra. Busy day?' said Jason obsequiously as she joined the two men in Greg's corner office. It was a wonderful space – B&B Italia furniture, walls painted a delicate shade of cornflower and fabulous views over the Thames, views

Greg rarely got to enjoy as he spent 90 per cent of his time in New York.

'How are you, Cassandra?' said Greg, neglecting to rise. Greg was a tall man and even sitting down he looked powerful and capable, a grey three-piece suit matching his swept-back hair and implacable eyes. He seemed very serious.

'Very well, thank you,' said Cassandra, giving him the full wattage of her smile. 'Now to what do I owe this pleasant surprise?'

'Don't screw around, Cassandra,' said Greg, an edge to his voice. 'You know what I'm here for. Jason has been good enough to bring me up to speed on the Phoebe Fenton situation . . .'

The snake, thought Cassandra, noting his smug smile.

'It's a wonderful issue, isn't it,' she replied evenly. 'Looks very strong on the news-stand and every major newspaper has carried at least part of the interview on their front page. It's too soon for EPOS figures,' she continued, referring to the weekly electronic sales figures the magazine received from newsagents using barcode-readers, 'but with this sort of publicity, I feel we have a chance of breaking *Rive*'s previous sales record.'

Greg laid one hand carefully on the table.

'That may be so, Cassandra,' he said, his eyes boring into hers. 'The problem is that we have Phoebe lawyers crawling all over us.'

'But, why . . .'

He lifted the hand briefly to silence her objections.

'Phoebe is claiming that we've "sexed up" the interview. They say that the journalist was creative with the facts and that any reference to Ms Fenton's depression was made to you in passing conversation and has been taken completely out of context.'

146

'I would dispute that,' said Cassandra coolly. 'If Phoebe's people . . .'

'I've taken the liberty of phoning Phoebe's people already,' interrupted Jason leaning forward in his chair, 'and they have made a proposal, a rather generous proposal in the circumstances, I would say. They say they won't pursue us for damages if we pulp the issue.'

'I don't need to remind you of the financial implication of pulping the issue,' said Greg. 'Not to mention the impact on the next circulation figures.'

Cassandra let them speak, determined not to lose her cool and intrigued to see how far Toxic was prepared to push it. *I can't believe he's actually using the magazine as a sacrificial lamb, undermining his own sales figures, just to twist the knife in me!* Cassandra knew she had underestimated the extent of his ambition. She looked across at him; despite his stern face she could tell he was enjoying it, enjoying having blind-sided her, enjoying being teacher's pet.

'Pulp the issue?' said Cassandra calmly. 'How can you call that a generous proposal? It is simply not an option.'

Greg brought his hand down on the desk, making both Jason and Cassandra jump. 'I will decide what is and is not an option for this company, Cassandra,' he said in a low voice. If nothing else, Greg Barbera was clearly pissed off at having been dragged to London to sort this mess out. 'Our legal department thinks it might be the best way forward and Jason seems inclined to agree. I, however, am keen to hear what you have to say on the matter.'

Cassandra paused, nodding slightly, before picking up the yellow Tanner Krolle handbag she had left next to her chair.

'I'm sure you are both aware of the libel laws in this country?' she asked, reaching into the bag. 'It's rather like the conundrum of the tree falling over in the woods: if no one is there to see her take cocaine, did it really happen?

147

The burden of proof, therefore, is on the publisher, i.e. Phoebe Fenton may well have a mental illness, but if we can't prove it, we are libelling her. If we can, however . . .'

Cassandra placed a small silver Dictaphone on the table and turned it on.

The voice was tinny but unmistakably the New York drawl of Phoebe Fenton.

'. . . I have bipolar disorder. It's been making me a little crazy.'

Greg's face softened with the smallest of smiles as she let the tape run.

'You make sure your back is covered,' he said approvingly.

Cassandra merely smiled. She had found the tiny buttonhole microphone she'd used to tape her conversation with Phoebe useful on numerous occasions. Greg Barbera's smile might not have been quite so wide if he'd been aware that Cassandra also had numerous tapes of her conversations with him: his promises of pay-rises and career advancement, his bitter attacks on his own company and indiscretions about his colleagues. It was all just ammunition – for now.

'But that's not all,' blustered Jason, trying to dig himself out of his hole. 'I called the head of media planning at the Emerald agency, just to see what they thought of the issue. She's not very happy either.'

'*You* called *her*?' asked Cassandra incredulously, unable to keep herself in check any longer. 'Whose side are you on?'

Greg looked at Jason, his expression suggesting that he too might like an answer.

'I was just gauging opinion,' said Jason weakly.

'Greg,' said Cassandra, turning her back on Jason, 'running the interview in exactly the way in which it was told to us was a calculated decision. I knew some of the more conservative advertisers wouldn't be happy but I suspect that when they see the circulation figure for that issue, they will applaud our bravery. Now is not the time to be "gauging opinion", it's a time to press our advantage, to go to the advertisers and guarantee them that *Rive*'s year-on-year circulation will rise by at least 5 per cent.'

'Guarantee?' spluttered Jason, 'But we don't even know how the issue is doing yet! April is never the strongest selling issue of the year.'

Cassandra turned and stared at him levelly.

'I predict by this time next week we'll be reprinting.'

'But our legal team says . . .'

'Fuck our legal department,' said Cassandra mildly.

Greg held up a hand to bring the sparring match to an end.

'OK. So how do you suggest we proceed?' He was pointedly asking Cassandra. Jason had already been dispensed with.

'Let me with deal with it,' she said confidently. 'I have already phoned my friend at Schillings to fire off a letter to "Phoebe's people",' she mocked Jason's words. 'And I will personally call all the major advertisers once we have the EPOS figures for the first week of sales.'

Greg seemed to be satisfied.

'Cassandra,' said Greg, his eyes unreadable. 'Just be careful.'

Cassandra smiled politely, knowing she was back in control, then looked at Jason who had the look of a wounded animal.

'Now if you'll excuse me I have a magazine to edit.'

She closed the glass door behind her and walked down the corridor, imagining with relish the pain Jason Tostvig was about to be put through. *That bastard!* She had been wrong to think he was harmless; it had almost been a costly slip. She had been right about one thing though; he was stupid – stupid enough to cross her. Cassandra stalked back into the same bathroom she had left only twenty minutes before and leant on the sink, taking in deep breaths. She reached up to curl her eyelashes and saw that her hands were shaking. *Pulp the issue indeed!* For all her reputation, Cassandra knew something like that wouldn't just be a black mark; it could be the loose thread which might start the whole thing unravelling. Even Diana Vreeland for all her brilliance and international reputation was ultimately dispensed with. That's what fashion was all about – dispensability.

For a second she felt a wave of profound doubt: the person on top of the mountain was on the thinnest ridge and had the longest way to fall. She suddenly turned and ran into the nearest stall and threw up. When the spasms had passed, she wiped her mouth carefully and, checking no one had been in the bathroom to see her shame, walked back towards her office, her head held high.

There was no turning back. She had so many balls up in the air, so much at stake; she couldn't afford to let up for a moment. Fashion was a game of poker: all about bluff and re-bluff, not who had the strongest hand. Cassandra had all her chips in the middle of the table, she couldn't back out now. As she turned the corner to her office, she saw Jason Tostvig coming out of Greg Barbera's office, his head bowed, his tie undone. Cassandra smiled. She would deal with him later.

11

'How are you bearing up?'

Roger popped a slice of tender Welsh lamb into his mouth and pulled a face.

'I can't say I've been delighted by the events of the last few weeks,' he replied sourly. Roger and William Billington were sitting in the dining room of Mark's Club, the establishment Mayfair restaurant where Roger had been coming since he was old enough to sign a cheque. William had been Milford's banker for more than twenty-five years, a role he had inherited from his father before him, but the two men were more than just business associates, and in fact Roger had dated William's sister for a while before he'd mistakenly double-booked her with a feisty deb one New Year's Eve. The resulting catfight was still fondly remembered by both men. Roger and William's relationship was based on something much more solid: a shared love of fine wines, food and money. Once a month they met up socially, taking it in turns to buy each other lunch in the best restaurants around London.

'Did you and Saul have a falling out?'

'Not at all,' said Roger, looking surprised. 'In fact the

whole family is in shock. Saul hadn't even seen the girl in the last three years, she was something of a black sheep to tell the truth. Never used to involve herself in family affairs, never summered with us at the house in Provence – not since she was a girl, anyway. Never joined us for Christmas in Gstaad. Strange girl; very closed off, I'd say.'

William chewed a mouthful of his steak thoughtfully.

'However, I heard that she's removed you from your position – a bit of a sideways move?'

Roger barked a hollow laugh.

'It's so transparent, isn't it? Some trick they've taught her at that management firm she was with no doubt. Make your mark, fire a few people, especially people more capable than yourself, who might make you look bad.'

'Hmm . . .' said William.

'More wine sir?' asked the sommelier, appearing at Roger's side.

Roger nodded, tapping the top of his glass.

'And she's replaced you with whom?' asked William.

Roger laughed cynically, wiping the corner of his mouth with a napkin.

'Ah, you haven't heard? Some twenty-six-year-old with no fashion college background and no track record bar some lowly position in a tacky Hollywood accessories company.'

William winced. 'Oh dear.'

'Indeed.' He scoffed, 'I'd almost understand it if she'd have got in a heavyweight designer, someone from Hermès or Bottega Veneta perhaps, but she's treating it as some sort of game. Trashed the entire new collection for no apparent reason, wasted thousands in the process. Now she has all these grand ambitions for expansion. I still have a 20 per cent stake in this company, William, and frankly I'm worried my shareholdings aren't going to be worth the paper they are written on by Christmas.'

William sat back and sipped at his wine.

'I have to admit that Emma's appointment came as a surprise to us all at Billington's. We all assumed that you were the natural heir.'

'Well, there we are in agreement,' snorted Roger. 'Saul never gave me the tiniest inclination it was going to pan out any other way.'

'Well, to be straight with you, Roger,' said William, 'Saul was a dear friend but you know I was getting concerned about his lack of focus with the business. It was never really in his blood. He enjoyed the trappings, but the nuts and bolts? Not interested.'

Roger felt no qualms about being disloyal to his brother. Saul had left him with nothing – well, nothing he wanted – so why not speak his mind?

'I totally agree,' he nodded. 'Meanwhile, you are aware Emma is looking for a capital injection of twenty million?'

William put down his glass.

'That much? We have an appointment in the diary for Friday so no doubt she will tell me more then.'

'And are you going to support her?' asked Roger, holding his friend's gaze.

'You mean are we going to support *her*,' said William with a smirk, 'or are we going to get behind *you*?'

Roger was glad he didn't have to make the purpose of their lunch explicit. He tapped his Limoges china plate with his fork for emphasis. 'I could do great things with the company.'

'I was looking forward to seeing it,' said William with a sympathetic smile. 'Of course no one knows what to make of her. She was a manager at Price Donahue so she obviously has some merit.'

Roger looked up. He had bargained on his friend's unwavering support and didn't like to hear Emma being talked about in such a positive manner. For a second he imagined Rebecca's response if the bank did decide to support Emma. Ever since the board meeting when Emma announced her intention to be CEO of Milford, Rebecca had been truculent and teary. The whole situation was having a detrimental effect on his wife's wellbeing and he wasn't going to let it continue.

'She's a number cruncher, William. Obviously that's no bad thing, and if Milford were a bank I'd be happier. But she has no experience in this sector, none at all. Plus she is naïve, her plans for expansion are foolhardy to say the least and they require a massive capital injection to proceed. I can't see how Billington's could possibly be prepared to support her.'

William nodded slowly, seeming to digest Roger's words.

'Well . . . the bank could refuse to support Milford's application with Emma as CEO. To lend money of that amount, we could impose certain stipulations. Such as an alternative CEO.'

Roger smiled into his crystal tumbler.

'However . . .' said William, pointing at Roger with his fork, 'she could dig her heels in. Then she could be removed by a directors' show of hands but as a 70 per cent shareholder she could call a special meeting and fire all the directors on the board and put her own stooges in place.'

Roger swallowed a mouthful of potato rather too quickly, which triggered a coughing fit.

'Could she do that?' he spluttered into his napkin.

William nodded.

'But what's more likely is that she would go quietly. Without the support of the other shareholders or financial institutions she'd have little choice but to roll over. There's no point hanging on to 70 per cent of a company which can't even get a fifty pound overdraft. I suspect she'd return to America and be happy to sell her shareholding to you – probably for a song.'

Roger licked his lips at the prospect.

'So . . . what does that scenario rely on?'

'First. When she comes to see the bank on Friday we make it clear that we are not prepared to back the company with her as CEO. We'll lend to Milford on the condition that a more experienced executive is in charge.'

'Me?' said Roger eagerly.

William's smile was sphinx-like. 'We could even make things doubly difficult and suggest there are a couple of loans that are dangerously close to being called in. It would put her in a very untenable position.'

Roger smiled and popped a spear of asparagus into his mouth.

'Of course,' mused William, 'we are assuming that no other bank will lend to her.'

The smile dropped from Roger's face.

'And how likely do you think that is?'

'Very. Banks can have a sheep mentality. They want to support who everyone else is supporting. If they know that Milford's existing bank isn't prepared to lend they will understandably be nervous. Emma's lack of experience in the sector and the appointment of a similarly inexperienced head designer won't help either. Frankly I'd be surprised if anyone else is prepared to back her.'

'So we wait for her to come to you.'

William tapped his glass against Roger's.

'You have my faith and my full support. Now, shall we order some dessert? The poached pear here is wonderful.'

12

She was almost there. Five miles into her six-mile jog, she picked up the pace, her eyes focused on the road as it went over a gentle rise and downhill. Every Saturday Emma took the same route in a long, wide loop around the village. She was particular like that. Back in Boston she had pounded the same route around Back Bay every day if she could; Mark used to laugh at her, said she had a touch of OCD and sometimes Emma thought he might be right. But she enjoyed the routine and the challenge, and each run she pushed herself faster and faster. She had an athlete's physique. Small breasts, long legs and lungs built for stamina, and she was now completing the course ten minutes quicker than when she first came to Chilcot. But today wouldn't count, because today she was taking a detour. Emma veered off her usual route and down a narrow lane, squeezing her hands into tight fists as she ran. Then she saw it: a bend in the road that made her shiver. It was a pretty stretch, dappled in the shade of an oak tree, but it was a bend that had changed her life forever, claiming the life of her father twenty-two years ago in a car accident. Emma had spent every day of the last two decades missing her father. Jack

Bailey had been an Economics Fellow at Oxford University. Brilliant and charismatic, at thirty-five he was destined for even greater things; government think tanks, a rumoured advisory role in the Treasury. Emma hadn't cared about any of that, of course, she'd just loved her father because he was gentle and funny. Emma was a classic daddy's girl. She was like him in many ways with her logic and intelligence, her thirst for knowledge. A big bear of a man, Jack had a big laugh and a fierce mind and Emma could still remember clearly their games of chess, the trips to zoos, castles and museums and the nuggets of information he'd scatter about to make them fascinating as well as fun. How the elephant is the only mammal that can't jump. How the Egyptians had invented paper aeroplanes. In the ink-black country sky they'd gaze at the stars through Jack's old telescope as he told her about the planets and pointed out the shapes: a bear, a plough, a dog. She slowed to a stop in front of the tree, looking up through its branches towards the cornflower blue sky. It had been a cold September night that had ended it all. She was seven years old. Tucked up in bed she'd thought nothing of the police sirens whizzing through the village until an hour later there had been a knock at the door followed by the sound of sobbing. Emma would never forget her mother coming to her bedside, not bothering to turn the light on. She could just make out her mother's tear-streaked face, just a shape in the dark telling her the news that her father had been killed, of how his Volvo had crashed into a tree on the outskirts of the village.

Today was his birthday. *Would* have been, she corrected herself. Jack Bailey would have been fifty-seven. Looking down, Emma noticed with surprise that there was a fresh bouquet of flowers by the oak tree. Emma wondered who could have put them there. Her mother? She'd seen her yesterday and she hadn't mentioned it. In fact Emma couldn't remember when the last time her mother mentioned Jack; with her new life with Jonathon it was as if she had forgotten the existence of her first husband entirely. Anger bubbled up, but she fought it down. That was no way to remember him. She walked over to the tree and put her ear against its bark. *Happy birthday, Dad. I wish you were here.*

She paused for a few more moments, then set off back towards Winterfold, the thought of a bunch of yellow chrysanthemums tied to a tree making her run faster. *Who had left them? Who had beaten her to it?* She veered off the road onto a wide grassy open space. In the distance she could see the edge of the village, the church steeple soaring into the sky. As she made for a path which would take her back towards the house, her foot caught on a rabbit hole and she stumbled forward, twisting her ankle. 'Ouch. Shit!' she muttered.

Her ankle was throbbing – not broken, she thought – but too weak to run on. A few feet away was a felled tree and she hobbled over and sat down on the trunk.

Emma took a swig from her water bottle and tipped her head back so the sun warmed her face. She was wriggling her foot around trying to loosen it up, when she heard footsteps behind her. She looked up, squinting into the sun. There was a man standing in front of her. He was wearing shorts and vest and she could see he had the firm physique of someone who worked out regularly. Tall, a strong chin, a crop of dark brown hair and narrow eyes, he was also out of breath.

'Are you OK?' he panted, hands on his knees. 'I saw you trip.' He was American: an East Coast accent, she thought. Not quite hard enough for a New Yorker or rounded enough for a Bostonian she thought trying to place it.

'No, no. I'm absolutely fine,' said Emma, 'My ankle went a bit wobbly there, but it's OK.'

'You're pretty fit,' said the man admiringly.

'I beg your pardon?' snapped Emma coldly.

'Just saying that you're fit,' said the man frowning. 'Have I said something wrong?'

Emma laughed. 'Oh, sorry. It's an expression we used to use as kids. Over on this side of the pond "You're fit" means "You're attractive", "You're sexy".'

'Dumb American,' he smiled, pointing to himself and shrugging. He pointed down to the heart monitor strapped to her arm.

It read sixty-five.

'Pretty good. For a woman.'

'For a woman?'

'You know. Women aren't as good athletes as men.'

'Actually there's very little between male and female athletes,' she said, surprised at the casual sexism. 'Some of the Chinese middle-distance runners will be beating most men soon.'

She wiped a few droplets of water off her lips while she tried to work out if she recognized him. Looking up and squinting in the sunlight his face didn't look familiar. He was definitely handsome underneath the red cheeks and sheen of sweat. It irritated her to think it.

'Rob Holland.' He extended a hand and she took it.

'Emma Bailey.'

'Ah. Local royalty.'

'Hardly,' she replied. 'How do you know my family?'

'Everyone in this village knows the local mafia.'

'Local mafia,' she said, trying to work out if he was joking. 'So you live in Milford,' she said slowly.

He sat down on the tree beside her and she felt herself flinch, the intrusion somewhat unwelcome.

'London actually. I live in Notting Hill in the week. Weekends I head west and come to this place. Do you mind if I have some of your water?'

She looked at him suspiciously. 'OK,' she replied, hesitantly handing him her bottle and watching him drain the water from it.

'Sorry,' he said handing her back the empty container.

He was beginning to rile her. It was a time to clear her head and here was some cocky American slagging off women and drinking her water!

'Which house?'

'None of the best ones, obviously. Your family has the monopoly of those,' he said playfully. 'I'm at Peony House. The owners are away in Australia so I'm renting it.'

'Mr and Mrs Parker's place.' She nodded thinking of the fine double-fronted Georgian house by the church. 'I heard they were away.'

'They have been. They come back in two weeks so there goes my weekend retreat. I've offered the Parkers 20 per cent over the value of the Peony House but they're not having it.'

'I could have told you they wouldn't sell.'

'You've not been around to ask,' he smiled.

'Anyway, I'm sure Notting Hill isn't that bad. I thought W11 would be more your scene.'

'It's full of people I see during the week. That's why I like coming here. To get away from the day-job.'

'Which is?' she said curiously. Whenever she met someone new she couldn't help herself size them up; guess what they did; create a mental picture in her mind of their life and past. It was probably why she had studied psychology at college.

'I work for a record company.'

'Argh,' she smiled. She should have guessed from the long baggy shorts that weren't much use for the serious runner. She had him pegged as something maybe in PR although he had that arrogance, that cocksureness that came with the young and very wealthy. Maybe it was family money.

'Shouldn't you be at crazy parties at the weekend?'

'Don't you know they happen in the week,' he laughed. 'I like my weekends for escaping from the music industry. Escaping from band managers, and people like John James.'

'Who's he?' Emma asked innocently.

'You've never heard of John James? Biggest rock act this decade. Fifty million album sales, the most downloaded artist in the history of downloading. You don't get out much,' he chided.

'I just don't really listen to music.'

'What about MTV?'

She looked at him. He must be mid to late thirties. Clearly a Peter Pan.

'Until a few weeks ago, until I came to Milford, I didn't have a television.'

'What? Why? Are you Amish?'

For a moment she thought he was flirting with her.

He was looking at her through thin, curious eyes.

'Not Amish. Just busy,' she replied quickly. 'When you work 18 hours a day there's no time for TV or music.' She had a vision of him lounging all over Peony House with MTV blaring in the name of work, surrounded by beer cans and pizza boxes and wondered what Mr and Mrs Parker would think of it all.

He raised an eyebrow. 'There's always time for music.'

The sun was beating down now on the common.

In the background she could hear the church bells pealing.

'I'm late. I've got to go.'

'Wait up,' he said grabbing her arm.

They both stood up from the tree and began walking back to the village.

'I wanted to talk to you today. That's why I'm here. Let me buy you lunch in the pub.'

'How did you know I'd be here?'

'I didn't have your phone number and anyway, I wanted to talk to you face to face. I noticed you come running every weekend and I thought it might be the only opportunity to speak to you,' he said, shaking his shoulders.

'You followed me!' she gasped.

He looked sheepish.

'You take the same route. Not wise by the way. Any weirdo could be lying in wait for you.'

'Tell me about it,' she replied flatly.

'I wanted to talk to you about Winterfold. I haven't got a clue if you planned to stay there. Make it your home. I know it's not for sale yet, but I heard talk in the village that you thought it might be too big for you. I can pay top dollar. If you would consider renting it out on a long-term lease I'm open to that too.'

She stared at him open-mouthed. The cheek of him. Following her here. Suggesting the house was too big for her as if she was some sort of mouse.

'You couldn't afford it,' she said, still angry at being monitored.

'Sweetheart. That's my problem,' he said coolly.

Of course he could afford it, she thought quickly. She didn't suppose record company executives made a great deal of money. Therefore it was definitely family money. The worst sort she thought, remembering the boys at Harvard with their sports cars and their country club memberships.

She started to walk away from him and then broke into a slow jog.

'Won't you at least think about it?'

'I'm not interested. Winterfold is my home.'

He trotted alongside her, his bare arm brushing alongside her and tickling her with its light down.

'Think about it. I could be useful to you. Word is you're trying to revamp the company and I know every celebrity

162

worth knowing over here and in the States. I can get Milford bags on the arm of every A-lister worth their salt. I can get them on the red carpet of the Grammies, the Oscars, MTV awards. You can't buy that kind of endorsement, that sort of visibility for the company. You help me, I'll help you.'

Rob Holland! Who was he? How did he know so much about her? He was creepy. And cocky.

'Who said I wanted that sort of pop culture endorsement, Mr Holland?'

'Don't be so pig-headed,' he said.

She began to quicken her pace.

'Hey, well forgive me for asking!' he shouted after her, throwing his arms into the air. Emma started pulling away from him, her ankle suddenly feeling much better. He slowed to a trot and cupped his hands around his mouth to shout after her.

'Well, call me if you change your mind.'

She didn't bother to look back.

13

In the luxurious bedroom of Alliance's Knightsbridge company flat, which was ostensibly kept for visiting senior management, Cassandra was doing her own brand of corporate entertaining. Kneeling between Oscar Braun's pale thighs she focused all her attention on his considerable cock. As her long fingers closed around the base of his shaft she slowly, expertly, moved her mouth from his velvety tip down its entire rock-hard length, feeling it pulse between her ripe lips. Hearing Oscar groan, she looked up over his gently undulating stomach. He was lying flat out on the bed, his face strained with concentration, close to the edge.

Time to get this over with, thought Cassandra, unfastening the white bra from the Forden lingerie collection she had worn specifically: Oscar was chief executive of the brand, and it was only right that he did a little market research every now and then. She tipped her toned body towards his face, dipping one erect nipple into his greedy mouth.

'Do you like it?' she whispered, guiding his throbbing cock into her, knowing she was taking him to the brink.

'If there's one thing you can do, Cassandra, it's fuck,' he panted in perfect English.

She rotated her hips, moving him deeper inside her, arching her back, her arms behind her, fingernails trailing up the inside of his thigh. Finally, he bucked into her, crying out in German, before collapsing back onto the sheets, barking out an amazed laugh.

Cassandra reclined on the buckwheat pillow, her firm breasts pointing towards the ceiling, and poured herself a glass of water from the bottle on the bedside table.

She had swapped business cards with Oscar at the Paris *Rive* party and had enjoyed playing phone-tag with the dark-eyed Austrian until he was next in London. But the breakfast meeting arranged at the Berkeley Hotel had not turned out exactly as Cassandra has hoped. Whenever Cassandra mentioned the thorny issue of Forden pulling their advertising budget, Oscar simply changed the subject.

By the time she had finished her pot of white jasmine tea, she had decided on a different tack and had started to brush her stockinged foot against his leg under the table. Three hours on from that breakfast, she had no complaints about Oscar's performance in bed; she'd genuinely almost come. For Cassandra, that was satisfaction. Slightly recovered, Oscar crawled up the bed to lie next to her.

'I shouldn't have expended so much energy,' she said, lighting a cigarette, 'I've got a busy day ahead of me. Getting Forden clothes into *Rive*.'

Oscar simply smiled and stroked her cheek.

'Incidentally,' she said turning to face him, 'Jason Tostvig said there might be a problem with Forden advertising in the second half of the year.'

Oscar paused slightly before answering.

'It's true we are cutting down on our advertising budget for that period,' he said distractedly. 'You'll have to speak to our marketing director to discuss it any further.'

'Really? I was under the impression that all orders came from you.'

He stepped out of bed, naked except for his chunky gold Rolex and started putting on his boxer shorts which had been jettisoned onto the chair.

'Honestly, Cassandra, if this little interlude has all been about advertising, then I think I've been right about moving the brand from *Rive*,' he said with cruel amusement. 'The editor is the embodiment of the magazine. I think it's starting to look a little cheap, don't you?'

'Cheap?' hissed Cassandra. 'Do you know how many pieces of editorial Forden have had in the last twelve months in *Rive*? Do you know how much that is worth in commercial terms?'

Turning around, he gave her a cool gaze. 'Darling, I really don't count those little mentions in the retail pages, or a tit-bit in the fashion news to keep us happy. How many times have you featured our skirts, jackets or pants in the main fashion stories?'

Well, perhaps if your stuff wasn't so hideous, thought Cassandra, *maybe there might be a few more*. It was true that Forden had barely featured in the magazine for years, but the bottom line in magazines was profit, over 70 per cent of which came from advertising. And Cassandra simply could not afford to lose a quarter of a million pounds worth of Forden's money, even if their clothes were laughably frumpy.

'How many times? Once,' said Cassandra, calmly stubbing out her cigarette.

'I see. Well, Cassandra my dear, we don't advertise for your good health, but my company's,' said Oscar evenly. 'Over the last five years we have spent 1.5 million pounds in your magazine and yet we have received only a handful of significant credits. Need I remind you that fashion advertising keeps your magazine alive? Editors who forget that tend to have a very short shelf-life.'

'You and I both know it's not that simple,' said Cassandra, shrugging off the threat. She eyed him shrewdly, however. If she had thought Oscar would be a pushover, she was wrong. 'Everyone knows that simply being in the pages of *Rive* is endorsement enough. Our readers more than any others come to our magazine for the advertising as much as the editorial – when they see Forden ads in *Rive*, they accept that we have chosen to run those ads because we are giving the products our tacit approval. We don't let any old brand buy their way into *Rive*.'

She wanted to tell him the truth, of course. That with the clothes his company was producing, he would simply be pouring those millions down the drain and that it would take more than pretty ads to be a Chanel or YSL. For that, you had to design and produce beautiful, luxurious things that people would kill to wear, but you also had to go even further, to create a fantasy world that would transform the wearer and transport them to a different place altogether. For that, you needed to have some style. But she thought she would save that information for a consultancy fee. Cassandra lay on her side and watched as Oscar dressed. If he thought he had won this particular battle, she would see how he dealt with this little broadside: 'Have a nice time with Karoline at the opera tonight.'

Oscar looked over at Cassandra, his eyes lingering on her naked skin.

'You're well informed.'

She saw the nervousness in his eyes at the mention of his wife.

'She told me when I spoke to her yesterday,' smiled Cassandra.

'Incidentally darling, I am chairing a Charles Worth exhibition at the V&A. We need a very connected committee of members and I thought Karoline would be perfect. I'm meeting her for talks on Friday. I told her to keep it all quiet until we'd firmed everything up.'

There was no mistaking Cassandra's implication. She let it sink in for a moment. Married men always took their lovers too lightly, thinking only with their poor neglected cocks until it was far too late. If there was one thing men feared, it was a vengeful wife and this was compounded in Oscar's case, as Forden was owned by his wife's family. While Karoline Braun preferred to devote herself to child-rearing in a big schloss near Salzburg, her husband had taken on the role of Chief Executive and he wouldn't want to lose that. Suddenly Cassandra felt aroused by the power she had over him and stretched out her legs longingly.

Oscar was quiet for a minute, busying himself in the mirror with a complicated tie knot.

'Now, what were we saying about the advertising?' he said calmly.

Cassandra's wide mouth twitched with just the suggestion of a smile. She walked up behind Oscar, undid his cravat and tied it for him again.

'I think you were saying that you were looking at increasing your spend substantially over the next year, possibly tying Forden into a long-term deal. Maybe a solus deal. I think you had realized that our two companies could have a special relationship. I think "special relationship" was the phrase you used.'

Cassandra gave his knot a final tug and stood back, satisfied with her handiwork.

'Now if you'll excuse me,' she said, walking naked into the bathroom, 'I must go and shower.'

Forty minutes later, Cassandra pressed the bell next to the door of a grand Belgravia townhouse. *I should have a fuck before every important meeting,* she thought, feeling her skin prickling with the power of sex. She was shown into a wide, light kitchen at the back of the house with a view of the long tree-lined garden through the French windows. This was the impressive London home of AtlanticCorp chief executive Charles Dyson, the man in charge of over fifty newspapers around the world. It was no secret that AtlanticCorp was launching a weekly fashion magazine in the States, a big-selling US equivalent of the weekly French *Elle*. And after Guillaume Riche had told Cassandra that the editor-in-chief heading up the project was about to be let go, she'd told Guillaume to use his contacts and leverage to let AtlanticCorp know that Cassandra Grand would be a superior replacement.

'I hope you don't mind meeting me at home,' said Charles, sitting down opposite Cassandra at a large, rustic kitchen table and pouring coffee. 'I get paranoid having meetings in hotels and restaurants. Even in the most obscure places you always seem to be spotted by someone. And it would never do for us to be seen together, would it?'

'Certainly not,' agreed Cassandra.

'I took the opportunity of ordering lunch. I hope you haven't eaten,' said Charles while a chef, complete with white uniform and tall hat, brought out lobster rolls and teriyaki beef. They made small talk, both gently flirting, politely probing, neither giving anything away. When the meal had been cleared, Charles pulled a large leather portfolio from behind his chair and placed it on the table in front of him.

'You know AtlanticCorp would be very interested in having you on board for the new launch,' he said, meeting Cassandra's gaze.

'What about Carrie?'

'Let's just say that's not your problem. Well, this is it: Project Diamond,' he said grandly.

Cassandra smiled. She was itching to see what they had developed. She lifted one finger towards the file, but Charles pulled it back protectively.

'You understand that I can't show you anything,' said Charles, frowning. 'Our team have spent six months putting this dummy together, it's top secret.'

Cassandra was not to be deflected so easily. She simply shrugged.

'Not so secret that you haven't already presented to advertisers,' replied Cassandra, 'and you know what big mouths they have.'

Charles knew full well that Cassandra had enough friends in the fashion community she could ask for a full written report from each of them on what they had seen at those presentations.

Cassandra lifted a glass of mineral water to her lips. 'Besides, you can't even begin to expect me to give up a job like UK *Rive* to jump ship to a completely unknown entity without seeing something. I'm happy to sign a non-disclosure agreement.' She smiled sweetly. 'In blood, if necessary . . .'

'Ink will be fine,' smiled Charles and pulled out a document – a single sheet of paper which Cassandra scanned quickly.

'All seems fairly standard . . .' she said pulling out her fountain pen and signing her name with a flourish. 'Now show me what you've got.'

She flipped through pages of shoes, bags, lipsticks, spas, and trend stories – most of it well executed but nothing that would get the industry ablaze with glaring originality. Cassandra frowned at a fashion spread featuring a stunning black model on a white horse.

'Who is the photographer here?'

'Arnold Marsaud.'

She lifted one eyebrow and looked up at him. 'I know

newspapers rather than magazine are AtlanticCorp's forte. Therefore you might not fully understand that using sub-standard photographers is a false economy. It's like trying to save money by buying cheap racehorses. They won't win the Kentucky Derby.'

Charles shifted in his seat. He wasn't used to having his projects criticized so openly.

'We have a good team,' he said defensively. 'The features team come from a wide range of prestigious titles.'

Cassandra was not impressed.

'Features? But this is supposedly a style magazine,' she said frankly. 'Fashion people are only interested in the environment the magazine produces. You have to get big-name fashion photographers in from the start or you're finished.'

Charles paused, looking at Cassandra shrewdly.

'I understand we seem to be having a few problems in that department.'

'Why?' asked Cassandra. 'This is a fashion magazine.'

'Which is why we are looking for someone with heavy-hitting fashion credentials to take over from Carrie's good work.'

Good work my arse. Admit it, you made a bad appointment, thought Cassandra.

'Well, Giorgio and Karl are very dear friends of mine,' said Cassandra. 'Guillaume Riche is like a father. And I've just had a very productive meeting with Forden and you know how difficult they are to please.'

'Which is precisely why we thought of you, Cassandra,' said Charles.

Cassandra looked at the spreads again, turning them over slowly, and then closed the portfolio.

'Well, Charles,' she said, 'it's extremely flattering that you thought of me. However, I can't just leave UK *Rive* for the editorship of Project Diamond. *Entre nous* the company has even bigger plans for me and I'd be a fool to leave them unless there was a considerable carrot being dangled under my nose.'

Charles's expression did not change as he flatly mentioned a high six-figure salary that made her stop and think.

'Well, I . . .'

'Plus share options, a driver and an interest-free loan to buy a property of your choice. Home ownership is so rare in Manhattan these days. New York is such a wonderful place to work.'

Charles knew he had pressed exactly the right buttons, but Cassandra forced herself to resist.

'I was deputy editor of US *Rive* for three years, remember,' she smiled. 'I love New York, but . . .' She was silent for a few moments as if she was giving it consideration.

'What I'd be really looking for is an editorial directorship, plus . . .'

She wrote a seven-figure number on a napkin and passed it over to him.

'. . . a remuneration package in this ball-park. And a seat on the board.'

Charles folded up the napkin slowly.

'That would be a considerable departure for us,' he said. 'As you know, magazines are a new media platform for us.'

'And I have to safeguard my career very carefully,' she said.

Charles nodded.

'I think we both need to go away and think about it.'

Cassandra smiled politely and pushed her chair back, offering her hand.

'I will *definitely* be in touch,' she said, holding his hand and his gaze for a fraction longer than was necessary. She knew by the way he smiled back at her that she had hit home. Mission accomplished. It had been a very productive day indeed.

172

14

'You're a little early, madam,' said Morton, opening Winterfold's double doors before Emma had a chance to put her key in the lock. She threw her car keys on the walnut console table, flopped into a deep wing chair and kicked off her shoes.

'Ooh, that feels good,' she said, wriggling her feet in the deep pile carpet. 'When it's eight o'clock and you're telling me it's early, maybe it's time to retire,' she smiled at Morton, glad to see his genial face, even more glad of the mug of hot tea he produced from nowhere. When Emma had first moved into Winterfold, she had thought having a butler was a terrible extravagance, some strange reactionary throwback to colonial times, but now she realized why Saul enjoyed having him around so much. The house felt far too big for her to live in alone and coming home to dark empty rooms would have had her reaching for the gin. With Morton in residence, however, Winterfold felt more like a home – a huge home, admittedly – but slightly more warm and cosy, slightly more alive. Plus, Emma enjoyed the old man's company; he was polite and deferential, however many times she asked him to treat her 'as a friend', but there was a twinkle in his eye and a wry smile on his lips. *I suppose that's what you'd need, looking after Saul for so long*, thought Emma.

'This arrived for you this afternoon, madam,' said Morton, carrying a large cardboard box through to the study. 'I think you'll be more comfortable in here. I've made the fire for you.'

'Morton, please call me Emma. And here, let me get that,' she said, standing and taking the package from him. Emma had no idea how old Morton was – seventy, nearing eighty? – but he was certainly too old to be doing heavy lifting.

'Whatever can this be?' she wondered, walking into the cosy study, warmed from the crackling fire. According to his butler, Saul had spent most of his time in this room and Emma could see why. It was one of the most welcoming in the house, with wood-panelled walls, acres of bookshelves and deep squashy sofas facing a home-cinema grade media system: plasma TV, state-of-the-art stereo, internet access, the works. Emma placed the box on a mahogany coffee table in front of the fire and knelt to open it. She pierced the top with a letter opener and sliced back the lid. She frowned as she pulled out the layers of bubble-wrap packing. Stacked inside were dozens of CDs. She pulled them out and spread them on the table: David Bowie, Marvin Gaye, Led Zeppelin, Oasis, John Coltrane. One by one she looked at them, having a foggy awareness of some names – The Beach Boys or John Lennon, of course – but most she had never even heard of. *I mean, who were the Velvet Underground? And surely there can't be a band called Niggers With Attitude?* As she reached the bottom, she noticed a business card which had fallen down the side of the box. She picked it up and had to suppress a smile at the hand-written message on the reverse. It read: *100 albums to listen to before you die. Enjoy. Rob x.*

Morton walked in carrying the teapot and a plate of biscuits. Placing them on the side, he bent and picked up a copy of Frank Sinatra's *Songs For Swingin' Lovers*.

'I have this on an LP. Oh, and this,' he said, picking up Bob Dylan's *Blood On The Tracks*. 'It's a good selection; whoever sent these has good taste.'

'Thanks, Morton,' said Emma, still smiling. 'I didn't know you were such a connoisseur.'

'Oh, in my youth, madam, in my youth,' he smiled, the twinkle back in his eye. 'Myself and Mrs Morton used to cut quite a dash through Soho, if I do say so myself.'

Emma giggled.

'You're a dark horse, Mr Morton.'

Emma crossed to the CD player and slotted a disc into the drawer. *The Beatles* by The Beatles. It seemed the safest choice to Emma, although *curious it doesn't have much of a cover*, she thought. She pressed the shuffle button, expecting a random jingly jangly Sixties pop song but instead was faced with a spiralling swirl of psychedelic guitars. Emma's mouth hung open and she scrabbled to look at the track-listing. 'While My Guitar Gently Weeps'? 'Ob-La-Di, Ob-La-Da'? 'Everybody's Got Something to Hide Except Me and My Monkey'? *What was all this?* But as the record carried on, Emma found herself swept up in it. It had a strange primal urge she liked. She settled in a big armchair by the fire and used the remote to flick through the tracks, finding everything from beautiful ballads to strange avant-garde soundscapes. The record seemed to be almost as big a revelation as the man who had sent them. Emma had googled Rob Holland the evening after they had met on the common. She hadn't meant to, but curiosity had got the better of her and she'd been surprised that he had his own Wikipedia entry. An even bigger surprise was that Rob wasn't just an executive of Hollander Music he was the European *chief* executive. The company itself was a subsidiary of Hollander Media, a huge NYSE company that owned thirty radio stations, a major Hollywood studio, and a TV station network, to just scratch the surface. It was a multi-billion dollar international company. His father Larry was chief executive and the family were still major shareholders, which made the Hollands one of the fifty richest families in America. *Rich enough to rent Winterfold?* thought Emma, recalling their conversation on the run. Rob Holland could probably buy Winterfold with the interest from his trust-fund alone.

Morton popped his head around the door.

'I was about to serve dinner, madam, but you have visitors.'

'Oh, really?' said Emma, surprised. 'Who is it?'

'Your mother, your Uncle Roger and Aunt Julia. Should I show them into the red room or would you rather stay here?'

'Here, I think,' said Emma, rising. She smoothed down her skirt and quickly looked in the mirror above the fire, suddenly unaccountably nervous.

'Hello. What a surprise,' said Emma as they walked in. Her unsettled feeling increased as she saw the cool look of purpose on their faces. She doubted they were popping round for a cup of sugar.

'I hope we didn't disturb you,' smiled Julia, taking off her scarf.

Emma shook her head. 'Of course not, please do come in. I was just . . . well . . .' she said, scrabbling for the remote to turn down The Beatles.

'Don't worry, we won't be long,' said Roger gruffly.

'Yes, I think we should cut to the chase here,' nodded Virginia, sitting in a chair without removing her coat.

'We're all a little worried, dear,' said Julia with a note of kindness, leaning against the desk.

'What about?'

'William Billington at the bank phoned Roger this afternoon to give him a heads-up that the bank are going to turn down Milford's application for a capital loan.'

'What's he doing phoning Roger?' said Emma feeling a hot flush of panic.

'I *am* a director of this company,' said Roger coolly. 'I've dealt with William for years. He was trying to let us down gently. Frankly it was all rather embarrassing, not to mention incredibly worrying,' continued Roger disapprovingly. He had walked over to the drinks table and began pouring himself a brandy.

Emma looked down at the floor. She thought her business-plan was convincing and at her meeting with Billington's she'd felt sure that she had their support.

She glanced at Roger wondering if he'd had anything to do with the bank's decision. After all, *he'd dealt with William for years.*

Emma was determined not to show her disappointment and fear.

'It's a set-back but I do have a few other meetings lined up and I'm confident that we'll get the money.'

'None of us share that confidence Emma,' said Roger, leaning back in the chair and sipping his drink.

'Oh? And who exactly is "us"?' asked Emma.

'The other directors. The factory. Have you spoken to the shop floor at all? They are aware that you want to decrease production and they all believe they are going to lose their jobs. So much for your expertise in management,' he sneered. 'The only positive thing you've done so far is to get a new designer onboard and she's a complete amateur. How old is Stella now exactly, sixteen?'

Emma felt the anger welling up in her, outraged that they had come into her own home and ganged up on her.

'And then there's the rumour that the directors aren't getting the end of year bonus,' added Julia softly.

Emma shot a look at her mother. That had to have come from her; Emma had only mentioned it to her briefly the day before. It was the final straw and she came out fighting.

'First off, Stella Chase is a very talented and successful designer,' she said firmly, 'we're damned lucky to get her and when she starts work on Monday, everybody had better make her feel like that. Secondly, I really don't think directors should get a bonus when the company accounts are running at record losses. How would that management strategy go down on the shop floor, Roger? And finally, whether you believe in me or not, I have had some very positive feedback from the banks and lenders I am meeting next week, and I maintain that I'm confident we will get the money we need.'

'The money *you* want for your hare-brained schemes,' said Roger petulantly, reaching for the decanter.

'Billington's will lend us the money if someone experienced is CEO,' said Julia.

'Someone like Roger?' said Emma cynically.

'Yes,' replied Virginia. 'Someone like Roger. This is for the good of the family you know, Emma,' said Virginia.

'Oh, you talk to her,' said Roger to Virginia, taking his glass and leading Julia towards the door. 'Perhaps you can talk some sense into her.'

For a minute Emma and her mother didn't speak, both staring into the fire, listening to it crackle.

'Go back to Boston, sweetheart,' said Virginia finally. 'You were doing so well out there.'

Emma felt she'd been punched in the stomach. She couldn't believe her own mother would betray her like this.

'So you don't think I can turn the company around?' she said, a waver in her voice.

178

'Oh, I think your intentions are good Emma, but look at the facts. Morale is low, our bank has turned against us and this is tearing the family apart. Personally I don't need the money, as Jonathon does very well. But Julia? Her gallery hangs on by a thread and Roger, well . . . Roger has his expensive wife.'

The two women exchanged a hint of a smile and Emma felt a spark of warmth towards her mother, then immediately extinguished it. More than anything Emma wanted Virginia to support her, but why should today be any different to the last twenty years of her life? Since Jonathon had come into the picture, Emma had felt more like an obligation than a daughter. No, there was never anything that would amount to neglect; Virginia sent polite letters to Emma at boarding school and had visited her once at Stanford University – although Emma remembered that the stay had conveniently coincided with a performance of *Rigoletto* at the San Francisco Opera that Virginia had particularly wanted to go to. And on the rare occasions that Virginia spent Christmas in Oxfordshire or at Saul's chalet in Gstaad, she would grudgingly invite Emma to join them. But that was the rarity. More often, she'd be on a Caribbean cruise or in a luxury bolt-hole in the Bahamas with Jonathon which meant that from the age of eighteen Emma had spent Christmas with college friends or alone. Did she love her mother? She wondered. Of course she did. But could she count on her? *No. Emphatically no.*

'Mum, Saul wanted me to do this,' said Emma as firmly as she could. 'I have another three appointments with three other lending banks this week. We'll get the money, I promise you.'

'Emma, if Saul were here now, he'd be much more concerned about you sorting out other areas of your life than saving the company.'

'Like what exactly?' asked Emma.

'Like your personal life,' said Virginia, pacing in front of the fire. 'You're thirty next birthday, Emma. You have no boyfriend, no time to see friends, no time to have a life. You're here living in a huge house with a man you hardly know, old enough to be your grandfather. Darling, you're paying for his company.'

Emma looked into her mother's eyes.

'I have to do this,' she said quietly.

Virginia shook her head ever so slowly, her lips in a line. Then she sighed and dropped her hands.

'If you must. After all, you can do whatever you want to do. But a word of advice, give everybody some good news. *Do* something and do it quickly.'

'Like what? Give Julia and Roger their bonuses when the rest of the employees haven't had a pay-rise in twelve months?'

'It might postpone a revolution,' replied her mother.

She kissed her mother on the cheek and said goodbye.

When her guests had gone, Emma wandered through the house to the kitchen. Morton had clocked off for the night but had left a note on the table informing her there was boeuf bourguignon in the oven. After the attempted ambush, however, she really didn't feel hungry and instead made a pot of coffee that she took back through to the study. Everything was still except for the noise of logs burning in the fire. She took a random CD from the pile and put it on, then flopped back onto the sofa and sipped her coffee. Perhaps coffee hadn't been the best idea when she needed to calm down; she felt fidgety and edgy and much more upset by the meeting than she should be. It was more than anger at their approach or the disappointment of not getting the loan or even the unfeeling attitude of her mother. No, when it came down to it, she felt lonely. Emma had decided

180

to take on this huge task on her own and had predictably ruffled the feathers of everyone she might have looked to for support. She was alone in her desire to modernize the company and alone too in this huge house. *What the hell am I doing here?* she thought to herself. Looking up, she saw Rob's business card propped up on the desk. Her mother was right. *She had to do something.* She grabbed the phone.

'Hi Rob, it's Emma. Emma Bailey.'

'And is that the sound of "Stairway to Heaven" swelling through Winterfold, I hear?' said a playful voice.

'No, it's your tinnitus,' she smiled, suddenly feeling better. Rob laughed.

'Thanks for the CDs by the way,' said Emma. 'It's going to be an education.'

'Well, no slacking off and listening to Chopin or something, because I'm going to test you next time I see you.'

She paused, wondering if she was about to do the right thing, nervous at the spontaneity of her decision to call him.

'I've been thinking about our conversation about Winterfold.'

'I was hoping you would.'

'Is that why you sent me the CDs? Is it a bribe?'

'No, I sent them because I wanted you to have them.'

She took a sip of coffee, stalling for time before she continued.

'Thing is, I'm thinking of moving out. Before I instruct an estate agent to look for a tenant I wanted to know if you were still interested.'

'So it *is* too big for you,' he laughed.

'The rental will be valuable income for the company,' she said seriously.

'So you don't want to sell it?'

'No,' replied Emma quickly. As Winterfold was a company asset and she was the controlling shareholder, she could

order its disposal if she wanted to. But it was too raw a
move, especially bearing Virginia's warning in mind.
Winterfold was the heart of the family and it had too much
of Saul in it. Emma could never bring herself to sell it. Not
yet anyway.

'How much do you want for a twelve-month lease?'

Emma took a deep breath and named a six-figure sum.
Not enough to save the business but enough to give everyone
in the company a very tiny pay rise.

He laughed. 'Emma! That's daylight robbery.'

'Rob, you know as well as I do that bog-standard houses
in good parts of London rent for far more than that.
Winterfold is a special place; beautiful, full of character and
close to London. I can name five wealthy Russians who
would offer me double the price I've just mentioned.'

'Well, why don't you ask them?' replied Rob with mock
petulance.

Emma giggled.

'Because they haven't given me a hundred CDs to listen
to before I die.'

There was a pause as Rob seemed to think about it.

'OK, how about I come over on Saturday to have a look
around? Maybe we could go for a run afterwards.'

'I run alone. Just come round to the house. Ten-thirty.
I'll see you then.'

She hung up smiling.

15

Giles Banks loved fashion. He loved it with a passion stronger than anything he had ever known. Clothes were his obsession and for the last two decades, they had been his life. Giles spoke five languages, had a first-class degree from Cambridge and had won a number of prestigious awards for his journalism; he really didn't need to spend his days debating ballet flats versus kitten heels. But Giles knew he had been blessed; unlike many people, he got to spend ever hour, every second of his day doing something he loved. Giles was also aware that his fervour was surprisingly rare in the industry. Fashion was populated by poor little rich girls and poisonous queens; the currency of the catwalk was gossip, the more toxic the better. To them, the clothes were just something else to laugh at. However much they air-kissed and declared things to be 'fabulous', more than anything, the fashion community loved to bitch. And Giles knew that they bitched about him. They called him the 'Cashmere Walker' because of his fondness for soft pastel jumpers and his constant presence by Cassandra Grand's side. Giles didn't mind; there were worse things to be called and worse people to spend time with. He adored Cassandra and loved working with her almost as much as he loved fashion. It was an un-requited love, of course, as Cassandra's drive and ambition meant that everyone and everything was dispensable.

Today Giles was escorting Cassandra to an appointment at Dior's office above their Sloane Street store. Although Cassandra respected Giles's fashion eye implicitly, she really didn't need him there. In fact, she didn't really need to see the Dior Autumn/Winter collection at all. She had already seen the catwalk show in Paris, followed by a private viewing at their headquarters on Avenue Montaigne, but Dior were one of *Rive*'s most important advertisers and etiquette dictated they see it again in London. Giles, however, never tired of visits to the fashion house: seeing the collection lined up on hangers and on mannequins, running his fingers over the exquisite fabrics, inspecting the workmanship, marvel-ling at the detail. Cassandra, meanwhile, spent their allotted thirty minutes being rather more aloof, regally accepting a little Nobu sushi from a very handsome waiter while politely viewing the collection and making assurances to prominently feature Dior's bag of the season in the September issue.

'I have a proposition for you, darling,' said Cassandra, holding onto Giles's arm as they descended the stairway onto the street. Outside, the sky was bright blue showing the first signs of spring, but it was still cold.

'What proposition? Where's the car?' asked Giles distractedly.

'I told Andrew to come back in thirty minutes,' said Cassandra, steering Giles down the road. 'Let's get a drink at the Mandarin Oriental, there's something I want to discuss with you.'

Giles felt a flicker of anxiety as they walked into the hotel. Cassandra ordered a coffee and an Earl Grey in the Mandarin bar and they took a seat.

'So, what is it?' asked Giles.

'Don't be so jumpy,' she smiled, 'It's nothing bad. In fact I think you'll find it rather good.'

Giles was instantly suspicious. Whenever Cassandra phrased anything like this, it was invariably good for Cassandra but not necessarily good for anybody else.

'As you know I've been commissioned by the publishers Leighton Best to write *Cassandra Grand: On Style*, but they've just sprung the most ridiculously short deadline on me. There's just no way I can do it justice as well as editing one of the biggest fashion magazines in the world.'

'So what are you going to do?' asked Giles, taking a sip of his tea.

She gave him one of her rare broad smiles, usually reserved for celebrities or chief executives.

'I thought maybe I could get someone I trust to help me.'

'Me?'

'Yes, you,' she said touching him lightly on the hand. 'You are the only person who can do this Giles. You're the only person who knows how I think and the only person with the knowledge and style to make it work.'

'Cassandra, your greatest talent is making a chore sound like the chance of a lifetime,' said Giles playfully.

'Chore? I thought you always wanted to write a book,' she said. 'What was it again?'

'*The History of Dior.*'

Cassandra pushed a manicured fingertip across the surface of the table.

'Strictly speaking Giles, *Rive* owns the copyright to everything you do, which *could* make writing books a little complicated. But once we get *On Style* out of the way, I'm sure we can look at your contract and iron that out. Plus, I can introduce you to the people at Leighton Best and get the Dior thing moving.'

Her implication was clear. If he didn't write *Cassandra*

Grand: On Style, he could forget writing his own book while he was still on the staff.

Giles thought for a moment.

'Will I get a credit?'

'Somewhere in the book, yes,' she said, waving a hand vaguely. 'But you have to understand that *On Style* is being sold on my persona in the industry.'

She reached into her Bottega Veneta tote and pulled out an envelope which she put on the table.

'Of course I will pay you a fee,' she said tapping the envelope. 'And you can take the rest of the week off to make a start.'

Giles looked at the envelope wondering how much was inside. Whatever it was, it was probably a drop in the ocean compared to the advance Cassandra had received. Still, she had him over a barrel, and a drop in the ocean was better than nothing. He looked at the envelope without saying anything and finally picked it up.

'Good,' smiled Cassandra. 'I knew you'd see what a wonderful opportunity it is for you. Now I've just made a few notes; Leighton Best keep phoning me demanding to see some copy so it would be great if we could get something to them pretty quickly . . .'

She reached into her bag again, pulled out a Dictaphone and a sheaf of papers and handed them to him.

'I've dictated some notes and done a chapter outline.'

She glanced at her watch and stood up without having touched her coffee. 'I think Andrew will be outside. Come on, let's go,' she said, the discussion over.

Giles stood slowly and followed behind her, feeling rather as if he'd been ambushed. He watched Cassandra stride towards the street, thinking how unsettling it was having a friendship that was underpinned by fear.

*　　*　　*

186

Across town, Emma and Stella were sitting in the reception area of Sheldon Saks, a small American lending bank with their UK headquarters on Threadneedle Street in the heart of the City. Emma idly picked up a copy of the *Economist* and leafed through it, trying to compose herself. Sheldon Saks were, quite frankly, her last chance and she was desperate not to show it. It had been a demoralizing week for Emma; bank after bank had refused her application for corporate finance. Of course, she could still go to the investment banks; through her time with Price Donahue she had good contacts there, but that was a road she really didn't want to go down. Investment banks meant giving away a slice of your business and once they'd got hold of that, it was usually the beginning of the end; either you did a good job and they forced you to sell for a profit or you did a bad job and they fired you and took all of your assets. Emma hadn't come this far to give up on the dream just yet.

'This really isn't what I had in mind for my second day of work,' said Stella, fiddling with the cuffs of her one smart black dress. 'I have to say I feel a bit more comfortable behind my drawing board.'

Emma looked at Stella with sympathy. She wished she didn't have to put her through this, but Sheldon Saks had asked to meet Milford's new head designer and besides, Emma wanted to show her off. She didn't have much to show for her time as CEO of Milford, but Stella was one of the things she was definitely proud of. Of course, Emma had tried to hide the desperation of the financing situation from Stella – how would *that* look when she had moved her life halfway around the world to join a new company – but Stella still looked nervous. Emma hoped she wouldn't crack under interrogation. Banks were intimidating places at the best of time.

'Listen, you'll be brilliant, just be yourself,' whispered

Emma as they were called into the office. 'Remember, this is where the Milford renaissance begins!'

Ralph Wintour was around fifty, with a standard-issue navy banker's suit that seemed at odds with his American Deep South accent. If Wintour was surprised to see two such young and attractive women in front of him to present their vision for a luxury goods company then he did not show it.

'Ms Bailey, good to meet you,' he said, shaking Emma's hand firmly. 'And Ms Chase? Please do have a seat and let me know how I can help you.'

Emma had prepared a document which she placed on the desk in front of him. It detailed Milford's stores and concessions worldwide, the company assets and debts with sales performance charts showing profits, both current and projected. There was an overview of the multi-billion-pound luxury goods market which explained how accessories accounted for up to 80 per cent of the sales for some of fashion's biggest household names. She included her own CV as well as those of Stella and Ruan and outlined the additions she would make to the team once additional financing was in place: an experienced marketing director, a full-time PR firm.

'Milford is a sleeping giant,' said Emma, meeting Wintour's gaze when he looked up from the document. 'Everybody thinks of Louis Vuitton as this ancient colossus of the fashion industry, but until the late 1970s it was just a small family luggage company with a couple of shops. A decade later and with good management, they had increased profits so much, they could afford to buy out two champagne houses and so created one of the world's most prestigious luxury goods companies.'

'And you believe you can do that with Milford?' said Ralph Wintour, his eyebrows raised.

'I believe there is a great deal of money still to be made in the luxury sector, yes. The short-term goal is to quadruple profits and then roll out the brand globally in the medium term . . .' To her surprise, Emma found herself confidently talking about the luxury goods market as if she had been working in the sector for decades. She told how Miuccia Prada and her husband Patrizio Bertelli had transformed Prada from a twenty-five-million-dollar business to a three-quarters-of-a-billion-dollar business in just six years. She explained how Tom Ford and Domenico De Sole had rescued Gucci from the verge of bankruptcy to become *the* fashion brand of the Nineties. She felt good, she felt confident. *She had to; there was nowhere else to go.*

Ralph Wintour sat back in his seat and regarded Emma and Stella silently.

'Well, I should tell you that I've had one of our luxury retail analysts look at Milford and their report back is good,' he said. 'Milford is underperforming considerably, but he believes with the right management team, it could be turned around quickly.'

'I think my professional credentials speak for themselves, Mr Wintour. I have just promoted Ruan McCormack to be my number two and he has fifteen years experience of working for Milford. Stella, here, was one of the top young designers in America before I approached her to make the move to us.'

'With your commercial background, Ms Bailey, I'm sure you know how nervous everyone is becoming of debt financing, especially in the current climate. Milford is already running at a loss so some banks would consider lending to you as highly risky without wanting a stake in the company and representation on the board.'

'We are running at a very small loss,' corrected Emma. 'But we also have considerable assets such as Winterfold and Byron House.'

'And would you be prepared to raise a mortgage on them?'

'Yes,' replied Emma coolly. Inside, however, her heart was pounding.

'Now Ms Chase?' said Wintour, taking a cursory glance at Stella's CV. 'I don't see any formal fashion training from this information? Why should Sheldon Saks risk their money on an untrained design director?'

Stella felt her cheeks warm under Ralph Wintour's gaze. She knew from the worn look on Emma's face that this appointment with Sheldon Saks was life or death, in fact she had suspected the company's finances were shaky when she had accepted the job. But she reasoned that if Emma was prepared to believe in her, she was prepared to return the favour. For once, Stella felt part of a team and she liked it. Besides this man was trying to frighten her, bully her into backing down. Well, what had her mother always told her to do in that situation? Fight back. Don't be intimidated and use words as a weapon.

'It's true, I studied sculpture at the Slade,' said Stella evenly. 'But then Tom Ford studied architecture. He wasn't a big-name designer before he got his chance at Gucci, but his designs transformed the company. Similarly, Miuccia Prada was a mime student before she inherited her family's luggage company. You'll also see from my CV that I have three years of experience building up a company from nothing into an award-winning multi-million-dollar business.'

Wintour made a note in a leather-bound book and Stella resisted the urge to wipe the palms of her hands on her dress. Emma looked over at Stella and smiled, but she felt exhausted and her hands were trembling. She carefully folded them into her lap.

'You'll be aware that we always do our homework at the bank before we lend large sums of money,' said Wintour. 'And I was most interested to read that you'd worked at Price Donahue. They have quite a reputation in the States.'

Emma felt a tightness in her throat. Who had he been speaking to? Daniel Davies? *Mark?*

'Turns out you actually met my brother Kevin a few weeks ago,' said Wintour, the hint of a smile on his lips. 'He's the CFO for Frost Industries. I hear PJ threw one of his legendary business brunches?'

Emma's heart flipped over, suddenly remembering Mark's story about her bursting into song. He *was* joking – *wasn't he*?

'Kevin said you impressed those old buzzards in Vermont, said you had one hell of a business brain. And d'you know? He actually bet me ten dollars that you'd have paid off the loan in full in three years.'

Wintour chuckled and spread his hands.

'Who am I to turn down a wager with my brother?'

For a moment Emma couldn't believe what she was hearing.

'So you'll lend us the money?'

Wintour nodded.

'I need to look through the facts and figures, see how it all stacks up. But I dare say we might be in business.'

To everyone's surprise, Stella jumped out of her chair, whooping. 'You rock, Mr Wintour,' she cried and before anyone could stop her, she leant over the desk and kissed him on the lips.

'Well, thank you very much,' said Wintour looking pleasantly flustered. 'Whoever said you English girls were reserved, obviously never met one.'

16

Unlike some companies, where the employees dreaded work-bonding and brainstorming sessions, the *Rive* international conference was always something the editors looked forward to. Held every year in April, the event saw the editors of all twelve editions of the magazine from around the globe, along with selected publishing directors, jetting off first class to a luxury resort, usually in the Caribbean. Once settled in their five-star accommodation and given free run of the spa facilities, they were then expected to exchange ideas and share problems, subsequently returning home brimming with ideas and fired with new-found enthusiasm. In reality, the *Rive* conference was three days of tanning, bitching and gossip, with each editor jostling to score points from each other and undermine their rivals in front of the directors. As a bonding session, it was a hopeless cause as each editor was in constant competition: for the same cover stars, the same advertisers and even in some cases, the same readers. So while on the surface the event appeared to be a dozen impossibly glamorous women air-kissing and exchanging endless compliments about each other's hair and swimsuits, beneath the surface it was a frenzy of political manoeuvring and back-stabbing. Cassandra always loved every minute of it.

This year's conference was being held at the Paradise Sands resort in the Bahamas' stunning Harbour Island, two hundred miles east of Miami. The hotel building itself was like a grand ivory plantation house from colonial times, while dotted around the lush grounds between the palm trees and frangipani bushes were twenty cottages painted in ice-cream colours, all commandeered by Alliance for the duration. The beach, metres away from each front door, was a perfect stretch of pale pink sand the colour of a ballet slipper, the clear, warm, Gulf stream waters lapping against it in a hypnotic rhythm.

From her lounger by the infinity pool, Cassandra could see Silvia Totti, *Rive*'s Italian editor, in a black maillot, getting an early start to her tan, the French editor Françoise Caron was scrolling through her BlackBerry and sipping a chai latte, while the Russian and Brazilian editors were still picking at breakfast on the terrace. Cassandra, meanwhile, was hard at work. She had spent the last hour reading the first twenty thousand words of *Cassandra Grand: On Style* which Giles had delivered to her before she left for the airport. It wasn't bad at all. Considering he'd had only a week to do it, Giles had managed to convert all her ideas into a smart, stylish read, peppered with just the right amount of autobiographical detail. *I must get him a little something when I get back,* she thought smiling. *Cartier, perhaps.* Noting that it was 9.40 – the first session was due to start at 10.00 – Cassandra put down the manuscript and finished off her freshly pressed watermelon juice.

'Didn't you know this is an unofficial editor's holiday?' said a voice. Cassandra looked up and saw *Rive*'s US editor Glenda McMahon. She was dressed in her Manhattan uniform of a charcoal shift dress and leopard print neckscarf, the only concession to the fact that she was on Harbour Island and not Manhattan Island was that she had swapped her Manolo heels for white leather thong sandals.

'I never like to bring too much work on these things,' said Cassandra, quickly zipping up her tote. 'But I wanted to read a hard copy of all the editorial for the July issue.'

Glenda raised an eyebrow to denote her disdain for any kind of work in such surroundings, but secretly, she was impressed.

'So, how's everything in New York?' Cassandra asked her former boss.

'Absolutely wonderful,' purred Glenda. 'We're doing so well this year, I can't tell you.'

Cassandra smiled to herself. She'd been taught a few lessons in self-promotion from Glenda over the years simply by observing her. She was always positive and bullish to her public; her house could burn down and she would spin it as a 'decoration opportunity' and feature firemen's helmets as next month's 'must have'. And you had to hand it to her, the strategy had worked. Glenda McMahon was not the most beautiful or intelligent woman in New York, but through sheer force of will, she had risen to the very top of Manhattan's society tree. Married to one of the top invest-ment bankers in America, together they were one of New York's glossiest power couples and divided their time between a townhouse on the Upper East Side and an estate in Bedford, New York.

However, as Glenda's former number two at US *Rive*, Cassandra had been privy to all her editor-in-chief's secrets; the speech coach employed to eliminate her Brooklyn accent, the image consultants hired to transform her into a fashion power-player. There were the expensive Japanese hair treat-ments which transformed her from mousey fuzz to sleek blonde bob and the coloured contact lenses which made her eyes feline and piercing. And then there were the skin laser sessions and vitamin shots, face-lifts, liposuction, tennis lessons, ski lessons, tutoring in French and Italian. Whatever Glenda had, thought Cassandra admiringly, no one could deny she had worked damn hard for it.

The two women walked from the pool through the shade of the palm trees around to Paradise Sands' conference room on the far side of the house. A long room with white clapboard walls and pale wooden floorboards, the whole eastern side of the room had concertina shutters which could be pushed back to reveal the glinting turquoise waters and allow the smell of the frangipani to waft in on the breeze. Glenda and Cassandra took their seats around a long table with the ten other editors and assorted directors, and at ten o'clock sharp a small man entered and sat at the head of the table. With his five-foot-six frame and clipped white hair, Isaac Grey looked rather timid, but in his case first impressions were far from the truth. As Chief Executive of Alliance Publications and majority shareholder of the NYSE-listed company, Isaac was a media powerhouse with a fearsome reputation. Having inherited the Alliance business from his father at the age of twenty-seven, he had spent the last forty years strengthening, launching and acquiring titles, until his company now rivalled Condé Nast as the most prestigious publishing house in the world. The floatation of Alliance five years ago had made him a billionaire and he still owned 51 per cent of the business.

'Some of you might think this is an unofficial holiday. It is not,' he began, pouring himself a glass of iced tea and looking around the table. Cassandra and Glenda exchanged a small smile.

'Yes, the annual *Rive* conference is meant to be fun, but it's also a valuable chance to exercise our considerable collective brainpower and confront the challenges of the year ahead. This year, as I'm sure you all know, we have a specific challenge coming our way and that's going to be the focus of today's forum. I want to hear brilliant ideas from everybody here,' he said with meaning.

Isaac then formally introduced the conference attendees for the benefit of international colleagues who had not attended the previous year. There were welcomes to the recently appointed South African Editor Charlize Marten, the editor and publishing director of the soon-to-be launched Indian edition and finally Jason Tostvig.

Cassandra could feel herself smarting just looking at Toxic. On the flight over from Heathrow, she'd been forced to sit next to him and listen to his inane chatter about his many professional triumphs and sexual conquests. He was particularly excited about the trip as Isaac Grey had called him *personally* – a word Jason emphasized, presumably to impress Cassandra – to invite him along. In the end, Cassandra had been forced to feign fatigue in order to shut him up. Pretending to be asleep, she could still hear him boasting to the flight attendants.

'This morning's session we are going to be considering the threat of Project Diamond, the AtlanticCorp magazine launching in the US in September,' continued Isaac, sounding more like a general addressing his troops than a publisher. 'Here's what we know: it's weekly and they are aggressively targeting our advertisers, so we can assume they will be stepping on our toes editorially. We also know they are supporting the new launch by advertising in their newspapers and on their cable channels, which makes them very dangerous. So I need your best thoughts on this one, people.'

'But I heard they were about to fire their editor,' interjected Glenda with the confidence of the most senior editor in the room. Isaac nodded – it clearly wasn't news to him. 'Which suggests they are having a few teething problems, but we have to assume that this is merely a blip. A company like AtlanticCorp is not going to launch anything which is not the best it can be,' he looked at Glenda meaningfully. 'It would be a fool who doesn't consider them a threat.'

Isaac then handed over to Greg Barbera who instructed the group that he wanted each of them to think of how their edition would cope with the threat of a Project Diamond launch in their territory.

'Go grab a fruit juice,' he said, 'find yourself a shady corner and go and "imagineer"! Brainstorm in pairs if you like, but I want you to present individually. We want to hear what *you* think.'

Cassandra was the first to leave the conference room. She walked through the early morning sun to her cottage where she freshened up and retrieved some notes she had brought with her. By the time she emerged ten minutes later, the grounds were dotted with *Rive* employees, an editor in the hammock under a palm tree, another under a thatched parasol on the pink sands. A couple of editors were working together but most seemed to be alone. *That figures*, she thought, as they would all be aware that this was less about safeguarding *Rive*'s position and more about showcasing their own talent.

'Jason,' she smiled. Cassandra's shadow fell across Tostvig's face and he squinted up at her from his sun-lounger. He had taken off his shirt and Cassandra couldn't help noticing he had a nice body. Lean and firm, with a rippled six-pack that was the distinct bronzed colour of St Tropez self-tan. Cassandra snapped her eyes away, angry with herself that she was becoming a little aroused. A waiter came over and put a beer on the table next to Jason's lounger.

'Working hard?' she asked, pointing at the blank pad next to the glass.

'Imagineering,' said Jason sarcastically, shielding his eyes.

'Well, I expect this is where your newspaper experience is going to come into its own for once,' said Cassandra tartly.

'What do you mean?' asked Jason, sitting up and putting on his sunglasses.

'Oh, you know; newspapers are good at this sort of added-value thing. Free CDs, DVDs, collect the vouchers and get your own library of Danielle Steele books, that sort of thing. Get the right item and you've got a guaranteed sales boost. Isaac was desperate for us to get free flights a couple of years ago, but nothing ever came of it.'

'Well, if you sit down and be a good girl I might tell you how we did it at the *Herald*.'

'I don't need your help, Jason,' said Cassandra coldly.

Tostvig smiled.

'Suit yourself. Oh, by the way, why don't you wear shorts more often in the office?' he asked, looking her up and down.

Cassandra knew she looked stunning in a pair of black cotton shorts and a white silk vest top with gold gladiator sandals weaving their way up her legs. For once she didn't mind his eyes raking over her body.

'I might, if you lend me your sunglasses for the next couple of hours.'

Jason took them off and frowned at them.

'What do you need them for?'

'Nothing . . .'

'Nothing you do, Cassandra, is for nothing.'

'Ain't it the truth,' she smiled, whipping the shades from his hand and walking away.

Fifty minutes later, Silvia Totti kicked off with her plan for freezing out Project Diamond.

'Without the raw materials, this magazine will be nothing. If they cannot use the best photographers, the best models, no one will take them seriously and their fashion advertising will dry up,' said the Italian editor with a half-smile. 'With the right pressure applied in the right places, AtlanticCorp could find that all the supermodels are booked. Photographers too, stylists, make-up artists,' she purred like some Machiavellian queen. For a second, the room nodded their approval at Silvia's master-plan until Isaac pointed out that if everyone started playing dirty, AtlanticCorp also owned a movie studio and could put an embargo on numerous Hollywood stars ever appearing in *Rive*. Silvia sat down quickly.

Sheri Ellison, the Australian editor, talked about budget cuts and producing less original material, even though the Australian issue already had a budget a third the size of the UK edition and used over 75 per cent of material from the US and UK editions. Glenda was nodding like some elder statesman. *Like she understands budget cuts*, thought Cassandra. As long as they didn't affect her.

Glenda's vision was radical: she proposed to turn *Rive* into a weekly. Overrunning the allotted five-minute presentation slot by twenty minutes, her proposal was sweeping and convincing; she had clearly done her homework, throwing in projected sales figures and promising a 40 per cent increase in profit within five years. Cassandra wasn't surprised she sounded more like a publisher than an editor. Glenda was a businesswoman first and foremost: that's why she had survived in the industry for so long. There was a long and heated debate after her presentation about whether the industry could sustain multiple fashion weeklies but Isaac had looked impressed and had been making notes constantly throughout. Cassandra knew she would have to produce something special to beat it.

'I started this exercise by putting my old newspaper executive hat on,' began Jason Tostvig, instantly captivating the largely female audience with the wattage of his broad white smile.

'In the line of attack, *Rive* needs to offer more value for money. At the *Herald* we found that everybody – rich and poor – loves a freebie.' He pulled a white linen laundry bag from under the table and tipped out the contents. Cassandra heard a couple of gasps from around the table and smiled when she saw Isaac's face pale. Jason, however, carried on confidently, unaware of the reaction.

'These are the sorts of covermounts which could run. Sunglasses, postcards, spa slippers,' he said holding up some flimsy towelling flip-flops that were given out free by the pool. 'The ladies love this sort of crap.'

He carried on for the full five minutes, boasting about his contacts in Taiwan and how he was confident he could source *Rive* sarongs for thirty pence a unit. 'And, Isaac, if you want a free flight offer, look no further. I can sort it out in a heartbeat.'

As he sat down and poured himself a glass of iced tea, Tostvig didn't seem to notice the silence in the room. Cassandra rose to her feet.

'Well, while I think that Jason is well-meaning with his, ahem, supermarket sweep for the front cover, I believe that if we start acting like a company under siege, the advertising community will start believing it,' she said. 'Project Diamond is a weekly but they don't intend to be direct competitors with *Rive*,' stated Cassandra boldly. 'The feel will be very middle market. You only have to look at their personnel: the features team is good but the fashion is very weak. I suspect they will struggle to get anyone decent to shoot for them and without the photographers, the model agencies will be nervous. No photographers and no models equals no fashion advertising.'

Cassandra was enjoying her moment, particularly when

she saw Glenda's face pale as she filled in the blanks from the information Charles had given her, without actually admitting she had seen the dummy.

'The point is,' said Cassandra, 'that people come to *Rive* for certain things. They come to us for luxury, for authority, for a badge of identity. They come to us for escapism. Far from price-cutting, free gifts and diluting our quality and size by going weekly, I propose we *increase* investment and we increase price. We make *Rive* magazine a luxury product in its own right, a beautiful accessory every woman has to buy every month. We add select brand extensions to extend our reach as a global multi-platformed media brand and here's how we start to make more profit . . .'

As Cassandra went into details, Isaac Grey felt his cock go hard. *Cassandra Grand,* he thought, *is a sensation.*

'That was a very impressive performance today, Cassandra,' said Isaac from the comfort of the Master Suite on the top floor of the house. Cassandra stood by the shutters enjoying the breeze on her face but kept out of direct view of the window: it wouldn't do to be seen in the chairman's bedroom. She had first met Isaac Grey at a party in the National Portrait Gallery in London, eleven years earlier. She was twenty-four and one of the most respected young stylists in the country. He was fifty-six, in a long, unhappy marriage and he had been knocked out by Cassandra's confidence, beauty and cut-glass English accent. He had offered her a lift back to her Notting Hill apartment and she had asked him in for a nightcap, both of them fully aware exactly where the evening was heading.

As soon as they had entered the hallway he had ripped off her silk slip-dress pushing her against the wall so she had burned the back of her legs on the radiator. She had made him pay for that. Leading him into the shower, she'd stripped him and soaped up his body, being meticulously careful not to kiss him or touch his erect manhood. When she knew he could take no more, she had lowered her lips onto his, letting his hands explore her soft tanned skin. Finally she had sunk to her knees, scarcely able to breathe as she let him come in her mouth with the shower water surging all over them. Back in the bedroom, they had fucked for two hours solid and Cassandra had enjoyed every second of the power she knew she had over one of the wealthiest media moguls in the world. She knew she had been as skilled as any of his lovers – from the budding starlets wanting to appear in his magazines to the high-class hookers he used on business trips around the world. Cassandra was good: she had to be.

'When am I going to see you again?' he had whispered at six o'clock the next morning as he pulled on his Brioni suit.

Cassandra had shrugged, feigning indifference.

'As you're going back to New York tomorrow, that's up to you.'

'I have to see you again,' he had pleaded.

'Things could be so much easier if I lived in New York,' she had replied.

A month later Cassandra Grand was senior fashion editor of US *Rive*.

I hope he's grateful for all I've done for him, thought Cassandra with a smile as she turned away from her view of the ocean.

'I take it the rumours are true then?' said Isaac, fixing his vivid blue eyes on Cassandra.

'And which rumours would they be?'

'The rumours about AtlanticCorp trying to poach you.'

'Wherever did you hear that?' she replied, pretending to be shocked. She had, of course, begun the rumours herself.

After her meeting with Charles Dyer, she had made sure that all the New York gossips had got to hear about her meeting with him. It was like the government 'leaking' sensitive documents. Not only had it got the industry buzzing, it had the side effect of prompting Charles Dyer to come back with an improved financial offer to come across to AtlanticCorp. Charles had, however, politely refused her demand to be made editorial director. Cassandra hadn't been surprised; she had known it was a long shot, and now it looked like she was going to get what she wanted out of her conversation with Charles anyway: leverage with Alliance.

'I knew it!' said Isaac through gritted teeth. 'I'll fucking kill Charles! You refused them obviously?'

Cassandra did her best to look shamefaced.

'Well, you might as well know that we have been in discussions about an editorial director's position at AtlanticCorp,' she said, choosing her words carefully. 'It was mooted as a board position. But no, for the minute we haven't taken it further. The door is still open, but I thought that we should have a conversation first before I did anything drastic.'

Isaac walked over to the drinks cabinet and poured himself a large bourbon.

'You know how much I want to keep you within the company.'

'No. How much, Isaac?'

'What will it take to make you stay?'

She could tell by the look in his eyes that he wanted her, but she vowed she'd never allow that to happen again. Their affair had ended years ago, twelve months after she had arrived in New York, in fact. By that stage Cassandra had convinced herself she could marry him; he would have been the perfect father-figure for Ruby. But Isaac had said that it would be too costly to leave his wife Miranda, so Cassandra had ended the relationship. Twelve months later, Isaac was having an affair with Geri Bergman, a twenty-three-year-old PR girl from Los Angeles. Six months after that he filed for divorce from Miranda. Another six months after that and Geri Bergman was Mrs Grey number two. Cassandra had to hand it to the girl: that was some ambush.

Wrapped up in her thoughts, Cassandra hadn't heard Isaac walk over. He reached out and touched her cheek. She stepped back.

'You're a terrible tease,' he said, grinning.

'How much do you want me to stay with the company, Isaac?' said Cassandra.

'What do you want?' he asked, sipping his bourbon.

'I want the American issue.'

Isaac looked at her.

'Does Glenda know that?'

'She'd be a fool not to suspect.'

'What about France? I can get rid of Françoise at the end of the conference.'

Cassandra tried to hide her frustration.

'I don't want the French edition.'

'Why not? It is the most influential fashion title in the world. Fashion is in your blood.'

'But it is not the company's biggest money-making and flagship title. That's where I want to be.'

Isaac swirled the bourbon around in his glass, looking troubled.

'Glenda is doing a good job,' he said flatly. 'Circulation is up 5 per cent. She is popular with the staff. There is no reason to get rid of her. Not yet anyway.'

Cassandra paused for one moment, letting the whirring sound of the ceiling fan fill the silence.

'But I do mean what I say,' said Isaac, 'I don't want to lose you. What will it take?'

'I want a written assurance that I will be the next editor-in-chief of American *Rive* when you finally *do* come up with a reason to get rid of Glenda. In the meantime, I want a one hundred-thousand pound pay rise.'

Isaac almost choked on his bourbon.

'I thought we were already very generous with your salary!' he spluttered.

Cassandra stared at him.

'I've got a call to Charles pencilled in on Wednesday.'

'Cassandra, you are impossible,' said Isaac, slamming down his glass.

'Oh, and there's one other thing,' said Cassandra. 'Jason Tostvig. I find him very difficult to work with. I think you saw today that we're not exactly on the same wavelength.'

Isaac nodded slowly.

'I'd agree with you there. What *was* he talking about? All those horrible free gifts, phone-lines and cheap flights. This is Alliance Inc he is working for, for heaven's sake!'

'And I suppose you heard what happened with Phoebe Fenton?'

He pursed his lips. 'I hear it caused a bit of a furore. What was the upshot?'

'All positive, of course,' she smiled. 'Sales up 30 per cent year on year, advertisers all happy when they heard it was our biggest selling April issue since launch.' Cassandra paused, deliberately failing to mention the 250 reader complaints.

'The problem was that Jason panicked,' she continued. 'He frightened the advertisers, then recommended we pulp the issue before he'd even spoken to me. I just don't think he's cut out for magazines, let alone *Rive*.'

'Perhaps we move him onto *Smile*,' said Isaac thoughtfully. *Smile* was Alliance Inc's big-selling young women's magazine. A successful title. A prestigious title.

Cassandra shuddered. 'Great. Put the wolf in the henhouse.'

'What do you mean?'

'Well, let's just say he makes me uncomfortable. Leering at women, making off-colour comments. In fact earlier he said I should wear shorts more often to the office. Just think of him at *Smile* with all those vulnerable girls.'

'I had no idea,' said Isaac, rubbing his chin. 'Maybe he'd be better off at *Rural Living*. The staff there are mainly over fifty and male.'

He will hate it! thought Cassandra with well-disguised glee. Urbane Jason, with his Gucci suits and love of London's nightlife, talking to the hunting set about fly-tying and carriage clocks!

Cassandra smiled and touched Isaac's shoulder.

'Let's get the ball rolling with all of this, then I'll put the call in to Charles and let him down gently.'

The gardens were dark when Cassandra came down the fire escape of the main house so she wouldn't be noticed. She could hear the rhythmic croak of frogs in the undergrowth and the background swoosh of the sea lapping onto the beach.

As she turned the corner of the path towards her cottage, she bumped into a tall elegant woman carrying a cocktail glass. It was Françoise Caron, *Rive*'s French editor. Cassandra smiled, thinking how close the woman had come to losing her job only minutes ago.

'Going to bed so early?' asked Françoise.

'I'm tired,' smiled Cassandra. 'It's been an exciting day.'

'Oh, we are all going to Glenda's for drinks. Did she not invite you?'

She had, but Cassandra had declined, having no desire to listen to a group of women compare salaries. But now she looked at Françoise and felt something. What was it? *Pity.* Isaac had clearly marked the French editor's card; he had axed editors in the most brutal and public ways in the past, and this time next year Françoise would probably not be coming to the conference. Still, she was well-connected and would probably go on to a job with a fashion house, but . . . *it never did any harm to network*, thought Cassandra. *You never knew when they might kick the chair out from under you.*

Silvia Totti, Charlize and Sheri were already on the veranda of Glenda's vanilla-coloured cottage when Françoise and Cassandra arrived. Glenda's accommodation had a jacuzzi and a long deck that looked out to the darkness of the ocean. They all sat around a table and helped themselves to Glenda's generous spread of drinks and canapés as they talked. Five of the most important women in fashion. They dictated to millions of other women what to wear, they had the power to make or break designers, fashion houses, whole brands. They were the focal point for an entire industry.

Throughout their conversation, Cassandra had noticed Glenda pouring herself generous measures of vodka. She had also filled her guests' glasses and put two bottles of champagne in buckets next to the table. Then Sheri had asked Glenda about Armani's latest collection and she had smiled thinly.

'Who cares?' she said, tossing back her drink.

Cassandra flinched. She knew that Glenda liked to drink, but only ever in private. Glenda was a master of image and Cassandra had never seen her mask slip once. At lunchtime meetings with PRs or advertisers she was strictly teetotal, even at parties in front of industry figures or staff, she stuck to Perrier. But safe in her inner circle, away from prying eyes, Glenda would let her hair down, usually via vodka and tonic. Cassandra had asked her about it once and she had shrugged. 'I'm from a big drinking family.' It was the only time she had ever referred to her past, a past that she had wiped away like a smudge on a piece of French linen.

But now, in front of the international editors, this was a serious slip. If she was showing weakness, that meant she didn't care. *What's going on here?* thought Cassandra.

'Come on ladies, drink and be merry!' said Glenda, a slight slur in her words. 'For tomorrow we die.'

The other women exchanged looks.

'What do you mean?' asked Silvia Totti.

'Haven't you heard? Alliance is up for sale,' said Glenda. 'Or will be soon. My husband works on Wall Street. Rumour has it that the company is looking for a buyer. Seems like Uncle Isaac wants to cash his chips in. So if we get bought by another company, little perks like this may well stop.'

Cassandra did not doubt what Glenda said, but she was bemused. She knew that it had always been Isaac's dream to overtake Condé Nast. The company had been doing very well over the past few years. It wouldn't be long until his dream became a reality; why would he sell now when he was so close?

'So do they have any interest?' asked Cassandra, cautiously.

'Someone said they are being courted by Girard-Lambert.'

As the women excitedly discussed the possibilities, Cassandra sipped at her pomegranate juice and considered Glenda's revelation. Yes, now she thought about it, it actually made sense. Isaac hadn't seemed overly concerned about the launch of AtlanticCorp's magazine and had shot down Silvia's suggested dirty tricks campaign. Normally he would have gone on the offensive with the enthusiasm of a pit bull terrier let off the lead. She kicked off her sandals and reached for the champagne.

'Well, we might as well enjoy it while it lasts.'

17

'Cam! It's so good to see you,' said Emma, embracing her friend warmly. She had been looking forward to Cameron's arrival for a week, counting down the days until she would be able to talk to a friendly face. Emma sat back down on the banquette and rearranged her napkin. They were meeting in Nicole's restaurant on Bond Street, convenient for Claridge's round the corner where Cameron was staying. She had flown over to speak at a convention on 'The Future of the Luxury Goods Market' and Emma had nearly snapped Cameron's hand off when she had suggested lunch. It wasn't every day you could pick the brains of a six-hundred-dollar-an-hour management consultant for the price of a Caesar salad.

'How was the conference?' asked Emma.

Cameron slipped off her jacket and nodded to the model-grade waiter to fill her glass with still water.

'Useful. Everyone was there; reps from Hermès, Gucci, Rolex. I honestly don't know why you didn't let me get you a slot speaking there; it would have been excellent exposure for you. You're such a good public speaker too, so I don't know why you wouldn't do it.'

'It's not that I can't talk in front of five hundred people,' said Emma frankly. 'It's just that I can't talk about the luxury goods industry in front of five hundred people. I'd be exposed as a fraud because the amount I know about the luxury goods industry can be written on a Smythson notelet.'

'Well, you're definitely learning fast,' laughed Cameron. 'Two months ago you wouldn't even have known what Smythson was.'

Emma smiled, but there was truth in Cameron's words. She was on a very steep learning curve and on her better days Emma merely felt like a little girl playing at running a handbag factory. On her bad days, she felt smothered by doubt and helplessness. It was like running through treacle.

Cameron reached out and touched Emma's hand, seeming to read her thoughts.

'So how are things with you, honey?'

Emma managed a weak smile.

'Oh, things aren't that bad. At least we've got our financing in place. I've promoted our head of merchandising Ruan McCormack to be my COO and he is fantastic. But my family hate me and I've had to fire seven people. I now need a bodyguard to go down to the village shop.'

Cameron nodded sympathetically.

'You've got to hold onto the positives, sweetie. How's your new design guru working out?'

'Oh, she's wonderful. She's been locked away in the studio since she started, but we've already run up some prototypes of her first designs – the benefits of having your own factory, I guess – and I think they're amazing.'

She reached under the table and grabbed a plain white paper carrier, handing it to Cameron. Inside was a mid-sized black leather handbag and Cameron held it up admiringly. It resembled a Gladstone bag, but with all the hard lines removed; its soft shape was emphasized by subtle quilting and a woven handle.

'This is hers?' she asked, looking at Emma with wide eyes. 'Honey, it's beautiful! I'd buy this in a heartbeat.'

She stood up and slipped the bag over her shoulder, checking how it looked in a mirror by the door. Then she clicked it open and examined the inside.

'Kid leather inside, all hand-stitched, solid brass hardware,' said Emma.

'Oh, I can see all that,' said Cameron, nodding. 'This baby's got class written all over it.'

She sat down again and looked at Emma. 'I think it's fabulous. Does Stella have any more like this?'

Emma laughed.

'I can barely stop her! She has a dozen designs as good as this if not better and she wants to put them all into production.'

Cameron raised her eyebrows. 'Well if they're this good, I'd say let her.'

'I hope the fashion magazines all react the same way as you have,' said Emma. 'We desperately need their support.'

'Well, I wouldn't count on the support of the magazines close to home,' said Cameron.

'What do you mean?'

Cameron paused awkwardly.

'Well, there was a guy named Claude Lasner at the conference, some sort of fashion recruitment guru, I think. Anyway, we got chatting and I mentioned you and he was very dismissive about Milford, said the company was a hair's breadth from bankruptcy.'

'That will explain why he gave me short shrift,' said Emma. 'I was trying to find a designer through him. My cousin Cassandra put me onto to him.'

211

'Yes, but I did some subtle digging and it turns out that he got his information from none other than Cassandra herself.'

'No!' gasped Emma, 'But why? Why would she say that? It's her family's business – her mother's a shareholder!'

Cameron took a sip of her water.

'Well, I don't want to say anything about your family . . .'

'No, please tell me,' said Emma, looking worried. 'As I said, they already hate me.'

'Well,' said Cameron slowly, 'I would say it does rather look like she wants you to fail.'

'But I don't understand. Why . . .'

'I'm only speculating here, but with my consultant's hat on, I'd say it was a fire sale strategy. Cassandra wants the company to go under so she can pick it up for a song.'

For a moment, Emma just gaped at her friend.

'*That bitch!*' she said finally. 'And after I went to her on bended knee to ask for her help! How could she? And who else has she been telling these rumours to?'

'Probably everyone,' said Cameron dryly.

Understatement of the decade thought Emma to herself, anger bubbling in her stomach.

'So who are you getting to do your shop refit? Peter Marino?'

'Who's he?'

'Emma!' scolded Cameron. 'He's only the best commercial interiors guy in the business! He does all the best shop designs: Donna Karan, Chanel, Fendi . . .'

'Well, in that case, we couldn't afford him.'

Cameron gave a small smile.

'So when are you reinstating womenswear?'

'There was a clothing line a few years ago but it got axed. Do you think we should do it quickly?'

'Well, you don't want to be an accessories company

forever,' said Cameron switching into professional mode. 'The mark-up in handbags is huge and I think you're absolutely right moving your accessories into premium luxury, but to make real money you need to branch out into more mass market areas: perfume, cosmetics, diffusion ranges, maybe even a home range. But for that you need to position yourself as a fashion house as quickly as possible. A ready-to-wear line helps give your company identity.'

Emma felt a flutter of panic.

'I was going to leave it a few seasons before we introduced womenswear.'

Cameron shrugged as she stabbed an anchovy.

'Perhaps, but as you're not introducing them − you're *reinstating* them I don't think you have to wait that long.'

The waiter came to clear away their plates and Cameron watched her friend's gaze linger on him.

They both cracked up giggling the moment he had left.

'Gorgeous,' smiled Emma.

'Gay,' replied Cameron.

'How do you know? You don't know him.'

'Oh honey, he *has* to be, no straight man was ever that pretty,' said Cameron watching his behind disappear into the kitchen.

'So how is he?'

Emma blurted out the question she'd been dying to broach ever since Cameron had told her she was flying in from Boston. Cameron was the only person at Price Donahue who knew about Emma's relationship with Mark. They'd even gone out once with Cameron and her banker boyfriend Billy. Mark had claimed to be so uncomfortable with the duplicity they had never done it again.

'Mark, I take it?' asked Cameron looking up.

Emma nodded, feeling a cold chill down her spine at the mention of his name.

'Working hard as usual, taking over the universe. Lonely as hell. Completely miserable, I'm sure,' said Cameron with an encouraging smile. She put her hand on Emma's.

'Sweetie, you know you're better off without him. And anyway, if you had stayed at PD, if you had got that partnership, you would never have made the move to Milford, would you? And although it probably doesn't feel like it right now, it's the best thing that could have happened.'

'*Was* it the right move?' asked Emma, a note of desperation in her voice. 'I've never felt so unsure of anything in my whole life. I don't even think I look the part.'

'Well, I'd agree with that,' said Cameron with a smile. 'What have you got on today? Brooks Brothers?'

Emma opened her jacket to look at the label. 'How did you know?'

'Look honey, Brooks Brothers is fine for the City, but fashion is a different beast. You can't go around like that.' She flapped a disapproving hand at Emma's suit and put her napkin on the table.

'Come on,' she said, standing and signalling to the maitre d' for the bill, 'I think we're going to have to get you some armour.'

'What do you mean?' frowned Emma.

'We're going shopping.'

Cameron looked at her friend as if she were sizing up a prize heifer.

'Hmm . . . personally I love Marni, but I think it's a little bold for you,' she said, turning Emma around. 'Dolce is too sexy for you but they do amazing trouser suits, not that your figure needs any help. We could do Prada or Helmut Lang but you can be too severe anyway.'

'Severe?' said Emma, putting her coat on.

'You're the MD. You want to be sharp and chic but I don't think you should look too ball-breaker-like. We need

214

some jersey and crêpe and maybe a touch of georgette to soften the lines. That would be wonderful on you; I'm thinking kind of Julie Christie in *Darling*.'

'Isn't that the one about the prostitute and the soldier?'

'No, it's the one about the floozy and the prince. But she looked amazing.'

Cameron squinted into a compact mirror and scribbled on the bill.

'Let Price Donahue get this one.'

Three minutes later, they were on Bond Street standing outside a shop full of black lacquer and silver mannequins.

'Yves Saint Laurent,' whispered Cameron taking her by the arm and leading her in. 'Chic for day. Sophisticated for night. This is the place.'

No sooner were they in the shop than Cameron had picked up two ivory silk shirts, an amethyst silk jersey cock-tail dress and a pleated navy pencil skirt. She threw them over her arm and led Emma into the fitting room.

'Come on, gorgeous, we're going to turn you into a fashion icon,' she smiled.

After buying half of Yves Saint Laurent, they visited Gucci and Gina for shoes and Alexander McQueen for a gorgeous slate-grey cashmere overcoat. Flushed with indulgence, they stood on the corner of Bond Street and Piccadilly.

'Here, now you're fit for the front row!' grinned Cameron, pushing the bags towards Emma, who staggered under their weight, but laughed with excitement.

'Oh, and one more thing . . .' said Cameron, flipping open her phone.

'Julian? It's Cameron. You too, darling, and thanks for the cut — it looks fabulous. Now I have a challenge for you: Emma, my close friend, needs some of your magic to bring her into the twenty-first century.' Cameron winked at Emma. 'Can you? This afternoon? You're a doll! I'll tell her, kiss-kiss.'

Cameron snapped her phone shut and handed her a card from her purse.

'Julian Coco, my London hair-stylist.'

'You have a *London* hair-stylist.'

'Of course,' she smiled. 'Julian is the *best*. His hair cut will change your life, I guarantee it.'

She took a step back to look at the old Emma one last time.

'From now on you're going to look the part, act the part and *be* the part,' said Cameron with a wicked grin. 'Milford is a sleeping giant, my sweet. And you're going to be the beauty to wake it up.'

18

'Why? *Why*, Emma? I just don't understand.'

Virginia stood in Winterfold's red room, fixing herself a large gin and tonic, watching her daughter pack her belongings into boxes. She couldn't believe Emma was leaving the grandeur of Saul's exquisite manor to move into the converted stable block on the edge of the estate. She looked around the room with its ruby wallpaper and elaborate classical cornices over the doors and tall, elegant windows. Why would anyone leave somewhere this beautiful to move somewhere so small, so poky, so *bleak*? Virginia shivered and took a gulp of gin. The truth was that the Stables brought back unhappy memories for Virginia; Saul had given the cottage to her as a favour after the death of her first husband Jack. It meant that Virginia could sell the Baileys' family home and swell her modest bank balance; but that whole three-year period, from Jack's death to when Virginia met her second husband Jonathon at a dinner party in Barnes was the darkest time of her life. Isolated, lonely and resentful, the romantic notions Virginia had once harboured when she'd married the poor but handsome academic Jack Bailey were completely gone. But that had been then, she thought quickly sipping her drink – a different time, a different person – here and now her daughter had a golden opportunity to live the life she had always wanted for herself. Why on earth wouldn't she take it?

Emma tried to remain patient, drawing a hand across her forehead and leaving a white dusty smear. 'What do I need a twenty-five-bedroom house for?' she said, briskly clapping dust from her hands.

'You could say the same about the royal family,' scoffed Virginia.

'That's not the point. It's not a question of *need*.'

Emma winced at the snobbery. Having tasted the loneliness of Winterfold she was quite looking forward to a smaller, more manageable home. When she had first opened up the Stables the previous weekend, it had looked and smelled a little unloved with dusty surfaces, grimy windows and a general air of neglect. But she had rolled up her sleeves and, with the help of Ruan and Abby, had given it a lick of paint and brought in some squashy sofas, big rugs and a new sleigh bed. And now her collection of books, pictures and photographs had arrived from Boston, the Stables was beginning to look more like home.

'Roger and Rebecca are furious, of course,' said Virginia taking a sip of gin. 'You know how much they wanted to live in Winterfold. They can cope with *you* being here, because that was Saul's wishes. But to lease it to a stranger – well, it's hurt them.'

'Moving out of Winterfold is really a matter of cost, Mother,' said Emma firmly. 'The way the company finances are at the moment, I need every source of income I can get. I doubt very much Roger would have been able to afford the rent I get from Rob Holland. Rob can afford to pay top dollar and he's promised to keep Morton on.'

'Why not just stay and fire Morton if you're watching

the pennies?' whispered Virginia, looking behind her in case the butler was listening.

'He's worked here forty years, Mother.'

'He *is* rather dishy,' said Virginia sinking back into a chair. 'He's got the village in quite a lather.'

'Morton?' said Emma frowning. 'He's about eighty!'

'Rob, silly,' said Virginia, raising her eyebrows. 'He'd be good for you.'

Emma gave a short laugh. That was *just* what she needed right now. She had no desire to complicate her life any more with a relationship; after Mark, she felt cut off from her desire. And besides, if Mark had turned out to be so unreliable and selfish, she could only guess what trouble a relationship with someone like Rob Holland would be.

Virginia poured herself another gin from the decanter and they both jumped as they heard the distant clanging noise of furniture being dropped.

'Hi, do you want this?' said a voice at the door. Emma looked up to see Julia brandishing a silver candelabra. Emma had asked her to come round to identity any semi-valuable antiques, furniture or pieces of art so they could be put in storage while a tenant was living in Winterfold.

'Take it,' said Emma, waving a hand at the candelabra. She still felt guilty that Saul's own sisters had received very little in his will. He had obviously drafted his will at a time when there was plenty of money sloshing around so that the 'remainder of his estate' gifted to his sisters would have amounted to something significant. In actual fact, Julia and Virginia were rumoured to have received less than £30,000.

'Actually, Julia, there's some stuff in the attic that needs restoring. I was wondering if you knew anybody good who could do it? I don't really want to leave anything around that might be of value.'

'Of course I know people,' she said, sounding offended.

'Could you pop up, have a look and then sort it out for me?'

'I could,' said Julia, 'if you might do one little thing for me?'

'Name it,' replied Emma, keen to repair relations within the family where she could.

'I hear that your friend Rob works in the music industry. I was wondering if he could help Tom. Everyone keeps saying how talented he is and he loves music, what with his DJing and whatnot.'

Emma smiled. Tom was one of her favourite people for all his faults, so anything she could do for him would be a pleasure, but she was well aware of Tom's many sudden changes of direction in career – not that Emma was one to talk – and knew of his reputation as something of a dilettante layabout. While she knew it was bad business to upset her tenant so soon, she also felt an impish glee at the prospect of foisting Tom onto Rob; it would be rather like throwing a spanner into the works.

'Well, I'm not sure I have that kind of influence over Rob Holland,' said Emma, 'but I will ask him if he has any openings. Leave it with me, Julia, I'll try my best.'

Julia smiled with relief.

'Oh, thank you so much, darling. Tom will be so grateful. And I'll go straight up to the attic now – I'll keep you posted.'

When Julia had gone, Virginia pulled a sour face. 'I hope you know Tom will be a disaster? Don't go upsetting Rob and ruin your chances of snagging him.'

It was Emma's turn to pull a face.

'Mother, if Rob Holland was the last man on earth, I wouldn't look at him twice. He's rude, self-obsessed, arrogant and . . . did I mention rude?'

'Beggars can't be choosers, darling,' said Virginia, waving her empty glass.

'By the way, seeing as you're giving things away, I don't suppose you'll be needing this decanter at the Stables, will you?'

For the first time in days, Emma laughed out loud.

Stella paced around the luxurious suite of the Soho Hotel, fussing about rearranging handbags on their plinths, knowing that the next three hours were make or break for the company. She was running on adrenaline, knowing that if she stopped she would close her eyes and probably not wake up for a week. Since her arrival in England almost a month earlier, Stella hadn't even had time to unpack and settle into her new house in Chilcot, a small barn conversion on the edge of the village that cost more than she could afford. She barely saw any daylight as she left home for the Milford offices at dawn and often didn't set off home again until midnight. She would spend the entire time in between hunched over her drawing board in the top-floor studio, designing handbags as if her life depended on it. The Milford archives had been a shambles, so Stella had fallen back on her own collection of vintage Milford handbags. She'd adapted the shapes, making them more contemporary, adding her own flourishes here and there, and spent hours with Ruan McCormack discussing the fine points of their manufacture. The result had been a small collection of twelve bags, samples of which had been made up in the softest leather ready for today's press show. Today was pivotal for the business. Here, in this hotel suite, they would unveil their first collection to the fashion press. They would either laud Milford as the hot new label or condemn the company to a slow and lonely death. *And if that's not pressure, I don't know what is*, thought Stella, looking around the suite. They had, however, done a pretty good job, even if she did say so herself. The room was darkened and each of the twelve bags had been placed on pink Perspex plinths, each lit from below and spot-lit from above, giving each handbag an otherworldly glow of pure luxury. In fact, the whole room looked like it was displaying the crown jewels of some far-off exotic state.

'But what if no one comes?' said Stella, eyeing the trays of canapés and rows of baby bottles of champagne lined up on a walnut table.

Emma looked at her watch. It was 12.30. The press invitation had stated a noon start and not one fashion editor had come within ten yards of the expensive suite.

'Then we are eating crab claws and drinking Moët for the next month,' she said nervously.

'Of course people are coming. They are just fashionably late,' said Zoe Miller the chic fashion PR whom Emma had hired for the launch of the Autumn/Winter line. It had been Zoe's idea to send the invitation to the press show in a Milford chalk-white leather passport holder. Emma had winced at the cost, but as Zoe had pointed out, Milford were hardly a huge noise on the fashion scene and they were in direct competition with numerous other, rather more mouth-watering press events that week. Without an example of Milford's new image, *without a small bribe*, there was a very real chance of them being totally ignored.

'So what happens after this?' asked Emma trying to fill in the awkward silence.

'We send celebrities, editors and magazine fashion directors the key bag of the season. So I guess they all get this one,' said Zoe holding up a large soft bag that was Stella's favourite. It was a slightly smaller version of the handbag Emma had shown to – and which had so impressed – Cameron at the café. It was exquisite, the design bold yet practical, the materials and craftsmanship unrivalled. The creamy-soft calf leather had been selected with the greatest care and made more supple by a method called press and boarding. The bag's jewel-like lock had been made by a local silversmith; the seams were all sewn by hand and folded over like the hems of a Hermès scarf. For Stella the love and skill that had gone into making the bags was a source of great pride, a far cry from the depressing Mexican sweat-shop used by Cate Glazer, where hundreds of women worked for a pittance to produce bags that would be sold for twice their monthly wage. When it was finished, Stella had chris-tened it the '100 Bag' after listening to Emma's theory about exclusivity. Milford were only going to make six hundred '100' bags; one hundred in six different colours that Stella had selected from the palette gleaned from the catwalks at the recent international collections. That had been one of the benefits of designing and producing their Autumn/Winter line so late; they could colour co-ordinate their accessories line with the forthcoming season's ready-to-wear.

'Fashion editors will get a less expensive bag, of course, while fashion assistants can get something like a key-ring,' continued Zoe, popping a canapé into her mouth.

'Do we really need to give so many away?' said Emma, instantly totting up the cost in her head. 'I bet Hermès don't give out hundreds of Birkins every season.'

'No, they don't,' smiled Zoe. 'They are an established vener-able brand and they don't need to seed,' she said referring to the marketing ploy of giving celebrities and taste-makers free bags every season.

'Well, good for them. I don't want Milford bags being seen hanging off the arm of every Tom, Dick and Harry celebrity. I'm not sure consumers at the very top end of the market are impressed by that.'

'But even Hermès has benefited from celebrities,' continued Zoe. 'In the 1950s Grace Kelly was snapped on the cover of *Life* magazine holding her Hermès shoulder bag in front of her pregnancy bump. Hermès renamed it 'The Kelly' and – Hey presto! – an icon was born.'

'But even if you send celebs a bag you can't be guaranteed they'll use them,' said Stella, remembering her time in LA. 'Cate Glazer sent an ostrich-skin bag to this big-time actress once and the next week it was spotted on the arm of her cleaner.'

'So, Emma. Who do you know?' asked Zoe, sitting on the arm of a long cream sofa.

'Oh, I'm best friends with Jennifer Aniston,' she said with an ironic smile.

'Marvellous! That's a great start,' chimed Zoe.

Emma shook her head, frowning.

'Zoe, I was joking.'

'Oh. Well, obviously I can send them to *my* contacts,' said Zoe, completely unfazed.

Stella looked at her suspiciously. Stella had encountered Zoe's kind – self-interested, mercenary – many times before at LA fashion parties. She wondered how many of their bags would end up in the back of Zoe's own wardrobe or on the arms of her friends. She made a mental note to tip off Emma.

'Otherwise we could get someone to endorse a product,' continued Zoe. 'But for the right celebrity, well, that fee could run into hundreds of thousands.'

Stella and Emma exchanged troubled looks.

Stella glanced at her watch. 12.45. Still no one. For the first time since she had arrived in England, Stella had time to think – and time to panic. Yes, life at Cate Glazer had many faults, she was taken for granted and overlooked, but at least it was secure. When Emma had knocked on her door, she had been ready for a change, a new challenge, but sitting in this big empty room, it all suddenly felt too reckless. She walked over to the walnut table and twisted the top off a mini-champagne bottle. 'Well, if no one else is going to have them . . .' she smiled. Just then, there was a slight creak as the door opened. Stella, Emma and Zoe all looked at each other as an elegant brunette in jeans and a beautifully-cut cashmere coat walked in and signed the visitors' book. Sophie North, *Vogue*. *She was from Vogue!* 'Oh, I love this,' said the woman, picking up the 100 Bag in the darkest aubergine. Zoe winked at Stella. *They were in business.*

19

Winterfold's walled garden was crowded with nearly a hundred people all talking, laughing and drinking cocktails. There was a model on a Lilo in the swimming pool, three naked women in the hot-tub and two rock stars drinking champagne out of an ice bucket. It was the first warm day of spring and everyone was enjoying the feel of the sun and the sense of liberation that comes with the end of winter. Everyone except the party's host, that is. Rob Holland sat in a pink rubber ring, looked around him and wondered why he wasn't enjoying himself more. Five years ago he would have loved this, basking in the glory of finally having a big country house with a pool and a lake, bathed in sun and surrounded by willing women and bubbly on tap. *So what was the problem?* OK, so Winterfold was rented, but his wealthy West London circle of friends neither knew nor cared as long as he invited them down for long weekends. This weekend he had Kowalski, the country's hippest hard-partying rock band as house guests. They'd brought a troop of friends and hangers-on, including half a dozen gorgeous models, one of whom was now waiting naked in the jacuzzi for Rob, and they were all going through his food and drink like a plague of locusts.

The truth was that at thirty-eight, watching people ten years younger – God, *twenty* years younger – glugging champagne and dancing to the music pumping from the huge speakers on the lawn, made him feel old. One minute he had been a crazy teen hooked on rock music and all its decadent charms, the next he felt like Grandpa Joe, hanging out with the kids at the chocolate factory. If he was honest, Rob had wanted this to be a quiet weekend, getting ready for the arrival of Polly, his six-year-old daughter who lived with her mother in New York and visited him every school holiday. But it hadn't worked out like that. He'd been forced to invite these over-styled, overgrown teenagers to his new home because there was mutiny at his record company. In the last months, two of the major acts on his record label had walked out and both had petulantly released material on their own websites within days. And it wasn't just happening to Rob, it was happening all over the industry. He'd never known a time when there'd been more disputes over back-catalogues and digital rights; it seemed as if every other band was going on strike or storming out. Rob was torn: he had always been a enthusiastic supporter of talent but when he had the Hollander money-men, his father's inner circle, breathing down his neck, suggesting redundancies and reduced marketing spends, what was he to do? In the case of Kowalski, one of Hollander Music's biggest-selling acts, Rob had done what he knew best. Their manager Tony Holden had begun to play hardball over their latest contract, so Rob had gone on a charm offensive, inviting them to his country retreat, plying them with booze and women and made them feel happy, special and loved. So far it seemed to be working. Tony had started talking about new studio sessions and tours, intimating that they might be ready to sign to the label long-term. Rob had smiled and responded enthusiastically, but inside he felt like the poor little rich boys at his elite prep school in Connecticut who curried favoured with the jocks and the popular set by doing their homework or paying them money. And he was doing exactly the same, ultimately to keep his father – and his father's money-men – happy.

He looked over to the jacuzzi where Trudy, the twenty-two-year-old blonde glamour model was waving at him. That didn't make him feel any better either. *What the hell is wrong with me?* he thought. Trudy was the third blonde model he'd slept with in as many months; the last two hadn't got beyond a second date. Inevitably, people called Rob a womanizer, but he called it pragmatic. He had a big job, a young child and a difficult ex-girlfriend. Not to mention his father. That was enough people making demands on him 24/7; he didn't need anyone else, and in the music business, there was always another pretty girl. It kept the loneliness at bay and the sex drive satisfied, so what was the point in getting involved unless it was with someone looking for the same things as he was? Now *that* was something the music business did *not* supply.

The door of the garden creaked open and Rob tipped his sunglasses down to see who it was. He groaned audibly when he saw Emma Bailey approaching across the lawn.

'Oh, shit,' he mumbled, struggling to get up and out of the rubber ring. He saw the expression on her face change from surprise to disapproval to fury.

'Emma. Great to see you!' he said quickly, turning on his most dazzling smile. 'New hair. I like it.'

'I don't believe it,' whispered Emma angrily. 'What on earth are you thinking . . .'

'Ah, let's go over to the gazebo, shall we?' said Rob, taking her by the arm and steering Emma away from his guests. She looked as if she was about to erupt and he didn't want a dressing-down in front of a load of rebellious youths.

The gazebo was at the end of the garden away from the pool. Honeysuckle climbed the white lattice walls, but the sweet, heady scent did nothing to calm Emma down.

'Who the hell are those . . . those *people*?'

'Don't worry, they're going in a few minutes,' said Rob, sheepishly.

'Well, it doesn't look like it,' spluttered Emma, as she watched two more people disrobe and jump into the pool screaming. Rob shrugged.

'Look, the lease doesn't say anything about not having parties.'

Emma was in no mood for technicalities.

'This is still my house!' she snapped. 'You've only been in it two minutes and what sort of respect are you showing my home? I know how these things end up, the place is trashed and a white Rolls ends up in the pool!'

'I thought you never went to showbiz parties.'

'I don't. *Oh, my God,*' she gasped. 'Someone over there is taking cocaine!'

Still wide-eyed with shock, Emma turned her head as someone shouted from the jacuzzi.

'Rob, are you coming in?' shouted Trudy, lifting herself out of the water, her bare breasts exposed above the foam. 'I'm getting out otherwise. I'm like a prune!'

At exactly the same time Morton walked into the garden, his shirt sleeves rolled up, holding a silver tray full of tubs of chocolate ice cream.

'Ooh, ice cream!' shouted Trudy, already distracted.

He watched Emma's lips harden into a tight line. Rob felt unsettled at the way she made him feel. He wondered how old she was. Probably not yet thirty and yet she acted a generation older than the people around him. Despite her anger she obviously felt awkward just being here. He felt sorry for her.

'Listen, I'm sorry about all this,' he said.

'Yes, well, I think your girlfriend wants you.'

'She's not my girlfriend.'

'Of course not.'

'Do you want a drink? An ice cream?' he added weakly.

She took a seat on a rattan chair and paused for a moment, breathing deeply.

'It's not a social call,' she said coolly.

'No, I didn't think it would be.'

'I've come to follow up on our agreement.'

Rob raised an eyebrow.

'Have I signed my soul away to the devil and don't even know about it?'

'Not quite,' she said, trying not to smile. 'Remember when you first asked me about renting this place?' she said, her eyes still glued to the action in the garden.

'How can I forget that sight of you in cycling shorts?'

He saw her flush pink. *Ah-ha, a little nick in her steel-plated, career-girl armour!* He couldn't help notice how pretty she was when she wasn't so uptight but he pushed away the thought as quickly as it had popped into his head. She was his *landlady*, not some girl in the jacuzzi.

'Yes, that occasion, when we were running,' she said with a little frown line between her brows. 'You said that you could get some of your celebrity friends to use our products, endorse them perhaps?'

From her red cheeks and stilted delivery, Rob could tell it was difficult for her to ask him for help. Now her hands were on her lap and she was playing with her fingertips.

'Celebrity endorsement,' he said seriously. 'That can get expensive.'

Emma looked up, her mouth open.

'You led me to believe they'd do it for free,' she said.

For a second Rob thought he could have some fun, string

230

it out. Emma was obviously easy to wind up, but the truth was Rob did want to help her. Emma Bailey might be his polar opposite – she was serious and formal and her idea of a good night was probably a nice game of Scrabble – but he recognized many of her weaknesses and anxieties so clearly it was like looking in a mirror. Rob thought back twelve years; when his elder brother was killed in a climbing accident. The family tragedy that meant Larry and Patricia Holland had gone from expecting nothing from their dilettante second son to expecting everything. Rob's easy, idle life had been turned upside down when he was thrown into a senior job in his father's media empire, where half the workforce cried *'Nepotism!'* and the other half just dismissed him as dead wood. Emma Bailey was just about to find out how lonely it was at the top – perhaps she already had. There were no such things as friends, just people who wanted things from you. Well, she was going to serve him his notice at Winterfold but the least he could do was try and give her a break.

'So you're asking for my help?' he teased.

She shook her head and got up to leave. 'I knew I shouldn't have come.'

'Hey, hey! Wait,' he said, touching her arm. 'I think I can help you.'

He handed her a drink and she took it.

'Ste Donahue: the guy that probably just got me kicked out of here. The guy who took the coke,' he said nodding towards the tall, skinny man wearing just jeans and dirty sneakers. 'See that girl on the Lilo? That's his girlfriend.'

Emma watched as the woman rolled off into the water, then pulled her long lean frame out of the pool, a tiny gold bikini barely covering her perfectly-proportioned body. She shook her wet tawny hair across her back and tilted her face to the warmth of the sun, revealing high cheekbones and green eyes.

'Gosh! Is that who I think it is?' gasped Emma. 'She's that model, isn't she? Clover Connor – even I know her. She's always on billboards in Times Square.'

Rob nodded, a sly smirk on his face.

'Exactly. I think she made $14 million dollars last year; catwalk, editorial, advertising. I think you could say she's big.'

Emma pulled a face.

'And Clover Connor goes out with *him*?'

Rob laughed. 'You really don't read the gossip pages, do you?'

'I can't believe someone like that, goes out with someone like that,' she repeated quietly.

'Ste is the lead singer of Kowalski, one the country's biggest rock acts who are breaking through in America. It's the classic celebrity pairing,' shrugged Rob. 'Model and rock-star. It doesn't matter that he's white and skinny and takes more drugs than a lab rat; in her eyes he's a poet, an artist with even more credibility and fame than she's got.'

'So are you telling me you can . . .?'

Rob smiled and touched her arm again. An unconscious intimate gesture, that made them both flinch slightly.

'I'll speak to her. She owes me a few favours, and she's angling for a recording contract. I'll see what I can sort out, OK?'

Emma smiled. It was weak, but it was a smile.

'I am pissed off, Rob, but you've bought yourself some time.'

'That's good enough for me, baby!' he said with a wink.

Emma turned back towards the gate.

'Oh and Rob? Don't call me baby.'

20

'Cassandra, are you ready? Fashion keep yelling for you,' said Lianne, as soon as her boss had walked through the door. 'They want to do the run-through.' Cassandra gave her assistant a rare smile.

'Certainly, I'm on my way.'

She was in a buoyant mood. She had just come down from Greg Barbera's office where he had confirmed Jason Tostvig's departure from *Rive* magazine to go and join *Rural Living* as its publishing director. According to Greg, Jason hadn't been seen in the office since Isaac Grey had announced his change of senior management although he had received a phone call from Jason's mother saying her son was seeing a doctor about stress and he might need to be signed off work indefinitely.

Cassandra strode into the fashion department for the monthly ritual of examining every bag, skirt, dress, shirt, hat, scarf and shoe that her editors intended to put in their fashion shoots. Not only was the run-through crucial for ensuring that every major advertiser was represented within *Rive*'s fashion pages, but Cassandra wanted every item in the magazine to have her personal seal of approval. She simply could not trust anyone else's fashion eye.

'So. Talk me through it,' said Cassandra running her fingers along the long rails of clothes.

Francesca Adams, the fashion director, cleared her throat to speak.

'As you know, I'm doing "Oligarch's Wife". Belle is shooting the Debutante's story and Laura is doing the suede story in Papua New Guinea.'

'Yes, how are we doing with the cannibals?'

Laura Hildon, her blonde aristocratic senior fashion editor popped her head around the rail.

'It's proving a bit tricky, to be honest. I thought we might just shoot Giselle next to a bunch of locals and get them to hold up a couple of human skulls but we think there might be trouble at customs if we try and take something like that through. I don't think Giselle will be too happy, either.'

'Well, you'd better find some genuine cannibals then,' snapped Cassandra. 'Belle. You'd better go first. It's obvious that Laura hasn't prepared her shoot properly.'

Rive's talented young fashion editor directed her boss towards the rail of clothes she intended to take to her shoot.

'As I said I'm going for the oligarch's wife in Sardinia vibe. Trash luxe. Lots of metallics. Lots of Cavalli and Dolce.'

'Will Abramovitch let us use his yacht?' said Cassandra thoughtfully. 'We could call it Roman's Holiday.'

'We're shooting at Cala Di Volpe. It's been arranged for weeks,' said Francesca cautiously, hoping Cassandra wouldn't make another one of her sudden changes. Cassandra rifled forensically through the rail, pulling out pieces she didn't consider suitable or up to scratch and handing them to a fashion assistant who was waiting behind her to catch the fall-out.

'I love this piece,' said Francesca holding up a violet Lycra jump-suit. 'It's perfect for hopping on and off a Gulfstream.'

'I'm teaming it with Roger Vivier pumps and the new

Milford 100 Bag which I adore,' said Belle. 'There's only one sample in the pewter ostrich. It's coming over from *Vogue* this afternoon.'

'Tell them not to bother,' said Cassandra coolly.

'I don't understand,' said Belle feeling the icy chill sweep through the fashion department.

'Tell them not to *bother*,' repeated Cassandra. 'The jump-suit and the pumps are fine but we need to find a replacement for the bag.'

Francesca usually bowed to her boss's better judgement but she felt she must stick up for her junior fashion editor, knowing just how hard Belle had worked on the story.

'But Cassandra, it's going to be the bag of the season,' she offered nervously. 'There's a lot of buzz around Milford right now. Everyone was going wild for them at the press launch.'

'I do not want Milford bags in this magazine,' said Cassandra flatly.

Belle looked as if she was on the verge of tears. 'The story is not going to work without it.'

Cassandra's happy mood had now disappeared completely. She carried on flicking through the clothes with noticeably more disdain than only a few minutes before.

'No. No. No,' she said curtly, discarding piece after piece. 'Where are the bloody advertisers? And what's this?'

She picked up a long, ivory evening dress, sparkling with a thousand encrusted crystals.

Belle looked at the editor, petrified.

'It's a Marc Abrams bespoke piece. The one he made especially for this shoot,' said Belle, clutching at the fabric. Cassandra vaguely remembered discussing it. It would have cost the up-and-coming London designer a fortune to make, knowing full well that exposure in *Rive* would be crucial publicity for his fledging brand. Well right now, she didn't give a fig how much it cost him. *What was she, a charity?*

'Do you know what?' said Cassandra pushing her mouth into a sullen pout. 'I don't think this story works at all.'

'But we're leaving for Porto Cervo on Friday,' said Belle, her voice almost a whisper.

'Well, you'd better think of a back-up plan, because I'm not going to press with a dozen blank pages.'

There's a lot of buzz about Milford. She couldn't stop the words ringing in her head. She turned and strode out of the fashion department to the sound of Belle sobbing.

21

'Tell me again how the hell Milford got Bret Alexander to shoot their ad campaign,' said Johnny Brinton, dragging on his cigarette and blowing the smoke in a cool stream towards Winterfold. 'I mean, he's only the hottest music video director since Spike Jonze. My agent says he's starting to cast his debut movie. Well, if he is, he'd better cast me. I tell you, there's got to be something in it for me today other than five hundred quid and doing you a bloody favour.'

Tom Grand puffed on his cigarette and smiled. It was typical of Johnny; his old school friend and sometime flat-mate was never satisfied with his lot. *Typical bloody actor*, he thought. Still, as they leant up against the location van smoking, Tom was feeling uncommonly pleased with himself; he still couldn't believe they'd pulled it off. When Emma had asked him to round up a dozen of his best-looking, high-profile friends and persuade them to be in a photo-shoot, he'd thought she was having a laugh – and anyway, why ask him? He always screwed things up. He was still feeling bruised from the *Rive* party debacle; he hadn't spoken to Cassandra since, he had zero job prospects and was increas-ingly reliant on his mother's hand-outs which, incidentally, had slowed right down to just a trickle. But for some reason, Emma seemed to have faith in him and when she had offered him two thousand pounds for his trouble, he'd leapt at it. He'd begged his friend Johnny, the son of rock legend Blake Brinton, to get involved and between them they had persuaded every rich, socially connected, good-looking, twenty-something bloke in the area to appear in Milford's ad campaign.

'I think Bret is a mate of Rob Holland's – the guy who's renting Winterfold from my cousin Emma?' said Tom, tossing his cigarette under the van. 'Apparently she said she'd terminate his lease if Rob didn't help her out.'

'I thought you said there'd be loads of models here,' grumbled Johnny, stamping his own cigarette into the emerald grass.

Tom looked around Winterfold's front lawns, which were humming with activity. As well as the lighting, wardrobe and the stylists teeming around the two location vans, Saul's classic car collection – *Tom's* car collection, he corrected himself – had been retrieved from storage and had been parked outside the house in a fan, like a gleaming peacock's tail. Tom and Johnny's ten other friends, all wearing jodhpurs, polo shirts and riding boots, were sitting in director's chairs having their make-up done in readiness for the next shot.

'Clover Connor is here,' said Tom. 'What more do you want?'

'She's not up for it though, is she? She's going out with that junkie Ste Donahue.'

'Come on,' smiled Tom. 'You know you can pull anyone if you try.'

It was true: Tom Grand was popular with the ladies, but it was nothing compared to Johnny. It helped that he was the son of a rock legend who lived ten miles away in a huge mansion rumoured to be the biggest private home in the county. It helped that he was an up-and-coming actor and constantly being name checked on every Hot List in the media as the new Jude Law. It helped that he was a staple of London's most glamorous social circuit and spent his evenings flitting between Nobu and launch parties. The annoying thing was that Johnny was handsome, charming and confident; he really didn't need any help bedding any woman who took his fancy. Just then a beautiful blonde girl stepped out of the main house, talking to Emma and Marcus who was art-directing the shoot. Tom's heart gave a little involuntary lurch: she was lovely. She had a broad sunny smile, an exquisitely pretty face, long legs in tight indigo jeans and what looked like a fine pair of knockers beneath a semi-transparent cream shirt.

'Who's *that*?' whispered Tom, squinting in the sun.

'Whoever it is, she's out of your league, sunshine,' smiled Johnny, pulling up his cream jodhpurs so they looked even tighter around the crotch. 'And anyway, I saw her first.'

'Uh-uh. I actually think I know her,' said Tom, the penny dropping.

'Who is she then? She's gorgeous.'

'Stella Chase. She's the designer here. The last time I saw her was about twenty years ago.'

'In that case then, you can introduce me,' said Johnny running his fingers through his tousled hair as he started to walk over. Tom's heart gave another lurch and he swore under his breath, knowing it wasn't worth getting into a competition with Johnny.

Since the afternoon of the pool party in Winterfold's walled garden, the Milford ad campaign had quickly snowballed, mainly due to the efforts of Rob Holland who had been keen to show Emma he wasn't the decadent layabout she had presumed him to be. Rob had enlisted Ste Donahue into his scheme and together, they had gently persuaded Clover to defy the advice of her agent and agree do the Milford shoot, in return for a 'mates rates' fee, the entire range of the company's Autumn/Winter line and an assurance from Rob that he would seriously consider her demo tape. Through Stella they had found Marcus Lynch, an old friend from her student days who was now the art editor of an achingly trendy French fashion magazine and he had agreed to art-direct the shoot. Emma thought she would have to hire one of the big advertising agencies to produce the campaign at mind-boggling expense but it turned out that this was the way fashion houses operated; working with a tight cabal of art directors and fashion photographers to produce their advertising imagery, only using media buyers at agencies to secure ad space in magazines. Because fashion was such a small world Emma had initially been wary of Marcus, wondering whether he might be a stooge sent by Cassandra to sabotage the shoot but she had worried unnecessarily. Marcus had once been fired by Cassandra as a young designer and he didn't have a good word to say about her. Emma was also encouraged when, despite his trendy sensibilities, Marcus agreed that they should cash in on Milford's English heritage to create their brand imagery – in fact it had been his idea to shoot at Winterfold and get a dozen handsome polo-clad extras. He'd also jumped on Rob's suggestion that they use a music video director to shoot it to stop it looking too soft and nostalgic.

'Whaddayathink?' asked Bret, showing Emma the latest digital shots on his laptop. There were three set-ups: one was a close-up of Clover framed by the majestic backdrop of the house. In the next, Clover was astride a shiny chestnut pony surrounded by Johnny, Tom and half a dozen other polo hunks. In the third she was climbing out of Saul's 1967 gun-metal Aston Martin, wearing a long white Grecian gown, slit from hem to thigh to show one long length of bronze leg. They were elegant, but sexy. They were fantastic.

'Absolutely beautiful,' said Emma softly. She looked at Bret and he grinned at her reaction.

'I aim to please,' he said. He was a big bear of a man with a loud belly laugh and a crooked smile, nothing at all like the pretentious fashion photographer Emma was expecting.

'But I'm not sure there's enough bag in the shot,' said Emma quickly, nervous that all she could see was a curved leather handle and the side of the 100 Bag.

Bret started laughing.

'Honey, fashion is all about building dreams. Ralph Lauren was a Jew from the Bronx, just like me, but it didn't stop him creating an empire based on a WASP way of living. You walk into a Ralphy shop, it's like stepping onto the freeking Great Gatsby set; it's goddamn genius. And it's what you got here. People don't want to see a bag, they want to see a fantasy they can buy into.'

'Are you sure?' asked Emma looking to Marcus for reassurance.

He nodded. 'And what you've got here is genuine, too. This is gen-u-ine blue-blood Britishness. Old money and elegance. Style not fashion.'

'*Style not fashion*. I love that,' said Emma. 'Can I use it for the slogan?'

Emma turned as a black 4x4 crunched down the gravel drive and stopped.

The door opened and a woman stepped out of the passenger seat. She had a glossy, buttery, blonde bob, large expensive sunglasses pushed back on her head and she was so slim and delicate that her kitten heels didn't seem to sink in the grass. At first Emma thought she might be another model for the shoot before Rob jumped out of the driver's side. Unless she'd had a radical makeover, this was not the naked girl in the jacuzzi at the pool party. *Not another one*, thought Emma. Then Rob went round to the back of the car and helped a little girl wearing pink stripy tights down and onto the grass.

'How's it going everyone? Hey, Bret, how are you?' Rob walked over to the group and shook the director's hand.

'If we don't shift a million handbags after this ad then I'm a fucking Chinaman,' smiled Bret, picking up his camera and heading back to Clover.

The blonde woman pulled a face and put a protective arm around the child. 'You'd think he'd tame his language in front of Polly,' she whispered to Rob.

'Emma, this is Madeline,' said Rob with a hint of awkwardness. 'And this,' he said, looking down at the girl with what could only be described as adoration, 'is my daughter Polly.'

Emma was stunned.

'*You* have a daughter?' she said before she could stop herself.

This time, Madeline gave a little tinkling laugh.

'That's how everyone reacts,' she said, putting out a delicate hand for Emma to shake. Emma caught Rob rolling his eyes and felt guilty; she didn't want to sound unkind. Rob had been incredibly generous with his time and contacts, even if she suspected his motives were to curry favour and buy time at Winterfold.

'Daddy, you said you'd show me the ponies again,' said the little girl.

Rob took Polly's small hand in his big one and looked at Madeline.

'Take her,' said Madeline briskly, 'I'll be fine here.'

Emma could feel herself redden slightly in the elegant woman's presence. She assumed Rob and Madeline weren't still together, but with someone like Rob, you never could tell. Had he been keeping a wife secreted away in New York while he'd been playing Hugh Hefner in England? He'd certainly kept the child quiet. Emma thought of the naked blonde in Winterfold's jacuzzi and suppressed a wince. Poor Madeline.

'So. You and Rob are . . .' Emma let the sentence hang politely.

Madeline smiled. 'We were together a long time ago. Polly was the result of that time.'

'Great! That's wonderful,' said Emma a little too eagerly.

'Polly and I live in New York,' said Madeline, not surprising Emma in the slightest. Madeline was so polished and groomed she reeked of the Upper East Side. 'Polly is on her Easter break, she's staying here while I go to Paris. My partner is doing some work over there.'

The conversation slipped into pleasantries. While Emma didn't find herself particularly warming to Madeline – she had a certain froideur not dissimilar to her cousin Cassandra – she couldn't help but be impressed by this woman's obvious accomplishments; she was a former lawyer, who had given it all up to raise Polly and in her own words fundraise an impressive roll call of causes from a ballet school for under-privileged African-American children to a theatre for disabled adults. Not Rob's type at all, she decided.

'So were you and Rob married?'

'No, thank God,' smiled Madeline, warming up slightly. 'I was just out of college when we met. Rob had just started working for his father's record company, which to my impres-sionable twenty-two-year-old mind seemed rather cool.' She half laughed, half winced at the memory. 'I stayed the night at his loft in Tribeca and never moved out. But by the time I was twenty-six I felt a different person. Rob is adorable but immature and our relationship was breaking up just as I found out I was pregnant.'

'Were you not tempted to stay together?'

'For the sake of our child?' said Madeline. 'He asked me but I knew we were doing the right thing for Polly by splitting up.'

Madeline paused and examined Emma critically.

'Are you and he . . .' Madeline wagged her finger between the two of them.

Emma shook her head, embarrassed that she had been asking so many questions. But she'd been interested to find out about the Rob Holland she hadn't so far seen. The man who proposed to his pregnant girlfriend even though they were not in love. The man who, unlike every other man on the shoot, was ignoring Clover Connor to run up and down the lawns with a little girl on his shoulders.

'I didn't think so,' said Madeline briskly. 'And take it as a compliment.'

Light was fading from the sky, the clouds were stung with pink while the spread of oak trees to one side of Winterfold looked as if they had been dipped in molten copper. It was a lovely evening. They'd been shooting for almost twelve hours but not even exhaustion could dampen Stella's mood. Today was the first day she'd really felt she had made the right decision moving back to England. After the fraught meetings with the bank, after the coldness Roger Milford and many of the factory workers had shown towards her, after spending 75 per cent of her time locked away in a studio, she finally felt as if they were getting somewhere. And more than that, Stella really felt that she was something to do with it all.

'That was wicked,' said Clover, handing Stella the tight tweed jacket she'd been wearing for the last shot of the day. 'Bret was fabulous, plus he told Ste he'd love do the next Kowalski video too, so you can imagine how chuffed *he* is.'

'Not as pleased as I am, the way the shoot has gone today. You were wonderful,' smiled Stella. Although Clover seemed down-to-earth with her Northern accent, chain-smoking and frequent cackles, Stella had been in the fashion industry long enough to know that talent had to be fawned over all the time and she was sure Emma was too naïve to do it.

'I'm going to Cannes for the film festival in a couple of weeks,' said Clover. 'Karl has made me this wonderful dress. You couldn't make me a bag to go with it?'

Stella's heart leapt, but she tried to keep cool. Clover asking *me* to make *her* a bag! She knew that Ruan would scream at her that the workshops were already at full stretch, but this was huge; it was gold-dust to have a big star walk the red carpet with one of your products. Stella knew Clover would look amazing, that the look would be dissected and talked about in a hundred magazines and newspapers around the globe and that her two-minute appearance outside Cannes' Palais des Festivals would be worth hundreds of thousands of pounds in advertising for Milford.

'Sure, babes,' she said casually, as Clover ran off to her trailer. As soon as she was out of earshot, Stella buried her face in the tweed jacket and screamed with delight.

'So what did you think?'

Stella was heading back into the main house, her mind fixed on the hot coffee that Emma had said was waiting there, when she heard the voice behind her.

Stella turned round to see Johnny Brinton who she had spotted as soon as he'd arrived with Emma's cousin Tom that morning. Her whirring overworked brain had registered then how ridiculously good-looking he was, but here and now, up close, without the distractions of the shoot, he was something else. Johnny was tall, rangy and tanned; the collar on his polo shirt looked brilliant white against his golden brown skin. His dark blond hair was swept back, showing off his enormous ice-blue eyes, while his cheekbones could cut paper. Back in LA, beautiful men just looked vain and overly pampered; Johnny had a casualness about him that was confident and incredibly sexy. Stella actually felt her knees shake. It was the first time in a long time she had felt that powerful lurch of instant sexual attraction. In the last three years she'd had one longish relationship with Ed, a surfer from Laguna Beach, who'd had the same sort of louche good looks as Johnny if not quite as exquisite. She had fallen deeply in love with Ed, but she was never entirely sure it was reciprocated. She'd put up with his dawn starts to catch the tide, the evenings spent on the beach playing touch football or smoking weed, even his regular disappearances with his surf crowd chasing the big waves and swells around the globe. She'd held on until there was nothing left to hold on to. And now she was ready for someone else; Stella knew that she wanted to fall in love.

'I thought you looked great,' said Stella realizing, too late, that in speaking her mind she'd sounded incredibly flirty. 'Sorry!' she gasped, blushing. 'I didn't mean that, although yes, you did look great. Oh, just ignore me. It's been a long day.'

A wide smile spread across Johnny's face and he touched her arm making her shiver.

'So which magazines is the campaign going in?' he smiled, 'I did this as a favour to Tom and he tells me nothing. For all I know it could be some jodhpur fetish magazine for bored country housewives.'

'Nothing so exotic,' smiled Stella. '*Vogue*, *Elle*, I'm not sure they have finalized the plan yet.'

'Well, you must let me know so I can tell my PR.'

'PR? What are you promoting?'

'Just myself,' he smiled. 'I'm in a film that comes out in a week's time.'

'Wow.'

'You should see it. I think the press, cast and crew screenings are finished, but the premiere's next Thursday. Would you like to come?'

Stella felt a rush of excitement at his choice of words. Would you like to *come*. It was a more personal proposition than asking her if she'd like to *go*.

'I'd love to.'

When Stella played the exchange back in her mind later that evening, it sounded like such a line. It was, of course, but Stella didn't care, she wanted to get swept up in it. He looked her age but had the confidence of someone older. She'd heard a rumour on set that he had a famous father. *Hey, who doesn't?* she thought.

'Here, give me your number,' he continued.

He fished his mobile out of his pocket and began punching the number in, then looked up at her.

'I'm Johnny, by the way. Why haven't we met before?'

'I'm Stella. And probably because I've just moved over from LA.'

'Well, we'd better start making up for lost time,' he said, his eyes dancing.

'How about Thursday?' asked Stella, feeling suddenly bold.

Johnny grinned.

'It's a date.'

'Is it?' asked Stella.

He winked and put his mobile back in his pocket.

Tom sat in the beautiful 1956 silver gull-wing Mercedes parked outside Winterfold, watching Stella and Johnny through the glass. *Well, that was a foregone conclusion*, he thought, watching their body language as they strolled along the grass in the pretty dusk light. They looked like young lovers in a Disney film. Tom cursed himself for not acting sooner. He'd had a brief chat to Stella earlier that day, sharing a laugh as they worked out they had once been naked together in the paddling pool in Provence, but it had been nothing beyond friendly chit-chat. For once, Tom's bravado had failed him and his cheeky-chappy sparkle failed to shine its brightest. Not that it would have made the slightest bit of difference if Johnny had decided he wanted to have Stella for himself. As long as Tom had known him, from the days when they'd first sat next to each other at prep school, Johnny had always got whatever he wanted, whether it was a place on the rugby team, admission to RADA or a swanky penthouse in Notting Hill, paid for by Daddy. Tom was happy for his friend, of course, although there was still a little nub of envy that he couldn't shake; a frustration at how one person could have so much luck, how everything so constantly and predictably always went his way. Tom was actually glad he and Johnny had drifted apart. In the last couple of months he'd crashed a few weekends in Johnny's spare room and they'd gone out to a few parties together, but that was about it. Once upon a time, they had been inseparable, but it had slowly dawned on Tom that having a friend like Johnny was the same as having a sister like Cassandra – bad for your self-esteem.

Someone tapped on the window and Tom opened the door. It was Jamie Curtis, one of Johnny's West London friends who had been an extra on the shoot.

'Nice car. Whose is it?' he asked, climbing in the tan leather passenger seat.

Tom smiled with undisguised pride.

'It's mine. Well, it will be in four years.'

'Four years? Tough luck, mate. Now's the time you need a bitch magnet like this one.'

'You're telling me,' sighed Tom. 'Still, I'm taking it for a run round the estate – want to come?'

Jamie smiled, nodding enthusiastically. 'Fire her up!'

Tom caught Emma's look of surprise as the thrumming engine turned over and they roared off down the drive. She was probably worrying if he was insured, but what the fuck – the car was his. If he wanted his little James Bond moment then he was sure as hell going to have it. The gravel drive coughed up little puffs of smoke as the car hit forty, fifty, then sixty miles an hour. He squeezed his foot down harder on the pedal, his anger and frustration at Johnny, at Cassandra, at everyone, turning to aggression.

'You mentalist!' shouted Jamie as they screamed round the lake at ninety. 'You got that right,' said Tom, then put his head out the window and whooped.

Twenty spine-tingling minutes later they were back in front of Winterfold. His mother was standing on the front step with a concerned expression.

'Uh-oh. I think someone's grounded,' teased Jamie when they had pulled to a stop.

'Grounded?' replied Tom wounded. 'I'm twenty-fucking-six not twelve.'

'Johnny said you were living back at home,' he laughed.

'It's purely temporary,' huffed Tom.

'In that case, why don't you come out to Ibiza in the summer?'

Tom looked at Jamie, oozing wealth with his ruddy good looks, upper-crust accent and chunky signet ring on his little finger, and felt bitter.

'I usually try and go but I can't afford it this year,' shrugged Tom. 'I haven't got a job and my mum is giving me grief for having to bail me out. Look at her now. She's practically breathing fire.'

'But would you like to go?'

'Of course,' said Tom getting out of the car. He pulled a cigarette packet out of his pocket and lit up straight away.

Jamie slammed the passenger door and walked round to him.

'Me and some mates are going over, you should come. We're gonna run a bar and a club night out there. Nothing too big but we want to get the right crowd so we expand next year. We need someone to come in and run the bar. It's just a little place but it's got a great location in Ibiza Town.'

'Me?' said Tom inhaling on his cigarette.

'Johnny said you might be up for it. Plus, he said you'd be perfect. You know everyone, you can sort out the music. We need someone who can talk the patter, know what I mean?'

Tom nodded, liking the sound of it.

'Well, I've done a bit of bar work before, but I haven't got any money to put in.'

Jamie patted him on the shoulder.

'Don't worry about the money. We've got that sorted.'

Of course you have, thought Tom. Jamie was part of Johnny's West London moneyed crowd. His family were Old Money and titled to boot.

'Obviously you'll get a smaller cut than the rest of us but so long as you make it work for us, I reckon you'll clear fifty grand for the summer.'

'Fifty gees. That sounds like it might be worth it.' Tom had to stop himself doing a cartwheel. *Fifty fucking thousand!* Where else was he going to make that sort of money, let alone running his own bar in Ibiza?

Jamie's mobile was ringing angrily.

'Hey, have a think about it, eh?' he said, picking up the call. 'Johnny has my number.'

'Tom, get over here!' hissed a voice to their left. They both looked to see Julia, her face like thunder, and Jamie smirked and rolled his eyes.

'TOM! I need to speak to you,' shouted Julia angrily.

Tom shrugged his shoulders sheepishly and made the 'I'll call you' sign to Jamie. *Ibiza*. It was a lifeboat. It was time to get a life, get out of the country and do it quickly. *Balearics, here I come.*

22

Cassandra pushed back in her chair and rubbed her tired eyes. She had just spent the last twenty minutes in front of her computer screen poring over the week's sales figures. Thursday afternoons were either heaven or hell for Cassandra. When they had good sales she felt on top of the world, but today she felt sick to the pit of her flat stomach. *Rive*'s June cover had been the worst-selling issue of the last twelve months. Sitting halfway through the fashion season, June was never a strong-selling issue for fashion magazines, which was why publishers often propped it up with holiday-friendly freebies taped to the cover – free flip-flops and make-up bags, the sort of tat Cassandra despised with a passion. But even taking the give-aways into consideration, *Rive* had done poorly. Cassandra reached up to the Scandinavian blonde wood shelf where all the recent issues were lined up and pulled down the June edition. She looked the cover over critically. The cover-lines were good, the features inside strong and the fashion shoots were some of the best they'd done in years. Which only left the choice of cover-star: Ludvana, the seventeen-year-old Eastern European beauty. Ludvana was fashion's newest superstar, six foot two, with straight ice-blonde hair falling to her waist and she had just landed campaigns with Gucci to Victoria's Secret. *Rive* had hired Patrick Demarchelier to shoot Ludvana as Lady Godiva riding through the streets of Manhattan on a horse. The shoot had cost them $100,000, not to mention weeks of wrangling with New York's City Hall to get permission to stop traffic and block streets – and for what? Sales figures were down 20 per cent on the Gwyneth Paltrow cover the month before. Cassandra had agreed to Ludvana against her better judgement and evidently, she had been correct. While Ludvana had made the right statement to the fashion industry, she was *so* hot, *so* new, that half *Rive*'s readership wouldn't even know who she was. It had been a classic case of not seeing the wood for the trees. The success of *Rive* was down to their breadth of readership, not just St Martin's fashion students or chic, urban twenty-somethings desperate to read about the latest trends. *Rive* also had to appeal to the chic yummy-mummy holding onto her youth and the elegant sixty-year-old with a closet full of vintage Halston. The *Rive* reader was anyone who wanted to aspire to the high fashion lifestyle of gloss, glamour and escapism the magazine served up month after month.

Cassandra sank back into her chair, biting her lip. To the outside world editing a fashion magazine was child's play, all you had to do was look fantastic, go to three parties a night and then wait for all the hot designers to send you free handbags. But magazine publishing was a business just like any other, and at the end of the day, it was figures that counted and this one bad issue would drag down the rest of the year's good sales, giving the impression of a mediocre year, when up until now, *Rive* had been doing very well.

'Mum! Mum! Listen,' said Ruby, bursting through the door without knocking.

'Sweetie, I'm busy,' said Cassandra sternly. 'I thought Laura was taking you on the London Eye?'

'We did that like, *hours* ago,' said Ruby, flinging herself down on an Eames chair and spinning around on it like a carousel. 'Anyway, I've just been in the art department. David Stern took a picture of me and turned it into a *Rive* cover. He's just printing it off now so I can see it. Isn't that cool?'

Cassandra sighed. Not for the first time, she doubted the wisdom of bringing Ruby to the office, but this time she didn't have any choice. It was half-term, Julia was busy in the gallery and Ruby had complained so much about being left at school with all the girls whose parents were in the forces that Cassandra had relented. Monday had been spent taking tea at Claridge's and shopping in Harvey Nichols, Tuesday afternoon Ruby had been taken to Hari's salon in South Kensington for a facial. But by Wednesday Cassandra could no longer stay away from the office. She had a lunch scheduled with Aerin Lauder, who was always charming company but as her family's company owned everything from Estée Lauder to Origins there was no way she could ask her to rearrange. So she had left Ruby alone in her Knightsbridge apartment, telling Gerald the concierge to check on her every hour. By the time Cassandra had arrived at her desk, there were already three increasingly frantic messages from Gerald, complaining that Ruby had set off the building's fire alarm, having tried to make a cheese toastie by jamming all the ingredients into her Kitchen Aid toaster. There was nothing for it but to bring her into the office.

'Ruby, please,' sighed Cassandra as Ruby swung her feet up onto the table and knocked a vase of calla lilies flying.

'Sorry,' said Ruby, looking anything but.

Cassandra glanced at her watch. It was already 6.30 p.m.

'So are you ready to go out?' she asked, getting up from behind her desk.

'Go out where?' asked Ruby with a suspicious frown.

Cassandra sighed. 'Darling, we went through your itinerary this morning. Giles is taking you for burger and shakes at Automat and then to see that new Disney movie. I promised Disney's chief exec I'd tell him what you thought. Then a car is taking you back to the apartment and Grandma is meeting you there as soon as she can get here from Oxford.'

'But I don't want to go,' whined Ruby.

'You *like* Giles,' said Cassandra, who had no time for a teenage tantrum. 'You had a great time yesterday when he took you to the Canaletto exhibition at the RA.'

'I don't want to go and see the Disney movie. I want to go and see that thing you're going to tonight.'

'Darling. It's a premiere, a work thing.'

'Johnny Brinton is in it, isn't he? He's gorgeous. Surely you can get me a ticket.'

'But it's a 15 certificate,' said Cassandra, her patience running out.

'Loads of people say I look eighteen.'

'You can't come.'

'Why not?' said Ruby, her voice now raised considerably. 'I want to see Johnny's film and I know there's a party afterwards. I want to *go*!'

'Stop it!' screamed Cassandra, smacking her hand on her desk. Her yell seemed to hang in the air, then she heard the sound of gentle sobbing from her daughter. Softening, Cassandra reached for her, but Ruby shook her head violently away.

'Sweetheart I didn't mean to shout. Come here.'

She pulled Ruby over to the soft leather sofa. Cassandra was not a demonstrative woman beyond the thousands of air-kisses she distributed each season, but she sat close to her daughter and rested her hand gently on Ruby's knee.

'You never want to spend any time with me,' sniffed Ruby, wiping her eyes with the sleeve of her cotton dress.

'Now you know that's not true,' said Cassandra firmly. 'We had a wonderful trip together during the Easter holidays, didn't we?'

A travel PR had arranged for Cassandra and Ruby to go to the latest luxury resort in the Maldives. Although Cassandra could barely afford the time out of the office, they'd spent five days in a deluxe water villa where she had topped up her tan and edited the manuscript of *Cassandra Grand: On Style*.

'No!' pouted Ruby, 'it was just where *you* wanted to go, just like you want to go to the premiere without me.'

'Sweetheart, I work very hard. When I go to a party it's not to have fun. I stay thirty minutes, talk to the most important people in the room, people who can help me, *help us*, and then I leave. I'm not trying to stop you from having fun when I say you can't go tonight but you have to understand what I do and why I do it. I don't have any choice.'

'You *do* have a choice,' said Ruby, sobbing, 'You always have choices. Like you choose not to see me most weekends when half the girls at school go home. You choose to give me presents instead of your time. You even have the choice whether to work so hard. What would happen that's so bad if you didn't stay at the office so late or go to all these parties? What would happen if you didn't have so great a job? Would we starve?'

'Ruby, stop it.'

'You say everything is to help us,' she said, her eyes blazing in hurt and anger. 'But how does it help *me* having a mother I never see? Did you stop to think about where *I* would like to go on holiday? Or whether I like going to a boarding school? Milly Steele goes to a day school.'

'Oh, and I suppose you'd prefer to be one of those sad media children like Milly Steele growing up in the Groucho or round a campfire at Glastonbury?' replied Cassandra tartly.

'At least her parents want her with them,' wailed Ruby, the tears flowing swiftly now. 'You just don't want me around. You buy me off and farm me out. What's wrong with me? Am I not pretty enough? Not enough of a perfect accessory? Don't you love me? Or maybe you just don't love me as much as you love your job!'

Ruby stared at her mother, a brave, challenging look that was part courage and part disappointment and Cassandra felt a strange mixture of both pride and sadness.

'Darling, it's not like that at all. You know I love you very, very much.'

'Do you?'

Cassandra stood up and strode over to her desk, picking up the phone.

'Giles? Could you step through please?'

Ruby bowed her head, shaking it gently.

'Giles,' said Cassandra as he walked into the office, 'there's been a change of plan.'

Ruby spun round and looked at her mother.

'I want you to take Ruby round to the fashion cupboard and sort her out with dress, bag and shoes.'

'It's a very pretty dress she has on,' smiled Giles.

'Yes, but tonight we're going to a very high-profile event, one where Ruby has to look at least fifteen. That dress that came in today, the aqua Dolce? I think that would look very nice with her skin tone.'

'I can go to the premiere!' squealed Ruby.

Cassandra gave a little half-smile. 'I'm giving Giles the night off, yes.'

Ruby ran round the desk and threw her arms round her mother.

'Darling, be careful not to mark the Balenciaga,' she said, carefully peeling her off. 'And Giles? Can you see if Lianne is still here and get her to clean up these lilies.'

23

Emma strolled along Oxford's High Street feeling a real pang of affection for the city. Although she had loved her student and subsequent professional life in Boston with its colonial elegance and cultural micro-climate so isolated from the rest of America, Oxford was steeped in a history Boston could only dream of, not to mention a gentle majesty few cities in the world could match. She'd spent the last couple of hours enjoying supper with Ernesto Pozzi, a professor at North Western University who was currently a visiting Fellow at Magdalen College. As Ernesto had been one of her father's best friends, Emma had made a point of keeping in touch over the past few years, although finding the time to make the journey to his house in Chicago had been difficult. Emma had been delighted therefore when the old man moved to Oxford, albeit temporarily; it made their meetings more convenient. Over a steak and chips supper in a brasserie full of students, they'd discussed literature and funny stories about students and Ernesto had pressed a huge pile of books on her, insisting she read them all. But mainly they'd talked about Ernesto and her father Jack's time together as students in Cambridge. Emma loved these stories more than anything.

Her mother did not like to talk about her father and as Emma had no brothers and sisters, meeting Jack Bailey's friends was a way of keeping him alive.

She stood for a moment in the road trying to get her bearings. She hadn't been to Oxford for at least five years and couldn't remember where she'd parked her car.

'Get out of the road, honey!' said a voice. A hand gripped her arm and steered her towards the pavement. 'If a bus comes along there won't be enough left of you to make a handbag.'

'Rob!' said Emma, looking around as a car tore past, its horn blaring. 'What are you doing here?'

'Picking up a painting,' he grinned, 'from your aunt's gallery actually. She managed to find me this great Bridget Riley lithograph I'm giving to a couple of friends as a wedding gift. I've just driven here straight from work; she kept the gallery open late so I could collect it.'

She looked at the large package underneath his arm.

'A Bridget Riley? Nice gift. Beats a Teasmaid.'

'What's a teas maid?' asked Rob, eyebrows raised.

Emma giggled. 'Some other time,' she said, noticing that they were heading towards Magdalen Bridge, both walking in step together without asking where the other was going.

'So, how did the shoot go?'

'Really well. The photos look beautiful.'

'I hope you and Madeline didn't do too much whispering about me. I saw you huddled together gossiping.'

'She's nice. An impressive woman. Doesn't strike me as your usual type,' said Emma with a crooked smile.

'Oh, and what's that supposed to mean?'

Emma laughed again.

'Just that she's quite different from Trudy.'

'I'll have you know Trudy has a chemistry degree. She's a very nice girl.'

'I'm sure she is. Does Polly like her?'

Rob paused before answering.

'Trudy's never met Polly. I don't like girlfriends meeting my daughter until, well, I think they're ready.'

Emma looked down at the books under her arm, feeling slightly uncomfortable. They fell silent as they came to Magdalen Bridge and stopped, leaning on the ancient stone, looking down into the water.

'Well, I'm sorry it didn't work out,' said Emma. 'You and Madeline, I mean. It must be hard living so far away from your daughter.'

'Yeah, I miss Polly like crazy. I feel like a bad father every day I don't see her which is about three hundred and thirty days of the year.'

Emma suddenly felt truly sorry for Rob, wondering if he regretted Madeline turning down his proposal of marriage. She looked up and saw that he was examining her face, as if he knew what she was thinking.

'When Maddy and I got together it was a pretty weird time for me. I don't think it was ever really going to work out between us and it was definitely for the best.'

'A weird time?'

He hesitated and Emma felt the discomfort again, as if she had pushed him further than he wanted to go.

'I'm a second son,' said Rob slowly, his eyes fixed on the River Cherwell gurgling beneath them. 'My family didn't have any expectations for me beyond keeping out of jail and maybe marrying someone pretty. I dropped out of college, formed a band, went to a lot of nightclubs. If we'd have met back then we'd have got on real well,' he smiled.

Emma grinned.

'Then, when I was twenty-five, my brother Sam died. He was five years older than me.'

'Oh, I'm really sorry,' she replied, very much regretting ever having started this conversation.

261

'Sam was this *brilliant* person, good at everything. He came to Oxford University actually. When he died it was a huge wake-up call for me. I was too ashamed to keep living the way I'd been before when my two young nephews suddenly had no father. I offered to join the family company, then met Maddie at a party in Connecticut. She was from a nice family; she was the *right* sort of girl.'

'But you weren't right for each other.'

She looked at him and they both smiled sadly.

There was a deep silence. Rob had a slightly startled look as if he regretted opening up to her in this manner. Emma was thrown; she'd never had Rob pegged as the sort of person who would do the right thing if it wasn't what he wanted, regardless of the circumstances.

'Yeah well, I would have been a crap rock star,' he said, in an attempt at levity. She realized that there probably weren't very many people he could talk to about this.

'So anyway, where are we walking to?' he smiled.

It was past eight o'clock and it had suddenly got dark, the pink sky losing its colour as if someone had turned down the dimmer switch. Streaks of sun still glinted in the river, but the street lights were beginning to flicker on.

'I'm in a car park about five minutes walk down there,' said Emma, pointing downstream.

'Come on, it's getting dark. I'll walk you.'

They walked down some steps and along a wide gravel towpath.

'It's really pretty, isn't it? Oxford.'

'When it isn't a little spooky,' smiled Emma, looking around at the dusk closing in. 'I'm really grateful for the help you've given us, by the way. The ad pictures are amazing and we couldn't have done it without you.'

'Does that mean you're not going to kick me out of Winterfold?'

262

'It means I owe you one. We really must take you out as a thank you. There's a really great restaurant in Sherby.'

'Well, that depends on who the *we* is.' He smiled.

'Myself, Stella, maybe Ruan,' she said, not wanting to sound as if she was asking him out. *Which of course she wasn't.* 'And Trudy is invited of course,' she added quickly.

'There's no need, really,' said Rob. 'I wanted to help.'

They turned away from the river along a narrow street, then round a corner and into the car park.

'Well, this is me,' said Emma as they stopped by her car.

'What are you doing this weekend?' Rob asked suddenly.

'Oh, I don't know. The usual I guess; go for a run, do some paperwork, read a bit. I might meet Stella for Sunday lunch.'

Rob was laughing.

'What's so funny?' she asked.

'Nothing.'

'Tell me what's so funny?' She was slightly offended. 'What do you expect me to do each weekend? Sky-dive? Pole dance?'

He held up his hands.

'Hey, I'm not laughing at you, but I don't think it would be such a bad idea if you did have some fun. Listen, this wedding I'm going to,' he said quickly, his words coming out in a rush, 'it should be lovely, it's in Wales, the bride's dad has a castle. Why don't you come?'

Emma was completely taken by surprise by his invitation.

'I don't think so,' she stuttered. 'I'd be in the way, wouldn't I?'

'In the way of who?'

'Trudy.'

'She's not coming,' he said, sounding mildly irritated. 'I don't want to give her the wrong idea. Anyway, stop mentioning her. She's not my girlfriend. It's just sex.'

She shot him a dirty look, feeling piqued at the way he confused her.

During the course of ten minutes, she had completely reversed her view of him, feeling empathy for his loss and respect for his efforts as a son and father. Then, with one comment, her view of him had come back, full circle: he was a sexist pig who treated women as nothing more than notches on his bedpost.

'It's very kind, but I'm so busy,' began Emma, opening the door of her car and putting her books on the passenger seat.

'Ah, come on, what else are you going to be doing?' asked Rob, craning his neck to see the books. '*Poetry and Romanticism, 1750–1840*?'

She threw her bag on top of the book, as if to protect Ernesto's books from him. 'You should read it,' she snapped. 'You might learn something.'

'Come on, Em. I don't really want to go alone but I don't want to take a girlfriend. And anyway, you said you owed me one. The bride's dad's an intellectual, so you'll be able to talk to him about poetry and stuff.'

'To think I thought *you* might want me for my company,' she said, feeling a little hurt.

'I'm leaving tomorrow afternoon,' said Rob. 'I think you'll have fun. We'll have fun.'

Emma knew he was right. A warm, sunny weekend had been predicted. So she loved her weekends pottering around Chilcot but it was hard to completely relax when there was a Milford employee at every turn. A wedding in a castle *did* sound like fun. As for Rob, well, what was she getting so worked up about? So he was a chauvinist. That wasn't exactly news, but she couldn't help admit that he was good fun.

'Maybe I'll call you tomorrow.'

'Separate bedrooms and everything, I promise,' he smiled, holding up three fingers like a boy scout.

Emma felt a sudden surge of spontaneity that was most unusual.

'In that case you have a deal.'

Stella had been to premieres many times before in LA, having occasionally been thrown a couple of tickets by Cate Glazer for the opening of one of her husband's films, but this was the first time she had ever gone alone. Stepping out of her taxi at the corner of Leicester Square, she felt a sudden knot of fear. *What the hell am I doing here?* she thought to herself. Meeting a man she hardly knew in a dark room surrounded by film stars? Just then she heard a mighty roar from a huge crowd squashed behind the crash barriers and police.

'Not quite what I had in mind for a first date,' she muttered under her breath as she walked towards the red carpet. Not that Stella was entirely sure she was even on a date. Johnny was going to the premiere separately with some of the cast, which was quite understandable. If he was seen walking the red carpet with any member of the opposite sex it would be a definite statement that they were together – and she and he had barely talked, let alone, well, done *anything* else. Johnny's arrangements about meeting afterwards were vague to say the least too. Her ticket had arrived with a bunch of fifty red tulips and a note that read simply 'See you at the party.'

But date or no date, Stella had wanted to look her very best, so she had decided to channel the 'sixties starlet at Cannes' look. Her favourite canary yellow chiffon dress, known by her friend Tash as 'the man-magnet dress', floated six inches above the knee and was cut dangerously low at the front. Her skin was tanned from the recent good weather, and silver Pierre Hardy heels and a vintage Milford clutch bag completed the look which was already getting her noticed. She was only a few feet onto the red carpet and already photographers had started snapping.

'Over 'ere, darling!'

'What's your name, love?'

A woman with a clipboard and a headset darted out and pulled Stella into an area in front of a paparazzi scrum. 'I think you're wanted,' hissed the PR woman, stepping out of shot. Stella was overwhelmed by the bright bursts of light and walked away dazzled and blinking.

'Ooh, fabulous dress,' said a voice. Stella looked up to see a man with a huge camera on his shoulder flanked by a glamorously-dressed journalist who was pushing a microphone into Stella's face. 'Fashion TV. Why don't you tell the viewers about your look?'

Stella gripped her clutch bag a little tighter. *Crikey. Why was anybody interested in her?*

After the film, select members of the audience moved on to the aftershow party at Asia de Cuba at the St Martin's Lane Hotel. Cassandra was standing in a roped-off VIP area with Johnny Brinton's stepmother Astrid. Astrid was one of Cassandra's closest friends, a former stylist who had met and subsequently married the rock star Blake when she had styled him for the cover of his first solo album. Her official age was thirty-eight but Cassandra reckoned she was a decade older. Even so, she looked remarkably good: she was wearing one of her many pieces of couture, a beautiful French navy Chanel cocktail dress.

From her elevated position, Cassandra could see the entrance and watched as Johnny arrived in a flurry of hysteria, the well-wishers and fans pushing past the bigger names to get to him. He was surrounded on all sides, he was pushed and prodded, but he took it all in his stride, signing autographs and cracking jokes. It took something special, some indefinable 'ingredient X' to get that sort of reaction, to rise above the hundreds of good-looking singers, actors, dancers, presenters and models that choked media land and Johnny had it. *Yes, that boy has star quality*, thought Cassandra.

'So how does Blake feel about being eclipsed by his son?' asked Cassandra, watching Johnny work the room with such finesse, it was as if she herself had given him a master-class. 'I think you will look back at tonight and pinpoint it as the night Blake became the second most famous member of the family.'

'Yes, he gave a wonderful performance in the film, didn't he?' smiled Astrid, 'but I have to say, I think there was a certain degree of inevitability about it all, don't you? Johnny's been acting up ever since I met his father.' She paused to accept a quail's egg and caviar blini from a waiter.

'And is Ruby enjoying herself?' asked Astrid, watching the girl trying to sip a glass of champagne in a very grown-up fashion.

'Urh,' groaned Cassandra, 'she told me on the way over here that she now wants to be an actress.'

'What happened to her wanting to be an archaeologist?'

'That was last year's little fad. She kept trying to persuade me to do a shoot at the Hanging Gardens of Babylon so she could come with me. It actually sounded like a rather good idea until I found out it was destroyed in an earthquake 2,000 years ago.'

Astrid giggled. 'Whenever did something like that ever stop you? I'm surprised you didn't tell Giles to *make it happen*.'

Cassandra rolled her eyes.

'Anyway, where are we on the exhibition?' she said. 'I know we have a lunch on Monday but you might as well give me the broad strokes.'

Cassandra and Astrid had begun to organize a grand charity dinner dance to rival the Met-Gala in New York. The theme was the works of the great couturier Charles Worth, the British designer who moved to Paris and kick-started couture and the modern day fashion industry as we know it. However, as vice-chair of the organization committee, it was Astrid's responsibility to arrange a venue and she had hit a solid wall. The plan was to have the exhibition-cum-dinner immediately after couture week in January but the Chambre Syndicale, who governed the biannual couture shows had yet to announce the dates, which made it impossible for her to confirm a venue.

'I've been tearing my hair out, darling, I really have,' said Astrid. 'I have another meeting with the V&A tomorrow and Karoline Braun has been a real find in drumming up corporate sponsorship, but . . .'

'Who is that stunning girl with Johnny?' interrupted Cassandra, surprised that she did not know every good-looking and important person in the room. 'Is she a model?'

'That's Stella Chase. I think she's Johnny's date tonight.'

Cassandra opened her grey eyes in surprise. 'Stella Chase the designer at Milford?'

'The same. She's a very pretty girl, isn't she? Too small to model but lovely all the same. The photographers have been having a field day with her tonight.'

Cassandra nodded unconsciously. Yes, she certainly had a certain something.

'How on earth did Johnny meet her?' she asked.

'He did some shoot for Milford the other day.'

Cassandra looked sharply at her friend.

'Johnny modelled for *Milford*?'

Astrid pulled a face and looked away.

'Now, darling, don't go all funny just because you're still pissed off about your cousin. I never told you because

268

I knew you'd react like this and frankly, Johnny could do with a high-profile advertising campaign.'

'High-profile? I doubt that,' snorted Cassandra. But she felt her good mood evaporate as she thought of Emma Bailey. *Just what is that little bitch up to now?*

'Can you believe people are talking Oscar-buzz already? Best fucking supporting actor! Can you imagine if I got it?' laughed Johnny when he had steered Stella into a quiet corner. Stella smiled politely, but she was not in the best of moods. Johnny had taken over an hour to come over and find her. Of course, he had been snowed under with journalists, producers and celebrities telling him what a fabulous performance he'd given. Buoyed by their attention, he was even more funny and charming than he had been at the Milford shoot, but still . . .

'If I was on the Academy I would vote for you,' smiled Stella, doing her best to sound witty.

Johnny took a flute of champagne and downed it in one.

'Can I just tell you how incredible you look tonight?' he said putting his hand on her shoulder. 'You could be having an Elizabeth Hurley moment in that dress.'

'Does that make you my Hugh Grant?' she said, suddenly feeling flirty.

'Something like that,' he said in a low voice, looking straight at her. His ice-blue eyes were incredible. 'So how about we get out of here?'

Stella nodded, her earlier annoyance melting away.

'I heard a few people are going to Bungalow 8?'

'What? And get mobbed again?' smirked Johnny, taking her hand. 'Come on, it's about time we made this into a proper date.'

'So it *is* a date?' she replied, feeling in a much better mood.

He smiled and lifted her hand to kiss her palm. It was an intimate, sexy gesture and Stella shivered.

'Well, maybe you should go first,' she said quickly, not wanting to ruin his image so soon.

'Oh no, you don't get away that easily,' he laughed. 'Shall we? He cocked out his arm playfully and she slid hers through.

The cameras went wild as they left the party. For Stella, it was ten times more frightening than having to walk the red carpet on her own three hours earlier.

They dashed through the flashbulbs and into the car which was waiting for Johnny.

'Westbourne Grove,' he ordered before settling back into the leather seat.

He put his hand on her bare thigh and watched as the London streets slipped by. They hardly spoke, just enjoying the tension that was crackling between them.

A thought nagged at Stella that she shouldn't be going back to his flat so soon – they had barely spent an hour in each other's company – and yet here she was with the hottest guy in London. *Correction,* she smiled, quoting one of the *Time Out* journalists at the party, *the hottest new guy in film.*

The car slid to a stop outside a white stucco-fronted mansion block. Johnny took her by the hand and ran up the front steps, hastily pushing open the front door.

Once inside, his hands cupped her face, his lips stroking hers, the kiss growing deeper and deeper in intensity until their hands were caressing each other's neck, cheeks, hair.

She was swept away in such a violent surge of lust that she could barely speak.

'Which floor?' said Stella, her breath already ragged.

'Top,' he whispered. Now she grabbed Johnny's hand and

pulled him towards the staircase, racing up the steps, laughing as they ran. When they reached the final flight, Johnny caught up with her, grabbed her hips, pulling her down. She was on her hands and knees, looking up at his front door, giggling, when she felt his hands reach under her dress. His fingers rested momentarily on her hips, before they hooked into the top of her panties, peeling them down. Johnny smoothly flicked her panties over her shoes and pushed the chiffon skirt up to the small of her back, leaving her lower half completely bare. She arched her back in desire as he caressed the curve of her ass, then gasped as she felt his tongue lick the length of her dark crease.

'I've only just started,' he whispered, climbing two stairs so he was right on top of her, pressing his hard cock against her. Leaving her panties on the step, he pulled her upright and pushed her gently against the door, his lips caressing her neck as he rattled the key in. The door swung open. Not bothering to turn on any lights, he urgently pulled at the dress zipper, but the vintage fastener was stuck.

'Just get it off,' panted Stella, almost blind with desire. She heard the faint tear of fabric before it floated to the ground. Standing in only her heels, he pressed her back against the wall, their lips smashing against one another's in their urgency. Then suddenly Johnny pulled away and, looking her in the eye, slowly licked two fingers and lowered them onto her warm belly. She was already wet between her thighs before his fingers dipped and curled, pushing inside her, massaging her ripe clitoris until she groaned. She moved her feet apart and lifted her arms above her head, where she grabbed onto a light fitting on the wall.

He curled his fingers, damp from her juices, around her right breast and almost took it whole into his mouth, before pulling back to bite her brown stud-like nipple so soft and sweetly, that she arched her back in pleasure.

271

'I didn't know pretty boys were so good at sex,' she whispered, the words gasping out. Her skin felt as if it was burning, sexual heat firing up every nerve ending.

'Only good? I can do better than that.'

They both laughed as Stella began unbuttoning his shirt, while Johnny lifted her into his arms and into the bedroom, tapping the door behind him with his foot so it closed with a gentle click.

24

The wedding of Laura Hildon, fashion editor of *Rive* magazine, and Max Carlton, one of the hottest young investment
bankers in the City, was held in Hildon Castle, a stately pile
set against the stunning backdrop of the Welsh mountains.
As Laura was Henry and Eleanor Hildon's only child and
they were one of the wealthiest families in Wales, they were
both determined to do her proud. Forty-eight hours of cele-
brations had been planned, kicking off with a themed party
on the lawns tonight, but that was just the appetizer. Over
the course of the weekend there would be the wedding
ceremony itself followed by a black tie dinner for six hundred,
then a midnight firework display rumoured to have cost a
quarter of a million pounds. It would all come to a polished
finish with a brunch for all the guests still left standing on
the Sunday. For such an event, only the very best wardrobe
would do, so Laura's Lacroix couture bridal gown, made
and modified under Cassandra's guidance, had arrived from
Paris the day before in the back seat of Henry Hildon's Bentley
which had been specially sent to collect it. At Laura's request
Cassandra and Giles had been the first guests to arrive at
Hildon Castle to oversee a private dress rehearsal with the

hand-picked hair and make-up artists. The two of them had spent the last hour walking around the grounds, supposedly to get some fresh Welsh air before the preparations began; but in actual fact, Cassandra was desperate to do a full inventory of the estate. Yes, Hildon Castle was absolutely in the middle of nowhere. Cassandra had chartered a helicopter to take them there, which she had intended to write off against a location scout fee, but apart from its distance from the metropolis – *any* metropolis – she was unable to find fault with it. The castle was surrounded by beds of lupins, peonies and delphiniums which softened its hard granite and slate edges. There was a crystal-clear lake and a thick pine forest that melted into the foothills and the house itself was dramatic with towers and narrow windows, and open and welcoming too.

'Love is in the air, darling,' said Giles dramatically, picking up a pale pink rose that had fallen to the ground and handing it to Cassandra. 'Perhaps tonight will be the night when we both find love.'

'For God's sake, Giles, you sound like the fool from a Shakespeare play.'

'A fool for love, methinks,' he smiled taking a sip of the fresh, iced lemonade he had been carrying around. 'As for you, my dear, you haven't had a decent relationship since last year's Spring/Summer collections. You're one of the most eligible women in the country and you behave like a nun.'

'I would be a very naughty nun,' smiled Cassandra, taking off her sunglasses and fixing them on her head.

There was nothing like a wedding to make a person reflect on their own love life and Cassandra was no exception. She had quietly turned thirty-six the previous weekend and had chosen to spend it alone at the Grove Spa just outside London. Most people assumed that because Cassandra threw

274

and attended a lot of parties in the name of work she was a party animal, but away from the office and the catwalk she was a very private person, preferring to rely on herself and her own company. *It was better that way*, she thought.

As they walked across the manicured pea-green lawns in front of the castle, they saw Laura and her mother Eleanor waiting for them at the grand entrance. Tall and slender, Eleanor Hildon was wearing long grey slacks, a cream geor-gette blouse and a long string of pearls that fell across her flat chest.

'Did you enjoy the grounds?' she smiled, revealing a set of blinding white teeth, slightly too large for her mouth.

'Oh, they're splendid,' replied Giles. 'They remind me of the Butchart Gardens in Canada.'

'And, Cassandra, how have you settled into the gardener's cottage? Laura said you might be sensitive to noise and I thought the castle might get a little rowdy later on. We have forty people staying here just tonight.'

Cassandra smiled politely. She had no desire to be painted as a delicate flower – she'd have to have words with Laura about that later – but if it meant she could slip away from the party unnoticed, it was worth it. Six hundred well-oiled revellers laughing and shouting inside the castle's stone walls would be an acoustic hell.

'I've had a complete nightmare with the seating plan,' continued Eleanor. 'According to Laura, everybody seems to hate somebody. Thank goodness tonight is a more casual affair. I thought the Wild West theme would be such fun, don't you?'

Cassandra smiled again, slightly less warmly. Laura caught the expression and quickly intervened.

'Well, you're just in time to meet Max. He called me a few minutes ago to say he'd arrived – Ah! Here he is now.'

They all turned to face the drive as a powerful car

thundered towards them and skidded to a halt in front of the house. A tall elegantly-dressed man jumped out, pushing his dark hair off his face as he did so. Wearing a Euro-Sloane uniform of polo shirt, chinos and Tod's loafers, his body was lean and fit and moved with a confident swagger. To her great surprise Cassandra felt a stir in her groin. Max Carlton was not the most handsome man she had ever seen, but he had a presence, a sensual aura she could feel herself responding to. Max kissed both his bride-to-be and his mother-in-law on the cheek before fixing Cassandra with a smile.

'And you must be Cassandra,' he said, putting out a huge hand. 'I'm Max.'

'I can't believe you two haven't met,' said Laura, flushed with pride.

'We have spoken on the phone,' said Cassandra calmly. 'I have been trying to extract details about the honeymoon, but it was a hopeless cause even when I told him I was co-ordinating your trousseau.'

'Well, I wish he'd tell me,' said Laura with coltish exuberance. 'I hate surprises.'

'Talking of honeymoons,' said Cassandra. 'Remind me when you're back in the office?'

'A week on Monday,' said Laura. 'We couldn't be away for too long: Max has a new job.'

'Atlantis, the Private Equity group,' he replied, locking his gaze on Cassandra.

'It's a partnership, so it's brilliant for him,' said Laura, rolling her eyes.

'I'm so happy for you,' Cassandra said quickly.

'Now that everyone's been introduced, let's go indoors for some lunch,' said Eleanor clapping her hands together. 'Marshall, our chef, does a wonderful pork with sloe-berry sauce made from fruit grown in the grounds. With a bit of luck we'll all be able to get to know one another much better.'

'Yes, that would be lovely,' said Cassandra. And she could feel Max's eyes boring into her.

'Rob, are you insane?' shouted Emma. 'How can you expect me to go?'

When Rob had casually revealed the identity of the bride halfway up the motorway, Emma had gone berserk. This was supposed to be a break, a stress-free weekend. But instead, Rob had invited her to the wedding of Laura Hildon – the fashion editor of *Rive*. That meant Cassandra would almost certainly be in attendance and that most definitely meant there was going to be a confrontation of some description. Cassandra's betrayal of Milford still stuck in Emma's throat and while she had resisted the urge to call Cassandra after Cameron had told her of her bad-mouth campaign, she couldn't – *wouldn't* – let the incident pass if they met face to face.

'I'm sorry, Em, I really didn't know,' said Rob, slowing his sports car to only slightly over the speed limit. 'Listen, if you really don't want to go, I'll take you home again. I had no idea it was going to be a problem.'

It was true of course. While Rob could be insensitive and immature, there was no way he could have known about her problems with her cousin – he would have assumed Cassandra would be a welcome friendly face for Emma. Taking a deep breath, Emma decided that if this weekend was about relaxing and enjoying herself, then that was what it was going to be. Besides, Rob had been charming and amusing company for the entire journey, during which they had talked about everything from music to politics, art to religion. It was a refreshing change for Emma, who spent the bulk of her time having conversations about work with either her family or colleagues. Emma had also spent the journey quietly taking in the magnitude of Rob's wealth. The supple cream leather in his gun-metal Aston Martin told her that it was a top-of-the-range prestige vehicle. There had been a call to his mobile from the pilot of his family's private jet, making arrangements for Rob's trip to New York on Sunday night – no queuing at Heathrow for Rob. And when they had called in to the country house hotel to drop off their bags, the hotel concierge had spoken to Rob as if he was visiting royalty. Emma had to admit it made her a little uncomfortable.

'So how do you know Laura again?' asked Emma as the castle loomed into view. Even from a distance it was a spectacular place. As the rich orange sun sank behind the hills, it showered the grounds with golden light and turned them the colour of spun gold. She could make out the festivities on the long lawns in front of the castle in the deepening dusk: a bonfire was glowing and strings of red and yellow lanterns hung from the trees.

'Old family friend,' said Rob. 'I'm really here as a proxy for my dad who's doing some deal in China. My dad and Laura's dad, Henry, met travelling round Europe when they'd both finished university. I think they ended up in Greece, skippering sailboats for rich tourists, or some such. Henry met Laura's mum out there, I think she was working in a bar. Anyway, they've all stayed friends ever since, so us kids occasionally got thrown together on holidays and visits.'

Rob pulled up in front of the castle.

'Wow! This is wonderful,' smiled Emma, climbing out of the car and standing on tiptoes to look at the party on the lawns. The air was scented with the smells of roasting food and the heavy smoke of the bonfire. Guests wandered around in fancy dress, weaving between the neon-lit sideshows – a rifle range, a coconut shy and a bucking bronco – while waiters dressed as cowboys handed out cones of nachos, smothered in sour cream and peppers. Three more pseudo ranch-hands were manning a huge hog roast and pouring cider into tankards from large wooden vats while somewhere in the distance, a country and western band was playing. She turned towards Rob, grinning.

'It's such a holiday atmosphere, isn't it?'

Rob laughed.

'Ah, so she knows how to have fun!' he teased. 'She has holidays!'

'Of course I have holidays.'

'Going to the library doesn't count.'

She slapped him on the arm.

'I do have holidays. In fact I'm thinking of going to Costa Rica in August actually. Apparently August is fashion's holiday month, but the shop launches in the second week of September so I can't be gone for too long.'

'Costa Rica. Nice,' said Rob, as they moved across the lawn towards the party.

'I have a friend who lives out there running a cave-diving operation.'

'A friend?' he said, eyebrows raised.

'Yes, a *friend*,' said Emma. 'Honestly, all you ever think about is sex.'

Rob chuckled to himself as he took a glug of cider from the stall.

'So there's no significant other?'

'No,' said Emma quietly. 'I had my fingers burnt at the start of the year, so I'm giving relationships a wide berth for a while.'

'And you go cave diving instead.'

She gave him a puzzled expression.

'How does that compare with having a boyfriend?' she asked.

'Because everyone has a reckless streak, even you. Most people use sex and relationships for excitement and – strangely – to make themselves vulnerable. Extreme sports is much the same thing. It's the only outlet for danger in your perfect, ordered life.'

'Charming,' she sniffed.

'Hey, don't shoot the messenger,' said Rob, with a smirk. 'And there were compliments in there somewhere, you just didn't want to see them. Now, how do you fancy a quick ride on the bucking bronco, danger girl?'

Cassandra's grey eyes turned a deep shade of green as she saw them together. *What was Emma doing with Rob Holland?* she thought enviously. *And at a wedding, too.* Of course, she knew that Rob was Emma's new tenant, but coming to a wedding together was a message. How on earth had she managed it? But then, while Emma was hopelessly over-dressed in a YSL lilac silk sheath dress – Cassandra could recognize it even from a distance – she grudgingly had to admit that Emma looked good. So where was the timid, pasty girl she had met in Paris? Her hair had been cut and coloured too. She was laughing happily as she watched Rob on the bucking bronco, clapping her hands. Cassandra bristled. *Who did Emma think she was?*

'Well, well, what a surprise. A fully-fledged member of the fashion set,' said Cassandra walking up behind Emma.

'Not quite,' said Emma with a weak smile. 'I'm a guest of Rob Holland. He's a friend of Laura's father's.'

'Yes, and Rob's quite a catch. It seems like it's your year for getting what you want.'

'We're just friends,' corrected Emma.

'Oh. I see. My mistake,' smiled Cassandra. Emma flushed. She felt awkward and foolish, just like she always had when her big cousin was around. Inwardly she cursed herself for having been caught off-guard. She simply hadn't been prepared for bumping into her so soon.

'So how's business?'

This is it, thought Emma. Time to stand up to the bully.

'Oh. I didn't think you cared.'

Cassandra pulled back with a note of surprise.

'What an odd question. Of course I care. My mother has a stake in the business.'

Emma pursed her lips and looked straight at Cassandra. 'Which is why I thought it was strange that you'd been bad-mouthing Milford all round the industry.'

Cassandra's face coloured ever so slightly.

'Don't be absurd.'

'Seeing as you ask,' continued Emma politely, 'everything is going better than we could have possibly expected. The revamped store opens next month just in time for delivery of the new stock. It's a soft launch – we're having a bigger opening party in September. I'm not sure whether *Rive* have shot the Milford 100 Bag for their September issue but don't worry. Everyone else has. *Vogue*, *Elle*, *Harpers*, they're all doing something substantial.'

She felt a little swell of triumph as she said the words.

The mouse that roared, thought Cassandra, smarting. Of course, she had heard from her mother about Emma's little successes at Milford and she had to admit that the shoot with Clover Connor had been quite a coup – she'd had serious words with Clover's agent about that one. The family appeared to have been placated a little for the moment but Cassandra knew that they could easily be swayed the other way in a heartbeat. All it would take was the right pressure.

'I could lie to you, Emma,' said Cassandra quietly. 'I could say that we haven't featured Milford in *Rive* because everyone knows my connection to the company and I don't want accusations of nepotism.'

Cassandra turned her head and looked directly in front of her where Rob Holland was clambering off the bucking bronco to rousing applause.

'The truth is that *Rive*'s seal of approval is a very potent sales force indeed. I vet every single word, picture and product in my magazine and the reason your 100 Bag won't be featured is because I don't believe in either you or the company.'

'You have absolutely no justification for that,' said Emma, determined not to wilt under the force of Cassandra's confidence.

'Don't I?' she said cruelly, turning to glare at her cousin. 'Oh, I think I do. You've taken the company so far upmarket you're trespassing in a world you neither know nor understand. You're in my world now, sweetheart.'

'You're wrong,' said Emma.

'I think not. Deep down, you know you're the little trier who never really *could*. We all know why you're here. You never got your partnership, your boyfriend in Boston dumped you and you're running away and hiding, playing at being the boss of a company you know you don't deserve.'

Emma glared at her, wondering how she knew about Mark, about the job. She had only told her mother.

'And now you dare to criticize *me* for questioning your judgement and not blindly supporting you?'

Emma just looked at her; her delivery had been brutal. She felt mauled, a kitten face to face with a vicious alley cat.

'Ah, Miss Bailey,' said a voice to Emma's left. She turned to see a small wiry man wearing red moleskin chaps and a leather vest. 'I thought I'd take this opportunity to introduce myself,' he said, extending a hand. 'Larson Quinn. I'm coming to Milford on Tuesday for the interview for the *Tribune*.'

Emma smiled, trying to blink back a tear. 'Oh. How nice. And what a coincidence.'

Larson looked at Cassandra, waiting for an introduction.

'Larson. Cassandra Grand, my cousin.'

Cassandra smiled thinly. She was vaguely aware of the man. A regular on the party circuit, a vicious little queen who took lovers of both sexes – whoever could be the most useful to him – she thought he had just been made redundant after the closure of *Men's Style Monthly*.

'Your cousin? Really, how interesting,' said Larson, sensing the tension between them. 'You must have had such fun in the dressing-up box together.'

'Hey, Em, what did you think?' said Rob, grinning from ear to ear as he emerged from the bronco pen. 'Three minutes and still sitting pretty,' he said, slapping his thigh and giving a cowboy yelp.

'Yes, well done,' said Cassandra smiling warmly as she held out a hand to him. 'You're the star of the show.'

'You're Cassandra, aren't you?' said Rob, shaking her hand enthusiastically. 'There's a few photos of you at Winterfold.'

'Perhaps I'll see you in Chilcot some time,' she replied.

'That would be great,' grinned Rob.

Cassandra turned to Emma and gave a small triumphant smile.

'Come on. We're going,' said Emma, grabbing Rob's arm and pulling him away.

'Hey! What's got into you?' he hissed as she dragged him across the lawn, leaving Cassandra and Larson behind.

Emma tutted, shaking her head vigorously.

'You! Simpering in front of Cassandra, flirting like a schoolboy, thinking with your sex rather than your brain as usual.'

'My *sex*?' he laughed. 'You can say the word "cock" in front of me,' he whispered dramatically.

Emma flushed slightly but she was angry and wanted to lash out.

'Cassandra is a complete bitch,' she ranted. 'She uses people, manipulates them, treats people like dirt just because they don't throw out last season's designer wardrobe when it's not in fashion. Which, incidentally, is what will happen to you if you even think about getting involved with her.'

'What are you going on about?' asked Rob, completely taken aback by Emma's outburst.

'Cassandra. She's spiteful, hurtful and evil. I knew I should have gone back to Chilcot when you told me who the bride was. But no, I listened to you.'

A tear slipped down her cheek but Rob didn't seem to notice it.

'I don't want to accuse you of overreacting, but that's awfully what it sounds like from where I'm standing,' said Rob, as he walked towards the bar. 'Everyone I've spoken to who knows her says she's really charming. In fact she seemed perfectly OK just then.'

'Who's everyone?' snapped Emma unable to stop herself. 'Your media crowd? I'm sure they are great judges of character.'

Rob spun round towards her, flapped his arms helplessly.

'You can be really dismissive, you know that?'

'What's that supposed to mean?' she replied getting increasingly upset.

'You are so fast to judge people who are not as quick as you, as sharp as you or as moral as you. *Cassandra is a bitch, Trudy is a bimbo. My friends are shallow.* You can't go through life having such contempt for other people just because they don't match up to what you think and believe.'

Emma felt bewildered and off-balance. She had expected Rob to be supportive, to notice she was upset at the very least, but instead he was attacking her.

'Forgive me if I think Cassandra is trouble,' she said trying to keep her voice measured. 'Forgive me if I think you sell yourself short with women. I'm sure Trudy is a very nice girl but I just wonder what a successful, intelligent guy like you has in common with a topless model?'

'Well, we didn't stay in doing the crossword, did we?' he said sarcastically.

'Didn't?' asked Emma quickly. 'Oh, it's past tense now. So Trudy's past her sell-by date already? Roll on the next simpering beauty who'll massage your ego. Cassandra's single but I dare say she bites.'

'Well, remind me not to come knocking on your door.'

'If you thought I found you remotely attractive, I'm sure you would.'

Rob glared at her.

'I think the pressure is getting to you. Look, the rifle range is over there. I suggest you go and shoot some ducks and get whatever this is out of your system before you say something we both might regret.'

Rob thumped his cider tankard down on a table and stalked off into the dark.

'So what do you make of your cousin's revamp of Milford?' asked Larson Quinn casually sipping his champagne, determined to make his few minutes' audience with Cassandra Grand count. 'I hear the reaction after the press shows was fantastic.'

'Was it really?' said Cassandra with a small laugh. 'I don't know who you've been talking to.'

'So what do you think honestly?' he replied. 'Hit or miss?'

'Oh darling, it breaks my heart to say it, but it's just not going to work. To be in charge of a luxury brand, you have to understand what the fashion brands represent and you have to know how to service your audience. With the new ultra-premium price tag Milford are aiming at the couture customer, women who fly private and take eight dresses for two nights of parties. You've seen Emma Bailey: does she look like she represents that sort of brand?'

Larson's eyes were sparkling as she spoke; he sensed he was getting an exclusive here. Word on the fashion grapevine was that Emma and Cassandra didn't get on because Cassandra had wanted the company for herself.

'Can I quote you on that?' asked Larson, 'it would be great for my piece.'

'Not if you ever want to work for *Rive*,' replied Cassandra with a hint of menace in her voice, before turning the mega-watt smile back on.

'As I matter of fact I've sent you my CV a few times,' he said obsequiously. 'You really do have the most special magazine.'

'Well, it just so happens that I have a fashion features writer vacancy. Why should I recruit you?'

'Because I'm good,' he said simply.

'Well, that remains to be seen,' she purred, accepting a glass of champagne from a waiter. 'Why don't you send me your Emma Bailey interview when you've done it. Let me see if you have the *Rive* perspective on the industry.'

Cassandra smiled as Larson nodded. He clearly understood what she was asking him to do. If he pleased her, he might stand a chance of getting the job on *Rive*. In reality, she had no intention of ever doing any such thing. But he didn't need to know that quite yet.

Rob couldn't find Emma anywhere. *Why the hell do I even want to?* he thought angrily, downing his glass of champagne in one. He'd met some pretty high-maintenance women in his time, but Emma Bailey took the biscuit. The real kicker was that he had foolishly thought she was different. When she wasn't fretting about work or her jogging times, Emma was sweet and funny, her fierce intelligence offset by an endearing naivety that made him somehow want to protect her. But tonight – tonight she had shown another side and had turned on him liked a caged tiger. He was angry because she had disappointed him. Angry because her words, however unreasonable they might have sounded at the time, had more than a ring of truth about them. Rob knew he was used to women who hung on his every word, women who treated him like a king. It was exactly what his therapist had told him in the years after his brother Sam had died; his therapist had put it down to Rob's family; Sam had taken all the attention and affection from his parents, so Rob sought the adoration he craved elsewhere. And as a child of ultra-rich parents, used to getting whatever material things he wanted, Rob had a sense of expectation that meant he believed no woman would ever turn him down.

If you thought I found you remotely attractive . . .

The words had stung and he wasn't even sure why. Emma wasn't even that hot. Not like her cousin Cassandra who he certainly wouldn't mind getting to know better. Ah, maybe it was just a bruised ego, he reasoned. All men wanted to be desired and a rebuff by anybody, well it was gonna hurt. He took a deep breath and tried to calm down. As he wandered around the grounds looking for Emma, he kept stumbling across the teepees that had been used earlier in the day for 'Indian Head massages', whatever *they* were. Now in the darkness, they seemed to have been transformed into tiny dens of naughtiness, where the faster ends of Laura's fashion crowd and Max's banker friends had retreated to be out of the disapproving gaze of the Welsh aristocracy. There were giggles and clinking glasses coming from some, strange aromas and moaning from others. Rob doubted that

287

Emma would be inside any of the tents, but he had looked everywhere else and he was starting to become a little anxious. He had invited her here and as such he felt a sense of responsibility. Rob bent down to the tent furthest from the bonfire and peeked inside. There, to his surprise, he saw a beautiful redhead sitting on a cowskin rug smoking a joint.

'Hello there, what brings you out this far?' she said with a flirtatious smile.

'Same thing as you,' he said smiling. 'Avoiding the cowboys and the blue-bloods.'

'Well, in that case come and join me. My name's Jessica, by the way. 'Want some?' she asked, holding up the joint. Rob watched a thin spaghetti strap fall off one bare shoulder and smiled to himself. Yes, Emma probably needed some more time to cool off. In the meantime, he was going to stay here and have some fun.

Emma had spent the last forty-five minutes looking for Rob. What a bitch she'd been! Rob had only ever been generous to her and how had she repaid him? By being a cow. So he had terrible taste in women, but when had that ever been a crime? Why had she been so mean to him? She ran their conversation over and over again in her mind wondering how she could have been so volatile and rude. Cassandra, that's how, she thought grimly. Her high and mighty cousin had wound her up so tightly that she had taken it out on the first person she had seen. Rob didn't know the things Cassandra had said and done against the company, so no wonder he thought Emma was being overly hostile to her.

Emma's mind was a whirl, trying to work out her feelings, his feelings, overanalysing every angle. Was Rob right when she said the pressure was getting to her? What about her mother's theory that she needed a boyfriend as another layer to herself? Was she just fooling herself when she thought she could do it all alone? Emma had gone through life convincing herself that she didn't need anyone, but her experience at Milford suggested quite the opposite: without the help and support of Ruan, Stella and Rob, she would have ground to a halt months ago. *And this is how I treat my friends!* she thought miserably.

Emma had now walked in a huge circle right around the party looking for Rob and there was nobody else here she knew. She had had a brief conversation with Giles – *was that his name?* – Cassandra's colleague she had met in Paris and while he was charming and pleasant he was much less friendly than the first time they'd met. Obviously Cassandra had got to him too. Feeling thoroughly wretched, she just wanted to find Rob to apologize. The only place she hadn't checked was inside Hildon Castle itself, which seemed to be out of bounds, and a group of wigwams on the perimeter of the party. She poked her head inside the first one she came to and was hit by the smell of alcohol and marijuana. A man and a woman were sitting on a rug, laughing, their hands inches apart on the ground. Emma pulled back, feeling as if she had intruded on something intimate, before she realized the man was Rob.

'Em! I was looking for you!' he cried, jumping to his feet.

'Sorry for disturbing you,' she stuttered, dimly aware of how oddly formal she sounded.

'Nonsense, come and sit down. There's a warm glass of some potent brew if you want it. This is Jessica, by the way. She's a stylist, lots of celebrity clients. Maybe you two should talk about Milford.'

'I don't think tonight's the night for business,' she smiled, trying to stop the tremor in her voice. 'I just wanted to say that I was thinking about going. Apparently there's a coach going back to the hotel in about ten minutes.'

'Oh. Well, I'll come then,' said Rob. Emma was quick enough to catch the glance between Rob and Jessica that made it clear neither wanted the party to end.

'No, no, you stay,' said Emma. 'It's not even midnight, you don't want to miss a quarter of a million pounds worth of pyrotechnics.'

'There is another bus at one,' said Jessica helpfully, touching Rob softly on the leg. Rob and Emma looked at each other, the second's silent pause seeming to drag on and on, before Emma conceded she had no claim over Rob that evening – or any evening.

'You stay and have fun,' said Emma, forcing an encouraging smile. She turned and walked away from the scene as quickly as possible, hoping and praying that she would hear Rob's footsteps behind her. But they never came and two minutes later she was sitting at the back of the bus, completely alone.

Cassandra stood in the shadows watching the country and western hoedown with amused disdain. She wasn't sure whose idea a Wild West party had been, especially as all Laura's friends came from the super-poised fashion set, but at least the macho banker crowd seemed to be having a good time whooping and swinging their partners.

'Not joining in?'

She looked up to see Max holding two glasses of wine, his handsome, craggy features accentuated by the dim tawny light from the bonfire. She had known he would come. When they had sat next to one another at lunch, the chemistry between them had been instant although she hoped not obvious; it wasn't exactly good form to be seen openly flirting with the groom-to-be. However, she had taken particular attention with her appearance at the party and studiously avoided Max to see if he would come and look for her. *Some men are so predictable,* she thought, smiling to herself.

'I don't dance,' said Cassandra.

'Oh, I'm sure you do,' smiled Max. 'Although I suspect the do-si-do isn't quite your thing.'

'Not yours either?' she said, looking into his deep blue eyes.

'Hey, I'm only the groom,' he said. 'I don't have anything to do with actually planning the wedding, all I have to do is turn up.'

'Speaking of which, shouldn't you be with your fiancée?'

'Actually, no,' he said with a small smile. 'In fact I'm not supposed to see her at all.'

'Ah yes, that's right. Whatever happened to having the stag do the night before the wedding?'

Max laughed. It was throaty and deep and Cassandra felt it in her stomach.

'It's a safety net, isn't it? Now if your bollocks get shaved, you have time to grow them back again in time for your wedding night. We went to a gun club in Prague, firing ex-Commie Kalashnikovs: every young boy's dream.'

Cassandra shivered. There was a rough edge to him; he hid it well underneath the Savile Row suits, but there was something raw about Max Carlton, something that had her off-balance. Cassandra was used to going home with the most powerful or the most handsome in the room. In a party full of multi-millionaires, landed gentry and male models, Max Carlton was neither. And yet, she had a desire for him she hadn't felt in years.

'Well, here's to the dying hours of freedom,' said Max, raising his glass.

'You'd better make them count.'

'Got any suggestions that don't include cowboys and nachos?'

Their eyes locked and he moved a little closer to her, his arm brushing hers. If either of them thought about the morality of what they were about to do on the eve of Max and Laura's wedding, they didn't voice it.

'I have some Cristal in my room,' said Cassandra quietly. 'I'm in the gardener's cottage.'

'It's the best offer I've had all day,' he replied with a grin. 'I'll meet you there in a few minutes?'

Cassandra nodded and walked away from the party.

The cottage was five hundred metres from the main party and hidden by a wing of the house. There was no one to see Cassandra slipping in through the front door and slowly closing the curtains, shutting out the lights of the bonfire. Picking up a beautifully wrapped oblong box, a wedding gift from the *Rive* office to Laura, she ripped off the paper. She could replace it. No one bothered to look at their wedding presents until after they got back from honeymoon anyway.

A few moments later there was a knock. She opened the box and took out the Cristal, tearing off the yellow Cellophane as she walked to the door.

'Now this is much more civilized,' smiled Max, taking the bottle from her.

'What's the bet there are no champagne flutes,' said Cassandra walking into the tiny farmhouse kitchen. As she reached up to open a cupboard, she felt him behind her, the whole length of his body pressing against hers. At first he kissed her so lightly on the nape of her neck, she could feel his breath on her skin, then she turned her head until his lips were on hers.

'Max, we shouldn't,' she whispered, not meaning a word of it.

'Why not? This is my stag night, remember,' he mumbled as his lips brushed along her neck.

'Well, I don't want to disappoint you,' she whispered, her skin starting to prickle with need. She felt his hands grip her hips and turn her around.

'I've been thinking about you since the second I saw you,' he growled, lifting a finger up to her cheek.

'And what have you been thinking?' she asked with a wicked look on her face.

'I've been thinking about what it would be like to taste your cunt.'

Cassandra gasped. She had never felt such a sweet, violent intensity of lust.

'Don't just think it,' moaned Cassandra, '*do* it!'

Then his fingers were unzipping her dress, the feather-weight fabric sliding to the floor. He rolled his hands down her slim hips so her chocolate lace thong slid down in one movement.

He lifted her onto the kitchen table, spreading her legs wide and pushing the lace cup of her bra back, his lips descending on her beige nipple, which ripened in his mouth. With her head thrown back in ecstasy, she felt him slowly trace a wet line down over her firm, flat stomach until he reached her thin damp strip of hair. Lifting her legs in the air, he pushed his tongue into her, withdrawing to blow on her clitoris, before burrowing once again for slow rhythmic laps of her swollen nub.

'Now! We have to do it, now!' she whispered throatily. He uncurled himself, reached into his pocket for a condom, and after fumbling with the buttons of his trousers, pushed them urgently to the floor. He wrapped his firm hands behind her buttocks, and pulled her to the very edge of the table. She felt his thick cock, *that thick, sweet cock so wasted on poor little Laura* inch into her, then stop, letting her feel it inside her, filling her. Then he began to move, sliding all the way out then in, quickening both the pace and intensity of his thrusts. As she began to pant, he pulled her legs even wider, plunging so deep that she screamed out with desire. She pulled him closer, grabbing at his hair as she felt the sweet swell of orgasm gathering at her centre before igniting into such a sweet, violent, explosion the background noise of the party faded into nothing and all she could see, taste, feel and hear was Max. He pulled out of her and buried his head in the curve of her neck. They were silent for a few moments before she raised her head and spoke.

'We've just been very, very naughty.'

Max laughed, his breath still coming in pants.

'Don't worry, it was just sex. Just incredible fucking sex,' he said cupping her chin in his hands, pulling her close, the sweat from Cassandra's skin dampening his T-shirt. She nodded, but as they lay there, entwined on the kitchen table, the fireworks began popping and banging around them and they both knew it was something much more powerful indeed.

25

'Are you sure you want me there?' said Johnny, changing into his fourth outfit. The previous three lay discarded on the thick carpet of his bedroom.

'Well, are you sure you want to come?' teased Stella as she watched him dress. 'I know that the whole meeting the parents thing is a bit scary, especially after, you know, we've only been seeing each other a few weeks.'

'Scary?' he asked, finally settling on a navy polo shirt and cream trousers. 'I think I can cope with an evil stepmother,' he looked up and grinned. 'Well, as long as you're not a bunny boiler who just wants to get me introduced to Daddy so he can give us his blessings.'

Stella's heart did a belly-flop. No, she wasn't thinking of marriage quite yet, but it was hard to believe that their relationship had come so far so quickly. It had all been such a whirl; they hardly seemed to have been apart in the three weeks since their first date, helped in part by Johnny's break between projects. Not due to start rehearsals for his next film until the end of June, and with promo work for *This Country of Ours* out of the way, he'd spent his time shuttling between Chilcot and Notting Hill. And the more she saw him, the more Stella was falling for him. *And who could blame me?* she thought, watching him slip on his loafers. Yes, he was sexy and gorgeous, but Johnny was also dynamic, rich and generous, plus he had a worldliness and sophistication far beyond his years. Stella would only admit to herself that she liked him very much but what scared her, *thrilled her*, was that it could easily develop into something more intense.

'Chessie isn't exactly evil,' said Stella grudgingly. 'It's nothing to do with what she's like. It's how my father is around her.'

Christopher Chase's wives had long been the fly in the ointment in her own relationship with her father. With the exception of her mother, his partners had treated him terribly; two had left him for richer, more impressive men, while Stella was convinced Chessie was only sticking around for what little money her father had left. What frustrated Stella madly was that Christopher couldn't or wouldn't see it, even when they left him for a wealthier model. And if Stella breathed a word against any of them, he refused to speak to her for months. Stella was left with the choice of being honest and estranged or frustrated and impotent as she watched these women suck the life out of her father.

'Well, just say the word if you want me to beat her away with a broomstick,' said Johnny, jumping over and planting a kiss on Stella's neck. 'By the way, you look gorgeous.'

'Do I look OK?' she blushed. In an apple-green sundress and silver sandals she looked like a sixties Biba model. Johnny grabbed the keys to the Porsche.

'Alright then, let's go slay the dragon!' he chuckled.

'I'm so glad you're coming,' smiled Stella, taking his hand.

'Are you kidding?' he laughed. 'I wouldn't miss this for the world.'

*　　*　　*

Christopher and Chessie had wanted to meet at China Tang, the glamorous, decadent-looking restaurant in the basement of the Dorchester which, Stella suspected, was Chessie's suggestion rather than her father's. The maitre d' spent a great deal of time fussing round them, which Stella had found was par for the course whenever she was out with Johnny. Sometimes, like today, the attention was welcome but at other times it was unwanted and intrusive. She didn't mind when he was stopped for autographs, but increasingly women would touch his bum or demand a kiss, as if he was somehow fair game just because they had seen him in *Heat* magazine. They had a drink in the lovely Art Deco bar and then went to their table. They were alone for a few minutes before Christopher and Chessie arrived. Stella found that she was unaccountably nervous, worrying not only about how her father would behave, but even more about how *she* would behave in front of him. She so wanted to make a good impression on Johnny, but Stella knew that her father's ambivalent attitude towards her was her Achilles heel. She knew how he was: wrapped up in his own little world and seemingly disinterested in everything else, including his daughter, but each time it hurt, each time it opened up fresh wounds and Stella would often find herself overreacting to the smallest comment or imagined slight. It wouldn't have mattered so much if she didn't constantly worry about him, but she did. She couldn't help it; she loved her father despite everything. When he finally did arrive, shuffling in bent over a cane, Stella was shocked. She hadn't seen her father for two years and was taken aback by how stooped he had become. His fingers were now so badly knotted with arthritis that Stella audibly gasped. Chessie on the other hand looked radiant in a fitted scarlet dress that showcased a pair of magnificent breasts, noticeably more magnificent than when Stella had last seen her. Chessie was ten years older than Stella which made her 36 and she was at the height of her beauty. She had long chestnut hair, the colour and glossiness of a red setter, the upright posture of a dancer, and the slight uptilt of her nose suggested she was surveying all around her with disdain. A former life model, she had met Christopher when she had sat for him for a series of sculptural nudes, shortly after his third wife Sandrine had run off with a New York art dealer. Six months after their first meeting Christopher and Chessie were married in a quiet ceremony attended by only two witnesses whom they barely knew. What surprised Stella was that it had only taken them six months. Chessie of course no longer modelled yet seemed to be frustrated living in Christopher's beloved Trencarrow, a large farm on the outskirts of St Ives. She had thus persuaded him to buy a flat in London's Connaught Square and seemed to Stella to spend more time in *Tatler*'s party pages than in Cornwall. Stella had an idea how it was all going to end up but she'd daren't voice those fears to her father.

'It's good to have you back, darling,' said Christopher, taking the seat opposite Stella. She smiled politely, but inside she smarted at the words; she'd been in the country three months and this was the first time he'd been to see her. Despite her hectic workload she had tried to arrange to go down to Trencarrow but her father and Chessie were always away on some trip. The last time she suggested it, Chessie's mother was down from Derbyshire, which apparently made a visit from Stella impossible. Stella took a deep breath and bit her tongue. *Come on, Stella, don't kick off so soon*, she thought, aware she was perhaps reading far too much into her father's perfectly pleasant comment.

'This is my friend Johnny Brinton,' said Stella. At the mention of his name, Chessie instantly became more animated. 'Not *the* Johnny Brinton?' she asked, touching his hand. 'I came to see *Death of a Salesman* at the Old Vic, I thought you were wonderful. I had no idea you were a friend of Stella's.'

'I'm glad you enjoyed it,' he replied and went on to tell her about the great reviews for *This Country of Ours*.

Stella sat back and watched the familiar pattern. Chessie was a model of politeness and charm to Johnny, whilst barely acknowledging Stella's presence. She was willing for Johnny to hate her as much as she did but apparently he too was caught under the spell. They talked a little about Johnny's forthcoming film project, the latest goings-on at Milford and the current exhibition at St Ives Tate Gallery. Her father barely spoke and only picked at his food.

'How's your mother?' said Christopher finally, looking half-heartedly at the dessert menu.

'I saw her just before I left LA,' said Stella. 'She's well. She has two shops now in San Francisco.'

'Grocery stores, aren't they?'

'Health food,' said Stella, gritting her teeth at the lack of interest he showed in his former wife.

'Well I'm so pleased you're back over in England and working for Saul's old company. My goodness, Emma impressed me.'

Stella smiled. 'She's very good.'

'Yes, Chessie's youngest sister Amy is doing terribly well too. She's an architect, and she's just been taken on by Norman Foster's firm.'

Stella found herself getting upset again as Christopher told them about Amy's skyrocketing architectural career; he barely mentioned her own achievements at Milford.

'Anyway, we have some wonderful news,' said Christopher after the waitress appeared with some green tea. Stella looked up sceptically.

299

'Chessie is pregnant,' he said, beaming. 'It's very early days. Chessie didn't want to tell anybody til twelve weeks but we had to tell someone.'

Johnny reached across the table and put his hand over Chessie's.

'I'm so happy for you both. Mr Chase, that really is wonderful news.'

'Well, it is at my age,' he chuckled. 'It turns out I can still do something after all.'

'Yes, congratulations to you both,' smiled Stella, willing herself to be happy.

'Me, a mother,' laughed Chessie. 'I guess we'd better get the mini-breaks in while I still look good in a bikini.'

'Well, make sure you're around the third week in September,' said Stella. 'It's the Milford launch party, during London Fashion Week.'

'It's my birthday then,' said Chessie mournfully.

'What? All week?' said Stella, unable to hold it in.

'We were planning on going away,' replied Christopher with a note of reproach.

'You have a lot of holidays,' said Stella trying to sound light-hearted.

'I'm just enjoying my retirement,' said Christopher. 'And with the baby on the way, I think we need a bit of fun while we still can.'

'But you will try and come?' pressed Stella.

'We'll certainly try,' smiled her father.

Chessie's slim white hand went proprietorially over her husband's.

'Or maybe we can pop down to the shop next time we're in London,' she said. 'If there's anything I fancy do you do family rates on the handbags?'

Stella managed to remain composed while Christopher paid the bill. He looked forgetful as he searched every pocket trying to find his wallet and Stella felt a simultaneous pang of sadness and anger.

'We're staying at the hotel tonight,' he said when they'd finally paid up.

'Why don't you stay in the Bayswater flat?' asked Stella. 'I thought that's what it was there for.'

'I don't come up to London very often,' said her father, seeming to ignore the disapproval in her voice. 'Chessie wanted it to be a treat.'

'Of course,' said Stella thinly, trying hard to keep the smile on her face. They all rose and Christopher kissed his daughter on the cheek. They moved into the hotel lobby, where Stella and Johnny congratulated them once again on the news about the baby and they turned away to go to their room. Suddenly Stella felt herself well up with tears she could no longer contain. She covered her face and sobbed into her hands.

'Stella! What the hell's the matter?' asked Johnny, looking around to make sure no one was watching them.

'Nothing.'

'Of course there's something the matter. Tell me.'

He pulled her into a quiet corner of the lobby, sitting her down on a chair.

'It's just . . . Why do we bother meeting up? He hasn't got more than a passing interest in my life, but anything that comes out of Chessie's mouth he considers of life and death importance.'

'Come on baby, you're being dramatic.'

'No, every time I see him, I hope that things have changed,' she said determined to get it all off her chest. 'He's not a bad man but he's so wrapped up in her. I think my presence only reminds him about a past, a life he wants to forget.'

'Stel, she's his wife. You are his daughter but you barely

301

see each other so, honestly, it's not surprising you don't have the closest relationship.'

He pulled her into a tight hug and she enjoyed smelling the cotton of his shirt and the smell of lime cologne.

'Well then, I'm going to try harder,' she said using the back of her hand to wipe away her tears. The unexpected news that he had another child on the way kicked in some strange competitiveness she didn't understand.

'Come on. Should we go for a drink?' said Johnny briskly.

'I just want to go home,' she said sadly.

As they stepped out onto Park Lane, she noticed a photographer loitering on the pavement in front of them. 'Oh shit, not now,' she moaned, but it was too late.

The paparazzo had already advanced towards her, pointing a lens only feet away from her face.

'Look, just piss off!' she shouted angrily waving her arm in front of her, slapping the camera back into the photographer's face. Startled, he lost his footing and his camera rattled to the ground.

'Fucking bitch!' he shouted, picking it up and chasing the two of them down the road, the motor drive of his camera whirling until they jumped into a taxi and sped off into the night. All in all, it hadn't quite been the game of happy families Stella had hoped.

26

Emma sat in her sunny office looking at the month's press clippings with mixed emotions. For one thing, it was a fairly slim file. Zoe, Milford's publicist had offered exclusives to the *Tribune* and to *Vogue* which meant that the bulk of the Milford coverage would be running in the September issues – she hoped. Still, the August issue of *Vogue* had just hit the news-stands, and their glowing two-page profile on Stella had been absolutely fantastic. But Emma's *Tribune* interview with the strange little man she'd met at the wedding had been quite the opposite; the feature questioned Emma's fashion credentials, sniped at Milford's stuffy image and ridiculed the designs. Zoe was mystified. She had told Emma she usually had a good relationship with the journalist and couldn't offer up any explanation why their piece had been so damning.

'Hey Em, why so glum?' said Stella, popping her head around Emma's office door.

Emma smiled. Nothing seemed to be able to get Stella down.

'Oh nothing, just work stuff,' she said.

'Forget about all that,' said Stella, waving her hand

dismissively. 'Think about happy things like this: we're going to a festival tomorrow afternoon. Want to come?'

'What sort of festival? Opera? Cheese?'

'Cheese?' said Stella, flumping down on Emma's leather office sofa.

'Cheese is the new wine, or so I've been reading,' smiled Emma.

'That might be so. But I'm talking about a rock festival.'

'You mean like Glastonbury?'

'A bit like Glastonbury but this one has posher loos and fewer drugs. Come on. It will be fun. Rob's getting us tickets so it will be rude to turn him down.'

Rob. Emma smarted at his name. They had barely spoken to each other since the Hildon wedding. Emma had packed her stuff the morning after the Wild West party and, too afraid to interrupt a possible sex-fest with him and the redhead, had stuck a note under the door of his suite, claiming a work emergency had called her back to Chilcot. She'd got the train home and since that weekend she'd kept her distance. She had just about managed to convince herself that the arrangement suited her fine, so why then was she so irritated that Rob was now apparently such good friends with Stella?

'In other news, have you seen this?' said Emma quickly, handing the cuttings file to Stella.

'The *Vogue* piece? It's wicked.'

'No,' said Emma. 'The *Tribune* story.'

Stella flicked through the stories, lingering on Larson Quinn's hatchet job of Emma. She handed them back with a half-smile.

'It's disappointing, but not that many fashionistas read that newspaper anyway.'

'Just their handbag-gift-buying husbands,' replied Emma.

'Anyway, talking of the press, I saw the pap shot of you crying in the *Sunday Mirror*,' she said softly. 'Is everything OK?'

Stella shrugged. 'I've already told you my dad's wife is pregnant, haven't I? The paparazzo caught me just after he'd told me. I was upset at the time, but it's fine now, honestly, I was being silly. I didn't think it was a story but clearly it was.'

Emma looked at her kindly. 'Now you're going out with Johnny I guess everything's a story.'

At the mention of his name, Stella's face broke into a beaming smile.

'He's so great, Emma, I so want you to meet him.'

'I met him at the shoot.'

'Meet him *properly*. That's why you should come to the festival tomorrow.'

Emma felt glad for her friend's obvious happiness, but she wasn't at all keen about spending the day in a muddy field surrounded by hippies. And she wasn't all that keen to see Rob either.

'I'll think about it,' she said quietly.

'Well, don't get upset about the cuttings,' said Stella, suspecting that's why Emma was in a bad mood. 'Remember *Elle* are doing me "At Home" and there's the double page spread in *Tatler*'s Accessories Special. *Grazia, Marie-Claire, In-Style, Red, Harpers* – everyone's featuring us.'

'The future sounds so rosy,' smiled Emma displaying her usual caution.

'So you'll come to the festival? There's a big group of us. Rob, Johnny and some of his mates, Ruan too. It's going to be a laugh.'

'OK, OK, I'm in, I'm in,' said Emma, holding her hands up in surrender. 'Can you pick me up after my run?'

'Sure thing, boss,' said Stella as she headed for the door, 'although I'm not sure sweaty Lycra is entirely appropriate for a festival.'

She ducked, squealing, as Emma threw the cuttings at her.

27

For the first time in her life Cassandra Grand had found a great passion other than her work. Almost immediately after he returned from his honeymoon, Max and Cassandra had begun a full-blown affair, meeting for snatched afternoons in discreet hotels and at her apartment. To her complete surprise, Cassandra found she couldn't get enough of him. Work appointments, lunches, dinners were cancelled if the chance arose to be with him. For Cassandra, who had never been addicted to anything except power and success, Max Carlton was a compulsion. He was the only person she had ever been with where she felt empowered simply being in his company. Conversation was electric, sex was fantastic and she didn't even need his physical presence to be aroused. He'd call her at 3 a.m. from the quiet of his study, instructing her where to touch herself, making her come with the sound of his voice and his intimate knowledge of her body. If Cassandra hadn't known better, she would have said she was head over heels.

Three weeks after they'd first met she had invited him to Les Fleurs. It was only the second time since she had inherited the beautiful Provençal villa that she had managed to get down there. It had required some intricate planning: in particular, sending Laura away to LA to style a hastily arranged beauty shoot. She hadn't felt guilt, just faint pity that Laura couldn't even vaguely satisfy her groom so soon after their wedding vows.

In Provence, the lavender fields were in full bloom and the sun was liquid fire. Cassandra and Max had spent the last two days in bed, only getting up to take a dip in the pool or make a little food. The only time they had ventured out of the house for a dinner at the Grand Hotel du Cap Ferrat, they had been forced to beat a hasty retreat after both seeing someone they knew. On the vast, antique sleigh bed, Max rolled himself off Cassandra, lying on his back and pulling her into the crook of his arm.

'Have we got anything to drink?'

'Get it yourself,' she growled, feeling too exhausted to move.

'Hey, I'm a guest in this house,' he said, pulling the white crumpled sheet down to his six-pack to cool his sweat-sheened body. 'Come on, mistress of the house, get me a drink and I'll be your willing sex-slave for the rest of the trip.'

'I thought I was getting that for nothing.'

After a moment's stand-off Cassandra stepped from the bed, grabbed a silk sarong from the chair and tied it loosely around her breasts.

'I don't do this for anyone,' she smiled, shaking her dark hair over her shoulders. 'In fact I do it for no one but you.'

Walking downstairs she enjoyed the feel of the cool stone tiles on her bare feet, in fact Cassandra loved the way she was feeling altogether. She was more relaxed than she had been in years, despite – or perhaps because of – the sneaking around they had had to do over the last few weeks. Returning with two tumblers of iced water, she found Max propped up in bed on the pillows.

She jumped up beside him and her sarong fell open. He gulped at the water while his hand lazily stroked her thigh.

'Why have you never got married?' said Max suddenly.

She looked at him curiously and then shrugged against the pillow.

'Marriage just isn't a compelling enough idea for me. I don't need companionship; every minute of my day is full and I barely have time to see my own daughter. I get enough sex. I'm financially independent. I only have time to be alone.'

'So if you don't want a husband, what is it you want?'

She knelt on the sheets, facing him.

'I want to be fashion's biggest name,' she said frankly.

He looked at her seriously.

'And how do you intend to do that?'

She took a deep breath before she told him. No one knew the true extent of Cassandra's ambitions. She admitted little to Giles and nothing to Ruby, Astrid or her mother but she felt as if she could open up to Max as he was a separate, secret pocket of her life, hidden from the world. Besides, she knew Max would understand – his ambitions were as fierce as hers.

'For a long time I thought I was going to inherit a luxury goods company,' she began slowly. 'I thought that would be my base.'

'The company was Milford and it went to your cousin Emma Bailey,' said Max.

'How do you know?'

'I keep up,' he said with a small smile.

'I was promised it and I *will* have it,' she said flatly. She paused, then she told him everything. How she had warned Claude Lasner not to touch the company so that Emma could not get a big-name designer in place. How she had threatened photographers and art directors not to work with them,

309

banned Milford products from *Rive*, whispered among the big retail buyers that the new Milford range was a dud. She didn't want the company to get off the starting blocks and while she killed time she was going to become the US editor of *Rive*.

Max was smiling as she recounted her back-stabbing and double-dealing and it irked her enormously.

'What's so funny?' she snapped, totally unused to someone not only challenging her, but *mocking* her.

'Darling, I know you think you've been running this clever campaign of industrial espionage, but all you've been doing is taking pot-shots. And not very effective ones at that,' said Max.

'Pot-shots!' said Cassandra, widening her eyes.

'Let me guess,' said Max, running his hand up and down his firm belly. 'You went to see the banks to find out if you could borrow the money to buy out Emma, yes? They refused because you have no retail or real business experience. Yes, you understand publishing better than anyone in the business, but that isn't particularly relevant to running a luxury goods company, no matter how famous a journalist you are. So you thought laterally: if you continue to undermine Milford with your considerable influence, maybe in twelve months the company will be worthless and then Emma will want to sell. As editor of US *Rive* you'll have a bigger global pull, the banks might take notice and back you this time. But wait! You're worried. You might be next in line but you might have to wait years to get the job. And what if Emma surprised everyone and made a success of the company. Then you can never afford it.'

Cassandra sat looking at him, her eyes glowing with fury. She had exposed herself to him, she had trusted him and he'd made her plan seem so amateur and haphazard that her cheeks stung hot with ridicule. The hurt she was feeling was because his assessment was so devastatingly accurate.

'Get out,' she said quietly, unable to stop her voice quavering.

'No,' said Max, having the confidence not to move an inch. 'Forget Milford. What do you really want, Cass?'

She got off the bed and started pacing around before she spoke.

'To build a Cassandra brand. And Milford would be the perfect base to build from.'

'But that ship has sailed for the moment,' said Max brutally. 'What are you going to do now? And similarly, what would becoming editor of US *Rive* achieve? Make you a tiny bit more famous than you already are? It's a blind alley. You should forget that too.'

Cassandra went to the window and leant against it. She felt weak with frustration.

'What then? Forget my whole career?' she said sarcastically.

'You should be building up *your* brand, not *Rive*'s.'

'Well, I have the *Cassandra Grand: On Style* book coming out in September.'

'Fantastic!' said Max. 'Now you're thinking about *you*. This time next year you want your name to stand for a whole lifestyle. Like Kelly Hoppen, Donna Karan, Martha Stewart, Donna Hay. They all say something. Start thinking about what Cassandra Grand stands for, not *Rive*. *Rive* is yesterday's news, a stepping stone to a real career.'

'So do you think I should start a fashion line?' she said, suddenly feeling excitement growing in her belly.

He shook his head. 'Takes too long. You need to make the biggest splash in the smallest space of time. Your field of expertise is magazines so let's start there.'

'Launch my own magazine? That's expensive unless I wanted to start small – and small's not my thing.'

'No, private equity won't look at start-ups,' continued Max, ignoring Cassandra's look of disappointment.

'So what do you suggest?' She was so unfamiliar with asking for help that her voice was almost a rasp.

'Launch *Grand* magazine on somebody else's money but take a stake – 50 per cent ideally. Time Warner backed Martha Stewart who later bought out their shareholding. That's where you start.'

She looked at him. He was so sure, so confident, so brilliant. What did he see in someone as timid as Laura?

'Next you use the magazine company to spin off into other areas: clothes, cosmetics, interiors, using private equity cash. That's where I can help you,' he smiled. 'In the meantime, if Milford stalls, you'll have more business credentials and collateral to raise the cash to buy her out.'

She felt a surge of an unfamiliar feeling.

'You believe in me,' she said feeling aroused.

'You are beautiful, you are smart and you are *hungry*. And *Grand* magazine is where it all starts.'

He said the word 'hungry' as if it was their special word.

'I want this to work for you,' he said, stepping off the bed before coming round to hold her from behind. She leant back into him and took a breath. His words had been cruel, but they had been a wake-up call. She groaned, feeling his lips on her neck. Sunshine streamed in through the shutters, warming their bodies and speckling their skin with light. Max Carlton was the other half of her circle. She didn't just want her brand. She wanted it all. She wanted him.

28

Even though Tom Grand was of a generally optimistic disposition, life as the manager of Ibiza Town's Sugar Bar was turning out better than even he could have hoped. He had pretty girls lining up to sleep with him, a cellar full of cold beer and he got to sleep in until noon; it was as if some genie had granted him three wishes without bothering to ask. He swivelled the pink Plexiglas stool away from the bar and sat back, sipping a cool San Miguel and letting the late afternoon Mediterranean sun warm his face. Not for the first time in the four weeks he'd been in Ibiza, Tom looked around him and offered up a prayer of thanks. The Sugar Bar was tiny, but it was in a perfect position. On the corner of the harbour front and the wide lane leading to Ibiza Town's main square and beyond it, the castle, it was the ideal place to catch the party crowd as they geared up for a night in one of the big clubs outside town. Tom's bar had a small seating area inside, but the main action was focused on the wide, red neon bar that faced onto the street. With a DJ spinning the party sounds, frozen daiquiris lined up on the bar and the inevitable gaggle of babes-in-hot pants surrounding Tom, the Sugar Bar acted like a honey pot attracting bees: it had been crammed every night, often with hundreds of happy clubbers gathering outside in the lane. And all Tom had to do was chat up the girls and count the money at the end of the night. Well, that wasn't strictly true; he'd had a hard afternoon of it today, auditioning promotions girls. The set-up was that the Sugar Bar acted as a 'feeder' bar for Spice, the club night his partners Jamie and Piers ran at Desire, a brand new superclub in Ibiza Town's marina. Accessible only by a boat known locally as 'the disco tub', Spice was achingly exclusive and aimed at the fashion and jet-set crowd. Jamie had ambitions for it to be the new Pacha and had spent a fortune on refurbishing the place in gold and black, complete with an ergonomic 'floating' bar. The trouble was that so far, Spice had proved far too exclusive for its own good. It was certainly a beautiful crowd, but there simply weren't enough of them to compete with the real Pacha, despite Jamie and Piers's extensive London contacts. Their contract was for a twelve-week run from the end of June to the closing week parties at the end of September and with Spice only running at half-capacity Tom had been given the task of funnelling more glamorous high-rolling punters their way.

'Give us a twirl, darling,' said Tom, as Melena, a pneumatic pole dancer from somewhere in the Baltic States arrived to try out for the promo gig. Frankly, all the girls had to do was walk up and down wearing go-go boots and a tight T-shirt emblazoned with the word 'Spice', but Tom liked to be thorough with the recruitment process. Currently, he'd narrowed it down to Peaches, the former Manumission podium dancer and Suki a vivacious blonde with the biggest silicone tits he had ever seen. *But then again, Melena's ticking all the right boxes too*, thought Tom with a smirk. Unfortunately, Melena didn't speak very good English, so sadly she was ruled out – for the promotions job, anyway.

'I'll give you a call, babe,' he said, thinking that he'd do exactly that. Tom had quickly found that as manager of the bar he had a never-ending supply of gorgeous women desperate to get in to bed with him in return for getting on the guest list to one of the big clubs; he just couldn't miss out here. Plus there was always someone willing to supply him with drugs on the never-never. It was something like paradise.

He was distracted by the sound of a scooter pulling up outside the bar, tooting its horn as it approached. Jamie pushed his sunglasses off his face and balanced the bike on its kick-stand.

'Wotcha.'

'All right, Jamie? Just sorting out the promotions girls. Have you got the flyers sorted yet?'

Jamie pulled a face and took Tom's beer, knocking it back.

'No, they've been held up in customs, or some such rubbish,' said Jamie. 'I don't know why someone on the bloody island couldn't do gold-leafing, but this is the shit I have to put up with. Now I'll have to go down there and bribe the fucking customs to get them released. I hate this fucking place sometimes.'

'Hey, maybe we could . . .' began Tom.

'Yeah, and "maybe you could" shut up,' he snapped. 'Honestly Tom, running a business is not all just leaning on the bar and banging the barmaids, you know. While you're twatting about down here, Piers and I are working our arses off dealing with much bigger financial matters.'

Tom looked at his friend and noticed for the first time that he had dark bags under his eyes. The truth was, Tom had no idea what the other two were doing most of the time and he had even less of a clue how the finance worked. All he knew was that the bars themselves were owned by a Spanish businessman, rumoured to own a sizeable chunk

315

of Ibiza Town. Jamie and Piers had put the money up front for a lease on the bar and the club, while Tom was a partner in name only. For this arrangement Jamie and Piers were to get 45 per cent of the net profits to Tom's 10 per cent at the end of the season. In the meantime Tom was working for a basic salary which was enough to rent a small apartment on the outskirts of town. Clearly there was more to it than that, but looking at Jamie's frowning face, Tom was glad he wasn't involved.

They both jumped at the sudden blare of a car horn. Tom turned to see a battered and dusty delivery lorry parked by the rear entrance to the bar.

'Doors are open!' yelled Tom to the driver who waved and jumped down from his cab. They had a deal with the Spanish owner to provide the bars with cheap alcohol which was a gift for Tom. In the weeks before he arrived he'd heard all sorts of scare stories about the island being overrun by Russian and Romanian gangsters, but if it were true, they had been left alone so far.

'We're off back to London on Tuesday so you'll be manning the fort until Friday,' said Jamie. Tom looked at him in surprise.

'You're going again?'

'We *are* working over there, you know,' said Jamie, finishing off the beer. 'Which is actually what I wanted to speak to you about. We've got a big meeting with the PR next week because we've got a bunch of dance journalists coming out. We're pulling out all the stops, putting them up at the Hacienda Na Xamenda. You know how fucking demanding journalists can be so I want you to plan some sort of sexy itinerary for them. Nude beaches and girls in the day, drugs and girls all night. Maybe throw in a boat-trip to Es Vedra, that freaky pagan islet down south; you know, tell them it's spiritual and shit, give them some acid. Make it memorable.'

'Bloody hell, how much is all that setting us back?'

'Enough,' said Jamie with an expression that suggested argument was not wise. 'But we need the publicity.'

Tom was about to reply, but the van driver nudged his arm and pushed a clipboard in front of his face.

'*Puede usted firmar para esto?*'

'*Que?*' asked Tom.

Jamie rolled his eyes. 'He's asking if you can sign for it.'

'Oh sure,' smiled Tom, scribbling on the page.

As the man walked away, he looked over at the truck which had its rear doors open, loaded to the roof with beer crates and boxes of spirits.

'Man, that's a fuck of a lot of booze.'

'Well, I hate to tell you this Tom, but people drink at bars,' said Jamie, irritably, before softening his expression as another curvaceous blonde walked up to the bar. Tom held up two fingers to her and motioned for her to sit at the bar.

Jamie's eyes lingered on the girl as she jiggled onto a seat, then turned to Tom.

'Now can I count on you to pull this rabbit out of the hat? We need a big night.'

'You can count on me, boss,' said Tom, doing a mock salute.

'Well, I certainly hope so,' smiled Jamie, climbing back on the scooter.

'Don't worry,' shouted Tom over the harsh roar of the engine, nodding towards the girl at the bar, 'I think this one's going to be the best ever!'

29

Pierre Desseau sat at his walnut desk, glancing at his watch impatiently. Pierre was not accustomed to being kept waiting. He was the chief executive of Girard-Lambert, the second biggest publishing company in the world. Pick up any book or magazine from anywhere in three continents and there was a strong chance his company had produced, printed and distributed it. He was rich and powerful, and yet here he sat, drumming his fingers, waiting for Cassandra Grand. She swept in dressed in the dark Dior suit she had worn for the couture show earlier that day. She carried a leather folder under her arm and wore a professional expression on her face.

'Pierre,' she smiled, offering her hand.

'Miss Grand, sit down.'

For a man of fifty, Pierre was very attractive. His nose was long and straight, his eyes were dark and searching. His crisp blue shirt looked just a little brighter beside his tanned skin. But Cassandra was also aware of his gaze from the other side of the desk. She knew she was looking beautiful, as she sat there in her crisp white shirt. She knew it gave her an edge.

'I was intrigued by our conversation the other day,' began the Frenchman, recalling their meeting at the start of the week. Cassandra had cornered him at a cocktail party after the Chanel couture show and informed him that she had a proposition that could make his company the number one publishing company in the world. 'Shall we cut to the chase?'

Cassandra nodded and put her folder on the edge of his desk.

'I wasn't sure if you were aware that Isaac Grey had recently sounded out a number of media brokers regarding a possible sale of the business?' she began cautiously. She certainly did not want to insult him. As a leading figure in the publishing industry she supposed he made it his business to be aware of every movement within his field; after all, if Glenda McMahon's husband was aware of it, the news must be buzzing all over the financial and business communities. But she couldn't be sure and wanted to put herself in the driving seat from the very start of the meeting.

'And?' said Pierre, giving away nothing, coaxing her to divulge more information. *It's a game of poker*, thought Cassandra.

'He didn't instruct anyone,' she said with a shrug.

'Meaning that he has changed his mind about a sale of the company?' said Pierre. He flicked a switch on the coffee machine behind him and pulled out two demitasse cups. Cassandra sat back in the chair and crossed her long legs, aware that his eyes were following her movements.

'Everyone knows there are inheritance issues in the Grey family,' she continued. 'Isaac has a wife but no children. He's not close to his nieces or nephews and he's almost seventy. Everyone has been presuming for years that he'll sell his stake in the company.'

Pierre laughed. 'He has also been emphatic for years that he will *not* sell.'

Cassandra felt her nerves jangle. It was a game of poker all right, a dangerous, high-stakes game where she had wagered all her chips. For all she knew, Pierre could be best friends with her boss and if Isaac got wind of anything discussed in this meeting, she would certainly lose her job and possibly even face criminal charges. But when the rewards were so high, you had to take big risks, so she opened her briefcase and pulled out a sheaf of papers.

'I know that you made a move for Alliance eighteen months ago.'

Pierre nodded.

'I tabled a friendly bid, yes.'

'Five billion euros,' said Cassandra flatly.

'You've done your homework.'

'Five billion is a lot of money, but then it's a glittering prize. With the exception of Condé Nast there isn't a publisher who has a more prestigious portfolio of up-market magazines. You want Alliance Corporation. Most publishing companies do.'

Pierre paused.

'But everyone knows the money is in the mass-market sector. What makes you think I would prioritize the high end of the market?'

'One word: advertising. Access the top end of the advertising – fashion, autos, beauty – and your profits will skyrocket. Oh, and there's this . . .'

Cassandra produced a clipping from the *Wall Street Journal* which she put on the desk in front of him.

'Your most recent interview, dated March this year, in which you say you'd love a slice of Alliance if it ever became available.'

Pierre did not smile.

'What is it you want, Miss Grand? I am the CEO of a publishing company, not a detective agency. If it was the latter I would certainly give you the job of my right hand man. As it is . . .'

'Isaac knows he must sell,' interrupted Cassandra, 'but his heart rules his head. That's why he won't let go until he has to.'

'Carry on,' said Pierre.

'Isaac owns 70 per cent of the company. The rest is floated. But if a single shareholder acquired 25 per cent of the company they could make life so difficult that he'd be given no choice but to let it go.'

'What you are essentially suggesting is a hostile takeover,' said Pierre, rubbing his chin. 'Without the cooperation of the Alliance board, due diligence would be impossible. Much as I admire the company as a CEO, I would not be prepared to take the risk of buying into the company blind. Yes, the portfolio is prestigious, but Alliance titles are also plagued with rumours of poor advertising yields, bulk sales propping up various titles, astronomical expenses, and a troubled online division. Without knowing if that's true, well . . .' he shrugged his shoulders. 'The odds are too high.'

Cassandra nodded. She had anticipated his reaction. Now she had to take the biggest gamble of her career.

'But if you had somebody on the inside of Alliance, someone senior, they could do much of the due diligence for you. They could certainly provide enough information for you to take a considered view about whether you'd want to buy such a large volume of shares.'

Their eyes met and she felt a surge of electricity run through her; it was the thrill of dealing with an industry giant on equal terms, but also the adrenaline rush of betting every penny you owned on one spin of the wheel.

'You're taking a big risk, Miss Grand,' said Pierre, his face impassive. 'I could put a phone call in to Isaac Grey as soon as you leave this room.'

'Do you think I got where I am today without taking any risks?'

He smiled. He had bright white teeth and a lip that curled slightly upwards. 'You and me both, Miss Grand. So seeing as we have such a great deal in common, why don't you level with me? What do you want? An editorship of a flagship title?'

She shook her head slowly.

'It's hardly worth taking such big risks for little more than you already have. No. I was thinking the currency of my information would be worth a great deal more than that.'

'How much more?'

Cassandra's heart was pounding, but her face remained calm, composed.

'I want my own magazine.'

Pierre frowned.

'But you're already an editor.'

'You misunderstand,' she smiled. 'I want a magazine. In my name. I want it to be called *Grand* and I want it to be run from a satellite company, half of which would be owned by Girard-Lambert itself; the other 50 per cent shareholding would belong to me.'

Pierre took a sharp breath.

'That's a big ask.'

'It's a big get,' she replied coolly.

Pierre Desseau looked at the gorgeous woman in front of him with respect. He was glad he'd waited for Cassandra Grand now.

'Let me think about it,' he said finally.

Cassandra stood up and flipped her folder shut.

'You have seven days and the clock's ticking now.'

30

On the hottest day of the year, Dugdale Court, a two-thousand-acre estate in the heart of Wiltshire, looked stunning. As the location of a two-day music festival it was nothing like Emma had imagined; there were no muddy fields, no bead-wearing hippies and no giant pink drug cloud hanging overhead. In fact it was lovely. Shimmering in the distance, past the swarms of happy people, was an old stately home not unlike Winterfold. Music from some faraway stage wafted through the air, pleasantly muffled as if played through a pillow, whilst a hot-air balloon floated overhead in a cloudless blue sky carrying an advertising slogan that read 'Smile'. The whole scene was so full of life and fun it was impossible to be in anything but a good mood.

'Who owns this place? It's incredible!' asked Emma, fixing her sunglasses on her head as the four of them – Stella, Johnny, Ruan and Emma – meandered through the crowd.

'Some rich lord who's mad about music,' replied Ruan laughing. 'Look at all these people. It's got to be a money-spinner. Maybe you could do a heavy metal festival at Winterfold.'

She tapped him on the arm, happy that she was getting better at being teased.

'Don't joke. I'm sure Rob has already thought about it. You'd better keep an eye out for roadies when my back is turned.'

'Hey, there's Rob now,' said Stella, pointing towards the champagne tent.

They wandered over towards him. He was wearing the off-duty rock uniform of jeans, T-shirt and sunglasses but he looked anything but relaxed as he talked forcefully into his mobile phone. When he saw the group drawing near he hung up and smiled.

'Sorry, Kowalski are headlining tonight and I'm just checking everything is OK. They have to be closely monitored at all times,' he said with a half laugh, tucking his phone back in his pocket.

'Thanks so much for getting everyone tickets,' said Stella, giving him a kiss on the cheek. 'I think it deserves a drink. Or several. Champagne or beer and who's coming with me?'

'Shit, one of my old friends is over there,' said Johnny. 'I'm just going to say hi.'

'I'll get the beers in,' said Ruan.

'Then I'll do the 'poo run,' smiled Stella. 'Who wants what?'

'I have a drink coming,' said Rob distractedly.

Before Emma could even think about what was happening, Ruan, Stella and Johnny dispersed, leaving her alone with Rob. They looked at each other and then at their feet.

'Hey.'

'Hi.'

'I didn't know you were coming, I would have got you a ticket,' said Rob after a moment.

'Well, here I am anyway,' she said breezily despite feeling

so awkward. The uncomfortable look on Rob's face when he had seen her told Emma all she needed to know: the tickets Rob had given to Stella weren't meant to include her.

'I didn't think you liked rock concerts,' he said with sly smile, 'or rock music for that matter.'

'Well, yes, you're right, there. I've never been to one. Nothing like this anyway.'

'But you were a student for about a million years. How can you have been a student and not gone to a festival?'

Emma was in no mood for friendly banter, not if he didn't want her there.

'Rob, don't ask questions you already know the answer to,' she said coldly.

Rob nodded and pulled a face.

'Well, I think you'll enjoy it,' he said gently. 'Dugdale Court is as nice as a festival gets. Pimm's, champagne. There's a jazz tent, world tent, music, comedy.'

Emma relented a little. No reason not to be civil, she thought, he *was* making an effort.

'Just give me the rock. That's why I'm here,' she smiled.

'Well, that can be arranged,' he replied. 'There's one of our new signings on in a few minutes. I'll get you a laminate so you can go backstage; it'll save you from the mosh pit.'

'The mosh pit?'

'I can see I'm going to have to educate you.'

He smiled again and Emma felt a little of the ice between them thaw.

'Listen, I wanted to apologize for the way I behaved at Hildon,' said Emma. 'There was a reason why I was so bloody angry and I guess I should have told you that first before I set on you like a rabid dog.'

'It's fine, honestly,' smiled Rob, his dark green eyes crinkling in the sun. 'It's all forgotten.'

Emma felt frustrated. She wanted to talk about it but he seemed to want to move on.

'No really, Rob, I . . .'

'Rob! ROB!'

They both turned round as they heard a voice calling him. Emma saw a tall, slender figure waving.

'Rob! Did you want bubbles or Pimm's?' shouted the woman. As Emma's eyes adjusted to the glare of the sun, she could make out the long mane of dark red hair.

'Jessica from the wedding,' said Emma, forcing herself to smile.

'Yes. Everyone wanted to come this weekend,' said Rob obtusely.

Suddenly Emma felt stupid for having tried to explain herself to Rob and for a few seconds they didn't speak. Rob pulled the mobile out of his pocket and looked at it as if he was waiting for it to ring. Emma's eyes followed Jessica as she moved from the tent towards them holding two flutes of champagne. She was wearing a short, white, wispy kaftan and silver gladiator sandals; even though she must have been pushing thirty Jessica had legs as good as a nineteen-year-old supermodel.

Jessica handed Rob his glass and slipped her free hand around Rob's waist possessively.

'We meet again,' said Jessica to Emma. 'Sorry, I can't remember your name, but it's lovely to see you. I didn't know you were coming.'

'Another person who didn't,' muttered Emma, instantly regretting it as she saw Rob look away.

Rob's mobile started ringing and he answered it. 'Shit,' he said, covering the mouthpiece, 'I have to go backstage. Listen, Emma, do you still want that laminate?'

'I don't know, maybe I'll try the mosh pit,' said Emma seriously.

Jessica let loose a peel of laughter.

'Oh honey, no, take the laminate, I've got one,' she said pulling the pass from around her neck.

Emma could feel her cheeks flush.

'No, no, I'll get you a laminate,' said Rob firmly. 'I'll be back in ten minutes.'

Emma saw his eyes trail between herself and Jessica before he walked away.

Emma looked around for Stella anxiously, but she could see her running giddily towards the main stage where a band were just plugging in. Johnny was signing autographs for a group of pretty teenagers and Ruan had vanished into the beer tent. There was no one left to save her.

'What a pretty top.'

'Thank you,' said Emma feeling extremely uncool in shorts and an embroidered vest she'd found in Faneuil Market in Boston.

'What happened to you at the wedding?'

'I was only ever coming to the Friday night party.'

'Really?' said Jessica, tilting her head. 'Rob said you had to rush off for some emergency. Anyway, you missed a fabulous weekend. I was so pleased when I found out you and Rob weren't *together*,' she said lowering her voice dramatically. 'I'd clocked him as soon as I got to the party.'

'Have you seen a lot of each other since Laura and Max's wedding?' asked Emma casually.

'We're both incredibly busy but we've been out a few times, yes. Have you seen his house in Notting Hill? Just incredible.'

'No. I haven't.'

'Working in fashion, you kind of give up hoping to meet someone as great as Rob. Most of the men I meet are gay or total arseholes.'

Emma just nodded, silently sizing the girl up. Jessica was

loud and sexy and confident. Emma wanted to despise her, but she knew her anger was nothing to do with Jessica.

'I must have a long chat with Johnny and Stella,' said Jessica, 'I would love to style them both.'

'I'm not sure Stella needs styling. She does a pretty good job herself.'

'Well, let me loose on Johnny then,' she smirked, 'He is *so* sexy. Not that I'd want to date him,' she added quickly. 'A friend of a friend went out with him for a little while. Screwed around on her something rotten.'

They both turned to look at Johnny who was having his picture taken with a pretty teen in pixie boots and hot pants.

'You might want to tip Stella off, but if she's in the first flush of love maybe you should keep it under your hat,' she smiled.

Jessica squeezed Emma's hand and drained her glass.

'Toodle-pips. I'm going to find Rob. And just a word of advice: stay away from the mosh pit.'

In the VIP tent Stella was having her photograph taken yet again and telling a journalist for about the tenth time that day that she was wearing a vintage dress. *Why did they want to know? Who cared that she'd just pulled the old thing from her cupboard this morning?*

Ever since the premiere when she and Johnny had been snapped exiting the after-party, there seemed to be a photographer's lens pointed at her wherever she turned. *This Country of Ours* had been a smash hit and had pushed Johnny into the spotlight, turning his minor son-of-star celebrity into the latest media obsession. There were profiles of him everywhere from *Grazia* to *Heat*, and everybody wanted to know who the stylish blonde was at his side. When word spread that she was not only a fashion designer, but Christopher Chase's daughter to boot, her profile began to mushroom too. Stella was beginning to realize that the number of genuine UK celebrities on the ground was actually quite thin so the star-hungry press were always eager to create new ones in order to sell their papers.

But while Johnny appeared to be in his element with all the attention, it wasn't something that she wanted. She had spent four years in LA surrounded by waiters, busboys, pool attendants, barmaids, and personal trainers all of whom were all in Tinseltown chasing the dream of becoming famous. It had never once appealed to Stella. She liked leaving the house in sweatpants and no make-up. She liked being able to visit the local shop or take out her rubbish without being photographed or asked to justify what she was doing, wearing or eating. She had seen the paparazzi at work in LA but in London they seemed to be even more relentless. It was scary and, for Stella, most unwelcome. She looked over at Johnny who was being interviewed for a local TV station. *Still, it wasn't all bad,* she thought. *At least I get to go home with him.*

The light was seeping out of the sky, but the evening still had a balmy warmth. Stella looked around to see Emma walking over, holding a half-empty glass.

'There you are,' said Emma, 'You've been missing in action for hours.'

'I saw you with Ruan,' replied Stella, actually feeling a little guilty. 'I thought you were OK so I went to watch a couple of bands and then I chilled out here for a bit. Why? What's wrong?'

She looked at Emma and wished her friend would lighten up a bit, maybe relax a little. Emma was a lovely person, she was smart and kind but she seemed to be in a perpetual state of anxiety.

'Oh, I was just a bit embarrassed earlier on. Rob didn't know that one of the tickets he gave you was for me.'

329

'I kind of assumed he would. You two have been as thick as thieves lately, haven't you. Why would he mind?'

'No reason,' shrugged Emma lamely. She hadn't told Stella about going to the Hildon wedding, fearing her exuberant, loved-up designer would read too much into it.

'So what do you think of Jessica?' asked Stella, sipping her drink thoughtfully.

'I haven't given her a great deal of thought.'

'I wanted to hate her because she's so pretty, but actually she's quite nice,' said Stella. 'It turns out she styles loads of famous people. She said she'll get Milford bags onto the arms of as many of the rich and famous as she can.'

'Oh, that's nice of her,' replied Emma mustering up as much enthusiasm as she could.

'And she's so slim. Johnny says he's heard that she's on these Mexican diet pills. He says she styled an actress friend of his who just couldn't get into any of the sample sizes so Jessica gave her a bag of these pills just so she could get her into this amazing Dior. Apparently it works; she looked incredible.'

Emma grimaced, wondering why anyone would want to shovel barbiturates down their neck in order to fit into a dress.

'I used to think he was in love with you,' said Stella swirling round her mojito.

'Who?' said Emma suddenly snapping back to attention.

'Rob, of course. I mean he's done so much for us.'

'Don't be stupid,' said Emma. 'Can you imagine me going out with someone like Rob?'

'Anyway, that's why I invited Ruan. To make Rob jealous.'

'What?!'

'To make him jealous,' repeated Stella with an angelic smile. 'I mean, when was the last time you had a shag? I really think it would be good for you.'

'Stella!' said Emma, aghast.

'Anyway, I think it might be working. Did you see the way Rob was looking at you before? You'd been talking to Ruan for ages and his face was like thunder. Then I got to thinking that maybe you rather fancy Ruan. I mean he is very, very sexy in a sort of Heathcliffe way. And he's single. Unless he's gay. Which he very well might be because I've never seen him show any interest in women.'

Emma looked at Stella's glass, convinced that she must be drunk.

'Stella, Ruan isn't gay just because he hasn't got a girlfriend. And the only reason I was talking to him for so long is because he's practically the only person I know here.'

But Stella wasn't listening.

'The more I thought about it the more I thought you're better suited to Ruan than Rob anyway,' she continued breezily. 'I mean, you're both so serious about work and you told me once you used to have a crush on him. I think you should just shag him.'

Stella giggled at Emma's blushes. Right then Johnny came over and kissed Stella on the back of her neck.

'Who's shagging who?' asked Johnny, grinning.

'Emma and Ruan. Possibly,' declared Stella.

'Ooh, spicy!' said Johnny, his grin getting even broader.

'You two are impossible,' said Emma, stalking off towards the beer tent.

'Give Ruan our love!' called Stella after her.

Rob was having a bad day. He'd foolishly agreed to be interviewed by a music journalist who only seemed interested in discussing rumours that more bands at Rob's company were about to defect to other labels. It was a headache Rob really didn't need; only that morning his father had grandly delivered a memo demanding that millions be shaved off

331

their budget for next year. That meant redundancies, cutting advances to artists and reducing marketing spend right across his roster of three thousand musicians. Not only would that mean more defections, it was a PR nightmare waiting to happen. This had been the worst year of his professional life. When he'd joined Hollander Music he'd surrounded himself with talented executives who had years of music industry experience and as much enthusiasm as he had. Profits had risen. Their label scored a bumper crop of Grammies. He'd been made Vice President of the US company before being appointed CEO of UK and Europe eighteen months ago. But his arrival had coincided with one of the most uncertain times in the record industry's history. CD sales were down and the new technology of online downloads was not sufficiently geared up to recoup the difference. It was a daily fight just to keep the company above water. His father didn't understand the industry, just the bottom line and he seemed to believe the change in fortunes was down to his feckless son. Rob felt isolated. If he were to talk mammoth budget cuts with his management team of old school musos he would be branded a corporate sell-out. But if he didn't make difficult decisions the company would face possible disaster. He felt sure that Emma Bailey would have an opinion on this. *Of course she would have an opinion on it.* He didn't want to think about her either. He hadn't invited Emma to the festival because he hadn't wanted her to be there – it was as simple as that. He knew she'd see him with Jessica and she'd say something, or give him one of those looks that would make him feel that what he was doing was completely wrong. And don't even mention the fact that Jessica had become annoyingly possessive and clingy when she had seen Emma. He sighed: *Broads, man.* Suddenly Rob had a moment of clarity; it was like the sun bursting through the clouds.

For the first time in a long while, all he wanted to do was go and get completely smashed.

Emma looked at her phone and frowned. She had just received a message from Ruan saying that *everyone* was in Kowalski's tour bus, whoever *everyone* might be. *We're in Area B*, Ruan had said. Area B? Where was that exactly? Festivals were perfect places for losing people. It was like the Labyrinth at Knossos thought Emma, wondering in which direction to go. She wandered away from the VIP area into the back-stage parking area, a higgledy-piggledy assortment of coaches, lorries and sleek Winnebagos, all so high it was impossible to see into the next row, let alone spot your own vehicle. This is hopeless, she thought crossly. It was dark, she was lost and as their driver wasn't picking them up until 1 a.m., she had another hour and a half to kill. She was about to call Ruan asking him for better directions to Area B when she heard a familiar voice and a high-pitched giggle. She stopped behind a long silver Winnebago and peeked around the corner. Illuminated by a shard of moonlight, she could see a couple laughing; Johnny Brinton and the girl in pixie boots whom she'd seen with him earlier. They weren't kissing or even touching, but there was an intimacy about the way they were standing that reminded her of when she first saw Rob and Jessica at the wedding. Suddenly Johnny turned and looked into the dark in Emma's direction. She jumped back, not knowing if he had seen her and quickly moved off back the way she had come. A burly man stepped out of a trailer and almost knocked her down.

'Are you lost, love?'

Emma tried to keep her voice low.

'I'm looking for Area B.'

'It's over there,' he said, pointing a torch away from Johnny and the Pixie.

'Thanks!' she hissed and set off at a run. It had suddenly turned very cold and the thin sweater she had brought wasn't keeping her warm. Finally she found a white tour bus with a card in the window that read 'Kowalski'.

'There you are,' said Ruan. 'I went to meet you in the comedy tent but you'd gone.'

'It wasn't very funny,' smiled Emma.

To Emma's surprise it was not particularly glamorous or luxurious inside a rock band's tour bus. There were a couple of bench-type sofas, cramped bunk beds and a long kitchen area with a chipped Formica table that jutted out at right angles. There was a faint smell of alcohol, sweat and marijuana, but no rock stars. The band had only finished their storming set on stage twenty minutes ago and had yet to appear. Stella was lying back like Ophelia on one of the bunk beds, her eyes closed, and after what she had just seen, Emma was glad she was asleep. Ruan was slumped on one sofa while Rob, sitting with his back to the window next to Jessica, was drinking champagne out of a large plastic cup.

'Well, better late than never,' smiled Jessica handing Emma the bottle of Moët.

'How was the mosh pit?' asked Rob, his eyes looking a little glassy.

'I gave it a wide berth,' she smiled. 'I managed to see one of Hollander's new bands though – The Constants. They were fantastic. Their last song reminded me of something on that Beatles album you gave me.'

A slow grin spread across Rob's face.

'You're learning, kiddo.'

Emma caught Jessica carefully watching them both and then give a sour smile. For Emma, who had spent her undergraduate years studying psychology because she wanted to understand human behaviour, it was telling. At that moment she knew she didn't like or trust Jessica.

'I don't know about anyone else but I need a pick-me-up before the driver comes,' said Jessica, reaching into her handbag. She took out a little paper envelope, unfolded it and then tipped some of the white powder onto the table. She took a credit card out of her purse and expertly chopped it into four fat lines, inhaling one through a rolled-up twenty pound note.

Emma felt deeply uncomfortable. She had never been a drug user, not out of any great moral fortitude but simply because the idea had never appealed, but she knew enough to know that doing drugs was a short cut to being 'cool', to being part of this world. Once again Emma felt like she was the geek in the playground, the square, the bore. As if sensing her discomfort, Jessica nodded in her direction.

'Want some?'

'No thanks, I was actually just going back outside,' she answered, flushing slightly.

'So soon?' replied Jessica. 'Is it another *emergency*?'

'No, there's still something on in the comedy tent we wanted to see,' said Ruan quickly, following Emma out of the trailer.

'Have fun,' trilled Jessica.

Rob frowned as he watched them go, unable to put his finger on why he suddenly felt uncomfortable. The amount of booze he'd consumed might have had something to do with it. After he'd decided to get rightly sozzled, he had entered the champagne tent at a run and poured half a bottle of Moët into a plastic pint glass, knocking it back like lemonade. He was now comfortably numb, but not so numb that he couldn't feel Jessica's hand stroking his crotch under the table. That certainly wasn't the thing that was wrong — he was most definitely enjoying what she was doing. Jessica was a world-class fuck, she was also funny and smart, albeit street-smart. She was definitely a cut above the girls he usually met on the party circuit. But still, he couldn't concentrate, something was nagging at him. He brushed Jessica's hand away from him and stood up.

'Where are you going?' asked Jessica, surprised.

'I'll be back in a minute.'

'You're not going after Emma, are you?' she said, standing up and holding onto his arm.

'*No,*' he snorted, as if she had said something ridiculous. 'There's a band manager I need to speak to. I'll just be a few minutes.'

'Come back soon,' she whispered into his ear. 'I'm horny and I want to fuck you into tomorrow.'

Rob walked into the dark. The music from the stage had stopped and instead there was just the distant sound of cheering. Without thinking, he found his feet leading him towards the comedy tent. She was standing in the dark at the back, small and slim next to the tall, brooding figure of Ruan. They were both laughing and she was tapping her foot in time to the music until the final act came on. She didn't look awkward now. She looked softer, happier. Not the bristling angry wound-up little thing from the wedding, not the stressed-out workaholic he would see jogging around Chilcot. *Happier than when she was with him.* Rob realized that he'd come to find her because he had hated the situation in the trailer, the look on her face when Jessica had offered her drugs. It wasn't disapproval, just awkwardness and a little panic, an emotion Rob would never have associated with Emma; she always seemed so capable, so in control. But he shouldn't have worried; she was OK. *Too* OK. He shook his head and turned around, slowly heading back to the bus. He wasn't even looking forward to the world-class fuck that was waiting for him there.

31

The San Pellegrino bottles lined up on the tables glinted in the sunlight. It was a blazingly hot day and Cassandra stood up to close the blinds as the *Rive* staff settled themselves around the boardroom table. When she took her seat, she was surrounded by almost the entire staff of the magazine, all looking at her expectantly.

'Any idea what next month's ABC figures are going to look like?' asked a voice from the back.

Cassandra nearly smiled; she knew what was on their minds. The ABC figures – the official industry circulation figures released twice a year – were about to be announced and they were the only real way magazines could tell how their sales compared against their rivals. With the exception of the most senior staff, the team were only privy to the figures when they were published in February and August and they were powerful numbers. Poor ABC figures could lose a magazine a vital advertising campaign and they would certainly destroy a staff's morale; even a tiny downturn could send them into a depression. And that was Cassandra's problem. She already knew that *Rive*'s figures would be static: no rise, no fall. The Phoebe Fenton cover and the resulting controversy had given the circulation a big push, but a poor selling March issue and the dreaded Ludvana cover had had an impact on sales. It was bad news in any event but following her conversation with Pierre Desseau, it was a disaster. Cassandra needed to show him that she was one of the top editors in the world and mediocre sales figures just weren't going to do that. It was extra pressure she just didn't need. Pierre had called her back six days after their meeting to say he was interested, but he told her he needed more before he would consider agreeing to his side of the bargain. He wanted hard proof she could access Alliance's figures and plans. Cassandra told him she could play hardball too: *No* Grand *magazine*, she said, *no insider information*. It had been like the hard slog of a grass-court tennis match. Eventually the Frenchman had conceded, but had insisted that Cassandra prove she was worthy of the job. He had set her a list of targets, the biggest of which was that she had to out-perform US *Rive*. Not at the news-stand – that was impossible – but in industry standing. And while they could massage the figures slightly, there was no hiding the fact that Cassandra's performance this year was beginning to look a little lacklustre.

'We are expecting a very tiny uplift in figures,' said Cassandra, taking a sip of water. 'As you know we have had some incredible sales in this period, but it's a very competitive market out there right now. That said, our market share is excellent: we remain the number one choice for premium fashion advertisers and our covers are some of the most talked about in the business. Which,' she paused and placed her manicured hands flat on the table, 'is why we're here.'

At the back of the room, Lianne flipped a switch and the covers from *Rive* over the last six months flashed up. Next came *Vogue*'s covers, then those of *Class* magazine.

What was noticeable was the regularity with which the magazines' cover-stars were repeated. If Angelina was on one cover one month, she'd be on somebody else's the next – in many instances, the same actress or singer was on two or three magazines the same month. Deborah Kane, *Rive*'s entertainment editor, leant forward. Deborah was in charge of liaising with celebrity publicists and securing the celebrities for the magazine.

'It's getting more and more difficult, Cassandra,' said Deborah. 'Increasingly we can only get a star to agree to be in *Rive* when they are promoting something. And I can name five top LA and New York publicists who won't agree to exclusivity, so you get Jennifer turning up on three covers in one month. It's the same problem for everybody.'

'We *aren't* everybody,' snapped Cassandra. 'We have to provide our readers with exclusivity. We have to get them the un-get-able.'

'Well, what about using more models?' suggested Deborah.

'With the exception of Clover Connor and Summer Sinclair, models just don't work as well for us as celebrities,' said Giles, folding his arms.

'Besides, as some of you here may know,' said Cassandra, 'I want to refresh the magazine for our March issue.' The March and September issues were the two most important issues of the year because they launched the new fashion season and would be full of advertising for the new lines from every fashion house.

'You mean redesign?' asked Jeremy, her features editor.

She glared at Jeremy, fully understanding his implication. The dreaded 'R' word – a redesign – was the industry's tool for propping up an ailing or stagnant magazine.

'Not a redesign, Jeremy,' she said, icily, 'a re*fresh*. I don't expect you to be aware of the subtler nuances of magazine publishing, but we need to mix things up for the reader. So what do we have so far?'

Giles cleared his throat. 'We have an entertaining slot

pencilled in: Cavalli has agreed to throw a lunch on his yacht. He'll get lots of celebrities there although, obviously, they'll have to be wearing Cavalli. We also have an art special . . .' he said, pushing across a 1930s cover of French *Vogue* which featured a beautiful watercolour of a model. 'Lagerfeld is doing some exclusive illustrations for us along these lines. I think they'll be fabulous.'

Cassandra nodded her approval. 'Art and fashion. Very *Rive*,' she said.

Francesca, her fashion director, looked efficiently through her notes. 'We obviously won't know our stories until after the shows but I think Mert & Marcus are on board to shoot twenty pages of trends, which will be a studio shoot. For our location shoot, I'm thinking somewhere edgy and *difficult*. Maybe a knitwear shoot in Sierre Leone or perhaps guns and couture in Darfur.'

David Stern grimaced as Cassandra glanced over at Lianne to make sure she was taking full notes.

'I like it. Features?'

'I thought of the cover-line 'Fashion Muses Compare Notes,' where we do a big photo-shoot with everyone from Amanda Harlech to Stella Tennant and Sophia Coppola,' said Jeremy, feeling less bold after his dressing down.

'Salman Rushdie wants to do an essay for us. He's thinking of appropriate subject matter.'

'Nothing too contentious,' replied Cassandra raising an eyebrow.

'"Botox Beneath the Burka" is a report we wanted to do on plastic surgery in the Middle East. And of course we have the "At Home" special.'

'Continue,' Cassandra nodded. 'At Homes' were the holy grail of features. Voyeuristic and usually sumptuous, they offered an insight into the celebrity's world you just couldn't get from a straightforward interview.

340

'Who have we got so far?'

'George Clooney's Lake Como villa . . .'

'Gorgeous but done already by *Vanity Fair*,' Cassandra snapped. 'Come on, work harder, I want exclusives here.'

'Well, Catherine Zeta Jones at her Bermuda house fell through.'

'Why?'

Deborah Kane had the pinched look of someone who was sucking a lemon.

'A clash with filming,' she shrugged, 'plus I think she really wanted to be shot in a studio.'

'I don't want excuses,' said Cassandra, struggling to control her temper, 'I want results. What *Rive* needs for its March cover is something special, something *extra* special, something that has never been seen before in the pages of a magazine. We need to be the ones to deliver the unbelievable.'

She thought of the Princess Diana pictures shot by Mario Testino, images that were still being talked about over a decade later, or Demi Moore naked and pregnant, a pose that had been copied by dozens of magazines around the world. She needed something to make the readers sit up and notice. *That would make Pierre Desseau sit up and notice*, she thought. She looked round the room and was met by a sea of blank faces.

'Meredith. Give me a name,' said Cassandra pointing at her beauty director.

'Julia and Cameron don't do much. It'd be good to get them.'

'Are you people not listening to me?' she said, her voice raised. 'We want somebody we have never seen on the front cover of a magazine. Somebody new, somebody exciting.'

Deborah Kane shuffled uncomfortably in her chair.

'When you think about it Cassandra, there are only so

many celebrities in the world and everyone has taken a bite out of them. We could look at doing an ensemble cover, maybe? Five of the hottest new actresses breaking through. Do it as a gate-fold?'

'And copy *Vanity Fair*'s annual Hollywood issue?' said Cassandra. 'Come on, we are *Rive*, we lead, we do not follow. Who else?'

There was a long, uncomfortable pause, while all the staff avoided her gaze.

'Where did we ever get with Georgia Kennedy?' Giles said finally. *Now that was a name*, thought Cassandra. Georgia Kennedy was the twenty-first century's Grace Kelly. An Oscar-winning actress, her acting talent was only matched by her beauty and her sense of style. She'd burned brightly in Hollywood in the early Nineties, scoring half a dozen near-legendary leading lady roles in some of the biggest hits of the decade. She had been a true superstar. But five years ago, at the peak of her fame and desirability, she had met and married Sayed Jalid, the ruling prince of oil-rich country Sulka, and had effectively disappeared from view. There were occasional photographs of her doing charity work, visiting land-mine victims in Angola or orphanages in southern Africa, or a rare appearance at a gala dinner or royal wedding but, in celebrity terms, that made Georgia Kennedy a recluse.

'Now we're talking,' said Cassandra, the hint of a smile on her lips. 'I want her on our March cover. And not just the cover. I want Georgia Kennedy — At Home.'

Deborah stifled a surprised little laugh and Cassandra immediately rounded on her.

'You find this funny, Deborah?'

'No, I'm sorry,' she said, 'but you're asking for the impossible. I've tried at least a dozen times to get her and it's always a polite no. There's a reason she hasn't been on a single magazine cover in the last five years – she doesn't want to be. She doesn't do photo-shoots and she doesn't do interviews, not even about her charity work.'

'I don't want to hear this!' spat Cassandra. 'All I'm hearing is "can't" and "won't" and all I'm getting is excuses and easy options. Doesn't anyone in this room have any ambition? Any passion? Doesn't anyone want *Rive* to be the best fashion magazine in the world? Well, I do. In fact, forget fashion, I want *Rive* to be the best magazine in the world! Now get out there and get me Georgia Kennedy.'

The other members of staff looked nervously at each other as Cassandra closed her notebook to signify the meeting was over.

'Perhaps we should have a back-up plan as well?' said Giles politely.

'And perhaps we need to rethink various members of staff if they can't deliver,' said Cassandra, already walking to the door.

32

Cassandra Grand was not a woman to take chances, not unless she had no choice. She knew she had to make *Rive* as talked-about as Pierre wanted but she had little faith in her staff to pull a world-class exclusive out of the bag. Which was why she was sitting in a velvet booth in a quiet bar in St James's, facing a man who did not look as if he belonged in SW1. Nick Bowen was a retired New York cop who had married a Brit and left the States – and the force – for better-paid work in the private sector. He specialized in divorce cases: following the billionaire husbands of stay-at-home wives who were hungry for fat divorce settlements. He had strong international connections and a reputation for delivering whatever you wanted at any cost. She had called him the day after her editorial meeting and given him two weeks and an unlimited expense account.

'Please tell me you have something of interest,' said Cassandra, waving away the waiter.

'If you're looking for dirt on Georgia Kennedy then you're going to be disappointed. She's as clean as a whistle,' said Bowen, trying hard to avert his eyes from Cassandra's cleavage. One thing he liked about high-level divorce work was the good-looking women. The wives of rich men were almost always gorgeous. Too skinny for his liking, of course and they had the sort of attitude he could only stand in ten-minute, well-paid bursts but *damn*, it sure beat pulling stiffs outta the Hudson.

'There must be something,' frowned Cassandra. 'You don't get to be big in Hollywood without doing something underhand or illegal to get there. Casting couch? Drug parties?'

Bowen shook his head.

'Two weeks isn't a long time for a comprehensive report, Ms Grand.'

'Well, it should be, the money I'm paying you,' snapped Cassandra.

Bowen's face was impassive. He'd taken abuse from professionals; another pissed-off broad didn't dent his armour.

'Ms Grand,' he began patiently. 'One of the reasons Sayed Jalid took her as a wife is because her closet is skeleton-free. She was an honours student in Missouri. Worked her way up through adverts and bit parts in films. No reputation of the casting coach. No scantily-clad magazine shoots. Very professional, very focused. Two long-term boyfriends, both respectable, both drug-free. Then she married Jalid and since then, no playing around and by all accounts they have a very happy marriage.'

'Shit,' said Cassandra quietly, tapping her fingers on the table. 'What about him?'

'He's a decent guy. Oxford scholar, Sandhurst. Georgia is the second wife, his first died in childbirth. Besides, even if we had something we can't touch him. He's super-protected 24/7 and surrounded by the sort of powerful friends and associates who could make any scandal disappear before you typed the first word.'

'So you're saying I've wasted my money?'

'Not exactly,' said Bowen with a crooked smile, placing

a brown envelope on the table. He pulled out a large black and white photograph of a handsome young man. 'Sayed has a daughter and a younger son from his first marriage. This is Alex Jalid, the son. He's 20, an English student at Brown University. A good scholar, but lazy, bit of a party boy. And very extravagant, he flies student friends to New York on nights out in his father's private jet.'

He put another photograph on the table in front of Cassandra. It was a girl with exquisite features and a long tumble of pale hair.

'This is Tania, Alex's girlfriend. She's a model in New York with a small agency called Mode.'

Cassandra tutted suggesting her patience was wearing thin. 'A playboy prince with a model? That's hardly the most scandalous story I've ever heard of.'

Bower smiled slowly. He took another photograph out of his briefcase and put it on the table.

'And who's this?' asked Cassandra curiously.

'This,' replied Nick Bowen, 'is where it starts to get interesting.'

She smiled as he began explaining the photograph's significance to her.

'I'm sorry that's all I could get in two weeks,' he said, after he'd finished, looking at her face for approval.

Cassandra touched his calf with her bare foot under the table, smiling as she saw his eyes widen.

'It's enough, Nicholas. It's more than enough,' she said with a surge of excitement. Her plan was about to come together.

It was the hottest summer in a decade and with the heat came a wave of positivity at Milford. The company's advertising campaign was everywhere and Clover Connor was papped carrying a 100 Bag in Ibiza. The refurbishment of the Bond Street store finished on time, a crack sales team was headhunted from other designer stores and the Milford Autumn/Winter line was delivered. It looked fantastic.

For Stella that meant twice the pleasure. Satisfaction of a job well done and the opportunity to start the creative process all over again, dreaming up new designs that women would be clamouring to buy in six months' time. Of course, her earlier designs would live on; Emma wanted the 100 Bag and the Milford clutch as perennial pieces to be repeated in each collection in new leather and colourways. However each season there were to be six new designs to underline Milford as a fashion house and to increase profit potential as women wanted to add to their collection of bags.

That summer Stella had found the perfect place to dream up new ideas: the roof terrace at Byron House. Strictly speaking, it was just a flat expanse of roof reached by a fire exit door that led off from her studio, but it was a sun-trap, a perfect place to take vintage magazines, source books and a cold lemonade to enjoy the weather, especially when Emma wasn't due in the office all week.

Lying out on a towel she had found in a store cupboard, Stella was enjoying the uninterrupted quiet and sun on her face when she heard Emma's voice echo round the studio.

'Stella?'

'Out here,' she called, surprised.

Emma poked her head out onto the roof.

'Can I have a word?'

'Sure.'

'Inside,' said Emma. 'It's a deathtrap out there.'

Stella climbed back into the studio and joined Emma at a round table in front of Stella's mood board, an enormous expanse of cork tiles onto which she had pinned magazine tears, postcards of old films, photographs and swatches of fabric.

'I thought you were supposed to be in Costa Rica this week,' said Stella, dabbing at her forehead with her towel.

'Cancelled. But I've been in London all morning.'

'Hardly Central America,' grinned Stella.

'I've been down to the store,' said Emma, frowning.

'What's wrong?'

'Oh, nothing. In fact, quite the opposite.'

Emma took a spreadsheet from her briefcase and handed it to Stella.

'Sales from the Bond Street store in one week.'

To Stella it was just a jumble of tiny numbers in little boxes.

'Is this good?'

Emma took a drink of water from the bottle on the table.

'It's 400 per cent up on what we were projected to be doing and we haven't even officially launched yet. Bond Street has already called in with a stock order for more products.'

She took a breath.

'Which is why I want to launch a collection of womenswear next season.'

Stella just gaped at her.

'You're not serious? You want to launch a ready-to-wear line in six months?' she said, feeling a spike of fear. 'That's crazy!'

Emma looked at her determinedly. 'There's a real momentum building here, I can feel it. A year is a long time in fashion and I don't think we can leave it another couple of seasons. I always saw Milford as a fashion and luxury goods company like Hermès or Louis Vuitton, rather than one that simply makes handbags and luggage. If results are this good, then I think it makes sense to expand quickly.'

'How big a collection were you thinking?' asked Stella with a sinking feeling. It didn't take much to work out that Emma's new plans had direct implications for her.

'Small and exclusive,' she said firmly. 'It has to be in line with our brand message for the bags which are practically made to order. There seems to me to be a gap between haute couture and ready-to-wear and that's where we should fit in.'

Stella smiled thinking how far Emma had come in the literacy of fashion. Six months ago she didn't know a Tod's from a Toblerone; now she was proposing to break the mould and create an entirely new fashion market. Now Emma even looked the part in her camel Armani shift dress and Louboutin heels, her hair like a flaxen horse's tail, swinging elegantly with every move of her head.

'So you're thinking sort of limited edition pieces,' said Stella, beginning to get excited about the idea, despite herself.

'Absolutely; an artisan line if you like,' said Emma. 'I'm thinking a 20-piece capsule wardrobe with a cap on the number of pieces in production. We do this for three or four seasons then we can think about a full ready-to-wear line at a slightly more accessible price point.'

'You want womenswear for next season,' said Stella, still shaking her head in disbelief.

Emma nodded.

'You do think it's possible?' she asked, with a note of reservation in her voice. 'If we're going to do it, we have to do it properly.'

Stella remembered a similar conversation with Cate Glazer, who had also been in a hurry to expand her empire after a couple of hit bags. Cate had had much bigger resources at her disposal than Milford and even more bullish confidence. The fashion press had doubted such a fast expansion at the time but Cate had pulled it off and their first show during New York Fashion Week had graduated them from a bag company to a lifestyle empire.

'Well, anything's possible,' said Stella. 'But who's going to design it?'

Emma pulled a face.

'Me? Come on, Em, I'm flattered but how can I do both? I'm flat out as it is.'

Emma smiled and looked towards the roof. 'Looked like it.'

'OK, OK, but I want a team. I know a guy from St Martin's who's worked at Donna Karan and another girl who has experience on Savile Row. Although strictly speaking, design isn't the problem,' she said, now thinking out loud. 'Fabric's the big hitch. It's one thing turning up at Premiere Vision – that's the big textile trade fair in September – but the very best suppliers will have exclusive contracts with the top fashion houses.'

'Can we cut a deal?'

Stella tapped a thoughtful finger on her lips.

'I know an excellent textile mill in Bologna who might do something with us, but we'll have to go out to Italy for some heavyweight schmoozing. Then there's manufacturing – we won't be able to do it here. Gosh, there's so much to think about! Where were you thinking of showing?'

'Paris would be incredible, but that's unlikely given our lack of track record and the time span. Anyway, I think we should show in London. Given the heritage of the brand it feels only right. I've already spoken to the British Fashion Council. We'll get a professional show-producer, top models . . .'

Stella listened to Emma's words, but had already begun to drift off into her own thoughts. What Emma was suggesting . . . it was every designer's dream, but did she really have what it took to pull it off? Tom Ford had transformed Gucci in practically one season with his legendary 1995 collection of sexy velvet hip-huggers and satin shirts but he had both a gargantuan talent and a steely commercial brain. There were days when Stella thought she was just playing at the fashion business. Before Emma came along she never had anyone to cheerlead her ambitions. Her talks with her mother never got beyond lightweight chit-chat and the only time her father had ever pushed her to do anything was when he was trying to get her to follow him into sculpture. As if reading her thoughts Emma looked her directly in the eye.

'I know what a great job you can do with it. Look what you did with the accessories line in a matter of weeks.'

'No pressure then,' said Stella a touch sulkily.

'I've had a lawyer looking into the share structure of the company. I want to give you stock in Milford, Stella,' said Emma firmly. 'Ruan too, actually. You both deserve it more than I can say.'

Stella wasn't sure how to respond.

'Wow. That's great news,' was the best she could manage.

'I believe in you, Stella,' said Emma simply.

Stella walked over to the office coffee pot and poured two black coffees.

'So. When do we start?' she asked, handing Emma a cup.

'Straight away.'

'Well, as soon as I get back from holiday,' corrected Stella. 'Johnny's parents have this house in Cap Ferrat and I thought I'd go for a couple of weeks. We're going to drive down. Stay in some chateaux along the way. Johnny starts filming in Wales for two months soon so we wanted to spend some quality time together.'

'Stella, you can't just go away for two weeks whenever the mood takes you,' said Emma, a note of warning in her voice. 'I don't want to sound like your boss, but you had five days off last month.'

'Johnny had a photo shoot for *Tatler* in the Maldives! He paid for me to go out there.'

Emma leaned towards her, her eyes steely.

351

'Stella. We – no, *you* – have a real opportunity here. You're on the verge of being the next big thing. Don't squander it chasing after a man.'

Stella felt like screaming. *How dare Emma say such a thing!* Yes, of course she'd been spending as much time as she could with Johnny, but why shouldn't she? She didn't want to end up an old spinster like Emma, too cynical and angry for a relationship with anything other than her career.

'Take a look at the press cuttings, *boss*,' she said, her voice dripping with sarcasm. 'I think I'm doing fine.'

'That all depends on whether you want to be known as a great designer or as half of an It-couple.'

Stella slammed her coffee cup on the table, all the excitement of launching her own womenswear line and becoming a Milford shareholder completely forgotten.

'Jesus, Emma!' she cried, 'all I'm asking for is two measly weeks off. I've been working my arse off for this company and I think I deserve a break.'

Emma looked intently down at her coffee mug before speaking.

'I'm just saying be careful,' she said softly.

'Careful of what?' shouted Stella, too upset to hold it in. 'Careful of getting a life? Careful of not devoting every waking minute of my time to the bloody company?'

'Of course you're entitled to time off. As your boss and your friend I'm just concerned about how long and who with. You know Johnny has a bad reputation. I don't want you to waste your time or energy on someone who might not be worthy of you.'

'How dare you?' snapped Stella, enraged. 'You hardly know him. And you know *nothing* about our relationship!'

'Do you trust him?' said Emma.

Her words stung. In some corner of her mind, Stella registered the implication of the question and noted the solemn expression which suggested Emma knew more, but she was too wound-up to pay heed.

'What's *really* wrong, Emma?' said Stella, her voice cracking. 'Are you jealous? Jealous that I manage to get the job done *and* have a life? Or are you jealous that all the press is about me?'

Emma was shaking her head. 'Stella, don't be ridiculous.'

Stella snorted. 'Am I? Am I really?'

Emma slowly gathered her things and stood up.

'Take a week off,' she said.

'Forget it,' said Stella coolly. 'Let's just get back to work. Because that's all there is, isn't there?'

'Stella . . .' said Emma softly.

'Let me have those deadlines,' she said, brisk and businesslike. 'Don't worry, I'll get it done.'

She walked back out onto the roof. Suddenly, despite the heat, she felt stone cold.

33

August is the fashion industry's playtime, a small window of opportunity for pleasure between couture and the final preparations for the Spring/Summer collections held in September. Most years Cassandra spent two weeks of August holidaying in the same destinations as the rest of the fashion crowd: the hillside villas of Ibiza, the hip hotels along the French Riviera or on one of the magical islands that pepper the Italian coast – Stromboli perhaps, where Dolce & Gabbana had their own luxurious villa, or Pantelleria, a favourite with Giorgio Armani. But for the last two years Cassandra had spent her time on Guillaume Riche's 175-foot motor yacht *Le Soleil* which, from the second the designer had launched it, had become one of the most sought-after August invitations for Europe's rich, famous and fashionable. Its luxury had already taken on mythical proportions for those not lucky enough to have sailed in her. People whispered about the hand-painted silk paper and Hepplewhite furniture in the staterooms, about the former Michelin-starred chef in the galley and of service so particular and exacting that each guest would have their bedsheets washed and ironed twice daily, once in the morning and once after their siesta.

As *Le Soleil* slid through the blue Aegean waters, mooring just off Mykonos Town, Cassandra sat on the walnut deck knowing the great yacht was all this and more. She was one of the few people who could be guaranteed their annual invitation; Guillaume was known for his eclectic mix of guests so that no one, except his very closest friends, could be absolutely sure they'd be asked on board until their hand-written invitation arrived by courier. Not even Ruby had secured an invitation this year, although that had been at Cassandra's request. Although she felt pangs of guilt at having spent the last two weekends in Provence with Max, she still didn't want her daughter on board *Le Soleil* when there was so much work to be done. And just because that work was going to be done in the super-chic clubs and bars of Mykonos Town surrounded by Guillaume's beautiful people it didn't mean she was any less busy.

'What an absolutely glorious night for a party,' said Serena Balcon, holding the hand of her fiancé actor Tom Archer as she daintily stepped out of the tender that had brought them into the harbour. It was no surprise that Serena was on board *Le Soleil*. Every designer was currently courting the aristocratic actress, each one desperate to design her wedding dress, despite knowing it would be tough to wrestle the honours from Serena's old friend the French/Tunisian couturier Roman Le Fey.

All safely ashore, the group from *Le Soleil* stepped into the golf carts that were waiting to transport them through the whitewashed streets of Mykonos up to a villa situated at the top of town. Dusk was falling, the pink sky spilling a peachy glow over the sugar-cube houses clinging to the hill.

'Whose party is it again?' asked Tania Squires excitedly as they approached an enormous white villa.

'Leopold Mancini, one of the industry's top manufacturers,'

replied Cassandra. 'Italian, I believe. He has a big party in Mykonos every year. It's a must for anyone in the Cyclades.'

Cassandra eyed the New York model, not for the first time on the trip. Tania had an innocence that was quite charming and unexpected in the fashion world so it had not surprised Cassandra to hear, when they were sunbathing together on the top deck of the yacht earlier that day, that she had only moved from West Virginia to New York six months earlier. Tania was the sort of girl who advertised breakfast cereal; an extremely pretty girl, with long, champagne-blonde hair and a face of remarkable symmetry, although her features lacked anything memorable that would mark her out for the very top flight of modelling. Cassandra had already considered and rejected Tania for editorial in *Rive*, as she felt sure most of the other top fashion editors had done before her. It was why she still behaved like an eighteen-year-old, having not yet acquired the knowing, world-weariness that typified successful model teens. Still, there was something refreshing about Tania's wide-eyed wonder that not even Ruby with her routine exposure to the best things in life could match. Cassandra saw Tania take a deep breath of warm Greek air, shut her eyes and smile to herself.

'It's so wonderful to be here. I couldn't believe it when my agent got the invitation from Guillaume.' She opened his eyes. 'It's just crazy, isn't it? *Me* and Clover Connor are the only models on board!'

'He's probably just after my mother's couture business,' came a voice from the seat behind her. Cassandra turned to see the very handsome face of Alex Jalid, Tania's boyfriend and Georgia Kennedy's stepson.

'Guillaume doesn't work like that,' said Cassandra. 'It doesn't matter how rich you are, how famous you are. Guillaume simply wants a mix of interesting people he can have a wonderful time with.'

'I suppose so,' said Alex sullenly, turning to watch *Le Soleil* which had anchored outside the bay. 'This had better be a good party, then.'

'Oh, it will be,' said Cassandra with a smirk. 'I can guarantee that.'

Leopold Mancini held his annual party during the same week of August every year, at his enormous villa, one of the chicest in the whole group of Greek islands known as the Cyclades. It had a reputation of being one of the most flamboyant and decadent parties of the year; Mykonos was a favourite destination for both the fashion set and the glamorous gay community, both of whom had a reputation for partying hard. Leopold also had the money to do it justice. He was one of the invisible men of fashion; not a designer or a high-profile CEO of a luxury goods company, but still one of the most important men in the industry. His company Leopold was one of the industry's most respected manufacturers and with his vast profits came the luxury of being able to stage the most spectacular and lavish events.

This year, as it quietly coincided with his fiftieth birthday, Leopold had decided to pull out all the stops. In the sumptuous courtyard was a life-size ice sculpture of Michelangelo's David and a twelve-foot champagne fountain spilling over with Krug. Semi-naked waiters circulated with trays piled high with delicacies known for their aphrodisiac qualities: rock lobster, Galway Bay oysters and tiny truffle tartlets. There was even a rumour that George Michael was going to do a thirty-minute set.

Clover Connor drained her fifth flute of champagne and lay back on the day bed to watch her boyfriend Ste Donahue lean against the wall strumming his guitar. They had found a quiet corner at the back of the villa facing away from the sea and into the interior of Mykonos which, in the shimmering

357

darkness, Clover thought looked like the surface of the moon. The party was picking up around them but she had no desire to venture out of Ste's air-space and into the accusing stares and curious glances. Clover read the tabloids, she knew people criticized their relationship but what did she care? Every date she'd ever had since she was seventeen had been in the papers, it was the normal state of things for her. Besides, most of her previous boyfriends had been musicians because it was a combination that worked; their itinerant lifestyle, the adoration, the money and temptations that they both encountered meant the rock star and the model both understood and needed one another. It was mutually supportive. But Ste was the most fascinating and sexiest musician she had ever encountered. His lean sinewy body, unruly dark hair and handsome, haunting features were the sort she used to dream about when she was growing up in Newcastle. He wrote her songs and sang her to sleep. He was clever, fun and knowledgeable and was hailed in the rock press as a genius. OK, so he enjoyed drugs – they both did. But the drugs helped him create those poetic lyrics that had set the album chart on fire. Anyway, what if he was dangerous? His kisses made her weak. Ste Donahue wasn't just the love of her life, he was an obsession.

Clover stood up and wandered over to the wall where she could see the party in full swing. She remembered the days when it frightened her to come to parties like this. Ten years ago when she had first arrived in Paris to model she had been taken to some grand townhouse near the Bois. Coke was being snorted off every surface and the sounds and smells of sex – gay sex, straight sex, group sex – was all around her. Somebody had given her an ecstasy tablet and, too afraid to do anything else, she had taken it. Clover laughed to herself. How funny and naïve she was back then. Ste produced a crack pipe and lit it, the familiar sickly smell mushrooming around him. He inhaled the fumes, closing his eyes in pleasure and then passed it to Clover. A nagging voice in her head told her she shouldn't. She'd done some coke on the yacht as well as at the party and had drunk almost a bottle of Krug. But then as Ste smiled over lazily, she just wanted to climb into his skin. She loved him, loved him, loved him. The very least she could do was to take his hand and join him in that sweet heaven.

Cassandra and Giles stood on a balcony in the west wing of the villa enjoying the fresh air and peace away from the party. It was a wonderful night out there. Although it was now dark, it was still almost 80 degrees. Cassandra loved coming to Mykonos, she loved its stark aesthetics: the sugar-cube buildings, the blue and white churches with their cerulean domes, the startling blue of the Aegean against the dark, dusty volcanic soils further inland.

Giles was staring out at the black curtain of the sea. Only the flashes of silver light caught by breaking waves showed that there was anything out there but emptiness. 'You know that the island straight out there, Delos, is at the exact centre of the earth?' said Giles. 'Legend has it that Delos was an invisible floating island until the god Poseidon anchored it at the centre of the four points of the compass using chains made from diamonds.'

'Why on earth would he do that?' asked Cassandra.

'Because his brother Zeus had got a young lady in the family way and the gods forbade her to give birth anywhere on the earth. Delos wasn't considered earthly – still isn't. The Greeks still believe it is a sacred place. You can't stay there overnight and it's illegal to give birth or die there.'

Cassandra giggled.

'Darling, how do you *know* these things?'

'Benefits of a classical education,' smiled Giles. 'The only

359

thing worth going to a public school for. Well, that and the divine boys.'

A waiter approached them. He was naked except for a white thong and after he had handed them some champagne and turned away, they could see a tattoo on his right buttock that said 'This way, please.' They both burst out laughing.

'So. Has it been a useful trip?'

'What *do* you mean?' said Cassandra coyly.

'You never let a little thing like being on holiday get in the way of work. Have you persuaded Serena Balcon and Tom Archer to do a cover?'

'Giles, you do insult me,' she chided.

He raised a groomed eyebrow. 'Am I not correct?'

Cassandra laughed.

'Not both of them together – couples just don't sell. But yes, Serena has indicated that she might like to do something special for us. Of course I will leave it up to you to think of what that something special should be.'

She glanced at her Cartier watch. It was almost eleven o'clock. At some point she wanted to slip away and call Max but right now there was a more important phone call to make.

'I'm just going to the bathroom,' she smiled, handing Giles her glass of champagne.

She moved through the villa admiring Leopold's fabulous art collection; a Bacon, some Keith Harings, a couple of Hockney pool-scapes. Whilst they were a joy to behold, they only served to remind Cassandra that she was not yet operating at the most lucrative end of the fashion industry. She went to the bathroom; she always felt more powerful with a slick of red on her lips.

Finding the room empty, she was refreshing her make-up when the door burst open. Clover Connor staggered in and, grabbing the hem of her skin-tight white Alaia dress, wriggled it over her head and dropped it on the floor, leaving her completely naked.

'Clover! Are you OK?' asked Cassandra. The model was swaying like a willow in the breeze, her eyes completely glassy.

'I need a pee, I need a pee,' she repeated, before slumping to the ground.

'Clover! Clover! Are you all right?' asked Cassandra leaning over her. 'What have you taken?' Clover's drug use, which was an open secret in the fashion industry seemed to be sliding from recreational to something much worse. Cassandra wasn't so much concerned for the girl's physical or moral wellbeing. No, she was more worried because an addicted model was an unreliable one and Clover was one of the few models whose presence on a cover always guaranteed a sales uplift. Concerned that she might get vomit on her ivory Le Smoking, Cassandra ran out of the bathroom to look for Giles. She found him coming down the corridor towards her.

'Quickly, come with me,' she ordered.

'I was just looking for you,' replied Giles quickly. 'Leopold says Ste Donahue is totally strung out on the balcony in his bedroom. He's been looking for Guillaume to remove him but I think he has already left for the yacht. There are wagging tongues everywhere, we need to do something quick.'

Tania bounded towards them holding a flute of champagne aloft. She had stripped down to just a white string bikini.

'What's wrong?' she trilled.

'Ste isn't feeling too well,' said Giles diplomatically.

'I was going to say the same about Clover,' said Cassandra through her teeth.

Giles grasped the situation immediately.

'Where is she?'

'In a bathroom, on the next floor.'

'What's the problem? We're not going already are we?' said Alex, strolling up to the group.

'Possibly,' murmured Giles. 'Alex, can you go and get Security? Failing that, someone big and muscly. You shouldn't have a problem around here.'

'But I was just on my way back to the pool,' he replied, a note of whine in his voice.

'Just *go*!' snapped Giles, his usually gentle voice now clipped and firm.

'Now, Tania, get someone with one of those golf carts round to the front.'

'Mmm, Giles. You can be so butch when you want to be,' smiled Cassandra approvingly.

He took off his white jacket and turned towards the bathroom. 'Let's just go and find her, shall we?'

Clover was lying spreadeagled on the bathroom floor when they found her, vomit trailing from the side of her mouth. Tania followed them in, and gasped when she saw her idol in such a state.

'Is she dead?' she gulped, both hands flying to her mouth.

Giles turned on her. 'Didn't I tell you to go and get a golf cart?' he barked. 'And has Alex gone to get Security?'

'I think he's gone to the bar.'

Giles was too distracted to get angry.

'All right, stay here and help me,' he said in a low voice that left no room for argument. Giles pulled a towelling robe from a cupboard and folded it around Clover's naked body.

'Help me lift her,' he said to Tania.

Meanwhile, Cassandra had left to find Leopold to help locate Ste and get him out of the party. Ten minutes later, two security guards dressed in white loaded Ste's limp body into a golf cart before helping to put Clover in beside him too.

'I'll go back with them to the yacht,' said Giles.

'Tania. Why don't you go too?' said Cassandra. 'I'm sure Clover will be really grateful for your help.'

Tania looked at Alex who had just come from inside the villa.

'Are you going to come?'

'There's no point us all going,' said Cassandra, touching Alex's shoulder.

'I agree,' he replied, after viewing the events with the superiority of a Roman emperor watching lions and Christians.

By the time they reached *Le Soleil*, Guillaume had already been woken and he had alerted the deck hands to help Tania and Giles bring Clover and Ste on board. Guillaume was out on deck in his long, navy, silk dressing gown. His mouth distorted into an expression of distaste and then disbelief as Clover crouched down on her hands and knees and puked onto the deck.

'Get her off this boat as soon as possible,' he whispered to the captain.

'We'll throw them in the hold to cool off,' said the captain.

'And get one of the crew to hose them down,' added Guillaume, picking an imaginary fleck of dust from his robe. 'And remind me next year to be more careful with the guest list.'

Back at the party Cassandra took her mobile out of her white clutch bag and propped it under her neck. Everything was turning out more beautifully than she'd hoped. She'd had one agenda for this evening but this was like a bonus prize.

'Can I have the entertainment desk, please?'

'Jacqui speaking. How can I help you?'

'I have a story that I think might be of interest,' she said, looking at her watch. It would only be 8 p.m. in London; perhaps not too late to make the late edition of the Sunday papers.

'Who about?' asked the journalist.

'Clover Connor and Ste Donahue.'

'Keep talking.'

'They are on Guillaume Riche's yacht in Greece taking enough cocaine to build a snowdrift. Tonight the pair of them collapsed at a fashion party after overdosing and have been forcibly removed. Clover was completely naked when they dragged her out.'

'Without decent pictures I'm afraid we can't offer you much.'

'Money is not necessary,' said Cassandra shortly. 'Just make sure you mention in the copy that Clover Connor is the new face of Milford.'

She flipped down the phone and tossed it into her bag. Spotting a silver atomizer inside, she spritzed her body. Then she shrugged and fished the mobile out again. *While she was at it she might as well call Page Six.* Just a quick call, she couldn't be long. She had other things to attend to tonight.

On the other side of the villa, Alex Jalid knew that the party was just getting started. Most of the people from the *Le Soleil* delegation had already gone back to the yacht, so now it was really time to have some fun. He had been eyed up all evening by an outrageously good-looking brunette who was now naked except for a slim-fitting pair of white trousers. When their eyes locked again, Alex realized it was a call to action. His senses blurred by alcohol, he knew there was no turning back as the stranger began to walk towards him smiling. It was now dark, and the mood of the party had changed; it was now prickling with sex and promise. The handsome stranger took hold of Alex's hand and whispered into his ear. There was a discreet little club in a backstreet not too far away where they could really enjoy themselves. They took separate golf carts into town; you couldn't be too careful and he was right. When they stumbled out of the club two hours later, his arms draped around his companion, he was too drunk to be cautious, too high to hear the gentle whir of a camera shutter. He was too driven by lust to notice anything else as he spent a sexually-charged ten minutes in a doorway saying a passionate goodnight to his new friend.

'Good morning, Alex,' said Cassandra, taking a small sip of freshly-pressed raspberry juice. 'And where is the lovely Tania today?'

Alex slid into the booth opposite her and took a crois-sant off a bone-china plate. It was indeed a beautiful morning and the sun was already beating down on the deck canopy under which they were being served breakfast.

'Still in bed, where I'll be in about five minutes, but I'm starving so I had to surface for some food. I waited five minutes for room service and nothing happened. I wouldn't get that back home.'

'Well, it's fortuitous that you're here because I want to talk to you.'

'Really?' said Alex in a bored voice, pushing a pair of sunglasses down over his bleary eyes.

Cassandra took a moment to look at him. Alex was such a good-looking boy. Dark brown hair, strong elegant features and liquid chocolate eyes. His bare chest was tanned and toned, his six-pack rippling over the top of his surfer shorts.

'Why don't you come with me?' said Cassandra, briskly dabbing her mouth with a napkin.

'Can't you see I'm busy?' he said petulantly, tearing his croissant in half.

'Alex, I think you'll find this is important,' she replied, meeting his gaze.

Sighing, he pulled himself up and followed Cassandra down to her stateroom and flopped into a leather club chair in the corner.

'So what is it?' he asked impatiently.

'As you might guess, as an editor-in-chief of a major magazine, I never switch off. My mobile is on 24/7. I check my emails every day even on holiday.'

Alex looked at her as if she were a halfwit.

'And?'

What a pompous little prick, thought Cassandra.

'And this morning a set of images was sent to me by my friend Gary. He owns a photographic agency which deals largely in red-carpet events, but occasionally freelance snappers approach Gary with more scurrilous stuff.'

'If there's a point, I hope we're coming to it soon,' said Alex, rolling his eyes.

'It seems this trip has been targeted by various paparazzi,' said Cassandra boldly. She took a brown A4 envelope from the dressing table and handed it to Alex. 'There's a few long-lens bits and pieces of Clover sunbathing on deck. Some of Serena and Tom when we went to Santorini and of me getting off *Le Soleil* last night. It's all pretty harmless stuff except the pictures in that envelope.'

Alex opened the envelope, tipping the contents on his lap. There were a dozen 10 x 12 inch snaps that had been printed off in *Le Soleil*'s communications room, and as Alex shuffled through them, his face crumpled in shock and horror.

'At first I wasn't sure it was you,' said Cassandra. 'The quality could be better after all, but I think when you look at them from a certain angle it's quite clear, don't you? Not to mention the fact that that jacket you're wearing – that you *were* wearing – is quite distinctive. Gary wanted me to tell him who the person in the photographs is. I suspect he already knows and simply wants me to confirm.'

Cassandra had the curious sensation of being able to read someone else's thoughts simply from watching his face. First Alex had that look of someone being caught out, swiftly followed by a glistening sweat trickling down his brow. She could see every emotion, shame, fear and panic written across every inch of his handsome face.

She took the prints from him and looked at them as if she was considering them for the first time. In the first shot she could see Michaelis, the Greek rent boy she had hired to do the job, threading his arms around Alex's waist as they came out of a discreet Mykonos Town gay bar. The next two pictures showed them kissing. In the fourth photograph Michaelis was on his knees in front of Alex. The grainy image was poor quality but the photograph could not disguise Alex's face twisted with delight.

'I don't know who this is,' said Alex finally putting the pictures calmly back in the envelope. *Ah, now the denial phase*, thought Cassandra and had to stop herself from grinning with glee. The photographer had produced better pictures than she could have hoped considering they were taken from a distance and as for Michaelis, he had worked wonders getting Alex so out of it that he'd made an intimate moment in a semi-public place possible. It had helped immeasurably that Tania had been taken out of the picture by the sheer fluke of Clover and Ste's timely collapse.

'Come now,' said Cassandra firmly, 'to anybody who knows you, who knew what you were wearing that night, it's obvious it's you.'

Alex sat silently on the chair, his face white.

Cassandra knew Michaelis wasn't Alex's first gay lover. Nick Bowen had uncovered a more long-standing relationship with a New York model-bartender called Bradley Mathis. Bradley and Alex had been together for six months before Alex had called it off at the beginning of summer, fearing his tony college friends might have got wind of it. Nick had shown him a photograph of Bradley; tall, dark and handsome. At least Cassandra had known his type.

'What do you want me to tell Gary? You can see what sort of position this puts me in.'

'It's not me!' said Alex, his voice raised.

'Alex, if I say I don't know who these pictures are of, who knows who else Gary might ask? Someone who doesn't know you, someone who doesn't understand how your family might react.'

'Do you think he's asked anyone else?'

Cassandra shrugged. 'I'm guessing he's sent them to me to confirm because he thinks he knows who it is, he knows I'm on *Le Soleil* with you and he knows the shit he'll be in if he gets it wrong. But if I don't respond to him quickly he'll certainly snoop around. Believe me they'll find your friend in the photograph and give him a big cheque to talk.'

'My father can buy your friend's company,' snorted Alex, his face in an angry scowl. 'My father can make anything go away.'

Cassandra went up to him and touched his shoulder.

'The question is, do you want your father to know?'

Alex ran his hand through his hair and exhaled, his eyebrows knotted together in concentration. It was several seconds before he spoke.

'OK. Yes, it is me in the photograph,' he said quietly. 'Yes, I'm gay. Yes, I have silly, star-struck girlfriends who don't ask too many questions to cover up the fact that I am gay.'

He stood up and faced Cassandra. 'Being gay might not

be such a big deal in your world of fashion but to my family it would be a very big deal indeed. Do you know that there are still laws against homosexuality in over a third of countries around the world today? My country is one of them. Do you think I want to be gay? Do you think I want to wear it like a badge?'

'So your family don't know,' said Cassandra, making her voice sound as sympathetic as possible.

'My stepmother suspects I'm sure but my father doesn't know. As a matter of honour my father will cut me off without a penny.'

He walked to the bar, twisted open a bottle of mineral water and gulped heavily, tears falling down his cheeks.

For a second Cassandra felt guilty. He was a playboy, he was careless and arrogant, but he couldn't help his sexuality. Then she remembered what a little prick he had been earlier and pushed away any feelings of sympathy.

'I can get back to Gary and tell him he's mistaken and that it's just a couple of male models, nobody of interest. It might generate a bit of gossip but nobody will be surprised this goes on in Mykonos in party season. It's a nothing story.'

Alex looked up, his face full of hope.

'So you'll help me?'

She nodded and smiled. 'I'll help you Alex. Who knows? One day you might be able to help me.'

34

No one could believe it. The guests at the Milford relaunch party were genuinely taken aback at how fantastic the company's revamped Bond Street store looked. It was a reasonable reaction, especially from the few who had ever ventured inside the dusty original. It had been so faded and unremarkable, even the most regular visitors to Mayfair's famous shopping street would be hard pressed to remember it even being there. Now the Milford store was the talk of London Fashion Week; journalists whispered it was the work of uber-architect Peter Marino, the king of the luxury goods store who had redesigned everything from Barneys to the Dior store on Avenue Montaigne, while fashionistas wondered if, in the Milford bag, they had finally found an alternative to their beloved Hermès Birkins.

Up on the mezzanine floor, Emma looked down on the packed shop floor below her, sipping a flute of champagne to take the edge off the adrenaline buzz coursing round her body. It really did look like a different place compared to the shop she had first encountered six months ago. Now it was sleek, chic and luxurious, the perfect embodiment of the new Milford brand. In actual fact it hadn't been overhauled by Peter Marino – the cost of a superstar architect would have broken the bank. Instead, Emma had drafted in a small but creative firm of architects who had followed her brief to the letter; keeping the elegance you'd expect from a brand with Milford's British heritage, but giving it a much more edgy, contemporary feel. Now the store felt like a colonial country club with its walnut panelling, brass ceiling fans and wooden floorboards. A sweep of staircase, lavishly carpeted in white, led to the mezzanine floor where they had created a private salon for bespoke clients with velvet tiger-print chaises longues and a bar dispensing drinks. Even empty, the shop looked glamorous but with the hundreds of wide-eyed fashion players crammed inside, not to mention the string quartet who were playing in a corner and the white-tailed waiters dispensing raspberry martinis, it looked like a scene from *White Mischief*.

'I hope you're feeling pleased with yourself,' said Ruan, climbing the stairs to join Emma at her lookout post.

'You do realize that this is the first party I've ever thrown in my life?'

'Well, what a way to start,' he laughed. 'According to Zoe, simply *everyone* is here.' To give credit where it was due, Zoe had done an amazing job with the guest list; the right mix of money, celebrity and press. Apparently she had secured the attendance of several key society people by promising them a Milford bag and once they were on board, the rest of London Fashion Week had followed as word trickled out that it was the week's hot party.

'I'll be honest with you, Ruan,' whispered Emma. 'I haven't a clue who anyone is.'

'Well, you know Clover Connor,' said Ruan, nodding over at the model who was looking stunning in a white Grecian mini-dress.

'I'd rather Clover had kept away,' said Emma, wincing.

The face of Milford was apparently on her first night out after a short spell in rehab. Emma had nearly died when she'd read a story in the tabloids a few weeks earlier about a supermodel caught naked and completely out of her head at a party in Mykonos. The piece had been a blind item, but although the model was unnamed it was clear it was referring to Clover.

'Don't be daft,' laughed Ruan. 'Clover is like Teflon. No scandal ever sticks. In fact whatever she does seems to make her more famous, more sought-after.'

'I hope you're right,' laughed Emma nervously.

'How's the family?'

'If you mean have Roger and Rebecca fired any barbed remarks my way, then no, they seem to be on their best behaviour tonight.'

'I see Cassandra won't be coming.'

'I assume not, but how do you know for sure?'

'She's throwing a party tonight as well. Apparently it's to launch her book.'

'God, she is absolutely impossible!'

Ruan put his hand on her shoulder.

'Em, it doesn't matter any more. Look down there: we've made it. And if you needed any reassurance, I think you'll find the last 100 Bag has just been sold.'

He pointed to an expensively-dressed woman leaving the party carrying a chocolate-brown cardboard bag, festooned with a turquoise ribbon. They had spent a long time redesigning the packaging, making the Milford brown more rich and chocolaty and the blue more vivid and crisp. The carrier bags were almost as desirable as what was inside.

Emma watched the woman go and turned to Ruan, her mouth open.

'Really? You're kidding, right?'

Ruan shook his head.

'We've sold out in every colour. That's six hundred bags each, selling at over two thousand pounds each.'

'No!' she gasped, quickly doing the maths in her head, 'Even with the ones we gave away, that's . . . Ruan, this is brilliant!'

'Plus, Eugenie Vlodsky – she's the wife of that Russian oligarch – has just made enquiries about a "comprehensive" bespoke luggage set in antelope skin: I bet her definition of comprehensive is pretty ample. And Em, that's just the start, we've had thirty-five appointments for our bespoke services put in the book just tonight.'

Emma felt like doing a cartwheel, but restrained herself and instead leaned over and gave Ruan a kiss on the cheek.

'Thank you,' she said simply, squeezing his hand. 'I couldn't have asked for a better right-hand man.'

Emma finished her champagne and walked back down into the main throng of the party. Eyes looked up approvingly as she descended. She felt embarrassed under scrutiny although she knew she looked fantastic. Her bottle-green Lanvin silk dress was simple yet stunning, cut just below the knee with bracelet sleeves and a generously scooped neckline. Her hair had been blow-dried so it fell in soft waves around her shoulders. She wore no jewellery except for her watch and a pair of pearl earrings; she didn't need any. She was the CEO of a luxury goods company and the patina of power and glamour finished off her look without her even knowing it. Emma no longer needed guidance to look good. She would never be an intuitively stylish woman like Stella who seemed to be able to throw a quirky necklace onto an otherwise unremarkable dress to create something memorable and unique, but she had acquired a low-key, elegant style all of her own.

Over the other side of the room she could see Rob Holland and Jessica arrive. *Still going strong, I see*, thought Emma, before realizing that she'd actually forgotten to invite him. It had been almost two months since they had seen each other at the festival; they'd spoken a few times on the phone about Winterfold, about rent and repairs and so on, but that had been about it. Looking at him towering over the crowd, it made her a little sad. Even though he could be absolutely infuriating, she had at one time thought she and Rob could become good friends. Still, maybe he was genuinely happy with Jessica; she shrugged as he caught her eye and made his way over, kissing her on both cheeks.

'Stella called me to see if I wanted to pop down,' he said answering the unspoken question. 'Said I could come on the proviso I got some of my acts to come.'

'She didn't!' Emma said, lifting her hand to her mouth.

He grinned. 'Sounded like a fair enough trade-off to me.'

He popped a canapé in his mouth and turned round to look for Jessica but she was now having her photograph taken in a swarming mass of paparazzi by the door.

'I have to say, Em. This is officially a *great* party.'

'You say that with such surprise,' smiled Emma.

'You have many talents Miss Bailey, but I wasn't sure partying was going to be one of them. Next time I have one of my naughty rock acts in town I'm gonna tell them to give you a call.'

They both laughed.

'I haven't seen you in weeks.'

'I've been staying in London actually. Jessica's idea of *rural* is Holland Park, although this weekend I'm forcing her out of the Big Smoke.'

'Are you both coming out to Chilcot?'

'Norfolk actually. A friend of mine is lending me his house up there. It's on stilts right by the beach, a crazy-looking thing.'

'It will be absolutely beautiful. I love those long windswept

374

beaches like Brancaster on the north coast. The lavender fields might still be out too. I'm jealous,' she smiled.

'I think Polly will like it too.'

Emma looked at him curiously, remembering what he had said to her once about not introducing girlfriends to Polly until he was absolutely ready. She felt a stab of something unpleasant, not envy exactly. No, it was disappointment that Polly was meeting *Jessica*. She'd hoped it would be someone more deserving.

'Polly and Jessica?'

'A breakthrough, I know,' he grinned.

'I *knew* that's why you really wanted Winterfold,' she teased.

He looked at her curiously. 'I don't understand.'

'The huge family house. Actually half a dozen families could live quite comfortably in Winterfold, but the principle is the same – it's a nesting instinct, Rob Holland. Secretly you want to settle down.'

'Don't be silly.'

'So it's a coincidence Polly is meeting Jessica?'

'Actually, I double-booked,' he said grumpily.

'Whatever you say . . .'

He looked away, suggesting that he didn't want to talk about it any more. After a pause, he said, 'Seriously Emma, you did great. I always knew you were going to.'

She shrugged modestly.

'I never did buy you that drink to say thank you.'

'I suppose you'll be less crazy after tonight.'

'Uh-uh, fashion is a never-ending conveyor belt.'

'Well, when you are less busy give me a ring, we'll grab a beer at the Feathers.'

'That would be nice.'

Over the crowd, Emma could see Jessica looking around for Rob, a look of annoyance on her face. Rob followed her gaze and frowned.

'Listen, I've gotta go,' he said quickly. 'I think Jessica needs me.'

'I bet she does,' said Emma under her breath as Rob pushed through the crowd. 'I bet she does.'

'So do you think we're the hottest power couple in London yet?'

Stella looked at Johnny and laughed.

'The hottest *what*?'

'Power couple,' he said, entirely serious, before pausing to pose with Stella for a photographer. He didn't need to pose; from any angle he was easily the most handsome man in the room, even dressed down in jeans and a white shirt.

'If we were in New York it would be difficult but over here . . . I mean Sting and Trudi are getting on a bit and once the *Vanity Fair* piece comes out . . .'

The week before, Johnny's publicist had got a call from *Vanity Fair*'s London editor requesting an interview and shoot time with Johnny and Stella.

'We're not seriously getting the cover are we?'

'Not the US cover. Not yet, anyway,' he grinned. 'But if the US cover is some TV star no one's heard of over here, we might get the British cover. Remember that Patsy Kensit and Liam Gallagher 'Cool Britannia' cover? That was never a US cover but they stuck it on the British issue and it was still one of the most memorable magazine images of the last twenty years, wasn't it.'

'Well, let's just wait and see, huh, Liam?' smiled Stella. Secretly she was hoping they weren't on any *Vanity Fair* or any other cover, any time soon. Things had returned to normal with Emma after their showdown in the studio, and although her boss had made it clear she had no wish to be in the public eye, Stella was conscious not to steal any more of her boss's thunder. Her eyes darted around the room searching for a face.

'Why are you so edgy, baby?' asked Johnny.

'He's not here, is he?'

'Who?'

'My father.'

Johnny squeezed her hand.

'You kind of knew he wasn't going to be, didn't you?'

'Yes,' she sighed. 'But you always hope.'

Johnny turned her around and looked her in the eye.

'People are always going to disappoint you in life, Stella. So Chessie got her way and they're not here, but look around! Five hundred people are here to see you and the things that you've created. Are you going to let Chessie and your father ruin that?'

She nodded. Johnny was right. This was the biggest night of her life and she wasn't going to let anything or anyone spoil it.

'You'll never guess what,' said Jessica, snaking her hand around Rob's waist and pushing her mouth close to his ear.

'What? Sorry, I was miles away,' said Rob, rather startled to see her. While Jessica had spent the last half hour flitting around like a social butterfly, Rob had been thinking about Emma, or rather about what she had said. Was she right? Did he want to settle down? *Did he want to settle down with Jessica?* When he had first got together with Madeline, a friend had quipped that relationships were a question of timing. That had turned out to be correct: when Rob had met Maddy, he had been mourning his brother; he'd just taken a job in his father's company and had wanted to embrace a more stable and sensible way of life. Maddy had fitted the bill perfectly, but the more

377

he had got sucked into the record industry and the temptations that came with it, the more that relationship had faltered. But maybe now he was ready. As forty loomed, he was sick of transient relationships. He looked at Jessica smiling up at him. She was good company and beautiful. She knew his crowd, and didn't make too many demands on him, she fitted comfortably into his life. But was she really so different from any of the indeterminate blondes, brunettes and redheads who had shared his bed in the last decade? Maybe it was just timing after all.

'Sorry, Jess, got a lot on my mind at the moment,' said Rob, returning her embrace. 'What were you telling me?'

'I was telling you how much I love this party!' she gushed. 'First of all I get invited to Donatella's party on Sunday, then I speak to Eugenie Vlodsky who says he's going too and can give us a lift to Milan in his father's jet! Isn't that just so cool?'

Rob pulled away from her, frowning.

'You want to go to a fashion party in Milan this weekend? Have you forgotten what we're supposed to be doing?'

'Of course not, we're seeing Polly, aren't we?' said Jessica casually.

She grabbed a raspberry martini off a passing tray and continued talking in rapid-fire sentences.

'But Eugene isn't leaving until 2 p.m. on Sunday afternoon. If we have a car waiting at Linate airport, or better still, hop in Eugene's, that will give us enough time to get to the party. We can still go to Norfolk if we can get Polly back to her mum on Sunday morning.'

Rob looked at her, open-mouthed.

'What's the matter?' asked Jessica. 'Don't you want to go?'

'Any other weekend, of course I'd like to go to Donatella Versace's party,' he said, his back stiffening. 'But this weekend I'd like to see my daughter. I've arranged for the three of us to go to Norfolk. Besides which, Maddy is in England for a wedding and she won't be able to look after Polly. Not without enormous inconvenience to her anyway.'

He felt a sudden swell of loyalty towards Maddy. Whatever differences they might have had, however cold and patrician he thought she was, she took her parental responsibilities more seriously than anything else in her life. And for that he respected her a great deal. Jessica pursed her mouth, looking deep in thought.

'Well, how about I come back from Norfolk on Sunday morning? Can't you get your driver to pick me up? Eugene is flying out of Luton so that's really handy for East Anglia anyway.'

Rob ran his hand through his hair.

'Jess, why am I getting the feeling you don't want to come? Don't you want to meet Polly?'

'Of course I want to meet her. I bet she's adorable.'

'So . . .'

She didn't say anything for a few moments and then looked up at him with her enormous aquamarine eyes.

'Honey, this is a really great career move for me. Imagine how many celebrities, agents and PRs I'm going to meet. And the truth is you'll probably have a better time with Polly on your own.'

Rob blinked at her. Suddenly all the anger he'd felt building just drifted away.

'OK, Jess, you go to Milan.'

Jessica batted her eyelids and tilted her head.

'Are you sure you're not angry with me?'

He forced a smile. He didn't want to spoil Emma's party with a scene.

'Of course not.'

'In that case let me go and find us a couple of cocktails to celebrate.'

He watched her go, that perfect ass and those long, long legs. Just another woman passing in and out of his bed, another notch on the headboard. Except this one had got close. This time it had been a near miss.

In a stunning duplex apartment in Knightsbridge, the book-launch party for *Cassandra Grand: On Style* was also going strong. Looking sensational in a backless, sequinned Galliano cocktail dress, the author smiled for her audience, gliding around the party signing books and giving quotes to journalists, while secretly seething that this, *her* party, wasn't the only game in town.

'I can't believe you're going already,' whispered Cassandra to her mother.

'Darling, you know how much being here means to me but I have at least to show my face at Milford. I do part-own the company.'

'But this is *my* launch party,' she said angrily, struggling to keep a smile on her face in case someone should look over.

'I can stay another ten minutes but it's really most unfortunate scheduling. I wish the two parties hadn't been on the same night.'

The real reason for Cassandra's fury was not that her mother was leaving after two hours. It was that at least a dozen key guests including two broadsheet fashion editors, the MDs of three major fashion houses and several celebrities hadn't turned up at all. Max might have called it a *pot-shot*, but she hadn't been able to resist asking her publishers to have her book launch on the same night as the Milford party. That would wipe the smile off Emma Bailey's face, she had thought, when her company's big splash was like the *Mary Celeste*. But while her launch was well attended, Cassandra's anticipated victory was not quite as glorious as she had expected it to be. She was still cursing Emma for forcing her into such a tactical lapse, when Ruby trotted over to give her grandmother a goodbye hug. Ruby had obtained a special dispensation to come for the night and had brought along two friends from school, Pandora and Amaryllis, sisters whose father was a Greek shipping magnate. This particular news had pleased Cassandra no end, almost enough to forgive the girls' appearance. Overcome at being invited to a real fashion party, they had gone to town with their outfits, hair and make-up. Short skirts showed off their very long legs and no one would have guessed their ages.

'Ruby, are you going to be all right staying here?' said Julia kissing her grand-daughter on the forehead and trying to mask her concern. She had spotted men old enough to be their fathers, grandfathers even, eyeing up the girls all evening.

'Nah, it's fine. We're having a wicked time here,' said Ruby, taking a slurp of orange juice. Julia hoped that it was just orange juice in there. *One heard such stories.*

Cassandra watched her daughter run back into the thick of the party. As she turned, she glanced out onto the balcony and froze. Max and Laura were standing talking in the balmy night air. *What the hell was he doing here?* She certainly hadn't invited him but he had come anyway – and he had come with his wife. His daring sent a flush of lust along her skin; the sense of danger of having Laura at his side, oblivious to everything that was going on, only heightened Cassandra's emotions. As soon as she saw Laura head towards the ladies' room, she murmured an excuse to her mother and headed out onto the balcony.

'I assume you're not going down to the Milford party,'

whispered Max into her ear, the breath on her neck almost making Cassandra moan.

'Don't be ridiculous,' she snapped, pulling away and grabbing a flute of pink champagne. 'It will be full of scavengers on the hunt for a free bag. Emma's so tight they'll be lucky to get a spring roll and a glass of cava. But forget her, what are you . . .'

'Cassandra, darling!' said Alison Edmonds, interrupting. The tall, imposing managing director of publisher Leighton Best bustled over. 'I just had to tell you I think the book is *absolutely fabulous*,' she said, giggling at her own joke.

Cassandra smiled weakly.

'The Christmas book of this year, I don't doubt it.'

She grabbed a canapé and popped it in her mouth, leaving a few flakes of crostini on her top lip. 'Now, I know this was a one-book deal, I know you're incredibly busy doing other things but we see you as a very important author for Leighton Best. Jenny Barber said you've got a number of ideas up your sleeve. What was this idea she said you had about Christian Dior?'

Cassandra waved a manicured hand dismissively in the air.

'Let's not talk about work tonight.'

'Quel dommage,' she smiled. 'Fabulous venue, by the way. I wish all our authors could pull strings like you can. Anyway, mustn't keep you from all your friends,' she said with a wink, moving off again.

Cassandra turned to find Max gone. Instead, Giles was standing there looking at her, stony-faced.

'What's the matter?'

'The Christian Dior idea your publisher just mentioned,' he said quietly. 'Is that the one I'm writing?'

He had such a stiff upper lip. God bless the civilized English thought Cassandra, knowing he was unlikely to make any sort of fuss.

382

'Yes, a Christian Dior biography was something I mentioned to her,' she said briskly. 'They were pushing me for suggestions for book two. Anyway, it's hardly the most original idea in the world, is it?'

'So you think you will do it?'

Her eyes challenged him. Warned him.

'Perhaps.'

Giles simply nodded and she smiled. He knew that to do or say anything further was futile. He was one of the few anointed members of her court, but that status could be revoked at any given time. In time he would see that what was best for her, was best for both of them. She looked around for Max; he was a few yards away chatting distractedly to Alison Edmonds. While she helped herself to another canapé, he gave her a small smile and motioned gently with his head towards the stairs. Noticing that Laura was now deep in conversation with Giles, she slowly followed. There was a long corridor at the top and only one door was ajar. Looking both ways to check she hadn't been seen, Cassandra pushed the handle. Max was standing just inside and he grabbed her, forcing his lips down on hers, his hands caressing her bare back, his fingers slipping inside down the curve of her ass.

'Max, please,' she moaned, not wanting him to stop.

'Laura is going to some other party,' he whispered. 'I said I'd see her back at the house.'

She looked up, their faces inches apart, sharing the same air.

'What did you have in mind?' she murmured.

He smiled wolfishly. 'I think you know. When do you think you can get away from here?'

'Max. It's my party. Plus Ruby is here.'

'It's nine-thirty, the party is almost over. Can't Ruby go home with your driver?'

He rubbed the palm of his hand across her breast, feeling her nipple harden at his touch.

Suddenly nothing seemed as important as her own longing, ripping at every nerve ending.

'Where shall we meet?'

'I've booked a room at the Cadogan Hotel.'

'Sorry, darling, but I have to go and do some more work,' said Cassandra, slipping an arm around Ruby's shoulders and brushing aside a pang of guilt at the deliberate lie to her daughter. 'Andrew will take you back to the house. What's happening to Pandora and Amaryllis? Are their parents in London?'

'Yes and Amaryllis has just invited me to sleep over. Apparently their house is amazing.'

'I'm sure,' smiled Cassandra.

'So I can go?'

'Where's their house?'

'In Regents Park. Andrew could drop us off there instead.'

Amaryllis stepped forward and handed Cassandra a card. 'That's our address. Someone will bring Ruby back home tomorrow or she can come to Battersea heliport with us. Daddy's helicopter is taking us back to school.'

'Well, I think that all sounds in order,' said Cassandra briskly. She made a quick call to Andrew confirming the arrangements, requesting that he take her to the Cadogan Hotel first before he returned to collect the girls. Kissing her mother goodbye, Ruby headed to the bathroom with Pandora and Amaryllis, all of them giggling.

'Do you think she'll find out?' said Ruby, looking up into the wide mirror as Amaryllis applied a slick of red lip gloss.

'Find out what? You *are* staying at our house. We're just going clubbing first,' smiled her friend.

'Are you sure we'll get in?'

'Don't worry,' said Amaryllis, taking her eye-liner and applying a generous amount to the top of Ruby's eyelid. 'We're on the guest list and our parents won't be back until after midnight. No one is going to know any different.'

35

Cassandra sat at her suite in the Milan's Hotel Principe di Savoie reading a card from Donatella Versace. It was the start of Milan Fashion Week and she was surrounded by extravagant floral arrangements traditionally sent by fashion houses to welcome the editors to the collections.

There was a knock at the door and Francesca, *Rive*'s fashion director entered, looking fabulous in black tailored pants, white shirt, a long string of pearls and a sable mink shrug. She was, as she had told Cassandra earlier in the week, currently channelling Babe Paley and in Cassandra's opinion she looked even better than the Fifties society beauty herself.

'Have you got a moment?'

'Literally a moment,' said Cassandra glancing up from the pile of correspondence. 'The car is downstairs ready to take us to the Missoni dinner.'

Francesca took a seat in a pale blue wing-back chair. She was a self-assured woman but in Cassandra's company she seemed on edge.

'What is it?' said Cassandra briskly.

'I wanted to talk to you about Laura.'

Cassandra propped Donatella's card back against the vast spray of black orchids that had accompanied it.

'What about her?' she said, picking up the stiff white invitation from the writing desk and putting it in her clutch bag.

'It's about the number of overseas shoots she's doing. She's never in the office.'

Francesca paused for a moment as if she was summoning up courage.

'You're the fashion director. Sort it out,' said Cassandra simply.

'But you've specifically requested that she do them. The rest of the team are getting very upset about it and to be honest, when I'm the one commissioning the stories and then you go over my head, I feel it's undermining my position in the department.'

Cassandra looked at her critically, surprised that her fashion director had had the balls to speak up. Then again Francesca was one of her most impressive and committed members of staff. Unmarried and ambitious, Francesca Adams devoted her life to fashion and to the magazine. *Rive*'s most stylish ambassador, next to Cassandra herself, Francesca understood that fashion was about sacrifice; whether it was spending her entire life hungry so that she could be a perfect size eight, or clocking up big debts to look and act the part of a top fashion director. So extensive and deluxe was Francesca's wardrobe that Cassandra had always assumed that she was independently wealthy. But the one time she had dropped in on Francesca's Chelsea apartment she'd had a big surprise. It had the right SW3 address; but it was the smallest studio Cassandra had ever seen. No lightshade hung from the solitary light bulb. Two huge wardrobes, spilling out with this season's designer clothes, meant there was no room for any other furniture except a sofa bed that doubled up as somewhere to sit and sleep.

Cassandra admired Francesca's commitment to the fashionable cause. It was why she had turned a blind eye to Francesca taking garments from other editors' rails when they were preparing for shoots. She had known about it for months; Laura and other editors had complained incessantly about it. But Cassandra understood Francesca's desire to be and look the best. Francesca had passion. The same passion she had herself.

'Oh, come on Francesca, you're all griping because you want to do the shoots yourself,' said Cassandra pulling on her Prada fur.

'That's not true,' replied Francesca, fiercely defending her position. 'It's because Laura's shoots are very one note – she's our least creative editor and if she carries on doing so much location stuff the entire fashion section is going to start looking samey.'

'For goodness' sake. We have almost a hundred pages of fashion stories in *Rive* per issue. Laura's one twelve-pager is hardly going to spoil the mix.'

She found herself pausing for a moment, knowing in her heart that Francesca was right. She was sending Laura away so much because she wanted time with Max. She would never let anything compromise the quality of the magazine, but he was like a drug and she would do anything just to be with him.

'Anyway,' said Francesca narrowing her eyes like a cat, 'I also think she is moonlighting on the side for other magazines.'

'Laura would never do that. It's a dismissible offence. Besides, she hasn't got the gall.'

'I'm sure she's doing a shoot that isn't on any of the flat-plans,' added Francesca. 'There's a rack of clothes at the back of the fashion cupboard. Various coloured gowns. Really top-of-the-range stuff. Some couture pieces. We have never talked about doing that story.'

Cassandra tried to disguise her annoyance. Alex Jalid had been good as his word, and had greased the Sulka Royal Palace wheels to make sure a shoot with Georgia Kennedy was going to happen. There were conditions attached; *Rive* were to shoot in the family's summer lodge not the main palace and Georgia would only talk about her charity work, although Cassandra was confident they could extract some more personal stuff.

The Georgia Kennedy shoot was top secret. It had to be. If the Americans got wind of it they would try to muscle in and claim it as their own. There had been at least three instances Cassandra could recall when her entertainment editor Deborah had secured a celebrity for a shoot, only for the star to pull out and turn up in the US issue a couple of months later. So for the Georgia Kennedy shoot only Giles, Laura and the art director knew what was happening and it needed to stay that way.

'Really,' said Cassandra rubbing her bottom lips thoughtfully. 'I did ask her to call me in a gown for a benefit dinner in New York. Let me look into it. And Francesca. Thanks for telling me. I'm sure it's entirely harmless but if Laura has been freelancing for other magazines she'll be feeling my wrath.'

Cassandra nodded at Francesca, her cue for her to leave, and she vowed the next day, Laura was going to be in serious trouble for her indiscretion.

36

'This is one fucking-awesome party,' said Tom, taking a vodka shot from a passing tray and knocking it back. It was Sunday afternoon and in front of his eyes two hundred of Ibiza's most beautiful people were partying around a huge, turquoise, infinity pool, as if it was their last day on earth. In Tom's direct line of vision were two world-famous music producers, a hip Hollywood actress, and a smattering of West London socialites in various stages of undress. Roland Gonzalez, the white-hot techno DJ was at the decks watching as Alexia Dark, the super-model, was thrown into the pool by an Eighties rock star whose face was so rigid with cocaine, he couldn't even laugh.

The party was being held at the sumptuous villa belonging to Miguel Cruz, one of the richest men on the island. He was the owner of both the Desire nightclub and Sugar, the small Ibiza Town bar that Tom, Jamie and their other business partner Piers had commandeered for the summer.

'Of course it's awesome. It's the last weekend of the season,' replied Jamie distractedly, smiling over at a six-foot pneumatic blonde wearing a feathered head-dress and a tiny, gold, sequinned tunic. 'Shit, check her out, Tommy. I think she wants me.'

'Uh, I think *she* is a *he*,' laughed Tom, trying to keep himself alert with another vodka shot. He couldn't believe that he was going back to England at the end of the week. It had been a glorious, fun-filled summer; his bar had closed the night before and what a send-off it had been. Tom and sixty of his new best friends had drunk the bar practically dry and he'd celebrated by spending the night with Peaches, the Sugar Bar's stunning promotions girl, resulting in only two hours sleep before coming to this party. Piers, the third partner in Sugar and Spice Productions came striding around the pool. Dressed in long white Bermuda shorts and a stripey Hackett T-shirt that did little to disguise his girth, he was fiddling anxiously with the signet ring on his little finger.

'Whatsup?' asked Jamie tipping his sunglasses onto the back of his head.

'Miguel wants to see us in his office,' said Piers, frowning.

'Fine. Sure. Right,' said Jamie. Curious, Tom studied his face and was concerned to detect the same level of apprehension in Jamie's manner.

'What's going on, guys?' asked Tom.

'Nothing, it's fine,' said Jamie, 'Completely fine. Miguel probably just wants to sign some paperwork or something.'

But Tom caught the look that passed between Jamie and Piers and it did nothing to reassure him that Miguel wanted to clear up some admin. They looked scared.

They were led away from the pool and into the house by a besuited bald-headed man and through to an expensively furnished study, with long shutters opening onto a terrace on the other side of the house. Miguel Cruz, an impressive-looking man with a hooked nose and wiry grey hair, remained seated sat behind his desk when they entered the room, while the bald guy waited silently by the window, his hands folded in front of him. Tom felt as if he had been hauled in front of the headmaster. Miguel picked up a document from his leather-topped desk and considered it for a few moments.

'I have in front of me the accounts for the Sugar Bar and the Spice nightclub,' he said finally, looking at each of them in turn.

Not one for small talk then, thought Tom, feeling hot in spite of the cool mountain breeze blowing in through the shutters.

'I see Sugar and Spice Productions has made a €340,000 loss.'

'What? How can that be?' asked Tom, completely floored by the news. He took a step forward to try and peep at the papers in front of Miguel. 'But I did a bloody booming trade all summer!'

Jamie pulled him back and Tom saw the look of fear on his friend's face. Jamie and Piers were responsible for the accounting. Tom had given the books only the vaguest look. His administrative responsibilities had amounted to no more than cashing up at the end of the week and banking the proceeds. He knew that the Spice club hadn't been delivering the sorts of crowds that Jamie and Piers wanted, but €340,000 in debt! – they must have been haemorrhaging money. *Where had it all gone?*

'We've a heavy outlay to get established,' explained Piers nervously. 'Publicity, alcohol, venue refurb and so on.'

'I'm sure,' smiled Miguel, 'Many clubs have the same problem in the first season. I'm sure it will be better next year. However, it is in the terms of the contract that you must settle the balance within 28 days,' Miguel added coolly.

'That shouldn't be a problem,' said Jamie confidently. 'Perhaps we can talk again later in the week?'

'No need,' said Miguel taking a sip from his crystal tumbler of water. 'Deal with my business affairs manager Carlos as you have already been doing.'

He stood up and walked to the shutters. 'Now I suspect young men like yourselves would rather be out by the pool rather than in here with me.'

The three men stepped outside and into the strong September sun. They were all subdued; Miguel's calm acceptance of their explanation had been far more unnerving than if he'd shouted and made threats. When he was sure they were out of earshot of the office, Tom turned on his friends.

'Three hundred and forty thousand? Where the hell's all that gone?' he hissed angrily.

'You heard Piers,' said Jamie. 'It cost a fortune to refurb the club, I mean the barstools alone! Ostrich doesn't come cheap you know.'

'But that much? Miguel must have been screwing us on the booze. I knew we shouldn't have let him supply us.'

'You were the one who signed for most of the drink,' replied Piers tartly.

'That's because I was the only one who sold any!'

'Don't be a cock, Tom,' said Jamie, 'I was there when you took that delivery, remember? Do you have any idea what they were loading into your cellar? Did you check the paperwork? No – you were too busy sniffing around the tart in the mini-skirt!'

'Sod off, Jamie! I worked my arse off . . .'

'Chaps! Come on!' shouted Piers. 'This is getting us nowhere. The truth is we didn't make any money and now we owe serious money to some rather unpleasant people.'

'What do you mean, "unpleasant"?' asked Tom.

Jamie and Piers exchanged a look.

'Our friend Miguel has something of a reputation, shall we say?' said Piers. 'He doesn't like people who owe him money. He can get quite nasty.'

'Oh, bugger,' whispered Tom.

'Exactly.'

Tom thought for a moment.

'Can you really get €340,000 just like that?' asked Tom remembering Jamie's confidence in the study.

'I have a couple of trust funds that I'd rather not use,' shrugged Jamie. 'Otherwise I might be able to tap my father for a hundred gees.'

Tom gaped at him. Jamie was talking about hundreds of thousands of pounds as if it was pocket money. He looked at his friend in a new light.

'Well, a hundred grand isn't going to cover it,' said Tom sitting on a chair under a parasol. Jamie and Piers sat opposite him and took two drinks from a waitress.

'Three hundred and forty thousand euros is about two hundred and fifty thousand quid,' said Piers. 'It's less than ninety grand each. Personally I think it could have been a lot worse.'

'Ninety grand *each*?' hissed Tom. 'And I'm supposed to chip that in too, am I?'

'Of course you fucking are, you twat,' replied Jamie.

'But I'm not a proper partner! I was only supposed to be getting 10 per cent of the profits. QED I owe 10 per cent of the debt,' said Tom, knowing that 10 per cent of their debt was well beyond his reach, let alone a third. 'After all, Sugar has been turning a profit all season, I'm the one who's been making money. Why should I get screwed for you pair spending God knows how much on bloody ostrich-skin stools?'

'Come on, Tom!' said Jamie, slamming his drink down on the table. 'You are a partner of S and S Productions even though you didn't put a dime in up front. If Spice had made a million and your bar had flopped, you'd still have wanted your 10 per cent and you'd have got it.'

Tom's watched the giant disco ball twirl over the pool, wondering if he had a legal way out of this situation; his mother must know a lawyer.

But all he had was a one-page letter of engagement from Jamie and Piers. Off the top of his head he could barely remember what it said but he felt sure it was nothing more detailed than a confirmation of his partnership in S and S Productions and a 10 per cent slice of any profits. Tom shook his head and pushed his drink away. Suddenly he felt sick to the pit of his stomach.

37

'I can't believe you've come,' said Johnny, throwing down his script and gathering Stella up in his arms, swinging her round and planting kiss after kiss on her neck. 'Save me from this set of divas and neurotics.'

Stella beamed. She had driven out to the set of Johnny's film on a whim, not sure if he'd be available or whether he'd even want her there – these actors had to stay in character, didn't they? But when she'd knocked on the door of his trailer, the look on his face had been worth the effort.

'I can't stay long but it was a great day for a drive,' she giggled.

'Anyway the cast aren't that bad are they?' She peered out of the small window onto the set. It was like looking back in time. Johnny's film was a 1930s romantic drama, featuring a farmhand's torrid affair with the Nazi-sympathizing American wife of a rich English industrialist. Johnny, of course, was the farmhand. Actors were milling around the grounds of the location, a stately home in the Brecon Beacons, in tea-dresses and Veronica Lake curls or sombre three-piece suits and trilbies. Just being here had already sparked off a couple of ideas for Stella's latest Milford collection.

'What's Lisa Ladro like?' asked Stella referring to Johnny's glamorous co-star. Lisa was a 'showbiz' thirty-six, which made her at least ten years older. Certainly, she had a string of high-profile marriages and a cabinet full of Golden Globes behind her. Apparently she'd hand-picked Johnny especially for the role, which he took as a massive boost for his career as Lisa's latest husband was the Oscar-winning director Marv Houston.

'She's the worst of the lot,' he grinned. 'You should see her list of demands: macrobiotic meals served four times a day, Jo Malone candles by the truckload, Evian water to wash her hair, they've even had to install a bikram yoga studio next to her trailer, which has to be heated to, like, precisely 37 degrees. The list goes on. Do you think I should be more demanding?' he added seriously.

'No, I do not,' smiled Stella, stroking his cheek. 'Don't you go changing one bit.'

He pulled her onto the day bed and sat her on his knee. 'So how's my baby been this week?'

'Milford is taking off like you wouldn't believe since the party. Stylists for every big celebrity are on the phone requesting bags. Plus, I'm working like a madman to get this 20-piece collection done for the next London Fashion Week. A great Indian silk factory who work with Valentino are going to supply us, and I'm getting two assistants to help me. How's that for a start?'

'My little Tom Ford,' said Johnny, running his fingers through her hair. 'You and I are going to take over the world.'

She let herself sink back into him, smelling his faint musky cologne, feeling his strong muscular arms wrap themselves around her, and felt a sense of consuming bliss.

'Look, there's the first assistant,' he said pointing through the window to a man with a pair of headphones hanging around his neck. 'How do you fancy a tour around a movie set?'

'Only if the tour guide is you,' she said standing up and pulling his hand.

It was almost six by the time Stella left the set. Johnny went back to his trailer to re-read the script for a night scene the director wanted to get in the bag. He lay back on the day bed, propped his head up with a cushion and popped open a bottle of Peroni. There was a knock at the door, and he sat up, expecting it to be his call for make-up. The door opened and Lisa Ladro was standing there in a white towelling robe, her face freshly made-up. She tossed back her mane of copper hair as she stepped into the trailer.

'I'm not disturbing anything?' she said in her faint Southern accent.

'No, she's gone. Finally,' said Johnny smiling and putting down his beer.

'She seems sweet.'

'She is,' replied Johnny holding out his hand.

The actress locked the trailer door behind her, checked that the window blinds were down and unfastened her robe in such a seductive manner it made Johnny instantly hard.

She was fucking sexy for an older bird, he thought, his eyes raking over her bronzed naked body, in perfect condition except for a bit of cellulite on her thighs and a slight crepeyness around her cleavage. The fact that she'd fucked a load of Hollywood legends turned him on too. There had been chemistry since the first day on set. She'd flattered him and stroked his ego, comparing him to a young Paul Newman. By the end of week one of filming, she had been stroking something else entirely.

'Now why don't we finish what we started earlier?' she purred, walking over and straddling him on the bed. Johnny groaned as she unbuttoned his jeans and pulled down his trunks. His cock sprang free and she took it between two warm soft hands. For Johnny, networking had never been so enjoyable.

38

'That's it, Xavier has the shot,' said the photographer, stepping away from his tripod and tossing his grey hair back dramatically. Cassandra allowed herself a small smile. Putting aside the Frenchman's annoying habit of referring to himself in the third person and overlooking the small fact that *she* dictated when they had the right cover shot in the bag, Cassandra was still pleased. Standing there in front of them, framed by a backdrop of virgin rainforest, Georgia Kennedy looked like an exotic bird of paradise, her apricot couture gown iridescent in the fading afternoon light.

The shoot had gone even better than she had hoped – wonderfully, in fact – despite the fact that Sulka had caught her completely by surprise.

Although Cassandra knew the precise location of every YSL boutique in the Western world, geography was not her strong point. She knew little about the country, except that it was an oil- and gas-rich Muslim state and Georgia Kennedy was the ruling prince's wife. Picturing her *Rive* cover, she had imagined Georgia against a dramatic backdrop of tawny Arabian sand dunes. She had instructed Laura Hildon, who was styling the shoot, to bring dresses in shades of nude and

400

camel 'so Georgia looks dip-dyed in the sand'. It had been a rare oversight. After a 15-hour flight via Singapore, they had stepped out onto a lush, tropical island nestled in the Java Sea. The colour and texture of the jungle backdrop was going to make it difficult to put any cover-lines on the image at all, but Georgia's beauty and regal poise were such that Cassandra knew no words would be necessary.

'Georgia. You were absolutely wonderful,' said Cassandra, going over to the actress. She was about to give her the traditional air-kiss but catching the warning glance of a stern-looking courtier, she gave her a short respectful nod instead.

The shoot had taken place on the wide terrace of the Royal family's summer palace, an enormous wooden lodge that clung to a tropical hillside and which had views over the whole principality; thousands of acres of jungle, a grey stripe of sea, and the capital city of Sulka Town shimmering miles away in the hazy distance.

'I'm surprised how much I enjoyed that,' smiled Georgia, taking a sip of iced water, offered to her by a waiter from a silver tray.

'You should,' said Cassandra, 'the Ellie Saab couture looks divine on you.'

She had specially commissioned the gowns from Saab, not only because she loved the beautiful craftsmanship of his evening dresses but because the couturier worked out of Beirut, which she had assumed was just a short hop to Sulka. Instead the gowns had had to travel across an entire continent and had arrived by a Fed-Ex van grumbling out of the jungle minutes before the first shot. Georgia smiled. She had a few lines collecting round her eyes but otherwise she was still exquisite.

'My life may have changed but there is still a little bit of the girl from Kansas City in me who loves dressing up in wonderful gowns.'

Cassandra turned to see Giles waiting patiently behind them, ready to conduct his interview with Georgia. She was of course hoping that Georgia was about to give them an intimate portrait of palace life, but she suspected that the princess was too clever and dignified to do that.

'I'm also grateful that this shoot will highlight some of the causes close to my family's heart,' said Georgia, looking straight at Cassandra. 'And you know how much Alex is grateful. I'm so glad his new charity has given him some focus.'

Feeling the piercing gaze of this elegant woman, Cassandra suddenly felt a stab of fear that Georgia Kennedy knew exactly why and how this shoot had happened.

Surely not, she told herself, feeling rattled nonetheless. *Surely not.*

The *Rive* crew waited around the summer palace until Giles had finished his interview and Laura had packed away all the clothes, after which a 4x4 took them on the long bumpy journey through the jungle and back to the capital city.

'I might start writing this up while it's still fresh in my mind,' said Giles as they walked through the cool marble lobby of their hotel.

'Good idea,' replied Cassandra. 'I think I'll go for supper with Laura. Maybe you can join us in the bar for drinks later?'

Laura looked exhausted. Without the luxury of an assistant, which Cassandra had vetoed on the grounds of secrecy, Laura had had to carry, unpack, press and pack all the clothes herself, which she had done with very little grumbling – a remarkable achievement given her seniority; in the world of fashion, the chain of command was as rigid as the army and any deviation invariably ended in a hissy-fit.

'Supper?' said Laura wearily. 'I have rather a lot to do,' she said, glancing at the suitcases of clothes.

'You have an hour now,' said Cassandra glancing at her watch and turning towards the lift. 'Let's meet in the restaurant at eight.'

In her room, Cassandra stepped out of her clothes, damp and sticky from the humidity, leaving them on the floor as she walked into the shower, letting the steaming water run over her body until every nerve felt revived. She wrapped her hair in a turban, pulled on a fluffy white robe and flopped onto her four-poster bed. She was just reaching for the phone to call Max, when it started ringing.

'Did you get everything you need?'

Alex Jalid sounded eager and concerned.

'It was wonderful, Alex. I can't thank you enough for arranging this.'

'You can thank me by never repeating our conversation in Mykonos or anything that has gone before or after it.'

She gave a small smile as she replaced the receiver. She would of course keep her side of the bargain, but it was inevitable that Alex would be caught out again one day soon. He was too important, too careless, too arrogant not to be. For a second she wondered who would benefit from his indiscretions next time? A jilted lover? An opportunistic member of his court perhaps? She didn't care; he'd been useful to her this time – that was all that mattered.

Laura was already at a table in the hotel restaurant, rumoured to be one of the best eating establishments in the country and full of rich Sulkanese couples and American oil company executives dining on expense accounts. As she sat down, Cassandra examined Laura critically. Her hair was lank and her eyes rimmed red. She hadn't even changed; Cassandra could smell the hot sweat of the jungle from the other side of the table. Laura had already ordered an aperitif and lifted the cocktail to her lips, draining the glass in one.

'I needed that,' said Laura, motioning to the waiter for another. Cassandra merely lifted an eyebrow.

'So are you happy the way it went?' asked Laura.

Cassandra's smile was wide and genuine.

'It's the coup of the decade,' she said warmly, 'and I think Xavier definitely did it justice. I think the sales figures will go through the roof. The strongest covers are often the simplest, aren't they? Those 1960s *Esquire* covers – Andy Warhol in a Campbell's soup can or Muhammad Ali with his hands tied. Even that *Vanity Fair* cover of Jennifer Aniston after her break-up with Brad Pitt – just Jennifer in a man's shirt. The power of a picture was worth a thousand words.'

'Well, thank goodness the Ellie Saab dress arrived in time,' said Laura, taking another drink. Cassandra pursed her lips and let the jibe pass; she was not about to admit her mistake to Laura. She noticed that Laura had glanced twice at her watch in the last five minutes.

'Is everything all right?'

'Well, yes,' she said, shrugging when she realized Cassandra was waiting for a fuller answer. 'Actually, I was just keen to call Max. I haven't spoken to him in two days.'

'I'm sure he'll cope,' said Cassandra.

Laura gave a half-smile and flushed. Cassandra sensed that something was wrong.

'Tell me,' said Cassandra, hoping she had achieved the right note of professional firmness and personal concern. Laura finished her cocktail before she spoke.

'I'm not sure Max is happy that I'm spending so much time out of the country,' said Laura, her eyes darting to the table.

Cassandra felt a little stab of panic. After all, Max had never once complained to her when Laura was on a photo-shoot in LA, Paris or Peru if it meant they could spend a sex-charged night in a hotel or a lazy weekend in Provence.

'Did he actually say that?' she asked intently.

'No,' replied Laura, 'but he seems ever so distant these days. My mum calls it the "disapproving quiet".'

Cassandra felt a sudden short-lived light-headedness; a sense of glee and triumph not to mention wonder that Laura thought Max's distance from his wife was *disapproval*! She instantly imagined herself a fly on the wall in the Carlton household; Max's barely-disguised disinterest in his wife, the inevitable lack of sex in the bedroom – or anywhere else for that matter – their polite but stilted conversations over supper during which Max would feign a meeting in Brussels or Geneva to spend the night with his lover. It was all Cassandra could do to stop herself from laughing out loud.

'Isn't Max happy for all the wonderful professional opportunities you've been given?' asked Cassandra.

'I suppose so, but because he's away so much himself now . . .' Laura paused as her eyes started watering. 'I, we, don't want our marriage to suffer.'

Laura drew a napkin to her eye and dabbed it quickly.

'I'm so sorry, Cassandra. I'm just tired and emotional not to mention rather embarrassed,' she said with a small smile.

'Don't be,' replied Cassandra.

The waiter came over and Cassandra ordered two salads for them before snapping the menu shut. Laura looked at Cassandra hesitantly.

'I've been meaning to ask you, and this is probably as good a time as any . . .' She trailed off, wilting under Cassandra's gaze. 'I was wondering if I could cut back on the number of overshoots I've being doing.' She held her hand up in front of her apologetically. 'Cassandra, I am so grateful for the opportunities you have given me and I think I've been doing some of the best work of my career.'

'But?' asked her editor slowly.

'But for the sake of my marriage I'm not sure I can carry on working like this,' replied Laura, her voice barely a whisper.

Cassandra looked at the young woman sitting opposite her, despising her for her weakness, hating her for marrying the one man who had got under her skin; the very thought of him made her ache with desire. She glanced down at the table where Laura's left hand was resting gently on the stark white tablecloth; the wink of the flawless diamond on Laura's platinum wedding band, a symbol of fidelity and eternal love, seemed to mock her. Cassandra longed to tell Laura how Max felt inside her, how much she loved the taste of his cock, how he knew every intimate part of her body and how he desired it madly, even when they spoke on the phone. She bit her lip gently as she composed herself. In her experience the truth rarely got you what you wanted.

'Can I ask you something?' said Cassandra finally. 'Do you respect yourself?'

The question seemed to take Laura by surprise.

'Yes,' she answered cautiously.

'Then don't give up. Laura, you love fashion,' said Cassandra leaning forward and putting her hand over the younger girl's. 'I see it every day in your eyes at work. I've seen it on this trip. Fashion is in the blood that pumps through your veins. You know as well as I do that fashion isn't a career, it's a way of life. It's a way of expressing ourselves. We've both spent years on our hands and knees in fashion cupboards ironing clothes and sewing on buttons because we simply don't want to do anything else. Fashion is your passion; it's your life-force. Don't let a man take away a vital part of you.'

Cassandra took a small breath, wondering if she had over-done the melodrama.

'He's not a man,' said Laura, holding her head up straight. 'He's my husband.'

'Precisely,' said Cassandra coolly. 'Marriage is not something that takes over your life. It's something that fits into your existing one. A really good marriage is one where you both understand that and support each other's passions and ambitions.'

'I thought maybe I could become a contributing editor . . .'

Cassandra felt a jolt of anxiety. She felt sure it was only a matter of time before he ditched his mousey bride, but until then she needed Laura in a position where she could monitor and control her. She shook her head gravely.

'You can't give in now, Laura. I saw how you looked at each other at the wedding: your marriage is stronger than you think. You can ride out a little bumpiness. Think of it as short-term pain, long-term gain. You have raw talent and influential friends,' she lied. 'Work your butt off for the next two years. You'll be the next Venetia Scott or Katie Grand and then you can pick and choose your jobs. You'll get the best advertising campaigns, consultancies at fashion houses. Then you can do much less and you and Max can relax together. But if you give up now, you'll just be another lady who lunches who once had something to do with fashion but no one can quite remember what. Do you think Max is going to respect you for that?'

Cassandra saw Laura's eyes sparkle at that final mention of Max. How desperately she sought his approval!

'Do you think that's what Max wants?' asked Laura more brightly.

'I think he wants a wife he admires, a wife who forges her own destiny and doesn't rely solely on him for her identity. Remember Max is a self-made man. He has a fierce work ethic, I'm sure he wants a partner not a dependant.'

Laura was nodding slowly. 'You're right. Oh, Cassandra

I'm so sorry for bringing this up. I'm going to give *Rive* my everything and I don't want you doubting me for a minute.'

Cassandra sat back in her chair, a broad smile of relief on her face.

'I'm only glad I can help,' she said, raising a regal hand to summon the wine waiter. 'I think this calls for champagne.'

39

If Emma thought she had beaten Roger, she was mistaken; her uncle had simply changed his tactics. Since the summer, when it appeared that Milford might really begin to show a profit, he'd realized that his shareholding might actually be worth something in the very near future. So at Rebecca's suggestion, he had stopped trying to fight Emma in the open and instead had started to use his new position as head of bespoke to his advantage. It was a position that allowed for a lot of travel and more importantly, face-to-face contact with Milford's most important clients, so Roger would take any opportunity to visit the client rather than take an appointment at the Bond Street store. In the last two months alone he had been to Moscow, New York and Dubai to discuss the bespoke luggage requirements of several high-spending clients. He had sometimes taken Rebecca with him and always made sure he spent his company expenses liber-ally – dining in the finest restaurants which he had signed off as entertaining. Emma was in no position to complain; Roger had proved to be a natural at persuading rich people to part with their money and the bespoke division was booming.

His latest business trip was to Brazil and so far he was enjoying it enormously.

'I am so glad you could come all this way to see us,' said Ricardo Perez, extending a hand towards Roger as he stepped off the small plane onto the runway in São Paulo. Roger had taken a phone call from Perez's assistant a week earlier making noises about a 'substantial bespoke order', asking that as Ricardo's diary would not allow a journey to Milford's Bond Street store, would it be fine for the Perez family's Gulfstream to collect Roger from Luton to take him to São Paulo instead? Roger had graciously agreed and had quickly decided that flying private suited him very well. Now arriving at the Perezes' mansion he felt sure he preferred his new position to being Milford's creative director. He loved the travel, the luxury, the mingling with the very top strata of society. Not that he would ever admit that to Emma.

The mansion was fifty miles outside São Paulo, colonial in style, and it reminded Roger of the Raffles Hotel in Singapore. Set on a hillside, Roger could see a swell of eucalyptus trees stretching in a thick carpet of lushness behind the house. The grounds at the rear of the property sloped down to the ocean from where they could hear the sound of crashing Atlantic waves on the shore. A butler appeared from nowhere and offered Roger a cold glass of iced tea. He took a sip, gazed up at the ceiling fans and felt at home. *Yes, I could definitely get used to this*, he thought.

'So you think you can do something special with the new plane?' asked Ricardo, showing him the specifications for the family's latest jet.

Roger nodded emphatically, putting away this book of leather swatches.

'We will use the best leather, dye it in the Perez corporation colours. It's actually a very similar blue to a set of luggage Milford made for Princess Margaret in the Sixties.'

Ricardo was nodding. 'My mother will like that. And what do you think about using the crocodile skin for the luggage set?'

'Obviously it would be fabulous. Your family deserves the best,' said Roger, understanding that Ricardo was the sort of client who wanted to be flattered at every possible opportunity.

'The only downside is that it may take a little time to get the order to you.'

'How long?' asked Ricardo, frowning. He was also the sort of client who wanted everything immediately.

'A year, perhaps. Maybe more.'

'That sounds ridiculous!' said Ricardo, sitting up as if he had been insulted.

'Not really,' said Roger diplomatically. 'Like you, Milford demands perfection. We use the very best crocodile skins – the Australian *Crocodylus porosus* provides the finest, hardest-wearing leather and it can take the backs of three crocodiles to produce one small suitcase. To source so many skins that are free of teeth marks and other blemishes will take time.' Roger looked at Ricardo shrewdly. 'I could deliver them more quickly, of course, but then your luggage would not be the best in the world. You might not notice the skin blemishes but I would, and I want you to have the luggage you deserve.'

Ricardo looked pacified. 'Thank you for your honesty.'

'My pleasure. When they are finished you will have one of the most remarkable sets of luggage in the world.'

'And you can even do cases for my polo sticks?'

'We could make you a leather polo pony if you so wished,' laughed Roger, accepting another drink off a white-suited butler.

As the afternoon progressed the two men got on famously. By remarkable coincidence they had both even attended the

411

same public school – Stowe – although Ricardo had entered three years after Roger had left. The Perez family business had begun in tin, but they had expanded into many other areas including food, property and telecommunications, growing richer every year until they were one of Brazil's pre-eminent families. Most importantly to Roger, they had become a family in a position to order nappa leather upholstery for their private jet, a family who needed bespoke leather luggage to complement it.

Ricardo was the son of Juan Perez, the current CEO of Perez Industries. In his early forties, with a crown of patent black hair and a handsome, if weathered, face, Ricardo was an impressive figure. Roger hadn't been able to make out his exact role within the corporation, but he had quickly learnt that Ricardo was a keen polo player and largely spent his time overseeing corporate entertaining.

'Well, it's going to be a pleasure working with you,' said Ricardo, lifting his glass. 'My mother wanted to go with Hermès, but I can see we are going to have more fun.'

Roger lifted his glass towards Ricardo. 'To fun!' he cried and the two men laughed.

'Let's go,' said the Brazilian, pulling his car keys out of his pocket. 'I have some business to discuss with you.'

'I thought we were already talking business,' said Roger, following him out of the house and onto the long drive where Ricardo clicked open a Rolls-Royce Silver Shadow. The evening was drawing in and light was seeping out of the sky so that by the time they left the Perez family compound it was almost pitch black. It felt quite eerie listening to the sudden squawk of the lorikeets in the trees surrounding them, letting his imagination run riot about what other beasts could be lurking in the foliage.

'So, Roger, what do you think of Brazil?' asked Ricardo after a while.

'Well I can't see much of it right now,' he laughed, looking out into the thick forest, 'but what I have seen is incredibly impressive.'

'Precisely. We have the fifth largest population in the world, one of the world's largest reserves of nickel, uranium and iron, and São Paulo is the world's second biggest city. People talk about China and India as new economic superpowers but when a Mexican is one of the top three richest men in the world you know that Latin America is where it's at. And my family have interests in everything.'

'You don't need to convince me about the merits of Brazil or of your family,' said Roger, a little on edge at how dark and lonely it felt driving through thousands of acres of forest. Ricardo nodded.

'The reason why my family has flourished is because we move with the times,' he continued. 'We are expanding constantly and diversification is the mantra of our business.'

There was a large pothole in the middle of the road which Ricardo chose to ignore, causing even the mighty Rolls-Royce to shudder. Roger felt a stab of envy at a man who could treat a Silver Shadow like a rally car.

'Eco-tourism is a huge global boom area and where better than Brazil to experience it. I have my own company, which I am developing separately from the Perez Corporation, concentrating in eco-hotels.'

'Eco-tourism?' said Roger, surprised. He didn't think Ricardo with his gas-guzzling motor and demands for a 33-piece set of luggage made from crocodiles would know what the phrase meant. Ricardo gave a quick sideways glance as if to read his mind and laughed.

'It's just business, like everything else, Roger. I want to develop a chain to rival Aman and I've already found my first property in Bahia.'

Roger's eyes widened at the mention of Aman, a collection

413

of luxury resort hotels in Jackson Hole, Morocco, Phuket, and all points in between. It was a huge international luxury business.

'How come your father isn't involved?' asked Roger cautiously.

'He had his fingers burnt with hotels ten years ago and refuses to invest in them again. Plus he's getting older, more cautious. Anyway, it is something I need to do for myself, I need to have an identity beyond just being my father's son.'

'I understand that feeling,' said Roger staring out of the window into the blackness. 'I had to watch my older brother make many bad decisions with our family company. I had so many ideas but could implement few of them. It's only after his death that we've managed to return Milford to its true position as one of Europe's finest luxury goods houses.'

'You and me are the same, huh?' laughed Ricardo. 'The son, the brother who wants to do his own thing. Who *should* be doing his own thing.'

There was a long silence before Ricardo spoke again.

'How does my hotel sound to you?'

'It sounds wonderful,' laughed Roger. 'I'll be checking in as soon as it opens. My wife loves luxury. She's always wanting to jet off to an Aman hotel.'

'I think you could bring something much more to the project than mere patronage, Roger,' said Ricardo coolly.

Roger raised an eyebrow.

'What did you have in mind? I didn't think eco-resorts would be big on leather goods.'

Ricardo laughed.

'Perhaps not leather, you are correct. However, you understand the premium luxury goods market and the people who can afford those goods. Whether it's a Milford handbag or a $2,000-a-night hotel, we are talking to the

414

same demographic. They want the latest thing of good taste that mirrors their status.'

Adrenaline began to course round Roger's veins. This was the reason he had switched his focus away from the Milford boardroom and out into the real world where real deals were being done. Emma could keep her silly little bags — here was an opportunity to make some serious money.

'I'll be frank with you Roger. I'm looking for investors,' said Ricardo flatly. 'Partners, if you'd like. People with vision and flair in tune with my own and of course a little money,' he laughed.

'You were thinking of me?' queried Roger.

'I think we could talk about it. I read about you, I hear about you from friends in London. I know you don't control Milford but you want to. I hear you are ambitious and creative. Just like me.'

Roger felt his chest puff out.

'What level of investment were you thinking?' he asked. 'And for what return?'

'Ten million dollars for a 20 per cent stake. My business-plan outlines an investor's exit strategy after five years for a 35 per cent return. That's on conservative estimates. However I think eco-tourism is about to go through the roof. You could be buying into a slice of the world's most successful hotel chain at ground level.'

Roger had no idea if this was a sound investment or not but ten million dollars was certainly more money than he could get his hands on. He made the quick conversion from dollars to sterling and decided the only possible way to do it, *should he wish to do it*, was to sell his Milford shareholding.

'With your corporate experience, a board position would of course be open to you,' added Ricardo. 'You would enjoy that, yes? Why don't you bring your wife out to São Paulo? Stay at my home.'

415

'I'm sure she would enjoy that,' said Roger thoughtfully.

Ricardo reached over and thumped Roger's shoulder.

'To make money you have to take risks, my friend. And you have to be able to grasp the opportunities when they come along.'

For the first time in a long time Roger began to feel the heady excitement of business and it was intoxicating. Having spent the last year feeling emasculated and powerless as Emma transformed the company around him, paying casual disregard to his talents, he was enjoying the way Ricardo's proposal made him feel: back in charge of his destiny. Being a board director of the most luxurious eco-hotel chain in the world would give him even greater perks than the ones he had at Milford. It would be a bigger challenge and bring greater rewards. Plus Ricardo was such a compelling character. He saw much of himself in the Brazilian and felt pleased and flattered that Ricardo wanted to bring him into his venture.

'Who else is investing?'

'Maybe you won't know them,' shrugged Ricardo. 'Friends. People like me.' He rattled off a few names. Roger recognized most of them.

'Why me?'

'Because I have a good feeling about you, Roger. I think you can do big things. I think you believe that too, eh?'

They arrived at a set of large wrought-iron gates which opened after Ricardo had muttered quick-fire Portuguese into an intercom. It was a large plantation-style house.

'Here we are,' he said.

'And where is here?' asked Roger, a little apprehensively.

'A friend's, where we can have fun,' said Ricardo, slapping him on his back which felt sore from the sun. They climbed out of the Rolls and were admitted by a doorman in a black polo neck. Inside was a large parlour-type room with velvet sofas and a mahogany bar in one corner behind which a beautiful raven-haired girl was mixing a couple of caiprihinas. Roger instantly knew what sort of 'friend' Ricardo had. This was a high-class whorehouse, a pleasure palace where deals were sealed and not just in the bedroom. He had friends with high-powered corporate jobs in London and New York who had encountered places like this when doing business in certain parts of the world, but he had never been to one himself. Ricardo looked over at him with a small knowing smile.

'Fernandez is a great girl,' he said, tipping his glass towards the barmaid.

She was indeed; she could have been a supermodel or a Latino movie star. Thick black hair cascaded down her back and her eyes were the colour of Cognac. Roger had some experience with hookers – he'd had a regular girl in his thirties before he'd met Rebecca – but Roger felt a crushing sense of guilt as the luscious brunette sat close to him, the curve of her breast like a ripe peach spilling over her low-scooped dress. But his sex life with Rebecca had slowed of late and as Fernandez put her hand at the top of his thigh, he felt himself grow hard immediately.

'I'm going upstairs,' said Fernandez seductively. 'Come up when you're ready.'

Roger glanced at Ricardo.

'We travel to Bahia tomorrow and look over the business-plan. In the meantime I want you to have some fun.'

Roger pushed away his thoughts of Rebecca. After all, it was rude to refuse – it might even damage the deal. He stood up and headed towards the stairs, a small smile on his face.

40

Dressed in nothing but a cream silk Sabbia Rose dressing-robe that skimmed over every curve, Cassandra watched Max pour two glasses of wine, determined to make every minute of his flying visit to her apartment count. It was 9 p.m. on a Monday night and he'd already told her he couldn't stay much after midnight without Laura asking questions. Padding across the spacious living room she pressed a remote control so that the open fire set into the wall roared to life, feeling its warmth through her gown. She rarely drank alcohol at home but she was grateful for the Chablis that Max handed her. The last two months had been hectic. Not only had there been the Georgia Kennedy shoot to organize, she'd been busy planning her empire. Her latest project was researching the feasibility of a Cassandra perfume, for which she had visited a perfume manufacturer in Paris and flown out to visit their factory in Grasse, all of which had been written off as researching brand extensions for *Rive*. Max had taken off his shoes and tie and unbuttoned the top two buttons of his shirt. He picked up a black leather portfolio on the glass coffee table and flicked through. Inside were a dozen mocked-up covers for Cassandra's magazine, *Grand*.

'Just a few ideas I've been throwing around with an art director friend.'

She didn't need Max to tell her they were good. They were fabulous in every sense: classy, intelligent and commercial all at the same time. Cassandra was more excited about the prospect of having her own magazine than anything else in years. Except perhaps the prospect of getting Max all to herself.

'Speaking of work, come here,' said Max, fetching his briefcase and taking a document from it.

'What's that?' asked Cassandra, curious.

'A proposition for you.'

'Really?'

He strode over to her by the fire and Cassandra thought how glorious he looked in its glow: powerful thighs under fitted Brioni trousers, light casting shadows on his face so that he looked mysterious, almost feral.

'We've been tracking a medium-sized French holding company with a view to acquiring it,' he said.

Cassandra's interest began to wane.

'Darling, you're a partner in a private equity company. Isn't that what you do every day?' she sighed.

'This company is largely involved in the paper and timber industries; those are the divisions of the group we really want, but they have other interests − a tyre company, an insurance brokerage − things we'll probably sell on if we buy the holding group.'

Cassandra took a sip of wine to hide her yawn.

'Why are you telling me this? A share tip-off? Because being CEO of a tyre company isn't exactly what I had in mind.'

'The company has a textile division which contains a little jewel,' continued Max, his dark eyes boring into her. 'Clochiers. What do you know about it?'

Cassandra's eyes opened wide.

'Clochiers? Of *course*. They were a 1930s couture house, smaller, less influential than Schiaparelli or Madame Vionnet, but well known for their beautiful day dresses. Maria Clochiers died young before the label could ever really take off, but fashion historians believe that had she lived she could have been as big as Coco Chanel.'

Max grinned, swilling the Chablis round in the bottom of his glass.

'That's what my analysts told me too,' he smiled. 'I think you could do something special with Clochiers.'

'Me?'

She immediately thought of discussing it with Giles. He was an expert on French design houses of the 1920s and 1930s and would know all there was to know about Clochiers. Max nodded.

'It's still a working company, but clearly off fashion's radar, manufacturing small-scale evening wear – scarves and the like – to an aging client base. In the right hands I think it could be brought back to life.'

Cassandra was practically salivating. Clochiers! Her mind raced ahead, thinking of the things she could do with a brand of this heritage, of this class. *Who needs Milford?*

'What are you proposing?' she asked, trying to be as business-like as her semi-sheer robe would allow.

'When we break up the holding company, we could sell Clochiers to you. Obviously not you by yourself, unless you have large reserves of money I don't know about,' he smiled. 'You'll need to bring some equity yourself to the table, but I can arrange additional debt financing and I'll be an investor myself along with other well-matched partners.'

'It sounds very interesting,' she replied, trying to keep her cool.

Max placed his wine glass on the table.

'But that's enough talking shop for one evening.'

Cassandra smiled and beckoned him over.

'Well, are you just going to stand there or are you going to fuck me?'

'Beg me for it,' he said taking a step towards her and untying her gown so her round breasts sprang lose. He took his palm and placed it over her nipple, circling it slowly until it became rock hard.

'Beg me,' he repeated.

'Never,' she whispered, her pupils dilating with need. Right now she wanted nothing more than to feel his cock deep inside her. The excitement of the proposal still buzzing through her, she was desperately, painfully hungry for him.

He licked two fingers and she parted her legs in readiness. She groaned as his fingertips curled into her wetness, her breasts pressing against the cool cotton of his shirt as he planted soft butterfly kisses on her neck. She pulled him down onto the rug as he scrambled out of his clothes. His body positioned over her, his strong hands parted her legs so far apart she could feel cool air on her ripe clitoris. His hands moved up her body, gripping her hair and she could smell herself on his fingertips. After a few maddening moments he inched his cock into her, so slowly that she screamed out in frustration. And when he'd filled her entirely, he increased his thrusts faster and faster until she came in white-hot release, the climax still shuddering through her body as she felt Max erupt inside her. They didn't move for a few seconds afterwards.

'You do realize you're very stubborn,' said Max softly, pulling her into the crook of his arm. Cassandra didn't reply, biting her lip to stop herself from speaking, suddenly frightened by the force of the feelings that Max stirred to the surface, feelings that were fighting to make themselves heard.

'I love you,' she whispered, but her mouth was pushed against his shoulder and the words were lost in the folds of his cotton shirt.

41

The Feathers was unusually busy for a Saturday night, thought Emma as she stepped into the warm pub. She looked around anxiously – she hated going into pubs on her own. She saw that Ruan was at his usual corner table, a pint of Guinness in front of him, chatting to some boys from the factory. Standing behind them was Rob. Even in a room crowded full of people, bodies pressed up against each other, she could hear his voice and his laughter. He seemed to know everyone in the place; talking, winking or back-slapping everyone who walked past him. It irritated Emma. She hadn't been into the pub in weeks, whereas Rob had obviously been virtually living there. These days she seemed to spend Saturday nights asleep on the sofa, too weary to do anything except read or listen to music. She was certainly too tired to go out, especially when the nights were short, cold and debilitating. But tonight Stella had some friends down from London and attendance at the Feathers was apparently compulsory. So despite the fact that she'd been feeling under the weather all day she'd popped down, her cherry red jumper making her look more perky than she felt. She was at the bar vainly trying to get served when she felt someone squeeze in beside her.

'Do my eyes deceive me or is this Miss Emma Bailey in the pub?'

Rob casually waved at the barmaid who immediately stepped over.

'You make it sound like the passing of Halley's Comet,' said Emma after she had ordered. 'A once in a lifetime's sighting.'

'Well, you don't come down that often.'

'I come down plenty,' she said defensively. 'You're only here three nights a week so you're hardly in a position to monitor my every move.'

'I have my spies,' smiled Rob.

'Yes, I'm sure,' said Emma. Realizing he wasn't going to be so easily shaken off, Emma sighed.

'I think Stella's in the back snug,' she said. 'I hear she has some pretty London ladies in tow.'

'In that case, Ruan can fend for himself,' said Rob.

The back part of the pub was bursting at the seams. It was so hot that the windows were dripping with condensation and Irish music was playing loudly.

'Emma. Over here,' shouted Stella from a corner table where she was sitting with three beautiful girls who all had that fashionable metropolis polish, aided by the flattering addition of candlelight. Emma was not at all surprised when Rob went and squeezed himself in the booth next to Petra, Stella's prettiest friend.

'We're waiting for Johnny to drop in, then we're going over to his parents' place,' said Stella, pulling her hair up into a ponytail.

'What's it like?' asked Emma. 'Isn't it the biggest house in Oxfordshire?'

'Something like that. You can come and see for yourself.

424

His mum and dad aren't around his week and we're all staying over. Come.'

Curiosity tempted Emma, but her hands felt clammy and her heart seemed to be beating faster than usual.

'I'd love to, but I feel a bit crock,' she replied, taking a sip of wine and wishing it were water.

'Rob?' asked Stella.

Emma stole a look at him, willing him to turn them down. It wasn't as if she was interested in Rob, but she had come to know him and he was a more complex man than he pretended. She wished he could be something other than a womanizing Peter Pan when he was around her.

'I can't,' he shrugged. 'I have an early start tomorrow. I'm having to go visit a recording studio in Devon.'

'What? To see a band?' asked Petra, balancing her chin on her hand prettily.

'Yeah, actually. Kowalski.'

'Wow,' Petra's enormous aquamarine eyes lit up. 'That's impressive. Stel said you were a big cheese in the music biz. Can I come too?'

Emma glanced up to see Rob looking at her, giving her a complicit smile.

'Rob. You coming?' shouted a voice over the music.

They all looked up to see Ruan standing by the snug door. He was tapping his watch and motioning towards the exit.

'They want me to go to this pub music quiz somewhere,' said Rob, glancing longingly at Petra. 'Apparently I'm their secret weapon. Sorry, ladies.'

'Make him stay!' whimpered Petra as he left the pub. 'In fact, make that other good-looking one stay too,' she added, turning to look at Ruan through the window. Emma was feeling worse by the minute. A group of rugby players had moved into the snug and were cheering and singing songs. One of them stumbled over a stool and fell against Emma.

'Sorry, love,' he laughed, spilling beer over her jeans.

Emma's heart was racing now and she could feel her forehead bead with sweat. The pub walls seemed to be closing in on her and the jukebox music and songs echoed around her head.

'I just have to step outside,' she mumbled to the others, but they were gossiping and laughing and hadn't seemed to notice Emma's distress. She pushed her way through the crowd until a blast of cold outside air hit her. She staggered into the car park and sank down onto a freezing cold stone step, put her head between her knees and forced herself to take deep breaths. She felt a little better with cold fresh air in her lungs.

'Em. Are you OK?'

She looked up to see Rob leaning down to take her arm. He led her over to a bench opposite the pub.

'Sorry, I don't know what that was,' she said slowly, still trembling. 'It felt like a panic attack.'

Rob sat down on the bench besides her keeping his arm wrapped around her. Two men were climbing into a taxi and Rob waved them on, indicating for them to leave without him.

'A panic attack?'

'I don't know,' said Emma, squeezing her eyes shut. 'Maybe it wasn't. I feel like shit, though.'

'I think you're working too hard,' said Rob, shaking his head. 'Your body is crying out for you to stop.' The tone of his voice was stern but concerned.

'I'm fine, honestly, I'm fine,' insisted Emma. 'I shouldn't have gone to the pub, that's all. It was too noisy and busy and I just felt I was being crushed. You go to the pub quiz. I think I'll call a taxi home.'

'I'm worried about you.'

'Don't be, really. It's passed, whatever it was.'

426

'Seriously, Em,' he said, real concern in his voice. 'You need a break. Have you had a holiday this year? Stella said you never went on that Costa Rica trip.'

'I've been too busy.'

'And it's killing you.'

He dipped his hand into his pocket and called a taxi from his mobile. Feeling less wobbly now, Emma was actually enjoying the feeling of someone taking care of her. It was something she wasn't used to.

'You're right,' she said softly when he'd come off the phone. 'I think I do need a break.'

'Why is work so important to you?' he asked seriously, studying her face.

She shrugged.

'It's all I have.'

'OK, that's it. I'm picking you up at 10 a.m. tomorrow,' he said suddenly.

'I suspect I might be in bed.'

'If you're ill, then fair enough and I'll send Morton round with the Lemsips. If not, you're coming with me to Devon.'

'Devon?' laughed Emma weakly. Rob had such a decisive look on his face, she knew she was going to have to humour him.

'Kowalski are recording their third album. I usually swing by when my big acts are in session to see how things are going and I'm flying down tomorrow.'

'Don't be silly. I don't want to intrude on your work.'

'It's not really work. I just lurk in the background, checking they're not doing anything too experimental,' he grinned. 'Anyway, the studio is in a great spot, right by the river, and I know a fantastic place nearby for dinner. Before you ask, I have to be back in work for Monday too – that's why I'm taking the chopper. We'll be back for midnight and then you can carry on working yourself to death. Is it a deal?'

The taxi had arrived and was tooting its horn.

Emma put her hand nervously on Rob's and nodded.

'Are you feeling better?'

She nodded. 'A lot better. See you tomorrow.'

'So you're going to come to Devon?' he replied, a note of surprise in his voice.

'If some deadly virus hasn't got me in its grip, yes. I think Devon might be just what I need.'

'Consider it part of your continuing musical education.'

'In that case, count me in.'

The Brintons' Oxfordshire home, Greywood, was the most sumptuous property Stella had ever seen. Grander even than Winterfold, it was an enormous Jacobean mansion recently revived by a multi-million pound makeover courtesy of Astrid Brinton's design flair. The ground floor contained Greywood's most formal rooms including a wood-panelled library and a banqueting hall with beamed ceilings and a table that comfortably seated forty. A less formal wing of the property contained a billiards room, media room, farm-house kitchen, gym and playroom – there were even 'servants' loos', although Stella hadn't quite worked out if the term was a relic from a more distant era or whether that was how the Brintons regarded their vast team of home-help. And fittingly for the master of the house, there was a 48-track recording studio and a certified organic dairy in the grounds, which delivered ice cream, cheese and milk to the house.

Stella sat curled up on an egg chair in the playroom, a shag-piled pleasure palace that contained a bank of vintage video games and a 60-inch plasma television, wishing she was alone with her boyfriend. Johnny had only finished filming principal photography of his latest film two days ago, but instead of having a quiet weekend with Stella he'd invited his mates to Greywood and suggested Stella invite some of her own mates to make up numbers. The boys had arrived at the Feathers, just after Emma's abrupt exit, with two friends called Jamie and Piers, who had recently returned from a long hot summer in Ibiza and they had all quickly returned to Greywood to take advantage of Blake Brinton's extensive wine cellar. Now she was here, Stella was feeling uncomfortable. In the company of his posh London friends, Johnny had turned a little boorish, opening bottles of expensive claret at random and then leaving them uncorked and barely touched. It didn't help that Petra had been flirting so outrageously with Jamie; she thought they were going to have full sex up against the Space Invaders machine. It was already past 2 a.m. and Stella was feeling tired, with no desire to keep herself pepped up with the cocaine that was circulating around.

'I'm going to bed,' she smiled at Johnny, expecting him to take the hint.

'I'll see you up there in a little while, hon,' he said kicking back on the sofa, a bottle in his hand.

Against her better judgement Stella went upstairs. The Brintons still kept a bedroom for their son which had been redecorated as part of the house's tasteful overhaul. Grey silk wallpaper hung on the walls, along with a framed selection of magazine covers featuring Johnny. There was a vast, oak, sleigh bed against one wall and a claw-foot bath in a large bay window. Stella undressed, switched off the lights and slipped into bed in her bra and thong waiting for Johnny. She lay back on the pillow, her eyes wide awake, straining her ears for sound. *Where the hell is he?* Outside she could hear the screech of an owl. She struggled to stay awake, but the bath tap was dripping and its hypnotic sound pulled her eyelids closed.

Suddenly Stella awoke with a start. It was pitch black

and she turned over to find the bed beside her empty. She turned on the bedside lamp: 4 a.m. – Johnny should have been here hours ago. She slipped out of bed, pulled a towelling robe from a hook nearby the bath and went out into the corridor. The dance music that had been blaring through the house earlier was gone and now it was so still that she could hear a violent snoring coming from one of the guest bedrooms. Stella crept through the house feeling on edge, but angry. *Where the hell was he?*

The playroom was empty and dark, the kitchen too. Perhaps he was playing snooker, she thought, trying to remember where in this labyrinth of rooms the billiards room was. She thought she heard faint laughter and followed the noise, unconsciously walking on tiptoes. As she drew closer, she had a sudden sense of foreboding as she remembered what Emma had said about Johnny in the summer: *You know he has a bad reputation.* There had been other things too; a blind piece in the *Sun* about a hot young actor having an on-set fling with his older co-star. That couldn't have been Johnny and Lisa Ladro? She wanted to turn back and hide. The truth was what she feared most.

She pushed open the billiard room door a crack and saw Petra sitting on the edge of the pool table, her legs apart, Johnny standing between them, their faces were inches apart, Petra's head tipped suggestively to one side.

They sprang apart when they saw her.

Stella could feel her cheeks burning red with embarrassment and fury.

'I was just telling Petra the differences between billiards, pool and snooker,' said Johnny casually. Stella turned and fled. With nowhere to go – home was ten miles away and she was stuck without transport in the middle of one thousand acres of estate – she ran back to the bedroom and

430

locked the door behind her. Seconds later Johnny was banging on it furiously.

'Stella! You're being an idiot. We were just playing pool.'

'Playing away, more like!' screamed Stella, hot, furious tears flowing down her cheeks.

'Stella, if you don't open the door, I'm going to break it down.'

He banged on it insistently, the door rattling alarmingly in the frame.

'Stella! I mean it! Open it *now*!'

Reluctantly, she unlocked the door. Johnny ran in and tried to hold her, but she fought him off.

'Get away from me!' she shouted, slapping him across the face.

He pulled back and rubbed his cheek.

'I deserved that,' he said quietly. 'But she threw herself at me. I get that Stella, you know I do. But nothing happened.'

'Oh yes, it's so fucking tough, being Johnny Brinton, isn't it?' she spat.

He grabbed her shoulders and held her tight.

'I love you, Stella. Honestly, *nothing happened*.'

She wanted to believe him. They hadn't been actually kissing, or even touching. But it was enough. The tears started rolling down again.

'Do you know what people have been saying behind my back?' she sobbed, collapsing on the bed. 'Poor Stella. Johnny Brinton can't keep his dick in his pants.'

'This isn't those Lisa Ladro rumours again, is it?' he sniffed. 'For God's sake Stella, if you're going to be in the public eye, you're going to have to get used to people making up this shit.'

'And you expect me to trust you when you behave like that?'

431

They looked at each other in silence.

'I want you to trust me,' said Johnny. 'I want you to know you're the only girl in my life.'

'You don't want a girlfriend,' snapped Stella. 'You want a fan club.'

'Marry me,' he said quietly.

For a minute she wasn't sure what he had said but his eyes had a profound look.

'What did you say?' she said, wiping her tears away with the back of her hand.

He took her hand, gave her a long smouldering look, the sort of look that had made him a star. Then he got down on one knee.

'Stella Chase,' he asked, 'will you marry me?'

42

By helicopter the journey down to Devon's Camel Estuary took just under an hour. Rob was flying the helicopter while Emma sat in the seat next to him, watching the English countryside slip by, through a glass panel beneath her feet. She couldn't believe how, only twelve hours earlier she had felt so panicked and dizzy when she had been forced to leave the Feathers. Now she felt happy and carefree and was looking forward to the day with a sense of excitement. Finally they flew over Camel Studios, circling the area. The building was a converted stone watermill perched on the edge of a wide tidal creek fringed with golden beech forest. It was set in large grounds: as they landed, Emma could see goal-posts for a five-a-side football pitch and a jetty complete with small boat which took musicians and crew across the creek to the nearest road. Rob had requested an isolated studio for Kowalski's recording session: he felt it was the best way to protect his investment, not to mention the safety of the band members. After a disastrous holiday in the Greek islands, Ste Donahue and his girlfriend Clover had almost hospitalized themselves with a reckless drink and drugs binge. Ste had spent six weeks in the notorious Second

433

Chances rehabilitation facility drying out and although Sid McKenzie, Kowalski's manager, swore that Ste was off the drugs, Rob wanted to do whatever he could to keep him out of trouble. An inaccessible studio wouldn't prevent Kowalski bringing drugs in of course; over the years Rob had witnessed all manner of craziness during recording sessions, but at least it might keep any troublesome hangers-on away. That was his hope, anyway.

It was a glorious late morning as they ducked under the blades of the helicopter and walked towards the studio. The creek shimmered silver and bronze and although there were clouds on the horizon, for now they had been blessed with a window of warm sunshine. Rob led Emma through the building, past walls hung with dozens of gold and platinum albums, and straight into the control room, the studio's nerve centre. It was a surprisingly cramped space dominated by a huge mixing desk which featured rows and rows of tiny knobs and sliding faders, over which was a large glass window looking into the 'live room' where Kowalski were playing. Rob and Emma stood by the door and watched as two sound engineers and an intense-looking man Rob introduced as 'Chris the producer' worked busily at two computer monitors and a huge rack of electronic gizmos, all of which were connected by a tangle of coloured cables. As Rob spoke to Chris, Emma took a seat and absorbed the sights and sounds around her. Even for a relative pop music Luddite, Emma could feel the magic in the air and she had to stop herself from grinning. Rob certainly looked happy too. Every now and then he would comment on a certain phrase or riff and tell Chris how fantastic it was sounding; she could see passion pulsing in his veins and his face was creased in seriousness as he listened to the tracks play back.

'Nice one, Ste, let's take some time out,' said Chris into a microphone after the singer had done his vocals. They all went through into a room that adjoined the control room, a chill-out area that contained a table football game and some sofas. They said hello to the band, but Emma felt a little awkward until Ste walked over to her and smiled.

'Hi there, you wanna play?' he asked, the words muffled by the cigarette hanging out of his mouth.

At first Emma was alarmed, assuming he was referring to the guitars lying about the room until she saw he was pointing towards the table football.

'Sure,' she said cautiously.

Ste walked around the other side of the table and expertly flipped a ball onto the table.

'So you're the bag lady that Clover did some stuff for, right?' he said, spinning a handle so a line of plastic footballers whacked the ball down the pitch.

'Bag lady!' laughed Emma. 'Well, that's one way of describing me. How is Clover?'

'In New York working. Probably better that way for a while, seeing as we're both trying to keep clean.'

He looked up and motioned at Rob who was talking intently to Chris.

'So you with the boss now?' he asked with a cheeky smile.

Emma flushed. She felt a little exposed without Rob's protective presence.

'He's just a friend,' she said quickly, spinning a handle and ramming the ball into the back of the net.

'Does Rob have female friends? I've never known it,' smiled Ste.

'Ah, I see you know him then.'

Despite herself, she found herself warming to Ste. He was not the sinister strung-out poet the newspapers depicted him as.

'Yeah, well Rob is my fucking idol,' smiled Ste, knocking

the ball down to Emma's end of the table again. 'We'd still be playing in tiny pubs if it wasn't for him.'

'Did he discover you?'

He nodded and took a swig of black coffee from a poly-styrene cup.

'Two years ago we were some no-mark band on the road in a shitty tour bus that used to be my dad's old window-cleaning van. We were going nowhere and my dad wanted his van back.'

'The end of the dream,' giggled Emma.

'Yeah,' he laughed. 'So we cobbled together some cash to do a demo. Six or seven tracks which we'd put on a CD and sent to anyone we could think of: journos at the NME, DJs, record companies, you know. We put it on MySpace and sold shit-loads of the CD, but still, it's hardly playing Wembley Stadium, is it?'

Emma had stopped playing to listen to his story.

'Then some geezer made contact saying he loved our stuff and wanted to meet up. Said he was from a record company. We were like, "Yeah, *right*!", thinking it was a mate taking the piss. But it was Rob. He was working in America then, Vice President or something and he rolled up to see us in this pub in Manchester. He'd come all the way from fucking New York, can you believe it?'

'He must have liked you.'

'You don't get a fucking bog standard record company scout coming north of Highgate, let alone the VP of one of the biggest record companies in the world. Turns out Rob trawls MySpace, pubs and clubs all the time looking for new talent. It's not his job but he does it because he loves it. He *believes*, man.'

'Well, he certainly did you proud,' said Emma, knowing that Kowalski had just had a US Billboard top ten hit, a rarity for a British band. Ste looked over his shoulder before blowing a smoke ring.

'Our manager wanted us to move labels,' he said in a low voice, 'but I was having none of it. Rob cares about the talent and you'd be amazed how rare that is in this business.'

Emma turned to look at Rob laughing with the sound engineer. She felt so warm inside she felt her heart might melt. In that moment, she realized how much she was attracted to him. He was good-looking. That was obvious; *too obvious*, but that wasn't what was making her feel this way now. She liked their banter, their companionship. She enjoyed the way he made her laugh, challenged her and helped her beyond the call of friendship. And yes, she used to think he was frivolous. Yes, he had a worrying track record with women, but today she felt proud to be at his side. Today she respected him, admired him. Today she wanted to kiss him. *God, what's happening to me?* she wondered.

How she wanted to go home! From her relaxed happy mood as they had flown in, Emma now felt on edge, completely self-conscious and embarrassed, convinced that her feelings were transparent. After lunch every hour had seemed to drag by interminably. By 5 p.m., she was jumpy with nerves, anxious about Rob's plan to have dinner at his secret fabulous restaurant. She knew she should be excited and if she had been more confident with the opposite sex it might have been easier to interpret Rob's invitation to Devon as sexual interest, especially when she'd found out Jessica was out of the picture. But with a sinking feeling, Emma rationalized that he was simply being nice to her, just as he had been all year. Rob gave Ste a bear hug, the singer so thin and slight he almost disappeared in Rob's embrace. The goodbyes complete, everyone headed back inside the mill and Rob led Emma back to the helicopter, speaking to someone on his mobile as they went.

'Do you know what, honey?' he said as he hung up.

Honey! thought Emma, her heart lurching again.

'. . . I think we might have to skip dinner.'

'But I thought you said they were the best steaks in the west.'

'They are,' said Rob with a frown. 'But there's bad weather on the way. If we leave now and don't stop off at Lucknam Park we should just miss it. I have to fly to New York tomorrow afternoon. The last thing I need is to get stuck here.'

Emma tried to hide her disappointment, hoping that he might even suggest staying at the studio overnight.

'Well, I don't fancy being up there in a storm,' she said pointing towards the sky. 'It is getting dark.'

'You mean am I night-rated?' he grinned handing her a pair of headphones to block out the noise of the flight.

'Night-rated?'

'Qualified for flying in the dark. Don't worry, you're in safe hands.'

The whoop-whoop of the blades grew into a roar and the helicopter pulled away from the ground, dipping and bobbing until the studio grew smaller and smaller in the growing dark. They flew low and rain began spotting on the window. Rob had a frown of concentration between his eyebrows and she felt a rush of lust.

It was five-thirty and the ground was almost invisible except for the odd twinkle of a village beneath them. The clouds in the sky looked very big now, like thick puddles of tar. For twenty minutes the journey was fairly smooth. Despite the chugging of the blades overhead, Emma felt remarkably peaceful, as if she were floating in a little bubble. Then she felt a jolt from under her seat, followed by a mechanical clunking sound. She looked at Rob and saw anxiety on his face.

Emma was not easily scared but her hands gripped the edge of her seat.

'What was that?' she asked.

'Nothing to worry about,' said Rob's voice crackling through the headphones, not sounding too convincing. 'Just turbulence.'

The wind was now whipping furiously around the helicopter so it was bobbing around like a cork at sea. When it suddenly dropped thirty feet Emma felt her breathing almost stop.

Rob's eyes scanned the instrument panel in front of him. 'I'm going to have to land,' he said, his voice calm despite the danger. Emma scrunched her eyes tightly and prayed.

They were now only a hundred feet from the ground and Emma squealed involuntarily as the wheels of the helicopter clipped the top of a tall tree. She saw a dark open field spin below them, the craft swinging violently as the strong winds swirled around it, then the glare of the landing lights on the grass that was blown flat by the helicopter. And then they were down. She exhaled several quick, sharp breaths and Rob reached over and grabbed her hand.

'It's fine, honey. It's fine,' he said, his face pale. 'We're on the ground.'

Rob cut the engines and the blades slowly whirled to a stop. Suddenly they were wrapped in an eerie silence.

'Where are we?'

'In a field,' said Rob with the hint of a smile. 'I'd guess somewhere in west Somerset, we weren't blown too far off course.'

He got out of the craft and went round to her side, helping her out onto the damp grass, the rain and wind biting at her legs.

'This is where we get killed by a raging bull,' said Emma grimly, looking around for signs of life.

'Are you OK?' asked Rob.

She nodded and he pulled her close then took her hand

and they began walking towards some lights, the mud squelching all over her shoes. After a few minutes they reached a small farmhouse. The door opened immediately and a man of about fifty in a thick coat and Wellington boots stepped out.

'What the bloody hell has happened?' he blustered.

'I'm sorry, I had to emergency-land my helicopter in your field,' said Rob politely. 'My mobile has no reception and I need to call for help.'

A lady with grey fluffy hair popped her head around the doorframe.

'Come in, it's filthy out there. This is Alan and I'm Joan. Now what did you say? You've crashed your helicopter?' she asked with wide-open eyes.

'Not crashed exactly,' said Emma as they stepped inside the warm house. 'But we won't be able to take off again in this weather.'

'If we've crushed any of your crops I will pay for any damage, of course,' said Rob.

'. . . bloody think so too,' he mumbled after Rob disappeared to make some calls. The woman was much more welcoming however, plying Emma with sweet tea laced with brandy. Rob reappeared.

'Turns out Babington House is about twenty miles away. They said they can arrange for a car to pick us up.'

'What about the helicopter?' asked Emma.

'I want to get it checked out before I even think about flying it anywhere.'

He turned to the farmer and his wife.

'I'm going to move it out of your field as soon as I can. As I said I'll happily paid for any inconvenience.'

Joan pressed a mug into Rob's hand.

'Hot cider,' she smiled. 'You must need it. Now did I hear you're thinking of going over to Frome? We won't hear of it, will we, Alan? Not in this weather. See that barn you walked past on the way in? Well, we use it as a B&B in the summer. It'll do you just right. No charge, not after what you two have just been through.'

Emma caught Rob's eye and managed a smile. 'I don't mind if you don't,' he shrugged.

Joan tightened the belt of her dressing-gown further around her ample waist.

'That's settled then. Let me go and make the bed up.'

Bed *singular*. Emma felt another rush of panic – just what she needed.

The B&B was surprisingly cosy. Just one room with a tiny *en suite*, containing some simple furniture and an iron bed covered in a vast patchwork quilt, but the carpet was thick underfoot and the wooden shutters blocked out the hostile weather. Joan lit the fire and left them with a terracotta pot of hot cider. Emma gratefully took off her wet shoes and sat on the bed, trying to rub the dirt off with some tissues sitting on the bedside table. She dared not look up at Rob in this confined space and emotionally charged atmosphere. *Or is it all in my head?* she wondered.

'Well, you can't say I don't know how to show a girl a good time,' said Rob. 'Believe me, I'm usually better than this on a first date.'

'First date?' replied Emma, feeling a chug of butterflies.

'To think I brought you here to help you de-stress out,' he said, avoiding her question.

'We're in one piece,' smiled Emma. 'Plus I've been to the famous Camel Studios. All in all, a good day.'

Rob sat on a threadbare chaise longue in the corner, looking drained.

'Ste loves you, you know,' said Emma, putting down her shoe.

441

Rob smiled.

'He'll be one of the world's biggest stars within the next three years if the drugs don't kill him.'

'He seemed OK today.'

'Hmm. For now.'

'Why did you come all the way from New York to meet a band you'd only ever heard on MySpace?'

'Is that what he told you?' he asked, raising an eyebrow.

'He also told me that he won't move record labels while you're still in charge.'

'He told you *that*?' said Rob, looking brighter. 'I wish all my artists would share his point of view.'

'Are you having problems?' said Emma gently. If she recognized anything, it was the voice of an anxious senior executive. Rob shrugged.

'The industry is really tough at the minute. It's one of the reasons I'm off to New York tomorrow: a showdown with my dad about the company's bottom line.'

'Profits are down?'

He nodded and moved over to the bed, slowly telling her of his *annus horribilis*; defections, redundancies and loss of morale. How he was under pressure from New York – and his father – to continue with more cost-cutting to keep profits stable. And of his feeling of isolation, and of how he felt he was a lone voice championing the music.

'Because it's suddenly all about the money.'

'But it seems to me . . .' Emma hesitated before she spoke, out of her commercial comfort zone, but eager to help if she could. 'It seems to me that you need to invest not cut corners. Your industry relies on talent. Creatives, *the artists*, don't care about the bottom line, they care about companies caring about *them*.'

Rob looked at her curiously. 'So what do you suggest?'

'You're not a money-man Rob, you're passionate about

442

music. Ste knows it and I bet the industry knows it. Hollander should become the company that champions the artist, encouraging creativity, investing heavily in new talent, not cutting back on it. Perhaps you need to decentralize the company; form new semi-independent labels for new talent, hothouses if you like. Because if you can get back your reputation as the company who loves the art not the profit, chances are you'll attract the best new talent *and* a decent proportion of the established talent. Think about it; you say disgruntled bands are leaving other labels, well they've got to go somewhere. Incentivize them to sign to you. In bad times, good companies with good management can profit. It's like the clever property developers buying up all the great land in a recession. CD sales may be down, but now's the time to invest to increase your market share. Besides, from a purely business point of view, a shift from CDs to downloads is surely a good thing because there are no production or distribution costs involved. All you have to do is pay the artists and the shareholders – and I bet they'll both like that idea.'

She sat back and took a breath. Rob just gazed at her.

'You're incredible,' he said quietly.

The atmosphere in the room had suddenly changed. Emma shifted awkwardly on the edge of the bed, wishing she had the sexual confidence to know what to do next. In every other aspect of her life she knew how to lead, but now she felt as if she was floundering out of her depth; she was afraid to take the next step.

'Just ignore me. I don't know anything about the music industry.'

'Just like you didn't know anything abut the fashion industry and now you have one of the hottest luxury goods labels in Europe.'

'Now I'm embarrassed.'

443

He paused and looked softly at her. 'You do know I've spent most of this year trying to impress you?'

Emma laughed quietly. Compliments made her nervous, especially when they came from someone she'd spent all afternoon thinking about.

'Believe me, I was never the girl that boys wanted to impress.'

'Well, I was never the boy who kept getting turned down.'

Emma laughed again. 'I've never turned you down.'

Their eyes locked across the bed and Emma forced herself not to look away. A nagging voice told her to leave the room now, she couldn't trust him; he was a womanizer and a rogue. OK, so he was sexy and fun and kind but all she would be was just another notch on his bedpost. But still . . .

Oh, let yourself be happy, she cursed herself.

Rob stood up and began to walk around the bed towards her. Emma let him come. He put his hand out and took her fingers, pulling her in until their lips met in a soft, gentle kiss, growing deeper in intensity until she was aware of nothing else except the warmth of his body against her and a flood of delirious happiness washing over her. His hand slipped under her cashmere sweater to caress the curve of her back. She lifted her arms so he could slip the garment off, wet lust stirring between her thighs. He lowered his head to kiss the soft skin of her shoulder, before unhooking her bra so her breasts sprang free. He cupped one, caressing her hard nipple with his tongue as she almost laughed out loud in pleasure at his expert, exquisite touch. She unzipped his jeans while he hastily removed his navy cotton sweater. Sinking onto the bed they moved more urgently, touching and kissing each other, their need rising.

'You're so beautiful,' he murmured, his hot breath against her neck. For once she didn't challenge him, happy to let him peel off the rest of her clothes until they were both naked. As his lips went down on her, she almost flinched at his touch, and when she thought she could take no more he drew his firm body on top of her, savouring the moment as he slid himself into her, parting her thighs wider and wider. She came before he did, biting his shoulder as the sweet violent pulse tore through her body. He followed a few seconds later, collapsing on her, a smile of satisfaction on his lips and she lay back in his arms exhausted, surprised and contented. It was Rob who spoke first. 'What the hell took us so long?' he laughed.

Emma woke slowly. Weak sunlight forced its way through cracks in the shutters and for a moment she had absolutely no idea where she was. Turning, she could feel a warm body breathing gently beside her and the events of the previous night flooded back.

'Good morning,' said Rob, his voice all croaky with sleep.

Anxiety flooded over her as she waited for his next move. Would he move away from her or shuffle closer in? She examined his face, waiting to see the flicker of regret. But there was none.

'What a night,' he said.

'Not every night you have to land a helicopter in a blowing gale.'

'That's not what I'm talking about,' he said with a lazy smile.

He pulled her into the crook of his arm and she was flooded with relief, lying there as he kissed her hair.

'How cold do you think that bathroom is?'

'Very. Maybe we need some more of that hot cider.'

He pulled away and propped himself up with a pillow. 'Listen, I'm flying to New York this afternoon. I've got some business over there to sort out, then it's Thanksgiving.'

He rolled his eyes and grinned. 'If I don't turn up to the family gathering my dad will cut me off without a cent.'

'We wouldn't want that, Rockefeller,' replied Emma, feeling happy and relaxed.

'So I think we'd better think about getting back.'

That was the test she thought to herself. He would be nice to her lying in the bed where they had just had sex, but what would it be like when they got back to Chilcot? Would they forget it had ever happened, or would it be something more significant? Looking at his ruffled bed-hair squashed against the pillow she knew which one she wanted.

'I'm back next Monday. How about we do something?'

'Maybe something a little less rock and roll,' she smiled.

'I'm all for that. How about dinner?'

'Hot date at the Feathers?'

'If you're lucky!' he laughed, then hesitated and, for a minute, his bravado had gone.

'Or how about you come up to London for the night?'

He touched her cheek and she felt the reassuring complicity between them.

There was a knock at the door and a grumbling of keys.

Joan the farmer's wife bustled in with a tea tray.

'We didn't make arrangements for breakfast last night,' she said, 'so I thought I'd bring it to you. I know you love-birds like breakfast in bed.'

Rob and Emma grabbed the quilt around their bodies as Joan put a tray of croissants and apple juice on the bedside table.

'Don't be so coy, lovies,' she smiled, taking her time to pour the tea. 'I've seen it all before.' As she turned, she gave them a long wink. When the door closed, Rob and Emma looked at each other, then roared with laughter.

43

'I have Glenda on the phone for you,' said Lianne, calling through to Cassandra.

Cassandra twizzled her Eames chair so she was looking out of the window and picked up the receiver.

'Glenda. What can I do for you?' she asked, rolling her gold pencil between her fingers.

'You've got Georgia Kennedy,' said an irate, barely controlled voice down the receiver.

Cassandra was momentarily floored. *How the hell did she know?*

She paused before speaking.

'We've entered into a dialogue with her people,' she said coolly. 'But frankly it's unlikely. As we both know, it's a pretty impossible get.'

'Entered into a dialogue?' repeated Glenda, sounding astonished. 'Don't give me that crap! You shot her in Sulka. She's your March cover. I *know* what happened.'

Cassandra felt her face flush with anger, wondering furiously how there could have been a confidentiality breach. Laura was too timid to ever disobey Cassandra's instructions; Giles she could trust. As for the photographer and hair and make-up team, she had made it perfectly clear they would never work in fashion again if word of the shoot got out. Was Glenda bluffing? Cassandra knew she could carry on denying it, but there was a certainty in Glenda's voice that suggested the woman was telling the truth – she knew.

'Glenda. This is our exclusive. We have gone to a great deal of effort, time and money sorting this out. It came through a personal contact and Georgia only wants to do UK *Rive*, that was part of the deal.'

'We've both been trying to get her for two years. How come you've suddenly got the coup . . .'

'You're wasting your time, Glenda. She is our cover. End of story.'

'I hope you know this is career suicide!' yelled Glenda, causing Cassandra to jerk the phone away from her ear. She was well known for ruling her office with fear. Glenda was no grande dame of fashion who operated with icy froideur; she could scream, shout and intimidate like an Eighties Wall Street trader.

'Perhaps you could use Georgia for your April cover,' said Cassandra, unable to resist the barb. She knew Glenda would rather stab herself in the eye with her Blahnik heel than run the same cover as the UK edition a month later. But Glenda had already put the phone down on her.

Forty minutes later Cassandra checked her emails. There was a message red-flagged from Glenda.

We need to talk. My PA has arranged for you to be on the 8 a.m. tomorrow morning to JFK. A car will pick you up to take you to Isaac's. Town not Country.

This time, Cassandra knew she had to obey.

The limousine met her at JFK to take her to Isaac Grey's Upper East Side home. As she sat back in the leather seats she ran through the inevitable showdown in her head, predicting how Glenda would scream and bawl and threaten, resolving that she would stand her ground and then when Glenda had blown herself out, make Isaac increase the clothing allowance she received with her salary. It was the least he could do to make up for the dreadful inconvenience.

Isaac's home was one of the most spectacular on Fifth Avenue, a stunning triplex in one of the most prestigious condos in the city with direct views over Central Park. During their affair several years earlier, Cassandra had been there many times. His Anglophile tastes were reflected in the decor; it was done out to resemble Chatsworth in miniature.

A maid in a grey uniform answered the door and Cassandra was irritated to see Glenda had arrived first. She could hear her laughing in the drawing room with Isaac. The head of the company was in his off-duty clothes; a pair of navy blue trousers, white shirt and a shapeless brown cardigan. He looked like a retired metro worker from Brooklyn, not a media tycoon worth over two billion dollars, a man who had recently sent his private jet from New York to London to pick up a briefcase he'd left in Claridges. Although he was over sixty, he walked across the room like a tiger, his shoulders rolling.

'Come in, Cassandra. Sit down. Miki has fixed some lunch.'

A walnut table by the window looked out over the park, the noise and energy of New York a whisper on the street below.

'You don't need me to tell you what a good job we all think you're doing at UK *Rive*.' He glanced at Glenda as if to include her in the reference.

'And we're amazed yet again at your resourcefulness in getting Georgia Kennedy At Home. I don't know how you got it.' He held up a hand. 'I won't ask. However you know the US has to run first with exclusives of this magnitude.'

He paused to let Miki serve them razor-cut beef carpaccio as Cassandra silently fumed. She thought that Isaac was her ally.

'The US edition has been after Georgia for a long time,' said Glenda. 'I have even had lunch with the ambassador. When they acquiesced to your cover request we feel sure that Ms Kennedy's office was under the impression she was doing the cover for us.'

'I can assure you that's not true,' snapped Cassandra. 'And where is the written rule that says the US has to run first with exclusives? We generate our own covers practically every month and I don't see you clamouring to pick those up.'

'They weren't Georgia Kennedy,' said Glenda flatly.

Isaac turned deliberately in his chair to face her. His head was slightly cocked as he spoke to her as if he was directing his speech to a small child.

'US *Rive* is the flagship magazine of this company. We have to send a message out to the industry. The best writers, the hottest exclusives. Where US *Rive* leads, other editions follow.' His sharp, dark eyes seemed to penetrate hers.

'Great, thank you,' said Cassandra sarcastically. 'Thanks for supporting our efforts.'

'You should also be aware, Cassandra,' said Glenda, leaning forward in her Biedermeier chair, 'that *Style* magazine has launched and to be frank, it's faring a little better than we expected. US *Rive* needs to be head and shoulders above the competition if we are to ring-fence our position with advertisers. I feel you have stolen our thunder on this one a little, Cassandra.'

Miki came to fill Cassandra's cup with Lapsang Souchong.

She put the cup on the saucer, touching her finger against the Sèvres porcelain to stop it from rattling.

'Given the circumstances,' said Isaac, coughing lightly, 'perhaps you could run the cover simultaneously. Why don't you both have Georgia on the March cover?'

Both Glenda and Cassandra glared at him.

'That's simply not acceptable,' said Cassandra coolly. 'Georgia Kennedy's people won't allow it.'

'Actually I spent all last night on the phone to her private secretary,' said Glenda. 'The Royal Palace are happy with the arrangement.'

Cassandra bit her lip trying to keep her cool. She knew she had pushed her luck as it was and that Isaac could fire her on the spot if he chose. Anyway, she thought, if her plan came to fruition, this entire meeting would be irrelevant. It wouldn't do any harm to step back gracefully.

'So you will pick up half of the cost of the shoot?' said Cassandra eventually.

Glenda nodded. 'I'll arrange for that straightaway.'

'See, I knew you ladies could come to an agreement,' smiled Isaac.

They finished their lunch making stilted small talk and said their goodbyes.

'So, Glenda,' said Isaac, seeing them both to the door. 'Will I see you at the opera tonight?'

Cassandra fell silent as they talked, knowing she was biding her time.

She and Glenda walked to the lift together, tension prickling between them.

'No hard feelings?' smiled Glenda coolly.

Cassandra shrugged as she pulled on her fox fur coat.

'I'm obviously not delighted.'

The lift pinged open and they walked inside, both studiously avoiding each other's gaze.

'Out of interest,' said Cassandra, still looking forward, 'how did you find out about the Georgia shoot?'

'Oh, you know, industry gossip.'

Cassandra turned to face her.

'I doubt that.'

'If you must know,' smiled Glenda sweetly, 'it was Giles Banks.'

Cassandra looked back at the lift doors to hide her surprise and fury.

'I doubt that also,' she said, keeping her voice level.

'Really? I spoke to him in the summer about a job. We've been in touch ever since. I don't think he meant to tell me,' said Glenda with relish, her mouth twisting cruelly. 'But you know, I can be very persuasive.'

The lift doors slid open and Cassandra turned to face Glenda, her eyes blazing.

'Now *that* I believe,' she said. 'But you know, Glenda, I can be very persuasive too.'

As she turned to leave, her heels clicking on the marble of Isaac's lobby, Cassandra was sure she could hear Glenda laughing softly.

44

'I was thinking about maybe Ibiza next August,' said Stella, beaming at Johnny sitting opposite her. They were having dinner at the Panton House restaurant just outside Chilcot and all evening, Stella had been unable to talk about anything else but wedding plans.

'There are some amazing villas out there,' she said licking the last of her raspberry sorbet from her spoon. 'Or maybe even your mum and dad's place in St Jean? We could invite everyone over. It would be more like a holiday than a marriage.'

Johnny shrugged.

'If we have it overseas, all our guests will want to hang around for days afterwards,' he said moodily. 'Call me a crazy romantic but do we really want one hundred and fifty people on our bloody honeymoon?'

He nodded at the waiter to request the bill.

'Anyway, I've got some good news to tell you.'

'And you've kept it quiet all through dinner, you fox,' said Stella, trying to hide her disappointment that he didn't seem as enthusiastic about the wedding planning as she was. *Still, he was a man.*

'I've got a couple of auditions in LA next week,' he said, pausing for effect, 'and one of them is with Ridley Scott!'

'That's great news,' smiled Stella. Johnny had signed to the William Morris agency in LA six weeks earlier and he was already generating a great deal of interest.

'Ridley-fucking-Scott, man!' he said, smiling to himself. 'The man's a bloody legend! I don't know why I didn't get an LA agent sooner. I can't bloody wait to get out there. Which is why we need to talk . . .'

He put his hand over Stella's and looked into her eyes.

'I've been talking with the agency and they reckon that if my career is going to take off Stateside then I need to decamp over there for a little while. I mean it makes sense, doesn't it? I've no idea how Jude Law managed to be so bloody successful living in London.'

Stella looked at him aghast, her happy mood starting to crumble.

'LA? But what about us? You know my work is here!'

'I've been thinking about that,' he said handing his black AMEX card to the waiter. 'What about going back to Cate Glazer?'

She jerked her hand away from his, sending a dessert fork clattering to the floor.

'First, leaving Milford isn't an option,' she snapped, 'and second, you know how miserable I was at Cate's.'

'What about my career?' he pouted, 'in twelve months I'll be rich enough for you never to have to work again.'

'Aren't we the progressive husband?' she said tartly.

'Fiancé,' replied Johnny. 'We're not in any rush to get married, are we?'

Stella glared at him.

'The way you've been acting tonight it's as if you don't want to get married at all.'

'Don't be ridiculous. I just think with my career taking

off, there's no big hurry is there? And anyway, you know how birds get if they think their heart-throb is completely off the market. At least if you're only engaged they still think they're in with a chance. We want to keep the box-office receipts rolling in, don't we?'

Stella stood up, throwing her napkin down on the table.

'I'm going home,' she said shaking her head incredulously.

'Keep your voice down,' he hissed. 'I'm coming with you.'

They drove back to Stella's house in silence. Once inside, Johnny took off his coat, flung it over the sofa and flopped down in an armchair.

'You do understand where I'm coming from,' he said finally. She looked at him and almost laughed at his beautiful, insolent good looks. He was so self-assured, so self-confident, so *selfish*. He really didn't think she would mind.

'Of course I understand,' she said quietly, too tired and disappointed to argue with him any longer. She walked into the kitchen to make some coffee and noticed her answer-phone was flashing red. She pressed the button.

'Stella, it's your father. Please call me.'

Stella looked at the machine, puzzled.

'What's wrong?' asked Johnny, kicking off his shoes.

'My dad,' she replayed the message. 'He sounded upset. I should call him back.'

Johnny swung his feet onto the coffee table and switched on the TV.

'Sure, babe, bring us a beer first, eh?' he called, not taking his eyes off the screen. Stella threw him a bottle, slightly harder than was necessary, and took the cordless phone into the kitchen.

'Dad. It's me. Sorry it's late but I think you called earlier. I forgot to take my mobile out with me.'

There was a long silence.

'She's left me, Stell.'

Stella felt a flood of panic. 'Who's left you, Dad?' knowing the answer to her question before she'd even asked.

'Chessie,' he croaked.

'But she's seven months pregnant,' said Stella, doing a quick calculation on her fingertips. 'She can't leave you now.'

'She can and she has and she wants half the house. I'm going to have to sell Trencarrow.'

Stella felt a hot flush of rage.

'She can't have Trencarrow!' she snapped. 'You've been there forever, it's your home! God, she's such a gold-digging cow.'

'Stella, please. That's unfair.'

'Whose side are you on?' she exploded. 'She's trying to take you for every penny you have and you're defending her?'

She could hear a faint echo down the phone; either it was a very poor line or he was crying.

'Dad, please. Come on, everything is going to be all right,' she said, feeling helpless, guilty and sad, wishing she could be there with him to nurse him with a hot toddy and a hug.

'Yes,' he said so faintly she could barely hear it.

'I'm going to come down tomorrow.'

'Please don't. I want to be on my own.'

'Dad. I'm coming. I'll call you tomorrow. You just try to get some sleep, OK? I love you.'

Stella hung up the phone gently, thinking of her father all alone in his dark farmhouse in Cornwall.

'What did he want?' asked Johnny, taking a long swig of beer and glancing away from a boxing match on television.

'Chessie's left him,' said Stella softly.

Johnny looked up and seeing the expression on her face, turned down the sound.

'Shit. What does that mean?'

'It means he's heartbroken,' snapped Stella. 'It means he's going to lose the house he loves.'

'Well, I hope it doesn't mean that you're going to have to look after him.' He took another swig of beer and turned back to gaze at the TV. 'I'm dreading it when my folks start getting really old, although my dad took so many drugs in the Seventies he'll probably cark it before he's sixty.'

She sat down on the arm of the sofa and looked at Johnny. It was just typical of him to turn the conversation around to himself.

'Well, I'm going to have to go to him,' she said. 'He sounded distraught.'

'What about his other kids?'

'My stepbrother and -sister live in Scotland. I haven't seen them in ten years. I'll speak to them tomorrow but they are both pretty useless. They see Dad less than I do.'

Hearing the wobble in her voice, Johnny finally put down his beer and moved over to her, putting an arm around her shoulders.

'But baby, it's only fair you share the load, you can't take the weight of everyone's troubles on your shoulders. Just because you're a wonderful person, don't let people take advantage of you.'

'He's my father and his wife has left him,' said Stella firmly. 'That's hardly taking advantage.' She was beginning to realize that Johnny wasn't thinking about the situation entirely altruistically. She looked at him, her eyes pleading.

'Can we drive down tomorrow in your car? Mine is in the garage having a service.'

'To St Ives?' said Johnny, frowning. 'Out of the question, honey. It's at least four hours each way and it's my mum and dad's dinner party tomorrow night. Sam Mendes is going to be there, I can't miss that, can I?'

Stella stood up, shrugging his arm off. She was losing patience rapidly.

'You don't have to come,' she said. 'Can't I just borrow the car?'

'But I need you to come to the dinner,' said Johnny, a little whine entering his voice, 'my mum will get so pissy if you don't come, she wants to hear all about the *Vanity Fair* shoot. Surely we can drive down to your dad's on Monday? I'll be free for the week then unless I get a recall for filming.'

'You selfish bastard,' snapped Stella. 'A dinner party! You think a bloody meal's more important than my father?'

Johnny stood up and moved towards her, his arms open.

'Stell, come on. You're upset. We'll go first thing Monday and I'll stay as long as you like.'

'Oh, just leave me alone,' she said shaking her head angrily as she stalked towards the bedroom. 'I'm going to bed – you can sleep in the spare room.'

'For fuck's sake,' he muttered under his breath, turning the television back up again. 'Moody, bloody women.'

It was pitch black when she awoke. Stella turned on the lamp and glanced at her watch. Four a.m. Her head was pounding and her mouth was dry. Desperate for a glass of water and an aspirin she got out of bed, peeping into the spare bedroom before she went downstairs. Johnny was fast asleep, snoring lightly, a long, tanned leg peeking from under the duvet. She longed to climb under the covers with him but shook the thought off. *If he thinks he can get around me that way, he can think again.*

She walked into the kitchen, now fully awake and feeling unaccountably anxious. Knowing she wouldn't be able to fall back to sleep, she drank the water and went over to the computer in the living room to check train times to St Ives.

She kept all the lights off except for a small lamp; she didn't want to wake Johnny and spark another confrontation. After a few minutes she heard a low insistent beep coming from somewhere in the room. She tracked it down to Johnny's coat on the sofa: the beep indicating an unread text. Curiosity needled her. Who would text Johnny in the middle of the night? Knowing it was wrong, she pressed the 'read' button on the phone.

Left you a message. Must speak to confirm a few details before we run story. Elsa x

She stared at the phone, feeling nausea rising from the pit of her stomach. Elsa? What story? *Elsa. Elsa.* She'd met a reporter called Elsa at the Dugdale Festival in the summer, a pretty showbiz writer for the *Sunday Herald. Elsa x.* That kiss was familiar: far too familiar for her liking. Feeling guilty at the intrusion, but needing to know, Stella dialled 1-2-1 to listen to his messages.

'Message left at 1.35 a.m., 25 November.'

'Hi Johnny, Elsa here,' said a bouncy voice. 'Listen, great to speak earlier. Stella's dad divorcing – wow! So sorry, but it's a great tip-off and you know that if you look after us, we'll look after you. I hope to get the story into Monday's issue. We want to be the first on this one, so it will probably go in the main paper rather than the showbiz pages. I'm rambling. It's late. Call me first thing. Need to know how long Chessie and Chris were married for, plus a few details on how cut-up Stella is: "A close friend revealed", you know the sort of stuff. Anyway, call me. Ciao.'

Stella sat there, stunned in disbelief. If he wanted to peddle stories about himself that was fine, but deeply personal stories about her and her family? *The bastard!*

'Get up!' she hissed, standing over his bed. Johnny groaned and turned away.

'I said GET UP!' she yelled, pulling his pillow from under his head.

'Hey!' he protested, rolling over and blinking at her, 'What's happening?'

His bed-head hair was sexy and tousled, his pale blue eyes squinted at her sleepily.

'You've told the papers about my *father*,' she growled, fury building inside her.

'What?' he replied groggily. 'What are you talking about?'

'Don't bother fucking denying it!' she shouted. 'You phoned that tart Elsa at the *Herald*! You told her! And what else have you told her? I suppose the pap turning up outside China Tang was your work too? Plus all the other little details of our relationship that seem to get out on a weekly basis.'

Johnny sat against the bedstead and rubbed his face.

'Don't be so bloody naïve and hypocritical, Stella,' he said sharply. 'You're quite happy to be one part of the new hot couple, aren't you? You love the attention, the party invites and the free holidays. And you love being called the new Stella McCartney and getting all that free publicity for Milford. How do you think it happens? Simply by being talented? *Grow up*. The media creates stars and you have to give them a helping hand. When we're big enough, established enough, then we hire a publicist to keep the attention away from us but we're not A-list yet. We *need* the attention right now, any way we can get it.'

'Get out,' she snarled. 'I'm sick of it – sick of you, sick of your selfishness and sick of your self-obsession.'

He laughed nervously.

'You're kicking me out?'

'It's over.'

'Over! What about *Vanity Fair*?'

'Get out!' she screamed, pulling the silver band off her

wedding finger, the stand-in ring for the engagement rock he hadn't quite got around to buying, like all the other things he had never got around to doing, not when there was his career to consider.

'And by the way,' she added, 'your cock is tiny.'

She threw the ring at his chest and stormed out.

After Johnny had called a taxi and retreated to his parents, Stella went back to bed, unable to do anything but cry.

When she finally arose at 11 a.m., red-eyed and exhausted, she went downstairs, opened the French windows and stood outside inhaling the air, oblivious to the cold.

The last thing she felt like was a long train trip to Cornwall; it was going to take nine hours with the sketchy Sunday service. But now she needed to see her father more than ever.

She poured herself a glass of red wine from the bottle that had been left on the coffee table from last night. She was all out of tears. Sinking into an armchair she looked around her; Johnny's scarf in a corner, the coffee cup he had drunk from the night before, the faint outline of his body on the sofa cushion. Tiny painful reminders of how things were, tiny reminders of how things could change so quickly.

The door bell rang. She took a deep breath and rubbed her eyes before she opened it, expecting it to be Johnny.

Tom Grand was standing at the door. She'd seen him at the Feathers on Friday night and they'd made a vague plan to all have Sunday lunch.

'I hope I've not disturbed you.'

'No, come in,' she said with faux verve.

'I was just passing. Johnny's not answering his mobile. I was wondering if we were still on for lunch today.'

His smile made her feel less alone.

461

'Are you OK?' said Tom, finally examining her face.

'Yes.'

'You're not.'

'You're right,' she laughed sadly, puffing out her cheeks so they looked like little round apples on her face.

Tom made coffee while she told him what had happened. She didn't spare a single detail. She knew Tom was Johnny's friend but it was cathartic, and anyway, she had always considered Tom to be kind and fair if one of the flakiest men she'd ever met.

'Johnny's a twat,' said Tom angrily, swigging his coffee. 'As for this Chessie character. Why would she leave her husband, seven months pregnant?'

They both looked at each other. 'Someone else.'

'Typically my car is in the garage and the trains are going to take forever.'

'I can drive you if you want,' Tom said, shrugging.

'Are you sure?' She didn't know Tom well and it was a big ask, especially as he was Johnny's friend.

'You promised me Sunday lunch. We can get it on the way to St Ives.'

45

Cassandra touched back down again in London on Sunday evening and immediately directed her driver to take her straight to Giles's apartment on a tree-lined street in Chelsea.

'Cassandra. This is a surprise,' said Giles, opening the door with a glass of wine in his hand. Over his shoulder, Cassandra could see a grey-haired forty-something man hovering at the kitchen door.

'This is Stephen, my friend from Norfolk,' said Giles smiling. 'We were just about to eat. Squid-ink pasta and scallops: there's enough for three.'

There was a delicious smell permeating around the flat, but she was in no mood to eulogize about his delicious cuisine.

'Whatever you're cooking, I think you'd better turn it off. I'm here to talk not eat.'

'Is there something wrong?'

She ignored his question and instead walked into the small, immaculately furnished living room, taking a position by the large bay window. Glancing at his friend, Giles followed her and shut the door behind him.

'Cassandra, what on earth is wrong?' he said, now looking very concerned.

She stood quietly for a moment, arms folded in front of her chest.

'You're fired,' she said finally.

Giles's mouth dropped open.

'Are you joking?' he stuttered, his face paling.

'No, Giles, I am not,' she said simply, picking up a photo from the window-sill and examining it. Giles sank into a blue leather wing-chair.

'But why?'

She looked at him, his eyes welling with tears, and felt no pity. She had helped him, trusted him, and this is how he repaid her. It only confirmed to her that her philosophy of life had been correct all along: trust absolutely no one.

'You knew the Georgia Kennedy shoot was confidential and yet you told Glenda McMahon.'

'I did not,' he said quietly. 'I never would do that.'

She snorted. 'You were in New York last week. Look me in the eye and tell me you did not visit US *Rive*.'

Colour had stained his cheeks and his aristocratic façade was visibly shaken.

'Yes, I went in to see Alannah, the features director. But she's my friend. We met to go for coffee.'

Cassandra met his gaze full on.

'Of course,' she said walking to the door.

Giles sprang from his chair and grabbed her by the arm.

'I swear I did not tell a soul about the Georgia Kennedy shoot. After all our time working together – after our years of *friendship* – you should believe me.'

Cassandra snorted. 'After all my time in the industry, Giles, I believe no one.'

She looked down at his restraining hand until he finally released her, his arm flopping by his side.

'Goodbye, Giles,' she said. 'Enjoy your squid.'

46

Tom drove Stella down to Trencarrow in Julia's car, fearing his own beaten-up Mini might not make it past Bristol. Stella winced every time Tom lit one of his red label Marlboros, trying not to breathe the noxious fumes that filled the car. But she knew she was in no position to complain. It had been so nice of him to drive her down to her father's farm in St Ives and he seemed more than willing to listen to her relationship traumas as they hurtled down the A303. It wasn't until they were passing Stonehenge that Tom finally noticed Stella's polite coughs.

'Sorry, are my ciggies bothering you?' Tom asked, frantically rolling down the window. 'God, I'm such a selfish pig.'

'Don't worry about it,' she smiled. 'I feel so on edge, I've been tempted to bum a fag off you ever since we left Chilcot, even though I haven't smoked since I was fifteen.'

'Well, I wouldn't weaken now. Filthy habit,' he grinned.

Despite his occasional thoughtlessness, Tom was good company, thought Stella affectionately. He seemed able to read her mood, making jokes and singing along to the radio to make her forget her problems, but keeping quiet when he could see a troubled, thoughtful expression on her face.

'You know I'm going to be an emotional wreck by the end of the day,' smiled Stella looking at Tom's profile. 'I just want to say thanks for putting up with me.'

'Your dad's wife has run off with someone and your boyfriend, *my friend*, has proved himself to be a complete arsehole. I think that's more than a decent excuse if things get a little watery-eyed.'

'Of course I'm upset about Johnny, but I don't know why I feel so upset and responsible about my father,' said Stella tracing her finger along the car window. 'It's not as if we're close.'

'But he's still your father,' said Tom turning his head to look at her. 'My dad moved to South Africa about twenty years ago and yet I still hope he'll turn up for my birthday, or Christmas, or phone me when he hears something good has happened in my life, rare though that may be. I used to get the occasional card with a twenty quid note but even those have stopped. Even though I expect nothing from him, I still get disappointed.'

'Does Cassandra?' asked Stella, although it was hard to imagine Tom's ball-busting sister having a vulnerable side.

'Nah,' he smiled. 'That's the thing about rejection. It either fucks you up or toughens you up.'

It was dark by the time they approached Trencarrow and that only added to the drama of the setting. The house stood on a grassy headland a few miles outside St Ives, only a hundred metres away from the cliff edge. Seagulls wheeled around overhead; the steely grey sea glinted in the distance. Tom slowed the car down. Gradually the road had been getting more and more narrow, until it was just a bumpy farm track and he could hear thick mud churning under the wheels. They turned the corner to see Trencarrow silhouetted against the sky; only one leaded window glowing orange.

'Let's get in quickly,' said Stella as she stepped out of the car and buttoned up her coat. 'It's starting to rain.'

They knocked at the front door, flipping up their collars and hunching against the wind which had suddenly whipped up. The door creaked open to reveal Christopher Chase in a tartan dressing-gown and a pair of Aran socks, looking every one of his seventy-three years. There was a scratch of white hair on his chin as if he hadn't shaved in days and Stella was sure he was even more bowed since the last time she had seen him in June. For someone who had always looked so vibrant and stylish, even in his advancing years, it was a shock.

'Stella!' he said. 'Well, this is a surprise.'

She put out her arms to embrace him. 'I told you I'd come.'

'I didn't think you would,' he replied.

She introduced him quickly to Tom.

'Ah, little Tommy,' said Christopher with a sad smile. 'Oh, I remember you as a wee mite on your mother's knee. Do come in, both of you.'

Christopher led the way into the dark living room, which was only lit by a single lamp. Stella sat down on a leather Chesterfield, glad when Tom came to sit beside her. Her eyes darted around the room while Christopher fixed them a glass of whisky each from a bottle that was three-quarters empty. Trencarrow was far more expensively furnished than she remembered – like a country boutique hotel. There were at least half a dozen photographs of Chessie dotted around the room. Idly, she wondered what had happened to the childhood photos of herself, Andrew and Nancy, her half-brother and -sister from Christopher's first marriage. At one time, they had filled the stone mantelpiece.

'Do you know where she is?' asked Stella when her father had settled into his wing-back chair.

'Chessie? In London somewhere,' he replied with the wave of a hand. 'That's where she met *him*.'

'Who is he?' asked Stella cautiously.

'Her bloody new boyfriend, of course! I gather he's got one of those fancy townhouses in Connaught Square near our flat.'

'It's not Tony Blair is it?' piped up Tom suddenly. 'He's got a gaff around there.'

Stella shot him a look and the impish grin fell from his face.

'He's called Graham,' said Christopher, staring at the rain on the dark window. 'Apparently they've been carrying on together for the best part of a year. She says she was going to end it with him when we got pregnant, but it turns out she *loves* him,' he said, spitting out the words.

'And are you sure it's your baby?'

Stella regretted saying it as soon as the words came out of her mouth but Christopher looked too defeated to be angry.

'She says it is, although that might be just so she can get the farmhouse. But even so, I want to believe it's our child.'

He fell silent. Stella looked to Tom for support, then turned back when she heard the sound of gentle sobbing.

'I'm going to have to get rid of the farmhouse, you know,' said Christopher through the tears, covering his mouth with one gnarled hand. 'I'm going to lose Trencarrow on top of everything else.'

Stella moved over to him, feeling a fierce wave of anger towards Chessie, and sat on the arm of his chair putting an arm across his shoulder. It was funny how concentrating on her father's problems was making her forget her own.

'I devoted myself to that woman,' he said, looking up at her. 'I didn't go to Saul's funeral because she was getting breast implants, did you know that? I missed my best friend's funeral just to be with her.'

Stella felt a sudden impulse to laugh at the image of Chessie thrusting her silicone breasts in front of Christopher and banning him from going to Chilcot. But she was quite sure her father wouldn't see the funny side of anything at that moment.

'Surely you don't have to sell the farm,' said Tom, frowning. 'After all, *she* left *you*.'

'I'm not sure that's how the lawyers will see it,' sighed Christopher. 'We've been married eight years and she's carrying our child. She'll want something, probably everything. But the truth is I've got nothing to give her. Nothing except the house.'

Stella didn't need to see his bank statements to know he was telling the truth. The expensive refurbishment of Trencarrow, the swish Bayswater apartment and Chessie had the best car and clothes and an expensive London social life. She really had bled him dry.

'What about selling some of your work?'

'I haven't worked in years,' he said quietly. Stella noticed he was now directing his conversation at Tom, as if it was easier to talk to a relative stranger.

'Well, can't we sell some of your old stuff?'

'Have a look around,' he replied sweeping an arm around the room. 'There's not much left. I must have sold about fifty pieces over the last ten years. High-maintenance wives can be expensive you know,' he said with a small smile.

It was something that had been nagging at Stella since they had arrived: how few of Christopher's sculptures were dotted round the house. In many ways her father had been a victim of his own success. Twenty, thirty years earlier, his Mayfair art dealer Bartholomew Davies would sell his sculptures as fast as Christopher could produce work, but now the famous bronze curves had gone and so too had the income.

'I'm an old fool, Thomas,' said Christopher. 'A fool for love. I've lost count of the pieces I gave away – seduction tools as it were,' he smiled. 'And the rest have gone on divorce settlements and holidays. The only thing still left is Byzance.'

Stella's heart fluttered. Byzance was her favourite piece. A six-foot bronze in the shape of a sail that took pride of place in the garden behind the house, sheltered from the sea and the rain. There was no way she was going to let him sell that.

'Tell me, Thomas, do you like art?' asked Christopher. Tom walked over to two brightly-coloured paintings by the door. They were vaguely nautical. Tom thought he could make out a boat and a lighthouse.

'These are great,' he said.

Christopher nodded.

'A great friend of mine and Saul's did those, Ben Palmer. You won't have heard of him. Poor sod didn't have two brass farthings to rub together, couldn't even afford materials. He used to hang around the Porthmeor Studios, using paint left over from other artists' sessions. That painting on the left is done on a piece of chipboard that was put over a broken window.'

'What are the Porthmeor Studios?' asked Tom, genuinely interested. This was a part of his Uncle Saul's life that he'd never heard about.

'Oh, the studios are a piece of Cornish history,' he replied. 'Everyone worked out of there at some point. Sandra Blow, Patrick Heron, even Francis Bacon for a few months.' Christopher shrugged. 'Sadly Benjamin didn't quite take off in the way they did. I'd sell those pictures if I thought they'd raise anything. But I'm quite happy to look at them every day though.'

Stella felt tears welling up. She had grown up listening to her father's stories of the St Ives art movement and she knew how much her father treasured Ben's paintings. It broke her heart to see that he was prepared to get rid of them so readily.

'It's late,' said Christopher grabbing onto the arms of the chair to pull himself up. 'Do you mind if I turn in?'

'It's not that late,' replied Stella, wanting to stay up and talk despite feeling emotionally exhausted herself.

'It is for me, darling,' he said, rising with difficulty, gently squeezing her arm.

'Don't blame Chessie,' he said quietly. 'She's a young woman like you. What does she want with an old man who goes to bed at seven o'clock?'

Tom and Stella watched him leave the room.

'Can you believe he's making excuses for her?' asked Stella when he had gone.

Tom shrugged. 'When a relationship ends, sometimes it's easier to believe it was your fault.'

Stella suddenly thought of Johnny and her heart felt raw. The tears began to come again. She leant into Tom and he put a fraternal arm round her shoulders.

'It will get better you know,' he said, giving her a gentle squeeze.

She nodded her head sadly. 'I had a narrow escape with Johnny, I'm sure of it. Yes, it hurts like hell, but I'm sure it's more painful after marriage and kids.'

She stood up and started pacing around the room to stop herself dwelling on her own problems.

'Tom, I can't let him sell Trencarrow.'

'Maybe those paintings *are* worth something,' said Tom, pointing to the Ben Palmer oils.

'It's worth asking your mother,' said Stella.

Tom had walked over to the big bay window and was staring out into the darkness, wondering vaguely how much Trencarrow was worth and how much Chessie would get her claws on.

471

'What's that big building out by the cliffs?'

'The barn? It's dad's studio.'

'Can I have a look?'

'There's not a lot to see. As he told you, he's given up. There's probably just a load of rusty chisels and dust in there now. I'm sure he'll walk you down after breakfast tomorrow.'

'Come on,' he said with a grin. 'It looks spooky . . . It's a fine old night to be scared.' He made a weak attempt at a werewolf's howl and started pulling on his coat. Stella started laughing.

'Tom, it's pitch black out there! And it's pissing down.'

'You must have a torch, come on! It won't seem quite as romantic in the morning.'

'Romantic?' said Stella, feeling a little awkward.

'Not like that,' he grinned.

'If I fall flat on my face in the mud you're paying for the dry cleaning.'

'You'll be lucky, love. I'm a penniless fool,' he said spreading his hands to the sky.

She laughed but she was already reaching for her coat. She found a torch by the door and then reached into a ceramic jug to pull out a set of keys.

'Creature of habit. Still keeps them in there after all these years.' The back door creaked as it opened and a gust of chilly air rushed into the house. As Stella pulled up the collar on her coat, she could hear the low swoosh of the sea unseen below. Outside, the sky was mottled in a thousand shades of black and as she felt Tom's protective hand on the small of her back, she suddenly felt excited by this little adventure, even when the reassuring amber spilling from Trencarrow's windows grew faint and the barn loomed ominously in front of them. Stella handed Tom the key and whispered, 'You go first.'

'Wimp,' he hissed, fumbling the key in the lock and

opening the heavy wooden door. He flashed the torch up the wall, flicked a switch and flooded the barn with light. Stella gasped. She had been expecting to see an empty, desolate space, forgotten and forlorn, but the barn was full of sculptures, some small and exquisite, some five feet high. Although some looked rough and unfinished, many were polished and complete. Stella felt the familiar rush of excitement when she saw good art – *no, great art*, she thought. Right in the centre of the room was a large stone sculpture, obviously recently worked on. There were some tools on a table next to it: chisels, hammers and a smaller clay model of the larger work. It was amazing.

'*Shit . . .*'

'What's wrong?' asked Tom, walking slowly around the room, gazing at the sculptures. Stella walked over to the large stone and ran her hand across its surface.

'Nothing's wrong, far from it. It's just a surprise that Dad's still working on stuff,' she said quietly.

'I thought he said he wasn't.'

'He was lying,' she said, looking at him sadly.

Behind them the door swung open sending droplets of rain sweeping into the barn. Christopher was standing at the barn door, still in his dressing-gown, his shoulders wet.

'What are you doing in here?' he said. His voice was stern, a mixture of anger and alarm.

'Tom wanted to see the studio,' said Stella nervously, recognizing the disapproving expression on his face.

'You told me you'd stopped working,' she said, walking slowly towards him as if approaching a cornered animal.

'I have,' he said, looking away from her.

'Well, what's this?' she said, pointing to the large sculpture in the middle of the room.

'It's rubbish,' he said stiffly.

'Dad. This is not rubbish, it's amazing, I've never seen . . .'

'I said it's *rubbish*!' he shouted. 'Can't you understand plain English?'

He strode over to the table and swept his arm across it, sending his tools and the model flying to the floor.

'Dad! What the hell are you doing?' cried Stella, lunging for the sculpture, picking it up, the knees of her jeans covered with dust.

'Get out of here! OUT!' roared Christopher, striding through the open door out into the night. Her head whirling, Stella dropped the small sculpture and ran to follow him. It was raining hard outside. She caught up with her father and pulled at his arm, turning him so she could see the rain splashing on his face, hard and cold.

'Why didn't you tell me?' she shouted above the wind.

'Tell you what?' he snapped, pulling his arm away. 'The work in there is nothing to boast about.'

'Dad, they *are*! They're wonderful!' said Stella fiercely.

She could see rivulets of water running down her father's face and wasn't sure if it was rain or tears.

'You don't know what it's like to have a talent that the whole world looks up to you for, a talent that people will befriend you for, even marry you for. A talent that gives you fame and money and self-worth. And then to lose it all!'

He met his daughter's gaze directly.

'What nature gives you, it can take away,' he said, holding up his twisted hands. 'I still have a head full of ideas but I can barely hold a chisel. I don't want anyone to see my work now. I can hardly look at it. I don't want people to pity me and think "Oh what a shame! He used to be so good, but now this is all the old man can do." I want people to remember my work as it was.'

'Art isn't for museums, Dad!' shouted Stella. 'You told me that yourself once. It's a living thing, it keeps moving

474

forward. So maybe it's not your best work, but even your worst stuff is still touched by genius. People still want to see it, touch it, pay good money for it. Don't be a victim, Dad! Find a dealer, put on a show!'

'Don't be stupid, girl!' he yelled back. 'That's all in the past, let it go.'

Stella suddenly felt a surge of anger and she grabbed his arm again.

'I'll tell you what stupid is: sitting in your farmhouse wallowing in self-pity with the bailiffs knocking on the door. Because that in there,' she said pointing into the barn, 'is your way of keeping Trencarrow.'

He looked at her, his eyes dead.

'You'd better go back to your friend,' he said, his voice noticeably hoarse. 'Is he your new boyfriend?'

Stella shook her head absently as she took her coat off and put it over his sodden dressing-gown shoulder.

'Get inside, Dad.'

He looked out in the distance where the black melted into the sea and sky.

'I've missed you.'

'I've missed you too, Dad.'

She stood in the dark watching him go inside. She heard Tom approach behind her. He'd found an old golf umbrella in the barn and held it over both of them.

Stella started sobbing uncontrollably.

'I can't help him, Tom,' she said thickly, as Tom pulled her close with his free arm. She buried her head in his jumper which smelt of smoke and cologne. Tom gently led her back towards the house.

'We can help him,' he said in a firm voice. 'Let me speak to my mother; she knows every top gallery owner and collector in London. There's more than enough for a small show here. He'd sell out.'

'But what if he's right?' asked Stella. 'What if it's not as good as his old stuff?'

'It doesn't matter. A Picasso is still a Picasso. And your father is still one of the most famous British sculptors of the last century. With the right PR, at the right gallery, the art world will still see his genius.'

She looked up at him.

'Do you really think so?'

'I'm no expert, but my mother is. And I bet she can't wait to get her hands on him.'

47

Roger looked enviously around the grand Hampstead home of his friend Alan Parker, desperate to get the pleasantries over with so that they could talk business. He had little in common with his old school pal and talk at the dinner table of Alan's life in his City firm of solicitors and the renovation of their new Umbrian villa had almost driven Roger to tears.

'That was splendid, Beatrice,' smiled Alan, looking fondly at his wife as she cleared away the remains of the pannacotta.

'Coffee for everyone?' said Beatrice, clearly eager to busy herself with more domesticity.

'Rebecca, why don't you go and help?' said Roger. 'I just have to go and discuss a few matters with Alan.'

Rebecca pulled her mouth into a tiny pout before acquiescing. Roger had called Alan several days earlier for some off-the-record legal advice about the eco-hotels proposition. He hadn't yet mentioned it to Rebecca – she would have got too excited – without knowing first if he could afford to jump in with Ricardo, both financially and legally.

'So, to business,' smiled Alan, walking out of the room

and returning with a manila folder and a decanter of brandy. He shut the dining-room door and returned to his seat.

'You have a 20 per cent shareholding in Milford that you want to get rid of,' he said, pouring Roger and himself a generous measure. 'Is that correct?'

'That's right. A superb business opportunity has come my way so I want to liquidize a few of my assets,' said Roger a little boastfully.

'Do you have to sell the Milford shares?' said Alan taking a sip of his claret.

Roger bristled at Alan's implication.

'Of course not,' said Roger blustering. 'but frankly, now Saul is no longer with us I'm losing interest in the company. I feel my money would be better tied up elsewhere.'

Alan pulled a slight face that irritated Roger immensely. A look that said: *I disagree with you.*

'Well, I'm no expert in the luxury goods sector but from what I read in the business pages, your niece appears to be turning the company around nicely. Perhaps if you held off on selling them for another year or so . . .?'

'I shouldn't be saying this,' said Roger, leaning forward as if to share a secret, 'but Milford is all smoke and mirrors. A party in a shop and a few bags hanging off the arms of celebrities does not a corporate renaissance make.'

Alan nodded.

'In which case, you should take a look at this.' Alan opened the file and pulled out a thin document which had various paragraphs of text highlighted.

'Thank you for getting me copies of Milford's Articles of Association and Memorandum. Have you actually ever read them?'

Roger shook his head.

'It's what we pay lawyers to do,' he blustered.

'Everything looks very straightforward, nothing too

onerous – except paragraph four of the attached share-holders agreement.'

He handed it to Roger whose eyes scanned the page.

'So other shareholders have a first refusal option on the shares?' he said, looking up at Alan.

'Do you think they will want them?' replied Alan.

Roger shook his head condescendingly. 'My sisters Julia and Virginia who each have 5 per cent have neither the desire nor the money to do so. But Emma is on such a power trip that perhaps she will be sniffing around them.'

'She'll almost certainly want them,' agreed Alan taking a sip of brandy. 'Buying your shareholding would take her over 75 per cent and she could control the passing of special resolu-tions. Essentially it would put her in an unassailable position.'

Roger snorted, his face looked pinched. He hated the thought of Emma claiming an even bigger prize.

'Well, she might *want* the shares but I seriously doubt she could personally raise the money to buy them. Milford might be a donkey but to somebody who knows what they're doing, it's a potentially valuable business. What do you reckon it's worth then?'

'I have no idea. I'd need to see the accounts, assess company debts, its assets,' replied Alan. 'It's a recovering company but it's hardly Gucci.'

'Ball-park?' said Roger eagerly. 'Fifty million? Which would make my shareholding worth nearly ten mill.' He had stood up now and was pacing around the room. 'I figured about ten million,' he muttered as if he was talking to himself. 'Emma couldn't afford that. So we'd throw it open, maybe get a few companies interested. I was thinking LVMH or the Richemont Group, or maybe one of those private equity organizations. That would push the price up – there's plenty of people prepared to pay top dollar for a heritage company like ours.'

'Possibly,' said Alan sagely. 'But in my opinion, in the light of the favourable press she's been getting, Emma might be able to raise the funds to buy you out even if a company valuation went higher than fifty million pounds.'

'Well she's going to have to pay me top-whack, same as everybody else.'

Alan looked awkward.

'Ah, well, there's your problem, Roger. Should Emma or any other shareholders wish to buy your shares they can do so on the "fair valuation" principle. It's a fairly standard clause in family-owned companies.'

Roger stopped pacing and looked at Alan.

'So we fix a mutually agreeable price?'

'In principle, yes. However, fair valuations in my experience tend to be at a rate far below the price you would get on the open market. Because as you yourself point out, the company has only just turned a corner, Emma could get them for a steal.'

Alan puffed out his cheeks and looked up to the ceiling. 'If the company did have a valuation of fifty million, to sell a 20 per cent shareholding to a fellow shareholder . . . I don't know. I suspect she'd be looking to pay about two million quid.'

Roger looked at him in horror. 'For 20 per cent of the company! I thought you said *fair valuation*! That doesn't sound bloody fair to me!'

Alan put up his hands.

'Don't shoot the messenger, old boy. You've come to me as a friend, Roger, and I'm telling you how it is – or could be.'

A cloud of anxiety crossed Roger's face. He thought of Rebecca in her St Tropez villa or at the penthouse suite in Ricardo's Bahia development or the Chelsea townhouse, all the places they'd always talked about owning when they finally realized their money. *But two million?* Two million quid wouldn't even buy them a three-bedroom flat in Cadogan Square, let alone the beautiful Glebe Place mews Rebecca had her eye on.

'So what should I do?'

'If you want the maximum worth of your shareholding, the last thing you want is for Emma to buy them. You need to persuade the other shareholders to sell, to off-load Milford lock, stock and barrel to a luxury goods conglomerate or a private equity house.'

'And how do I do that?'

Alan laughed.

'Put the feelers out to the big boys on the quiet. If the price is right, I think the shareholders will snap their hands off – it could even tempt Emma. However well Milford is doing at the moment, it's a volatile business and if one of the big luxury firms comes knocking she'd be crazy to turn them down.'

For a moment, Roger smiled, thinking of the prospect of all that money, but then he remembered Emma and her ludicrous ideas of running a business and his smile faded. It might take a bomb to shift her from that chairman's seat.

'Thanks, Alan,' said Roger, raising his glass, 'you've given me an excellent idea.'

48

Rob didn't call Emma the Monday she knew he was returning from New York. He didn't call her on Tuesday, Wednesday or Thursday, by which point the silence was hurtful and distracting. Analytical by nature, Emma ran through in her head the reasons why she had not heard from him. There was a slim possibility he was still in the States, but as hope paled into disappointment, the likely explanation was that he was avoiding her and that in his mind at least, the night in Somerset had been a grade A mistake.

It was almost ten o'clock on Thursday night and she was still at work. She loved the security of her office, a space where she felt in control, and vocation filled the loneliness.

Closing down her computer, she yawned and slipped on her coat, knowing the last few hours hadn't been especially productive and mocked herself; she was the CEO of a company, why couldn't she do something as simple as call him? But the thought of the conversation, of Rob's apologies and polite excuses, made her squirm. The truth was, she'd been stupid. She knew Rob's reputation and his limited attention span with the opposite sex. She should have known better and now she had to deal with it, wondering how best to do that as if she were stamping out a business problem.

Her phone went as she strode out of the foyer.

'Emma,' she said briskly.

'It's Rob. Sorry it's late.'

She felt a surge of pleasure.

'How are you?' she said as casually as possible.

'I got back from New York yesterday. It's been hectic.'

'How's your father?'

'We had a few difficult meetings,' he said, his voice sounding on edge.

There was a long yawning pause.

'So are you around this weekend?'

'Mostly,' she said cautiously.

'I thought we could have lunch on Saturday at the house.'

Her first thought was that she didn't want to see Morton in what could be construed as a first date. Her second thought was that it was lunch. Not dinner as he had suggested at the cider farm.

'From your silence you don't fancy lunch at Winterfold.'

'I was thinking.'

'So how about we go for a ride?'

'Very well,' she said, unable to stop herself smiling broadly into the receiver. 'I'll see you on Saturday after my run.'

Winterfold's stables, on the west perimeter of the estate, had been leased to a local riding school for several years. Rob kept a horse there, a sixteen-hand chestnut, and had arranged for Emma to ride a beautiful strong-looking bay. They had agreed to meet there; Emma was late, having changed clothes three times before deciding that her cherry-red sweater and tight cream jodhpurs were perhaps just a little too sexy but they were, at least, appropriate.

Rob had already saddled up and was sitting astride his horse without a riding hat, looking cavalier and certain.

'I never had you as the equestrian type,' she smiled, wedging her foot in the stirrup.

'You know I like to keep you on your toes.'

She bit her tongue, feeling they were already on the verge of some teasing banter. She wanted today to be easy and already she felt as nervous as a teenager.

'Where do you want to go?'

She knew immediately. The lake in the northern corner of the grounds. It was quiet and pretty and romantic.

They barely spoke on the way up there and were just content to take in the magnificence of the Winterfold estate. It never failed to take her breath away no matter how often she saw it. Today bright winter sunshine skimmed the long grass, turning it blonde like champagne.

The lake dazzled silver. There was a diving board at one end which looked as if it hadn't been used in a decade. They dismounted and tied the horses up to a tree and went to sit on an old gnarled log by the water's edge.

Their hands were inches away from each other's resting on the log. The sunshine on her face was making her feel bolder. She reached her fingers along the log until they touched his, feeling deliriously contented for one split second before he edged his hand slowly away.

That tiniest of movements was like a slap across the face.

'I'm sorry,' he said, pushing his fingers back clumsily towards her.

Emma gave a low, cynical laugh. The look on his face was transparent. Embarrassment, regret, kindness. She shuddered. Or was it *pity*?

'It was a mistake,' she said before she could think. She meant it to be a question, but self-preservation meant it came out more a statement of fact.

'You think so?'

How maddening language could be, thought Emma, trying to read the subtleties in his voice, subtleties that change how one was understood. Had he emphasized the word *you* which suggested that he didn't think it was a mistake?

'You're embarrassed about Somerset, aren't you?' she said finally.

'Embarrassed, no.'

'But it was a mistake.'

'In so much as I can't commit to anything right now.'

Her eyes didn't leave his face. Was he totally clueless or completely insensitive? Either way, she was angry. Angry with him for bringing her out for a romantic ride only to let her down. Angry at him for spoiling her special spot on the Winterfold estate. Angry at herself for learning that Rob couldn't commit to any woman and for allowing herself to think that it would be different between them. Emma was not a naturally gifted actor; even as a young child she had found lying awkward, not just because of her integrity but because she knew she would always get found out. But this time, needs must.

'You and me both,' she smiled with as much brightness as she could muster. 'It's such a relief you said it.'

'Right,' he smiled slowly.

He kissed her on the cheek. It felt like a brief goodbye. There certainly felt like no reason to stay by the lake.

Untying their horses he shouted over to her.

'Race you back to the Stables.'

As she galloped along, her horse edging in front of Rob's, the cold, fresh air slapping against her face, two small tears raced down her face and she convinced herself it was just the wind.

49

Cassandra set about finding Giles's replacement immediately, even though she knew the task would be a difficult one. After all, it was hardly the sort of job she could advertise in the Media *Guardian*. *Rive*'s editor-at-large needed incredible natural flair and an enormous Rolodex of contacts. More importantly they needed to understand what made Cassandra Grand tick.

Well, let's see what this one is made of, she thought as she strode through San Lorenzo towards one of the best tables in the house. Jessica West was already waiting for her. Cassandra's eyes darted over her, inspecting the cut of her shirt, the brand of her bag, noting her manicured nails, freshly blow-dried hair and discreet make-up. Cassandra smiled inwardly. Jessica West had passed the first test. The stylist had only recently come to Cassandra's attention. She had already met her of course – at the Versace party during Milan Fashion Week – and Cassandra remembered thinking that Jessica was bright and confident. She had been making a name for herself dressing celebrities; so much so that several big names had been requesting that she style them when they were being shot for *Rive* magazine. She was very beautiful, extremely thin – even slimmer than Cassandra – which she both admired and resented. It was a fine line.

'As you know there is the possibility of an editor-at-large position at *Rive*,' said Cassandra, cutting straight to the chase. 'I'm looking for someone with excellent social contacts and an unparalleled knowledge of fashion. It is a job traditionally held by a talented writer, editor and features visionary, shall we say. But I am willing to change the job description for the right person.'

'Would it involve any styling?' asked Jessica. She had deliberately sought out Cassandra at the Versace party and was glad her hard work was paying dividends. And to think she almost hadn't gone.

Cassandra arched an eyebrow. Jessica was no Giles. She doubted whether the girl could string a sentence together but it wouldn't do any harm to have an additional member of staff on board who had a knack of charming celebrities; after all, Deborah Kane was hardly coming up with the goods these days.

'We could be flexible. Tell me about yourself.'

'I've dressed loads of stars for all the big red carpet events this year. I've been in New York a lot since the summer so I have great contacts with the East Coast publicists. Plus I have excellent music contacts – I went out with Rob Holland the CEO of Hollander for a long time.'

'Rob Holland?' asked Cassandra, suddenly curious. 'Rob rents our family home Winterfold.'

'What a coincidence,' smiled Jessica. 'I adore Winterfold.'

'Funny I never saw you in the village. When did you split up?'

'Oh, it petered off a couple of months ago,' said Jessica vaguely. 'We're still friends though,' she added quickly.

This was the other reason Cassandra had wanted to meet Jessica apart from her growing reputation as a celebrity stylist. When she had met Jessica at the Versace party she knew she had seen the striking redhead somewhere before. It eventually dawned on her that it had been at Laura Hildon's wedding; she had been sitting next to Rob in church and had danced cheek-to-cheek with him at the black tie dinner.

'Rob is quite close to my cousin, Emma,' said Cassandra with a small smile. 'I never could work out what was going on between them.'

'Emma?' She searched Cassandra's face, and seeing she had found an ally began to talk more openly.

'She's just his landlady. I'm sure she fancied Rob, probably still does but he wasn't interested.'

'And how do you know that?' asked Cassandra.

She saw a split second look of distaste cross Jessica's face.

'Aside from the fact that she's hardly his type,' she said, her mouth turned downwards, 'I don't think anyone will ever get a look in with Rob's ex-girlfriend Madeline and child hovering in the background. I mean, Rob even spent Thanksgiving with them. Plus I saw him and Madeline together in New York at Sant Ambroeus and they looked very cosy. I'd say they were definitely back together.'

'That *is* interesting,' purred Cassandra. 'I hope you're not too disappointed.'

'Disappointed? Of course not,' said Jessica quickly. 'We're just good friends.'

'Just like Rob and Emma,' replied Cassandra, smiling. 'Just like Rob and Emma.'

50

Tom was in love. He realized it on the M4 heading out of London towards Oxfordshire. The clues were all there: the Kensington townhouse he was house-sitting was luxurious – silk sheets, basement pool, home cinema – yet here he was, making the journey out to Chilcot for the weekend in the slim hope of bumping into Stella in the Feathers. *Stella* he thought with a ridiculous grin on his face as he pressed down the accelerator of his ancient Mini. Just her name was enough to get his heart leaping. She felt so good for him, so right and now she was single. And it didn't help that she was gorgeous, of course. He had fallen in lust with her the minute he'd first laid eyes on her at the Milford shoot. Not that he'd been silly about it; he'd still slept with at least a dozen stunning women in Ibiza, but the point was that he'd found it difficult to shake Stella from his mind. Yes, her luminous beauty beguiled him, but having got to know her and spend time with her through her recent traumas, it was her strength and kindness that had really won him over. After the smoky journey to Cornwall, Stella had presented him with a gift-wrapped box of nicotine patches. It was an affectionate joke, but he had not

489

smoked in two weeks. He'd been off the drugs too – all right, so he could barely afford them – but it was more than that, it was because Stella had given him something else to look forward to.

Tom flexed his frozen fingers; they were nearly numb and the Mini's heating couldn't have picked a colder night to give up the ghost. Despite the weather he was in a good mood as the car chugged off the motorway, onto the A-roads and finally down the winding country lanes towards Chilcot. The night before he had seen a fantastic band, Red Comet, play at one of his favourite pubs in Camden. He'd chatted to the band at the bar and after a number of drinks had convinced himself they were the next big thing. Now Tom was keen to catch up with Rob Holland to pass on their CD and see if he was as excited by them as he was. Suddenly Tom's smile faded. *I've got to find some way of hitting the big time*, he thought.

Rain was now spitting on the windscreen and visibility was poor.

His mother's house was on the edge of the village and as he approached, he ducked his head to peer through the smeared windscreen. Dammit! Her car was already on her drive and there wasn't another parking space within a hundred yards of her house; by the looks of it there was some function going on at the Feathers. He drove past the house and turned into a lane that led off towards the common. He got out quickly, zipping his jacket up to his chin and started walking briskly back towards the house.

Tom barely felt the blow; it all happened too quickly. Something solid cracked hard against the back of his head and his body simply slumped to the ground. Instinct told him to raise his hands to his face, and between his fingers he could make out the shape of a boot coming towards him again and again. His nose cracked and he could feel the blood pour down his face. Blows were raining down all over his body, pain everywhere. Finally he was jerked upwards and a strong hand lifted him by the collar of his jacket.

'You know why we're here, doncha, sunshine?' growled a voice, close to his face. 'If we don't get what we want, we will be back. And next time, we'll cut your balls off.'

The man released Tom, letting him drop, his skull banging against the pavement.

Tom curled into a ball, expecting more kicks, feeling the raw pain all over his body but he didn't dare cry out in case he provoked more violence. He only began to moan when he heard a car engine gun and roar away. Wincing, he reached into his pocket but realized he'd left his mobile in the car. He rolled over and dragged himself off the ground but was only able to walk doubled-over in a crouch. It was only fifty yards to Julia's house, but it might as well have been a thousand. He could feel blood dripping down his cheek onto the pavement. Vomit was rising in his throat. *Not much further*, he told himself, willing his body to move forward. He fell against his mother's front door. Time seemed to stretch out as he pushed the doorbell.

'Tom!' screamed Julia as she opened the door and watched her son fall towards her. 'Darling, what's happened?' She knelt on the ground and rested his head in her lap, blood smearing over her skirt.

'Who did this?' she asked, weeping.

It was a minute before Tom could even open his bruised mouth to speak.

'I owe some people money, from Ibiza. A *lot* of money, Mum. And now they want it back.'

51

Christmas was one of Cassandra's favourite times of the year, in spite of being a hectic time in the office. Production of *Rive* shut down for ten days over the holiday season which meant that not only did they have to have the February issue finished and at the printers, but they also had to have completed most of the March issue as well. The pill was, however, sweetened by the glut of presents that came flooding in from grateful advertisers and fashion houses all thanking her for a 'wonderful year'. The cream B&B Italia sofa in Cassandra's office was already piled high with gifts: a set of Prada skis, a large monogrammed suitcase from Louis Vuitton, an Alberta Ferretti cashmere coat, fourteen handbags and a beautiful card from Dolce & Gabbana instructing her to go into the shop and pick anything she wanted.

These were what Cassandra called her A-division presents, gifts she would keep for herself or possibly put in Ruby's Christmas stocking. On another pile on the Perspex table were the B-division presents: bottles of champagne, leather purses, a Tiffany key-ring, an assortment of kitchen appliances, three Smythson diaries, a Roberts radio and a certificate for a course for six micro-dermabrasion sessions. These were presents destined for her mother, favoured members of staff or to be 're-gifted' to friends not in the fashion industry who wouldn't suspect that they were free. Perched on an office chair by her desk were offerings so gross that Cassandra could barely comprehend how they could come from anyone working in the fashion industry: cheap chocolates or low-grade scented candles. Cassandra snatched up a nasty-looking red passport holder and smelt it. *Not even leather!*

'Who the hell is this from?' she said, thrusting it at Lianne who was cataloguing the gifts ready for thank you notes. Her assistant pulled a face.

'That's from Glenda McMahon.'

Cassandra was about to give her opinion on the kind gift when she saw Jeremy Pike, Francesca Adams and David Stern at the door.

'What's this? A military coup?' said Cassandra, sitting back in her chair.

'We hate to disturb you,' said Jeremy, eyeing the gifts with undisguised envy, 'but the whole office is really worried.'

'What is it?' asked Cassandra, tossing the wallet into her drawer.

'There's a story on the Media *Guardian* about Alliance being sold.'

So the wheels were in motion, she thought, trying to keep her face impassive.

She'd had several meetings in the last few weeks with Girard-Lambert boss Pierre Desseau at his smart Neuilly townhouse. By necessity, they had met in complete cloak-and-dagger secrecy as this was nothing less than industrial espionage. Cassandra had fed Pierre everything she knew about her company: its plans to launch new magazines, its

493

digital strategy, the planned and actual marketing spend, plus the holy grail for a competitor – their unmassaged sales figures. In return, Pierre had outlined his plans for the takeover. She had been aware therefore that he was about to buy up Alliance stock which was floating on the open market in preparation for his bid, but she wasn't aware that he had yet approached Isaac Grey to make his offer. Cassandra felt adrenaline flood into her system: the game was afoot. A sales rumour probably meant the hostile bid might be imminent but it might also make the deal vulnerable to other media sharks smelling blood. She hoped against hope that it was the former because she only had a week. The deal had to be done before Christmas or her moment of glory would be in jeopardy.

'To my knowledge Isaac Grey doesn't want to sell,' said Cassandra evenly, meeting the anxious gaze of her team.

'But is it possible? What about our jobs?'

'What about our *expense accounts*?' asked Francesca. 'Isaac really understands our needs, but it's a nightmare at some companies. They won't let you take taxis, let alone helicopters.'

'Everything is going to be fine,' said Cassandra, smiling confidently. 'Stop worrying about it. It's Christmas! Why don't you all help yourselves to something from the table?'

Jeremy took some champagne. David took the radio.

'You know I have enough of this stuff myself,' smiled Francesca politely.

'Quite,' replied Cassandra, pleasantly.

52

In the nick of bloody time, thought Cassandra, putting down her black coffee as she read the headline in the *Financial Times*. She buzzed Lianne.

'Get me Eileen Donald, I don't care where she is – just find her. And cancel the ten o'clock meeting.'

Cassandra hung up and read the story again, more slowly this time. So Girard-Lambert had managed to push the takeover through two days before Christmas, she smiled, taking a sip of her coffee. A *'multi-billion dollar deal'* reported the *FT* excitedly, singling out *Rive* as *'publishing's crown jewels'*. Well, in the nick of time it might be, thought Cassandra, but the timing couldn't have been better.

She looked up at the magazine flat-plan which was pinned to the wall next to her desk. The February issue was due at the printers the following day. The magazine printed in sections but the cover was due to go to press that evening. Well, there was about to be a change of plan. If Glenda thought she was running simultaneous Georgia Kennedy covers with UK *Rive*, she could think again.

She saw her telephone flash red and Eileen Donald's number flashed in the LCD reader. Eileen was *Rive*'s production manager, the person responsible for making sure everything went smoothly between the text and pictures leaving the *Rive* office and the magazines rolling out of the printers.

'Cassandra. Your PA said it was urgent,' said Eileen in her crisp, efficient voice.

'It is,' replied Cassandra, leaning back in her chair. 'There's been a change of plan with the February cover.'

'You're kidding?' said Eileen. 'Cassandra, we print tonight! Has something fallen through?'

'Quite the opposite,' said Cassandra coolly. 'We've got hold of something absolutely wonderful.'

There was a long silence down the phone. Eileen was a no-nonsense woman and one of the few people in the company who dared say what she thought to Cassandra.

'If it's a new cover, we haven't a hope in hell of getting it retouched and over to the printers in time for this evening.'

Cassandra pulled the Georgia Kennedy cover from the locked drawer besides her.

'Eileen, darling, it's already been done.'

Cassandra smiled to herself. The Georgia Kennedy cover had been ready to go for a month. Every blemish, every line had been removed from Georgia's face. Her skin tone had been warmed up, her already svelte image trimmed with the power of digital retouching. She looked like a goddess.

'In that case, it shouldn't be a problem. Shall I warn the printers there's another file on the way?'

'You do that. Oh, one other thing,' purred Cassandra into the receiver. 'I need you to arrange an increase in the print-run by one hundred thousand. The issue is going to sell out instantly with what we currently have out there.'

She heard a faint splutter down the phone.

'I haven't got time to organize a huge hike in the print-run. What about additional paper stock? Do you know how much extra paper is needed for one hundred thousand extra issues?' said Eileen with panic in her voice.

'Just do it,' said Cassandra with steel in her voice. 'Borrow from our allocation for next month's issue if you have to, or take it from *Rural Living* magazine. They'll thank you for it when they see this issue.'

'Cassandra, I'm going to have to get authorization from Greg Barbera for this.'

'Greg doesn't need to know. These orders have come from Pierre Desseau, the chief executive of Girard-Lambert – our new boss in case you don't read the papers. I'm reporting directly to him. If you can't carry out his orders, then you'd better have a think about what corporate takeovers invariably mean; redundancies, sometimes even dismissals.'

'I understand,' said Eileen quietly.

'And Eileen, Pierre wants absolute discretion on this one. We want to take the industry by surprise with our big splash. Tell no one about the new cover or the additional print-run. And I mean *no one*.'

She slammed down the phone and glanced into her still-open drawer to see the nasty passport holder sent by Glenda sitting there. She picked it up and threw it in the wastepaper bin next to her desk.

Choke on that, Glenda, she thought smiling, before turning her thoughts to what she was going to wear for the Christmas party.

53

The sprawling luxury hotel Panton House was only five miles away from Chilcot. Built from beautiful honey-coloured stone, it boasted architecture by Robert Adam, grounds by Capability Brown and a kitchen managed by a more modern-day genius, Raymond Sancerre, the irascible Michelin-starred French chef. Rich Londoners often made the journey to dine there, but for most Chilcot locals it was generally off limits due to its prohibitive prices. So when Emma had decided to throw a big Milford Christmas dinner dance as a thank you for the hard work put in by her employees, Panton House was a natural venue to make the whole evening feel like a real treat. It was two days before Christmas Eve and the huge restaurant looked fabulous; it had been decorated with pine boughs and holly from the Chilcot woods and the staff were aglow with the spirit of the season.

'So, exactly how much is this setting the company back?' asked Roger, dabbing the last of his date and pecan pudding from the corner of his mouth with a napkin. Emma sighed inwardly; she had been expecting this all night. She had deliberately arranged the seating plan so she was seated next to Roger on the top table. It was a peace gesture and so far he had been polite, almost charming.

'We got a good deal,' she smiled. She explained how she had ruthlessly negotiated with Jocelyn Bentham, the owner of Panton House, by playing on his weakness for beautiful things. Emma had offered Jocelyn a brand new, entirely handmade bespoke set of luggage in return for an assurance that they could bring their own wine to the restaurant and not be charged corkage – a move that had saved them thousands of pounds.

'I've also paid for a third of the catering charges myself,' said Emma. 'Julia is also in the process of selling several pieces of art from the Winterfold collection that I hope will pay for necessary corporate expenses like this party.' Emma knew she was playing on Roger's weakness: his reluctance to look at the company accounts, because despite the discounts, the party had still been incredibly expensive to host, especially for a company that was only just moving into the black.

Roger nodded slowly, swirling his claret around in its glass.

'I know we've had our differences this year,' he began awkwardly, 'and I still don't agree with some of your decisions. But . . .' he hesitated, 'we're finally getting results. And as the head of the family I would like to thank you for that.'

Despite herself, Emma felt a warm glow course through her. She knew how painful that must have been for Roger to say, but she was grateful for his words.

'Thanks Roger. I only ever wanted to do the best for everybody.'

'Well, you know we all want you to come to Gstaad,' he said referring to the annual Milford family trip to Switzerland. As Roger had been gifted the chalet in Saul's will, the duty of being Christmas host had fallen to him. 'Let's think of it as a new start, eh?'

Emma smiled and nodded, but inside she was groaning. While Emma was glad of the thaw between her and the family, the prospect of five days with Roger, Rebecca, her mother and God forbid, *Cassandra*, seemed too much to bear.

'Well thanks so much for the invitation, Roger, but I'm not sure I'll be able to make it. After all, it's Christmas Eve the day after tomorrow and I haven't booked a flight. Besides, I've already stocked the fridge for Christmas dinner.'

'Rebecca has already looked into flights,' replied Roger generously. 'There's still business class flights available from Heathrow to Geneva. We have a wonderful chef at the chalet and I know how much you like to ski. Surely that's preferable to spending Christmas alone in the Stables?'

'Oh don't worry, I won't be alone. I've been invited to lots of Christmas drinks and Len's threatening to have a lock-in at the Feathers. Anyway, I've mentally prepared myself for staying at home,' she smiled. She touched his hand. 'Honestly Roger, thanks so much for thinking of me, but I think I'd better get to my feet and say a few words of thanks to the staff.'

After coffee, the Milford employees dispersed from their tables and filtered through into Panton House's giant conservatory, where a jazz band had just begun a Cole Porter medley. Emma had been walking through to join the dancing herself when she'd spotted Rob Holland hovering by the door, conspicuous in his jeans and a navy sweater in the sea of suits and cocktail dresses.

He came over and kissed her on the cheek.

'Emma.'

'Rob? What are you doing here?' she asked, feeling unnaturally irritated. Since their showdown in the woods, she'd spent the last month determinedly avoiding him and trying to put him out of her mind. It had been easier than she'd expected. She hadn't seen him around the village all month and the whole Somerset episode and his brush-off at the Winterfold lake had just left her feeling angry and used.

He shrugged and motioned with his thumb towards the other side of the hotel.

'I was having a drink in Panton's bar with a friend. There's a big notice-board in the lobby saying that the Milford dinner dance was in the Gainsborough restaurant and, well, I just wanted to come and say hi.'

'Well, hi,' she said curtly, unconsciously smoothing down the thin black velvet of her cocktail dress, then stopping herself.

'So how've you been?' said Rob after a pause.

'Busy.'

'I'm sure,' said Rob with a nervous laugh. 'Me too, I haven't even been to Chilcot for a couple of weeks.'

'Yes, the Christmas party season must be hectic,' she said, unable to stop it coming out like a barb. Rob looked like he was about to reply, then thought better of it. Instead, he said, 'I've been in New York quite a lot. It was Polly's birthday among other things.'

Emma did not want him to spoil her night and she was cross with both Rob and herself that his presence at the party was doing just that.

'Look, I'd better go,' said Emma, looking across the dance floor.

'OK, sure. Listen, I heard you were staying in Chilcot for Christmas. I'm off to Courchevel on Boxing Day but I'm around on Christmas Day if you fancied a festive drink at the Feathers?'

'I really don't know what my plans are yet,' she lied,

wondering who he was going to Courchevel with. Another glamorous blonde, no doubt.

'Well, whatever you do, I hope it's fun,' said Rob, giving Emma his playboy smile. Suddenly it had lost all its charm.

'And if you want to have some fun together, just give me a call and I'll . . .'

'Rob, don't,' she snapped, cutting him off.

'Don't what?' he frowned.

'Don't flirt with me.'

'Why not?'

'You truly are an insensitive bastard, you know that,' she replied shaking her head.

'What?'

'You heard,' she said, already walking away from him.

He pulled her arm.

'Look, Emma, there's something you should know.'

At that moment Virginia appeared behind Emma.

'Darling, I need to talk to you,' she said, putting an arm around her shoulders. For once, Emma welcomed her mother's interruption. Whatever Rob wanted to tell her, Emma felt sure it wasn't going to be good news.

'Oh, hello, Rob,' said Virginia with little warmth. 'I'm just trying to persuade Emma to come to Gstaad with us. Roger positively insists she come along and I think it will be so good for the family.'

'I agree with you,' nodded Rob.

Emma glared at him, not welcoming the interruption. Her life was none of his business.

'I'll see you in the New Year, Rob,' said Emma finally.

'I'd better get back to my friend,' replied Rob stiffly and turned away.

'I do think it's wonderfully generous of Roger to invite you to the chalet,' said Virginia, guiding Emma to the bar. 'Particularly as you started the year by firing him.' Emma looked at her mother. She looked great, perhaps twenty years younger than her sixty years in a long-sleeved grey silk cocktail dress worn with a simple string of pearls.

'Cassandra's going too,' continued Virginia. 'Julia tells me there's been some bad blood there as well so I think you can resolve a lot of differences if you can be bothered to make it.'

Emma was suddenly in no mood for her mother's sly digs.

'Oh, Mother, stop it!' she snapped. 'Can't you give your own daughter the benefit of the doubt for once? You make it sound as if I'm the one that's been in the wrong all year.' Emma didn't want to tell her mother about Cassandra's scheming; after all, business was good and if Cassandra had been trying to further sabotage the company, she hadn't been successful. Emma hoped her cousin had got the message that she was only hurting Julia's shareholding; perhaps she had just got bored and had turned her destructive urges elsewhere. Before Virginia could respond, they were interrupted.

'Great speech, Em. I think you've won a few more hearts and minds tonight.'

She looked up to see Ruan, looking disturbingly handsome in a midnight-blue tux. His dark hair curled on his collar and buoyed by good food and drink, he seemed a little less intense.

'You two should go and dance,' said Virginia, motioning towards the packed dance floor. 'The shop floor just don't know how it's done.'

They all looked towards Albert, the factory janitor, who was twirling his arms around like a helicopter, his large dickie bow flopping round his neck like a dead bird. Emma rolled her eyes at her mother's snobbery. Albert wasn't quite Fred Astaire, but he was having a good time and desperately trying to catch the eye of Abby Ferguson, Milford's marketing executive. Just then, the music changed pace as the singer began to croon Sinatra's 'I've got you under my skin,' to a slow, swinging beat.

'Come on then, lady-boss, show us your fancy footwork,' smiled Ruan pulling Emma towards him and turning her in time to the music. She squealed as he dipped her to the floor and felt herself blush as Ruan expertly whirled her around the floor, suddenly enjoying both the levity and the attention.

'Why, Mr McCormack, I had no idea you were so accomplished,' grinned Emma.

'Just one of my many talents,' murmured Ruan into her ear as he turned her smoothly.

'Oh? And what are the others, pray tell?'

Ruan's mouth was smiling, but his dark eyes were more intense than ever. 'That would be telling.'

Emma felt a blush spread down her neck and across her chest. It wasn't an entirely unpleasant sensation. As the music finished and they turned to clap the band, she snuck a sideways glance at Ruan, a curious smile on her face.

By midnight the crowds were dispersing. The remaining guests were laughing in Panton House's bar and the noisy chugging of taxis outside was almost drowned by out-of-tune but good-natured Christmas songs being sung by partygoers queuing for their lifts.

'I'm getting a cab to Chilcot. Want to share?' asked Ruan, flipping up the collar of his charcoal overcoat.

Emma nodded. 'Yes, please.'

They climbed into the back seat and the taxi grumbled along the road. Ruan and Emma sat in silence, just watching the village slip past. Emma could see the silvery clock face of the church hovering above a line of shadowy trees like the moon. Ruan had a large honey-coloured cottage right at the end of the village. Emma remembered his parents living there and how the track down the side led to a pond in which they would swim in the summer.

'Do you know all this time I've been back in Chilcot I have never been inside your house?' said Emma, overcome by nostalgia.

'Well, come in then,' said Ruan. 'Albert got me a bottle of good Scotch for Christmas that needs drinking.'

'You've already opened your Christmas presents?' said Emma with mock-shock.

'That one, yes. It was bottle-shaped and wrapped in Santa Claus paper so the element of surprise was gone,' he smiled.

Ruan let them in with a key he kept under a flowerpot on the window-sill. *Innocent country ways*, thought Emma with a smile. Inside, there was a stone floor covered with a huge brown rug and the living room was furnished in cosy, if masculine, style. Without thinking Emma decided it needed a female touch. She was embarrassed that she had never been here before. She considered Ruan a friend, but the truth was she barely knew him out of the workplace.

'I can't believe you haven't got a Christmas tree,' she laughed.

'Why put something up, only for it to have to come down a week later?'

'Spoilsport', she said. 'I think we need to do something about that, Scrooge.' She turned and disappeared out of the front door, returning with a twig sprouting leaves and berries which she pushed into the top of an empty wine bottle on the dining-room table.

'What's that?' laughed Ruan.

'Festive cheer,' she smiled.

Ruan chuckled and crouched down by the fireplace, busying himself with the task of lighting the coal. Emma flopped onto the sofa and gazed at him breaking up fire-lighters and arranging kindling.

505

'I couldn't have done it without you, you know that, don't you?'

'Don't be daft,' he said, turning around. 'You're the business brains and Stella is the design wizard. The sisters did it for themselves.'

'But I couldn't have understood the industry so quickly without you being there every step of the way, not judging me for my mistakes. In those early days I think I might have given up and gone back to Boston if you hadn't been there.'

Satisfied that the fire was burning well, he crawled over and sat on the rug near Emma's feet.

'Listen, Em, Milford meant everything to my parents and my grandparents before them. My family has worked for Milford for generations and now it means everything to me too. I've always wanted the company to do as well as you have and if you'd have been around ten years ago we might already be the British Hermès.'

'Ten years ago I was twenty years old,' she grinned. 'The only thing I'd have been good for at Milford is making cups of tea.'

'Why did you leave?'

'England?' she asked, surprised.

'One summer you were there, the next you'd gone. I thought you'd got a place at Oxford or something, but then I heard you'd gone to Harvard.'

'America suited me better,' she said, smirking at the thought that Ruan had taken a vague interest in her whereabouts. Had she had known that as an eighteen-year-old she'd have been doing cartwheels – perhaps she might even have taken up her place at Oxford. She lay back on the sofa, her eyes closing.

'Ruan, I think you'd better call me a cab. I'm completely beat.'

He picked up the phone and made a call.

'There's no taxis for at least forty-five minutes. They're all at Panton Hall ferrying everyone home,' he said finally putting down the receiver.

'Then I'll walk.'

Ruan laughed.

'Don't be mad! You don't want to go walking through the estate at this time of night. I saw Rob at the party. Maybe he's still there and could pick you up on the way past.'

'No!' she shouted.

Ruan looked surprised and then gave a low laugh.

'I did hear a rumour.'

'What rumour?' said Emma feeling her cheeks blaze pink.

'You and Rob?'

It felt wrong to lie to him, especially in his own home.

Finally she shrugged. 'It was a one-off. A mental aberration. I knew he was a bit of a bastard and I thought I'd be the last person to get caught in his web.'

'You women, you're so predictable,' he tutted. She picked up a newspaper from the sofa and hit him with it.

'That's right, rub it in. I'm a sucker for a handsome face and a fat wallet.' She sat back in the sofa and sipped the whisky he had offered her. 'Anyway, what about you? You were the heart-throb of Chilcot. Sorry, the whole of Oxfordshire; I thought you'd have settled down years ago.'

'Well, I almost did. I got engaged about three years ago,' he said frankly.

'I didn't know,' she said, suddenly curious about what sort of woman Ruan would be interested in. 'So . . .?'

'So she left me for someone else.'

'Handsome face, fat wallet?' smiled Emma sadly.

'Something like that. And the last woman I fell for was married. So here I am. Still single. I guess you could say I haven't had the best of luck.'

He gave her a long penetrating look which unnerved her

considerably, but she was too tired to try to get up. All she could do was sit there, thinking how good-looking he was and what a waste it was that he was alone. Certainly Ruan was more handsome than Rob and Mark, but they had been able to arouse great passion in Emma, a passion that had taken her out of her comfort zone and had made her feel alive, whether it was deliriously happy or prickling with rage.

Ruan was another sort of man entirely. More stable, more solid. Hard-working and serious, in many ways he reminded her of herself. He had consistently been her friend and supporter and she was terribly fond of him.

Suddenly she felt Ruan take off her shoes and put them to the side of the fireplace. The small, intimate gesture sent a jolt through her and she sat up.

'Let me pull out the sofa-bed for you,' he said softly.

He pulled himself up onto his knees and as he did so, his face passed within inches of Emma's. Before she could even think about what she was doing she reached forward and put her hand on his cheek, guiding him down until their lips pressed gently together. Her eyes closed and she enjoyed the soft, natural sensation of their kiss. She felt him pull away gently and her split second of pleasure was replaced with an unbearable awkwardness.

'I'm drunk,' she smiled, trying to make light of it.

'You're my boss,' he corrected quietly. 'Otherwise it might be different.'

'Look, I'd better go,' she said quickly, moving to get up.

'You're drunk and tired,' he said with a low laugh. 'Crash here. I'll just get you a blanket.'

As he brought over a tartan wool throw their eyes locked and she felt herself flush.

'I'm not embarrassed if you're not,' said Ruan and Emma smiled gratefully.

She remembered him turning off the living room light and the gentle padding of his feet as he went upstairs. The next thing she knew her eyes were open and dawn light was cracking through the cottage window. She squinted at her watch: 8 a.m. Ruan was still asleep and the Milford office had officially closed for Christmas. She was desperate for a cup of coffee but there was no time to hang around – she swung her legs off the sofa, moaning as she felt the pain in her head. Speaking in a low voice, she called a taxi and went across to the chair where her coat had been flung. She winced at the memory of last night as she spotted her shoes by the fireplace where Ruan left them, a small but potent reminder of what had happened. *How could I have been so bloody stupid?* she thought. Tomorrow was Christmas Eve and the thought of staying in Chilcot and bumping into either Rob or Ruan made her cringe. But there was another option and as she heard the taxi toot outside Ruan's cottage, she made up her mind. She was going to take the lesser of the two evils. She was going to Gstaad.

54

Sitting outside one of Gstaad's most popular cafés, Tom unzipped his ski jacket, took a sip of black coffee, and watched the Gstaad wonderland go by. Tom was usually unmoved by anything Cassandra loved, but he had to admit that the gingerbread houses with their powdered sugar snow twinkling in the fading afternoon light was enough to convince anyone that Gstaad was the prettiest village in the world. And to think he almost hadn't come. Not that it had been plain sailing. The bruising around his eye had already prompted difficult questions from Virginia and Roger and he'd almost rather face those goons again than have another showdown with Cassandra, who was due to arrive at the Milford chalet any second. His sister had consistently refused to take his phone calls since that stupid party in Paris. It was ludicrous! Nearly a year had passed and yet she was still behaving as if he'd killed her puppy or something. But then, even with that little pleasure hanging over his head, somehow the sights and the smells of Gstaad made it all seem worthwhile.

'Emma! Hey, Emma, over here!'

Emma was looking good. Fresh off the slopes, she had a

healthy pink-cheeked glow and her smile was wide as she hoiked her skis off her shoulder and sat down next to him.

'Tom! I didn't know you were coming!' she cried, reaching over to give him a kiss with genuine affection. 'I could have done with some company on the Wasserngrat.'

'I'm out of action,' shrugged Tom. He was reckless by nature, but even he wasn't convinced his knees would be strong enough to snowboard after being hit with a baseball bat two weeks earlier. 'I think the booze and cigarettes are finally catching up with me.'

'Oh yes? Stella told me you were trying to quit.'

'You've been talking about me behind my back then, have you?' he replied, secretly pleased.

'I've been curious since the second I heard you'd both been down to St Ives to see her dad,' she nudged him in the ribs.

'We're just friends,' he said quickly.

'I'm glad. She needs cheering up. Johnny Brinton is a viper. I saw him all over some woman at the Dugdale Festival. I tried to tell Stella but she didn't want to hear it at the time. I don't blame her. When you're in love who wants to hear it?'

'Viper? He's a worm. No, he's lower than a worm. He's a slug!'

'Just friends, hey?' smiled Emma sensing the fierce, protective tone in Tom's voice.'

'Stella's great.'

Emma started laughing quietly.

Tom sat bolt upright in his chair.

'Emma Bailey! You work in fashion for two minutes and already you've become this terrible gossip. What's happened to you?'

'I heard about Chessie,' said Emma, more seriously.

'Did Stella tell you what else happened at Trencarrow?

It turns out that Christopher has been sculpting all this time. I'm going to have a word with my mum to see if she can introduce him to a big gallery in London.'

It was only then that Tom realized with a sinking feeling that he still hadn't asked Julia about Christopher. After all she had done for him, it somehow felt rude asking her to suggest a big London gallery for Christopher. But then Tom had to admit he wasn't really doing it for Christopher; he was doing it for Stella.

He glanced at his watch.

'Come on,' he said. 'We'd better go and face the music.'

Emma pulled a face.

'Don't worry, I don't think they'll be back yet,' he said, patting her hand. 'They're still at the Eagle Club having lunch. Apparently Cassandra's gone straight up there to meet all her terrible Eurotrash friends. She finds it terribly embarrassing that Roger goes up there. My heart bleeds.'

Emma giggled. She was so relieved to have an ally over Christmas.

'A pact,' she said, squeezing his fingers. 'Let's stick together.'

Tom stood up. 'All for one and one for all,' he said, making an elaborate bow. 'Lead on, D'Artagnan.'

Le Chalet Anglais was an eighty-year-old traditional Savoyese chalet set back on a hill behind the town with beautiful views of the Palace Hotel's Rapunzel turrets. The main living room was a long high-beamed loft in aged pine lit by two chandeliers with a roaring stone fireplace at one end. The sumptuous dining area had a long rustic wooden table set with silver and bone china next to a huge open-plan kitchen area. By the time Emma had taken a hot shower and come back downstairs, everyone had arrived back at the chalet while a pretty chalet girl – who Emma predicted would end

512

up in bed with Tom by the end of the festive season – was pulling a huge Beef Wellington from the oven. It smelled delicious.

'Bloody awful snow,' said Roger, sipping a G&T in a velvet club chair in front of the fire. 'Global warming is going to put this town out of business if we're not careful. Ah, Emma,' he said, rising to his feet. 'Glad you could make it.'

'Thanks for inviting me. Actually, the snow wasn't too bad on the slopes today although on Boxing Day I think I'm going to Les Diablerets if anyone wants to come?'

'I will,' said Ruby, putting her hand in the air. 'I want to go skiing with Emma.'

Emma laughed. She didn't see Ruby a great deal; only in the school holidays when she stayed with Julia, but had enjoyed getting to know the young teenager who was fun, feisty and clever.

Standing next to the fireplace in skinny jeans, a white T-shirt and a red fox fur gilet, Cassandra viewed her daughter narrowly.

'You are not going to Les Diablerets with Emma. She's bound to go off-piste and leave you.'

'Emma's always been a wonderful skier, haven't you?' said Roger, handing her a glass of claret. 'Did you keep it up when you went to America? Jackson Hole has some decent skiing, I hear.'

'The Aman resort out there is wonderful,' piped up Rebecca.

'I sometimes got up to Maine,' said Emma, 'but to be honest, Gstaad was probably closer to Boston than Jackson Hole.'

Emma was relieved that the atmosphere was not as tense as she'd anticipated. Still, such a change in Roger's attitude towards her couldn't simply be festive spirit, could it? She mused, eyeing him carefully.

*   *   *

The chalet girl was serving the food in big earthenware pots in the middle of the table, so Roger clinked his ring against his glass.

'Before we start the meal I'd like to give a little toast to Saul, who's made this all possible tonight and I'm sure is up there right now delighted that we're all here together to enjoy it.'

'Hear, hear!' cried Tom, who seemed to be holding up his part of his pact with Emma by hitting the advocaat.

They all settled down around the table. Roger made a point of holding Emma's chair for her and then he sat down next to her.

'So I hear things are going well in your department,' said Emma.

Roger nodded enthusiastically, as he glugged wine into both their glasses.

'The wife of this *very* rich Eastern European came in a few days ago, didn't she Roger?' said Rebecca flicking a sheath of hair over her shoulder. 'She ordered a 50-inch crocodile bag with real eagle feathers. It's going to cost her £120,000 and apparently she didn't even blink. Isn't fashion crazy sometimes?'

'That's not fashion, that's money laundering,' said Cassandra cynically.

'All I could think of was: where are we going to get a croc big enough for a 50-incher?' said Roger, shaking his head.

As the meal progressed, Emma could not help but think that anyone listening to the laughter and banter around the table would believe they were watching a happy close-knit family sharing a warm Christmas together, rather than a collection of warring factions jostling for position inside a business balancing on a knife-edge.

When finally there was a lull in conversation, Roger put

down his glass as if he was preparing to say something important.

'Now we're all here,' he said, raising his voice to include everyone, 'and in such convivial surroundings, I think it's time I brought something up.'

'Roger,' said Julia. 'It's Christmas Eve.'

He shook his head and wiped his mouth with a napkin. 'It's good news, Julia. Or at least I think it is.'

Emma put down her fork and looked at Roger, suddenly feeling in her gut that she wasn't going to like what he was going to say.

'I was having dinner with Victor Chen a couple of weeks ago and, well, he's expressed serious interest in Milford.'

'Who's Victor Chen?' asked Tom, refilling his glass.

'He owns VCT, the luxury goods company,' said Cassandra with authority. 'I use the word "luxury" loosely because half of his company's products are now made in China.'

'I think that's rather uncharitable, Cassandra,' said Roger. 'I believe you could say the same about many high-fashion brands too. Just because something is made in the Far East doesn't meant to say that the quality is inferior.'

'That depends on your definition of "quality", Roger,' said Cassandra icily. 'If Milford moves production to Taiwan, you're in danger of destroying the brand altogether.'

'Come now, Cassandra . . .'

'How interested is he in Milford?' interrupted Virginia. 'Are we talking about a minority shareholding or something much bigger?'

'Oh, the whole thing,' said Roger blithely. 'Naturally the renaissance of the company is making waves in the industry and everyone is saying we're the new Burberry and Emma here is our Rose Marie Bravo, guiding our company from the ashes back to the top of the fashion tree. Of course people are going to see Milford as a good investment.'

Emma and Tom glanced at each other.

'Have you any idea of how much he'd be willing to pay?' asked Virginia.

Roger shrugged.

'Who's to say without a valuation, and anyway, a company is only worth as much as somebody is prepared to pay for it. Look at the sale of J Crew. Sold for four billion dollars off the back of profits of only four million dollars. The value is the brand. And our brand is back in business.'

People started talking amongst themselves and an excited twitter ran around the table.

'Hang on, hang on,' said Emma raising a hand slightly.

Roger's smile began to fade.

'VCT's interest is flattering but immaterial. I don't want to sell. Serious interest from a big group like VCT is a greater indicator that we're doing something right, but that's all. I think we've got something really valuable here – we're just at the start of our journey.'

'But surely we should at least wait to see what the offer is, darling?' said Virginia, a note of reproach in her voice. 'You can't be saying no to a sale full stop?'

'Yes, I am,' said Emma firmly. 'For the foreseeable future at least. I have a five-year plan I want to see through. The plan is to build the business, not prime it for sale.'

'Do you appreciate how much I am doing for this company?' said Roger, unable to hide his anger. 'I'm going to great lengths to sound out interest and follow up leads.'

'No one has asked you to do that, Roger,' said Emma calmly.

Roger got up from the table and stalked across the room, going outside onto the balcony.

'Look what you've done, Emma. It's Christmas, you know,' said Virginia.

'The subject is closed,' said Emma, meeting her gaze. 'We're not interested.'

'How can you be so damned stubborn!' cried Virginia, throwing up her hands. 'You have no idea what they are even offering. Perhaps you should consult a few other people before you start making such sweeping statements as "We're not interested". The *nerve*! This isn't *your* company alone, Emma.' She glared at her daughter for a moment before continuing.

'As we're talking about this and as you seem to have destroyed the atmosphere, I might as well tell you that Jonathon was talking to Harry Wilcox, a lawyer friend of his, and *he* recommended that we go public. We are hot news and we may never get any hotter. Harry said something about us being over-valued which, in share terms, means a very good return for us.'

'And why would we want to go public?' said Emma, raising her voice just slightly. 'Having to answer to so many shareholders? Do you really want that, Mother? We need to have a longer-term strategy to build a valuable luxury goods empire instead of selling out at the first opportunity. We should be trying to build something that could be worth ten, twenty times as much in ten years. And we should be building it our way. The Milford way.'

'*Your* way,' said Rebecca, sarcastically.

'Look!' said Emma, rapping her knuckles on the table and sending her glass of water flying. 'We are *not* selling the company to VCT or anyone else right now. We are not going to float the company either. I'm sorry if that spoils your Christmas but that's the way it is.'

Out of the corner of her eye, Emma felt sure she had seen Cassandra smirking, but when she looked around, the expression had gone. Julia looked at her watch and sighed.

'Look at the time. Let's go to church.'

Emma was glad of the break and found the tranquillity of the church soothing after the confrontation at dinner.

She wasn't religious but it felt like a safe haven, somewhere she could be alone with her thoughts away from the accusing stares of her family.

After Mass the rest of the family drifted out slowly and Emma hung back, hoping to avoid another argument. Unfortunately for her, so many people were eager to exchange Christmas pleasantries with the priest, the church doorway became a bottleneck and when she finally stepped out into the night, Emma found herself walking next to Cassandra. Her cousin was wrapped up in a long sable mink fur and black boots, like a ghost from a more glamorous age. They walked in silence, the others moving on ahead until all that Emma could hear was the soft crunch of Cassandra's boots in the snow.

'Why did you stick up for me at dinner?' asked Emma suddenly. It had been bothering her since Cassandra had spoken; it was so out of character.

Cassandra thrust her hands in her pockets and shrugged.

'It wasn't a question of sticking up for you. I'd simply hate to see Milford products being made on a conveyer belt in the Far East.'

'Well, I appreciated it; thank you.'

Emma wasn't sure she entirely believed Cassandra; her cousin never did anything without a motive; everything was calculated to benefit her. But then, Emma could do with every ally she could get at the moment. She had been nervous about coming out to Gstaad before this sudden outbreak of inter-family warfare and now she felt completely isolated. *It won't kill you to be civil, Emma,* she told herself.

'So how's work?'

'Very good actually,' said Cassandra. 'I've just taken Jessica West on as a contributing editor, I believe you know her? Used to go out with Rob Holland. It was quite serious at one point I think.'

'Yes, I think he liked her,' said Emma honestly, though it pained her to do so. 'But I think she was a little too ambitious. I don't think having stepchildren, playing happy families with Rob's little girl, figured in her immediate master-plan.'

Cassandra smiled.

'Yes, she told me that's why she finished with him. According to her, he was very cut up about it and went running back to his ex – Madeline, isn't it? Apparently Jessica saw them together in New York at somewhere glamorous like Sant Ambroeus. Sounds like they're well suited, anyway. For all his rock 'n' roll credentials, Rob is really just a Connecticut WASP.'

Emma stared down at the ground, dazed. While there was probably no way Cassandra knew about herself and Rob, her words were still designed to wound and they had had the desired effect, stabbing Emma in the heart like barbs. It all made sense. That was why Rob hadn't phoned after their night in Somerset: he'd got back with Madeline in New York. Her mind whirled, desperate to think of some other explanation. *It couldn't be true, could it? Rob didn't love Madeline and she didn't love him either.* But of course, love didn't need to come into it. Rob was back with Madeline for the sake of Polly, to be a family because Polly was the most important thing in his life. She felt a tear slip down her cheek. Just one. It was an act of rebellion: telling her that her head and heart were in conflict.

'Oh dear,' said Cassandra with a quiet look of triumph. 'Have I said something I shouldn't?'

Emma turned swiftly on her cousin.

'What is wrong with you Cassandra?' she spat.

Cassandra turned and smiled, pulling her mink coat tighter around her body.

'Oh dear, what's rattled your cage? It's not Rob Holland,

519

is it? He's slept with half of London, darling, so don't waste your time.'

'It's not Rob, it's *you*. You spread lies about me around the industry, you throw a party on the same night as the Milford launch, you even got that little creep from Laura's wedding to do a hatchet job on me! And now you think you can wind me up with stories about Rob.'

'I'm only saving you from getting hurt, being foolish enough to fall for some cad like Rob Holland.'

'Do you think I'm stupid?' replied Emma angrily. 'You don't give a hoot about me. It's all about Milford. It's all about getting even.' Emma took a deep breath and tried to compose herself.

'I never asked for Milford, or even wanted it, but it's mine now and I want to make it into the best thing I possibly can. Stop blaming me, Cassandra. Stop hating me. Please just leave me alone to get on with it. Take out your frustrations elsewhere.'

Cassandra's mouth curled viciously. She wasn't a woman who was accustomed to having people say things to her face. She stared at Emma with a look of disgust.

'For all that blue-chip education, and those fancy letters at the end of your name, you really don't know anything, do you,' she said, her voice a low, cold whisper.

'I know enough, Cassandra.'

'Do you?' she barked a hollow laugh, 'I really doubt that, Emma.' She stopped in the street and faced her cousin squarely.

'But you're right about one thing. I do blame you. But not for being given the company, although I'm sure you must have manipulated Saul somehow. Emma, I've been blaming you since I was thirteen years old.'

Cassandra paused, her breath puffing in white clouds.

'I've blamed you since the day your father destroyed my family.'

Emma actually gasped. She was rooted to the spot and could only stare at the woman, her head in the air, her slim, straight nose held aloft like a bloodhound.

'I don't understand you,' she whispered.

'It's very simple,' said Cassandra, her voice dripping with venom. 'Your father had an affair with my mother. Did you know that, Emma? Is that one of the things you "know"? My father found out and he left her. He left *us*. Do you know how that feels, Emma? Do you?'

'Cassandra, please.'

'Oh yes, you probably think you *know* how it feels, Emma, because your father is dead. But it's really not the same as someone *leaving* you. Mine didn't want us any more and you'll never know how that rejection makes you feel.'

Her cold confession had stunned Emma. She had been completely wrong-footed.

'I'm sorry your father walked out on you,' she said, trying to keep her voice steady, 'but it's not *my* father's fault. My dad didn't have an affair with Aunt Julia. She's my mother's *sister*.'

'Another one of your certainties? Well, I saw it with my own eyes,' spat Cassandra. 'That first summer we went to Provence, the night of the party. Most of the kids were in bed, but I thought I was too old to be tucked up with the children. I walked out deep into the grounds, to that tool shed.'

Cassandra's voice trailed off, as if it was taking every ounce of will to keep herself under control.

'I saw my mother in there having sex with your father. Sex I didn't understand then, but which I recognize now. Wild and hungry sex. Sex that breaks up families because it's so exciting it's like a drug which makes everything that's gone before seem hollow and meaningless.'

'It was dark, it could have been anyone,' said Emma,

521

knowing how weak her argument sounded, but still desperate to deny her father's involvement.

'It was them,' said Cassandra. 'My father left us three months later. *Abandoned* us. Your father broke up our family. I came back from my first term at school and he had gone. I grew up without a father.'

The moonlight was shining a milky light down at them. Behind them the church bells rang out their midnight Christmas peal.

'So every kick you give me makes you feel a little better? Is that it?' said Emma softly. 'Well, it's not going to bring him back.'

Cassandra turned towards Emma so quickly, she slipped on the icy path.

'Don't you dare give me your pseudo-psychoanalysis!' she hissed. 'You think your father ruined my whole life because he couldn't keep his dick in his pants? You think I'm some heartbroken little girl who's using success to make up for Daddy not loving me? You've been watching too much Oprah, honey.'

Cassandra held up one hand, her fingers curling into a tight fist. 'This isn't about my hurt feelings, Emma. This is about *revenge*.'

Emma's eyes widened as she saw the fury in Cassandra's face.

'And believe me, darling, I've barely even begun.'

Cassandra turned and strode on ahead. Emma could do nothing but watch her go.

'Is it true?'

Emma was standing by her mother's bedroom door. Virginia had changed into her dressing-gown and was turned towards the dressing table mirror, putting on face cream. In the dim light, her mother's face was pale, almost ghoulish in the reflection.

'Is what true, darling?'

Emma came in and sat on the blue and white gingham bedspread.

'That Dad and Aunt Julia had an affair? Was that why Uncle Desmond left her?'

She watched her mother's face carefully but she didn't even flinch, she simply carried on with her task.

'Who told you this?' she said finally.

'Cassandra.'

Virginia turned round to face her daughter.

'Jonathon will be back in a moment,' she said, looking over Emma's shoulder. 'He's only gone to get some coffee.'

'Cassandra said she saw them,' insisted Emma. 'She saw them together the summer before Dad died. Uncle Desmond found out and that's why he left Julia.'

For a moment, Virginia had a faraway look in her eye as if her mind had drifted off somewhere else. Then her face tensed, as if she were about to deny everything, then her cool face saddened with emotion, as an old wound re-opened, raw and bloody.

'Tell me, Mum,' said Emma softly.

'Some of it's true, some of it isn't,' she said, walking over to the bedroom door and closing it. 'Yes, your father and Julia had sex in Provence. You're a grown-up, Emma, you know how it can happen. You're drunk, it's hot, you're on holiday and caution flies out of the window on nights like that.' Her voice had the edge of sarcasm and the hint of regret. It was as if she were reciting lines from an old play she had long ago ceased to enjoy.

'How did you find out? Who told you? Dad?'

'Saul,' said Virginia quietly. 'I don't know how he knew. He told me he "suspected". I suppose in the same way that I suspected. You can just tell you know, sometimes.'

Virginia closed her eyes for a moment, seeing it all as if

523

it was only yesterday. She told Emma about the way her husband Jack and Julia had begun to avoid each other on the holiday; about the way her hand used to spring back from his when he touched her at the breakfast table; about the way two people who try to force themselves to be natural in front of one another, just end up looking even more contrived and unnatural. Emma could see the sparkle of a tear slip down her face; she who was usually so cool and restrained, usually such a mask of control. Emma wondered if it had always been that way.

'Julia and Desmond's marriage was very rocky,' she continued. 'It had been since Tom was born when Julia became very depressed. Several weeks after the Provence holiday Desmond left her; Saul suspected that he had found out about Julia and Jack. So Saul called up Jack and asked him to come round to the manor for a conversation, a *man to man* chat.'

A small smile pulled at Virginia's lips. 'Saul was like that. He was dreadfully irresponsible in some ways but in other ways he really understood his position as head of the family. Anyway . . .' she puffed out her cheeks, '. . . that's when your father's crash happened. On the way to see Saul.' She gave a low, angry laugh. 'The irony was that Des didn't leave Julia because of any affair *she* was having. Julia and your father – that was a one-off on holiday. Julia told me that many years later. Des left her because he'd met Helen by then, the South African trollop he eventually went to Durban with. Julia hid it from the kids, she didn't want them to know that Des was in a serious relationship so soon after he'd left them. She wanted to protect them.'

Tears were now running down Emma's cheeks.

'But Cassandra thinks it was all Dad's fault.'

'It wasn't. And I don't think Saul ever forgave himself for the accident. A fateful intervention,' she continued with a slow sad smile. 'Saul used to tell me over and over again that he'd left you without a father.' She looked at Emma with a more controlled expression as if she was putting her mask back on again.

'I don't doubt that's why he left you the company, Emma. It was his way of trying to make things up to us.'

Emma nodded, taking a tissue from the dressing table and wiping her eyes.

'Who knows about this?' she asked.

'To my knowledge, no one apart from us and Julia.'

'Cassandra certainly doesn't.'

Virginia turned to her; the cold eyes were back and the shutters were down.

'And you must make sure it stays that way.'

'But she despises me. She's trying to destroy the company and ruin me because she wants revenge for something she's got the wrong way around!' protested Emma.

Virginia grabbed Emma's hand and squeezed hard.

'No, Emma. I know Cassandra is hard work sometimes, but she's suffered enough. Please, for me,' she said, searching her daughter's eyes, 'let sleeping dogs lie.'

In her attic bedroom, a tiny room she had been furious about being allocated, Cassandra was unable to sleep. She sat on the bed, looking over to the small single bed in the corner, where Ruby was fast asleep. She watched the rise and fall of her breath under the duvet and felt a tug of guilt somewhere distant inside her. Did her daughter deserve a father? Cassandra had always rejected marriage in favour of her own career, thinking it would be better that way. That way, you didn't get hurt. But was she right?

There was a decanter of port on her bedside table and she poured herself a small measure. There was no balcony in the cramped living space in the rafters, but there was a door leading to some narrow steps which led to the ground, a relic from when the chalet had servants living in the attic who needed to come and go without disturbing the family. Cassandra put on her cashmere robe and went out onto the wooden steps. She sank down, and breathed in the ice-cold air. So finally she had told Emma, had told someone. But instead of the sweet relief of sharing a secret she had kept for over twenty years, there was a terrible sense of emptiness – and she had to admit it, embarrassment. *I'm such a bloody cliché*, she thought, her cheeks flaming despite the cold. All that time, without even knowing it, she had used the pain and hurt to drive her onwards, to transform herself into something bigger and better than that bruised 13-year-old who felt so worthless. *If I make myself clever and pretty and successful, then maybe Daddy will come back*, she mocked with an ironic smile. But now it had been vocalized, it didn't seem like such a potent force. Now it just felt like what it was; pain and envy so fierce it stuck in her throat and made her want to choke. Despite all Cassandra's bluster and threats, Emma had been right on two counts: every kick she gave her did make Cassandra feel better; she simply wanted Emma to suffer the way she had. But Emma was also spot on when she had said it was futile: Milford was successful. She had achieved nothing.

She looked at the dark jagged edges of the mountains and took a deep lungful of air, trying to let go of all the tension so that she could finally sleep. She was about to go inside when she heard the low creak of a balcony door opening beneath her and voices.

'Come in, Rebecca,' said a man's voice. 'It's bloody freezing.'

Cassandra peeked over the edge, keeping in the shadows. From her lofty position, she could see the whole balcony beneath her. Rebecca and Roger were talking in low mumbled voices. Rebecca was trying to talk in a whisper but her anger made her words clear.

'Come on, darling,' said Roger, 'we'll get this sorted. I'll get the money for the Ricardo deal. Perhaps we can sell this place. That will be a start.'

Moving silently in her cashmere socks, Cassandra moved down two more stairs, cocking her head and holding her breath.

'I'm not selling Le Chalet Anglais to raise the money,' hissed Rebecca. 'People would kill for a place in Gstaad. It's the only decent thing we've got. Forget the Ricardo deal. Something better will come along. And it better bloody had. We have a second-rate house and a two-year-old BMW. Do you realize how embarrassing it is for me getting it valet parked? I'm sick of living like the wife of middle management.'

'Ricardo's business *is* the something better, darling. I want to make some serious money for us both. I want us to have a better life. One day soon you can have whatever house or car you want. We'll get her out of the picture. There's more than one way to skin a cat.'

Rebecca laughed mirthlessly.

'Or a bitch.'

They moved back inside their room and closed the French windows. Cassandra pulled her robe tighter around her body and hurried back up the stairs to the warmth of her room, knowing exactly what they were talking about.

Christmas Day passed quietly. Lunch was subdued after which Emma retreated to her room. By Boxing Day morning, she was desperate to get out of the chalet. Christmas had turned into a nightmare. Gstaad was still Gstaad of course, super-chic and chocolate-box pretty, but with all this pressure, Emma couldn't even enjoy the view. She was aching to get up onto the slopes where she could be alone and clear her head. When she came down into the living room, she found Tom watching the television in tracksuit bottoms, his feet clad in massive fluffy slippers, a Christmas gift from Cassandra which he suspected was a dig at his layabout status.

'I'm going up to Les Diablerets,' said Emma. 'Do you want to come?'

'Nah,' he shook his head, sending crumbs from the croissant he was eating showering onto his sweater. 'It's Boxing Day, Em. A holiday – you've got to take these things seriously.'

'This is a holiday for me – getting away from it all. And everyone.'

Tom pulled a sympathetic face.

'Well, don't wear yourself out too much. I'm taking you down to Greengos or Hush tonight. Your treat.'

Emma giggled. 'Why not? Maybe I can bag myself a Eurotrash prince.'

The drive to Les Diablerets only took twenty minutes. The roads had been salted so there was no need for chains on the tyres. Emma loved being out in snow, and as she left the car and headed for the lifts, the air was so crisp the inside of her nose tingled. Les Diablerets wasn't as smart or chic as Gstaad. There were no Hermès boutiques or world-class hotels, no tourists in fur coats and moon boots. She could never understand the snobbery and posturing attached to ski resorts: skiing was all about surrounding yourself with natural beauty and pitting your own body against the elements; it was not about the social scene. Consequently, Emma loved skiing on her own, going deep into the powder off-piste, feeling the wind in her hair, spray on her goggles, her thighs like pistons aching to stop. It was the same well-hidden streak

528

in Emma that made her love cave-diving, a recklessness tempered by reason: she would take herself to the edge of her abilities, no more. This was why Emma had arranged for a guide to show her the best skiing, but steer her away from the real dangers.

Johann was tall and lithe, a proud German-speaking Swiss mountain guide who knew every run, slope and crevasse in a thirty-mile radius. He was also devilishly handsome, observed Emma, taking in his chiselled, if wind-chapped, features.

'There is some fresh powder today,' said Johann. 'Avalanches are a possibility.'

Emma nodded; she had already seen the reports. Avalanche alert was on level 3 today: a threat but not dangerously so. Wasting no time on small talk, they stamped into their skis and Johann took off, Emma hard on his heels. Immediately, Emma's world shrank to the stretch of snow directly in front of her skis. The roar of air in her ears, the exhilaration of the speed, the concentration as Johann led her in a series of sharp turns, it all blew everything else from her head. At first Johann skied at a fair pace, occasionally glancing behind to gauge her ability, but within minutes he was carving through the snow at full speed, confident Emma could handle everything he threw at her. She was grinning as he scythed to a halt at the edge of a cliff. In front of them across a gorge, Emma could see the jagged edges of even higher mountains, white velvet slopes broken with grey exposed walls of sheer rock. The air felt crystal clear and Emma felt her body and mind respond: she felt sharp and clear, unburdened by business worries or petty feuds.

'You ski well,' said Johann.

'Thanks,' said Emma, feeling her cheeks blush. 'I've got a good guide.'

She stood drinking in the fabulous view for a moment more, trying not to notice Johann's blue eyes fixed on her. The fitted white salopettes and bright blue jacket may have covered Emma's slim, athletic body, but not even the fleece headband covering her ears and the large goggles could hide the striking angles of her face.

'It's quiet today,' she said to fill the silence.

'Holiday time. People come less for skiing and more for drinking,' he smiled, then flipped his goggles down and plunged down the slope. Emma shot down straight after him, adrenalin rushing around her body. She felt free. This was when she felt truly alive, not staring at a spreadsheet or hammering out deals, but here, barrelling down a sheer face at 100 kilometres an hour. She was a natural skier, having learnt on these very slopes at Saul's invitation throughout her childhood, and every time she took to the snow, she wished she could spend her whole life out here, surrounded by crisp white nothingness. Out here, she felt at home.

All too soon, the sun began to sink, the light was fading fast and the ink-blue sky was slashed with ribbons of gold and pink. Johann brought them back round to their starting point. As she stepped out of her skis, Emma considered it a day very well spent. The conditions and scenery had been perfect, plus Johann had made her feel good – capable and attractive. She pulled her goggles off and hung them over her arm.

'Can I tempt you to a glass of Gluhwein?' asked Johann.

Emma pointed to the car. 'Driving, I'm afraid.'

'Then perhaps a chocolat chaud?'

She almost licked her lips at the thought of it, imagining Johann's strong hands wrapped around the mug.

'I'm afraid my family have plans for supper,' she shrugged.

'Perhaps you will come up to Les Diablerets tomorrow,

then? Here is my telephone number,' he said, handing her a card. 'Any time, day or night.'

'I might just do that,' she smiled.

'Auf wiedersehen.'

She attached her skis to the roof of the car and took off her thick padded jacket to drive more comfortably. She pulled out and Johann lifted a hand to wave. *Why am I such an idiot?* she thought angrily. *Why am I running back to a family who are trying to pull me down, when I could have . . .*

'Damn,' she cursed herself. Maybe Rob Holland was right, maybe she didn't know how to relax and have fun. She grimaced. That thought only reminded her of the day at the recording studios and her foot pressed down on the accelerator angrily. There were a few farms and chalets along the side of the road and although Boxing Day was a popular day for tourists flying in to the French Alps for the run up to New Year, there was hardly any traffic and once she was out of Les Diablerets it was almost pitch black. Emma thought of the folklore that Saul had once told her about the area. How the name Les Diablerets means 'abode of the devil' and how legend had it that lost souls drifted around the mountainsides at night carrying their lanterns. Slowly she became aware of headlights closing in behind her. The snow had started to fall again, so Emma hung back, waiting for the vehicle to overtake her. Instead, it came closer and closer until she could no longer see its lights. Then she jolted forward as the car behind touched her bumper.

'What the hell?' whispered Emma, tightening her grip on the steering wheel.

The vehicle behind bumped her again, this time with more force. As her mind searched for a rational explanation, she glanced down to check her headlights were on: *maybe he hasn't seen me here.* Suddenly Emma's head whipped forward as her car was slammed from behind. Her heart lurched; there was no mistaking the stranger's intent, and in front of her the snow was coming down quite heavily now. She looked into the mirror, trying to make out the driver, but there was another shuddering crash and her car veered dangerously onto the gravel siding, as her bumper glanced off the crash barriers.

'Who are you?' screamed Emma. 'What do you want?'

But the dazzling lights behind gave her all the answers she needed. Whoever they were, they were trying to push her over the edge. They were trying to *kill* her. Desperately, Emma stamped her foot down on the accelerator, and pulled away from the car behind, her hands shaking on the wheel as she fought to keep her car steady round a bend. And then she saw it in her headlights: two hundred yards up ahead, the sturdy crash barrier disappeared, to be replaced by a flimsy wooden fence. That meant the drop was less severe, less *fatal* – surely? As she gunned the engine, the chasing vehicle caught up and crashed into Emma's car so hard that her head cracked against the steering wheel. Her car was suddenly wrenched over to the right and thrown into a skid; the rear end whipped round and caught the last section of the steel crash barrier. Emma jumped on the brakes with both feet; her car veered off the road and slammed into the rough timber fence, chunks of wood and metal flew at the windscreen like missiles. The car slid along at a crazy angle, the fence holding its weight for the moment; only a few slats of wood preventing it from rolling down the mountain. Emma knew she had to move. She unclipped her seatbelt and pushed all her weight against the door. It flew open and she used the momentum to throw herself up and out of the car, landing face-down into the gravel at the side of the road, tearing her hands and elbows as she did so. She rolled over just in time to see the fence finally splinter and the car plunge away into the dark. There was nothing but a rushing sound for a few long seconds and then a crash, followed by a *crump* and a white glow as the engine ignited. Emma scrambled away from the edge, clawing her way across the dark road and into the snow bank on the other side. The cold air stung her bruised and torn body. She lay back as she watched the car burst into flames. And then she felt nothing.

55

The first thing Emma saw when she opened her eyes again was the sterile white of the hospital ceiling. Slowly her vision adjusted and she became aware of a shape standing by her bed.

'Rob?'

'Hey,' he said in a quiet voice, a sad smile on his lips. 'Welcome back.'

'Why are you here?' she croaked. 'How did you . . . what's going on . . .?'

Emma closed her eyes again, struggling to make sense of it all, her confusion almost as acute as the throbbing pain coming from every part of her body.

Lifting her head with effort, she saw a coat over the back of the chair and a large bunch of lilies in a vase on the table.

'Have I been unconscious?'

Rob nodded. 'Since yesterday.'

'But why are you here?'

He looked down and gave her a smile.

'I called to say Happy Christmas. Your mother had your mobile phone and told me there'd been an accident.'

Emma's head ached.

'I don't understand. You came from Chilcot?'

'No, I was in Courchevel; the drive isn't too bad. Just being a good neighbour – brought you some grapes,' he joked.

She managed a weak smile.

'I feel dreadful.'

'You don't look too hot, either.'

Emma actually laughed at this, instantly regretting it as pain stabbed at her ribs.

'You know how to charm the ladies, Rob Holland,' she winced. 'Every one except me, anyway. So tell me: what's the damage? It feels bad.'

Rob paused a beat before replying and by the expression on his face she knew that it was serious. Their eyes locked and Emma felt a flutter in her chest.

'I think it could have been a lot worse,' he said quietly. 'Broken wrist, ribs, lots of cuts and bruises. The main thing worrying the docs is that you've been unconscious for so long. But it's good to have you back again now, slugger.'

Emma smiled again and Rob straightened up.

'Listen, I think your mum is in the hospital somewhere getting a drink,' said Rob. 'I'm going to find her – and a doctor. Don't you go anywhere, OK?'

She reached out her hand to touch his.

'Don't. Just stay with me a minute.'

Looking at Rob, she realized all her anger towards him had gone. They weren't a couple but the connection was still there. She felt safe with him. He squeezed her fingers and with his other hand stroked her gently on the cheek.

'Do you remember what happened?'

She gave the slightest of nods.

'Someone ran me off the road,' she whispered.

She saw Rob frown.

'No, honey. You were in a car accident.'

She shook her head.

'Someone tried to run me off the road deliberately.'

'Look, I think I'd better get a doctor,' he said, standing up.

'Please Rob.'

A tear slipped down her cheek.

'Someone tried to kill me, Rob. You've got to believe me. My family want me dead.'

She saw his face change from surprise to concern.

'You've had severe concussion, Em. You were in an accident.' He lowered his voice and glanced around. 'Honey, your family doesn't want you dead. They've all been at the hospital for the last twenty-four hours worried sick about you.'

She gave a tiny shake of the head. It was exactly what she would expect from them: Roger and Cassandra with their crocodile tears.

'Have the police examined the accident scene yet?' she asked, her voice rising. 'Have they seen the tyre tracks of another car trying to push me off the road? Paint scrapes on the rear bumper? What have they *said*?'

Rob touched her shoulder.

'Easy, Em, I don't know. I've only really spoken to your mom and Roger.'

Tears were flowing down the sides of her face now.

'Rob, listen to me,' she said, struggling to control her voice. 'I saw the car behind me, a black car. It came up close behind me, smashed into the bumper, again and again.' Her eyes closed as she recalled the whole horrific scene. 'I couldn't see who was driving, but they tried to run me off the road.'

Rob was holding her hand tightly and he could feel it becoming clammy.

'Why would someone want to kill you?' he asked softly.

She looked at him, her heart full of longing for him and fear for herself.

'For the company.'

He puffed out his cheeks and let out a long breath.

'Em, don't think like that. It's not good for you.'

'I need you to believe in me.'

'I do, of course I do, but . . .'

He turned around. Roger, Virginia and a doctor were standing at the door.

'Thank God you're OK,' said Roger, bulldozing his way into the room.

Emma squeezed Rob's hand as the doctor approached the bed and reached for his notes.

'You had a very lucky escape,' said the Swiss doctor rubbing his square jaw as he consulted the notes by the bed.

Emma looked at Rob, then at Roger.

'I know,' she said.

56

Emma refused to return to the chalet. The doctors wouldn't let her fly with an arm in a cast and instead Rob hired a car and offered to drive her back.

Her phone rang as they were approaching the outskirts of Paris.

'Grüezi. Is this Fraulein Bailey?' asked an accented voice.

'It is,' said Emma, stealing a glance at Rob.

'This is Inspector Beck of the Canton Bern police. An abandoned Mercedes has been found in Montbovond, about a fifteen-minute drive from Gstaad. I thought you would be interested to hear we discovered scrape marks all along the left-hand side, showing traces of red paint. I suspect they will match the red paint from your hire car that was run off the road.'

Emma had to bite her lip to prevent herself saying 'I told you so'.

'I suppose you have traced the owner of the car?'

'Yes. It belonged to a Mrs Suzanne Marcel, a socialite lady who lives in Gstaad,' said the policeman. 'However, that does not help us too much as she had reported the car stolen before your accident.'

'That car tried to run me off the road,' said Emma firmly. 'Whoever hit my car was trying to kill me, Inspector. Are there any forensic tests you can do on the car?'

There was a long pause. She wished she had stayed in Gstaad longer. She wondered how much of a priority her case would be now she was no longer there to pursue it.

'Miss Bailey, we feel sure it was, how do you say in English, *joyriders*. It was Christmas, the car was stolen, the drivers were drunk.'

She could tell what he was trying to say: if joyriding was their most likely explanation, then it certainly wouldn't be worth doing any expensive forensic tests on the vehicle.

'Inspector Beck,' said Emma, her voice rising, 'I am absolutely convinced that whoever ran me off the road was doing it deliberately and knew it was me in that car. Even if you don't believe me, one thing is certain: I was almost killed on that mountain. On that basis – attempted murder – I would hope that you and your police force might put a little more energy into finding the culprits, even if it was, as you say, *joyriders*.'

Beck sounded apologetic as he replied.

'Fraulein, there is very little evidence.'

'Well *find* some, Inspector!'

When she put down her mobile, Emma's hands were shaking. She rested her head wearily against the window.

'It wasn't joyriders,' she said quietly.

'It *is* the simplest explanation,' said Rob.

She looked at his profile and suddenly remembered the cider farm and how happy she had been that night. In the intimate confines of the car, there were so many questions she wanted to ask him. Why had it all cooled so suddenly after his Thanksgiving trip to New York? She didn't even know who he had been in Courchevel with. She didn't *want*

539

to know. In Rob's car she felt protected and safe, she wanted everything to stay that way for now.

'What a great start to the New Year this is,' she said, watching the French countryside slip by.

'Listen, I have an idea,' said Rob quickly. 'Your birthday is next month, right?'

'You have a good memory,' she said suspiciously.

'I'm not just a pretty face,' he grinned. 'And I also seem to remember that last year's celebration was pretty crappy too, wasn't it?'

She gave a low sarcastic laugh. 'Oh yes. Betrayed by my then-boyfriend, I should have known what sort of year it was going to turn out to be.'

'Well, this year, Miss Bailey, you are going to have a party. After all, it is your thirtieth. You need to push the boat out.'

'Oh, Rob,' she groaned.

'I won't take no for an answer. We'll have a party at the house: leave it to me to sort everything out.'

'Yeah, great,' she grinned. 'Coke, hookers. Happy birthday, Emma.'

Rob didn't smile.

'Hey, maybe you could let me be nice to you every once in a while.'

'Oh, I'm not being ungrateful, Rob. I'm just not, you know, the party sort of person.'

'You did OK at the shop launch.'

'That was different. That was for the shop, not for me. I don't like attention in that way and I just don't think there's anything much to celebrate.'

'Why not?'

'Someone tried to kill me, Rob. I know they did.'

'But who? Your family? They have no reason to want you dead.'

'They have every reason,' she said, remembering the

conversation at the Christmas Eve dinner. 'They want me out of the way so they can either sell the company or float it. I don't trust anyone, Rob,' she said quietly. 'No one at all.'

57

'Georgia Kennedy! I don't believe it. How? Tell me!' said Jeremy Pike, rushing into Cassandra's office almost breathless with excitement. It was the first working day of the New Year and Cassandra had only just taken her coat off. She was inwardly delighted at the reaction to Georgia Kennedy on *Rive*'s February cover, having seen the looks of wonder on the faces of her staff as she passed through the outer office.

'Everybody has been after Georgia Kennedy for years, *everybody*. Come on, how did you do it? Spill!'

She suspected Jeremy was irritated to have been excluded from *Rive*'s little editorial secret, but for now he was hiding it well. Cassandra enjoyed her moment. Lightly tanned from Gstaad, wearing a winter-white, one-shouldered dress that would have looked over-dressed on anyone but her she looked and felt like the most powerful magazine editor on earth. 'My lips are sealed, Jeremy, even for you,' she smiled.

David Stern came in behind Jeremy, grinning.

'I went into Victoria Station's WH Smith this morning and they were all sold out.'

'Yes, and Sky news have phoned three times,' added

Jeremy excitedly. 'The *Evening Standard, The Times*. Everyone wants to interview you about the piece.'

'And they will. In time,' nodded Cassandra. 'But for now, it's all ours.'

'What's Glenda had to say about it?'

Cassandra's smile was sphinx-like. She knew she had that confrontation to look forward to as soon as New York woke up. Glenda would be incandescent with rage that Cassandra had gone back on their deal to run Georgia Kennedy on the March cover of both US and UK *Rive*. Cassandra's bold decision to run it a month early against her wishes meant that Glenda had been well and truly trumped, despite her supposed power and influence. *Couldn't have happened to a nicer girl*, thought Cassandra.

'Nothing yet, but I'm sure she'll be sporting about it,' she said. 'Now, Jeremy, can you round up the 10 a.m. meeting? Obviously there's plenty to discuss.'

'Like the takeover of Alliance?' said David, raising one eyebrow. As the buy-out had happened on the penultimate day of business before Christmas many members of staff hadn't been briefed about the news.

'It's good news all round,' said Cassandra breezily. 'Girard-Lambert are a huge company and they're prepared to invest heavily in *Rive*. With this cover and Girard-Lambert's muscle behind us, I'd say that this is the start of something wonderful.'

Lianne popped her head round the door.

'I have Pierre Desseau on the phone for you. Says he wants to meet for lunch.'

Cassandra almost purred with contentment. It *was* the start of something wonderful.

Pierre was already sitting at their table at the Ivy when Cassandra walked in, his skiing tan set off by the crisp blue of his shirt. Under normal circumstances, Pierre might have been Cassandra's type, but since Max had come into her life she had no desire for other men, however powerful. She sat down and took a menu from the waiter and allowed him to pour some mineral water into a glass.

'So how does it feel being the new owner of Alliance?' asked Cassandra, glad she had worn the winter-white dress.

'There's a lot to do, but of course it's exciting.'

'Well, the Feb issue is already flying off the news-stand,' she said.

'I'm sure,' said Pierre coolly.

His tone of voice put Cassandra on guard.

'Cassandra, we need to talk,' he said, putting his glass on the white tablecloth.

'About *Grand* magazine. Yes we do,' said Cassandra. She lowered her voice. 'I'm sure you'll agree I kept my side of the bargain.'

'Actually, I want to discuss *Rive*.'

He paused and put the palms of both hands on the table.

'I believe the UK and the US editions were supposed to run simultaneous covers of the Georgia Kennedy shoot for March? As it is, the UK edition has gone early with it, leaving the US issue high and dry for one of their most important issues of the year.'

She felt her throat dry and took a swift sip of water.

'So Glenda has got to you.'

'This is not playground one-upmanship,' said Pierre icily. 'Her March issue is about to go to press and they have no cover.'

'They'll cope,' said Cassandra tartly. 'And if they have to use the Georgia cover in March, so what? Glenda is exaggerating the situation for her own ends. She's quite happy for US *Rive* to run a month early with a cover the same as ours without thinking twice about *our* credibility.'

'Your ego is fucking with your business sense,' said Pierre in a low voice. The tables were close together and Cassandra glanced around, paranoid they might be overheard. It was really the most public, inappropriate place for a dressing-down.

'Every minute of every day I think about nothing but UK *Rive*,' she hissed back. 'I devote my life to it. I have turned it around and made it the hottest, most profitable fashion magazine in the country. Wanting the very best cover for *Rive* – an exclusive that I spent months successfully brokering myself, incidentally – has nothing to do with my ego and everything to do with consolidating our position in the market. Anyway, you wanted me to out-gun US *Rive*. That was the brief, wasn't it? Well, that's what I have done.'

'Yes, but at what cost?' said Pierre.

The meal arrived. Pierre looked at his plate before reaching into the inner pocket of his navy suit and pulling out a neatly-folded letter. He put it onto the table between them without a word.

'What's this?'

'A press release that will be going out to the industry tomorrow.'

Cassandra picked it up and scanned it quickly. Her mouth dropped open.

Girard-Lambert incorporating Alliance magazines are sad to announce the resignation of Cassandra Grand as editor-in-chief of UK Rive *magazine. Cassandra, who has been with the title for over four years, is leaving the company to pursue other interests. Her replacement is to be announced shortly.*

'What's this?' she said, unable to stop the croak in her voice. 'I hope you're going to tell me this is a way of getting me off *Rive* so I can start *Grand*?'

'There will be no *Grand* magazine,' said Pierre coolly.

Cassandra looked around again to make sure no one was listening to this grotesque pantomime.

'We had an agreement,' she snarled.

'We did,' he said flatly. 'One that was checked out by your lawyer. He was apparently happy that my obligation would be null and void in the event of your gross professional negligence.'

She felt as if her lungs had been punctured.

'And in what way have I been *negligent*?'

'You are a maverick, Cassandra. Creative, yes. Talented, of course. But not a team-player. I can't trust you to behave professionally, respectfully.'

'For instance?'

'For instance, Phoebe Fenton's husband Ethan has just bought Artemis cosmetics.'

Artemis was one of the biggest cosmetics companies in the world, almost rivalling L'Oréal in size.

'Phoebe and Ethan reunited over the holiday period,' continued Pierre. 'Ethan has already informed me that no Artemis advertising will run in *Rive* so long as you are in charge. Your Phoebe story, I believe, was another instance of you thinking only of ambition and not of consequence.'

Cassandra snorted.

'Don't be ridiculous, how was I to know her husband was going to buy Artemis? If that's what you call negligent, why not throw these in: circulation is up; ad revenue is up; our profile is sky-high. The industry love me. Fire me and you'll have the biggest, noisiest unfair dismissal case you've ever heard of.'

'You really must keep that ego in check,' said Pierre quietly, 'it will get you into trouble one day.'

Cassandra narrowed her eyes.

'Don't threaten me,' she spat. '*Rive* is nothing without

me. You know I was the driving force in the US and when I left to relaunch *Rive* UK all Glenda did was copy *my* vision.'

'Actually, Glenda has presented a very exciting new vision to me for the future of *Rive*.'

'You're welcome to it,' she snarled, standing up and walking towards the door; a hundred faces turned to watch her as she left.

Cassandra's apartment felt unusually still in the middle of the day. Ruby was back at her grandmother's before returning to school and the chaos she'd left in her wake had been replaced with Cassandra's tasteful order – but suddenly she longed for Ruby's careless abandon. She paced around the open-plan flat, aimlessly straightening books and cushions, still in her coat, clutching it tight around her body like emotional insulation.

She didn't need *Rive*, she didn't need Pierre Desseau, she told herself. She was Cassandra Grand! Any magazine or fashion house would kill to have her on board. *So why do I feel like I'm walking to the gallows?*

She snatched up her mobile phone.

'Max, can you come?'

She hadn't seen him for two weeks or spoken to him for three days; she missed him so much it was like a physical pain. Right now she wanted him by her side more than she had ever wanted anything.

'What's wrong?'

'Nothing. I need to see you about something. I'm at home. Come as soon as you can.'

She poured a vodka and slimline-tonic and took it out onto the balcony. She stared out at the city, not really thinking, just being, watching the clouds and traffic. She had no idea how long she was out there but she had watched the grey afternoon fade and now it was getting dark. Her skin was ice cold; she liked that. She wanted to be numbed – it was her way of coping. Max came at five, letting himself in with the key she had given him weeks before. He put the key on the table and walked across to her. Cassandra lifted her fingers to touch his lips, cupping his face before kissing him.

'You're cold,' he said, frowning.

'And you're early,' she smiled, pleased that he had rushed to her side.

'I wanted to come early,' said Max going over to sit in the Barcelona chair opposite her. Watching him, in the half light, almost made her forget about *Rive*. She wanted to climb into him, as if he was a suit. She decided not to mention her troubles straightaway – she wanted to enjoy a little time together first.

'So how was New Year without me?'

'St Barts was OK.'

He seemed uneasy, distracted. Cassandra immediately felt nervous. The room felt charged like the air before a storm.

'You were supposed to say how much you missed me,' she said.

There was a long uncomfortable pause.

'Laura is pregnant. We found out two days ago.'

She bit her bottom lip painfully.

'You said you weren't having sex.'

'Cassandra, she's my *wife*,' he said fiercely.

She tasted blood on her lip and licked it away, pulling herself up into her most majestic stance.

'Well, let her have babies! That's what trophy wives do, isn't it?' said Cassandra tartly.

Max stood up and started pacing back and forth across the rug; the same rug they had made love on so many times, planning their future together.

'Cassandra, it's more than that. We are having a *family*,'

he said. 'Another little me, I have to give it a go. I have to *try* and give it a go. At least for now. This child is the heir to Hildon.'

Cassandra walked to the table and poured herself another vodka, ignoring the tonic. He looked at her.

'I'm sorry, Cass. You are a breathtakingly exciting woman. You are passionate and beautiful and sex is incredible. But . . .' He hesitated.

'That's all I am to you,' she said quietly, putting down the empty glass and walking towards him, 'Sex? An easy fuck when your wife's back is turned?'

He grabbed her hands but kept his distance.

'No. *No.* You and I, we are the same creatures. We enjoy the thrill, we *want* each other but we don't *need* each other.'

It was as if he'd punched her in the stomach. From that first night Cassandra had felt that she and Max were soul mates, that their similarities had linked them on a deep and intimate level, but Max had just managed to make their connection feel inconsequential, something he could take or leave whenever he felt like it.

She nodded slowly, determined not to show her feelings. She was Cassandra Grand. She didn't *cry*.

'What about Clochiers?' she asked, not daring to breathe.

Max shook his head.

'I don't think we should see each other any more. You tempt me too much.'

Their eyes met for a moment; then she looked away.

'Just go,' she said.

He hung by her side for a moment, for once unsure of what to do.

'I saw the Georgia cover,' he said. 'It looks incredible. You see, you really don't need me, do you?'

'Clearly not,' she replied.

He smiled sadly, looked at the key he had left on the table and walked out of the door. And for the first time in a very long time, she cried until there were no more tears left to shed.

58

The next two weeks seemed to pass in slow motion. To Cassandra, it was as if she were detached from her own life, watching it all unfold on a movie screen. Guillaume Riche was on the phone immediately after he heard of Cassandra's 'resignation', insisting she recuperate at his chateau. She politely declined, knowing he was knee-deep in preparations for couture, but she was grateful for the support. Astrid Brinton also offered the use of Greywood, but the gesture was slightly undermined by Astrid's insistence that Cassandra step down as chair of the Charles Worth exhibition and party at the V&A. 'We don't want to lose people because they feel awkward do we, darling?' she had said. Cassandra soon found that this was a common feeling among many of her so-called friends. When she'd been appointed editor-in-chief of *Rive*, there had been fifty-seven bouquets of flowers waiting in her office from people in the fashion industry. On the news of her 'resignation' there were none; just a yawning, embarrassed silence and a couple of regretful texts from David Stern and Jeremy Pike. No magazine executives called, desperate to sign her as an editor, no fashion houses begged her to add her vision to their brand. She was, at least for the moment, a pariah.

Cassandra wasn't entirely surprised. You couldn't spend your entire working life air-kissing and not be aware how shallow the industry was. What did shock her, though, was how hard it hit her. Her whole life had been built around fashion and now it seemed she was frozen out, with no one to lean on. But by far the worst thing was that she had to deal with the loss of Max completely alone. No one knew about their affair. Over the last six months the one person with whom she had shared all her problems was Max and now he was gone. Cassandra had always been self-reliant, happy in her own company, but now she felt more alone than she had ever been. Famed for going to three or four parties a night, she now sat at home in her cashmere joggers and socks, staring at the walls. She had never been depressed, there had never been time, there was always so much to do, so much to look forward to, but now she felt crushed by the weight of everything. What was the point? Who cared what happened to her, anyway? Deep down, she knew she was letting the waters pull her under and the old Cassandra reared up enough to finally get her out of the house, to visit the health club at the Berkeley hotel. She was sitting by its beautiful rooftop pool, staring at a magazine, when she took the next body blow: her phone rang.

'Cassandra, it's Guillaume.'

'Oh, hello, darling,' she said, vaguely. 'How are you?'

'Fine, fine. Just wondered if you had heard the latest from *Rive*?'

She stayed silent, not sure if she really wanted to hear.

'Well, the big news is that Francesca Adams is the new editor-in-chief,' said Guillaume, not waiting for an answer, 'and the magazine is going to go weekly.'

Cassandra sat and listened as Guillaume filled her in on the industry gossip. Glenda McMahon had been named editorial director over all international editions including UK

Rive and, as they were planning a September relaunch, Glenda had been in the UK for the last twenty-four hours, presenting her vision to the team.

'They all hate her, of course,' said Guillaume kindly. 'To be honest, it's just not the same for anyone. I really missed you at couture, darling. Le Grand Palais was a less glamorous place without you.'

'I'll be back,' whispered Cassandra and hung up, her hands shaking.

Suddenly, for the first time in weeks, her head was buzzing with thoughts.

How could she have been so stupid? Francesca was more ambitious and resourceful than she had given her credit for. Francesca had been suspicious about an 'off-flat-plan' shoot at the Milan collections and she must have seen an opportunity and gone digging deeper. Cassandra had warned Laura to be discreet, but she was a stupid, naïve girl and Francesca had found out. Francesca must then have told Glenda and cut a deal for the editorship. Cassandra took a deep breath and looked out over the pool. It was as if the anger had burnt away a fog surrounding her. She was seeing clearly now. Very clearly. Suddenly it occurred to Cassandra that the Berkeley was one of the favoured London hotels for the international fashion community and it was where Glenda always stayed when she was over for the London shows. *I'll bet that bitch is here now!* she thought, getting quickly dressed and marching down to the front desk.

'Ms McMahon, please. I believe she's staying in the Wellington Suite?' said Cassandra in her 'do-not-fuck-with-me' voice.

'Just a moment,' said the blonde clerk nervously, obediently turning to her computer.

'I'm afraid we don't have a Miss McMahon in that suite.'

'Well, can you try your other rooms? This is urgent.'

553

'I'm afraid Miss McMahon isn't staying with us at all at the present time,' said the girl. 'I'm sorry.' The look on her face told Cassandra she was telling the truth.

Retreating into the hotel's Caramel Room, she ordered a mint tea to calm her, before ringing Lianne. Her old assistant sounded uneasy speaking to her but confirmed that Glenda had been in the office but had already left. Apparently, Lianne hadn't been taken into her confidence over her sleeping arrangements.

Cassandra rang every top hotel looking for her, but failed to track Glenda down. Frustrated, she pushed through the revolving doors and jumped into a black cab. Then suddenly she had a moment of clarity. Of course! She would be staying at the Alliance company flat. It was so typical of a brownnosing company toadie like Glenda to stay there to show the new management how she was saving them money. She redirected the cab to the anonymous red-brick block behind Harrods and strode up to the door. Cassandra still had keys which admitted her to both the building and the flat. In the lift, however, Cassandra began to doubt her instincts – what if she walked in on some French family using the flat while their fat papa was out dealing with some paper crisis at the printers? With this scenario in mind, she knocked on the door several times but there was no reply. She was about to leave when she heard a muffled laugh coming from inside.

Suddenly sure she had been correct about Glenda, she slid the key into the lock and opened the door. She immediately recognized Glenda's fur cape hanging up in the hall. Her heart was pounding. She cautiously ventured farther into the flat, her ears searching for signs of life. There was a rustle coming from the living room doorway – then there she was, Glenda, dressed in a long silk kimono.

'Cassandra!' she almost squealed, then regained her composure, 'What the hell are you doing here?'

'Getting some answers,' said Cassandra, taking a step forward, her voice dripping with loathing. 'It was Francesca who told you about Georgia Kennedy, wasn't it? Not Giles at all. You just blamed it on him so I would get rid of my best member of staff.'

'Cassandra. You're being emotional,' said Glenda, backing up slowly, a look of real fear on her face. 'I'm sorry things didn't work out for you but you brought it on yourself. I'd love to talk about it more but I'm in a hurry, so I'd be grateful if you'd leave.'

Cassandra advanced on her, stabbing the air with her finger.

'What did you do to get Pierre Desseau on your side so quickly? Fuck him?'

Her voice was low and uneven. Until now she had ignored the sound of a shower running in the background, her instincts blunted by anger. The sound of gushing water stopped and Cassandra kept silent, her nerve endings prickling, knowing now that Glenda was not alone. The bathroom door at the end of the corridor opened and out stepped Pierre wrapped in just a towel. Without conscious thought, Cassandra screamed and, all sense of control completely gone, she hurled herself on Glenda, her fingers like talons, grabbing at her silk kimono and tearing it open.

'You scheming bitch!' she yelled, her manicured nails sinking into Glenda's face and neck, her hands clawing at her hair. Pierre leapt forward to separate the women.

'Stop this!' he shouted, struggling to restrain Cassandra who kicked and flailed, her whole chic façade completely gone. Pierre finally managed to grab Cassandra's wrists and push her against the wall, manhandling her into a bear hug. Realizing she was beaten, Cassandra gave one last primal scream, then went limp in his arms. With glassy eyes, she looked at Glenda cowering in her torn kimono, the front of her body exposed. She did not look good naked, she thought in a detached way. The skin around her belly was crumpled like chamois leather and her nipples, clearly the result of a botched boob job, were terribly uneven.

Cassandra laughed cruelly. 'Your tits. They look cross-eyed!' She giggled hysterically. Gasping, Glenda quickly pulled her kimono about her, fled into the bathroom and locked the door.

'You're mad, Cassandra, mad,' said Pierre, releasing her from his hold.

She straightened up and pushed her hair away from her eyes.

'I was mad for ever getting involved with you,' she replied as calmly as she could. 'You two deserve each other. Your weekly "vision"' – she spat the word – 'will flop by the way. You clearly have no understanding of why women buy *Rive*. But I'll let you learn that the hard way.'

She turned her back on him and walked out of the front door without looking back. When she got out onto the cold street she sank onto the step feeling hollow, raw and completely and utterly betrayed and wondered how things could possibly get any worse.

59

Stella's debut womenswear collection for Milford, held on the final day of London Fashion Week, was a sensation. She had channelled all her unsettled emotions into her work and the result was a clever yet sumptuous show that had made even the most jaded fashion editor sigh with joy. Reports of the show in the next day's broadsheets talked of Stella's spectacular use of colour and coined the phrase 'stealth-wealth' – Milford's clothes, they gushed, needed no garish logos or labels to show they were the best. Milford, they said, had redefined the words 'luxurious' and 'classic'. Stella's vision had worked. She had taken her lead from the masters and it showed; the gowns were cut as beautifully as the best Schiaparelli and floated round the body as fluidly as fresh air. The bouclé day jacket had its seams weighted with fine chains, like the finest Chanel couture, to ensure that it hung perfectly. More importantly, the whole collection was wearable. The clean-line dresses, skinny trousers and scoop-neck sweaters were just what every woman wanted because they would flatter any figure. Stella had used the very best fabrics: the gossamer-fine cashmere tank needed the barest of design twists to look exquisite while the pencil skirt in the softest midnight-blue nappa leather looked and felt like the last word in super-luxury. When Stella took a bow and the whole audience of Covent Garden's Paul Hamlyn Hall erupted, Stella felt as if her life was finally turning a corner. Emma launched herself backstage as soon as the show was finished. She hugged Stella tightly, the two women knowing that in years to come they would look back on this show as the defining moment in the company's history.

'We did it,' laughed Emma feeling light-headed with relief and glee, her own troubles temporarily put to one side.

'We've just got to get through tonight,' replied Stella. 'We get through tonight and then we know we've done it.'

Cassandra sat in the back seat of Astrid Brinton's Mercedes, biting on her thumbnail. She still couldn't believe that Astrid and her mother had persuaded her to come. When she had first heard that Emma planned to host a huge party at Winterfold the night of Milford's debut collection, she had scoffed. It was one thing for Valentino to persuade fashion's great and good to attend his sumptuous Louis XVIII chateau on the outskirts of Paris; it was quite another for a non-entity like Milford to expect people to make the 70-mile journey out of London. But Cassandra was out of the loop: Milford was no longer a nonentity. According to Astrid, it was the hottest ticket of London Fashion Week, with Clover Connor and Ste Donahue rumoured to be making their first party circuit appearance together following their stints in rehab. Kowalski were due to play an acoustic set and a fleet of Audis was bringing the guests from the fashion show to Winterfold. Cassandra checked her lipstick in her compact. She knew she looked stunning even if she didn't feel it. Her oyster duchesse satin cocktail dress matched her colouring and tiny waist perfectly. Her dark, blow-dried hair bounced down her bare back and her five-inch heels would make her stand above almost anyone else at the party. For once, however, that thought sent a shiver through her.

'Don't be nervous,' said Astrid as the car pulled through the gates.

'Don't be ridiculous,' said Cassandra her mouth dry with apprehension.

She looked at her friend, grateful that just being next to Astrid, the society giant, offered her some sort of protection.

'You had to come, remember?' continued Astrid sternly. 'There's absolutely no point slinking off into the shadows like a loser. You're not a loser, you are fabulous and you have to remind everybody just how fabulous you are. Because *everybody* is going to be here tonight.'

That last comment particularly irked Cassandra. Her own fall from UK *Rive* seemed to have been exaggerated by the apparently unstoppable ascent of Milford and she couldn't help but wonder if she could have done things differently; if she had contested the will or joined forces with Roger, perhaps she would now be in charge of this thriving empire.

'Actually, I'm surprised you two are coming tonight too,' said Cassandra. It had only been a few weeks since the tabloids had gone crazy over Johnny and Stella's dramatic split.

'It wasn't our bloody fault,' said Blake from the front seat adjusting his bow tie in the mirror. 'It's our son. He's a tart. As if everyone doesn't know he's shagging that old slag Lisa Ladro. He's such an idiot; when her husband finds out, neither of them will ever work in Hollywood again.'

'I'd forgotten what a beautiful house it is,' said Astrid as Winterfold loomed into view, the drive lined with torches, its windows glowing pumpkin. 'Do you think it's more beautiful than ours?'

'So I suppose now you want to move?' said Blake sardonically, turning round.

'I didn't mean that,' snapped Astrid. 'I was just saying how fabulous it is. But at least someone suitable like Rob Holland lives here now. It would have been frightful if Roger and Rebecca Milford had moved in.'

'What have you got against them?' asked Cassandra, feeling slightly defensive about her own flesh and blood.

'Dreadful social climbers, the pair of them,' said Astrid. 'Helen, our nanny, used to go to school with Rebecca – apparently she used to be so *common*. It's everywhere now though, isn't it? Such vulgarity. Everybody wants to become a billionaire without doing anything. Did you see some frightful nouveaux riches Russians have bought Wadham Court? I mean it's the fourth best house in the county after Blenheim, Greywood and Winterfold!'

Cassandra looked at her friend and almost smiled at her hypocrisy. Instead, she felt a terrible sinking feeling in her stomach: she knew this was just the start. It was going to be a night of furious social competition.

The party was glorious. Guests had come from London in their hundreds, by courtesy car or helicopter, with many staying in every country-house hotel in a 20-mile radius. Since the show, Stella had already had three job offers and had been lavished with praise from some of the top retails buyers in the world. Harvey Nicks and Harrods, Colette in Paris and Bergdorf's in New York, had all told her that despite the limited run of the collection – Stella had insisted that only 100 copies of each piece would be made available – they were all going to put in large orders. Standing under a heater on Winterfold's impressive parterre, Stella felt as if she was watching a glamorous Fifties movie, as if she were *inside* a glamorous Fifties movie. She took a deep breath of

560

night air and thought to herself that, for the first time in a long time, she couldn't be happier. *Well, with one big exception*, she thought darkly, but then shook all thoughts of Johnny from her mind as she reached out and held her father's hand. Christopher Chase's fingers felt knotty and hard like the top of an old walking stick. She felt closer to him than she had for years and that made up for everything; she was glad that he seemed to be coping with Chessie's disappearance so well. *He's been through it all before, I suppose*, she thought with a wry smile. Before Christmas Christopher had turned down Stella's offer to come and live with her, even on a temporary basis, but he had delighted her by turning up to both the show in London and the party in Chilcot.

'He seems to have grown into a nice young man,' said Christopher, nodding over to Tom who was chatting animatedly to Ste Donahue.

'He is nice. In lots of ways,' said Stella taking a contented sip of champagne.

'In the important ways?' asked Christopher.

'He's kind and decent and funny.'

'But?' said Christopher raising one bushy, white eyebrow.

'He's a bit directionless and irresponsible,' she replied, feeling slightly disloyal, especially as they were things she'd heard said about Tom second-hand.

'There are worse things to be, such as selfish, pompous and vain,' smiled Christopher and his reference to Johnny Brinton was crystal clear. 'Those people you can't help. Other people, people with a good heart, you can.'

'People can only help themselves, Dad.'

'You helped me.'

He put his arm around her and they both smiled. It was time to start helping each other.

* * *

Emma had come into the courtyard to get some fresh air. Her head was spinning; she had just spent the last ten minutes talking to Tom Ford. She had giggled and blushed like a schoolgirl, but suddenly she felt that whatever the last year had thrown at her, she could take it all on again if it gave her one ounce of the contentment and self-worth that she was feeling right now. It was cold outside and while her dress, a long column of bottle-green silk, made her feel like the subject of a Tamara de Lempicka painting, it offered no protection against the chill.

She turned round and saw a dark figure silhouetted in the light of the courtyard doorway. As he moved closer, she could see that it was Rob. Standing hidden in the shadows, she watched him for a moment as he took a gold cigar cutter out of his pocket and cut off the end of his Cohiba.

'You know you don't have to step outside to smoke?' she said, walking into the light. 'Saul used to chomp on cigars like they were going out of fashion.'

He looked up and laughed.

'Now you tell me,' he grinned. 'Happy birthday, by the way.'

'You know, with all the excitement of the day, I keep forgetting.'

He nodded, looking her up and down. He whistled.

'You look incredible tonight.'

'Aw, this old thing? These are just my usual work clothes,' she said, avoiding his eye. After her accident, they'd got their friendship back on track, but it still made her awkward to be complimented by him.

'Well, I hope this has been a better birthday than last year?' he asked.

She laughed. That evening in Boston, standing in the rain with Mark, seemed like such a distant memory it was almost as if it had never happened.

'Well, thanks for letting us have the party here.'

'Hey, it's *your* house.'

'The company's,' she corrected him, '. . . although for how much longer I'm not sure.' She looked up at him. 'The truth is, I've been thinking about selling Winterfold.'

Rob stamped out his cigar and frowned.

'I thought you said you'd never sell. Hasn't your family had this house for like a hundred years or something?'

'I never said "never". I mean, what do we need it for? It's vanity. Ego.'

'You could look at it like that, I suppose. Personally, I'd say it was history, your family's heritage.'

Her family. While she loved Saul and was grateful for the opportunity he had given her, she was still bitter about the way the rest of the family had treated her – and on top of that, there was the nagging suspicion that someone close to her had been involved in that attempt on her life in Gstaad. Until she had found out who had been driving the car which pushed her off the road, she couldn't trust a single member of her family.

'I'm not sure the family needs bricks and mortar to define itself,' she said diplomatically. 'Well, maybe some of them do,' she laughed.

'Roger you mean?' smirked Rob.

'I didn't say that, *you* did. No, I do love Winterfold but what's important is the business. The house is an extravagance. We still have the factory and the offices and a sale would get rid of a lot of the corporate debt.'

Rob raised his eyebrows.

'You're not one to let sentimentality get in the way of a decision, are you?'

'So if we do sell, would you be interested?' she asked directly.

'Ah, so you think my ego needs some place like this.'

They both grinned.

'You know I didn't mean it like that,' said Emma. 'As incumbent tenant I thought you deserved first refusal. You always said you wanted to buy it.'

'Ouch,' he winced. 'Is that what I've been reduced to: "incumbent tenant"?'

'You know I think a lot more of you than that,' she said quietly. Emma had drunk three glasses of champagne and she instantly regretted coming out with something so soppy and romantic. So far she had kept her dignity where Rob was concerned and had no intention of getting hurt again. Rob had been good to her after the accident but that's how their relationship should stay, supportive but platonic.

'I'm glad to hear it,' he replied. He moved closer towards her; their cold breath was making white puffs in front of them and merging into one big cloud.

He took off his jacket and wrapped it around her shoulders.

'Can't have you freezing to death on your birthday, can we?'

She could feel that tension building up between them just like the night in Somerset and took a small deliberate step away from him to defuse it.

'So?'

'So what?'

'Are you interested in Winterfold? I thought you'd bite my hand off. I know you Americans love all that lord of the manor stuff – well, here's your opportunity.'

He didn't smile back, in fact his blue eyes looked sad.

'You know how much I love Winterfold,' he said, 'but I'm not sure I'm going to be needing an English stately home for much longer. I'm leaving London.'

'You've leaving the London office?' she asked masking her disappointment. 'Are you being posted somewhere else?'

His eyes didn't leave her face.

He nodded. 'Back to New York.'

She felt a thickness in her throat, suddenly thinking about Cassandra's smug news that Rob had been seen looking cosy with Madeline at Sant Ambroeus. She remembered how he had started to tell her something at the Christmas party before she had been disturbed by her mother.

'But you've not been in London for even eighteen months.'

'Something's come up,' he said trying to smile.

'Madeline?'

He looked surprised. 'What makes you say that?'

'Cassandra saw you have lunch together at Sant Ambroeus.'

'She's the mother of my child, Emma, I am going to see her occasionally,' he said, a smile pulling at his lips.

'She said you were looking cosy,' added Emma, trying to sound teasing.

Rob smiled and shook his head slightly.

'We met up because she was telling me she's getting married again. If I kissed her on the cheek or hugged her or whatever it was simply to congratulate her.'

Emma felt an enormous rush of relief flood over her.

'Oh, I'm sorry . . . so why the move?'

'I shouldn't be telling you this, but an announcement is being made to Wall Street on Monday so . . .' he paused to draw breath. 'My father is retiring. Finally.' He said with a small smile.

'No way! I thought he was going to carry on forever!'

She thought back to a recent profile of Larry Holland in Forbes. *The power-house titan who will never retire.*

'He's ill.'

'I'm so sorry,' she said, putting her hand on his arm.

'Against all previous form, he has decided he wants me to take over. CEO. The big job.'

Emma gasped.

'Wow, president of Hollander Media? That's a serious position.'

'Yeah, well. I was born to the job; I'm not necessarily deserving of it.'

'You deserve it,' she smiled, feeling genuinely happy for him.

'Not only that, I've persuaded him to invest in the record division. After much consideration he thought it was the right thing to do. You could have told us both in thirty seconds. Actually, as I remember it, that's exactly what you did.'

'I thought you said I knew nothing about music.'

'You don't,' he grinned. 'But you know an awful lot about business.'

'So when do you think you're going?' Her disappointment was crushing but she was determined to hide it.

'Once the official announcement is made on Monday there's nothing really stopping me. I'm going to start attending meetings at our head office in Manhattan in a couple of weeks.'

'You're leaving in two weeks!'

'Well, yes and no,' he laughed softly. 'It will take me a while to make the transition. I'll be shuttling between the two cities for a time. My father has someone in mind to replace me in London but even so, I don't think I'll be moving to New York permanently until April, maybe May. I'll officially take up the position of CEO a little after that.'

He saw Emma glance to the floor.

'Hey, don't worry. I'm good for the rent until the end of the contract.'

She took a deep breath and stepped forward to kiss him on the cheek.

'Congratulations, Rob.'

Their cheeks brushed against one another, their touch lingering for just a split second longer than necessary. They pulled away, but Rob held on to her fingertips. She looked up into his eyes.

'That night at the cider farm . . .' he said softly.

'Hey, that's all forgotten, Rob. Don't worry about it.'

But Rob continued as if he hadn't heard her.

'You remember I went to New York the day after? Well, that's when my father told me. I couldn't tell you about his retirement at the time, it would have affected the share-price of the company and they were in the middle of some re-financing. When we were by the lake, when I said I couldn't commit to anything, that's what I meant. I knew I was returning to New York. I didn't want to start what I couldn't finish. Then when you said you didn't want a relationship . . .'

She felt the brief pulse of hope.

'I wasn't exactly honest that day either,' she said and then paused, watching him and wanting him with all her heart. 'I think I could make time in my schedule for a man,' she smiled.

'How do you feel about long-distance relationships?'

'What's changed your mind?' she whispered.

'I miss you.'

'In that case, what's 3,000 miles between friends when one of us has a private jet?'

They laughed gently, stepping together in unison, before his mouth met hers in a kiss of such deep, sweet tenderness she wanted it to continue forever.

'We'd better go back to the party,' she whispered finally, resting her head gently on his shoulder. He pulled her hand and drew her back inside.

'Come on. We've got plenty of stuff to celebrate.'

In Winterfold's ballroom, Emma was standing to one side as Rob congratulated Ste on a brilliant acoustic set, when she turned to see her mother crossing the floor. In a room full of beautiful people Virginia still stood out, striking and patrician in an elegant kingfisher blue silk sheath dress, her hair up in a chignon.

'What a wonderful party, darling,' she said, 'and on your birthday too. Are you having fun?'

Emma nodded, unable to stop a big grin lighting up her face as her eyes darted towards Rob.

'Yes, you two seem to be getting on well,' said Virginia icily.

'Mother! I thought you'd be pleased.'

'Well, do you trust him?' asked Virginia, examining her daughter through narrow eyes.

'You mean as a tenant?' asked Emma, surprised at her strange question.

'I mean after what happened in Gstaad.'

'What are you suggesting?'

'I thought he was at the hospital very soon after your accident.'

'He was in Courchevel, Mother. What *are* you suggesting?' she repeated.

Virginia paused and took a sip of her champagne.

'A police officer in Gstaad told me you were convinced someone had deliberately tried to kill you.'

'And you think it was Rob?' said Emma incredulously.

'Not necessarily,' she mused after a long pregnant pause. 'I just thought it was odd, *convenient*, he was around so quickly.'

Emma shook her head. She was used to her mother's arctic attitude towards life, but this was a new standard.

'I don't know what happened in Gstaad, Mum,' said Emma. 'What I do know is that it wasn't odd for Rob to be at the hospital at all. He's my friend and I trust him.'

'You sound like you're in love with him,' said Virginia with a note of disapproval.

'I like him a lot,' replied Emma, stony-faced.

'I'm your mother, darling. I only want to protect you.'

'Is that so?' said Emma sharply. It had been a day of emotional peaks and troughs; elation, worry, surprise, and Emma felt about ready to snap.

'When have you ever really cared about me or my life?' she hissed. 'You've never particularly supported me, or tried to understand me – do you even know me? Yes, I'm your daughter, but I'm hardly a priority, am I? I have always come such a poor second to your life with Jonathon that I barely even register. It might suit you now to suddenly start caring, but don't bother. For once, I'm really, really happy. Don't go trying to spoil it.'

Virginia's face had drained of all colour. Gently touching her daughter's arm, she drew her away from the crowd into a quieter alcove.

'Is that how you really feel?' she asked.

Dizzy with relief at having finally aired feelings which had been bottled up for so many years, Emma nodded. Virginia bowed her head. As she looked up her face looked softer, more vulnerable.

'Emma, whatever you think, you're my daughter and I love you.'

'So why have you spent the last twenty years behaving like you don't care?'

'Because you're so much like him,' she whispered.

'Dad?'

Virginia nodded, her eyes glistening with moisture.

'He had an affair with my *sister*, Emma. Can you imagine how painful that feels, how worthless it makes you feel? And then he died,' she said her voice racked with sorrow. 'I loved him so much and he died not loving me.' A tear trickled down her face, leaving a thin silver line of foundation.

Emma touched her mother's arm. 'But he did love you. You told me yourself that it was a mistake, just a summer fling.'

Virginia shook her head.

'That's why I've thrown myself 100 per cent into my marriage with Jonathon,' she said through sobs. 'I won't take my eye off the ball. I won't let it happen again.'

Emma put her arms around her, feeling her eyes fill with tears as she did so and leaned on her mother's shoulder.

'It's OK, Mum, I understand,' she whispered. 'I understand.'

'Did you know Cassandra was here?' said Stella, handing Emma a glass of pink champagne.

'I think it's pretty brave of her to come,' said Emma nodding. She actually found she had mixed emotions about her cousin. She'd heard all about Cassandra's high-profile departure from *Rive*; it had been spun as a resignation but everyone in the industry knew she'd been fired. Emma certainly knew how humiliating that would be for her. Cassandra was the sort of woman who was defined by her job and to have it taken away must have been devastating. Then again, Cassandra was ruthless and driven. Ruthless enough to run her off the road in Gstaad?

'Well, just don't go offering her my job,' smiled Stella.

Emma couldn't tell if her friend was joking but there was a flicker of insecurity in her eyes.

'As if, Stella,' she said, gesturing back towards the party. 'Do you think all these people would be here if it wasn't for you? This is your doing, Stell, your triumph. Why would I be so stupid as to change that? Besides, I need someone to make my tea.'

Stella burst out laughing and nudged her friend gently in the ribs.

'Just think, you might be moving back in here soon. It's so lovely!'

Emma frowned.

'Why on earth would I be moving back here?'

'Come on, Em, because I saw you holding hands with Rob. How long's this been going on?'

Emma blushed, embarrassed at being caught out.

'Just tonight. Well, actually that's a lie, something happened in November too. I didn't tell you because it didn't go anywhere, which is exactly what you'd expect considering his reputation, isn't it? I didn't want anyone to say "told you so".'

'A womanizer is only waiting for the right woman, sweetie. And he's clearly come to his senses.'

Emma flushed again.

'Well, we'll see.'

Stella clapped her hands together gleefully.

'You're in love with him! I knew it! Go on, get upstairs and tear all his clothes off before someone else does.'

'Stella!' gasped Emma.

'Gosh, you're such a lucky cow. Everything is coming together for you, isn't it?'

'Don't say that,' said Emma. 'That's usually the point when everything starts to come undone.'

Roger and Rebecca stood at the top of the stairs looking down on the action from on high.

'I can't believe Tom Ford's at Winterfold,' said Rebecca, playing with the Tiffany diamond star necklace around her delicate throat. 'What a coup.'

'Yes, it's all been a rip-roaring bloody success, hasn't it?' said Roger bitterly, sipping on his neat bourbon. 'Emma's never going to sell now, is she?'

He had to admit that the catwalk show that afternoon

had been amazing. He'd been staggered by the excited charge of anticipation in the audience before and the gushing praise that had rung around the venue afterwards. Of course, it was his success too, but it was that very success which was now standing in the way of his ambitions.

'Victor Chen's company were interested because they thought they could get Milford for a good price and after today, I'm not so sure they'll be so keen. I can't stall Ricardo for much longer, and how else are we going to get the money?'

'Darling, maybe it's just as well,' said Rebecca, stroking his arm. 'I've been speaking to friends about Ricardo and I'm not sure he'd be the most reliable business partner. Apparently he's a terrible coke-head.'

Roger rounded on his wife angrily – how dare she question his judgement?

'Darling, I'm doing this for us! Don't start fighting me!'

'All I'm saying is that it's not necessarily a bad thing to keep hold of the Milford shareholding. For now at least. You never know, this thing might make us rich after all.'

'Not as rich as her,' said Roger, looking over at Emma, hate blazing from his eyes.

'Well, I guess we'd better make the best of it. She's not going to go away, is she?'

Roger threw back his bourbon, still looking at Emma.

'No, I suppose not.'

Cassandra had been in the Orangery overlooking the court-yard when Emma and Rob were talking. She had watched their interaction with interest and had been genuinely shocked when she had seen them kiss. It had made her want to retch. As if she wasn't miserable enough without having to watch the charmed life of Emma Bailey being played out before her in glorious Technicolor. That bitch had stolen her life and her glory – and now she even had a relationship. It was as if she were deliberately rubbing her face it in. Cassandra tightened her fingers into a fist, pushing her nails into her palm. She was going to get even with Emma, whatever it took.

Right now, however, all she wanted to do was go home. Despite her recent emotional wobbles, Cassandra still had a thicker skin than most and when she'd arrived at the party she'd held her head up high. But soon the whispers of the party-goers – of the fashion executives, the PRs and journalists – soon, they became deafening. Even worse were the looks on the faces of the few who did come over to speak to her; people who'd once fawned at her every word now viewed her with pity when they all asked 'so what are you doing next?' Alone and drained by the emotional toll of the past two weeks, she had felt something unfamiliar at the party, something unpleasant. She felt like an outsider.

Cassandra drained the last of her champagne and it made her reel. She'd eaten nothing in the past thirty-six hours in order to fit into her sample-size Dior cocktail dress and to make matters worse, she'd accepted a fat line of cocaine from Astrid. Her friend had assured her it would make her feel better. It hadn't.

She grabbed on to a table to steady herself, then sat down heavily on a marble stool. Her head was whirling, her senses suddenly overloaded. The smell of the frangipani and the warm, humid atmosphere of the Orangery made her feel even more nauseous.

'Cassandra? Is that you?'

She looked up and saw Emma.

'Ah, the hostess. Let me congratulate you,' she said, her voice thick with sarcasm. 'You never struck me as a style maven but this party is exceptional.'

'Thank you, I think people are enjoying themselves. Listen, I was sorry to hear about *Rive*.'

'No you're not,' said Cassandra, slurring her words slightly. 'No one's sorry. Everybody loves hearing about other people's misfortune, because it makes them feel better about their own sad little lives.'

'I'd say that was a little cynical.'

'Well of course you would – from your gilded perch.'

'Cassandra, please. There's no need to be like that.'

Emma sat down on a bench opposite her.

'There's something I've been wanting to tell you since Gstaad,' she said.

'Hmm, Gstaad,' smiled Cassandra, more than a flicker of malice showing as she remembered Emma's accident. 'Well, you seem to have recovered.'

'More or less,' said Emma.

Cassandra twirled a hand indicating that she wanted Emma to get to the point.

'So what is this thing you want to tell me?'

'My dad was not having an affair with your mum,' said Emma.

Cassandra laughed.

'Emma, I saw them together. Don't you believe me?'

'Yes I do. But it wasn't an affair, it was a fling.'

'Oh grow up! What's the difference?'

'The difference is that you've spent half your life hating me because you blame my father and, by extension, me, for the break-up of your own family. But your parents' marriage was already over.'

'It was not!' she said through bared teeth. 'Without your father, my family would still be together.'

'Cassandra, my mother told me everything; your father already had a mistress, the woman he eventually married and moved to Cape Town with. Ask Julia if you don't believe me.'

574

Cassandra looked at Emma venomously. Even if what Emma was saying was true, how was it supposed to make her feel better? Emma's words were just designed to alleviate her own guilt and make Cassandra feel bad.

'I know none of that makes up for the fact that he abandoned you,' said Emma as if she had read Cassandra's mind. 'But I don't want you to hate your family on a misplaced belief. Don't fight me, Cassandra. Channel your energy and brilliance in a different direction.'

To her utter surprise, Emma realized that a teardrop was slipping down Cassandra's cheek.

'Do you think this is all about *you*?' said Cassandra fiercely.

'I think you've got something to prove,' said Emma softly.

'I've spent the last twenty years trying to prove something,' said Cassandra. 'To my mother, to make her proud. To my father, to make him hurt. To Ruby, to myself, to the whole world.' She looked at Emma, her grey-green eyes blazing with truth and sorrow and anger. 'Where do you think ambition comes from, Emma? It comes from the fear of being nothing.'

Emma suddenly understood. She understood the pain that had been driving Cassandra and eating her up. And for what? Here she sat, friendless, alone, her eyes rimmed red, her face pale.

'Where are you staying tonight?' asked Emma softly.

'At Astrid Brinton's.'

'Do you want me to go and get her?'

'And let her see me like this?' Cassandra laughed sarcastically.

'She's your friend.'

Cassandra gave a small laugh.

'You don't understand, I can't let anyone see me like this or I'm finished. Even *more* finished. Fashion is cruel, Emma. They love to see someone on their knees – and they'll stamp on your hands while you're down.'

Despite her misgivings, Emma felt a wave of compassion for Cassandra, sitting crumpled, tiny and doll-like in her beautiful cream gown.

'You should go. There's a way out over here,' said Emma, pointing to a door at the back of the Orangery. 'My house is in the grounds straight along the path outside the door. I'll ask a driver to take you there. Wait at my house until everyone is gone and you can stay until tomorrow if you want. There's a spare room and clean towels . . . come on, Cassandra, you're in no fit state to join the party again.'

With every ounce of energy in her body Cassandra wanted to refuse her offer. She was too proud to accept anything from Emma, even a bed for the night, but at the same time she did not want to stay at the party for another second. And the thought of Astrid having this social ammunition against her was just too much to bear.

'Very well,' she said in a voice so inaudible it was lost in the swell of music in the background.

'Wait here,' said Emma firmly. 'I'll get my keys. Everything's going to be fine.'

By 12.45 a.m. the party crowd was thinning. Mink shrugs, opera capes, cashmere overcoats were being pulled out of the cloakroom and guests were either retiring to the rooms in Winterfold, to their accommodation in the village or to their cars to drive back to London. A spectacular fireworks display closed the evening; sprays of red, white and amber shot into the black sky while Winterfold's grand entrance hall buzzed with the contented conversation of scores of people who'd all had a fantastic time. Emma was fondling her wine glass and saying a personal goodbye to as many people as she was able when she saw Ruan approach.

'Pleased with how it went?' he asked.

Emma nodded, pulling on her own cashmere shawl she had got from the cloakroom.

'Better than I could have hoped. I haven't seen you all night, though. Where have you been?'

'Having my photograph taken for *Tatler*,' he grinned. 'Me, in a society rag! Who'd have thought it?'

'I think it suits you,' she smiled.

'Are you going home, already?' he said, noticing that she looked ready to leave.

'I might hang around for a little while.'

'Until the morning,' he smiled.

'What do you mean?'

'Rob Holland . . . Don't worry, I'll get all the gossip from him.'

'Stop it!' she slapped him on the arm, before moving on. Her good mood was dampened, however, when she turned to see Roger, Rebecca and Julia standing in a line, sending off their guests like royal dignitaries. She had tried to avoid them all evening. In fact, she had tried to avoid them since Gstaad. When they were being nice to her, it made her paranoid and when Roger gave her one of his long disapproving looks, all she could see was a conspiracy to get rid of her, *to push her off the road*. She had tried hard to shake off the feeling; after all, what proof did she have? As Rob had explained to her countless times, the Mercedes that had rammed her had been stolen, so the most logical explanation was that it had been drunken joyriders. But in spite of the logic of Rob's argument, she still refused to trust any of her family, particularly Roger and Rebecca.

'It's been fabulous, Emma,' said Rebecca, embracing her in a cloud of perfume.

'Thank you,' said Emma.

'We'll get one of those courtesy cars,' said Roger, looking pleased with himself. 'Would you like us to drop you off?'

'I'm just saying my goodbyes. There are a lot of cars outside so I'll get one in a few minutes.'

Virginia pulled Emma off into the boot room.

'I haven't seen Cassandra in ages,' said Virginia. 'Julia seems to think she went home with Astrid Brinton but she's on the dancefloor. Cassandra is normally the last person I'd worry about but she has been awfully edgy tonight.'

'She's staying at my house tonight. She's had a little too much to drink. I'm sure she'll pop by to Julia's tomorrow,' said Emma, not entirely sure why she was making up an excuse for her cousin, but feeling the urge to protect her all the same.

Virginia smiled. For once it was a smile that reached her eyes.

'Well, I'm off home now too.' She touched her daughter gently on the arm.

'I'm glad we've got things sorted. I'm proud of you.'

'I love you, Mum,' replied Emma softly reaching over and giving her a warm embrace.

Emma walked through to the cosy library where Rob was sitting on a velvet sofa holding a glass of brandy and laughing with Jed and Gary from Kowalski. They all looked up when they saw her.

'Well, I'm off,' she smiled awkwardly pulling her shawl tightly around her shoulders. 'I hope you guys enjoyed yourselves.'

'Cheers, Em. Top party,' said Gary with a boozy grin, raising his glass to her.

Emma smiled, thinking of how, only weeks ago, she had been terrified of this group of hell-raising, drugged-up reprobates, but beneath their hardcore public face they were just pussycats and, in fact, really nice people. Then Emma caught Jed nudging Gary and pointing a thumb towards Rob.

'Ah, yes, I think we'd better be going along to the snooker room now,' said Gary, standing up.

'Yes, that's right,' smiled Jed, as they both gave Emma a big bear hug and left the room, shutting the door behind them.

'Where was it you said you were going?' asked Rob softly.

'Back to the Stables. Well, that's unless there were any better offers on the table?' she added boldly. 'I hope so, because Cassandra's crashing at my place.'

'I think I might be able to think of something.' He smiled, standing up. He kissed her neck, pushed her shawl down her arms and skimmed his mouth across the skin of her shoulders. As she groaned in pleasure he took her hand and led her to the door. Emma had been careful to keep public displays of affection with Rob to a minimum. He was high-profile and handsome; she wanted the Milford party to be talked about the next day for all the right reasons, not for who was seeing whom. As she ascended Winterfold's grand staircase, Rob placed his hand protectively in the small of her back. She turned around and saw Ruan standing at the door of the ballroom. He smiled and gave her a small thumbs-up sign; Emma laughed, knowing he was right.

Rob slept in Emma's old room, the master bedroom with the big bay window which overlooked the whole of the estate. Stepping inside, they did not turn on the light and the view from the window was of just a carpet of shadows broken by pools of moonlight. For the past few weeks she had been convinced that she should sell Winterfold, but for the first time ever it suddenly felt like home. She felt Rob behind her; he unzipped her dress which slithered to the floor with a ripple and his hard body pressed against her naked back.

'Happy birthday, Emma,' he said, placing a soft kiss on the back of her neck.

Facing away from him she grinned, then turned and took hold of his belt.

'I think it's time I opened my present, don't you?'

60

Outside the garage at the rear of the house, Tom took a long swig of beer and decided it was time to sort his life out. Since Christmas, since his trip to Cornwall with Stella, he'd tried hard to keep clean. OK, so there'd been a couple of lines of coke at a New Year's party and the odd joint here and there, but he was doing well and it was definitely giving him a clearer head. Much harder, however, was deciding what to do with his life. The Ibiza episode had put him completely off clubland; if his mother hadn't paid off the debt he owed to Miguel Cruz he might very well be dead. But music was still his passion just as fashion was his sister's great love. Tom loved trawling bars listening to unsigned bands; in fact he still had the Red Comets' CD in his coat pocket. He had to get it to Ste Donahue or Rob Holland to see if they thought the young upstart band were as good as he believed they were. He put his empty glass down on the gravel and took a deep breath of the night air. Just then he suddenly caugh the trace of a familiar smell: the sweet aroma of crack cocaine. Tom looked around and saw a dark figure lift out of the shadows.

'All right, mate. Want a bang on this?' said Ste Donahue, holding up a glass pipe.

Tom winced and shook his head. He'd heard that Ste was clean after a long stint in rehab, but the rumour was clearly out of date.

'Where's Clover?'

'Fuck knows. She's in a crappy mood. I've left her to it.'

Tom pointed to the pipe.

'I thought you weren't doing that shit any more,' he said boldly. He loved music and he liked Ste. He didn't want him to throw his life and his talent away. He'd heard from Stella how hard Rob Holland and his team had tried to keep Ste clean. Ste shrugged. 'I want to. It makes me feel good.'

'There are other ways,' said Tom softly, remembering the way he felt when he was with Stella, or the time he'd driven the gull-wing Mercedes around the Winterfold estate, feeling invincible as the speedometer touched 100 mph.

Ste snorted. 'Like what?' he said cynically, slurring his words. *Love?*

The way Ste spat out the word, it was clear that his bust-up with Clover had been a major incident.

'Look, come and see my cars,' said Tom, pointing into the garage where the collection was stored. 'They make me feel like James fucking Bond.'

As they walked across the courtyard Tom pulled the Red Comets' CD out of his pocket and gave it to Ste.

'You should listen to these. They're great.'

Ste took it and pushed it into his pocket.

The garage was a huge space, the size of a tennis court, split partly in two by a barn wall that stretched up to the roof where there was a hay loft. The cars were lined up, each one lovingly polished and gleaming. Only Rob's mud-splattered Range Rover and trail motorbikes looked out of place among the classic sports cars.

'Come around the other side and see the E-Type,' said Tom, excitedly. 'Just looking at it makes me weak at the knees.'

As they approached the other side of the garage, he was suddenly aware of the unmistakable sound of someone having sex. In the dim light, he could see a woman lying splayed out on the bonnet of a silver car; her dress was hitched up around her waist and a man was thrusting into her. His trousers had crumpled down around his knees and his white shirt was hanging loose.

'Shit – that's my fucking Ferrari!' shouted Tom.

The couple stopped and turned like startled rabbits. The woman curled up and slipped off the car, her long blonde hair falling behind her. Ste stepped from behind Tom and said in a confused voice, 'Clover?'

Tom saw he was right: the girl was Clover Connor and the man, Blake Brinton, who was desperately trying to pull up his trousers.

'You fucking whore,' screamed Ste, charging towards them.

Tom tried to grab Ste but he shook him off, running up to Blake and grabbing his shirt.

'You dirty old bastard!' he cried, trying to throw a punch. Ste's fury was not enough however: Blake had a body toned from years of yoga and gym-work and swatted him away like a fly. Ste fell onto the floor into a cloud of dust as Clover bent to her knees to pick him up.

'Get away from me, you slut!' cried Ste, tears streaming down his face.

'Ste, honey, please. I'm sorry. I'm so, so sorry. I still love you,' squealed Clover.

Ste ignored her, stood up and threw his entire body weight against Blake like an angry, floppy doll. Blake simply moved out of the way and let Ste land with a noisy thump on the bonnet of the Ferrari. Tom flinched again, praying there would be no dents.

'Calm down, mate. It's not worth it,' he said, pulling Ste to his feet and steering him towards the door. Clover, now sobbing, ran after them. 'I didn't want you to find out like this.'

'Watch your mouth, Clover!' said Blake sternly. 'My wife is at the party.'

'Oh yeah, it suits you to still keep it a secret, doesn't it?' she screamed, her perfect white teeth bared. Tom caught the expression on Ste's face as he realized this was not one-off party sex. He turned away and started running out of the barn.

'Oh, shit,' said Tom, sprinting to catch up with Ste, who was now halfway across the courtyard and making his way round the side of the house. For someone apparently so unhealthy, Ste was quick and nimble as an alley cat.

'Ste,' he shouted after him. 'Come back!'

One of the drivers had left his courtesy car with its engine running as he went to help a beautiful blonde woman in a floor-length mink coat into the back of the car. Seeing his chance, Ste nipped into the front seat, slammed the door and roared off, leaving the driver and the blonde standing there, coughing dust.

'Bollocks,' moaned Tom, watching the car swerve all the way up the drive, its red tail-lights fading into the blackness.

'My car,' shouted the driver, running fruitlessly down the gravel drive.

Tom got his mobile out and tried to phone Stella but it went directly to voicemail.

He ran into the house, bumped into Morton and asked where Rob was.

'Retired to bed, sir,' he smiled, before leaning in and whispering, 'and he has company.'

'Sorry, Rob,' muttered Tom, as he ran up the stairs, taking them two at a time, 'but this is an emergency.'

*   *   *

Emma rolled over onto the pillow and sighed contentedly. Sex second time round with Rob had been magical, somehow more sure and real.

'Promise me you're not going to leave town for New York tomorrow and then not speak to me for weeks?' she purred.

Rob turned to face her, propping himself up on his pillow.

'Next time I go to New York, you're coming with me.'

'What for?'

'Shopping . . .' he grinned.

Suddenly there was a lot of banging on the bedroom door.

'What the hell?' said Rob, pulling on a white towelling robe.

Tom was standing at the door, panting, his cheeks flushed.

'Tom, is everything OK?' asked Rob.

'Not really,' he gasped, mentally reminding himself to give up the fags as well. 'Can I come in?'

Emma sat up in bed and pulled the sheet around her breasts sheepishly.

'What's wrong?'

'Ste found Clover shagging Blake Brinton in the barn.'

'*You're kidding*,' replied Rob.

'Ste took off in a stolen car about five minutes ago.'

'Oh, Jesus,' said Rob.

'It gets worse: he's pretty pissed and he's taken crack too. Who knows what else.'

Rob was already on his mobile trying to reach Ste.

'No reply. So where's Clover now?'

'Having a screaming row with Astrid Brinton downstairs. Turns out she's been shagging Blake since the Milford launch party.'

Rob and Emma looked at each other. 'Quite a party,' said Emma.

Rob quickly pulled on a pair of jeans and a sweater.

'Where you going?' asked Emma.

'To find Ste, of course. Tom's right, he's a hazard on the road.'

'Shall we call the police?' asked Emma.

Rob shook his head.

'He's already on probation for a drugs charge.'

He grabbed a pen and some paper and scribbled something before handing it to Tom.

'I'm going to see if I can find him. Look, it's 1.15 a.m. Give me twenty minutes or so. Then call his manager, the number's on here.'

'Do you want me to come?' asked Emma sitting up on the pillow.

'No. You stay here. Most of the guests and press have gone, but let's try and keep this as low-key as we can.'

Cassandra opened her eyes and, for a minute, wondered where she was. The surroundings were unfamiliar, the room dark. Then she remembered how a driver had brought her to Emma's house, a converted stable block a mile away from the main house. There was silence; the moon filtered in through the windows and, lifting her head with difficulty, she saw that she was in the living room lying on a leather sofa. Her gown had crinkled and she had snagged the fabric on the corner of Emma's coffee table. *Damn. Won't be so easy to get dresses for free now*, she thought. She desperately wanted to be under her Pratesi sheets in her Knightsbridge home. She wanted to be back behind her Christian Liagre desk telling people what to do – like the old days. She heard a chinking sound outside, like a milk bottle falling over. She dismissed it, maybe it was a cat. She was too tired, drunk and emotional to care or be scared. Nothing could hurt her now anyway! The darkness was her friend, a comfortable black cloud where she couldn't be seen. Her head was pounding. She wanted to shut out the noise of people whispering about her at the party. Yes, she just wanted to sleep. *Sleep.* It would all be over in the morning. She dimly remembered Emma saying something about there being a spare bedroom and clean sheets. That sounded good. What harm would it do to stay here for just a few more hours? She could be gone in the morning before Emma could see her. She dragged her body off the sofa and walked up the stone staircase towards the back bedroom. As she shut the door and peeled off her dress to slip between the cotton sheets, she didn't hear the creak of the letterbox, or the splash of petrol being poured carefully through the slit. And she was fast asleep by the time the burning scrap of linen was thrown into the hall and the flames began to fill the house.

After Rob had roared off in his Range Rover, Tom went back into the garage and found the keys to Rob's motorbike. He kicked it into life and drove fast out of the grounds, but after a few minutes it was obvious he was on a futile mission. He pulled up and turned around. The main gates to Winterfold were about two miles behind him on B-roads, but he wasn't far from the East Gate that would take him back through the estate and straight to the house. It was only as he drove back into the grounds that he smelt the strong and pungent smell of wood smoke. At first he thought there was a problem with the bike's engine. But then he turned a corner and saw flames pouring from the windows of a building.

'Fucking hell! Emma's house.'

He pulled his mobile out of his pocket and called 999, shouting at the operator for the fire brigade.

'Is anybody in the property?' asked the dispatch officer.

'I don't think so,' said Tom, thinking of Emma in Rob's bed only thirty minutes earlier. He hung up and opened the bike's throttle, powering back towards Winterfold. As soon as he got there, he saw Rob stepping out of his Range Rover.

'No sign of him,' called Rob, angrily slapping the car door shut.

'Forget that! Get Emma quick,' shouted Tom. 'The Stables is on fire. I've called 999 already but it looks pretty bad.'

'Fuck,' shouted Rob, running back towards the car. 'Get in! Cassandra is in there and the fire station is ten miles away. They won't make it in time!'

It was the acrid, choking smoke seeping under her bedroom door that woke Cassandra. She felt dreadful. No hangover had ever made her head pound so hard and her limbs felt like lead. She opened her eyes and was suddenly wide awake: the room was filling with smoke.

She threw back the sheet and moved to the door. The bedroom had a wooden floor that was hot under her bare feet. She reached for the doorknob, but was doubled up in a coughing fit before she even got there. Cassandra grabbed a towel and held it over her face as she forced herself to think. She cautiously touched the door handle. Not too hot – she opened the door and gasped when she saw the landing. It was full of thick, black smoke and flames filled the whole opening at the top of the stairs.

Slamming the door shut, she realized that she had only seconds before her room would also be engulfed in flames. Her eyes darted to the window. Dare she open it? She had seen films where fresh air inflamed the fire. *Was that a back-draught?* She couldn't remember. Would flames rip through the door and burn her alive? Would the house explode? She had no more time to think – smoke was pouring under the door now and she was beginning to suffocate.

She began coughing so hard that she was forced to her knees. Outside, she could hear a car horn hooting violently.

She ran to the window and saw a black Range Rover screeching to a stop at the back of the Stables. The doors flew open and Rob and Tom jumped out. Tom could see his sister's face in the window thirty feet above him, her features twisted in fear.

For a second he felt paralysed. What could they do? Fire had ripped through the ground floor of the house and was leaping out of the front windows. Getting into the house to help her would be impossible.

'She's got to jump,' shouted Rob, running to the back of the car to open the boot. He pulled out a blanket covered in horse hair and ran over to Tom.

'Grab one end of this. I'll take the other and we can stretch it out. We won't catch her, but we should manage to break her fall.'

Beneath her Cassandra could see her brother mouthing words she couldn't hear but when she saw the blanket, she realized that they wanted her to jump. She knew she had no other option if she wanted to stay alive. All around her the house creaked and groaned as it struggled to still stand, its beams and joists twisted by the heat. Her hands shaking, she inched the old window open and put her face to the hole, greedily sucking in fresh air. Revived, she opened a space big enough to jump through and hoisted herself up, her feet gripping onto the windowledge. Savage flames were only two feet beneath her, licking up from a ground-floor window and Tom and Rob seemed to be standing a long way from the house.

'We can't come any closer, Cass!' shouted Tom. 'You're going to have to jump out as far as you can. Don't worry, we'll catch you.'

She had no time to think about whether she trusted them. The smoke was so thick she could no longer see anything inside the bedroom, apart from a square of scorching flame

589

where the door had been. She jumped, hurling her body out into the space in front of her as far as she could. She felt like she was floating, the air full of sparks and ash, her body suspended there in time, a last look around at the world before death took her. Then time was switched on again and she felt her body slam against something – first the blanket and then the ground.

'No. No. No!' screamed Emma rushing out of the bedroom and flying down the stairs. Rob had phoned her to tell her about the fire and that Cassandra was lying injured at his feet, alive but in pain. There were still about forty guests at Winterfold who were all wondering what the hell was going on. In the distance the sound of sirens was getting louder. Emma threw open the front door and looked towards the glow of the fire. She quickly called Julia.

'The Stables are on fire. Cassandra was in there but she's OK. Come as quickly as you can.'

Julia screamed down the phone.

'My baby!'

'Someone, give me some car keys!' shouted Emma as the guests ran down the stairs towards her. A waiter, just packing up the last catering things, threw her a jangling bunch. 'The white catering van. Go!'

Emma smelt the inferno before she could see it. The Stables were over a bluff, hiding everything but the orange glow in the sky, but as soon as she had cleared the rise, the night sky was pierced by orange flames. Tears flowed down Emma's cheeks as she pressed her foot hard down on the accelerator. Her tears turned to choking sobs as she managed to make out the silhouettes of Tom and Rob standing two hundred feet away from the fire. Next to them the door of Rob's car was open and Cassandra was sitting huddled in a blanket.

'Thank goodness, thank goodness,' said Emma under her breath.

Four fire engines roared up behind her and suddenly the whole area was buzzing with firemen rolling out hoses.

'There's a water supply in that outhouse,' shouted Emma pointing to a small building fifty feet away. She ran over to Rob who caught her in a strong embrace, crushing her to his chest.

'She's got cuts and sprains and she's coughing up black stuff, but I think she's OK,' said Rob quietly.

Emma walked over to her and the two women locked eyes. 'We've called for an ambulance,' Emma said softly, then gathered Cassandra into her arms and held her. For a moment Emma didn't know what to say. She felt over-powered by feelings of guilt, anger and then fear. *How the hell had the fire started? Had Cassandra dropped a cigarette? Or perhaps it wasn't an accident.* No one had known that Cassandra was in there, no one had seen her go into Rob's room – anyone would have assumed Emma was in there asleep. Emma had a sudden flashback to Gstaad, remembering the black Mercedes smashing up against the rear of her car. Had the driver come back to finish unresolved business? Despite the heat coming from the burning building, she shuddered. Someone wanted her dead, she felt *sure* of it. And they had almost killed Cassandra in the process.

'Let's go over this one more time,' said Detective Inspector Peter Sheldon. 'You think someone meant to burn down the Stables with you inside?'

It was 4 a.m. and Winterfold was in chaos. Word of the blaze had got around the village and Roger, Rebecca, Stella and Ruan had all returned to the house: Stella and Ruan to reassure various important guests staying in the house that everyone was safe, and Roger and Rebecca had come back to tut and fuss around. Julia and Tom accompanied Cassandra to Oxford's John Radcliffe hospital. Emma sat in Winterfold's library with Rob at her side, her hand in his as she answered the policeman's questions. For a brief moment she reflected that only three hours earlier she had been feeling happy and secure. Apprehensive, yes, but excited when Rob had kissed her. Now it was fear of another kind. The fear of being watched, hated, *hunted*.

'I know it sounds ridiculous but I do think someone might want me dead.'

Inspector Sheldon looked at her cynically, but indicated she should continue.

'I was in Switzerland over Christmas and a car tried to run me off the road. I ended up hospitalized.'

'Was it investigated?' asked Sheldon and Emma caught the slight tone of disbelief in his voice.

'Yes. The police thought the most likely explanation was joyriders.'

'I'm inclined to agree.'

Emma kept quiet knowing it was pointless to argue. Rob, however, wasn't going to let it drop so easily.

'All Emma is saying is that it's more than a little strange that in the space of six weeks she's been run off the road and then her house has been set on fire,' he said irritably. The policeman closed his eyes, as if he had heard it all before.

'We can take a statement off you next Mr Holland,' he said. 'The fire officer will be here soon so we'll know more then. In the meantime, do you mind if we have a look around the house? And we'll need the names and contact details of as many party guests as you can get hold of. If it is foul play, then we're going to have to follow up with everyone we can.'

They all stood and Rob began to lead Emma back to his room.

'Oh, and by the way,' said the detective. 'Don't go anywhere, either of you. No sudden business out of town or trips abroad.'

Emma looked at him incredulously.

'Are you saying that we're *suspects*?'

Sheldon's face was impassive.

'Until we get to the bottom of this mess, Ms Bailey, we just want everyone to co-operate.'

61

The newspapers went into overdrive with the story. Monday was a slow day for news and the Milford party made a big splash in every paper on the stand. The broadsheets reported the fire that almost killed 'top magazine editor Cassandra Grand'. The tabloids went heavy on Clover Connor and Blake Brinton's steamy affair, claiming the couple were having 'red-hot sex as media superstar Cassandra Grand was burning to death', and the story was accompanied by lots of flashy photographs of the famous party guests, including, to her horror, one of Stella.

News of Cassandra's 'critical injuries' were overstated. Cassandra spent the night in the John Radcliffe Hospital, suffering from smoke inhalation, a cracked rib and a sprained ankle from the fall. She had been furious to be papped leaving the hospital in a pair of royal blue jogging bottoms her mother had brought to the hospital for her, but the humiliation was slightly sweetened by the fashion industry's unexpected volte-face upon hearing of Cassandra's ordeal. Within forty-eight hours she had received extravagant blooms from every major fashion house. Isaac Grey sent a muffin basket. Gwyneth texted over the number of her

Pilates teacher and everyone wanted to treat her to lunch or supper when she had fully recovered. By Tuesday Cassandra was beginning to feel much better.

Emma was one of the first visitors to come and see Cassandra after she had discharged herself from hospital and gone home.

'What beautiful flowers,' said Emma, admiring an arrangement of one hundred pale pink roses.

'Everybody has been coming out of the woodwork,' smiled Cassandra cynically. 'Fashion loves a crisis, darling. If I'd died I'd have been named as Editor of the Year and some designer would have named a handbag after me.'

Emma looked over at her, lying regally on her long beige sofa. Somehow she looked smaller, less scary. Not that she had changed entirely. Her ankle was strapped and propped up on a pile of cushions and Emma couldn't help but notice her immaculately painted toenails. *Priorities*, thought Emma with a smile.

'So how are you feeling?'

'I'd have preferred Hervé Léger to do the bandage,' she said pointing at her foot with a small smile. 'But what about you? Did you manage to salvage any of your stuff?'

Emma shook her head. 'Everything's gone except the things I had with me at the party. A credit card and a lipstick.'

'What colour?' asked Cassandra automatically and they both smiled.

'Do you know anything more about how it happened?'

'The police strongly suspect it was arson,' replied Emma.

'Yes, some tiresome police inspector was around for over an hour yesterday: very rude, terrible haircut,' said Cassandra. 'He wanted to know if I had seen or heard anything that evening.'

'Did you?'

Cassandra shook her head. 'No, at least nothing I can

595

remember. And before you ask, it wasn't me. I didn't smoke, light a fire or touch anything in the kitchen.'

'The fire officer thinks it was deliberate.'

'How can they tell?'

'By the patterns and intensity of scorching around the house, apparently. They think something came through the letterbox.'

Cassandra nodded thoughtfully, pausing before she spoke.

'Emma, I should probably tell you the police inspector was asking lots of questions about you,' she said finally.

Emma felt a small rush of fear.

'What questions exactly?'

'He knew that there's been some animosity between us.'

'So what are they thinking? That I torched my own house with you inside it?' said Emma incredulously. She looked at Cassandra warily. She felt terrible about what her cousin had just been through but it didn't mean she entirely trusted Cassandra. What had she been saying to the police?

The truth was that the fire had really frightened Emma and in actual fact she had desperately wanted Cassandra to have been responsible. A careless cigarette down the back of the sofa perhaps, or a candle left too close to the curtains. The alternative, well, the alternative meant that someone really did want her dead.

In the penthouse of the St Martin's Lane Hotel, Stella finally relaxed, her photo-shoot for *W* magazine over. Still wearing the Milford aqua chiffon cocktail dress she had posed in, she quickly gathered up her things and made for the door.

'Are you sure you don't need a car?' asked the art director as Stella said her goodbyes.

'No thanks, I've checked in at the hotel tonight,' she said gratefully. It had been a snap decision an hour earlier; she was so exhausted she didn't think she could make the journey back to Oxfordshire. She had barely stopped to take a breath for weeks – no, months – running at full pelt to get the womenswear line finished in time for the show and then there was all the press to deal with. That meant endless photo-shoots and interviews along with all the draining attention of the blood-sucking journalists on the tabloids. As Stella pushed open her door, all she wanted to do was sleep for a week. Her room three floors below wasn't as impressive as the penthouse but its sleek lines of wood, Perspex and sexy lighting were still beautiful. But Stella was too tired to take it in; she just flopped onto the bed and was about to drift off to sleep when her mobile rang.

'Hello,' she said groggily.

'It's Tom.'

'Oh, hi there,' she smiled propping herself up with a pillow. She was surprised at how pleased she was to hear his voice. There was a pause as if Tom was unsure about what to say next.

'So . . . heard any more about the cause of the fire?'

'You probably know more about it than I do,' said Stella. 'I've hardly been to Milford since that night.'

'Well, I just wanted to call and say that my mother has finally arranged a meeting with Walter Maier about your dad's exhibition. He's very busy, very important, and very German. He's invited us for drinks tomorrow – schnapps, most likely. Can you make it?'

'Of course I can make it,' said Stella, perking up considerably. 'I'm in London tonight actually so I'll just stay another day. Will you come with me?'

'If you ask nicely,' and she could hear the smile in his voice.

'Look, I have to go,' said Tom quickly. 'I have to be in Charing Cross Road by 8 p.m. for a gig.'

'I'm at the St Martin's Lane Hotel,' she replied. 'You should pop in and say hello.'

'In that case, what are you doing in a hour?'

'What did you have in mind?'

'Meet me in the lobby. Don't dress up.'

Something had troubled Emma all the way back to Winterfold. Why had the police been so interested in why Cassandra and Emma didn't get on? How could they possibly think that Emma would want to torch the Stables with Cassandra inside? It was inconceivable. Yes, Cassandra had resented her and tried to sabotage the company, but she had failed – the roaring success of the show and the party were proof of that, so what possible motive could people think Emma would have? She drove slowly back through the estate. The soft, woody smell of smoke was still hanging in the air. Her hands trembled on the wheel as she thought back to the events of Saturday night. Nothing seemed real except the rather obvious certainty that she now had nowhere to live. All her earthly possessions were to be found in the small handbag that she had borrowed from the factory, which was presently sitting beside her on the passenger seat. Rob had insisted she move into Winterfold but she had felt uncomfortable and had asked to stay in the guest suite. He hadn't complained and instead had sent his assistant to go shopping for Emma. So Emma had found her wardrobe already full of jeans, T-shirts, white shirts and a black Jil Sander trouser suit. She'd really appreciated the gesture.

Emma parked her car and walked through the house and into the kitchen. It was Morton's afternoon off and the house was ghostly quiet. She wandered around noticing for the first time how much it had changed. It felt more homely, peppered with photographs of Rob's family and friends. She was looking at them, wondering who the women in the pictures were when she heard footsteps in the corridor behind her. Emma quickly moved away from the photos

598

and was sitting on the sofa looking nonchalant when Rob clattered in carrying a big stack of pizza boxes.

'I picked these up from the village,' he said from behind the boxes. 'I didn't know what you fancied, so I pretty much got everything.'

'Just what I need, comfort food,' said Emma, clapping her hands.

They sat on the rug in the library and Rob lit a fire. As it crackled, Emma felt herself thaw emotionally. For the first time since her belongings had gone up in smoke she felt at home, felt like she had something to hold onto. Outside it was dark and raining heavily. The pizza gone, Rob dimmed the lights and brought a mountain of cushions over to the hearth.

'I went to see Cassandra today,' said Emma as she lay in Rob's arms, his fingers stroking her hair.

'How was she?'

'She looked fabulous,' she smiled.

'I'm not surprised. I'm sure she's quite enjoying all the attention.'

Emma was quiet for a moment, playing with Rob's cuff.

'Rob, do you think someone wants me dead?' she asked quietly, turning to look at him.

'Honey, let's not go through this again,' he said gently. 'Let the police work it out.'

'But will they?'

'Chances are that the fire was started by kids.'

'Just like it was joyriders who pushed me off the road. I guess I must be pretty unlucky.'

'It was still probably pranksters.'

'Petrol was poured through the front door.'

'You're just feeling vulnerable. It can make people a little paranoid.'

She pushed herself upright and looked at him. 'Well how's

this for paranoid? Basically there are two possibilities: some-body wanted to kill me, or somebody knew Cassandra was staying at the Stables and wanted to kill her.'

Rob thought about it for a while and decided to run with it.

'Well, I know Cassandra is pretty unpopular in some areas, but who would want to kill her? Surely she was suffering enough already at that point?'

'Yes, I know. It's unlikely, isn't it, but I'm still convinced the accident in Gstaad was a deliberate act.'

She saw Rob frown, chewing it over.

'OK,' he said slowly. 'Let's go with this one for a moment. Who wants you dead and why?'

Emma had spent the last forty-eight hours thinking about it fanatically, her forensic brain sifting through the many scenarios. Her mother would inherit Emma's shares on her death; and she felt sure that in that instance Virginia would want to get rid of them rather than keep hold of the shareholding. The other shareholders could get them at a preferential rate which meant that Roger, Julia, Ruan or Stella could, in theory, benefit from Emma's death. (She refused to believe that her *own mother* would try and kill her.) But in Emma's mind there was only one obvious person with both motive and opportunity: her uncle.

'Roger has hated me from day one,' she told Rob slowly. 'He thinks I've sidelined him from the company, which of course I have. He seems to have lost interest in Milford in the last few months and over Christmas was pressurizing me to have a meeting with a luxury goods conglomerate and he seemed desperate to sell. It's logical: because of terms in the shareholders agreement, he'll get more for his share-holding if we sell the entire company to an outsider than if he sells his shares to me.'

'So what's his motive?'

'Money,' said Emma frankly. 'Roger owns 20 per cent of the company. With me dead, the shares pass to my mother. She'd definitely sanction a sale if he asked her. Twenty per cent of fifty, a hundred, million pounds is *a lot* of money. Even for Rebecca.'

She looked out of the library door and, as she did so, images of Saturday night's party came back to her with clarity.

'Roger thought I was going back to the Stables. He offered me a lift back in the taxi right there,' she said, pointing to the curve of the stairs they could just see through the doorway. 'I told him I was getting the next taxi. His house is five minutes drive from the Stables through the East Gate. He could have waited half an hour, then gone to my house, saw the lights were on, and well . . .' her voice tailed off and suddenly she felt uneasy looking at the fire in front of them.

Rob put his hand over hers. 'How about we have an early night?'

'It's only seven.'

'I can think of ways we can while away the time,' he said, taking her hand.

She felt her body freeze. She'd barely let him touch her since the fire; she couldn't bring herself to be close to anyone; it was as if she had physically and emotionally shut down. She couldn't explain it, didn't want it, but it was as if some instinct of self-preservation was trying to protect her by making her stay isolated and distant.

'Em, please,' he said quietly. 'I know what's happened has been awful but you don't need to put yourself in deep freeze.'

He reached over and she let him kiss her softly on the lips.

'Let's take it slowly? Please?'

'At least sleep in the bedroom tonight.'

She hesitated and was about to speak when there was a knock on the door.

'Were you expecting anyone?' she asked Rob, suddenly on edge.

Rob got up and walked to the front door. Emma listened to the male voices that floated into the house.

'Em. It's Inspector Sheldon,' said Rob, returning to the door of the library with a frown on his brow.

Sheldon extended a hand. 'I hope I haven't disturbed anything,' he said looking around the hallway. 'I heard you were staying here, Ms Bailey. I'm afraid we need you down at the station to answer a few more questions.'

'I feel as overdressed as Joan Collins at a Hell's Angels convention,' whispered Stella, still wearing the aqua chiffon dress in the small dark basement of the Helter Skelter record shop on Denmark Street.

Tom laughed. 'I said don't dress up. Don't worry. No one comes here to people-watch,' he said, aware of the irony that every man in the room had been clocking Stella, luminous in some wisp of a shimmering blue dress, since the moment she had walked in.

'Shit. They're coming on,' he nudged her as four guys in black T-shirts and jeans walked onto a makeshift stage so small it was more like a podium.

'Who are they again?'

'Red Comets. A student band from Kings College. I think they're brilliant: the new Coldplay. I've given their CD to a few people.'

Tom didn't hold out much hope that Ste Donahue would do anything for the band, especially as he had so many problems of his own, but he was secretly excited about Rob Holland. He'd sent Rob a copy of the CD and he'd promised to give it a listen; if anyone could give the band a leg-up, it was Rob.

'If they're so good why are they playing in this record shop?' asked Stella, keeping her voice low.

'They'll get spotted at the Helter Skelter. The owner has incredible taste in music.'

The band was playing an acoustic set. The lead singer's voice was deep, rich and wistful; the guitars were haunting, filling the air with beautiful melancholy. Stella took a deep breath; she was surprised by the power and emotion of the music and the lyrics.

She turned to watch Tom as he gazed at the band with the same love and wonder as she experienced when she watched a fashion show. He turned and gave her a smile, his eyes bright blue in the dimly-lit room.

She was suddenly overwhelmed by emotion. She had heard of love at first sight but this was something else. A moment of clarity, a connection between two people binding them together with more than mere physical attraction.

'What do you think?' he asked, moving closer to her side. As their bare arms touched she melted.

'I think I like it here,' she replied. She rested her head on his shoulder, unable to stop herself. It felt like the most natural thing to do.

She felt his arms drop to his side and carefully, cautiously, he took her hand.

'Come on,' he said quietly after the end of the second song. 'I've seen them loads of times before.'

They walked back out of the basement and through the record shop. And against a rack of old LPs he kissed her, filling her with such a sweet light-headedness she thought she might float all the way back to Chilcot.

* * *

603

Although he was hiding it well, DI Sheldon was a little flustered. He was not at all used to sitting opposite such an attractive woman in the police interview room. In his line of work, it was usually street punks on GBH charges or pub brawls over money or women, not arson and attempted murder involving famous magazine editors and luxury goods companies. He knew he was lucky to be assigned the case and was desperate to make his mark. He wanted to join the Met within the year at the level of Chief Inspector.

He had spent the last three days making phone calls and talking to as many people who had been guests at the party as he could track down.

A joint investigation between police, fire and forensic services was pointing towards arson. The intensity of heat and burning around the kitchen door was almost conclusive that petrol, most likely diesel-oil fuel used in motorbike engines, had been poured through the letterbox.

The gravel approach to the Stables had been contaminated by rain and the water used to extinguish the flames and from the emergency vehicles that had turned up at the Stables so that the SOCO officers had found no useable foot or tyre prints.

'I want to talk about your relationship with Cassandra Grand. I've heard from a number of sources it was difficult.'

'We'd had a few disagreements,' said Emma honestly. 'But I didn't hold anything personally against her. She's my cousin.'

'Is it true that you think she's been trying to sabotage the success of your company?'

'I've had my suspicions, but . . .'

'You were heard arguing at around midnight during the party.'

'We didn't argue. Cassandra was upset. She'd been having a very difficult night and didn't want to go back to the party.

I said she could stay at my house and arranged for her to go out the back.'

Sheldon wrote something in his notebook before he spoke again.

'Cassandra said you insisted she sleep at the Stables.'

'She was upset and didn't want to see anyone at the party. You know what fashion people can be like.'

'Actually, I don't,' said Sheldon shortly. 'How come you weren't sleeping at the Stables? It's within the Winterfold grounds.'

'I was with Rob Holland.'

'Is he your boyfriend?'

'No. Not really.'

'Rob Holland said he left you in his bed at Winterfold at around 1.15 to go and look for Stephen Donahue. Tom Grand discovered the fire at around 1.30. Nobody appears to have seen you between 1.15 and 1.45.'

'I was in bed. Look, where are you going with this?' asked Emma, afraid of the accusatory tone in his voice.

Sheldon went to the telephone, made a call and within a minute an officer appeared holding a plastic evidence bag.

'Have you ever seen this before?' asked Sheldon putting on plastic gloves and pulling a black cashmere shawl out of it. 'It was found fifty feet from the Stables.'

'It's mine.'

'Can you explain what this petrol is doing here?' he asked, pointing at a dark black smudge along one edge.

'I don't know. I haven't seen the shawl since the party,' she said trying to keep cool but her skin prickling with anxiety and fear. 'What are you accusing me of here?'

Sheldon shrugged.

'I don't think I'd better say anything further until I speak to a solicitor,' said Emma.

DI Sheldon put the shawl back into the plastic bag and took off his rubber gloves. 'Under the circumstances I think that's probably a good idea.'

They lay in Stella's bed at the St Martin's Lane Hotel; crumpled sheets were pushed back over their bare legs. Stella lay in the crook of Tom's arm and traced her finger down the long scar down his neck.

'I hope this isn't just a thank you for sorting out the Walter Maier meeting,' he said contentedly.

'I hope you don't think I'm just after another bad boy.'

He sat up with a look of alarm on his face.

'Is that what you think?'

'No.' She thought about it for a moment. 'Although it did worry me for a while. I think that's why nothing happened sooner between us. I was protecting myself,' she said, their nakedness making her honest.

'I haven't had a joint since Christmas. I don't want to. I don't need to. Not with you around.'

She stroked his head.

'Everything was so shit for me last year, but you seem to make things so much better,' he continued softly. 'With a bit of luck, that fire and what happened to Cassandra will be the end of the run of bad luck.'

'Things aren't that bad, are they?' she asked. She glanced at his scar. She'd asked about it once and he'd said something vague about a mugging.

'If it wasn't for you and my mum it would be worse.'

'Your mum?' said Stella.

He took a long breath before he spoke.

'I've not wanted to tell you this, because I know you think I'm a bad boy, because you'll judge me and I'm trying to change. I don't want to make any more stupid fucking decisions in my life. But I have to tell you everything now because I want the slate to be clean. I don't want you to find out through someone else and then hate me.'

Stella had a sinking feeling in the pit of her stomach. What could it be? Was it criminal?

'Remember when I got mugged?'

She nodded slowly.

'It wasn't just someone random. I knew who it was. Well, I knew who ordered me to be beaten up.'

He paused and wiped his mouth nervously.

'I ran up big debts when I had the bar in Ibiza last summer. My side of the business was fine, but it was a partnership. My partners couldn't pay the debts. I couldn't pay them either. I can't sell my vintage cars because they're in trust till I'm thirty. I didn't want to ask anyone for help. I thought I could come back to England and it would all go away.'

'And it didn't?' said Stella softly.

Tom shook his head.

'They tracked me down. The interest had quadrupled. They invented all sorts of other money that I owed them. Damage to the building etcetera. The bottom line? A ninety thousand debt became almost a quarter of a million quid.'

'Shit,' whispered Stella.

'When they had me beaten up, when I was in hospital, I knew I was in real trouble. I told my mother and she found the money to pay them off.'

'How?'

He looked away, his face full of guilt, shame and sadness.

'It was every penny she had, every ounce of credit she could raise. It was money she wanted for a lease on a new gallery. I didn't want to take it but I had to. Otherwise I'd have been dead.'

He made a strange guttural choking noise and Stella realized he was beginning to cry.

She pulled him close to her and stroked the top of his head with her fingertips.

'Ssh,' she whispered. It's all over now. Everything is going to be all right.'

62

'*Arrested Emma!* That's impossible. What the hell do they have on her?'

Virginia listened to Emma's solicitor before she put down the phone trembling.

She sank into the nearest chair and looked at Jonathon standing by the living-room door. 'Emma's been arrested in connection with the Stables' fire.'

'Surely not,' replied her husband. His expression clouded over before he spoke again. 'What's that going to do to the company? How's it going to look? That luxury goods company won't be so interested in Milford if we're tarnished.'

'We'd better phone Roger,' said Virginia, her face pale. 'And then I have to see Emma.'

'*Arrested? Emma?*' Rob felt a swell of nausea on speaking to Richard Harrod, Emma's solicitor.

'They think it's arson and that she's responsible. They could go for attempted murder as well.'

'Do you think they will charge her?' asked Rob, horrified.

Richard Harrod cleared his throat.

'It's possible. Finding Emma's shawl covered in petrol wasn't exactly good news. Arson with intent to endanger life is a very serious charge.'

'There are a dozen reasons why her shawl had petrol on it! All sorts of farm vehicles drive through the estate; maybe there was diesel fuel on a tyre that ran over it.' He was losing his temper and his faith in the solicitor; he intended to bring someone in from London as soon as he got off the telephone.

He paced around the room, raking his fingers through his hair.

All he could think about was her conviction on the journey home from Gstaad that someone wanted to harm her. She was suspicious and desperate to work it all out with her fierce, clever mind, but she could do nothing now.

He made a few phone calls until he had found Cassandra Grand's home and mobile number and tried them both.

Arrested, wept Emma as she was led down to a cell after eight hours of questioning. Consumed by a sense of unreality, her head pounded, her throat was dry with panic. Her whole life seemed to be collapsing around her. How could everything have gone so utterly, hideously wrong. She had done nothing. Had they not checked with the Swiss police? The police seemed to be assuming that because Cassandra had almost died in the fire, she had been the intended victim. But it was Emma's house. *She* should have been sleeping there. Someone wanted Emma dead. To her it was obvious.

63

Cassandra felt her luck was finally beginning to change when Rob Holland phoned her to suggest dinner. She secured a table at Petrus and chose to wear a scarlet Donna Karan jersey dress that didn't restrict movement around her chest which was still incredibly sore from her cracked rib. Her face was perfectly made-up to enhance her natural beauty: a sweep of blusher swept across her cheeks, mascara widened her eyes and a peach gloss made her plump lips look even more luscious. She was still limping, but took painkillers so she could squeeze her feet into a pair of heels. She headed off with almost a spring in her step.

Rob was already at the table when she got there; he looked anxious but that could not distract from his sexiness. She observed him for one moment, self-assured, masculine and handsome in a crisp blue shirt and jeans. For the first time since Max, Cassandra felt a shot of lust curl in her groin.

He shook her hand before she sat down.

'This is a pleasant surprise,' said Cassandra her lips curling into her sexiest smile. She had seen his eyes flick up and down her body as she approached the table and knew he couldn't help but be attracted to her.

'How are you feeling?'

'Better for seeing you.'

Rob averted his eyes from the table and summoned the sommelier.

'I assume you've heard about Emma?'

Cassandra nodded.

'This can't be good for business,' she said, taking a menu from the waiter.

'I think that's probably the last thing on her mind at the moment.'

'The business is never the last thing on Emma's mind,' she replied with a small smile. 'Anyway, all this publicity with her arrest might not be a bad thing. No publicity is bad publicity. This is the biggest fashion crime story since Maurizio Gucci got gunned down outside his house in '95. Everybody must know the name Milford now.'

She ordered her food and folded her slender tanned arms in front of her.

'What did you want to speak to me about?'

'We need to talk about the fire, and Emma.'

For a second she thought of the quiet, studious girl on the steps of Les Fleurs all those years ago; it was laughable that the same person could be a killer.

She took a sip of the excellent Bordeaux that Rob had ordered.

'I used to think that people would kill for my job. But seeing as I don't have it any more it seems inconceivable that anyone would want me dead. So yes, I think it's unlikely that Emma set fire to the Stables to harm me. The likeliest explanation is that it was simply pranksters.'

'Did you see anything that night?'

'Rob, darling,' she said laughing slowly. 'Who do you think you are – Jonathon Hart?'

'Cassandra, please,' he said, fixing her with his most charming, persuasive stare.

She gave a little sigh. 'I've told the police everything. I was a little drunk, fell asleep and heard nothing until I woke up and the whole place was on fire. I wasn't exactly taking notes.'

'Who knew you were at the Stables?'

Cassandra shrugged. 'The guy who drove me there. Unless someone else saw me.'

'What do you think happened, Cassandra?'

She couldn't deny she'd given it a lot of thought. Cassandra was desperate to find out what had happened; after all, she was a victim whether it was intentional or otherwise. More importantly, she was naturally manipulative and scheming. In her own experience, accidents did happen, but more often than not things happened for a reason.

'You know Roger is desperate to sell Milford and Emma is adamant she won't get rid of the company.'

She paused, remembering what she had heard on the steps of the chalet in Gstaad.

'I think there's another business Roger wants to invest in.' She was loath to say any more. After all, she was closer to her uncle than to Emma. 'I heard him talking at Christmas. He needed the money quite quickly.'

'Emma doesn't exactly trust Roger either.'

'Have you ever thought there might be a third option?' said Cassandra, enjoying the fact that she had Rob's full attention. 'Someone wanted to kill me, but frame Emma.'

Cassandra thought about the many nights she had spent planning her empire with Max. Max had obtained a copy of Milford's Articles of Association and had gone through it with a fine tooth-comb to equip himself with all the facts. She still had a copy of the Articles somewhere in her apartment.

'Who would want Emma out of the way?'

'Anyone who wants control of the company.'

'Can I have a look at the Articles?'

'I have them somewhere.'

They finished their meal and Rob went to pay the bill.

As they left the restaurant she exaggerated her limp and Rob put out his arm to support her.

She leaned into his body, enjoying his scent.

'Can I give you a lift home?'

'Thank you. I'm just a couple of minutes away.'

He stopped outside her appointment, went round to open her passenger door and helped her to the front door.

'Do you want to come in?' she whispered. 'We could go through the Milford Articles together.'

Rob looked at her a moment longer than was necessary and then nodded.

'OK. Quickly.'

They went into her apartment and Cassandra switched on a solitary lamp. Soft, flattering light spilled around the room. Cassandra opened a bottle of wine and pulled out the Milford Articles and Memorandum from a box file.

'I think I'd better go,' said Rob, picking the documents up.

'You've not touched your drink.'

He shrugged uncomfortably and Cassandra understood immediately.

'You're in love with her,' said Cassandra with a small smile.

He nodded. 'I think I am.'

Leaving Cassandra's apartment he did not notice a lone paparazzo across the road. The photographer took his picture and immediately phoned the story through to his boss.

Emma was released without charge after twenty-four hours, but had been told to keep police informed of her whereabouts. When she left Oxford police station a reporter stopped her on the steps and thrust a Dictaphone under her nose.

'Can I get a comment about this?' said the reporter, pushing a copy of the *Mirror* under her nose.

The pages were flipped back to page seven: there was a grainy shot of Rob getting into his Range Rover next to a head-shot of Cassandra taken at London Fashion Week five months earlier. The headline read: *Record Mogul's Secret Tryst with Tragic Cass.*

The reporter immediately turned her attention to Rob who was standing by Emma's side. 'Is it true you are having an affair with Cassandra Grand?'

He hadn't read the paper but had received a phone call from his assistant warning him about the story – that he had been spotted coming out of Cassandra's apartment in the middle of the night.

It took every ounce of willpower he had to stop himself from grabbing the woman's Dictaphone and smashing it to the ground.

'Get back on your broomstick and piss off,' he growled, angered that Emma hadn't heard it from him.

They got into the Range Rover and Emma sat in the front seat shaking.

'So. Is it true? Did you sleep with her?' asked Emma, her voice cracking.

'Of course I didn't,' said Rob angrily.

'I was in a prison cell and I can't believe you would do this.'

'This is ridiculous! We went out for dinner. Yes, I dropped her off at her apartment and I gave her a kiss on the cheek as I said goodnight.'

Emma desperately wanted to believe him but she'd already had a lifetime of being let down by men. And Cassandra was a man-eater, a wounded one at that, who would no doubt milk her near-death experience for all it was worth. Why would Rob resist her charms especially when Emma knew she'd been behaving like a frigid old woman?

'She gave me these,' said Rob, his voice still wounded, and pulled some documents out of his glove compartment.

He gave her Milford's Articles and Memorandum, which he had marked up in yellow highlighter pen.

Emma felt a pang of guilt. 'I'm sorry.' She longed to kiss him but she could sense that a barrier had risen up between them.

'Have you read these things lately?' he smiled a little more warmly. 'It took me about two hours to wade through it all. Dull as ditchwater. Why do lawyers use five words when one will do?'

'So they can charge more!' she laughed.

'Read page five. No director of the company can serve on Milford's board if he or she has a criminal record.'

'So obviously if I was in jail I couldn't be CEO any more,' Emma said slowly, feeling angry that she hadn't made the connection herself.

'Would Roger finally get the job he wanted with you out of the way?'

'Not necessarily,' said Emma as Rob started the car.

They drove into Chilcot and to the Milford offices. It was 6.30 p.m. and most people had left for the day.

They took the lift to the third floor and walked silently into her office where Emma switched on a single lamp.

'Here. Have a look at this,' she said opening the filing cabinet and pulling a letter out of a drawer labelled *Contracts of Employment*.

'Ruan's?' said Rob quietly.

He could see Emma's eyes scanning the document.

'As COO, contractually he gets to deputize in my absence.

It doesn't specify for how long. So if I went down for arson for five or six years, Ruan would install himself as CEO.'

'But the board could get rid of him.'

'They could,' said Emma thoughtfully, 'but Ruan would already know that he has my backing as majority share-holder, which still counts even though I'm in jail.'

Rob sank back into the black Barcelona office chair.

'Has Ruan ever struck you as sufficiently power-crazed to frame you for murder?'

Emma shook her head vigorously. 'No. No, not at all.'

'So if we rule Ruan out, then who are we looking for?' asked Rob.

Emma pushed the filing cabinet closed with a clang.

'I say it brings us back to Roger.'

64

Sitting in Milford's boardroom, in her chair at the head of the long walnut table, Emma felt the same fear she had experienced on her very first day in the office. Back then it was nerves and a fear of the unknown. Today it was the more unsettling fear that, increasingly, she was losing control of the whole situation. And there was still the nagging feeling that perhaps someone in this room actually wanted her dead. Emma cleared her throat and looked at the shareholders around the table. Not one of them met her gaze.

'You know why we're all here,' she said. 'I believe Roger called this meeting in order to have me removed as CEO due to my supposed criminal activities.'

There was a deathly silence.

'So what are you going to do, Emma?' asked Virginia finally.

She pointed to the grey-haired man on her left.

'Magnus Anderson, Milford's company lawyer, is attending on my instructions. Magnus?'

The solicitor looked up and nodded deferentially to Roger.

'Roger is quite correct, the Articles of the company clearly state that a convicted criminal cannot be a director of the company.'

There was a murmur around the table as people whispered to their neighbours.

'But,' Magnus held up his hand, 'the key word is convicted. At this point, Emma hasn't even been charged.'

'But she has been arrested over some very serious allegations,' insisted Roger. 'The story is all over the media and it paints the company in a very bad light.' He looked around the table, appealing for support. 'Isn't the point of the board to make decisions based on what is best for the business?'

Emma looked at Roger, feeling her flesh crawl, wondering if it had been him driving the car, him who had poured the petrol through the letterbox? Whether he'd tried to kill her or not, there was something very dark and deceitful about him. But she just couldn't argue with what he had just said. What would her colleagues at Price Donahue, what would she, recommend to a tarnished CEO? At best, she would tell them to lie low and ride out the storm. Ideally, she would recommend that they quietly step aside and wait for the scandal to pass. She smoothed down her skirt nervously and glanced at Ruan who smiled encouragingly.

'Very well. In the best interest of Milford, I will take a two-week leave of absence from the company. By then the police should have further results of forensic tests and I'm confident I will be fully cleared. In the meantime, Ruan will be acting CEO.'

Everyone turned to look at Roger anxiously.

'A strong decision, Emma, best for everyone all round,' he said, with an oily smile. 'I'm sure everyone will join me in giving Ruan our full support at this difficult time.'

Suddenly everyone started talking at once, asking Emma questions, congratulating Ruan, calling for more information from Magnus.

Roger held up a hand and the hubbub died down.

'Actually, there is something else I wish to discuss since all the shareholders are here,' he said, pausing for a moment. 'I would like to sell my shareholding in Milford.'

Every face in the room turned to him, every mouth open in surprise.

'In accordance with our shareholders' agreement, I am giving you twenty-eight days notice to buy them,' continued Roger. 'Then I will be looking for other buyers on the open market.'

The uproar began again and Roger looked over at Emma triumphantly. He knew that as a suspect in an arson and attempted murder case, Emma would be unable to raise such a large amount of money and with her out of play, a sale of his shares to an outsider would bring a windfall of millions.

'Very well,' said Emma quietly, cursing herself for being out-manoeuvred. She declared the meeting closed. The shareholders filed out excitedly, unable to believe what they had just seen and heard.

65

Stella and Tom walked down Oxford's High Street holding hands; the cold air nipped their noses, but they were enjoying the warmth of each other's touch. In preparation for their meeting with Walter Maier to discuss the feasibility of a Christopher Chase exhibition, Stella had asked to meet up with Julia to get the lowdown on the German gallery owner. She was keen to make the best possible impression – both on Walter and on Tom's mother. Stella was excited but nervous as they turned off the High Street where Julia's little gallery The Hollyhock nestled in a quiet, scholarly mews.

'How does your mum feel about not showing my father's exhibition herself?' asked Stella, cuddling up against Tom, trying to shelter from the arctic wind.

'I think she was a bit disappointed when she heard you wanted to go with a big London gallery,' said Tom honestly. 'But she agreed it was probably for the best; she hasn't really got the client-base to make a success of such a show. Plus, I think she's trying to negotiate some commission with Walter so she gets something out of it.'

'Good for her,' said Stella. She had been feeling guilty

about the arrangement, especially after hearing how Julia had bailed Tom out of his Ibiza debts. But at the same time, her opinion of Tom's mother had increased enormously. A bell tinkled as they walked into the gallery and a forty-something man dressed in black came over to them.

'Thomas. How are you?' he said with a distinct lack of enthusiasm.

'Fine, thanks, Jacques. Is my mother around?'

'Sorry, she went to London first thing this morning. She said she'd be back by 3 p.m., but that appears not to be the case,' he said tartly.

Tom disliked the implication as he knew Julia treated her staff very well. *Poisonous little queen*, he thought.

'I imagine she'll be visiting my sister,' said Tom in a mild tone. 'I don't know if you heard, but she was almost killed a few days ago. Perhaps you'll excuse her if she has more important things to worry about, especially when she pays you a great deal of money to manage the gallery for her.'

Jacques tutted loudly.

'Do you mind if we wait here a little while? She might be back at any time and I need to pick her brains.'

'Very well,' said Jacques rolling his eyes. 'But you might prefer to stay in the back,' he added, looking pointedly at Tom's jeans and old parka. 'Hélène Brose is coming in at 4 p.m. She's a very important art consultant and I'm sure she would prefer to see the space without any encumbrances.'

Stella suppressed a smile.

'Let's go and get a cup of tea somewhere,' she whispered.

'There's a coffee machine in the office,' said Tom. 'Jacques. We're going upstairs for ten minutes.'

'If you must.'

Upstairs was just like any other office. There was a large, glass desk strewn with catalogues and photographs, a pot of pens and a big Rolodex. There were a few photographs on the wall of Julia at various art fairs, smiling with bigwigs from the art world whom Stella vaguely recognized. On the window-sill was the largest photograph of all. It was a framed picture of Julia, Tom and Cassandra taken with Winterfold in the background. Stella walked over and touched the frame, looking at the younger Tom and smiling.

'Was it hard being brought up by just your mum?'

'No, she did a great job,' said Tom, as he busied himself making the coffee. 'Look at the way she went running off to see Cassandra. She dotes on us. We couldn't have asked for more, honestly.'

Stella picked up a Hollyhock gallery brochure and leafed through it.

'She's had some good shows recently.'

'Want a private view?' said Tom, nodding towards a door behind her. 'That's where she keeps pieces from previous exhibitions that haven't sold or are waiting to go to their new owners.'

'Are we allowed?'

'Not really,' said Tom, opening the desk drawer and taking out a key. 'But seeing as it's you . . .'

Behind the door was a cramped storage room crammed with oil paintings, lithographs and sketches, some swathed in bubble wrap, some propped against the walls or on shelves.

'It's usually grouped into exhibitions,' said Tom, moving a large canvas out of the way to get to the back of the room.

'Here we go: a Terry Frost signed lithograph.' He pointed to the pencil mark in the corner next to the signature. '"A/P" – that means that this one is the artist's proof of that particular lithograph; it's one of the ones he kept for himself or to give to friends. I'd say it's a good investment.'

'I'm too poor to be investing in art,' smiled Stella. 'I'm

not Tom Ford yet, you know. Gosh, there must be hundreds of thousands of pounds worth of stuff in this room,' she added excitedly.

'Not really. That Frost lithograph is about as expensive as it gets. She mostly deals with stuff under a thousand pounds. I think me and Cass and then Ruby got in the way of making Hollyhock a more important gallery than it is now. She always put us first.' He fell silent for a moment, and Stella knew he was thinking about how his mother had bailed him out yet again at a cost to her own ambitions. Then Tom suddenly looked up, laughed and pointed to a low door at the back of the room which was set into the slope of the roof.

'Still, I bet my mum wouldn't let me play in here any more.'

'What do you mean?'

'When I was little and Mum had to bring me into the office with her, I used to play in here and hide in that little cubby-hole. I'd call it my space shuttle.'

'Ahh, sweet,' said Stella, stroking his arm affectionately.

Tom crouched down and lifted up a loose flap of carpet. Underneath was a key. Tom grinned at Stella and unlocked the little door.

'Fancy playing doctors and nurses in the space shuttle?' he asked. Stella giggled as Tom bent over and popped his head inside. 'Hmm . . . might be a little dusty for that . . .'

He was straightening up again when something caught his eye: a large painting leaning against the wall.

'Hang on,' he said and then reached into the space and pulled it out.

'Hey, do you recognize this?' he asked, beckoning Stella over. 'I think this is by the same guy as that stuff at your dad's house.'

'You mean Ben Palmer?' said Stella nodding. 'Yes, I'm

sure it's by him – the colours and shapes, the little boat, that red sky are all right. No, it couldn't be anyone else, I've been looking at those paintings in Trencarrow for years now. The style is identical.'

'What on earth is it doing in here?' he said, holding it aloft by its frame.

'Hang on, there's something on the back,' said Stella.

Tom turned it over.

'Another painting,' said Stella. 'I don't think that's Ben Palmer, it's too messy. Maybe it's by another artist?'

The picture on the back wasn't completely finished, but they could see that it was painted in a more brutal style: energetic brushstrokes and thick daubs of dark paint were emphasized with bright flesh tones and bottle greens.

'That's odd, isn't it? Why would someone paint on the back?'

Stella thought for a moment.

'Do you remember Dad saying that Ben Palmer was really poor? Didn't he say he used to paint on anything he could find lying around the studios? Why don't we show this to him? I bet he'll be interested.'

She reached into her bag, took out the camera she carried everywhere and snapped both sides of the painting.

'He loves Ben Palmer's stuff. When he gets some money from his exhibition maybe he could buy it.'

Tom put the painting back in the space shuttle. 'It's stuffed in here so she probably won't want much for it. He's got a computer, hasn't he? Why don't you send over the photos and see if he likes it?'

She turned and gave him a long kiss.

'What's that for?'

'For being nice about Dad. And for the space shuttle.'

Tom beamed.

'OK, enough romance, let's scarper,' he said quickly.

'Jacques will get all queeny if he thinks we've been mucking about in here.'

Stella was spending a relaxing evening in front of the fire with Tom after their chilly Oxford trip. They were just reading magazines and sharing a bottle of Chardonnay when the phone rang.

'Hello, Stella, it's your father,' said a rich baritone at the other end of the line.

'Oh, hi, Dad. How are you?'

'Muddling through,' he said grumpily, but Stella could detect a slightly more upbeat tone in Christopher's voice.

'Have you heard from Chessie?' she asked gently.

'A few letters from the lawyers,' he sighed. 'Nothing I can't handle. I'll be OK, sweetheart, don't you worry.'

'I'm glad,' said Stella, smiling into the phone. 'Anyway, did you get the images I sent you?'

'Yes, I did and that's what I'm calling about,' said Christopher. 'Where did you find this painting again?'

'In Julia's gallery. We thought it might be by the same artist as the ones you have at Trencarrow.'

'Yes, I'm sure it is; I'm certain it's Ben Palmer. Have you asked Julia about it?'

'Not yet. Did you like it?'

'First of all, are you entirely sure it is Julia's to sell?'

'As I said, we haven't spoken to her about it. Why?'

'Well, if it's Ben's work, then I'm certain it belonged to Saul,' said Christopher cautiously. 'Bless him, but Ben didn't sell very many paintings, so I doubt they're from the open market. I certainly know Ben gave Saul some paintings at about the same time as me in about 1959 or 1960. I'm convinced this is one of them.'

Stella moved off the sofa and went to sit on a chair by the window, out of earshot of Tom.

'Do you think Julia was willed them in Saul's estate? Or perhaps Emma has given them to Julia to sell.'

'Well, whoever owns that painting has something very valuable on their hands; something very valuable indeed,' said Christopher.

Stella frowned and glanced over at Tom, who was engrossed in his magazine.

'You've always said that the Palmer painting is only valuable for sentimental reasons.'

'*My* Palmer painting, yes. But the work you sent me . . .' and he paused. 'You saw the painting on the back?'

'Yes.'

'I'm sure it's the work of Francis Bacon.'

'*The* Francis Bacon? Really?'

'Yes. Bacon worked in the Porthmeor Studios in St Ives for a short period around the same time as Ben gave us his paintings. Ben was very hard up and used to paint on whatever he could find: boards, card, even other artists' canvases. Bacon was famous for destroying or throwing away anything he wasn't happy with and I'm sure he's painted on some of Bacon's discarded work.'

'Why would he give a valuable Bacon painting away to Saul? If Ben was so hard up, why didn't he keep it for himself?'

'Who knows? Ben never thought much of Bacon's work, called him a "dauber" and anyway, he might not even have identified it as Bacon's work. Bacon was in quite an experimental stage when he worked in St Ives and the painting is barely finished. Certainly, none of us had any idea how valuable his paintings would become decades later.'

'So you think it *is* valuable?'

She heard her father laughing slowly down the phone.

'The price of Bacon's work has gone through the roof. Ten, twenty million or more. As I said, Bacon's work in

627

St Ives was an important experimental period for him, so even though it's unfinished, it's of huge cultural and developmental significance. Even if it doesn't get authenticated by the Bacon estate, I'm sure someone, somewhere, will pay a fortune for it.'

66

Cassandra had spent the day quietly, reading and thinking; thinking about the past and particularly about the future. The fire had been a wake-up call for her in too many ways to count. She realized now that losing her job had hit her harder than she'd been able to admit. Before that terrible moment in the Ivy, Cassandra Grand had been indestructible, a goddess on her throne; nothing could touch her and everything she did turned to gold, assuming, that is, that gold was the colour of the season. She had spent so long going up, up, up, that when her wings melted, her fall was wounding and complete. She hadn't just lost her job, she'd lost Max, she'd lost her dream of building a Cassandra Grand empire and most importantly, she had lost her elevated place in the world. And now, looking back at it from the ruins of her once-glittering life, she realized that she had lost a lot more along the way. She'd lost her friends, her family and a little piece of her soul. But Cassandra was a survivor and nothing had made her realize that more than the Stables inferno. She'd survived *literally*. It was surely a sign that she had to pick herself up and get back on track. Cassandra had settled down into the sofa with a notebook and a Mont

Blanc pen to begin planning her fightback when the phone went.

'Miss Grand. It's Miss Broughton at Briarton School,' said the anxious voice of Ruby's head teacher.

'Is everything all right?'

'I'm afraid Ruby has disappeared from her room,' said the teacher.

'Well, where has she gone?' snapped Cassandra, her heart suddenly beating faster.

'Nobody has seen her since supper. Her friends Amaryllis and Pandora are also missing.'

'And have you phoned their parents?'

'Yes. They are in Athens and had assumed the girls were at school.'

'Well, I'm assuming they're not, otherwise you wouldn't be calling me,' snapped Cassandra.

'We think they might have slipped out of the grounds . . .'

'Can't you look after your pupils properly?' Cassandra shouted down the phone.

'We have procedures that usually work,' said Miss Broughton sounding unusually flustered. 'Of course we can't keep the girls on a twenty-four hour watch.'

'Have you called the police?'

'It's only been a couple of hours.'

Cassandra inhaled sharply to compose herself. She thought back to her own time at school. In every year there were the fast girls in class; the ones who smoked before everyone else, partied before everyone else, had sex before everyone else. She shuddered. Ruby was only just fourteen.

'I don't know if this is relevant,' said Miss Broughton cautiously. 'But we've interviewed all the girls' friends and apparently Amaryllis had been talking about going to "the

Brits"?' She said the last phrase as if she was trying to pronounce an obscure town in Africa. 'I believe it's some sort of musical shindig or something.'

'It's the Brit Awards tonight,' said Cassandra quickly.

'Perhaps they've gone up to London,' offered Miss Broughton weakly.

'Leave it with me,' said Cassandra, slamming down the phone and calling Rob Holland.

Stella didn't tell Tom what her father had said. Instead, she made an excuse about needing to check something at work and drove straight to Winterfold.

'Sorry Emma,' she said, embracing her friend who came to the door looking pale and drained. 'I know it's late, but I had to speak to you.'

'Is everything OK?'

Stella glanced around.

'Where's Rob?'

'He's at the Brit Awards tonight but he's coming back to Winterfold later. He insists on driving back to Chilcot every night from the office. You know he's usually only here at weekends.'

'Protecting his girl. Sweet,' smiled Stella.

'Without sounding a coward, I've been glad. I've been quite jumpy being here in this big house on my own.'

They went through into the kitchen and Emma began to make them coffee.

'So have you heard from the police again?' asked Stella.

'No, not yet.'

For a split second Emma glanced at Stella suspiciously. *Why was she asking? What was she trying to find out?* Then she turned back to the kettle and shook her head. *Stop being so bloody paranoid*, Emma scolded herself. *Stella is your friend.*

631

Emma was sure she was going slowly crazy, doubting everyone, looking for hidden meanings or motives in everything everyone did or said.

'I was in Oxford with Tom this afternoon,' said Stella.

'Tom?' said Emma, her eyebrows raised. 'Anything I should know about?

'Actually, yes,' said Stella with a smirk. 'I pounced on him on Tuesday. And before you ask he's a very good kisser.'

Despite her gloom, Emma laughed.

'Well, I'm glad to hear it. Does that make up for the fact that you disapprove of his lifestyle choices?'

Stella took a sip of warm, rich coffee.

'He says he's only had one joint since Christmas. And I think I believe him. Anyway, that wasn't what I wanted to talk about.'

There were a few moments of silence before Stella spoke again.

'We went to Julia's gallery and I saw a painting that I think you should take a look at.'

Stella reached in her handbag, feeling a stab of guilt. Julia was Tom's mum and had been very good to him, plus she was helping out her father with the exhibition, but she had to know if her suspicions were correct. She handed Emma the digital camera and scrolled to the picture she had taken in Julia's gallery.

'Do you recognize this? It was in the store room.'

Emma nodded, a faraway look in her eye as if she were trying to remember.

'It's Saul's. Yes, definitely. We had a huge clear-out before Rob moved in. Julia took away several things from the attic to be restored and valued. I made an inventory, although I suppose it was lost in the fire. After my accident I forgot all about it, but I do remember that painting. The colours . . . I don't exactly have a photographic memory for art, but this I do remember.'

Emma looked up at Stella.

'But why are you showing this to me now? It's not as if she stole it or anything.'

Stella felt a sinking sense of dread, thinking of Tom and how he would hate her if she was right. For a split second Stella was going to hold her tongue, but then she caught sight of the long scar on Emma's arm from the accident. Her friend was a shadow of her former self. She had lost so much weight since the accident that her jeans were hanging off her around the waist. The elegant, polished, successful woman had gone and had been replaced by a thin, nervy shadow. *No,* thought Stella, *the most important thing is the truth.*

'Did you ever see the back of this painting?'

Emma shook her head.

'No. It was in a horrible old frame. I think it was one of the ones Julia took away to reframe.'

'Well, this painting is by Ben Palmer, a Cornish artist and an old friend of Saul and my father's,' explained Stella. 'Ben gave both of them some of his work as a gift when they helped him out financially. Apparently the paintings themselves are worth very little, however, on the back of Saul's – *yours* – is a half-finished work by Francis Bacon. My father reckons it could be worth a lot of money, like maybe millions.'

Emma whistled.

'Are you sure the painting is yours?' said Stella, hoping that perhaps it was all a big mistake. 'Maybe Julia had a similar one. Maybe she knew Ben too?'

But Emma wasn't listening. She was staring out of the window into the darkness.

'It was Julia,' she said softly. 'In the black car in Gstaad. And it was Julia who torched the Stables because she wants me dead. No one knew she had that painting except me, and with me dead, it's hers.'

Emma fell silent, turning it over in her mind.

'But why now? She's had the painting for almost a year.'

'Because she needed the money,' said Stella quietly.

She stared down into the black liquid in her mug.

'She used every penny she owned to bail Tom out of trouble. Apparently she'd scrimped and saved over the years to open a new gallery, but some gangsters were threatening to kill Tom because of the debts he'd run up at his bar in Ibiza. She needed money to save her son.'

'She needed more money so she could save her son and get the gallery she wanted,' said Emma. 'So she thought she'd kill me, pocket all the proceeds from the painting and nobody would ever know any different.'

For the first time in weeks, Emma felt her anxiety and fear fall away, to be replaced by feelings of anger and betrayal. Her own aunt had tried to kill her, she felt sure of it. She looked at Stella suddenly.

'I can prove she was the driver in Gstaad.'

'How?'

'Get the Swiss police to re-examine the Mercedes,' said Emma. 'There must be traces of hair, something that we can link to Julia.'

'Em, I've watched enough CSI to know that it'll be hopelessly contaminated by now.'

Emma closed her eyes and nodded, her mind flashing back to the scene at the side of the road.

'You're right. And anyway, it was weeks ago, the car will have been mended and valeted, maybe even sold by now.'

Stella shook her head sadly.

'Money. It destroys everything,' she said.

Emma intuitively knew what Stella was thinking.

'Not everything, Stell. Tom can't blame you for something his mum did, he'll understand. If we're right about this, Julia almost killed her daughter too, remember?'

'God, this is going to tear the family apart.'

Emma nodded. She was right – and they were going to hold her responsible.

Ruby was scared. Far too late, she realized it had been a terrible mistake to come up to London. She knew she was going to be in dreadful trouble with school, with her mother, with her grandma, and what for? So far, it had been a miserable evening, nothing like Amaryllis had promised. Her glamorous older school friend – sixteen, she was practically an adult – had a new boyfriend called Wesley. He was apparently a famous jet-setting record producer which had impressed Ruby enormously, especially when he had promised he could get the girls into one of the exclusive after-show parties at the Brits. And of course Ruby had felt very grown up borrowing one of Amaryllis's Cavalli dresses, sneaking out of school and getting a taxi to London. Best of all, they were going to a fabulous showbiz party that had nothing, absolutely nothing to do with her mother. But it had all gone downhill the second they had stepped into the Sanderson's Long Bar, which was noisy and crowded and intimidating. Amaryllis and Pandora had blended seamlessly into the crowd and although they hadn't exactly left Ruby to fend for herself, she felt completely out of her depth. She'd breathed a sigh of relief when Amaryllis had said they were leaving, but instead of returning to the girls' parents' house, or better still, back to school, they had gone to Wesley's apartment in West London to carry on partying.

The atmosphere in the beautiful Notting Hill flat felt hostile and cliquey. Amaryllis had gone directly into a bedroom with Wesley and Pandora had attached herself to some long-haired man she'd met at the Sanderson. In an attempt to fit in, Ruby accepted a joint from a man called Danny, the only person in the room who had bothered to speak to her.

She'd inhaled too deeply, felt immediately nauseous and five minutes later was in the bathroom puking up the red wine she'd been downing throughout the evening.

Danny was waiting for her when she came out of the bathroom. She'd brushed her teeth using her finger and some toothpaste but she still felt wretched.

'Is everything all right?' asked Danny.

Ruby nodded, too weak to do anything except take his hand. He led her into a bedroom and she perched on the edge of the bed.

'Do you want to go home? Shall I call a taxi?'

She nodded. 'I want to go to Knightsbridge.'

While Danny went off to make the call, Ruby began to feel worse. The room was spinning and her hands felt tingly. Oblivious to her state, Danny picked up a guitar that was propped up by the window. He began playing and singing; the melody was like a lullaby and it was sending her to sleep.

The next thing she knew his body was over hers and his lips were brushing hers with a kiss. He smelt sweet and his eyes were beautiful, thought Ruby looking up and stroking his cheek.

'Good girl,' he whispered running his hand lightly down her bare arm. Danny's hand crept slowly up her thigh pushing back the fabric of her dress until his fingers were curling under the rim of her cotton knickers.

'No! Stop it,' said Ruby, suddenly feeling her cheeks flush with shame.

'Come on, let's have a little fun,' said Danny with a sexy grin.

She was really frightened now; afraid that the whole situation was about to tumble out of control.

'I'm fourteen!' she screamed, pushing him away from her and scrambling off the bed.

'Shit, oh shit!' mumbled Danny, recoiling away from her. 'You should have fucking told me!'

'I know,' said Ruby sadly. 'I'm sorry. Please, I just want to go home and see my mum.'

Cassandra pushed her front door open and flung her car keys on the table. She felt completely helpless. She had spent the last three hours trawling round every single Brits party in London. It had been a godsend that Rob Holland had been leaving the awards ceremony with his phone on when she had called. When Cassandra had filled him in on the story, he had roared straight round to pick her up in his Range Rover and had ferried her to a dozen pubs and clubs, even a tent in a railway arch. But no luck. Even so, she was certain Ruby and her two friends were somewhere in London partying, especially when the school had phoned confirming that a local cab had taken three Briarton girls, fitting Amaryllis, Ruby and Pandora's description, on a two-hundred-pound cab journey to London. Cassandra sank on the sofa and put her head in her hands. She imagined her child out in the city, God knows where, with those slags. Cassandra had been quick to blame Ruby's older friends and her school, but the terrible feeling of guilt in her chest told her otherwise. *It's all my fault*, she thought. She had barely seen her daughter in the last six months. During Ruby's October half-term Cassandra had been in Sulka. Yes, mother and daughter had been together in Gstaad, of course, but days had been spent skiing, evenings had been full of parties, and once Emma had had her accident the whole family was in a state of chaos. Time spent together in a hospital waiting room barely counted as 'quality'. She remembered Miss Broughton's cautionary words on the day of Cassandra's career talk to the school: 'I've always felt thirteen is a watershed age . . .', '. . . the cusp of womanhood . . .', '. . . she needs her mother to guide her along the right path.'

And had she been a good mother? Had she been there for her daughter at this difficult time? No, she had not.

Just then, there was a soft tap on the door. Cassandra sprang to the door, praying it wasn't the police. For a moment, she didn't recognize the exotic creature standing in the hallway. Ruby looked like a catwalk model, her hair long and glossy, the dress tight and black, giving her a spectacular cleavage. She looked about twenty-one. Cassandra felt sick.

'RUBY!' she yelled, her fear suddenly turning to anger. But her daughter flinched like a frightened puppy and she noticed that her eyes were raw from crying.

Cassandra jumped forward and gathered her into a big hug.

'Darling,' she whispered, still holding onto her tightly. 'Where the hell have you been?'

She led Ruby into the flat, feeling her shake in her arms.

'Amaryllis has got a new boyfriend,' stuttered Ruby, 'some record producer guy. He got us invited to some Brits after-show party so we slipped away from school.'

'Amaryllis is sixteen years old,' said Cassandra, not knowing whether she wanted to throttle Ruby's older, wayward friend or feel fiercely protective of a pretty young girl who had been taken advantage of by some man who should know better.

'Well, he thinks she's eighteen,' said Ruby, wiping the corner of her eye.

'I went to every party in London looking for you,' said Cassandra. 'What happened to you?'

'It was horrible,' said Ruby, sitting on the sofa and beginning to cry.

'There was a guy. This guy called Danny. Mum, I think

he wanted to have sex with me.'

Cassandra shut her eyes, not daring to imagine what happened next. She was not naïve: of course fourteen-year-old girls could be sexually active.

'I didn't, Mum. I promise.'

'I believe you, sweetheart,' she said holding her daughter's hands. 'But why did you run away from school to go to the party? Did you not think it would end up in trouble?'

Ruby looked at her mother for a long time before she spoke.

'Amaryllis and Pandora are the richest, most popular girls in school and they wanted to be my friends. It made me feel special just being with them.'

'You are special, Ruby. You don't need those girls to make you feel it.'

'I don't feel special,' Ruby said, quietly. 'I feel lonely.'

Finally, tears started to fall from Cassandra's eyes. She sat there on the sofa, hugging her precious daughter, sobbing into her hair, feeling more wretched and selfish than she had ever felt in her whole life.

67

'Hello, Emma, what a nice surprise. What can I do for you?'

Although it was only eight o'clock in the morning when Emma called at Julia's house, her aunt was up and ready for the day ahead. She led Emma through into the conservatory where breakfast had been set: two slices of toast, a glass of freshly-squeezed juice, a china pot of tea and a linen napkin were sitting next to the *Daily Telegraph*, and the whole homely scene was lit by the early morning sunshine flooding through the glass.

'Sorry for not calling before,' said Emma, 'but I saw your car and thought you'd be in.'

'What are you doing up and about so early?'

'I had to collect a friend from Heathrow.'

'Anyone I know?'

Emma shook her head and looked away.

'Well, can I offer you some tea?'

Emma stayed silent.

'I know, Julia,' she said slowly. 'I know what you did.'

Julia picked up her cup and saucer and smiled at her niece.

'Know what, darling?'

Emma knew that saying the words would rip their family apart. She knew how much it would hurt Cassandra and Tom, but she had to get to the truth or she thought she would go mad.

'I know that you drove me off the road in Gstaad,' she said calmly.

She watched Julia's mouth do a down-turn as if in slow motion.

'What a *wicked* thing to say,' she whispered, putting down her tea cup with a rattle.

Emma took a piece of paper out of her handbag and passed it to her aunt.

'I think you'll recognize that car.'

It was a grainy faxed photograph of a black Mercedes.

'I've never seen this car in my life.'

'I think you have and I think you've driven it,' said Emma. 'On Boxing Day, the day of my accident.'

'You evil girl!' said Julia, her hand flying to her mouth. 'What are you suggesting?'

Emma took a deep breath, trying to compose herself, trying to keep cool.

'The car wasn't yours, of course,' she continued. 'It belonged to Suzanne Marcel. Inspector Beck said her car had been stolen. I called him up to ask where it was stolen from. Apparently Mrs Marcel had driven to Diane Solomon's party in Gstaad and her car had got stolen from there while she was enjoying herself inside. Julia, I knew you had gone for drinks with Cassandra on Boxing Day but it turns out that you were at Diane Solomon's party too. You knew I was going to Les Diablerets. You knew what time I would be coming home. You stole Suzanne Marcel's car keys and tried to run me off the road.'

Julia had adopted a superior expression.

'I hate to point out the obvious, Emma, but it is you who

641

has recently been arrested for arson and for almost killing *my* daughter. Personally, I was prepared to give you the benefit of the doubt. I just didn't think it possible that you could have tried to kill your own flesh and blood. And how do you repay my support? You blame me, try and implicate me in your nasty little hit-and-run story. How could you? How *dare* you!' Her voice was getting more raised and more angry as she spoke.

A cloud floated over the sun and the light dimmed in the conservatory.

'I also know why you did it,' said Emma, and although her nerve was beginning to fail her, she was desperate not to lose her momentum now.

'You wanted me dead so that you could take possession of the Ben Palmer painting. With me out of the way, nobody knew you had the painting. You needed the money because you paid off Tom's Ibiza debts.'

'I had the money to pay off Tom's debts,' she said more coolly. 'Not that it is anything to do with you.'

'Yes, money you'd put aside for the Cork Street gallery you so dearly wanted. Money you felt you deserved back.'

Julia stood up.

'Oh, this is just nonsense, Emma!' she said, beginning to tidy away the breakfast things. 'I wasn't even going to sell that painting, it's by some unknown provincial artist and basically worthless.'

'Not when it has an important work by Francis Bacon on the back of it.'

Julia stopped in her tracks, her face draining of colour.

'Samples of your DNA are on their way to a police lab in Switzerland. I think we both know they are going to match forensic samples taken from Suzanne Marcel's Mercedes.'

Of course Julia had no way of knowing Emma was bluffing

with that last sentence. The rest of Emma's information was almost certainly correct, so Julia would have no reason to doubt her. But it was a gamble: Emma's only hope of finding out the truth was to force a confession from Julia.

'I hate to disappoint you with your conspiracy theories, Emma, but I might have borrowed Suzanne's car to run some errands,' said Julia.

The words were delivered confidently, but Emma instantly knew from the look on her face that Julia was lying.

'Julia, red paint on Suzanne's Mercedes matches the red paint on my hire car that you ran off the road.'

Julia sank into the white wicker sofa behind her.

For a few moments she didn't speak and then her upper body seemed to collapse onto her lap.

'It was for my son,' she said quietly, her voice trembling. 'Those gangsters were going to kill my son. I needed to get the money. I'll do anything to save my children.'

'You did it for yourself, Julia. The money you used for Tom's debts was for the gallery. You wanted to pay for both.'

Emma paused. 'The reason I was at Heathrow this morning was to pick up Inspector Beck.' She walked back through the living room and opened the front door to reveal a smartly dressed forty-year-old man. She had called the detective as soon as Stella had told her about the painting and had begged him to fly out to England. She had even paid for his airline ticket herself. She looked at Inspector Beck before pulling open her coat to reveal that she had been wired up. Julia started sobbing at the knowledge that her confession had been caught on tape and in spite of everything, Emma felt a pang of sorrow and regret.

'I'll take it from here,' said Inspector Beck, looking at Emma.

'I understand you have been involved in an investigation by the Oxford Police about a fire at your home,' he continued in perfect English. 'We should let the investigating officers over there know about Ms Grand.'

Julia looked at him in horror.

'Do you think I set fire to Emma's home?' she said in a high-pitched shrill voice. 'My daughter was in that house. I would never, never, never do a thing to hurt my children.'

'But you didn't know she was in there,' said Emma slowly.

Emma desperately wanted to believe that Julia had also torched the Stables but a nagging voice at the back of her mind told her that not everything was quite sorted, yet.

68

Cassandra and Tom were walking through Hyde Park, not talking, just trying to enjoy the view and the milky sunshine. The buds on the trees were beginning to burst and the breeze had lost its chill and smelt sweet and fresh. Spring was coming, for all of them. Cassandra had been unsettled when Tom had phoned to suggest they meet. The two of them had barely spoken in a year; even in Gstaad they had kept their distance, and while the whole childish spat seemed slightly ridiculous after everything that had recently happened, Cassandra was still angry that if Tom hadn't been so stupid and irresponsible then he wouldn't have got into the debt that had incurred such tragic consequences.

Cassandra puffed her cheeks out in the breeze. Since Ruby's disappearance, she had spent days examining her life and planning how to make amends, hoping and praying that the nuclear dust of her own personal explosion had all finally settled and she could at last get on with life. Her mother's ordeal – she had willingly returned to Switzerland to face her charges – weighed heavily on her, but Cassandra was determined to help her by instructing the best Swiss legal team she could, even though she was concerned about the cost.

Cassandra was still hobbling a little and as they crossed the little bridge overlooking the Serpentine, Tom took the arm of her grey Dior coat to steady her. In a past life, she would have glared at him, perhaps summoned a driver in a golf cart. Today, she simply let him.

'I'm sorry, Cass. I'm sorry for everything. My bar in Ibiza was successful. I just got a bit stitched up. Mum said she had the money.'

'Let's hope you've learnt a lesson. A painful one.'

'So do you think Emma will testify?' asked Tom as they sat on a bench and gazed out over the silvery water.

'I expect so,' Cassandra said bitterly. She had such conflicting emotions about her cousin that she felt nauseous just thinking about her. In her more reflective moments after the fire, Cassandra had felt herself soften towards Emma. She could now see she had got some things slightly askew: for years she had blamed Emma's father for splitting up their family. It wasn't true, and yet she had hated her cousin passionately on the shakiest of evidence because she had wanted to blame someone for her father leaving them.

But now there was a real reason to blame Emma for ruining her life. In the past weeks, Cassandra had come to terms with many things and one of them was that she loved her mother unconditionally. If Emma testified against Julia, she would rob Cassandra of a parent who loved her dearly, and whom she loved back, just at a time when she needed her mother most. On the other hand Julia had tried to *kill* Emma. However ruthless Cassandra knew she could be, she could never sanction or condone anything like that.

'What are we going to do?' asked Tom.

For the first time in her life Cassandra couldn't see the clearest path through.

'I don't know,' she said softly.

'Whatever it is, let's do it together,' said Tom, nudging her gently.

For a moment she let herself enjoy the feeling of her brother standing next to her; it felt reassuring. She did not feel alone.

She looked at him intently.

'Whatever you do next, you have to promise me that it involves getting a job,' said Cassandra resolutely.

'I don't need to sponge off you any more,' replied Tom sheepishly. 'Rob is going to sort me out with an A&R role at Hollander Music.'

'So now you're sponging off Rob?' she said, a ghost of a smile on her wide red lips.

'Watch it, cheeky. No, I'll be working for a living this time. Rob says I'm going to make him a lot of money. He's about to sign the Red Comets, that band I discovered in a dingy Camden dive.'

They both felt the mood lighten slightly.

'Well, how about lunch to celebrate you saving my life and finding a career?' replied Cassandra.

Tom looked at his sister. So strong, so determined. She was smart, beautiful and she could even be funny when she wanted to be. They were all good qualities that somehow had got lost in the rush for success and power.

'Listen, big sister. Seeing as I'm the one with the job how about I treat you to Starbucks?'

'Starbucks?' said Cassandra in mock horror. 'Don't you know who I am?'

They both looked at each other and laughed. Tom threw his arm around her shoulders and they headed off in the direction of the nearest latte.

*   *   *

Emma had been slowly falling apart. She was still losing weight, her skin had become blotchy and pale but she refused to slow down, no matter how often Rob asked her to. The gorgeous, generous woman he'd fallen in love with was becoming more withdrawn every day, despite the fact that the threat of attack had been lifted with Julia's arrest. In desperation, Rob had taken Emma to Lyme Regis where they'd checked into a boutique hotel by the cliffs. It was out of season and they had taken a coastal walk, through a beautiful wood where the trees would occasionally part to give glimpses of the sea shimmering in the distance, like a long, platinum ribbon.

In the last forty-eight hours things had moved quickly. Julia was being investigated by both the Swiss and UK police who were re-interviewing her in connection with the Stables fire. Walking along the coast with the wind in her hair, one hand stuffed affectionately in Rob's coat pocket, Emma was determined that she was going to try and put everything behind her and move on with her life.

Rob's company was definitely helping. It had been the first time in days that they had talked properly about things other than solving the crime. They talked about Rob's news plans for Hollander Music, about Ste Donahue and how well he was doing in his latest stint in rehab. They talked about Clover Connor who had maintained a dignified silence over the Blake Brinton affair but who had said that she and Ste were planning a commitment ceremony in Thailand as soon as he had finished his treatment. Tired from their climb, they sat down on a fallen tree in a sunny clearing.

'I wanted to take you to our house in Sag Harbor this weekend,' said Rob, 'but I thought we should wait until this has all blown over. It really is going to be all over soon, honey.'

His voice had a calm confidence that reassured Emma, but unconsciously Rob had put his finger on the root of Emma's anxiety: it *wasn't* over yet.

'It just seems like it will never be over,' she said sadly. 'I think everyone forgets that Julia is my aunt. What I'm doing is tearing my family apart.'

'Em, she tried to run you off the road!' said Rob. 'It's not what you're doing that's tearing your family apart; it's what *she's* done. Never forget that.'

She picked up a leaf and started picking at it.

'Who burnt down the Stables, Rob?'

'Bloody Julia,' said Rob flatly.

'You know I almost believed her when she said she didn't do it.'

'Emma! Listen to yourself. She wanted you dead.'

'Maybe we'll never know,' she said, with a shot of fear.

'I'm going back into the office on Monday,' she said, almost to herself. 'I've taken enough time off already.'

'Emma, you have to chill out.'

She shook her head defiantly.

'I *have* to. There's so much to do, so much damage to repair.'

Rob looked at her and sighed.

'So are you going to buy Roger's shareholding?'

Emma shrugged.

'After what's happened I don't know if the banks will be on-side enough. Although it might not be a bad idea to get someone like Victor Chen on board in some minority shareholding capacity. I think we need all the credibility we can get.'

'I could always lend you the money.'

'Rob. We're talking millions of pounds.'

'You know I have it.'

'Maybe,' she said, with a grateful look, squeezing his hand.

But this was another problem Emma was struggling to come to terms with, one that made her feel as if she was on the edge of a cliff looking down. Rob had to leave for New York permanently in a matter of weeks. She had found someone she loved and cared for and now he was going to leave her. Inevitably Emma had analysed the situation to death and she knew that the chances of their relationship surviving were slim. So no, she could not take money off him and be bound to him when she could see that there was an inevitable finality about their affair.

'I'm going to miss you so much,' she said looking up at him, her eyes moist.

'Come,' he said bluntly. 'Come and live in New York – what's the worst that can happen? Let Ruan run things over in England, you expand the US business. I have a great house in the Village. It's not quite the Oxfordshire country-side but I think you'll like it.'

She looked at him, her heart desperately wanting to say yes but knowing it was an impractical and reckless suggestion; she had people relying on her.

'Rob, come on,' she sighed. 'We've barely got the business started over here. I need to be here.'

Rob nodded.

'Will you at least think about it? Maybe you could come to New York to mull things over.'

'When it's all over,' she whispered. 'When it's all over.'

69

Astrid Brinton had a reputation for throwing fabulous parties, a reputation which crossed international borders and time zones. Whether it was a clambake at their Hamptons beach house, a cocktail party in their Cap Ferrat mansion or a post-Grammies shindig at their LA home, Astrid had a talent for entertaining that bordered on art. It was convenient that Blake had an enormous back catalogue of work that still sold in their thousands, and the recent reunion tour of his band Human Nature had sold out in stadiums around the world, raking in millions. For the Brintons' latest dinner party, held at their Henley-on-Thames Gothic mansion, no expense was spared, although the twenty-four exclusively selected guests sitting around their oval ebony dining table would all have turned up even if Astrid had announced that she was serving Pringles. After the delicious scandal involving Blake, Clover Connor and the bonnet of a Ferrari, sheer curiosity meant every one of the assembled guests had dropped whatever they were doing to attend. Even so, the meal was exquisite: Iranian caviar, Wagyu beef air-freighted straight from Japan and poached pears accompanied by tiny clouds of mascarpone sorbet. Each course was served with a perfectly matched wine costing at least a thousand pounds a bottle. After the finest Jamaican Blue Mountain coffee was brought in, Astrid jumped to her feet and tapped a Christofle teaspoon against a wine glass for attention.

'I know you've all been wondering why we've invited you here tonight,' said Astrid, radiant in ivory Chanel couture. 'Well, Blake and I wanted to share some very special news with our closest friends.' She paused dramatically.

'Blake and I are going to renew our wedding vows,' she announced gleefully, bouncing excitedly as a ripple of applause went round the table like a Mexican wave and the waiters appeared bearing vintage Dom Perignon.

'I got off the phone this morning from Frégate Island in the Seychelles and you're all invited. Watch this space, darlings!'

Johnny was the first to move around to congratulate his parents. He had flown in from LA that afternoon where he was playing the second lead in a Tom Cruise movie. His latest girlfriend – a pretty bible-belt blonde hung on his arm and simpered in all the right places.

'Who'd have thought it?' whispered Molly Sinclair, seated to Cassandra's left. Molly was an old friend of Astrid's from her modelling days. 'I thought Astrid would have been straight to the divorce lawyers after the Clover Connor episode.'

'And give up all this?' smiled Cassandra, touching the top of her champagne glass for the waiter to fill. 'Would you?'

'You're so right, darling,' purred Molly. 'Infidelity goes with the turf. I bet half the people in this room have fucked one another.'

Speak for yourself, thought Cassandra, knowing Molly's terrible reputation as a gold-digger around the society circuit.

'Speaking of which,' continued Molly, 'you'll never guess who I saw a few weeks ago in a very discreet little restaurant in Chelsea.'

'Who?'

'Your uncle's wife with a man who most definitely was not her husband. I must say they looked *very* cosy.'

'Rebecca?' replied Cassandra, completely surprised.

Molly put her hand over Cassandra's. 'Sorry, darling, I probably shouldn't have said anything, it being family and all. But I have to say he was a complete dish; looked a bit like that actor Rufus Sewell.'

Cassandra's mind began to work overtime. *Rebecca having an affair? Who with? What can she be playing at – is it just sex or is she thinking of an upgrade?* Cassandra had spent her entire working career manipulating people and turning situations to her own advantage. It had made her look for the angle in every situation. *There's no such thing as an innocent lunch*, she smiled to herself.

'Time for a little digestif,' said Astrid, leaving the room and coming back holding a beautiful porcelain dish on which stood a trembling pile of cocaine. Across the table, Johnny's girlfriend's eyes widened in disbelief.

'Meissen,' said Molly.

'Sorry?' said the pretty blonde.

'I noticed your surprised expression, darling. The dish, it's Meissen. Don't you have it in America?'

Cassandra left the table to freshen up in the bathroom. Greywood was a sumptuous palace, a labyrinth of complete luxury and she always enjoyed walking through the corridors admiring a Miro here, a Brancusi there. She was about to go back into the dining room when she saw a little boy waving at the top of the main flight of stairs.

'Hello, Josh,' she waved back at Astrid and Blake's five-year-old son. He was a cute little thing with a crop of floppy blond hair and stripy blue pyjamas, like a cover star from *Vogue Bambini*.

'Cassandra, come and see my new car,' he called, beckoning through the bannisters.

She wavered, a little embarrassed. *Weren't kids supposed to be able to detect adults who didn't like children?* Cassandra sighed, she supposed Josh was used to her being around by now and he decided the matter by running to the bottom of the stairs and tugging at her hand. She patted him awkwardly on the head.

'Not tonight, Josh. I have to go back in there and talk to your Mummy and Daddy. And they'll be very cross if they know you're not in bed yet.'

'First come and see my car. It's a BMW.'

She rolled her eyes. 'OK, but just for two minutes, OK?'

She carefully removed his sticky hand from the fabric of her Balenciaga pencil skirt and allowed herself to be pulled upstairs. They were met at the top of the stairs by Helen, Josh's nanny.

'I'm so sorry, Cassandra,' she said with an anxious expression. 'The television was on in my room. He was asleep twenty minutes ago and I didn't hear him.'

'Well, perhaps you shouldn't be watching the television when you should be watching Joshua?' said Cassandra tartly.

'Car! Car! Car!' shouted Josh, bouncing up and down.

Helen guided Josh towards his room.

'OK, let's show Cassandra your car quickly and then you must go back to sleep, deal?'

'OK!' said Josh, dashing off. The boy's room was like a fantasy playhouse created by interior designers. His bed was in the shape of a fort, but there was a Hockney over the fireplace next to colourful drawings by Josh. Josh got inside a miniature black BMW and began pedalling furiously around the room.

'Astrid tells me that you went to school with Rebecca Milford,' said Cassandra to the nanny. Helen nodded and then smiled gratefully once she realized that Cassandra was just making polite conversation.

'Yes, it seems a lifetime ago. We were in the same year actually, although I know you wouldn't think it to look at us,' she said.

Cassandra almost nodded in agreement. Helen looked as if she hadn't been to the hairdressers in years. Her hair was flecked with grey and the undersides of her eyes were puffy.

'Rebecca was always a beauty, though. You could tell she was always going to do well for herself. You know: marry well.'

Cassandra smiled, thinking it was all relative. She wouldn't be happy with someone twenty years older than herself unless he was one of Forbes 400 wealthiest. But for a poor girl from the village, she supposed Roger would have to do.

'Funny she ended up being Ruan McCormack's boss though,' said Helen.

'What do you mean?' asked Cassandra, intrigued.

'Oh, she went out with Ruan for about two years when we were at school. He was a couple of years below us but he was very good-looking even then. Funny how she owns the company Ruan works for. Although it's not surprising she ended up with Roger. Our PE teacher would take us running past the hall and she'd always stop and say, "I'm going to live there one day".'

But Cassandra wasn't listening. Suddenly something that had been staring her in the face seemed all too obvious. It was just as if bright stadium lights had gone on inside her head.

'Helen, does Astrid keep her old magazines?'

'You mean like *Rive* and *Vogue*? I don't think so. But I do, what do you want?'

'Do you have *Tatler*? About three issues ago. I want party pictures from the Milford launch party.'

'Oh yes, I've definitely got that one,' said Helen, leading

Cassandra down the corridor to her room. 'It's not often I actually know people at a party in a magazine. And Jude Law was there, wasn't he?'

'Yes, yes,' said Cassandra distractedly, as Helen rifled through a pile of magazines and found the right issue.

'There,' said Helen, flipping to the well-thumbed party section. 'Is that what you wanted?'

Cassandra scanned the pages and, finding the picture she wanted, carefully tore it out and handed the magazine back to Helen.

'Now I think you'd better get Joshua back to bed before he has a mini pile-up,' she said, scooting back towards the party as Helen stared after her with a look of total confusion.

Back at the party, Cassandra found Molly glassy-eyed and talkative, a trace of white powder around her nose, but when she showed the party pictures to Molly, she instantly confirmed that Ruan McCormack was the man she had seen Rebecca with at the Chelsea restaurant.

'I wouldn't forget those eyes anywhere,' she smiled. 'Just gorgeous, very rugged and intense.'

The dinner guests adjourned into the library, but despite the convivial atmosphere Cassandra could not shake her feeling of disquiet.

'Got somewhere else to go?' asked Molly sipping an expensive Chateau D'Yquem. 'If it's another party, I'm coming with you. There's not one single man here tonight. With the exception of you and me it's all bloody couples. I'm not surprised. Astrid must be feeling *frightfully* insecure.'

Cassandra looked at her but didn't take in a word Molly Sinclair was saying. Her mind had been mulling over what an affair between Ruan and Rebecca could mean. After Emma's arrest Ruan had been made acting CEO of Milford. If she had been charged and convicted he would have got the job permanently. Rebecca was having an affair with Ruan; would she leave Roger and achieve her dream of living in the 'big house'? Was burning down the Stables with herself in it some plan for Ruan and Rebecca to run Milford together too? Cassandra tried to look at every angle of it, secretly hoping that the driver who had forced Emma off the road in Gstaad would turn out to be Ruan or Rebecca and not her mother. *But then Mother confessed, didn't she?* She reminded herself. It was all too much: she felt a sudden urge to speak to Emma.

She excused herself from Molly and went over to Astrid who was sitting on a sofa on her husband's knee, her arm wrapped proprietorially around his neck.

'Sorry darling, I have to go,' said Cassandra, bending to kiss her on both cheeks.

'Don't be ridiculous, sit down,' demanded Astrid, 'I want to tell you all about Frégate.'

'Sorry. Can I call a cab?' said Cassandra firmly.

'To get back to London?' asked Astrid.

'No, I'm going to Chilcot.'

'In that case my driver can take you. Just let me give my husband a big snog and then I'll get him.'

Emma looked at her desk clock. It was 10 p.m. and she was alone in the office. In fact, the whole factory was dark and silent. Emma couldn't sit still at home though, not when there was so much to do. She knew she had promised Rob that she would ease herself back into work gently, but these days she found herself driven by some sort of strange nervous energy. It was as if her mind was struggling to work something out. Regain authority at work? Fix her relationship worries? Deal with the whole Julia situation? *God knows there's enough to sort out,* she thought. She turned back to her computer and clicked

657

through complicated spreadsheets – profit and loss, cash flow, product orders and production schedules – none of it seemed to be able to hold her attention.

She heard footsteps in the corridor and looked up in surprise to see Rebecca. Her hair looked freshly blow-dried; she was wearing jeans and an expensive looking cashmere overcoat.

'Hello Rebecca,' she said curiously. 'What are you doing here? Looking for Roger?'

Cassandra had asked Astrid's driver to make the twelve-mile journey to Chilcot. Before descending on Winterfold, she had wanted to call ahead to Emma, but realizing she didn't have her cousin's number in her phone phoned Rob Holland instead.

'Cassandra?' he said as he answered. 'Listen I'm a bit busy . . .'

'I was just wondering if Emma was with you?' she interrupted.

'No, I'm just on my way back to Winterfold. I spoke to her half an hour ago. I think she's still at the office. Why? Is everything all right?'

'Rebecca and Ruan are having an affair. Is it me or is it too bloody suspicious?'

'Suspicious?'

'I have a theory,' said Cassandra flatly. 'I'll meet you both at Winterfold and do me a favour and hear me out.'

Rob felt a sudden fear and didn't want Emma to be alone. 'How about I meet you at the Milford offices?'

'Very well,' said Cassandra. 'I should be there in ten minutes.'

Rebecca looked at Emma and there was something in her eyes that instantly put Emma on edge. Rebecca moved into Emma's office and carefully closed the door behind her.

'Rebecca?' asked Emma, now unnerved.

'I heard all about Julia,' said Rebecca, walking slowly towards Emma, 'and it's all worked out nicely for you, hasn't it? You've managed to wriggle off the hook yet again.'

Emma just stared at her, unsure what she expected her to say.

'Rebecca, what are you saying?' she said, all her instincts telling her something was wrong.

'I suppose this means you'll be CEO again,' said Rebecca, staring straight at Emma. 'Putting Ruan to one side yet again. You do know that without him this company would have been bankrupt under Saul?' Her expression turned to a sneer. 'And without him, you wouldn't have had a clue where to begin, would you?'

'We all value Ruan in this company,' said Emma slowly, moving to one side of her desk, but Rebecca closed her exit off.

Ruan? she thought desperately. *What does Rebecca have to do with Ruan?*

'We tried to make it easy for you, you know,' she said. 'We didn't want you dead. At least, *he* didn't.'

'What are you talking about?'

'I actually think Ruan cares for you in some small way. That's why I have had to come here alone tonight, to finish this. But he doesn't care for you as much as he loves me – how could he? He has been head over heels in love with me since he was fourteen. He'll do *anything* for me, you know.'

Emma's heart was beginning to race now. The offices were empty. She knew Ruan had still been in the adjoining factory an hour ago and usually said goodnight before he went home. *But like he'd help her.*

She looked around her, desperate to find a way out. Finding none, she lunged forward, trying to barge past Rebecca.

'Sit back down!' commanded Rebecca. She had pulled a gun from her coat and was pointing it at Emma's chest. It looked old, but sleek and definitely lethal.

'Rebecca, don't be so stupid,' said Emma, her voice tight. Rebecca laughed coldly. 'Yes – this is one of Saul's old guns and yes, it works.'

Emma stared at the gun, her heart hammering. She glanced at the telephone, but Rebecca saw her and smiled, shaking her head.

'Shame you couldn't stay in prison really,' said Rebecca conversationally, perching on the edge of the desk only feet away from Emma. 'Then Ruan would be CEO plus you'd be under terrible pressure to off-load your shareholding as well. I mean, it doesn't look good for a luxury goods company to have a dangerous criminal as its majority shareholder does it?'

'So what then?' said Emma, suddenly realizing that she had to keep Rebecca talking. 'So I sell my shares? Neither you or Ruan has the money to buy them.'

Rebecca laughed. It was mocking laughter that sounded empty and brittle.

'You gave him a 1 per cent shareholding, remember? He can now buy at the price of a shareholder's valuation and the banks love him. He's solid, experienced, reliable. Plus I'm about to take Roger for half of everything he's got.'

'So Roger knows nothing of this?' asked Emma, genuinely curious. *All that time I suspected Roger and it was his innocent little wife!*

'You're the first to know,' said Rebecca, giggling. 'I'm actually doing Roger a favour with the divorce. He's about to lose everything anyway, investing in Ricardo Perez's hare-brained hotel venture. Do you know Ricardo?'

Emma shook her head slowly.

'Terrible coke-head. I did my homework because Roger

wouldn't bother. Ricardo's father has side-lined him in the business because everything he touches turns to shit, just like Roger.'

Emma suddenly remembered the night of the Christmas party. *The last woman I fell for was married,* Ruan had said.

'So you set fire to the Stables. You wanted to frame me for the fire and for almost killing Cassandra,' said Emma working everything out.

'No, darling. I didn't do the actual torching. As I said, Ruan will do anything for me.'

Boastfully, she continued. 'Ruan and I had been talking about getting rid of you for ages. But I was the one who saw the opportunity. On the night of the party, Ruan knew you were staying at Winterfold. You told your mother that Cassandra was at the Stables. We got a taxi into Chilcot with her and she told us in the taxi. I then phoned Ruan with a plan. That simple. It was easy for Ruan to slip off to the Stables, siphon some diesel from a car or bike and pour it through the letterbox.' She laughed a cold brittle laugh and her beauty took on a cruel, hard edge.

'And I'd left my black shawl in the library,' said Emma.

'Yes, you did. After the fire, we all went back to the house and I found it on the sofa. Wiping some diesel on it and throwing it near the Stables when we all went to watch the blaze was easy.'

Emma felt beads of sweat run down her temple. She glanced over to the door but Rebecca saw her.

'Anyway, storytime's over,' she said, standing up and pointing the gun towards the door. 'We're going upstairs now. I think we'll take the stairs. Move it.'

Rob's Range Rover pulled up outside the Milford offices only seconds after Cassandra had climbed from Astrid's car.

'She must be here,' he said, seeing Emma's Audi. 'Still

working at ten o'clock. I tell her not to work so hard but she doesn't listen,' he said grimly.

'Has she answered her phone?' asked Cassandra, concerned.

'No, which is strange,' replied Rob.

'And whose car is that?' asked Cassandra, pointing to a soft-top BMW.

'Rebecca's,' said Rob. 'Oh, shit.'

Rebecca marched Emma up the stairs to the studio floor, pushing the muzzle of the gun into her back as she did so.

'Over to the fire escape there,' she ordered.

'The roof?' said Emma, trying to turn to look at Rebecca. She knew she was strong enough to overpower Rebecca – but when she was holding a gun there was no way she could risk it – not yet anyway. Rebecca jabbed her cruelly with the gun.

'There's been a change of plan,' she whispered in Emma's ear. 'If you're not going to jail, then I'm afraid you're better off dead.'

The cold, detached way Rebecca spoke made Emma's stomach turn over. *She really is crazy.*

'I can give you money, my shareholding, just tell me what you want,' babbled Emma, panicking as Rebecca pushed her through the fire escape door, onto the flat area of roof.

'Get out,' she snapped.

As her feet scuffed on the roof's surface, for a split second Emma thought of happier times when she and Stella had sunbathed out there one really hot July afternoon. Then she thought of Rob on the night of her birthday, smiling at her with love, holding her hands. And for a moment, despite the very real threat of death, it made Emma feel warm.

'Now, here's what you're going to do,' said Rebecca

662

matter-of-factly. 'You're going to jump off this roof. The newspapers will report how you were depressed. Everyone knows how *weird* you've been since the fire. And now having to testify against your aunt, well, people will understand why you did it, Emma. Your shares will pass to your mother. Your mother will sell them cut-price to Ruan. And well, we all live happily ever after. Except you, of course.'

'You're mad,' whispered Emma, her mind whirling. She had to think of something, she had to catch Rebecca off guard.

'No, not mad. Just as ambitious as you are. Except I didn't get the breaks, did I? The fancy schools and the high-flying jobs,' she snarled.

'Why are you doing this?'

'Why? Because ever since I was a little girl I looked at Winterfold and knew my life would be better if I lived in it. Winterfold was supposed to be *mine*. Now walk.'

There was a noise behind Rebecca and she spun round to see what it was.

Emma felt a split second of hope before she could make out that it was Ruan standing in the doorway of the fire exit.

'Rebecca. What the hell is going on?' he said, his voice raised and panicked.

'Run along, darling,' she said in a flat, emotionless voice. 'I'm trying to finish something off here.'

Ruan took a cautious step towards her, reaching out towards her.

'Rebecca. Stop it.'

Even in the darkness, Emma could see fear in his face.

'Give me the gun. This has fucking got out of control.'

'Don't be a coward, Ruan,' she screamed. 'We have to get the job done. For both of us.'

Ruan and Emma exchanged a brief, frantic look. At that moment she knew that no matter what he had done at the Stables he did not want to see her killed.

'Hand me the gun, Rebecca,' he replied, his tone now pleading. 'Think about what you're doing. Thing about what's going to happen.'

'Rebecca. Listen to Ruan,' said Emma, trying to keep her voice calm and steady. 'He cares about you. This has gone too far but we can stop it right now.'

'Emma. Walk. Now!' screamed Rebecca pointing the gun at Emma's head.

'Rebecca, don't,' shouted Ruan surging forward to try and grab the gun.

Without time to think, Emma flung her body away from them. There was a loud crack; it was the sound of a bullet being fired.

Rob and Cassandra ran through the fire escape onto the roof. Rob saw a gun lying on the asphalt and kicked it off the building with his foot. It was only then that he noticed there was a body slumped on the floor.

For the second time in a fortnight Detective Michael Sheldon had to make a late-night visit to Chilcot.

Two ambulances were outside Byron House by the time his Ford Mondeo pulled up to the Milford headquarters. Ruan McCormack was in one of them; a gun-shot wound in his right shoulder had caused considerable loss of blood but, according to the paramedics, he'd live. Rebecca Milford was having her makeshift handcuffs transferred over to the real thing. Rob had been quite impressed with his handi-work. After restraining Rebecca on the rooftop he'd used yards of fabric from Stella's studio to bind her wrists together until the squad cars had arrived. According to Cassandra the fabric felt like India's finest silk and had never been put to a better purpose.

Emma sat trembling on a sofa in the Milford boardroom.

'Are you all right?' asked Sheldon sitting down next to her and putting a reassuring hand on her shoulder.

'So now do you believe me?' she said quietly, unable to look him in the eye.

Sheldon simply nodded.

'You know on the night of the party there was a second call put in to the fire services telling them that the Stables was on fire? We'd traced the number back to Winterfold.'

'You thought I'd made the call?'

'I didn't know what to think. Now I believe it was Ruan. He was still at the party.'

'He didn't want to kill Cassandra, did he?'

Sheldon smiled. 'Emma, tonight I think you deserve to have the day off from thinking about it all.'

'Does that mean I can go home?'

Sheldon looked over the room where Cassandra was standing at the bar pouring vodka and tonic into a crystal tumbler. 'I think you all need to go home. We can finish off statements over there.'

Rob had found Emma's coat and draped it over her shoulders.

'Come on, let's go.'

'What about Cassandra?'

'Go and ask her.'

Emma approached the bar. Cassandra's tumbler was empty.

'Do you want to come back with us to Winterfold?'

'You know what happened last time you invited me to stay at your house.'

The two woman looked at each other for a moment; every feeling of anger, distrust and resentment they'd ever felt for each other was put to one side and they slowly smiled.

'Come on,' they both said in unison. 'Let's go.'

It was proving impossible to find Giles's home. *It's a windmill, for heaven's sake!* she thought, annoyed. *How hard can it be to find a building with enormous blades?* For an early April morning, the North Norfolk coastal road was clear and bright, enough so that she could pull down the convertible roof of the car. And despite the cold on her cheeks – *good for the complexion, darling* – for the first time in a long time, Cassandra was feeling pretty good. Ever since their rooftop drama at Milford a month earlier, the job offers had been coming in thick and fast: launch editor of a new luxury newspaper supplement in New York; editorial director of one of the biggest publishing companies in the UK. But the most intriguing offers had come from outside the magazine industry: consultancy posts and styling jobs for the biggest-name fashion houses. These were jobs that meant she could indulge her passion for clothes at the actual source; they were jobs which meant she would be flexible and could therefore spend more time with Ruby. Her daughter was sitting in the passenger seat, enjoying the drive. She was about to start a new day school in Kensington and had moved into Cassandra's apartment permanently. They had both agreed it was best if Ruby left Briarton; she'd got caught up with the wrong crowd and had paid the price. In life, Cassandra had told her daughter, there were some friends you had to cherish and hang onto and there were others who pulled you down; friends you needed to keep away from.

'There,' screamed Ruby, pointing to a large cylindrical house.

'That's not a windmill,' said Cassandra, annoyed.

'I bet you it is, I bet you,' insisted Ruby. 'It just hasn't got any blades.'

'Well, what if you want to make flour or something?' asked Cassandra.

Giles Banks opened the door to the windmill. Cassandra had first called him earlier in the week and it had been one of the most difficult calls she had ever had to make. It was a phone call of apology and regret. At first Giles had been offhand; gradually he had thawed but it wasn't until that precise moment that Cassandra knew she had been forgiven.

For a few moments they just stood there and looked at each other, then Cassandra spread her arms and they embraced, a warm, genuine embrace that felt good to both of them.

'Darling,' said Cassandra with a touch of reproach in her voice. 'You said it was a windmill.'

'It is,' said Giles.

'So where are the blades?'

'Not since about 1897.'

'Typical,' said Cassandra with a wink. 'All style over substance.'

It was a beautiful home. The curved walls were painted ivory with big windows that let in lots of light. Giles introduced Cassandra and Ruby to Stephen, the man Cassandra recognized from the night she'd fired Giles. She didn't say anything – there was nothing she could say. On an austere-looking desk by the window, there was a photograph of Giles and Cassandra taken outside a couture show the previous year and Cassandra looked up at Giles, a lump growing in her throat.

'Hey, Ruby,' said Stephen quickly, 'would you like to help me mix a fruit punch? Come on over into the kitchen, we've just had it redone.'

Giles led Cassandra out through a door onto a decking

area that had a splendid view over the fields to the sand dunes and the sea beyond.

'I'm sorry about everything that's happened in the last three months,' said Giles kindly.

'Thank you,' said Cassandra. 'But actually in a funny way I'm glad of it all. It was horrible at the time but I've learned an awful lot: about myself, about what I want and what I need. And you know what I needed the most?'

He shook his head.

'A friend,' said Cassandra softly.

He put his arm around her shoulder and she rested her head on his. One day soon she wanted to be held by a man she was in love with and who was in love with her. Right now, she'd settle for the embrace of a man whom she loved.

Giles looked inside the house at Ruby and Stephen throwing oranges and raspberries in a blender.

'I'm glad Ruby's come,' he said.

'Oh, why didn't someone tell me what I've been missing out on?'

'What's that?'

Cassandra waved a hand towards Ruby and Stephen, the windmill, the view.

'All of *this*. Fun. Love. Contentment,' she smiled and looked at her daughter lovingly. 'We're going to Paris for Easter.'

'Are you staying at Guillaume's chateau?'

'No. Disneyland Paris,' she laughed.

'Disneyland Paris?' said Giles, a horrified hand flying to his mouth.

'Then two nights at Le Meurice,' she laughed in her familiar glamorous tinkle. 'It's so handy for the Louvre. You know in all the times I've been to Paris, I've never seen the *Mona Lisa*.'

'There's a first time for everything,' said Giles. 'I hear she's very chic.'

They both fell silent, content in one another's company again.

'You know it was Francesca who told Glenda about the Georgia Kennedy shoot,' said Cassandra after a pause.

He nodded. 'I figured that out when Francesca got the editor's job.'

'I'm sorry for doubting you.'

'Well, you did me a favour.'

'Really?' said Cassandra, surprised. She knew he was finally writing his Dior biography, but she felt sure he missed life at *Rive*.

'That old life? It was tyrannical,' said Giles. 'Do you know how long it used to take me to get dressed in the morning?'

'You always looked fabulous,' she laughed, but she knew what he meant.

She couldn't have a favourite handbag because it had to be replaced every season. Even the most beautiful, exquisite dresses could only be worn once. After that they had to be archived until it was safe for them to be called vintage. Everything had to be the best, the latest, the hottest. It was no wonder she could barely sustain a relationship with a man; in her disposable and judgemental world, she wasn't even allowed to form a bond, a relationship, with a handbag.

'How's everything in Chilcot?' asked Giles. He had been taking a keen interest in the story that had been running in the papers for weeks. Rebecca Milford and Ruan McCormack were currently on remand for arson and attempted murder. Julia was still being investigated by the Swiss police; formal charges were expected any day.

'Emma has offered me a non-executive directorship of Milford,' she said, looking out to the strip of silver sea in the distance.

'So you've finally made your peace?'

She smiled. 'It turns out for both of us that we weren't really the enemy.'

In the last month, since the night of the drama at the Milford offices, she and Emma had met up several times. They might never be the best of friends – the situation with Julia, the car accident and the painting wouldn't allow it – but they had begun to recognize in each other a mutual respect and understanding that might one day become a bond.

'Are you going to take it? The directorship, I mean?'

She shrugged. 'What do you think?'

'I think you should,' said Giles honestly.

'Why?'

'I think you and Emma are different sides of the same coin. And, darling, just think what fun you could have with all those bags.'

Stephen brought them out glasses of his punch and they walked down the steps at the side of the deck into a wide country garden. To their left by an old stone wall was a bed of freshly-turned soil.

'What are you doing there?' she asked.

'I'm just finishing some planting.'

'Can I help?'

Giles handed her a trowel. 'I don't think lunch is for another half an hour.'

Cassandra sank down into the flower-bed; clawing her fingers into the dirt she enjoyed the feeling of the soil as it ran through her fingers, clogging up under her nails. She felt dampness seep through the knees of her Celine trousers. It felt good.

'Are you staying over tonight?'

'We'd love to,' she said, feeling the emerging sun warm her face.

*   *   *

'Mind if I knock off early?' asked Stella, popping her head around Emma's office door. It was five-thirty and it was still light; a peach sun was beginning to descend down a hazy blue sky.

'Of course not,' replied Emma, smiling. 'And you're not in tomorrow, are you?'

'No. It's the big day. I'm helping Tom move in, remember.'

'How could I forget?' grinned Emma.

'Yeah, well, it's not such a big deal, because he's hardly going to be there, is he? As a scout for Hollander Music he's going to be travelling all around the country. Did you know that the Red Comets, that band he discovered, have been signed to Rob's label?'

'Of course I do,' said Emma, 'I've already been to see them play.'

'*You've* been to a gig?'

'I'm looking on it as personal growth,' said Emma, with a straight face.

'Well, send my love to Rob.'

'Actually he can't come over this weekend after all,' she said, trying to hide her disappointment. 'He's had to fly to LA for a round of meetings with the studio.'

'Well, why don't you come round to mine for dinner?'

'And disturb the newly cohabiting lovebirds? No way.'

'Don't be silly, my dad is going to be there too. Tom and Christopher get on like a house on fire . . .' Stella blushed. 'Oops, I mean they get on brilliantly. Think about it anyway, yeah?'

Emma spun her chair around so she faced the window, watching Stella run happily across the car park to her car and drive off in the direction of Chilcot.

Turning back towards the office, it felt empty and hollow. Emma had to admit it: she felt terribly lonely here. Rob had finally moved out of Winterfold two weeks ago and was

671

now living in New York full time. At first, it hadn't been so bad. He still kept a wardrobe full of clothes in the master bedroom and his photographs were still dotted around the house. Every day she would find something of his that made her smile: a running shoe behind the curtain, cufflinks in a drawer, a sock that had lost its other half. They spoke to each other every night on the phone of course and the arrangement was that one of them would make a transatlantic trip every month, which meant they would see each other every fortnight. Yet here they were; this was the first weekend he was due to visit and they had tripped up at the first hurdle.

She grimaced; shouldn't this be the time when she could finally enjoy her success? Milford's sales were certainly soaring, exceeding even her most optimistic hopes and the business page analysts were hailing it as the greatest corporate fashion recovery since Fendi rejuvenated their fortunes with the baguette bag. Milford was the new watchword for super-luxury and the six-month waiting list for their bags only further enhanced the brand's appeal. And to cap it all, that morning, Cassandra had called to confirm that she was going to take up the non-executive directorship. Emma wasn't sure how it was going to work out; Cassandra wasn't the easiest person to deal with, but what Emma did know was that her cousin's flair and talent would be good for Milford. The challenge the company faced was to make sure it wasn't just enjoying a brief moment in the sun. They needed to roll out a lasting brand that straddled both classic style and fashion. That was Cassandra Grand in a nutshell and that was why Emma knew she had made the right decision by inviting her on board.

So with everything going so well, why did she feel so desolate? It was crushingly obvious. All her fears about her relationship with Rob were coming true: he wasn't there when she needed him, he wasn't there to hold her at night and he wasn't there to make her heart flutter with a shared look or a smile. What was the point of all these achievements and successes if you had to experience them on your own? She wanted Rob to be there to discuss the day's little triumphs and disappointments, she wanted work to be part of her life, not to define it so absolutely that it excluded everything else. Emma spun round in her chair again. *Come on, Emma*, she told herself, *you didn't go through all this to give up now.*

Twelve months. That's all they had to get through. Twelve months of long-distance love. Already she had identified a retail space on Madison Avenue that would be ideal for a new US Milford store. Then perhaps, maybe – *definitely* – she would base herself for part of the month in New York. And just then, Emma had a sudden, clear thought of what she wanted to do. She picked up her phone and called Spencer Fairfield, a senior fashion industry executive with over twenty years' experience at YSL, Gucci and Bottega Veneta and whom she had just appointed as her number two to fill the hole left by Ruan.

'Spencer, something's come up,' she said. 'I won't be in the office Monday to Wednesday. Will you be all right?'

After he confirmed that he was quite capable of holding the fort in her absence, she flipped through her Rolodex and dialled a number. Janine Colman was a travel agent Milford kept on a retainer to sort out flights, hotels, cars for the Fashion Week shows and other trips to source leather or fabric.

'Hi, Janine,' she said. 'It's Emma Bailey. Can you get me on a flight to LAX tomorrow morning?'

'I'm sure I can, but it will cost you.'

'I don't care. Please, just try and make it happen.'

Emma put down the phone, feeling light-headed but free,

and moved towards the door, grabbing her coat. Suddenly, she heard footsteps coming down the corridor and she froze, momentarily flooded by memories of a woman in a long coat holding a gun.

'Hey, stranger,' said a deep voice.

'Rob!' cried Emma, running up and wrapping herself around him. Rob dropped his bag on the floor with a thump and cupped her face in his hands, smothering her questions with kisses.

'Rob, what the hell are you doing here?' she asked breathlessly when he finally released her.

'I could say the same about you. It's gone 8 p.m. and I'm cooking you dinner.'

She looked at him bemused. 'But shouldn't you be in LA tomorrow morning?'

'Someone else is dealing with it. William Conran, the new CEO.'

'But *you're* the new CEO.'

'No, I was going to be the CEO. I've decided to stay at Hollander Music UK,' he smiled, taking her hands in his.

'Why?'

'For us. For you.'

She felt panic and guilt clutch at her heart.

'Rob, don't throw away your career for me!'

'I'm not throwing anything away,' he said, his eyes honest and bright. 'Look at me.' He was in a conservative dark blue suit, his new corporate image a world away from the laid-back jeans and T-shirted Rob Holland she had fallen for.

'Looks pretty good to me,' she laughed, threading her arms around his neck.

'I'm thirty-eight years old,' said Rob steadily. 'Do I want to be CEO of Hollander Media? Absolutely, *one day*. But the truth is I'm not ready for the boardroom and the golf course – I'm still crazy for the music. William Conran is more than capable of running the company; in fact he's been Dad's right-hand man for twenty years. I'd trust him with every cent I own. He's sixty-two this year and when he steps down, well then maybe, hopefully, I'll be in the position to take the job. *If*, that is, I'm done with the music and if you're ready to head up Milford in the States.'

Beaming at his wisdom, generosity and – whatever he said – his willingness to make a sacrifice for their relationship, she felt a surge of love that overpowered her with its intensity and fat tears of happiness began to roll down her cheeks.

'Hey, you do know there's more to life than just work?' he said stroking her hot cheek with his finger.

She nodded. 'I know. I've just booked a flight to LA to be with you.'

He held her close, breathing the same air.

'I love you, Emma Bailey. I love you more than all the love songs there ever were.'

'*She loves you, yeah, yeah, yeah,*' she whispered.

'You're definitely learning,' he said giving her a cheeky grin. 'But I think we've got a long way to go.'

She took his hand, grabbed her coat and they walked up the lane towards the glowing lights of Winterfold. Towards home.

What's next?

Tell us the name of an author you love

| Tasmina Perry | Go ▶ |

and we'll find your next great book.